ONE FALSE MOVE

FADE AWAY

Myron Bolitar Mysteries

ONE FALSE MOVE

FADE AWAY

by
Harlan Coben

Mystery Guild
Garden City, New York

FADE
AWAY

For Larry and Craig,
the coolest brothers a guy could ever have.
If you don't believe me, just ask them.

The author wishes to thank the following for their help: Anne Armstrong-Coben, M.D.; James Bradbeer, Jr., of Lilly Pulitzer; David Gold, M.D.; Maggie Griffin; Jacob Hoye; Lindsay Koehler; David Pepe of Pro Agents, Inc.; Peter Roisman of Advantage International; and, of course, Dave Bolt. Any errors—factual or otherwise—are totally their fault. The author is not to blame.

Chapter 1

"Just behave."

"Me?" Myron said. "I'm always a delight."

Myron Bolitar was being led through the corridor of the darkened Meadowlands Arena by Calvin Johnson, the New Jersey Dragons new general manager. Their dress shoes clacked sharply against the tile and echoed through empty Harry M. Stevens food stands, Carvel Ice Cream carts, pretzel vendors, souvenir booths. The smell of sporting-event hot dogs—that sort of rubbery, chemically, yet nostalgically delicious aroma—wafted from the walls. The stillness of the place consumed them; there is nothing more hollow and lifeless than an empty sports arena.

Calvin Johnson stopped in front of a door leading to a luxury box. "This may all seem a bit strange," he said. "Just go with the flow, okay?"

"Okay."

Calvin reached for the knob and took a deep breath. "Clip Arnstein, the owner of the Dragons, is in there waiting for us."

"And yet I'm not trembling," Myron said.

Calvin Johnson shook his head. "Just don't be an ass."

Myron pointed to his chest. "I wore a tie and everything."

Calvin Johnson opened the door. The luxury box faced midcourt. Several workers were putting down the basketball floor over the hockey ice. The Devils had played the night before. Tonight was the Dragons' turn. The box was cozy. Twenty-four cushioned seats. Two television monitors. To the right was a wood-paneled counter for the food—usually fried chicken, hot dogs, potato knishes, sausage and pepper sandwiches, that sort of stuff. To the left was a brass cart with a nicely stocked bar and minifridge. The box also had its own bathroom—this so the corporate high rollers would not have to urinate with the great unwashed.

Clip Arnstein faced them, standing. He wore a dark blue suit with a red tie. He was bald with patches of gray over both ears. He was burly, his chest still a barrel after seventy-some-odd years. His large hands had brown spots and fat blue veins like garden hoses. No one spoke. No one moved. Clip glared hard at Myron for several seconds, examining him from head to toe.

"Like the tie?" Myron asked.

Calvin Johnson shot him a warning glance.

The old man made no movement toward them. "How old are you now, Myron?"

Interesting opening question. "Thirty-two."

"You playing any ball?"

"Some," Myron said.

"You keep in good shape?"

"Want me to flex?"

"No, that won't be necessary."

No one offered Myron a seat and no one took one. Of course the only chairs in here were the spectator seats, but it still felt weird to stand in a business setting where you're supposed to sit. Standing suddenly became difficult. Myron felt antsy. He didn't know what to do with his hands. He took out a pen and held it, but that didn't feel right. Too Bob Dole. He stuck his hands in his pockets and stood at a weird angle, like the casual guy in the Sears circular.

"Myron, we have an interesting proposition for you," Clip Arnstein said.

"Proposition?" Always the probing interrogatory.

"Yes. I was the one who drafted you, you know."

"I know."

"Ten, eleven years ago. When I was with the Celtics."

"I know."

"First round."

"I know all this, Mr. Arnstein."

"You were a hell of a prospect, Myron. You were smart. You had an unbelievable touch. You were loaded with talent."

"I coulda been a contenda," Myron said.

Arnstein scowled. It was a famous scowl, developed over some fifty-plus years in professional basketball. The scowl had made its first appearance when Clip played for the now-defunct Rochester Royals in the forties. It grew more famous when he coached the Boston Celtics to numerous championships. It became a legendary trademark when he made all the famous trades ("clipping" the competition, ergo the nickname) as team president. Three years ago Clip had become majority owner of the New Jersey Dragons and the scowl now resided in East Rutherford, right off Exit 16 of the New Jersey Turnpike. His voice was gruff. "Was that supposed to be Brando?"

"Eerie, isn't it? Like Marlon's actually in the room."

Clip Arnstein's face suddenly softened. He nodded slowly, giving Myron the doelike, father-figure eyes. "You make jokes to cover the pain," he said gravely. "I understand that."

Dr. Joyce Brothers.

"Is there something I can do for you, Mr. Arnstein?"

"You never played in a single professional game, did you, Myron?"

"You know very well I didn't."

Clip nodded. "Your first preseason game. Third quarter. You already had eighteen points that game. Not bad for a rookie in his first scrimmage. That was when fate took over."

Fate took the form of big Burt Wesson of the Washington Bullets. There had been a collision, a searing pain, and then nothing.

"Awful thing," Clip said.

"Uh huh."

"I always felt bad about what happened to you. Such a waste."

Myron glanced at Calvin Johnson. Calvin was looking off, arms crossed, his smooth black features a placid pool. "Uh huh," Myron said again.

"That's why I'd like to give you another chance."

Myron was sure he'd heard wrong. "Pardon?"

"We have a slot open on the team. I'd like to sign you."

Myron waited. He looked at Clip. Then he looked at Calvin Johnson. Neither one was laughing. "Where is it?" Myron asked.

"What?"

"The camera. This is one of those hidden camera shows, right? Is this the one with Ed McMahon? I'm a big fan of his work."

"It's not a joke, Myron."

"It must be, Mr. Arnstein. I haven't played competitive ball in ten years. I shattered my knee, remember?"

"All too well. But as you said, it was ten years ago. I know you went through rehabilitation to rebuild it."

"And you also know I tried a comeback. Seven years ago. The knee wouldn't hold up."

"It was still too early," Clip said. "You just told me you're playing again."

"Pickup games on weekends. It's a tad different than the NBA."

Clip dismissed the argument with a wave of his hand. "You're in shape. You even volunteered to flex."

Myron's eyes narrowed, swerving from Clip to Calvin Johnson, back to Clip. Their expressions were neutral. "Why do I have the feeling," Myron asked, "that I'm missing something here?"

Clip finally smiled. He looked over to Calvin Johnson. Calvin Johnson forced up a return smile.

"Perhaps I should be less"—Clip paused, searched for the word—"opaque."

"That might be helpful."

"I want you on the team. I don't much care if you play or not."

Myron waited again. When no one continued, he said, "It's still a bit opaque."

Clip let loose a long breath. He walked over to the bar, opened a small hotel-style fridge, and removed a can of Yoo-Hoo. Stocking Yoo-Hoos. Hmm. Clip had been prepared. "You still drink this sludge?"

"Yes," Myron said.

He tossed Myron the can and poured something from a decanter into two glasses. He handed one to Calvin Johnson. He signaled to the seats by the glass window. Exactly midcourt. Very nice. Nice leg room too. Even Calvin, who was six-eight, was able to stretch a bit. The three men sat next to one another, all facing the same way, which again felt weird in a business setting. You were supposed to sit across from one another, preferably at a table or desk. Instead they sat shoulder to shoulder, watching the work crew pound the floor into place.

"Cheers," Clip said.

He sipped his whiskey. Calvin Johnson just held his. Myron, obeying the instructions on the can, shook his Yoo-Hoo.

"If I'm not mistaken," Clip continued, "you're a lawyer now."

"I'm a member of the bar," Myron said. "I don't practice much law."

"You're a sports agent."

"Yes."

"I don't trust agents," Clip said.

"Neither do I."

"For the most part, they're bloodsucking leeches."

"We prefer the term 'parasitic entities,' " Myron said. "It's more PC."

Clip Arnstein leaned forward, his eyes zeroing in on Myron's. "How do I know I can trust you?"

Myron pointed at himself. "My face," he said. "It screams trustworthiness."

Clip did not smile. He leaned a little closer. "What I'm about to tell you must remain confidential."

"Okay."

"Do you give me your word it won't go any farther than this room?"

"Yes."

Clip hesitated, glanced at Calvin Johnson, shifted in his seat. "You know, of course, Greg Downing."

Of course. Myron had grown up with Greg Downing. From the time they had first competed as sixth graders in a town league less than twenty miles from where Myron now sat, they were instant rivals. When they reached high school, Greg's family moved to the neighboring town of Essex Fells because Greg's father did not want his son sharing the basketball spotlight with Myron. The personal rivalry then began to take serious flight. They played against each other eight times in high school, each winning four games. Myron and Greg became New Jersey's hottest recruits and both matriculated at big-time basketball colleges with a storied rivalry of their own— Myron to Duke, Greg to North Carolina.

The personal rivalry soared.

During their college careers, they had shared two *Sports Illustrated* covers. Both teams won the ACC twice, but Myron picked up a national championship. Both Myron and Greg were picked first-team All-American, both at the guard spots. By the time they both graduated, Duke and North Carolina had played each other twelve times. The Myron-led Duke had won eight of them. When the NBA draft came, both men went in the first round.

The personal rivalry crashed and burned.

Myron's career ended when he collided with big Burt Wesson. Greg Downing sidestepped fate and went on to become one of the NBA premier guards. During his ten-year career with the New Jersey Dragons Downing had been named to the All-Star team eight times. He led the league twice in three-point shooting. Four times he led the league in free-throw percentage and once in assists. He'd been on three *Sports Illustrated* covers and had won an NBA championship.

"I know him," Myron said.

"Do you talk to him much?" Clip Arnstein asked.

"No."

"When was the last time you spoke?"

"I don't remember."

"Within the last few days?"

"I don't think we've spoken in ten years," Myron said.

"Oh," Clip said. He took another sip. Calvin had still not touched his drink. "Well, I'm sure you heard about his injury."

"Something with his ankle," Myron said. "It's day to day. He's in seclusion working on it."

Clip nodded. "That's the story we gave the media anyway. It's not exactly the truth."

"Oh?"

"Greg isn't injured," Clip said. "He's missing."

"Missing?" Again the probing interrogatory.

"Yes." Clip took another sip. Myron sipped back, not an easy task with Yoo-Hoo.

"Since when?" Myron asked.

"Five days now."

Myron looked at Calvin. Calvin remained placid but he had that kind of face. During his playing days, his nickname had been Frosty because he never displayed emotion. He was living up to his name now.

Myron tried again. "When you say Greg is missing—"

"Gone," Clip snapped. "Disappeared. Into thin air. Without a trace. Whatever you want to call it."

"Have you called the police?"

"No."

"Why not?"

Clip gave him the wave-off again. "You know Greg. He's not a conventional guy."

The understatement of the millennium.

"He never does the expected," Clip said. "He hates the fame. He likes to be on his own. He's even disappeared before, though never during a playoff drive."

"So?"

"So there's a good chance he's just being his usually flaky self," Clip continued. "Greg can shoot like a dream, but let's face facts: the man is a couple of sandwiches short of a picnic. You know what Downing does after games?"

Myron shook his head.

"He drives a cab in the city. That's right, a goddamn yellow taxi cab in New York City. Says it keeps him close to the common man. Greg won't do appearances or endorsements. He doesn't do interviews. He doesn't even do the charity thing. He dresses like something out of a seventies sitcom. The man is a nut job."

"All of which makes him immensely popular with the fans," Myron said. "Which sells tickets."

"I agree," Clip said, "but that just underlines my point. If we call the cops it could damage both him and the team. Can you imagine the media circus if this got out?"

"It would be bad," Myron admitted.

"Exactly. And suppose Greg is just hanging out in French Lick or whatever hickville town he goes to in the off-season, fishing or something? Christ, we'd never hear the end of it. On the other hand, suppose he's up to something."

"Up to something?" Myron repeated.

"Hell, I don't know. I'm just talking here. But I don't need a goddamn scandal. Not now. Not with the playoffs coming up, you know what I'm saying?"

Not really, but Myron decided to let it go for now. "Who else knows about this?"

"Just the three of us."

The work crew rolled in the baskets. Two extras were kept in storage in case someone pulled a Darryl Dawkins and shattered a backboard. They then began putting down additional seats. Like most arenas, the Meadowlands holds more seats for basketball than hockey—in this case around a thousand more. Myron took a another sip of Yoo-Hoo and let it roll around his tongue. He waited until it slid down his throat before he asked the obvious question. "So how do I fit in?"

Clip hesitated. His breathing was deep, almost labored. "I know something of your years with the FBI," he said finally. "No details, of course. Not even vagaries really, but enough to know you have a background in this kinda stuff. We want you to find Greg. Quietly."

Myron said nothing. His "undercover" work for the feds, it seemed, was the worst kept secret in the continental United States. Clip sipped his drink. He looked at Calvin's full glass, then at Calvin. Calvin finally took a sip. Clip turned his attention back to Myron. "Greg's divorced now," Clip went on. "He's basically a loner. All his friends—hell, all his acquaintances—are teammates. They're his support group, if you will. His family. If anyone knows where he is—if anyone's helping him stay hidden—it's got to be one of the Dragons. I'll be honest with you. These guys are a major pain in the ass. Spoiled, pampered prima donnas who think our purpose in life is to serve them. But they all have one thing in common: They see management as the enemy. Us against the world and all that crap. They won't tell us the truth. They won't tell reporters the truth. And

if you approach them as some, uh, 'parasitic entity,' they won't talk
to you either. You have to be a player. It's the only way to get on the
inside."

"So you want me to join the team so I can find Greg."

Myron heard the echoes of hurt in his voice. It was unintentional,
but he saw that both men heard it too. His face flushed in embarrassment.

Clip put a hand on his shoulder. "I meant what I said, Myron. You
could have been great. One of the greatest."

Myron took a deep swig of his Yoo-Hoo. No more sipping. "I'm
sorry, Mr. Arnstein. I can't help you."

The scowl was back. "What?"

"I have a life. I'm a sports agent. I have clients to tend to. I can't
just drop it all."

"You'll get the player's minimum prorated. That's two hundred
thousand dollars less whatever. And there's only a couple of weeks
left until the playoffs. We'll keep you on till then no matter what."

"No. My playing days are over. And I'm not a private investigator."

"But we need to find him. He could be in danger."

"I'm sorry. The answer is no."

Clip smiled. "Suppose I sweeten the pot."

"No."

"Fifty-thousand-dollar signing bonus."

"I'm sorry."

"Greg could show up tomorrow and you'd still get to keep that.
Fifty grand. Plus a share of playoff money."

"No."

Clip sat back. He stared at his drink, dipped his finger into it,
stirred. His voice was casual. "You say you're an agent, right?"

"Yes."

"I'm very friendly with the parents of three guys that will go in
the first round. Did you know that?"

"No."

"Suppose," Clip said slowly, "I guarantee you that one of them
signs with you."

Myron pricked up. A first round draft pick. He tried to keep his
expression cool—to do like Frosty—but his heart was thumping.
"How can you do that?"

"Don't worry about how."

"It doesn't sound ethical."

Clip made a scoffing noise. "Myron, don't play choirboy with me.

You do me this favor and MB SportsReps gets a first round draft pick. Guaranteed. No matter how this thing with Greg plays out."

MB SportsReps. Myron's company. Myron Bolitar, ergo MB. Representing sports people, ergo SportsReps. Add it together: MB SportsReps. Myron came up with that name on his own but still no offers came in from major advertising companies to use his services.

"Make it a hundred-thousand-dollar signing bonus," Myron said.

Clip smiled. "You've learned well, Myron."

Myron shrugged.

"Seventy-five thousand," Clip said. "And you'll take it so don't bullshit a bullshitter."

The two men shook hands.

"I have a few more questions about the disappearance," Myron said.

Using both armrests Clip rose and stood over Myron. "Calvin will answer all your questions," he said with a nod toward his general manager. "I have to go now."

"So when do you want me to start practicing?"

Clip looked surprised. "Practicing?"

"Yeah. When do you want me to start?"

"We have a game tonight."

"Tonight?"

"Of course," Clip said.

"You want me to suit up tonight?"

"We're playing our old team, the Celtics. Calvin will make sure you have a uniform by game time. Press conference at six to announce your signing. Don't be late." Clip headed toward the door. "And wear that tie. I like it."

"Tonight?" Myron repeated, but Clip was already gone.

Chapter 2

After Clip left the box, Calvin Johnson allowed himself a small smile. "I warned you it would be strange."

"Serious strange," Myron agreed.

"Finished with your nutritious chocolate beverage?"

Myron put down the can. "Yeah."

"Come on. Let's get you ready for the big debut."

Calvin Johnson walked fluidly, back straight. He was black, six-foot-eight, thin but not gawky or disproportionate. He wore an olive Brooks Brothers suit. Perfectly tailored. Perfectly knotted tie. Perfectly shined shoes. His tightly kinked hair was receding, making his forehead overly prominent and shiny. When Myron matriculated at Duke, Calvin had been a senior at North Carolina. That made him around thirty-five years old, though he looked older. Calvin had enjoyed a solid pro career over eleven seasons. When he retired three years ago, everyone knew he'd end up in the front office. He started off as an assistant coach, moved to player personnel, and just recently was promoted to vice president and general manager of the New Jersey Dragons. These however were just titles. Clip ran the show. General managers, vice presidents, player personnel, trainers, even coaches all bent to his will.

"I hope you're all right with this," Calvin said.

"Why wouldn't I be all right?"

Calvin shrugged. "I played against you," he said.

"So?"

"You were the most competitive son of a bitch I ever faced," Calvin said. "You'd stomp on someone's head to win. Now you're going to be a pissant bench-warmer. How's that going to sit with you?"

"I can handle it," Myron said.

"Uh huh."

"I've mellowed over the years."

Calvin shook his head. "I don't think so."

"No?"

"You may think you've mellowed. You may even think you've got basketball out of your system."

"I have."

Calvin stopped, smiled, spread his arms. "Sure you have. Just look at you. You could be the poster child for life after sports. A fine example to your fellow athletes. Your whole career crashed down around your ears, but you rose to the challenge. You went back to school—at Harvard Law nonetheless. You started up your own business—a growing company in the field of sports representation. You still dating that writer?"

He meant Jessica. Their togetherness seemed to always be an iffy thing but Myron said, "Yes."

"So you got the education, the job, and the gorgeous girlfriend. Yep, on the outside you're happy and well adjusted."

"On the inside too."

Calvin shook his head. "I don't think so."

Everyone's Dr. Joyce Brothers. "Hey, I didn't ask to be put on the team."

"No, but you didn't argue much either—except to up your price."

"I'm an agent. That's what I do. I up the price."

Calvin stopped and looked at Myron. "Do you really think you have to be on the team to find Greg?"

"Clip seemed to think so."

"Clip is a great man," Calvin said, "but he often has ulterior motives."

"Like what?"

Calvin did not respond. He started walking again.

They reached the elevator. Calvin pressed the button and the doors immediately slid open. They stepped inside and began to descend. "Look me in the eye," Calvin said. "Look me in the eye and tell me you never think about playing again."

"Who doesn't *think* about it?" Myron countered.

"Yeah, but tell me you don't take it one step further. Tell me you never drift off and dream about making a comeback. Even now, when you're watching a game on TV, tell me you don't sit there and do a slow burn. Tell me you never watch Greg and think about all the adulation and fame. Tell me you never say, 'I was better than him,' because it's the truth. Greg is great. One of the top ten players in the league. But you were better, Myron. We both know that."

"Long time ago," Myron said.

Calvin smiled. "Yeah," he said. "Right."

"What's your point?"

"You're here to find Greg. Once he's found, you're gone. The novelty will be over. Clip will be able to say he gave you a chance, but you weren't up to the challenge. He'll still be the good guy with the good press."

"Good press," Myron repeated, remembering the upcoming press conference. "One of his ulterior motives?"

Calvin shrugged. "Doesn't matter. What does matter is that you understand you don't have a chance. You're only going to play during scrub time and we rarely win or lose by a lot so that doesn't happen and even if it does, even if you play spectacularly, we both know it's scrub time. And you won't play well because you are such a competitive son of a bitch, you need the points to mean something to the outcome of the game or you don't play your best."

"I understand," Myron said.

"I hope you do, my friend." Calvin looked up at the numbered lights. The lights flickered in his brown eyes. "Dreams never die. Sometimes you think they're dead, but they're just hibernating like some big old bear. And if the dream has been hibernating for a long time, that bear is going to wake up grumpy and hungry."

"You should write country songs," Myron said.

Calvin shook his head. "Just giving a friend fair warning."

"Much obliged. Now why don't you tell me what you know about Greg's disappearance?"

The elevator stopped and the doors opened. Calvin led the way. "Not much to tell," he said. "We played against the Sixers in Philly. After the game Greg got on the bus with everybody else. When we got here, he got off the bus with everybody else. The last time anyone saw him he was getting into his car. The end."

"How did Greg seem that night?"

"Fine. He played well against Philly. Scored twenty-seven points."

"And his mood?"

Calvin thought about it. "Nothing I noticed," he said.

"Anything new going on in his life?"

"New?"

"Changes, that kind of thing."

"Well, the divorce," Calvin said. "It's been nasty. I understand Emily can be quite difficult." He stopped walking again and smiled at Myron. The Cheshire cat smile. Myron stopped but did not return the smile.

"Something on your mind, Frosty?"

The smile spread a bit farther. "Weren't you and Emily an item at one time?"

"A lifetime ago."

"College sweethearts, if I recall."

"Like I said, a lifetime ago."

"So," Calvin said, starting to walk again, "you were even better with the women than Greg."

Myron ignored the comment. "Does Clip know about my so-called past with Emily?"

"He's very thorough."

"So that explains why you chose me," Myron said.

"It was a consideration, but I don't think it's too important."

"Oh?"

"Greg hates Emily. He'd never confide in her. But since this whole custody battle started there's definitely been a change in Greg."

"How so?"

"For one thing, he signed a deal with Forte sneakers."

Myron was surprised. "Greg? An endorsement deal?"

"It's very hush-hush," Calvin said. "They're supposed to announce it end of the month, right before the playoffs."

Myron whistled. "They must have paid him a bundle."

"A bundle and a half, I hear. Upwards of ten million a year."

"Makes sense," Myron said. "A popular player who has refused to endorse any products for more than a decade—it's an irresistible draw. Forte does well with track and tennis shoes, but they're fairly unknown in the basketball world. Greg gives them instant credibility."

"That he does," Calvin agreed.

"Any idea why he changed his mind after all these years?"

Calvin shrugged. "Maybe Greg realized he wasn't getting any younger and wanted to cash in. Maybe this whole divorce thing. Maybe he got whacked on the head and woke up with an iota of sanity."

"Where's he been living since the divorce?"

"In the house in Ridgewood. It's in Bergen County."

Myron knew it well. He asked for the address. Calvin gave it to him. "What about Emily?" Myron asked. "Where's she staying?"

"She and the kids are with her mother. I think they're in Franklin Lakes or thereabouts."

"Have you done any checking yet—Greg's house, his credit cards, bank accounts?"

Calvin shook his head. "Clip thought this thing was too big to trust to an agency. That's why we called you. I've driven past Greg's house a few times, knocked on the door once. No car in the driveway or garage. No lights on."

"But no one's checked inside the house?"

"No."

"So for all you know he slipped in the bathtub and hit his head."

Calvin looked at him. "I said, no lights on. You think he bathed in the dark?"

"That's a good point," Myron said.

"Some hotshot investigator."

"I'm a slow starter."

They arrived at the team room. "Wait here," Calvin said.

Myron took out his cellular. "Mind if I make a call?"

"Go ahead."

Calvin disappeared behind the door. Myron turned on the power and dialed. Jessica answered on the second ring. "Hello?"

"I'm going to have to cancel dinner tonight," Myron said.

"You better have a good excuse," Jessica said.

"A great one. I'll be playing professional basketball for the New Jersey Dragons."

"That's nice. Have a good game, dear."

"I'm serious. I'm playing for the Dragons. Actually, 'playing' is probably not the right word. Might be more accurate to say I'll be getting fanny sores for the Dragons."

"Are you for real?"

"It's a long story, but yes, I'm now officially a professional basketball player."

Silence.

"I've never boffed a professional basketball player," Jessica said. "I'll be just like Madonna."

"Like a virgin," Myron said.

"Wow. Talk about a dated reference."

"Yeah, well, what can I say. I'm an eighties kinda guy."

"So, Mr. Eighties, you going to tell me what's going on?"

"No time now. Tonight. After the game. I'll leave a ticket at the window."

Calvin stuck his head back in. "What's your waist? Thirty-four?"

"Thirty-six. Maybe thirty-seven."

Calvin nodded and withdrew. Myron dialed the private line of Windsor Horne Lockwood III, president of the prestigious investment firm of Lock-Horne Securities in midtown Manhattan. Win answered on the third ring.

"Articulate," Win said.

Myron shook his head. "Articulate?"

"I said articulate, not repeat."

"We have a case," Myron said.

"Oh yippee," he drawled in that preppy, Philly Main-Line accent of his. "I'm enthralled. I'm elated. But before I completely wet myself, I must ask but one question."

"Shoot."

"Is this case of your customary charity persuasion?"

"Wet away," Myron said. "The answer is no."

"What? No moral crusade for brave Myron?"

"Not this time."

"Heavens be, do tell."

"Greg Downing is missing. It's our job to find him."

"And for services rendered we receive?"

"At least seventy-five grand plus a first round draft pick as a client." Now was not the time to fill Win in on his temporary career change.

"My, my," Win said happily. "Pray tell, what shall we do first?"

Myron gave him the address of Greg's house in Ridgewood. "Meet me there in two hours."

"I'll take the Batmobile," Win said and hung up.

Calvin returned. He held out a purple-and-aqua Dragon uniform. "Try this on."

Myron did not reach for it right away. He stared at it, his stomach twisting and diving. When he spoke his voice was soft. "Number thirty-four?"

"Yeah," Calvin said. "Your old number at Duke. I remembered."

Silence.

Calvin finally broke it. "Go try it on."

Myron felt something well up in his eye. He shook his head. "No need," he said. "I'm sure it's the right size."

Chapter 3

Ridgewood was a primo suburb, one of those old towns that still calls itself a village, where ninety-five percent of the students go on to college and no one lets their kids associate with the other five percent. There were a couple of strips of tract housing, a few examples of the mid-sixties suburban explosion, but for the most part Ridgewood's fine homes dated from an earlier, theoretically more innocent time.

Myron found the Downing house without any problem. Old Victorian. Very big but not unwieldy, three levels with perfectly faded cedar shingles. On the left side there was one of those rounded towers with a pointy top. Lots of outdoor porch space with all the Rockwellian touches: the kind of double swing where Atticus and Scout would share a lemonade on a hot Alabama night; a child's bicycle tipped on its side; a Flexible Flyer snow sled, although it hadn't snowed in six weeks. The required basketball hoop hung slightly rusted over the driveway. Fire Department "Tot Finder" stickers glistened red and silver from two upstairs windows. Old oak trees lined the walk like weathered sentries.

Win hadn't arrived yet. Myron parked and rolled down a window. The perfect mid-March day. The sky was robin-egg blue. The birds chirped in cliché. He tried to picture Emily here, but the picture would not hold. It was far easier to see her in a New York high rise or one of those nouveau-riche mansions all done in white with Erté sculptures and silver pearls and too many gaudy mirrors. Then again he hadn't spoken to Emily in ten years. She may have changed. Or he may have misjudged her all those years ago. Wouldn't be the first time.

Funny being back in Ridgewood. Jessica had grown up here. She didn't like coming back anymore, but now the two loves of his life—Jessica and Emily—had something else in common: the village of Ridgewood. That could be added to the list of commonalities between the two women—stuff like meeting Myron, being courted by Myron, falling in love with Myron, crushing Myron's heart like a tomato under a stiletto heel. The usual fare.

Emily had been his first. Freshman year of college was late to lose one's virginity, if one were to listen to the boasts of friends. But if there had indeed been a sexual revolution among American teenagers in the late seventies/early eighties, Myron had either missed it or been on the wrong side. Women had always liked him—it wasn't that. But while his friends discoursed in great detail on their various orgylike experiences, Myron seemed to attract the wrong girls, the nice girls, the ones who still said no—or would have had Myron had the courage (or foresight) to try.

That changed in college when he met Emily.

Passion. It's a word bandied about quite a bit, but Myron thought it might apply here. At a minimum, unconfined lust. Emily was the type of woman a man labels "hot," as opposed to "beautiful." See a truly "beautiful" woman and you want to paint or write a poem. See Emily and you want to engage in mutual fabric-ripping. She was raw sexuality, maybe ten pounds bigger than she should have been but those pounds were exquisitely distributed. The two of them made a potent mix. They were both under twenty, both away from home for the first time, both creative.

In a word: *kaboom.*

The car phone rang. Myron picked it up.

"I assume," Win said, "that you plan on having us break into the Downing residence."

"Yes."

"Then parking your car in front of said residence would not be a sound decision, would it?"

Myron glanced about. "Where are you?"

"Drive down to the end of the block. Make a left, then your second right. I'm parked behind the office building."

Myron hung up and restarted the car. He followed the directions and pulled into the lot. Win leaned against his Jaguar with his arms crossed. He looked, as he always did, as if he were posing for the cover of *WASP Quarterly.* His blond hair was perfectly in place. His complexion slightly ruddy, his features porcelain and high and a little too perfect. He wore khaki pants, a blue blazer, Top-Siders *sans* socks, and a loud Lilly Pulitzer tie. Win looked like what you'd picture a guy named Windsor Horne Lockwood III to look like—elitist, self-absorbed, wimpy.

Well, two out of three ain't bad.

The office building held an eclectic mix. Gynecologist. Electrolysis. Subpoena delivery service. Nutritionist. Women-only health club. Not surprisingly Win was standing near the entrance to the women-only health club. Myron approached.

"How did you know I was parked in front of the house?"

Keeping his eye on the entranceway Win motioned with his head. "Up that hill. You can see everything with a pair of binoculars."

A woman in her early twenties wearing a black Lycra aerobics suit walked out carrying a baby. It hadn't taken her long to get her figure back. Win smiled at her. The woman smiled back.

"I love young mothers," Win said.

"You love women in Lycra," Myron corrected.

Win nodded. "There's that." He snapped on a pair of sunglasses. "Shall we begin?"

"You think breaking into that house will be a problem?"

Win made his I'll-pretend-you-didn't-ask-that face. Another woman exited the health club; sadly, this one did not warrant a Win smile. "Fill me in," Win said. "And move away. I want to make sure they can see the Jag."

Myron told him all he knew. Eight women came out in the five minutes it took to tell the story. Only two of them were awarded The Smile. One wore a tiger-striped leotard. She was treated to the Full-Wattage Smile, the one that almost touched Win's eyes.

Win's face did not seem to register anything Myron said. Even when he told him about taking Greg's temporary slot on the Dragons, Win went on staring hopefully at the health club door. Normal Win behavior. Myron finished up by asking, "Any questions?"

Win bounced a finger against his lip. "Do you think the one in the tiger-striped leotard was wearing any underwear?"

"I don't know," Myron said, "but she was definitely wearing a wedding band."

Win shrugged. Didn't matter to him. Win didn't believe in love or relationships with the opposite sex. Some might take this for simple sexism. They'd be wrong. Women weren't objects to Win; objects sometimes got his respect.

"Follow me," Win said.

They were less than half a mile from the Downing house. Win had already scouted it out and found the path with the least chance of being seen or arousing suspicion. They walked in the comfortable silence of two men who had known each other a long time and very well.

"There's one interesting aside in all this," Myron said.

Win waited.

"Do you remember Emily Shaeffer?" Myron asked.

"The name rings a bell."

"I dated her for two years at Duke." Win and Myron had met at Duke. They had also been roommates for all four years. It had been Win who had introduced Myron to the martial arts, who had gotten him involved with Feds. Win was now a top producer at his Lock-Horne Securities on Park Avenue, a securities firm that had been run by Win's family since the market had first opened. Myron rented space from Win, and Win also handled all money-matters for MB SportsReps' clients.

Win thought a bit. "Is she the one who used to make the little monkey noises?"

"No," Myron said.

Win seemed surprised. "Who was the one who made the little monkey noises?"

"I have no idea."

"Maybe it was someone I was with."

"Maybe."

Win considered this, shrugged. "What about her?"

"She used to be married to Greg Downing."

"Divorced?"

"Yep."

"I remember her now," Win said. "Emily Schaeffer. Built."

Myron nodded.

"I never liked her," Win said. "Except for those little monkey noises. They were rather interesting."

"She wasn't the one who made monkey noises."

Win smiled gently. "The walls were thin," he said.

"And you used to listen in?"

"Only when you pulled down the shade so I couldn't watch."

Myron shook his head. "You're a pig," he said.

"Better than a monkey."

They reached the front lawn and proceeded to the door. The secret was to look like you belonged. If you scurried around back, hunched over, someone might take notice. Two men in ties approaching the door does not normally lead one to think thief.

There was a metal keypad with a little red light. The light was on. "Alarm," Myron said.

Win shook his head. "Fake. It's just a light. Probably bought it at Sharper Image." Win looked at the lock and made a tsk-tsk noise. "A Kwiktight brand on a pro basketball player's salary," he said, clearly disgusted. "Might as well use Play-Doh."

"What about the dead bolt?" Myron asked.

"It's not locked."

Win already had out his strip of celluloid. Credit cards are too stiff. Celluloid worked much better—known as 'loiding the lock. In no more time than it would take with a key, the door was open and they were inside the front foyer. The door had a chute and the mail was all over the place. Myron quickly checked some postage dates. No one had been here in at least five days.

The decor was nice in a fake-rustic, Martha Stewart sort of way. The furniture was what they called "simple country" where the look was indeed simple and the price outrageous. Lots of pines and wickers and antiques and dry flowers. The smell of potpourri was strong and cloying.

They split up. Win went upstairs to the home office. He turned on the computer and began to download everything onto floppy disks. Myron found the answering machine in a room that used to be called a "den" but now went by such lofty titles as the "California room" or "great room." The machine announced the time and date of each message. Awfully convenient. Myron pressed a button. The tape rewound and started playing. On the first message, which according to the digital voice was received at 9:18 P.M. the night Greg vanished, Myron hit bingo.

A shaky woman's voice said, "It's Carla. I'll be in the back booth until midnight." Click.

Myron rewound and listened again. There were lots of noises in the background—people chatting, music, glasses clinking. The call had probably been placed from a bar or restaurant, especially with that back-booth reference. So who was this Carla? A girlfriend? Probably. Who else would call that late to set up a meeting for even later that night? But of course this had not been just any night. Greg Downing had vanished sometime between the time this call was made and the next morning.

Strange coincidence.

So where did they meet—assuming Greg had indeed made their back-booth liaison? And why did Carla, whoever she might be, sound so shaky—or was this just Myron's imagination?

Myron listened to the rest of the tape. No other messages from Carla. If Greg hadn't shown up at said back booth, wouldn't Carla have called again? Probably. So for now, Myron could safely assume that Greg Downing had seen Carla sometime before his disappearance.

A clue.

There were also four calls from Martin Felder, Greg's agent. He seemed to grow more perturbed with each message. The last one said, "Jesus, Greg, how can you not call me? Is the ankle serious or what? And don't go incommunicado on me now, not when we're wrapping up the Forte deal. Call me, okay?" There were also three calls from a man named Chris Darby who apparently worked for Forte Sports Incorporated. He too sounded panicked. "Marty won't tell me where you are. I think he's playing a game with us, Greg, trying to up the price or something. But we had a deal, am I right? Let me give you my home number, okay, Greg? How bad's this injury anyhow?"

Myron smiled. Martin Felder's client was missing, but he was doing all he could to turn it into a positive lever. Agents. He pressed the mode button on the answering machine several times. Eventually the LCD screen scrolled to reveal the code number Greg had set to call in for messages: 317. A fairly new trick of the trade. Now Myron could call in anytime, press 317, and hear what messages had been left on the machine. He hit the redial button on the phone. Another fairly new trick. Find out who Greg called last. The phone rang twice and was picked up by a woman saying, "Kimmel Brothers." Whoever they were. Myron hung up.

Myron joined up with Win in the upstairs office. Win continued copying onto computer disks while Myron went through the drawers. Nothing particularly helpful.

They moved on to the master bedroom. The king-size bed was made. Both night tables were cluttered with pens and keys and papers.

Both.

Curious for a man who lived alone.

Myron's eyes swept the room and landed on a reading chair that doubled as a dressing dummy. Greg's clothes were strewn over one arm and the back. Normal enough, Myron guessed—neater than Myron, in fact, though that wasn't saying much. But looking again, he noticed something a tad strange on the other arm of the chair. Two articles of clothing. A white blouse and a gray skirt.

Myron looked at Win.

"They might belong to Miss Monkey Noises," Win said.

Myron shook his head. "Emily hasn't lived here in months. Why would her clothes still be on a chair?"

The bathroom, too, proved interesting. A large Jacuzzi on the right, a big steam shower with a sauna, and two vanities. They checked the vanities first. One contained a can of men's shaving

cream, a roll-on deodorant, a bottle of Polo after-shave, a Gillette
Atra razor. The other vanity had an open make-up case, Calvin Klein
perfume, baby powder, and Secret Roll-On. A sprinkling of baby
powder was on the floor near the vanity. There were also two disposable Lady Schick razors in the soap dish next to the Jacuzzi.

"He's got a girlfriend," Myron said.

"A professional basketball player shacking up with some nubile
lass," Win remarked. "Quite a revelation. Perhaps one of us should
cry out, 'Eureka.' "

"Yes, but it raises an interesting question," Myron said. "If her
boyfriend had suddenly vanished, wouldn't said lover have reported
it?"

"Not," Win said, "if she were with him."

Myron nodded. He told Win about the cryptic message from
Carla.

Win shook his head. "If they were planning on running away," he
said, "why would she say where they were meeting?"

"She didn't say where. Only in a back booth at midnight."

"Still," Win said. "It's not exactly the kind of thing you do before
you disappear. Let's say that for some reason Carla and Greg decide
to vanish for a little while. Wouldn't Greg know where and when to
meet her before the fact?"

Myron shrugged. "Maybe she was changing their meeting place."

"From what? Front booths to back booths?"

"Damned if I know."

They checked the rest of the upstairs. Not much doing. Greg's
son's bedroom had racing-car wallpaper and a poster of Dad driving
past Penny Hardaway for a layup. The daughter's room was done in
Early American Barney—dinosaurs and purple. No clues. In fact
there were no other clues until they reached the basement.

When they turned on the lights, Myron saw it right away.

It was a finished basement, a brightly colored playroom for the
kids. There were lots of Little Tikes cars and big Legos and a plastic
house with a sliding board. There were scenes from Disney movies
like *Aladdin* and *The Lion King* on the wall. There was a television
and a VCR. There was stuff too for when the kids got a little older—
a pinball machine, a jukebox. There were small rocking chairs and
mattresses and knock-around couches.

There was also blood. A fair amount of it in drips on the floor. Another fair amount smeared on a wall.

Bile nestled in Myron's throat. He had seen blood many times in
his life, but it still left him queasy. Not so with Win. Win approached

the crimson stains with something akin to amusement on his face. He bent to get a better look. Then he stood back up.

"Look at the bright side," Win said. "Your temporary slot on the Dragons may become more permanent."

Chapter 4

There was no body. Just the blood.

Using Glad sandwich bags he found in the kitchen, Win collected a few samples. Ten minutes later they were back outside, the lock on the front door reengaged. A blue Oldsmobile Delta 88 drove past them. Two men sat in the front seat. Myron glanced at Win. Win barely nodded.

"A second pass," Myron said.

"Third," Win said. "I saw them when I first drove up."

"They're not exactly experts at this," Myron said.

"No," Win agreed. "But of course, they hadn't known the job would require expertise."

"Can you run the plates?"

Win nodded. "I'll also run Greg's ATM and credit card transactions," he said. He reached the Jag and unlocked it. "I'll contact you when I have something. It shouldn't take more than a few hours."

"You heading back to the office?"

"I'm going to Master Kwon's first," Win said.

Master Kwon was their tae kwon do instructor. Both of them were black belts—Myron a second degree, Win a sixth degree, one of the highest ranking Caucasians in the world. Win was the best martial artist Myron had ever seen. He studied several different arts including Brazilian jujitsu, animal kung fu, and Jeet Kun Do. Win the Contradiction. See Win and you think pampered, preppy pantywaist; in reality, he was a devastating fighter. See Win and you think normal, well-adjusted human being; in reality, he was anything but.

"What are you doing tonight?" Myron asked.

Win shrugged. "I'm not sure."

"I can get you a ticket to the game," Myron said.

Win said nothing.

"Do you want to go?"

"No."

Without another word, Win slipped behind the wheel of his Jag, started the engine, peeled out with nary a squeal. Myron stood and watched him speed away, puzzled by his friend's abruptness. But then again, to paraphrase one of the four questions of Passover: why should today be different than any other day?

He checked his watch. He still had a few hours before the big press conference. Enough time to get back to the office and tell Esperanza about his career shift. More than anyone else, his playing for the Dragons would affect her.

He took Route 4 to the George Washington Bridge. There was no waiting at the tolls. Proof there was a God. The Henry Hudson however was backed up. He swung off near Columbia Presbyterian Medical Center to get on Riverside Drive. The squeegee guys—the homeless men who "cleaned" your windshield with a mixture of equal parts grease, Tabasco sauce, and urine—were no longer at the light. Mayor Giuliani's doing, Myron guessed. They had been replaced by Hispanic men selling flowers and something that looked like construction paper. He asked once what it was and had gotten an answer back in Spanish. As much as Myron could translate, the paper smelled nice and spruced up any home. Maybe that was what Greg used as potpourri.

Riverside Drive was relatively quiet. Myron arrived at his Kinney lot on 46th Street and tossed Mario the keys. Mario did not park the Ford Taurus up front with the Rolls, the Mercedes, Win's Jag; in fact, he usually managed to find a cozy spot underneath what must have been a nesting ground for loose-stooled pigeons. Car discrimination. It was an ugly thing, but where were the support groups?

The Lock-Horne Securities building was on Park Avenue and 46th, perpendicular to the Helmsley building. High-rent district. The street bustled with the doings of big finance. Several stretch limos double-parked illegally in front of the building. The ugly modern sculpture that looked like someone's intestines stood pitifully in its usual place. Men and women in business attire sat on the steps, eating sandwiches too hurriedly, lost in their own thoughts, many talking to themselves, rehearsing for an important afternoon meeting or rehashing a morning mistake. People who worked in Manhattan learned how to be surrounded by others yet remain completely alone.

Myron entered the lobby and pressed the button for the elevator. He nodded to the three Lock-Horne Hostesses, known to everyone else as the Lock-Horne Geishas. They were all model/actress wannabes, hired to escort high rollers up to the offices of Lock-Horne Securities and look attractive while doing it. Win had brought the idea home after a trip to the Far East. Myron guessed this could be more blatantly sexist, but he wasn't sure how.

Esperanza Diaz, his valued associate, greeted him at the door. "Where the hell have you been?"

"We need to talk," he said.

"Later. You've got a million messages."

Esperanza wore a white blouse—an absolute killer look against her dark hair, dark eyes, and that dark skin that shimmered like moonlight on the Mediterranean. Esperanza had been spotted by a modeling scout when she was seventeen, but her career took a few weird turns and she ended up making it big in the world of professional wrestling. Yes, professional wrestling. She'd been known as Little Pocahontas, the brave Indian Princess, the jewel of the Fabulous Ladies of Wrestling (FLOW) organization. Her costume was a suede bikini, and she was always cast as the good guy in the morality play that was professional wrestling. She was young, petite, tight-bodied, gorgeous, and though of Latin origin, she was dark enough to pass for Native American. Racial backgrounds were irrelevant to FLOW. The real name of Mrs. Saddam Hussein, the evil harem girl in the black veil, was Shari Weinberg.

The phone rang. Esperanza picked it up. "MB SportsReps. Hold on a moment, he's right here." She flashed the eyes at him. "Perry McKinley. It's his third call today."

"What does he want?"

She shrugged. "Some people don't like dealing with underlings."

"You're not an underling."

She looked at him blankly. "You going to take it or not?"

Being a sports agent was—to use computer terminology—a multitasking environment with the capability of performing a variety of services with but a click of a button. It was more than simple negotiating. Agents were expected to be accountants, financial planners, real estate agents, hand-holders, personal shoppers, travel agents, family counselors, marriage counselors, chauffeurs, errand boys, parental liaisons, lackeys, butt-kissers, you name it. If you weren't willing to do all that for a client—to be what is known as a "full service agency"—the next guy would be.

The only way to compete was to have a team, and Myron felt he had assembled a small yet extremely effective one. Win, for example, handled all the finances for Myron's clients. He set up a special portfolio for each player, met with them at least five times a year, made sure they understood what their money was doing and why. Having Win gave Myron a big leg up on the competition. Win was a near-legend in the financial world. His reputation was impeccable (at least in the financial world) and his track record unmatched. He gave

Myron an instant "in," instant credibility in a business where credibility was a rare and heady concoction.

Myron was the JD. Win was the MBA. Esperanza was the all-purpose player, the unflappable chameleon who held it all together. It worked.

"We need to talk," he said again.

"So we'll talk," she said in a dismissing tone. "First take this call."

Myron entered his office. He overlooked Park Avenue in midtown. Great View. On one wall he had posters of Broadway musicals. On another there were movie stills from some of Myron's favorites: the Marx Brothers, Woody Allen, Alfred Hitchcock, and a potpourri of other classics. On a third wall were photographs of Myron's clients. The client wall was a bit sparser than Myron would have liked. He imagined what it would look like with an NBA first rounder in the middle.

Good, he decided. Very good.

He strapped on his headset.

"Hey, Perry."

"Jesus Christ, Myron, I've been trying to reach you all day."

"Good, Perry. And you."

"Hey, I don't mean to be impatient but this is important. You get anything on my boat?"

Perry McKinley was a golfer on the fringe, no pun intended. He was a pro. He made some money, but he wasn't a name anyone but big golf fans would recognize. Perry loved to sail and was in need of a new vessel.

"Yeah, I got something," Myron said.

"What company?"

"Prince."

Perry did not sound thrilled. "Their boats are just okay," he whined. "Nothing great."

"They'll let you trade in your old boat for a new one. You have to do five personal appearances."

"Five?"

"Yep."

"For a Prince eighteen-footer? That's too many."

"They originally wanted ten. But it's up to you."

Perry thought about it a moment. "Ah, shit, okay the deal. But first I want to make sure I like the boat. A full eighteen-footer, right?"

"That's what they said."

"Yeah, all right. Thanks, Myron. You're the best."

They hung up. Bartering—an important component in the agent's multitasking environment. No one ever paid for anything in this business. Favors were exchanged. Trading products for some form of endorsement. Want a free shirt? Wear it in public. Want a free car? Shake hands at a few car shows. The big stars could demand serious payments in exchange for their endorsements. The lesser-known athletes happily seized the freebies.

Myron stared at the pile of messages and shook his head. Playing for the Dragons and keeping MB SportsReps afloat—how the hell was he going to pull it off?

He buzzed Esperanza. "Come on in here please," he said.

"I'm in the middle—"

"Now."

Silence.

"Gosh," she said, "you're so macho."

"Give me a break, huh?"

"No, really, I'm very frightened. I better drop everything and immediately do your bidding."

Her phone fell. She sprinted in, feigning fear and breathlessness. "Fast enough?"

"Yes."

"So what is it?"

He told her. When he came to the part where he'd be playing for the Dragons, he was once again surprised to see no reaction. This was strange. First Win, now Esperanza. The two of them were his closest friends. They both lived for ridiculing him. Yet neither one of them had taken advantage of the obvious opening. Their silence on the subject of his "comeback" was a tad unnerving.

"Your clients aren't going to like this," she said.

"*Our* clients," he corrected.

She made a face. "Does it make you feel better to be patronizing?"

Myron ignored the comment. "We have to turn this into a positive," he said.

"How?"

"I'm not sure," he said slowly. He leaned back in his chair. "We can say that the publicity of all this will help them."

"How?"

"I can make new contacts," he said, the ideas coming to him even as he spoke. "I can get closer to sponsors, learn more about them. More people will hear about me and indirectly my clients."

Esperanza made a scoffing sound. "And you think that's going to fly?"

"Why not?"

"Because it's bullshit. 'Indirectly my clients.' Sounds like trickle-down economics."

She had a point. "What's the big deal really?" he asked, palms to the ceiling. "Basketball will only be a couple of hours a day. I'll be here the rest of the time. I'll have the cellular phone with me all the time. We just have to emphasize that I won't be there long."

Esperanza looked at him skeptically.

"What?" he asked.

She shook her head.

"No, I want to know. What?"

"Nothing," she said. She looked him straight in the eye, her hands resting on her lap. "What does the bitch say about all this?" she asked sweetly.

Her pet name for Jessica. "Will you please stop calling her that?"

She made a suit-yourself face, for once not arguing. There had been a time—long, long ago—when Jessica and Esperanza had at least tolerated each other. But then Jessica left, and Esperanza saw what it did to Myron. Some people held grudges. Esperanza internalized them. It didn't matter that Jessica had come back.

"So what does she think?" Esperanza asked again.

"About what?"

"About the prospects for peace in the Middle East," she snapped. "What do you think I mean? Your playing again."

"I don't know. We haven't had a chance to talk about it much. Why?"

Esperanza shook her head again. "We're going to need help in here," she said, closing the subject. "Someone to answer the phones, do some typing, that kind of thing."

"You have someone in mind?"

She nodded. "Cyndi."

Myron blanched. "Big Cyndi?"

"She could answer the phone, do some odd jobs. She's a good worker."

"I didn't even know she could talk," Myron said. Big Cyndi had been Esperanza's tag-team wrestling partner, fighting under the name of Big Chief Mama.

"She'll take orders. She'll do shit work. She's not ambitious."

Myron tried not to wince at the thought. "Isn't she still working at the strip joint as a bouncer?"

"It's not a strip joint. It's a leather bar."

"My mistake," Myron said.

"And she's a bartender now."

"Cyndi's been promoted?" Myron said.

"Yes."

"Well, I'd hate to sidetrack her burgeoning career by asking her to work here."

"Don't be an ass," Esperanza said. "She works there nights."

"What," Myron said, "Leather and Lust doesn't do a big lunch crowd?"

"I know Cyndi. She'll be perfect."

"She scares people," Myron said. "She scares me."

"She'll stay in the conference room. No one will see her."

"I don't know."

Esperanza rose smoothly. "Fine, you find somebody. I mean, you're the boss. You know best. Me, I'm just a pissant secretary. I wouldn't dare question how you handle *our* clients."

Myron shook his head. "Low blow," he said. He leaned forward, his elbows on his desk, his hands holding up his head. "All right," he said finally, releasing a deep breath. "We'll give her a try."

Myron waited. Esperanza stared back at him. After several seconds passed, she said, "Is this the part where I jump up and down and say thank you, thank you?"

"No, this is the part where I leave." He checked his watch. "I got to talk to Clip about those bloodstains before the press conference."

"Have fun." She headed for the door.

"Hold up," he called out. She turned and faced him. "Do you have class tonight?" Esperanza took night classes at NYU. Law school.

"No."

"You want to go to the game?" He cleared his throat. "You can, uh, bring Lucy, if you'd like."

Lucy was Esperanza's latest love. Before Lucy she had dated a man named Max. Her sexual preference seemed to vacillate. "We broke up," she said.

"Oh, I'm sorry," Myron said, not knowing what else to say. "When?"

"Last week."

"You didn't say anything."

"Maybe because it's none of your business."

He nodded. True enough. "Well, you can bring a new, uh, friend, if you'd like. Or you can go yourself. We're playing the Celtics."

"I'll pass," she said.

"You sure?"

She nodded again, left the room. Myron grabbed his jacket and headed back to the lot. Mario tossed him his keys without looking up. He took the Lincoln Tunnel and hopped onto Route 3. He passed a huge and fairly famous appliance and electronics store called Tops. The billboard featured a giant nose jutted out over Route 3. The caption: Tops Is Right Under Your Nose. Very lifelike. The only thing missing were the giant nose hairs. He was only a mile or so from the Meadlowlands when the car phone rang.

"I have some preliminaries," Win said.

"Go ahead."

"None of Greg Downing's accounts or credit cards have been accessed in the past five days."

"Nothing?"

"Nothing."

"Any cash withdrawals from his bank?"

"Not in the past five days."

"How about earlier? Maybe he grabbed out a lot of money before he vanished."

"It's being worked on. I don't know yet."

Myron took the Meadowlands exit. He considered what this all meant. So far, not much, but it wasn't really good news. The blood in the basement. No sign of Greg. No financial activity. It wasn't really promising. "Anything else?" Myron asked.

Win hesitated. "I may soon have an idea where dearest Greg had that drink with fair Carla."

"Where?"

"After the game," Win said. "I'll know more then."

Chapter 5

"Sports is folklore," Clip Arnstein told the room full of reporters. "What captures our imagination is not simply the winning and losing. It's the stories. The stories of perseverance. The stories of sheer will. The stories of hard work. The stories of heartbreak. The stories of miracles. The stories of triumph and tragedy. The stories of comebacks."

Clip looked down at Myron from the podium, his eyes properly moist, his smile his most grandfatherly. Myron cringed. He fought back an intense desire to duck under the conference table and hide.

After a proper pause Clip turned back to the front. The reporters were silent. An occasional flashbulb burst forth. Clip swallowed several times as though summoning some inner resolve he'd need to continue. His throat slid up and down. He raised his moist eyes to the audience.

A little hammy, Myron thought, but all in all a fine performance.

The press conference was more crowded than Myron would've thought. Not a free seat and many reporters standing. Must have been a slow news day. Clip took his time, regaining his seemingly lost composure. "A little over a decade ago, I drafted an exceptional young man, a player I believed was destined for greatnesss. He had a great jumper, a well-honed court sense, mental tenacity, and on top of all that was a fine human being. But the gods had other plans for that young man. We all know what happened to Myron Bolitar on that fateful night in Landover, Maryland. There is no reason to dredge up the past. But as I said when I opened this press conference, sports is folklore. Today the Dragons are giving that young man a chance to weave his own legend into the lush tapestry of sports. Today the Dragons are allowing that young man to try and recapture what was so cruelly snatched away from him all those years ago."

Myron started squirming. His cheeks flushed. His eyes darted about, seeking a safe haven and finding none. He settled for looking at Clip's face, as per the media's expectations. He zeroed in on a cheek mole, staring so hard his vision began to mercifully blur.

"It won't be easy, Myron," Clip said, turning now and addressing

Myron directly. Myron kept his vision locked on the mole; he couldn't meet the gaze. "No promises have been made to you. I don't know what happens from here. I don't know if this is the culmination of your story or the commencement of a brave new chapter. But those of us who love sports can't help but hope. It is in our nature. It is in the nature of all true combatants and fans." Clip's voice started to crack.

"This is reality," he went on. "I have to remind you of that, Myron, much as I'd rather not. On behalf of the New Jersey Dragons I welcome you, a man of class and courage, to the team. We wish you nothing but the best. We know that no matter what happens to you on the court, you will bring honor to the entire Dragon organization." He stopped, tightened his lips and managed a quick, "Thank you."

Clip held out a hand to Myron. Myron played his part. He stood to shake Clip's hand. Clip however had other ideas. He put his arms around Myron and pulled him toward him. The flashbulbs increased to the point of being a disco strobe. When Clip finally pulled back, he wiped his eyes with two fingers. Sheesh, the man put Pacino to shame. Clip held out an arm, ushering Myron to the podium.

"How does it feel to be back?" one reporter yelled out.

"Scary," Myron replied.

"Do you really think you have what it takes to play at this level?"

"No, not really."

The moment of honesty stopped them for a second. But only a second. Clip laughed and everyone else in the room followed suit. Figuring it was a joke. Myron didn't bother correcting them.

"Do you think you still have three-point shooting range?" another asked.

Myron nodded. "I have the shooting range," he said. "I'm just not sure I have the making range." A stolen joke but what the hey.

More laughs.

"Why the comeback so late, Myron? What convinced you to come back now?"

"The Psychic Friends Network."

Clip stood and warded off further questions with a raised hand. "Sorry, gang, that's it for now. Myron has to get suited up for tonight's game."

Myron followed Clip out. They hurried down the corridor and into Clip's office. Calvin was already there. Clip shut the door. Before he sat down Clip asked, "So what's the matter?"

Myron told him about the blood in the basement. Clip visibly blanched. Frosty's fingers tightened against the armrest.

"So what are you trying to say?" Clip snapped when he finished.
"Say?"

Clip gave an elaborate shrug. "I don't get it."

"There's nothing to get," Myron said. "Greg is missing. No one has seen him for five days. He hasn't used his ATM or credit card. And now there's blood in the basement."

"In his kids' playroom, right? That's what you said before. The kids' playroom."

Myron nodded.

Clip looked a question at Calvin then turned his palms to the sky. "So what the hell does that mean?"

"I'm not sure."

"It doesn't exactly add up to foul play, now does it?" Clip continued. "Think it through, Myron. If Greg were murdered, for example, where is his body? Did the killer or killers take it with them? And what do you think happened here? The killers—what?—surprised Greg? Alone? In his kids' playroom where, I guess, Greg was playing with his little dolly? Then what happened? They killed him down there and dragged him out of the house without leaving traces of blood anywhere but in the basement?" Clip spread his hands. "Does that make sense?"

The scenario had bothered Myron too. He sneaked a glance at Calvin. Calvin seemed deep in thought. Clip stood.

"For all we know," Clip went on, "one of Greg's kids cut himself playing down there."

"Hell of a cut," Myron said.

"Or a bloody nose. Christ, those things gush like mad. Could be nothing but a bloody nose."

Myron nodded. "Or maybe they were slaughtering chickens," he said. "Could be that too."

"I don't need sarcasm, Myron."

Myron waited a beat. He glanced at Calvin. Nothing. He glanced at Clip. Nada. "It's getting opaque in here again."

"Pardon?"

"You hired me to find Greg. I'm tracing down a major lead. Yet you don't want to hear it."

"If you mean I don't want to hear that perhaps Greg has met with foul play—"

"No, that's not what I mean. You're afraid of something and it's not just that Greg may have met with foul play. I'd like to know what."

Clip looked over at Calvin. Calvin nodded almost imperceptibly.

Clip sat back down. His fingertips drummed the desktop. The grand-father clock in the corner ticked an imitating echo. "Understand," Clip said, "that we have Greg's best interests at heart. We really do."

"Uh huh."

"You know anything about hostile takeovers?"

"I was alive in the eighties," Myron said. "In fact, someone re-cently remarked on what an eighties kinda guy I am."

"Well, I'm undergoing one now."

"I thought you were a majority owner."

Clip shook his head. "Forty percent. No one else owns more than fifteen percent. A couple of the minority shareholders have gotten to-gether and are trying to oust me." Clip made two fists and put them on his desk like paperweights. "They say I'm too much a basketball mind and not enough a business mind. I should only be handling players and the on-court affair. They vote in two days."

"So?"

"So right now the vote is very close. A scandal and I'm done."

Myron looked at both men and waited a beat. Then he said, "You want me to sit on this."

"No, no, of course not," Clip said quickly. "I'm not saying that at all. I just don't want the press going berserk over what might be noth-ing. I can't afford to have anything unsavory uncovered now."

"Unsavory?"

"Right."

"Like what?"

"Hell if I know," Clip said.

"But Greg might be dead."

"And if that's the case, a day or two isn't going to help—cold as that might sound. And if something did happen to Greg, there might be a reason."

"A reason?"

Clip threw up his hands. "Hell, I don't know. You lift up a corpse or even a man in hiding and worms start to crawl out. You know what I mean?"

"No," Myron said. But Clip went on.

"I don't need that, Myron. Not now. Not till after this vote."

"Then you are telling me to sit on this," Myron said.

"Not at all. We just don't want an unnecessary panic. If Greg is dead, we can't do him any good now anyway. If he's vanished, well, then you are his best hope to avoid media glare or to save him."

They were still not telling him everything but Myron decided not to press it just now. "Do you have any idea why someone would be watching Greg's house?"

Clip looked puzzled. "Someone is watching his house?"

"I think so, yes."

Clip looked over to Calvin. "Calvin?"

"No idea," Calvin said.

"I don't know either, Myron. Do you have any thoughts?"

"Not yet. One more question: did Greg have a girlfriend?"

Again Clip looked toward Calvin.

Calvin shrugged. "He played around a lot. But I don't think there was anyone special."

"Do you know any of the women he played around with?"

"Not by name. Some groupies, stuff like that."

"Why?" Clip asked. "You think he ran off with a broad?"

Myron shrugged and stood. "Guess I better get to the locker room. It's almost game time."

"Wait."

Myron stopped.

"Please, Myron, I know it sounds like I'm being cold, but I really do care about Greg. Very much. I want him found alive and well." Clip swallowed. The wrinkles in his skin looked more pronounced, like someone had just pinched them out a bit. His color was not good. "If you can honestly tell me that revealing what we know to the public is best, I'll go along with it. No matter what the costs. Think about it. I want to do what's best for Greg. I care about him very much. I care about both of you. You're both fine young men. I mean that. I owe you both a great deal."

Clip looked like he was about to cry. Myron wasn't sure what to make of all this. He decided to nod and say nothing. He opened the door and left.

As he approached the elevator Myron heard a familiar, husky voice say, "If it isn't the Comeback Kid?"

Myron looked over at Audrey Wilson. She was wearing her customary sports-reporter garb: dark blue blazer, black turtleneck, what they called "stone-washed" jeans. Her makeup was either light or nonexistent, her nails short and unpolished. The only splash of color could be found on her sneakers—bright aqua Chuck Taylor Cons. Her looks were completely unspectacular. There was nothing wrong with her features but nothing particularly right about them either. They were just there. Her straight black hair was cut short in a pageboy with bangs. "Do I detect the scent of cynicism?" he asked.

Audrey shrugged. "You don't really think I buy all this, do you?"
"Buy what?"
"Your sudden desire to"—she checked her notes—"weave your
own legend into the lush tapestry of sports." She looked up, shook
her head. "That Clip can sure talk some shit, huh?"
"I have to get dressed, Audrey."
"How about giving me the lowdown first?"
"The lowdown, Audrey? Gee, why not ask for a 'scoop'? I love it
when you reporters say that."
She smiled at that. It was a nice smile. Full and open. "Kinda de-
fensive, aren't we, Myron?"
"Me? Never."
"Then how about—to coin yet another cliché—a statement for the
press?"
Myron nodded, put his hand to his chest in dramatic fashion. "A
winner never quits, and a quitter never wins."
"Lombardi?"
"Felix Unger. It was on *The Odd Couple,* the one where Howard
Cosell guest starred."
He turned and walked toward the locker room. Audrey followed.
She was probably the top female sports reporter in the country. She
covered the Dragons for the East Coast's biggest newspaper. She had
her own radio show on WFAN in a coveted time slot with huge rat-
ings. She had a Sunday morning round-table talk show called *Talking Sports* on ESPN. And yet, like almost every other female in this
male-dominated profession, there was something tenuous about her
station, her career always a half-step from toppling over no matter
how big she became.
"How's Jessica?" Audrey asked.
"Good."
"I haven't spoken to her in a month," she said with a singsong
tone. "Maybe I should give her a call. Sit down and have a heart-to-
heart, you know."
"Gee," Myron said, "that won't be transparent."
"I'm trying to make this easier on you, Myron. There's something
strange going on here. You know I'm going to find out what it is.
Might as well just tell me."
"I really don't know what you're talking about."
"First Greg Downing leaves the team under mysterious circum-
stances—"
"What's mysterious about an ankle injury?"
"—then you, his old nemesis, takes his place after being out of

commission for the better part of eleven years. You don't find that strange?"

Great, Myron thought. On the job five minutes and already someone was voicing suspicion. Myron Bolitar, master of the undercover. They reached the door to the locker room.

"I gotta go, Audrey. We'll talk later."

"Count on it," she said. She smiled at him with a gentle mocking sweetness. "Good luck, Myron. Knock them dead."

He nodded, took a deep breath, and pushed open the locker-room door.

Show time.

Chapter 6

No one greeted Myron when he entered the locker room. No one broke stride. No one even looked at him. The room did not go quiet like something out of an old Western where the sheriff pushes open the creaking door and sashays into the saloon. Maybe that was the problem. Maybe the door needed to creak. Or maybe Myron had to work on his sashay.

His new teammates were sprawled about like socks in a college dorm. Three of them were draped over benches, semidressed and seminapping. Two were on the floor, a leg being held in the air by assistants, stretching quads and calves. A couple others were dribbling basketballs. Four were hobbling back to their lockers after getting taped. Almost all were chewing gum. Almost all were also listening to Walkmans, the tiny speakers jammed in their ears and blaring so loudly that they sounded like competing floor models at a stereo store.

Myron found his dressing area pretty easily. All the other lockers had bronze plaques with a player's name engraved on it. Myron's did not. It had a piece of white adhesive tape above it, the kind used to tape ankles, with the letters M. BOLITAR scrawled in black marker. It hardly inspired confidence or spoke commitment.

He glanced around for someone to talk to, but the Walkmans were the ideal room dividers. Everyone was in their own private space. Myron spotted Terry "TC" Collins, the team's famed whining superstar, sitting alone in a corner. TC was the media's newest poster boy for the spoiled athlete, the guy "ruining" the genteel world of sports "as we know it," whatever that meant. TC was a hell of a physical specimen. Six-ten, muscular, wiry. His cleanly shaven head glistened in the fluorescent light. Rumor had it TC was black though it was hard to see any trace of skin through the work of his tattoo artist. The obscure ink images blanketed almost all available somatic sites. Body piercing too appeared to be more of a lifestyle with TC than a hobby. The man looked like a nightmare version of Mr. Clean.

Myron caught TC's eye, smiled, and nodded a hello. TC glared daggers and turned away. Making chums already.

His uniform was hung where it should be. His name had already been sewn on the back in block letters. BOLITAR. He stared at it for a moment or two. Then he quickly snatched it off the hanger and put it on. Everything caused bouts of déjà vu. The feel of the crumbly cotton. The shoelacelike tie-string on his shorts. The slight elastic tug at the waist when he put them on. The slight tightness of the top as it went over his shoulders. The practiced hands tucking in the tail. The lacing up of his high-tops. It all caused pangs. It was getting harder to breathe. His eyes blinked something back. He sat and waited until the feeling went away.

Myron noticed very few of the guys wore jock straps anymore, preferring those tight, Lycra shorts. Myron stuck with old dependable. Mr. Old Fashioned. Then he strapped a contraption onto his leg that was loosely labeled a "knee brace." Felt more like a metal compressor. The last thing he put on was his warm-ups. The bottoms had dozens of snaps up and down the legs, so a player could dramatically rip them off when called to go into a game.

"Hey, kid, how's it going?"

Myron stood and shook hands with Kip Corovan, one of the team's assistant coaches. Kip wore a plaid jacket that was about three sizes too small. The sleeves inched up to the forearms. The gut jutted out with great defiance. He looked like a farmer at the semiannual square dance. "I'm doing fine, coach."

"Great, great. And call me Kip. Or Kipper. Most people call me Kipper. Sit down, relax."

"Okay." Kipper?

"Great, happy to have you with us." The Kipper pulled over a chair, turned it so the back faced Myron, and straddled it. His pants inseam didn't look happy with the move. "I'll be honest with you, Myron, okay? Donny wasn't thrilled about this. Nothing personal, you understand. Just Donny likes to pick his own players. He don't like interference from upstairs, you know what I'm saying?"

Myron nodded. Donny Walsh was the head coach.

"Great, good. Donny's a straight guy though. He remembers you from the old days, liked you a lot. But we got a team heading for the playoffs. With a bit of luck we can lock up home-court advantage throughout the playoffs. It took a while to get the ducks all in a row. It's a balance, you know. Got to keep the ducks on an even keel. Losing Greg really knocked the wind from our sails, but we finally got those ducks back up. Now you come along, see. Clip doesn't tell us why, but he insists we add you to the roster. Fine, Clip is the big chief, no question. But we worry about getting our ducks back sailing straight, you see?"

The mixing of metaphors was making Myron dizzy. "Sure. I don't want to cause any problems."

"I know that." He stood, put the chair back with a sweeping motion. "You're a good guy, Myron. Always were a straight arrow. We need that now. A team-comes-first kinda guy, am I right?"

Myron nodded. "A straight-sailing duck."

"Great, fine. See you out there. And don't worry. You're not going to get in unless it's a blowout." With that the Kipper hoisted his belt up over the gut and sauntered—almost sashayed—across the room.

Three minutes later, the Kipper shouted out, "Gather round the board, boys." No one paid any attention. He repeated this several times, tapping Walkman-entranced players on the shoulders, so that they would hear. It took a full ten minutes to get twelve professional athletes to move less than ten feet. Coach Donny Walsh strode in with great self-importance, took center stage, and began spilling out the tired clichés. This didn't mean he was a bad coach or anything. You play over a hundred games a season it's hard to come up with anything new.

The pep talk lasted a full two minutes. Some of the guys never bothered turning off their Walkmans. TC was busy taking off his jewelry, a task that took great concentration and a team of well-trained technicians. Another minute or two passed and then the locker-room door opened. Everyone removed their Walkmans and headed out. Myron realized they were heading for the court.

Game time.

Myron stood at the end of the line. He swallowed deeply. A cold rush swept through him. As he made his way up the ramp he heard a voice over the loudspeaker scream, "And nowwwwww, your New Jersey Dragons!" Music blared. The jog quickened into a full trot.

The ovation was thunderous. The players automatically split into two makeshift lines for the lay-up drill. Myron had done this a zillion times before, but for the first time he really thought about what he was doing. When you were a star or a starter, you warmed up casually, loosely, unhurriedly. There was no reason to press it. You had the whole game to show the crowd what you could do. The scrubs— something Myron had never been—handled the warm-ups in one of two ways. Some went all out, slamming reverse dunks, doing windmill moves. In a phrase: showing off. Myron had always found this behavior sort of desperate. Others hung around the superstars, feeding them the ball, playing the mock defender like a boxer with a sparring partner. Cool by association.

Myron got to the front of the lay-up line. Someone passed him the ball. When you're warming up, you are subconsciously convinced that all eyes in the arena are on you, though in point of fact, most people were settling in or chatting or getting food or checking out the crowd and those that were watching couldn't care less what you did. Myron took two dribbles and laid the ball against the glass and in. Sheesh, he thought. The game hadn't started yet and already he didn't know what to do.

Five minutes later the lay-up lines disintegrated and players began to free shoot. Myron glanced into the stands for Jessica. She was not hard to spot. It was like a beacon hit her, like she came forward and the rest of the crowd stepped back, like she was the Da Vinci and the rest of the faces were but a frame. Jessica smiled at him and he felt a warmth spread through him.

With something close to surprise, he realized that this would be the first time Jessica had seen him play in anything but pickup games. They'd met three weeks before Myron's injury. The thought made him pause. And remember. For a brief moment his mind dragged him back. Guilt and pain washed over him until a ball careened off the backboard and smacked him in the head. But the thought remained:

I owe Greg.

The buzzer sounded and the players moved to the bench. Coach Walsh blurted out a few more clichés and made sure each player knew whom they were covering. The players nodded, not listening. TC still glared. Game face, Myron hoped, but didn't really believe it. He also kept an eye on Leon White, Greg's roommate on the road and closest friend on the team. The huddle broke. The players from both sides approached the center circle, greeting one another with handshakes and hand slaps. Once out there, the players on both teams started pointing around, trying to figure out who was covering whom since no one had listened thirty seconds earlier. Coaches from both sides were up, yelling out the defensive assignments until the ball was mercifully tossed in the air.

Basketball is normally a game of momentum shifts, keeping things fairly close until the final minutes. Not tonight. The Dragons cruised. They led by twelve after one quarter, twenty points by halftime, twenty-six by the end of the third period. Myron started getting nervous. The lead was big enough for him to get in. He hadn't really counted on that. Part of him silently cheered on the Celtics, hoping they could stage enough of a comeback to keep his butt on the aluminum chair. But it was a no-go. With four minutes remaining the Dragons led by twenty-eight points. Coach Walsh shot a glance down the bench. Nine of the twelve players had already gotten in. Walsh whispered something to the Kipper. The Kipper nodded and walked down the bench, stopping in front of Myron. Myron could feel his heart beating in his chest.

"Coach is going to clear the bench," he said. "He wants to know if you want to go in."

"Whatever he wants," Myron replied, while sending out telepathic messages of no, no, no. But he couldn't tell them that. It wasn't in his nature. He had to play the good trooper, Mr. Team-First, Mr. Dive-On-The-Grenade-If-That's-What-The-Coach-Wants. He didn't know how else to do it.

A time-out was called. Walsh looked down the bench again. "Gordon! Reilly! You're in for Collins and Johnson!"

Myron let loose a breath. Then he got mad at himself for feeling such relief. What kind of competitor are you? he asked himself. What kind of a man wants to stay on the bench? Then the truth rose up and smacked him hard in the face:

He was *not* here to play basketball.

What the hell was he thinking? He was here to find Greg Downing. This was just undercover work, that's all. Like with the police. Just because a guy goes undercover and pretends he's a drug dealer doesn't make him a drug dealer. The same principle applied here. Just because Myron was pretending to be a basketball player didn't make him one.

The thought was hardly comforting.

Thirty seconds later, it started. And it filled Myron's chest with dread.

One voice triggered it. One beer-infested voice rising clearly above all others. One voice that was just deep enough, just different enough, to separate it from the usual cacophony of fandom. "Hey, Walsh," the voice cried out. "Why don't you put in Bolitar?"

Myron felt his stomach plummet. He knew what was coming next. He had seen it happen before, though never to him. He wanted to sink into the floor.

"Yeah!" another voice crowed. "Let's see the new guy!"

More shouts of agreement.

It was happening. The crowd was getting behind the underdog, but not in a good way. Not in a positive way. In the most blatantly patronizing and mocking way possible. Be-Nice-To-The-Scrub time. We've won the game. We want a few laughs now.

A few more calls for Myron and then . . . the chant. It started low but built. And built. "We want Myron! We want Myron!" Myron tried not to slouch. He pretended not to hear it, feigning intense concentration on what was happening on the court, hoping his cheeks weren't reddening. The chant grew louder and faster, eventually disintegrating into one word, repeated over and over, mixed with laughter:

"Myron! Myron! Myron!"

He had to defuse it. There was only one way. He checked the clock. Still three minutes to go. He had to go in. He knew that wouldn't be the end of it, but it would at least quiet the crowd temporarily. He looked down the bench. The Kipper looked back. Myron nodded. The Kipper leaned over to Coach Walsh and whispered something. Walsh did not stand up. He simply shouted, "Bolitar. In for Cameron."

Myron swallowed and rose to his feet. The crowd erupted in sarcasm. He headed for the scorer's table, ripping off his sweats. His legs felt stiff and cramped. He pointed to the scorer, the scorer nodded and sounded the buzzer. Myron stepped on the court. He pointed at Cameron. Cameron jogged off. "Kraven," he said. The name of the man Myron would defend.

"Now reporting for Bob Cameron," the loudspeaker began. "Number 34. Myron Bolitar!"

The crowd went absolutely wild. Hoots, whistles, screams, laughs. Some might think they were wishing him well, but that was not really the case. They were wishing him well the same way you wish a circus clown well. They were looking for pratfalls and darn gone-it, Bolitar was their man!

Myron stepped on the court. This was, he suddenly realized, his NBA debut.

He touched the ball five times before the game ended. Each time it was met with cheer/jeers. He shot only once, from just inside the three point line. He almost didn't want to, knowing the crowd would react no matter what happened, but some things are just too automatic. There was no conscious thought. The ball went in with a happy swish. By now there were only thirty seconds left and thankfully most everyone had had enough and were heading to their cars. The sarcastic applause was minimal. But for those brief seconds when Myron caught the ball, when his fingertips found the groove, when he bent his elbow and cradled the ball half an inch above both palm and forehead, when the arm smoothed into a straight line, when the wrist flowed into a front curl, when the fingertips danced along the ball's surface and created the ideal backspin, Myron was alone. His eyes were focused on the rim, only the rim, never glancing at the ball as it arched its way toward the cylinder. For those few seconds there was only Myron and the rim and the basketball and it all felt very right.

The mood in the locker room was far more animated after the game. Myron managed to meet all of the players except TC and Greg's roommate Leon White, the one man he wanted to get close to most. Figures. He couldn't push it either; that would just backfire. Tomorrow maybe. He'd try again.

He stripped down. The knee began to tighten up, as though somebody had pulled all the tendons too taut. He slapped on an ice pack and fastened it with a stretch wrap. He limped to the showers, dried off, and was just finishing dressing when he realized TC was standing over him.

Myron looked up. TC had his various pierce-jewelry in place. Ear, of course. Three in one, four in the other. One in his nose. He wore black leather pants and a black cut-off mesh tank top, giving one an excellent view of the ring on his left nipple and the one in the belly button. Myron couldn't make out what the tattoos were. They just looked like swirls. TC wore sunglasses now, the wraparound kind.

"Your jeweler must send you a hell of a Christmas card," Myron said.

TC replied by sticking out his tongue and revealing another ring near the tip. Myron almost gagged. TC looked pleased by his reaction.

"You new, right?" TC said.

"Right." Myron held out his hand. "Myron Bolitar."

TC ignored the hand. "You gots to get thumped."

"Excuse me?"

"Thumped. You the new guy. You gots to get thumped."

Several other players started chuckling.

"Thumped?" Myron repeated.

"Yeah. You the new guy, right?"

"Right."

"Then you gots to get thumped."

More chuckling.

"Right," Myron said. "Thumped."

"There you go." TC nodded, snapping his fingers, pointed at Myron, left.

Myron finished dressing. Thumped?

Jessica was waiting for him outside the locker-room door. She smiled as he approached, and he smiled back, feeling goofy. She hugged him and gave him a brief kiss. He smelled her hair. Ambrosia.

"Ah," a voice said. "Now ain't this just too sweet?"

It was Audrey Wilson.

"Don't talk to her," Myron said. "She's the Antichrist."

"Too late," Audrey said. She put her hand through Jessica's arm. "Jess and I are going out now to have a few drinks, talk over old times, that kind of thing."

"God, you are shameless." He turned to Jessica. "Don't tell her anything."

"I don't know anything."

"Good point," Myron said. "So where are we going?"

"*We* are going nowhere," Jessica said. She made a motion behind her with her thumb. Win was leaning against the wall, completely still and at ease. "He said you'd be busy."

"Oh." Myron looked over at Win. Win nodded. Myron excused himself and made his way over.

Without preamble, Win said, "The last cash transaction Greg made was at an ATM machine at eleven oh three P.M. the night he vanished."

"Where?"

"Manhattan. A Chemical Bank near Eighteenth Street on the West Side."

"It makes sense," Myron said. "Greg gets a call at nine eighteen P.M. from Carla. Carla tells him to meet her in the back booth. So he drives himself to the city and picks up cash before he sees her."

Win looked at him with flat eyes. "Thank you for that analysis of the obvious."

"It's a gift really."

"Yes, I know," Win said. "Moving right along, there are eight saloons within a four block radius of this particular ATM. I limited my search to those. Of the eight only two have what one might term a 'back booth.' The others had tables or dining facilities sans booths in the rear. Here are the names."

Myron had long since gotten past asking how Win did it. "You want me to drive?"

"I can't go," Win said.

"Why not?"

"I'm going away for a few days."

"When?"

"I leave from Newark airport in an hour," Win said.

"This is sudden."

Win didn't bother responding. The two men headed out the players' entrance. Five kids ran up to Myron and asked for his autograph. Myron obliged. One kid who looked to be around ten years old took back the paper, squinted at Myron's scrawl, and said, "Who the hell is he?"

Another kid said, "Some scrub."

"Hey!" Win snapped. "That's Mr. Scrub to you."

Myron looked at him. "Thanks."

Win made an it's-nothing gesture.

The first kid looked at Win. "You anybody?"

"I'm Dwight D. Eisenhower," Win replied.

"Who?"

Win spread his hands. "Our blessed youth." He walked away then without saying another word. Win was not big on good-byes. Myron reached his car. When he put the key in the door, he felt a slap on the back. It was TC. He pointed at Myron with a finger holding more jewelry than a Gabor-family reunion. "Remember," TC said.

Myron nodded. "Thumped."

"Exacto."

Then he, too, was gone.

Chapter 7

Myron arrived at MacDougal's Pub, the first bar on Win's list. The back booth was empty so he grabbed it. He sat there for a moment, hoping a psychic force would tell him if this was the place where Greg had met up with Carla. He felt nothing—positive or negative. Maybe he should hold a séance.

The waitress came over slowly, as if the effort of crossing the floor was synonymous with wading through deep snow and she should be rewarded for it. Myron warmed her up with one of his patented smiles. The Christian Slater model—friendly yet devilish. Not to be mistaken for the Jack Nicholson model which was friendly yet devilish.

"Hi," he said.

She put down a Rolling Rock cardboard coaster. "What can I get you?" she asked, trying to toss up a friendly tone and falling way short. You rarely find a friendly barmaid in Manhattan, except for those born-again waitresses at chains like TGI Friday's or Bennigan's where they tell you their name and that they'll be your "server" like you might mistake them for something else, like your "legal consultant" or "medical advisor."

"Got any Yoo-Hoo?" Myron asked.

"Any what?"

"Never mind. How about a beer?"

She gave him flat eyes. "What kind?"

Subtlety was not going to work here. "Do you like basketball?" he asked her.

Shrug.

"Do you know who Greg Downing is?"

Nod.

"He told me about this place," Myron said. "Greg said he was here the other night."

Blink.

"Did you work last Saturday night?"

Nod.

"Same station? I mean, this booth?"

Quicker nod. Getting impatient.

"Did you see him?"

"No. I got tables. Michelob okay?"

Myron looked at his watch, faked shock. "Whoops, look at the time. I gotta go." He gave her two dollars. "Thanks for your time."

The next bar on the list was called the Swiss Chalet. Not even close. A dive. The wallpaper was supposed to trick you into believing that the place was wood paneled; the effect may have worked better had the wallpaper not been peeling in so many spots. The fireplace had a flickering, Christmas-light log in it, hardly giving the place the desired ski-lodge warmth. For some reason there was one of those disco mirrored balls in the middle of the bar. No dance floor. No lights. Just the disco mirrored ball—another staple of authentic Swiss chalets, Myron surmised. The place had the stale smell of spilled beer mixed with just a hint of what might have been vomit, the kind of smell only certain bars or frat houses held, the kind where the odor had seeped into the walls like rodents that ended up dying and rotting.

The jukebox blared "Little Red Corvette" by Prince. Or was it by the Artist Formerly Known As Prince? Wasn't that what he called himself now? But of course when "Little Red Corvette" had been released he had been Prince. So which was it? Myron tried to reconcile this crucial dilemma, but it began to confuse him like one of those time paradoxes in the *Back to the Future* movies so he gave up.

The place was pretty empty. A guy with a Houston Astros baseball cap and bushy mustache was the sole patron seated at the bar. There was a man and woman seminecking at a table in the center of the room—the most conspicuous table in the place, as a matter of fact. No one seemed to mind. Another male patron skulked around the back like he was in the adult movie area at his local video store.

Again Myron took the back booth. Again he struck up a conversation with a far more animated waitress. When he reached the part about Greg Downing telling him about the Swiss Chalet, she said, "Yeah, no kidding? I only seen him in here once."

Bingo.

"Would that have been Saturday night?"

She scrunched up her face in thought.

"Hey, Joe," the waitress shouted to the bartender. "Downing was in here Saturday night, right?"

"Who the fuck wants to know?" Joe shouted back from his spot behind the bar. He looked like a weasel with mousy hair. Weasel and mouse. Nice combination.

"This guy and me, we was just talking."

Joe Weasel squinted with beady, ferret eyes. The eyes widened. "Hey, you're the new guy, right? On the Dragons? I saw you on the news. With the dorky name."

"Myron Bolitar," Myron said.

"Yeah, right, Myron. That's it. You guys gonna start hanging out here?"

"I don't know."

"We get a pretty exclusive celebrity clientele," Joe said, wiping the bar with what looked like a gas station rag. "You know who was in here once? Cousin Brucie. The disc jockey. Real regular guy, you know."

"Sorry I missed that," Myron said.

"Yeah, well we've had other celebs, right, Bone?"

The guy with the Astros hat and bushy mustache pepped up and nodded. "Like that guy who looked like Soupy Sales. Remember him?"

"Right. Celebrities."

"Except that wasn't really Soupy Sales. Just someone who looked like him."

"Same difference."

Myron said, "Do you know Carla?"

"Carla?"

"The girl Greg was with."

"That her name? No, never got a chance to meet her. Didn't meet Greg either. He just kinda ducked in, cognito-like. We didn't bother them." He sort of puffed out his chest like he was about to salute. "At the Swiss Chalet, we protect our celebrities." He pointed at Myron with the dishrag. "You tell the other guys that, okay?"

"Will do," Myron said.

"Fact, we weren't even sure it was Greg Downing at first."

"Like with Soupy Sales," Bone added.

"Right, like that. Except this was really him."

"Guy looked like Soupy though. Great actor, that Soupy."

"And what a nickname."

"Talent all the way round," Bone agreed.

Myron said, "Had he ever been in here before?"

"The guy who looked liked Soupy?"

"Moron," Joe said, snapping the rag at Bone. "Why the fuck would he want to know about that? He's talking about Greg Downing."

"How the fuck was I supposed to know? I look like I work for one of those psychic networks or something?"

"Fellas," Myron tried.

Joe held up a hand. "Sorry, Myron. Believe me, this don't normally happen here at the Swiss Chalet. We all get along, right, Bone?"

Bone spread his arms. "Who's not getting along?"

"My point exactly. And no, Myron, Greg isn't one of our regulars. That was his first time here."

"Same with Cousin Brucie," Bone added. "He only came in that one time."

"Right. But Cousin Brucie liked the place, I could tell."

"He ordered a second drink. That shoulda told you something."

"Right you are. Two drinks. Coulda just had one and left. Course, they were only Diet Cokes."

Myron said, "How about Carla?"

"Who?"

"The woman Greg was with."

"What about her?"

"Had she been here before?"

"I never seen her here before. Bone?"

Bone shook his head. "Nope. I woulda remembered."

"What makes you say that?"

Without hesitation, Joe said, "Serious hooters."

Bone cupped his hands and stuck them in front of his chest. "Major Charlies."

"Not that she was good looking or anything."

"Not at all," Bone agreed. "Kinda old for a young guy."

"How old?" Myron asked.

"Older than Greg Downing, that's for sure. I'd say late forties. Bone?"

Bone nodded. "But a first-rate set of ta-tas."

"Humongous."

"Mammoth."

"Yeah, I think I got that," Myron interrupted. "Anything else?"

They looked puzzled.

"Eye color?" Myron tried.

Joe blinked, looked at Bone. "Did she have eyes?"

"Damn if I know."

"Hair color?" Myron said.

"Brown," Joe said. "Light brown."

"Black," Bone said.

"Maybe he's right," Joe said.

"No, maybe it was on the lighter side."

"But I'm telling you, Myron. That was some rack. Major guns."

"Guns of Navarone," Bone agreed.

"Did she and Greg leave together?"

Joe looked at Bone. Bone shrugged. "I think so," Joe said.

"Do you know what time?"

Joe shook his head.

"Bones, you know?" Myron tried.

The bill of the Astros hat jerked toward Myron like a string had been pulled. "Not Bones, dammit!" he shrieked. "Bone! No S at the end. Bone! B-O-N-E! No S! And what the fuck do I look like, Big Ben?"

Joe snapped the dishrag again. "Don't insult a celebrity, moron."

"Celebrity? Shit, Joe, he's just a scrub. Not like he's Soupy or something. He's a nobody, a zero." Bone turned to Myron. The hostility was completely gone now. "No offense, Myron."

"Why would I take offense?"

"Say," Joe said, "you got a photograph? We can put your picture on the wall. You could autograph it to your pals at the Swiss Chalet. We should start like a celebrity wall, you know?"

"Sorry," Myron said. "I don't have one on me."

"Can you send us one? Autographed, I mean. Or bring it next time you come."

"Er, next time."

Myron continued to question them but learned nothing more except Soupy Sales's birthday. He left and headed up the block. He passed a Chinese restaurant with dead ducks hung in the window. Duck carcasses, the ideal appetite whetter. Maybe Burger King should hang slaughtered cows in the window. Really draw the kids in.

He tried putting the pieces together a bit. Carla calls Greg on the phone and tells him to meet her at the Swiss Chalet. Why? Why there of all places? Did they not want to be seen? Why not? And who the hell is Carla anyway? How does all this fit into Greg's vanishing act? And what about the blood in the basement? Did they go back to Greg's house or did Greg go home alone? Was Carla the girl he lived with? And if so, why meet here?

Myron was so preoccupied he didn't spot the man until he almost bumped into him. Of course calling him a man might be a bit of an understatement. More like a brick wall doubling as a human being. He stood in Myron's way. He wore one of those pectoral-displaying ribbed T-shirts under an unbuttoned flower-patterned semiblouse. A gold horn dangled between his near-cleavage. Muscle-head. Myron tried to pass him on the left. The brick wall blocked his path. Myron tried to pass him on the right. The brick wall blocked his path. Myron went back and forth one more time. Brick Wall followed suit.

"Say," Myron said, "you know the cha-cha?"

The brick wall showed about as much reaction as one might expect from a brick wall. Then again it wasn't one of Myron's better quips. The man was truly enormous, the size of your average lunar eclipse. Myron heard footsteps. Another man, this one on the large size but at least of the human variety, came up behind Myron. The second man wore fatigue camouflage pants, a popular new urban fashion trend.

"Where's Greg?" Camouflage Pants asked.

Myron feigned startled. "What? Oh, I didn't see you."

"Huh?"

"In those pants," Myron said. "You just blended into the background."

Camouflage didn't like that. "Where's Greg?"

"Greg?" Snappy retort.

"Yeah. Where is he?"

"Who?"

"Greg."

"Greg who?"

"You trying to be funny?"

"What, you think this is funny?"

Camouflage looked over at Brick Wall. Brick Wall remained completely silent. Myron knew that there was a very real possibility of a physical altercation. He also knew he was good at such things. He also knew—or at least figured—that these two goons were probably good too. Despite Bruce Lee movies, one man defeating two or more quality opponents was nearly impossible. Experienced fighters were not stupid. They worked as a team. They never rushed one at a time.

"So," Myron said. "You guys want to catch a beer? Chat this through."

Camouflage made a scoffing noise. "We look like guys who like to chat?"

Myron motioned to Brick Wall. "He does."

There were three ways to get out of a situation like this unharmed. One was to run, which was always a good option. Problem was, his two adversaries were close enough yet spaced far enough to tackle

and/or slow him down. Too risky. Second option: your opponents underestimate you. You act scared and cower and then whammo, you
surprise them. Unlikely for Myron. Goons rarely underestimate a
guy six-four, two-twenty. Third option: you strike first and hard. By
doing this you increase the likelihood of putting one out of commission before the other one can react. This action however required a
delicate balance. Until someone strikes, you really cannot say for
sure that a physical altercation could not be avoided altogether. But
if you wait for someone to strike, this option becomes null and void.
Win liked option three. Then again Win liked option three even if
there was only one opponent.

Myron never got the chance to make a selection. Brick Wall
slammed a fist into the small of Myron's back. Myron sensed the
blow coming. He shifted enough to avoid both the kidney and serious damage. At the same time he spun and delivered an elbow strike
to Brick Wall's nose. There was a satisfying, crunching noise like a
fist closing over a bird's nest.

The victory was short-lived. As Myron had feared, these guys
knew what they were doing. Camouflage Pants struck at the same
time, connecting where his comrade had failed. Pain erupted in Myron's kidney. His knees buckled but he fought it off. He doubled over
toward Brick Wall and threw a back kick, his foot snapping out like
a piston. His lack of balance threw off his aim. The blow landed on
Camouflage's thigh. It didn't do much damage but it was powerful
enough to push him away. Brick Wall was starting to recover. He
groped blindly and found Myron's hair. He grabbed and pulled up.
Myron pinned the hand with one of his own, digging his fingernails
into the sensitive pressure points between the joints. Brick Wall
screamed. Camouflage Pants was back. He punched Myron straight
in the stomach. It hurt. A lot. Myron knew he was in trouble. He went
down to one knee and bounced up, a palm strike at the ready. It connected with Brick Wall's groin. Brick Wall's eyes bulged. He
dropped like somebody had pulled a stool out from under him. Camouflage Pants connected with a solid shot to the side of Myron's
head. Numbness flowed into Myron's skull. Another blow landed.
Myron's eyes began to lose focus. He tried to stand up but his legs
wouldn't let him. He felt a kick land on a rib. The world began to
spin.

"Hey! Hey, what you doing? Hey, you!"

"Stop it! What the fuck!"

In his haze Myron recognized the voices. Joe and Bone from the
bar. Myron took the opportunity to scramble away on all fours. There

was no need. Camouflage Pants had already helped Brick Wall to his feet. Both men ran.

Joe and Bone quickly came over and looked down at Myron.

"You okay?" Joe asked.

Myron nodded.

"You won't forget about sending us that autographed picture, will you? Cousin Brucie never sent one."

"I'll send you two," Myron said.

Chapter 8

He convinced Joe and Bone not to call the cops. They didn't take much convincing. Most people do not like activities that involve law enforcement. They helped Myron into a taxi. The driver wore a turban and listened to country music. Multiculturalism. Myron spit out Jessica's Soho address and collapsed into the ripped cushions. The driver wasn't interested in conversation. Good.

Myron mentally checked over his body. Nothing broken. The ribs would be bruised at worst. Nothing he couldn't play through. The head was another matter. Tylenol with codeine would help tonight, then he could move down to Advil or something in the morning. There was nothing much you could do for head trauma but give it time and control the pain.

Jessica met him at the door in her bathrobe. He felt, as he often did around her, a little short of breath. She skipped admonishments, drew a bath, helped him undress, crawled in behind him. The water felt good against his skin. He leaned back on her as she wrapped washcloths around his head. He let loose a deep, totally content breath.

"When did you go to medical school?" he asked.

From behind him Jessica kissed his cheek. "Feeling better?"

"Yes, Doctor. Much better."

"You want to tell me about it?"

He did. She listened in silence, her fingertips gently massaging his temples. Her touch was soothing. Myron imagined there were better things in life than being in this tub leaning back against the woman he loved, but for the life of him he couldn't think of any. The pain began to dull and slacken.

"So who do you think they were?" she asked.

"No idea," Myron said. "I imagine they're hired goons."

"And they wanted to know where Greg was?"

"Seems so."

"If two goons like that were looking for me," she said, "I might disappear too."

The thought had crossed Myron's mind too. "Yes."

"So what's your next step?"

He smiled and closed his eyes. "What? No lectures? No telling me it's too dangerous?"

"Too cliché," she said. "Besides, there's something else here."

"What do you mean?"

"Something about all this you're not telling me."

"I—"

She put a finger over his lips. "Just tell me what you plan on doing next."

He settled back down. Scary how easily she read him. "I have to start talking to people."

"Like?"

"His agent. His roommate, a guy named Leon White. Emily."

"Emily. That would be your old college sweetheart?"

"Uh huh," Myron said. Quick subject change before she started reading him again. "How was your evening with Audrey?"

"Fine. We mostly talked about you."

"What about me?"

Jessica began to stroke his chest. The touch slowly drifted away from being merely soothing. Her fingertips caressed his chest with a feather touch. Gently. Too gently. She was strumming him like Perlman on a violin.

"Uh, Jess."

She shushed him. Her voice was soft. "Your ass," she said.

"My ass?"

"Yep, that's what we talked about." To emphasize the point her hand cupped a cheek. "Even Audrey had to admit it was edible, running up and down the court like that."

"I have a mind too," Myron said. "A brain. Feelings."

She lowered her mouth toward his ear. When her lips touched the lobe, he felt a jolt. "Who cares?"

"Uh, Jess . . ."

"Shhh," she said as her other hand slid down his chest. "I'm the doctor here, remember?"

Chapter 9

The ringing phone jabbed at the base of nerves in the back of his skull. Myron's eyes blinked open. Sunlight knifed through the slit in the curtain. He checked next to him in the bed—first with his hands, then with his eyes. Jessica wasn't there. The phone continued to blare. Myron reached for it.

"Hello."

"So this is where you are."

He closed his eyes. The ache in his head multiplied tenfold. "Hi, Mom."

"You don't sleep in your home anymore?"

His home was the basement of his parents' house, the same house in which he'd been raised. More and more he was spending his nights at Jessica's. It was probably a good thing. He was thirty-two; he was fairly normal; he had plenty of money. There was no reason to still be living with Mommy and Daddy.

"How's your trip?" he asked. His mother and father were on some tour of Europe. One of those bus tours that hit twelve cities in four days.

"You think I called at the Vienna Hilton's long distant rates to chitchat about our itinerary?"

"Guess not."

"You know how much it cost to call from a hotel in Vienna? With all their surcharges and taxes and everything?"

"A lot, I'm sure."

"I have the rates right here. I'll tell you exactly. Hold on. Al, what did I do with those rates?"

"Mom, it's not important."

"I had it a second ago. Al?"

"Why don't you tell me when you get home?" Myron suggested. "It'll give me something to look forward to."

"Save the fresh remarks for your friends, okay? You know very well why I'm calling."

"I don't, Mom."

"Fine, then I'll tell you. One of the other people on this tour—the

Smeltmans, very nice couple. He's in the jewelry business. Marvin, his name is. I think. They have a shop in Montclair. We used to drive by it all the time when you were a kid. It's on Bloomfield Avenue, near that movie theater. Remember?"

"Uh huh." He had no idea what she was talking about but it was easier.

"So the Smeltmans talked to their son on the phone last night. He called them, Myron. He had their itinerary and everything. Just called his parents to make sure they were having a nice time, that kind of thing."

"Uh huh." Mom was in decompensation mode. There was no way to stop it. She could go in a heartbeat from the modern, intelligent woman he knew her to be to something out of summer stock *Fiddler on the Roof.* Right now she was Golda heading toward Yenta.

"Anyway the Smeltmans brag how they're on the same trip with Myron Bolitar's parents. Big deal, right? Who knows you anymore? You haven't played in years. But the Smeltmans are big basketball fans. Go figure. Their son used to watch you play or something, I don't know. So anyway the son—I think his name is Herb or Herbie or Ralph, something like that—he tells them you're playing professional basketball. That the Dragons signed you. He says you're making a comeback or something, what do I know? Your father is so embarrassed. I mean, complete strangers are talking about it and your own parents don't even know. We thought the Smeltmans were crazy."

"It's not what you think," Myron said.

"What's not what I think?" she countered. "You shoot around in the driveway a little. Okay, no big deal. But I don't understand. You never even mentioned you were playing again."

"I'm not."

"Don't lie to me. You scored two points last night. Your father called Sports Phone. You know what it cost to call Sports Phone from here?"

"Mom, it's no big deal."

"Listen to me, Myron, you know your father. The man pretends it doesn't mean anything. He loves you no matter what, you know that. But he hasn't stopped smiling since he heard. He wants to fly home right now."

"Please don't."

"Don't," she repeated, exasperated. "You tell him, Myron. The man is loo-loo, you know that. A crazy person. So tell me what's going on."

"It's a long story, Mom."

"But it's true? You're playing again?"

"Only temporarily."

"What does that mean, 'only temporarily'?"

Jessica's Call Waiting clicked in. "Mom, I gotta go. I'm sorry I didn't tell you earlier."

"What? That's it?"

"I'll tell you more later."

Surprisingly she backed off. "You be careful with your knee."

"I will."

He changed over to the other line. It was Esperanza. She didn't bother with hello.

"It's not Greg's blood," she said.

"What?"

"The blood you found in the basement," she said. "It's AB positive. Greg's blood type is O negative."

Myron had not expected to hear this. He tried to reconcile it in his head. "Maybe Clip was right. Maybe it was one of Greg's kids."

"Impossible," she said.

"Why?"

"Didn't you take basic biology in high school?"

"Eighth grade. But I was too busy staring at Mary Ann Palmiero. What?"

"AB is rare. In order for a kid to have it, his parents have to be A and B or it's impossible. In other words, if Greg is O, then his kids can't be AB."

"Maybe it's a friend's," Myron tried. "Maybe one of the kids had a friend over."

"Sure," Esperanza said. "That's probably it. The kids have some friends over. One of them bleeds all over the place and nobody cleans it up. Oh and then by a strange coincidence Greg vanishes."

Myron threaded the phone cord through his fingers like his hand was a loom. "Not Greg's blood," he repeated. "Now what?"

Esperanza didn't bother responding.

"How the hell am I supposed to investigate something like this without getting anyone suspicious?" he went on. "I have to ask people questions, right? They're going to want to know why."

"I feel very sorry for you," Esperanza said in a tone that made clear she was anything but. "I got to get to the office. You coming in?"

"Maybe this afternoon. I'm going to see Emily this morning."

"Is that the old girlfriend Win told me about?"

"Yes," Myron said.

"Don't take any chances. Put on a condom now." She hung up.

Not Greg's blood. Myron didn't get it. As he drifted off to sleep last night he had worked up a neat little theory that went something like this: the hoods were searching for Greg. Maybe they had roughed him up a bit, made him bleed a little. Just to show him they meant serious business. Greg had reacted by running away.

It all sort of fit. It explained the blood in the basement. It explained why Greg suddenly took off. Yep, all a very nice and neat equation: One beating plus one death threat equaled a man on the run.

Problem was, the blood in the basement was not Greg's. Kinda put a damper on the theory. If Greg had been beaten in the basement, then it would have been his blood. Greg would have bled his own blood, not someone else's. In fact, it was very difficult to bleed someone else's blood. Myron shook his head. He needed a shower. A bit more deducing like this and the slaughtered-chicken theory would begin to pick up steam.

Myron soaped himself up, then turned his back to the shower and let the water cascade over his shoulders and down his chest. He toweled off and got dressed. Jessica was on the word processor in the other room. He had learned never to disturb her when the keyboard was clacking. He left a quick note and slipped out. He grabbed the 6 train up to midtown and walked to the Kinney lot on 46th Street. Mario tossed him the keys without glancing up from his paper. He picked up the FDR north at 62nd Street and took it to the Harlem River Drive. There was a slow down for right lane construction, but he made it to the George Washington Bridge in pretty good time. He took Route 4 through a place called Paramus, which was actually a giant mall pretending to also be a township. He veered to the right and passed the Nabisco building on Route 208. He was hoping for a factory Ritz-whiff, but today he got nothing.

As he pulled up to Emily's house, déjà vu swatted him in the back of the head like a father's warning blow. He had been here before, of course, during college breaks in their courting days. The house was brick and modern and fairly huge. It sat in a well-groomed cul-de-sac. The backyard was fenced. He remembered that there was a swimming pool in the back. He remembered that there was also a gazebo. He remembered making love with Emily in the gazebo, their clothes wrapped around ankles, the humidity coating their skin with a thin layer of sweat. The sweet bird of youth.

He parked the car, pulled the key out of the ignition, and just sat there. He had not seen Emily in more than ten years. Much had happened in the ensuing years, but he still feared her reaction to seeing him. The mental image of Emily opening the door, screaming "Bastard," then slamming it in his face was one of the reasons he hadn't worked up the nerve to call first.

He looked out the car window. There was no movement on the street. Then again there were only ten houses. He debated his approach and came up with nothing. He checked his watch, but the time didn't register in his head. He sighed. One thing was for sure: he couldn't sit here all day. This was a nice neighborhood, the kind where someone would spot him and call the police. Time to get a move on. He opened the door and stepped out. The development was at least fifteen years old but it still looked new. All the yards were just a little too sparse. Not enough trees and shrubbery yet. The grass looked like a guy with a bad hair transplant.

Myron walked up the brick path. He checked his palms. They were wet. He rang the doorbell. Part of him flashed back to earlier visits, his mind playing along with the long, still-familiar chime of the bell. The door opened. It was Emily.

"Well, well, well," she said. Myron could not tell if the tone was one of surprise or sarcasm. Emily had changed. She looked a little thinner, a bit more toned. Her face was less fleshy too, accentuating the cheekbones. Her hair was cut shorter and styled. "If it isn't the good one I let get away."

"Hi, Emily." Mr. Big Opening.

"Here to propose?" she asked.

"Been there, done that."

"But you didn't mean it, Myron. I wanted sincerity back then."

"And now?"

"Now I realize sincerity is overrated." She flashed him a smile.

"You look good, Emily," he said. Get Myron on a roll and it's one good line after another.

"So do you," she said. "But I'm not going to help you."

"Help me what?"

She made a face. "Come on in."

He followed her inside. The house was full of skylights and cathedral ceilings and white painted walls. Airy. The front foyer was done in some expensive tile. She led Myron to the living room. He sat on a white couch. The floors were beechwood. It was exactly the same as it was ten years ago. Either they had gotten the exact same couches again or their house guests had been exceptionally well behaved. There wasn't a spot on them. The only mess was a pile of newspapers in the corner. Mostly daily tabloids, from the looks of it. A *New York Post* front-page headline read SCANDAL! in huge 72 point print. Specific.

An old dog traipsed into the room on rigid legs. It looked like he was trying to wag his tail, but the result was a pitiful sway. He managed to lick Myron's hand with a dry tongue.

"Look at that," Emily said. "Benny remembers you."

Myron stiffened. "This is Benny?"

She nodded.

Emily's family had bought the overactive puppy for her younger brother Todd when Myron and Emily had first started dating. Myron was there when they brought the puppy home from the breeder. Little Benny had stumbled around with blinking eyes and then peed on this very floor. No one cared. Benny quickly got used to people. He greeted everyone by jumping on them, believing in a way only a dog could that no one would ever do him harm. Benny was not jumping now. He looked very old. He looked a brief step away from death. A sudden sadness swept through Myron.

"You looked good last night," Emily said. "It was nice seeing you back on the court."

"Thanks." The quips never stop.

"Are you thirsty?" she asked. "I could make you some lemonade. Like in a Tennessee Williams play. Lemonade for the gentleman caller, except I doubt Amanda Wingfield used a Crystal Light mix." Before he could answer she disappeared around the corner. Benny looked up at Myron, struggling to see through milky cataracts. Myron scratched the dog's ear. The tail picked up a bit of velocity. Myron smiled sadly at Benny. Benny moved closer, as if he understood how Myron felt and appreciated the sentiment. Emily returned with two glasses of lemonade.

"Here," she said. She handed him a glass and sat down.

"Thank you." Myron took a sip.

"So what's next on your agenda, Myron?"

"Next?"

"Another comeback?"

"I don't understand."

Emily gave him the smile again. "First you replace Greg on the court," she said. "Maybe next you'll want to replace him in the bedroom."

Myron almost gagged on his lemonade, but he managed to smother the sound. Going for the shock. Classic Emily. "Not funny," he said.

"I'm just having a little fun," she said.

"Yes, I know."

She put her elbow on the back of the couch and propped up her head with her hand. "I see you're dating Jessica Culver," she said.

"Yep."

"I like her books."

"I'll tell her."

"But we both know the truth."

"What's that?"

She leaned forward now and took a slow sip from her glass. "Sex with her isn't as good as it was with me."

More classic Emily. "You're sure about that?" he said.

"Very sure," she replied. "I'm not being immodest. I'm sure your Ms. Culver is quite skilled. But with me it was new. It was discovery. It was impossibly hot. Neither of us can ever recapture that rapture with anyone else. It'd be impossible. It would be like going back in time."

"I don't compare," Myron said.

With a smile and a tilt of the head, she said, "Bullshit."

"You don't want me to compare."

The smile was unfazed. "Come, come now, Myron. You're not going to give me that spiritual crap, are you? You're not going to tell me it's better because you share a deep and beautiful relationship and thus the sex is beyond something physical? That line would be so unbecoming on you."

Myron did not respond. He didn't know what to say and he didn't feel very comfortable with the conversation. "What did you mean before?" he asked, shifting gears. "When you said you wouldn't help me."

"Exactly what I meant."

"What won't you help with?"

Again the smile. "Was I ever stupid, Myron?"

"Never," he said.

"Do you really think I believed that comeback story? Or the one about Greg being"—she made quote marks in the air—" 'in seclusion' for an ankle injury? Your visit here just confirms my suspicion."

"What suspicion?"

"Greg is missing. You're trying to find him."

"What makes you think Greg is missing?"

"Please, Myron, don't play games with me. You owe me that much at least."

He nodded slowly. "Do you know where he is?"

"No. But I hope the bastard is dead and rotting in a hole."

"Stop mincing words," Myron said. "Tell me how you really feel."

The smile was sadder this time. Myron felt a pang. Greg and Emily had fallen in love. They'd been married. They had two children. What had torn that all apart? Was it something recent . . . or was it something in their pasts, something tainted from the beginning? Myron felt his throat go dry.

"When was the last time you saw Greg?" he asked.

"A month ago," she said.

"Where?"

"In divorce court."

"Are you two on speaking terms?"

"I meant what I said before. About him being dead and rotting."

"I'll take that as a no."

Emily nodded a suit-yourself.

"If he was hiding, do you have any idea where?"

"Nope."

"No summer house? No place he liked to get away?"

"Nope."

"Do you know if Greg had a girlfriend?"

"Nope. But I would pity the poor woman."

"Have you ever heard the name Carla?"

She hesitated. Her index finger tapped her knee, an old gesture so familiar to him it almost hurt to watch. "Wasn't there a Carla who lived on my floor at Duke?" she asked. "Yes, Carla Anderson. Sophomore year, wasn't it? Pretty girl."

"Anything more recent?"

"No." She sat up, crossed her legs. "How's Win?"

"The same."

"One of life's constants," she said. "He loves you, you know. I wonder if he's a latent homosexual."

"Two men can love each other and not be gay," Myron said.

She arched an eyebrow. "You really think so?"

He was letting her get to him. Bad mistake. "Are you aware that Greg was going to sign an endorsement deal?" he asked her.

That got her attention. "Are you serious?"

"Yes."

"A big one?"

"Huge from my understanding," Myron replied. "With Forte."

Emily's hands tightened. She would have made fists had her nails not been so long. "Son of a bitch."

"What?"

"He waited until the divorce had been finalized and I got squat. Then he signs the deal. That son of a bitch."

"What do you mean, squat? Greg was still wealthy."

She shook her head. "His agent lost it all. Or so he claimed in court."

"Martin Felder?"

"Yep. Didn't have a penny to his name. Son of a bitch."

"But Greg still works with Felder. Why would he stay with a guy who lost his money?"

"I don't know, Myron." Her voice was clipped and annoyed. "Perhaps the son of a bitch was lying. It wouldn't be the first time."

Myron waited. Emily looked at him. Tears welled in her eyes but she bit them back down. She stood and walked to the other side of the room. Her back was now to him. She looked out the sliding glass doors into the fenced-in yard. The pool was covered with a tarp; random sticks and leaves clung to the aqua. Two children appeared. A boy of about ten chased a girl who looked to be eight. They were both laughing with faces wide and open and a little rosy from either cold or exertion. The boy stopped when he saw his mother. He gave her a big smile and wave. Emily raised her hand and gave a small wave back. The children ran on. Emily crossed her arms like she was hugging herself.

"He wants to take them away from me," she said in a remarkably calm voice. "He'll do anything to get them."

"Like?"

"Like the sleaziest things you can imagine."

"How sleazy?"

"None of your goddamn business." She stopped. She still had her back to him. Myron could see her shoulders quake. "Get out," she said.

"Emily . . ."

"You want to help him, Myron."

"I want to find him. There's a difference."

She shook her head. "You don't owe him," she said. "I know you think you do. It's your way. I saw the guilt in your face back then, and I could still see it the second I opened the front door. It's over, Myron. It had nothing to do with what happened to us. He never found out."

"Is that supposed to make me feel better?" he asked.

She spun toward him. "It's not supposed to make you feel better," she snapped. "It's not about you. I'm the one who married him. I'm the one who betrayed him. I can't believe you're still beating yourself up about it."

Myron swallowed. "He visited me in the hospital. After I got injured. He sat and talked with me for hours."

"And that makes him a swell guy?"

"We shouldn't have done it."

"Grow up," she said. "It was more than ten years ago. Gone and forgotten."

Silence.

After some time had passed, Myron looked up at her. "Could you really lose your kids?" he asked.

"Yes."

"How far would you go to keep them?"

"As far as I had to."

"Would you kill to keep them?" Myron asked.

"Yes." No hesitation.

"Did you?"

"No."

"Do you have any idea why some goons would be looking for Greg?"

"No."

"You didn't hire them?"

"If I did," she said, "I wouldn't tell you. But if these 'goons' want to hurt Greg, I'll do all I can to help them locate him."

Myron put down the lemonade. "I guess I better get going."

She showed him to the door. Before she opened it, she put a hand on his arm. Her touch burned right through the material. "It's okay," she said gently. "Let it go. Greg never found out."

Myron nodded.

She took a deep breath and smiled again. Her voice returned to its normal tone. "It was good to see you again, Myron."

"Same here," he said.

"Come back again, will you?" She was trying so hard to be casual. Myron knew it was just an act, one he had seen before. "Perhaps we can have a quick fling for old times' sake. Couldn't hurt, right?"

One last grasp at the shock. Myron pulled away. "That's what we said last time," he said. "And it still hurts."

Chapter 10

"It was the night before they got married," Myron began. He was back at his office. Esperanza sat in front of him. Her eyes were on him, but he didn't know that. He stared at the ceiling, his fingers laced and resting on his chest. He had his chair tilted far back. "Do you want the details?"

"Only if you want to tell me," Esperanza said.

He told her. He told her how Emily had called him. He told her how she came to his room. He told her that they'd both had too much to drink. He said that last one as a sort of trial balloon, but a quick glance at Esperanza blew that particular old balloon out of the sky. She interrupted with one question.

"How long after the draft did all this take place?"

Myron smiled at the ceiling. She was so damned perceptive. There was no reason to answer.

"I assume," Esperanza continued, "that this little tryst occurred sometime between the pro draft and your injury."

"You assume correctly."

"Ah," she said with a small nod. "So let me see if I got the true picture now. It's your senior year of college. Your team won the NCAA finals—a point for you. You end up losing Emily and she ends up engaged to Greg—a point for him. The draft comes. Greg is the seventh overall pick; you are the eighth—a point for Greg."

Myron closed his eyes and nodded. "You're wondering if I was trying to even the score."

"Not wondering," Esperanza corrected. "The answer is obvious."

"You're not helping."

"You want help, go to a shrink," she said. "You want the truth, come to me."

She was right. He took his hands off his chest. Keeping the fingers laced, he placed them behind his head. He put his feet on the desk.

"Did she cheat on you with him?" she asked.

"No."

"You're sure?"

"Yes. They met after we broke up."

"Too bad," she said. "It would have given you a nice out."

"Yeah. Pity."

"So this is why you feel obligated to Greg? Because you slept with his fiancée?"

"That's a big part of it, but there's more to it than that."

"Like?"

"It's going to sound corny, but there's always been a bond between us."

"A bond?"

Myron's line of vision traveled from the ceiling to his movie-still wall. Woody Allen and Diane Keaton were enjoying a Manhattan moment in *Annie Hall.* Bogie and Bergman leaned on Sam's piano back in the days when Paris had been theirs. "Greg and I were once-in-a-lifetime competitors," he said. "And there is a special bond between competitors. Kinda like Magic Johnson and Larry Bird. You become defined by one another. It was like that with Greg and me. It was unspoken, but we both knew the bond was there."

He stopped. Esperanza waited in silence. "When I hurt my knee," Myron continued, "Greg visited me in the hospital. He showed up the very next day. I woke up from some pain medication and there he was. Sitting with Win. And I instantly understood. Win must have understood too, otherwise he would have thrown him out."

Esperanza nodded.

"Greg stayed around too. He helped with rehab. That's what I mean by a bond. He was devastated by the news because when I got hurt, it was like a part of him was gone too. He tried to tell me why it meant so much to him, but he couldn't put it into words. It didn't matter. I knew. He just had to be there."

"And you hurt your knee how long after you'd slept with his new bride?"

"About a month."

"Did seeing him all the time help or hurt?"

"Yes."

She said nothing.

"Do you understand now?" he asked. "Do you see why I have to pursue this? You're probably right. Sleeping with Emily was probably nothing more than payback for not getting drafted before Greg. Just another stupid battle. But what kind of way was that for a marriage to start? I owe Greg Downing. It's that simple."

"No," she said. "It's not that simple."

"Why not?"

"Because too much of your past is resurfacing. First Jessica—"

"Don't start with that."

"I'm not," she said calmly. Her voice was rarely calm when it came to Jessica. "I'm just stating a fact. Jessica crushed you when she left. You never got over her."

"But she's back now."

"Yes."

"So what's your point?"

"Basketball also crushed you when it left. You never got over it."

"Sure I did."

She shook her head. "First you spent three years trying every possible remedy to fix your knee."

"I just tried to get better," he interjected. "Nothing wrong with that, is there?"

"Nothing. But you were a pain in the ass. You pushed Jessica away. I'm not forgiving her for what she did to you. You didn't ask for that. But you played a part in her leaving."

"Why are you bringing this all up?"

She shook her head. "You're the one who's bringing it all up. Your entire past. Jessica and now basketball. You want us to watch you go through all this again, but we won't."

"Go through what?"

But she didn't answer. Instead she asked, "Do you want to know why I didn't go see you play last night?"

He nodded, still not facing her. His cheeks felt flush and hot.

"Because with Jessica, at least there's a *chance* you won't get hurt again. There's a chance the witch smartened up. But with basketball, there is no chance. You can't come back."

"I can handle it," he said, hearing those words yet again.

She said nothing.

Myron stared off. He barely heard the phone ring. Neither one of them moved to answer it. "You think I should drop this?" he asked.

"Yes. I agree with Emily. She's the one who betrayed him. You were just a handy tool. If what happened somehow poisoned their relationship, it was her doing. It was her decision. You don't owe Greg Downing a thing."

"Even if what you're saying is true," he said, "that bond is still there."

"Bullshit," Esperanza said. "That's just a load of pedantic, macho bullshit. You're just proving my point. There's no bond anymore, if there ever was one. Basketball hasn't been a part of your life for a decade. The only reason you think the bond is still there is because you're playing again."

There was a loud pounding on the door. The frame shook and almost gave way. Myron startled upright. "Who's manning the phones?" he asked.

Esperanza smiled.

"Oh no."

"Come in," Esperanza said.

The door opened. Myron's feet fell to the floor. Though he had seen her many times before, his jaw still dropped open. Big Cyndi ducked in. She was mammoth. Six-five and over three hundred pounds. Cyndi wore a white T-shirt with the sleeves ripped off at the biceps. Her arms were the envy of Hulk Hogan. Her makeup was more garish than it had been in the ring. Her hair was purple spikes; her mascara was also purple though a darker shade than her hair. Her lipstick was a red smear. Cyndi looked like something out of Rocky Horror Picture Show. She was the single most frightening sight Myron had ever seen.

"Hi, Cyndi," Myron tried.

Cyndi growled. She held up her middle finger, turned, stepped back through the door, closed it.

"What the—"

"She's telling you to pick up line one," Esperanza said.

"Cyndi's answering phones?"

"Yes."

"She doesn't talk!"

"In person. On the phone she's very good."

"Jesus Christ."

"Pick up the phone and stop whining."

Myron did so. It was Lisa, their contact at New York Bell. Most people think that only the police can get phone records. Not true. Almost every private eye in the country has a contact at their local phone company. It's just a matter of simply paying someone off. A month's phone record can cost you anywhere from one thousand to five thousand dollars. Myron and Win had met Lisa during their days with the feds. She didn't take money, but they always took care of her in some way or another. "I got what Win wanted," Lisa said.

"Go ahead."

"The call at nine eighteen P.M. came from a public phone located in a diner near Dyckman Street and Broadway," she said.

"Isn't that up near Two Hundredth Street?"

"I think so. You want the phone number?"

Carla had called Greg from a diner on 200th Street? Weirder and weirder. "If you have it."

She gave it to him. "Hope that helps."

"It does, Lisa. Thanks." He held up the paper to Esperanza. "Lookie what I got," he said. "A real live clue."

Chapter 11

To be fair, the Parkview Diner lived up to its name. You did indeed have a view of Lieutenant William Tighe Park across the street; it was smaller than the average backyard with shrubs so high you really couldn't see the landscaped garden within. A wire-mesh fence enclosed the grounds. Hung on the fence in several places were signs that read in big, bold letters: DO NOT FEED THE RATS. No joke. In smaller print the warning was repeated in Spanish: *No Des Comida a Las Ratas.* The signs had been placed there by a group calling itself the Quality of Life Zone. Myron shook his head. Only in New York would this be a problem—people who could not contain themselves from the seductive lure of feeding vermin. Myron glanced again at the sign, then the diner. Rats. Quite the appetite-enhancer.

He crossed the street. Two levels above the Parkview Diner, a dog squeezed his head through the grates of a fire escape and barked at passing pedestrians. The Parkview's green overhang was ripped in several spots. The letters were faded to the point of unintelligibility, and the support pole was bent so far that Myron had to duck to get to the door. There was a poster of a gyro sandwich in the window. Today's specials, according to a blackboard in the same window, included eggplant parmigiana and chicken à la king. The soup was beef consommé. There were permits from the City of New York Department of Buildings stuck on the door like car-inspection decals.

Myron entered and was immediately greeted by the familiar yet nonspecific smell of a Manhattan diner. Fat was in the air. Taking a deep breath felt as if it would clog an artery. A waitress with hair bleached to the point of straw offered him a table. Myron asked her for the manager. Using her pencil she pointed over her shoulder at a man behind the counter.

"That's Hector," she said. "He owns the place."

Myron thanked her and grabbed a soda-fountain stool at the counter. He debated spinning himself in the seat and decided the act might be viewed as immature. Two stools to his right, an unshaven, perhaps homeless man with black Thom McAn sneakers and a tattered overcoat smiled and nodded. Myron nodded and smiled back.

The man went back to his coffee. He raised his shoulders and huddled into the drink as though he suspected someone might try to swipe it in mid-sip.

Myron picked up a vinyl menu with cracked binding. He opened it but didn't really read it. There were a lot of worn index cards jammed into protective plastic cases announcing various specials. Worn was an apt description of the Parkview Diner, but it didn't fairly convey the overall impression. There was something welcoming and even clean about this place. The counter gleamed. So did the utensils and the silver milkshake maker and the soda fountain. Most patrons read a newspaper or gabbed with one another as if they were eating at home. They knew their waitress's name, and you could bet your last dollar she didn't introduce herself and tell them she was going to be their server when they first sat down.

Hector the owner was busy at the grill. Almost two P.M. It wasn't the height of the lunch hour, but business was still pretty brisk. He barked out some orders in Spanish, his eyes never leaving the food. Then he turned around with a polite smile, wiped his hands on a rag, and asked Myron if he could help him. Myron asked if he had a pay phone.

"No, sir, I'm sorry," Hector answered. The Hispanic accent was there, but Hector had worked on it. "There's one on the street corner. On the left."

Myron looked at the number Lisa had given him. He read it out loud. Hector did several things at the same time. He flipped burgers, folded over an omelette, checked the french fries. His eyes were everywhere—the cash register, the clientele at both the tables and the counter, the kitchen to his left.

"Oh that," Hector said. "It's in the back. In the kitchen."

"The kitchen?"

"Yes, sir." Still polite.

"A pay phone in the kitchen?"

"Yes, sir," Hector said. He was on the short side, thin under his white apron and polyester black pants. His nose had been broken several times. His forearms looked like steel cords. "It's for my staff."

"Don't you have a business phone?"

"Of course we do." His voice spiked up a bit now, as if the question was an insult. "We do a big takeout and delivery business here. Lots of people order lunch from us. We have a fax machine too. But I don't want my staff tying up the lines, you know? You get a busy signal, you give your business to someone else, yes? So I put a pay phone in the back."

"I see." An idea came to Myron. "Are you telling me customers never use it?"

"Well, sir, if a customer truly insists, I would never refuse him." The practiced politeness of a good businessman. "The customer must come first at the Parkview. Always."

"Has a customer ever insisted?"

"No, sir. I don't think any customers even know we have it."

"Can you tell me who was using the pay phone at nine eighteen P.M. last Saturday?"

That question got his attention. "Excuse me?" Myron started to repeat the question but Hector interrupted him. "Why would you want to know that?"

"My name is Bernie Worley," Myron said. "I'm a product supervising agent with AT&T." *A product what?* "Somebody is trying to cheat us, sir, and we are not happy about it."

"Cheat you?"

"A Y511."

"A what?"

"A Y511," Myron repeated. You start tossing the bull, your best bet is to just keep tossing. "It's an electronic monitoring device built in Hong Kong. It's new on the market, but we're onto it. Sold on the streets. Somebody used one on your phone at nine eighteen P.M. on March eighteenth of this year. They dialed Kuala Lumpur and spoke for nearly twelve minutes. The total cost of the call is twenty-three dollars and eighty-two cents, but the fine for using a Y511 will be at least seven hundred dollars with the potential for up to one year in prison. Plus we'll have to remove the phone."

Hector's face became a mask of pure panic. "What?" Myron wasn't thrilled with what he was doing—scaring an honest, hardworking immigrant like this—but he knew that the fear of government or big business would work in a situation like this. Hector turned around and shouted something in Spanish to a teenager who looked like him. The teenager took over the grill. "I don't understand this, Mr. Worley."

"It's a public phone, sir. You just admitted to a product supervising agent that you used the public phones for private use; that is, for your employees only and denying public access. This violates our own code, section one twenty-four B. I wouldn't report it normally, but when you add in the use of a Y511—"

"But I didn't use a Y511!"

"We don't know that, sir." Myron was playing Mr. Bureaucrat to the hilt; nothing made a person feel more impotent. There is no darker pit than the blank stare of a bureaucrat. "The phone is on your premises," Myron continued in a bored singsong voice. "You just explained to me that the phone was only used by your employees—"

"Exactly!" Hector leaped. "By my employees! Not me!"

"But you own this establishment. You are responsible." Myron looked around with his best, bored expression—the one he learned while waiting on line at the Division of Motor Vehicles. "We'll also have to check out the status of all your employees. Maybe we can find the culprit that way."

Hector's eyes grew big. Myron knew this would hit home. There wasn't a restaurant in Manhattan that didn't employ at least one illegal alien. Hector's jowls slackened. "All this," he said, "because someone used a pay phone?"

"What someone did, sir, was use an illegal electronic device known as a Y511. What you did, sir, was refuse to cooperate with the product supervising agent investigating this serious matter."

"Refuse to cooperate?" Hector was grasping at the possible life preserver Myron had offered up. "No, sir, not me. I want to cooperate. I want to very much."

Myron shook his head. "I don't think you do."

Hector bit down and set his polite meter on extra-strength now. "No, sir," he said. "I want to help very much. I want to cooperate with the phone company. Tell me what I can do to help. Please."

Myron sighed, gave it a few seconds. The diner bustled. The cash register dinged while the guy who looked homeless with the Thom McAn sneakers picked out greasy coins from a dirty hand. The griddle sizzled. The aroma from the various foods battled each other for dominance with none winning outright. Hector's face grew more and more anxious. Enough, Myron thought. "For starters, you can tell me who was using the pay phone at nine eighteen P.M. last Saturday."

Hector held up a finger imploring patience. He shouted something in Spanish to the woman (Mrs. Hector maybe?) working the cash register. The woman shouted something back. She closed the drawer and walked toward them. As she drew closer, Myron noticed that Hector was suddenly giving him an odd look. Was he starting to see through Myron's rather husky load of bull-dooky? Perhaps. But Myron looked back at him steadily and Hector quickly backed down. He might be suspicious, but not suspicious enough to risk offending the all-powerful bureaucrat by questioning his authority.

Hector whispered something to the woman. She urgently whispered back. He made an understanding "ah" noise. Then he faced Myron and shook his head.

"It figures," he said.

"What?"

"It was Sally."

"Who?"

"At least I think it was Sally. My wife saw her on the phone around then. But she said she was only on for a minute or two."

"Does Sally have a last name?"

"Guerro."

"Is she here now?"

Hector shook his head. "She hasn't been here since Saturday night. That's what I mean by, figures. She gets me in trouble and then she runs out."

"Has she called in sick?"

"No, sir. She just up and left."

"You got an address on her?" Myron asked.

"I think so, let me see." He pulled out a big carton that read "Snapple Peach Iced Tea" on the side. Behind him, the griddle hissed when fresh pancake batter touched down upon the hot metal. The files in the box were neat and color coded. Hector pulled one out and opened it. He shuffled through the sheets, found the one he was looking for, and frowned.

"What?" Myron prompted.

"Sally never gave us an address," Hector said.

"How about a phone number?"

"No." He looked up, remembering something. "She said she didn't have a phone. That's why she was using the one in the back so much."

"Could you tell me what Ms. Guerro looked like?" Myron tried.

Hector suddenly looked uncomfortable. He glanced at his wife and cleared his throat. "Uh, she had brown hair," he began. "Maybe five-four, five-five. Average height, I guess."

"Anything else?"

"Brown eyes, I think." He stopped. "That's about it."

"How old would you say she was?"

Hector checked the file again. "According to this, she was forty-five. That sounds about right."

"How long has she worked here?" he asked.

"Two months."

Myron nodded, rubbed his chin vigorously. "It sounds like an operative who goes by the name Carla."

"Carla?"

"A notorious phone fraud," Myron continued. "We've been after her for a while." He glanced left, then right. Trying to look conspiratorial. "Have you ever heard her use the name Carla or hear someone call her Carla?"

Hector looked at his wife. She shook her head. "No, never."

"Did she have any visitors? Any friends?"

Again Hector checked with his wife. Again the head shook. "No, none that we ever saw. She kept to herself most of the time."

Myron decided to push a little further and confirm what he already knew. If Hector balked at this stage, so what? Nothing ventured, nothing gained. He leaned forward; Hector and his wife did likewise. "This may sound insensitive," Myron whispered, "but was this woman large chested?"

Both nods were immediate. "Very large," Hector said.

Suspicion confirmed.

He asked a few more questions, but any useful information had already been culled from these waters. Before leaving, he told them that they were in the clear and could continue to violate code section 124B without fear. Hector almost kissed his hand. Myron felt like a louse. *What did you do today, Batman? Well, Robin, I started off by terrorizing a hard-working immigrant's livelihood with a bunch of lies. Holy Cow, Batman, you're the coolest!* Myron shook his head. What to do for an encore—throw empty beer bottles at the dog on the fire escape?

Myron exited the Parkview Diner. He debated going to the park across the street, but suppose he became overcome by a lustful need to feed rats? No, he couldn't risk it. He'd have to stay away. He began to head to the Dyckman Street subway station when a voice stopped him.

"You looking for Sally?"

Myron turned. It was the homeless-looking man with the Thom McAns from the diner. He sat on the pavement, his back leaning against the brick building. He had an empty plastic coffee cup in his hand. Panhandling.

"You know her?" Myron asked.

"She and I . . ." He winked and crossed his fingers. "We met because of that damn phone, you know."

"Really."

Using the wall for support the man stood. His facial hair was whiteish, not full enough to be a beard yet past the stage of a Miami

Vice wanna-be. His long hair was black as coal. "Sally was using my phone all the time. It pissed me off."

"Your phone?"

"The pay phone in the back," he said licking his lips. "It's right by the back door. I hang out in the back alley a lot so I can hear it, you know? It's kind of like my business phone." Myron couldn't guess his age. His face was boyish but leathered—from the passing years or hard living, Myron couldn't say. His grin was missing a couple of prominent teeth, reminding Myron of that beloved Christmas classic "All I Want for Christmas Is My Two Front Teeth." Such a nice song really. No toys, no Sega Genesis video game. The kid just wanted teeth. So selfless really.

"I used to have my own cellular," the man continued. "Two of them, as a matter of fact. But they got stolen. And the damn things are so unreliable, especially around the high buildings. And anyone can listen in with the right equipment. Me, I need to keep what I do secret, you see. Spies are everywhere. And they also give you brain tumors. The electrons or something. Brain tumors the size of beach balls."

Myron kept his face blank. "Uh huh." Speaking of tossing the bull.

"So anyway Sally started using it, too. It pissed me off, you know? I mean, I'm a businessman. I got important calls coming in. I can't have the line tied up. Am I right?"

"As rain," Myron said.

"See, I'm a Hollywood screenwriter." He stuck out his hand. "Norman Lowenstein."

Myron tried to remember the fake name he used with Hector. "Bernie Worley."

"Nice to meet you, Bernie."

"Do you know where Sally Guerro lives?"

"Sure. We used to be . . ." Norman Lowenstein crossed his fingers.

"So I heard. Could you tell me where she lives?"

Norman Lowenstein pursed his lips and used his pointer finger to scratch a spot near his throat. "I'm not real good with addresses and stuff," he said. "But I could take you there."

Myron wondered how big of a waste of time this was going to be. "Would you mind?"

"Sure, no problem. Let's go."

"Which way?"

"The A train," Norman said. "Down to One Hundred Twenty-fifth Street."

They walked toward the subway.

"You go to the movies much, Bernie?" Norman asked.

"Much as the next guy, I guess."

"Let me tell you something about movie-making," he began, growing more animated. "It's not all glamour and glitz. It's a dog-eat-dog business like no other, making dreams for people. All the back-stabbing, all that money, all that fame and attention . . . it makes people act funny, you know? I got this screenplay with Paramount right now. They're talking to Willis about it. Bruce Willis. He's really interested."

"Good luck with it," Myron said.

Norman beamed. "Thanks, Bernie, that's real nice of you. I mean it. Real nice. I'd like to tell you what my flick is about, but well, my hands are tied. You know how it is. Hollywood and all the theft out there. The studio wants it kept hush-hush."

"I understand," Myron said.

"I trust you, Bernie, it's not that. But the studios insist. I can't blame them really. They got to protect their interests, right?"

"Right."

"It's an action-adventure flick, that much I can tell you. But with heart too, you know? Not just a shoot-em-up. Harrison Ford wanted in, but he's too old. I guess Willis is okay. He's not my first choice, but what can you do?"

"Uh huh."

One Twenty-fifth Street was not the nicest stop in the city. It was safe enough during the day, Myron surmised, but the fact that he was now carrying a gun made him feel a tad more secure. Myron did not like "packing heat" and rarely did so. It was not that Myron was particularly squeamish; it had more to do with comfort. The shoulder holster dug into his armpit and made it itch like he was wearing a tweed condom. But after last night's soiree with Camouflage Pants and Brick Wall, it would be foolhardy to walk around unarmed.

"Which way?" Myron asked.

"Downtown."

They headed south on Broadway. Norman regaled him with tales of Hollywood. The ins and outs. Myron nodded and kept walking. The farther south they headed, the better the area became. They passed the familiar iron gates of Columbia University, then turned left. "It's right up here," Norman said. "Toward the middle of the block."

The street was lined with low-rise apartments that were mostly used by Columbia's grad students and professors. Strange, Myron thought, that a diner waitress would live here. But then again nothing else about her involvement in all this made sense—why should where she lived? If she lived here at all, and not, say, with Bruce Willis in Hollywood.

Norman interrupted his thoughts. "You're trying to help her, right?"

"What?"

Norman stopped walking. He was less animated now. "All that stuff about being from the phone company. That was all crap, right?"

Myron said nothing.

"Look," he said, putting his hand on Myron's forearm, "Hector is a good man. He came to this country with nothing. He works his ass off in that diner. He and his wife and son—they slave there every day. No days off. And every day he's scared someone's going to take it all away from him. All that worry . . . it clouds the thinking, you know? Me, I got nothing to lose so I'm not afraid of anything. Makes it easier to see some stuff. Know what I mean?"

Myron gave a slight nod.

Norman's bright eyes dimmed as a bit of reality swept through him. Myron looked at him, really looked at him, for the first time. He made his eyes stop sweeping by him with barely a notice of age or height or even species. Myron realized that behind the lies and self-delusion lay the dreams of any man, the hopes and wants and needs that are the sole reserve of the human race.

"I'm worried about Sally," Norman went on. "Maybe that's clouding my thinking. But I know she wouldn't just up and leave without saying good-bye to me. Sally wouldn't do that." He stopped, met Myron's eyes with his own. "You're not from the phone company, are you?"

"No, I'm not."

"You want to help her?"

"Yes," Myron said. "I want to help her."

He nodded and pointed. "In here. Apartment two E."

Myron walked up the stoop while Norman stayed on the street level. He pressed the black button reading 2E. No one answered. No surprise there. He tried the entrance door, but it was locked. You had to be buzzed in.

"You better stay there," he told Norman. Norman nodded, understanding. These buzzer-protected doors were mild deterrents to crime, but their true purpose was to prevent vagrants from coming in

and setting up camp in the lobby. Myron would just wait. Eventually
an occupant would leave or enter the building. While said occupant
opened the door, Myron would enter as though he belonged. No one
would question a man dressed in khakis and a button-down BD Bag-
gies shirt. If Norman stood next to him, however, that same occupant
might react differently.

Myron moved down two steps. When he saw two young women
approach the door from the inside, he slapped his pockets as though
looking for keys. Then he walked purposefully up to the door,
smiled, and waited for them to push it open. He need not have bothered with the dramatics. The two young women—college students,
Myron guessed—went through the portal without looking up or de-
celerating their oral activities. Both were talking nonstop, neither listening. They paid absolutely no attention to him. Amazing restraint
really. Of course from this angle they couldn't see his ass, so their
self-control was not only admirable but somewhat understandable.

He looked back at Norman, who thankfully waved him off. "You
go yourself," he said. "I don't want to cause a problem."

Myron let the door close.

The corridor was pretty much what he expected. It was painted
off-white. No stripes or designs. There were no wall-hangings other
than a huge bulletin board that read like a schizophrenic political
manifesto. Dozens of leaflets announced everything from a dance
sponsored by the Native American Gay and Lesbian Society to po-
etry readings by a group calling itself the Rush Limbaugh Review.
Ah, the college life.

He ascended a stairway lit by two bare bulbs. All this walking and
stair climbing were starting to take a toll on his bad knee. The joint
tightened up like a rusted hinge. Myron felt himself dragging the leg
behind him. He used the railing for support and wondered what the
knee would be like when he reached arthritis age.

The floor plan of the building was far from symmetrical. Doors
seemed to be placed in the wall as though at random. Off in a corner,
a good distance from the other apartments, Myron found the door
marked 2E. The positioning made the apartment look like an after-
thought, as if someone had spotted some extra space in the back and
decided to add an extra room or two. Myron knocked. No answer. No
surprise. He checked the corridor. No one in sight. He was thankful
that Norman was not here because he wouldn't want someone to witness him breaking in.

Myron was not great at the lock-picking game. He had learned a
bit over the years, but picking locks was a bit like playing a video

game. You work at it enough, and eventually you move up levels. Myron hadn't worked at it. He didn't like it. He really didn't have much natural talent for it. In most cases, he relied on Win to handle the mechanical stuff, like Barney used to do on *Mission: Impossible.*

He examined the door and felt his heart sink. Even for New York the dead bolts were nothing short of impressive. Three of them stacked intimidatingly from six inches above the knob to six inches below the top frame. Top of the line stuff. Brand new, judging by the gleam and lack of scratches. This was a tad odd. Was Sally/Carla the extracautious type, or was there a more aberrant reason for such security? Good question. Myron looked at the locks again. Win would have enjoyed the challenge; Myron knew that any effort he made would be fruitless.

He debated kicking in the door when he noticed something. He moved closer and squinted into the door crack. Again something struck him as being odd. The dead bolts were not engaged. Why buy all these expensive locks and not use them? He tried the knob. It was locked, but that one would be easy to get through with the 'loid card.

He took out the card. He couldn't remember the last time he had used it. It looked pristine. Maybe never. He jammed it into the opening. Despite being an old lock it still took Myron almost five minutes to find the right spot to push the lock back. He gripped the knob. The door began to swing open.

It was open barely six inches when the odor attacked.

The bloodcurdling stench popped out into the hallway like pressurized gas. Myron felt his stomach dive and swoop. He gagged a little and felt a weight on his chest. He knew the smell, and dread filled him. He searched his pockets for a handkerchief and came up empty. He blocked his nose and mouth with the crook of his elbow, as if he were doing Bela Lugosi in *Dracula.* He didn't want to go in. He wasn't good at this type of thing. He knew that whatever image lay behind the door would stay with him, would haunt his nights and too often his days too. It would stay with him like a dear friend, tapping him on the shoulder every once in a while when he thought he was alone and at peace.

He pushed the door all the way open. The rancid smell permeated his meager protection. He tried to breathe through his mouth, but the thought of what he was sucking in made that option unbearable.

Fortunately, he didn't have to travel far to find the source of the odor.

Chapter 12

"Whoa, Bolitar, new cologne?"

"Funny, Dimonte."

NYPD homicide detective Roland Dimonte shook his head. "Christ, what a stink." He was out of uniform, but you wouldn't ever call him "plainclothes." He wore a green silk shirt and jeans that were too tight and too dark blue. The bottoms were tucked into purple snakeskin boots; the color faded in and out with any angle change, like some psychedelic Hendrix poster from the sixties. Dimonte gnawed on a toothpick, a habit he picked up, Myron surmised, when he spotted himself doing it in the mirror and decided it looked tough. "You touch anything?" he asked.

"Just the doorknob," Myron said. He had also checked the rest of the apartment to make sure there weren't any other gruesome surprises. There weren't.

"How did you get in?"

"The door was unlocked."

"Really?" Dimonte raised an eyebrow and looked back at the door. "The door is set to lock automatically when you close it."

"Did I say unlocked? I meant, ajar."

"Sure you did." Dimonte did a bit more gnawing, shook his head. He ran his hand through greasy hair. Ringlets clung to his forehead, refusing to give ground. "So who is she?"

"I don't know," Myron said.

Dimonte scrunched up his face like a closed fist. Displaying very skeptical. Subtle body language was not Dimonte's forte. "Little early in the day to be pulling my hardware, ain't it, Bolitar?"

"I don't know her name. It might be Sally Guerro. Then again it might be Carla."

"Uh-huh." Toothpick chew. "I thought I saw you on TV last night. That you were playing ball again."

"I am."

The coroner came over. He was tall and thin and his wire-rim glasses looked too big on the elongated face. "She's been dead awhile," he pronounced. "At least four days."

"Cause?"

"Hard to say for sure. Someone bludgeoned her with a blunt object. I'll know more when I get her on the table." He looked at the corpse with professional disinterest, then back at Dimonte. "They're not real, by the way."

"What?"

He vaguely motioned toward the torso. "Her breasts. They're implants."

"Jesus Christ," Dimonte said, "you fiddling with dead bodies now?"

The elongated face sagged, his jaw dropping to somewhere around his navel. "Don't even joke about that," the coroner said in a stage whisper. "You know what rumors like that could do to a guy in my business?"

"Get him promoted?" Dimonte said.

The coroner did not laugh. He gave Myron a wounded look, then Dimonte. "You think that's funny, huh? Goddamn it, this is my career you're fucking around with!"

"Calm down, Peretti, I'm just playing with you."

"Playing with me? You think my career is some kind of fucking joke? What the hell is wrong with you?"

Dimonte's eyes narrowed. "Kind of sensitive about all this, Peretti."

"You have to be in my position," he said, back straightening.

"If you say so."

"What the hell does that mean?"

" 'The lady protests too much, methinks.' "

"What?"

"It's Shakespeare," Dimonte said. "From *Macbeth*." Dimonte looked over to Myron.

Myron smiled. *"Hamlet."*

"I don't give a shit who said it," Peretti protested. "You shouldn't mess around with a man's reputation. I don't think any of this is funny."

"Like I give a rat's ass what you think," Dimonte said. "You got anything else?"

"She's wearing a wig."

"A wig? No kidding, Peretti. The case is as good as solved now. All we need to do is find a killer who hates wigs and fake tits. This is helpful, Peretti. What kind of panties was she wearing, huh? You sniff them yet?"

"I was just—"

"Do me a big favor, Peretti." Dimonte made himself a little taller, hitched his pants. Signaling importance. Again the subtlety. "Tell me when she died. Tell me how she died. Then we'll talk about her fashion accessories, okay?"

Peretti held up his hands in surrender and returned to the body. Dimonte turned to Myron. Myron said, "The implants and wig might be important. He was right to tell you."

"Yeah, I know. I just like busting his chops."

"And the quote is, 'Methinks the lady doth protest too much.' "

"Uh huh." Dimonte changed toothpicks. The one in his mouth was frayed like a horse's mane. "You going to tell me what the fuck is going on, or am I going to drag you downtown?"

Myron made a face. "Drag me downtown?"

"Don't bust my balls on this, Bolitar, okay?"

Myron forced himself to look at the bloodied corpse. His stomach did back flips. He was starting to get used to the smell, the thought of which was nearly as bad as the smell itself. Peretti was back at it, making a small slit to get to the liver. Myron diverted his gaze. The homicide crew from John Jay was setting up, taking photographs, that kind of thing. Dimonte's partner, a kid named Krinsky, quietly walked around and took notes. "Why would she make them so big?" Myron wondered out loud.

"What?"

"Her breasts. I can understand the desire to enlarge them. All the pressures in this society. But why make them that big?"

Dimonte said, "You're shitting me, right?"

Krinsky came over. "All her stuff is in those suitcases." He motioned with his hand to two bags on the floor. Myron had met Krinsky on maybe half a dozen occasions. Talking was not the kid's forte; he seemed to do it as often as Myron picked locks. "I'd say she was moving out."

"You got an ID yet?" Dimonte asked.

"Her wallet says her name is Sally Guerro," Krinsky continued in a soft voice. "So does one of her passports."

They both waited for Krinsky to continue. When he didn't, Dimonte shouted, "What do you mean, one of her passports? How many does she have?"

"Three."

"Jesus Christ, Krinsky, talk."

"One is in the name Sally Guerro. One is in the name Roberta Smith. One is in the name Carla Whitney."

"Give me those." Dimonte scanned through the various passports.

Myron looked over his shoulder. The same woman was in all three pictures, albeit with different hair (ergo the wig) and different Social Security numbers. Judging by the amount of stamps, the woman had traveled extensively.

Dimonte whistled. "Forged passports," he said. "And good ones too." He turned more pages. "Plus she has a couple of visits to South America in here. Colombia. Bolivia." The passports closed with a dramatic snap. "Well, well, well. Looks like we got ourselves a nice, neat drug hit."

Myron mulled over that bit of information. A drug hit—could that be part of the answer? If Sally/Carla/Roberta was dealing drugs, it might explain her connection with Greg Downing. She was his source. The meeting on Saturday night was nothing more than a buy. The waitress job was a cover. It also explained her using a pay phone and maintaining powerful door locks—tools of a drug dealer's trade. It made some sense. Of course, Greg Downing did not appear to be a drug user, but he would not be the first person to fool everyone.

Dimonte said, "Anything else, Krinsky?"

The kid nodded. "I found a stack of cash in the bedside drawer." He stopped again.

Dimonte gave him exasperation. "Did you count it?"

Another nod.

"How much?"

"A little over ten thousand dollars."

"Ten grand in cash, huh?" That pleased Dimonte. "Let me see it."

Krinsky handed it over. New bills, held by rubber bands. Myron watched while Dimonte shuffled through them. All hundreds. The serial numbers were sequential. Myron tried to memorize one of them. When Dimonte finished, he tossed the packet back to Krinsky. The smile was still there.

"Yep," Dimonte said, "it looks like things are coming together in a nice, neat, drug-hit package." He paused. "Only one problem."

"What?"

He pointed at Myron. "You, Bolitar. You're messing up my nice, neat drug hit. What the hell are you doing—?" Dimonte stopped himself and snapped his fingers. "Holy shit . . ." His voice sort of drifted off. He slapped the side of his own head. A small spark in his eyes expanded. "My God!"

Again note the subtlety. "You have a thought, Rolly?"

Dimonte ignored him. "Peretti!"

The coroner looked up from the body. "What?"

"Those plastic tits," he said. "Myron noticed they were huge."

"Yeah, so?"

"How big?"

"What?"

"How big are they?"

"You mean like cup size?"

"Yeah."

"I look like a lingerie manufacturer? How the fuck would I know?"

"But they're big, right?"

"Right."

"Really big."

"You got eyes, don't you?"

Myron watched the exchange in silence. He was trying to follow Dimonte's logic—a most treacherous trail.

"Would you say they were bigger than a water balloon?" Dimonte continued.

Peretti shrugged. "Depends on the balloon."

"Didn't you ever make water balloons when you were a kid?"

"Yeah, sure," Peretti said. "But I don't remember how big the balloons were. I was a kid then. Everything looks bigger when you're a kid. A couple years ago I went back to my old elementary school to visit my third grade teacher. She still works there, if you can believe it. Her name is Mrs. Tansmore. I swear to God the building looked like a goddamn dollhouse to me. It was huge when I was a kid. It was like—"

"All right, moron, let me make this simple." Dimonte took a deep breath. "Could they be used for smuggling drugs?"

Silence. Everyone in the room stopped moving. Myron wasn't sure if he just heard the most idiotic thing in the world or the most brilliant. He turned toward Peretti. Peretti looked up, mouth open in fly-catching pose.

"Well, Peretti? Could it be?"

"Could it be what?"

"Could she stick dope in her boobs? Smuggle drugs through customs with them?"

Peretti looked at Myron. Myron shrugged. Peretti turned back to Dimonte. "I don't know," he said slowly.

"How can we find out?"

"I'd have to examine them."

"Then what the fuck you staring at me for? Do it."

Peretti did as asked. Dimonte smiled at Myron; his eyebrows did a little dance. Proud of his deduction. Myron remained quiet.

"Nope, no way," Peretti said.

Dimonte wasn't happy with this report. "Why the hell not?"

"There's hardly any scar tissue," Peretti said. "If she were smuggling drugs in there, they'd have to rip the skin open and sew it up. Then they'd have to do it again on this side. There's no sign of that."

"You're sure?"

"Positive."

Dimonte said, "Shit." Then he glared at Myron and pulled him into a corner. "Everything, Bolitar. Now."

Myron had debated how to handle it, but in truth he had no choice. He had to tell. He couldn't keep Greg Downing's disappearance a secret any longer. The best he could hope to do was keep it contained. He suddenly remembered that Norman Lowenstein was waiting outside. "One second," he said.

"What? Where the fuck you going?"

"I'll be right back. Just wait here."

"Like hell."

Dimonte followed him down the stairs and out onto the stoop. Norman wasn't there. Myron looked up and down the block. No sign of Norman. This was hardly a surprise. Norman probably ran when he saw the cops. Guilty or not, the homeless learn quickly to make themselves scarce when the authorities come calling.

"What is it?" Dimonte asked.

"Nothing."

"Then start talking. The whole story."

Myron told him most of it. The story almost knocked the toothpick out of Dimonte's mouth. Dimonte didn't bother asking questions, though he continuously stuck in exclamations of "Jesus Christ!" and "Frigging A," whenever Myron paused. When Myron finished, Dimonte sort of stumbled back and sat on the steps of the stoop. His eyes looked unfocused for a few moments. He gathered himself together, but it took some time.

"In-fuckin'-credible," he managed.

Myron nodded.

"Are you telling me no one knows where Downing is?"

"If they do, they aren't talking."

"He just vanished?"

"That's how it appears."

"And there's blood in his basement?"

"Yes."

Dimonte shook his head again. He reached down and put his hand on his right boot. Myron had seen him do this before. He liked to sort of pet the boot. Myron had no idea why. Maybe he found the feel of snakeskin soothing. Reminiscent of the womb.

"Suppose Downing killed her and ran," he said.

"That's a pretty big suppose."

"Yeah, but it fits," Dimonte said.

"How?"

"According to what you said, Downing was seen with the victim Saturday night. How much you want to bet that once Peretti gets her on the table we find the time of death around then?"

"Doesn't mean Downing killed her."

Dimonte increased the speed of his boot-petting stroke. A man on Rollerblades skated by with his dog. The dog looked out of breath, trying to keep up. New product idea: Dog Rollerblades. "Saturday night, Greg Downing and the victim get together at some gin joint downtown. They leave sometime around eleven o'clock. Next thing we know she's dead and he's vanished." Dimonte looked up at Myron. "That points to him killing her and running."

"It points to a dozen things."

"Like what?"

"Like maybe Greg witnessed the murder and got scared and ran. Maybe he witnessed the murder and was kidnapped. Maybe he was killed by the same people."

"So where's his body?" Dimonte asked.

"It could be anywhere."

"Why not just leave it here with hers?"

"Maybe they killed him someplace else. Or maybe they took his body because he's famous and they didn't want that kind of heat."

He scoffed at that one. "You're reaching, Bolitar."

"So are you."

"Maybe. Only one way to find out." He stood. "We got to get out an APB on Downing."

"Whoa, hold up a second. I don't think that's a good idea."

Dimonte looked at Myron as if he were something left unflushed in a toilet. "I'm sorry," he said feigning politeness. "You must be mistaking me for someone who gives a rat's ass what you think."

"You're suggesting putting out an APB on a major, beloved sports hero."

"And you're suggesting I play favorites because he's a major, beloved sports hero."

"Not at all," Myron said, his mind racing. "But imagine what happens when you call out this APB. The press gets it. You start getting that OJ coverage. But there's a difference here. You got squat on Downing. No motive. No physical evidence. Nothing."

"Not yet I don't," Dimonte said. "But it's early—"

"Exactly, it's early. Wait a little while, that's all I'm saying. And handle this one right because the whole world is going to look at everything you do. Tell those bozos upstairs to videotape every step. Leave nothing to chance. Don't let anyone come back later and say you tampered or contaminated something. Get a warrant before you go to Downing's house. Do everything by the book."

"I can do all that and still put out an APB."

"Rolly, suppose Greg Downing did kill her. You put out an APB, you know what happens? One, you look single-minded. You look like you got it in your head that Downing was the killer and that was it. Two, you got the press in your face—watching your every move, trying to beat you to the evidence, compromising and commenting on everything you do. Three, you drag Greg in here now and you know what bottom-feeders are stuck to him?"

Dimonte nodded and made a lemon-sucking face. "Fucking lawyers."

"A dream team's worth. Before you have anything, they're filing motions and suppressing whatever and, well, you know the routine."

"Shit," Dimonte said.

Myron nodded. "You see what I mean?"

"Yeah, I do," Dimonte said. "But there's some stuff you forgot, Bolitar." He gave Myron big-time toothpick gnawing. "For example, if I issue an APB your little team investigation goes down the toilet. You lose out."

"Could be," Myron said.

Dimonte studied him with a small, uneven smile. "That doesn't mean what you're saying is wrong. I just don't want you to think I don't see what you're up to."

"You read me," Myron said, "like Vasco da Gama reads a map."

Dimonte gave him hard eyes for a moment; Myron fought off the desire to roll his in return. "So here's how we're going to play it. You're going stay on the team and you're going to continue your little investigation. I'm going to try to keep what you told me to myself as long"—he held up a finger for emphasis—"as long as it benefits my case. If I find enough to haul Downing's ass in here, I put out the APB. And you are going to report everything to me. You are not going to hold back. Any questions?"

"Just one," Myron said. "Where do you buy your boots?"

Chapter 13

On the ride to practice, Myron placed a call from the car phone.

"Higgins," a voice answered.

"Fred? It's Myron Bolitar."

"Hey, long time, no speak. How you doing, Myron?"

"Can't complain. You?"

"A thrill a minute here at the Treasury Department."

"Yeah, I bet."

"How's Win?" Higgins asked.

"The same," Myron said.

"The guy scares the piss out of me, you know what I mean?"

"Yes," Myron said, "I do."

"You two miss working for the feds?"

"I don't," Myron said. "I don't think Win does either. It got too restrictive for him."

"I hear you. Hey, I read in the papers you're playing ball again."

"Yep."

"At your age and with that knee? How come?"

"Long story, Fred."

"Say no more. Hey, you guys are coming down to play the Bullets next week. Can you get me tickets?"

"I'll do my best."

"Great, thanks. So what do you need, Myron?"

"The wheres and why of about ten grand in hundred dollar bills. Sequentially wrapped. Serial number B028856011A."

"How fast you need it?"

"Soon as you can get it."

"I'll do my best. You take care, Myron."

"You too, Fred."

Myron held nothing back at practice. He let it all hang out. The feeling was awesome and overpowering. He entered his own zone. When he shot, it was like an invisible hand carried the ball to the cylinder. When he dribbled, the ball became part of his hand. His senses were heightened like a wolf's in the wilderness. He felt like he'd fallen into some black hole and emerged ten years earlier at the NCAA finals. Even his knee felt great.

Most of practice consisted of a scrimmage between the starting five players and the five who saw the most bench time. Myron played his best ball. His jumper was popping. He came off screens strong and ready to shoot. He even drove straight down the lane twice—into the teeth of the big men's domain—and came away the victor both times.

There were moments he completely forgot about Greg Downing and Carla/Sally/Roberta's mangled corpse and the blood in the basement and the goons who jumped him and yes, even Jessica. An exhilarating rush like no other flooded his veins—the rush of an athlete at his peak. People talked about a runner's high, a euphoria from a gland secretion when your body was pressed to its limit. Myron couldn't relate to that, but he understood the incredible highs and plunging depths of being an athlete. If you played well, your whole body tingled and tears of pure joy came to your eyes. The tingles lasted well into the night when you lay in bed with no chance of sleep and replayed your finest moments, often in slow motion, like an overzealous sportscaster with his finger on the replay button. When you played poorly, you were surly and depressed and stayed that way for hours and even days. Both extremes were way out of proportion with the relevant importance of jamming a ball through a metallic circle or swatting a ball with a stick or throwing a sphere with great velocity. When you played poorly, you tried to remind yourself how stupid it was to get so caught up in something so meaningless. When you hit that rare high, you kept your internal big mouth shut.

As Myron dashed back and forth in the wave of basketball action, a thought sneaked in through the back door of his brain. The thought stayed on the fringes, hiding behind a couch, popping into view every once in a while before ducking back down again. *You can do this,* the thought taunted. *You can play with them.*

Myron's lucky streak continued when it came to his defensive assignment: Leon White, Greg's roomie-on-the-road and best friend. Myron and Leon bonded a bit while playing, the way teammates and even opponents often do. Whispering quick jokes in one another's ear while lined up chest-to-chest for an inbounds pass. Patting the other guy on the back when he made a nice play. Leon was a classy guy on the floor. No trash talk. Even when Myron burned his butt on a fade-away eighteen-footer, Leon offered only words of encouragement.

Coach Donny Walsh blew the whistle. "That's it, fellas. Take twenty foul shots and go home."

Leon and Myron exchanged a half-handshake, half-high-five the way only children and professional athletes can. Myron had always loved this part of the game, the almost soldierlike camaraderie; he hadn't had that in years. It felt good. The players partnered themselves up in groups of two—one guy to shoot, one to rebound—and went off to different baskets. Myron lucked out again and hooked up with Leon White. They each snatched a towel and a water bottle and strolled past the bleachers. Several reporters were perched up there for the practice. Audrey was there, of course. She looked at him with an amused smile. He resisted the temptation to stick his tongue out at her. Or his ass. Calvin Johnson had been watching practice too. He wore a suit and leaned against the wall like he was posing for a candid picture. Myron tried to gauge his reaction during the scrimmage, but of course Calvin's expression remained unreadable.

Myron shot first. He stood at the foul line, feet spread shoulder length, his eyes on the front rim. The ball back-spun through the hoop.

"I guess we're going to be roommates," Myron said.

"That's what I heard," Leon said.

"Probably won't be for very long." Myron took another shot. Swish. "When do you think Greg will be back?"

In one motion Leon grabbed the bouncing ball and swooped it back to Myron. "I don't know."

"How's Greg feeling? The ankle doing okay?"

"I don't know," he said again.

Myron took another foul shot. Another swish. His shirt, heavy with sweat, felt right. He grabbed the towel and wiped his face again. "Have you talked to him at all?"

"No."

"That's funny."

Leon passed the ball to Myron. "What's funny?"

Myron shrugged, took four dribbles. "I heard you two were tight," he said.

Leon gave a half-smile. "Where did you hear that?"

Myron released the ball. Another swish. "Around, I guess. In the newspapers and stuff."

"Don't believe everything you read," Leon said.

"Why's that?"

He bounce-passed the ball to Myron. "The press loves to build up a friendship between a white player and a black player. They're always looking for that Gale Sayers–Brian Piccolo slant."

"You two aren't close?"

"Well, we've known each other a long time. I'll say that."

"But you're not tight?"

Leon looked at him funny. "Why you so interested?"

"I'm just making conversation. Greg is my only real connection to this team."

"Connection?"

Myron started dribbling again. "He and I used to be rivals."

"Yeah, so?"

"So now we're going to be teammates. It'll be weird."

Leon looked at Myron. Myron stopped dribbling. "You think Greg still cares about some old college rivalry?" There was disbelief in his voice.

Myron realized how lame he was sounding. "It was a pretty intense thing," he said. "At the time, I mean." Extra lame. Myron didn't look at Leon. He just lined up the shot.

"I hope this don't hurt your feelings or nothing," Leon said, "but I've been rooming with Greg for eight years now. I've never heard him mention your name. Even when we talk about college and stuff."

Myron stopped right before releasing the ball. He looked over at Leon, fighting to keep his face neutral. Funny thing was—much as Myron didn't want to admit it—that did hurt his feelings.

"Shoot already," Leon said. "I want to get out of here."

TC lumbered toward them. He palmed a basketball in each hand with the ease most adults palm grapefruits. He dropped one of the balls and did a handshaking/slapping ritual with Leon. Then he looked over at Myron. His face broke into a big smile.

"I know, I know," Myron said. "Thumped, right?"

TC nodded.

"What exactly is thumped?"

"Tonight," TC said. "Party at my house. All will be revealed then."

Chapter 14

Dimonte was waiting for him in the Meadowlands parking lot. He leaned out of his red Corvette. "Get in."

"A red Corvette," Myron said. "Why aren't I surprised?"

"Just get in."

Myron opened the door and slid into the black leather seat. Though they were parked with the engine off, Dimonte gripped the steering wheel with both hands and stared in front of him. His face was sheet-white. The toothpick hung low. He kept shaking his head over and over. Yet again, the subtlety. "Something wrong, Rolly?"

"What's Greg Downing like?"

"What?"

"You fucking deaf?" Dimonte snapped. "What's he like?"

"I don't know. I haven't spoken to him in years."

"But you knew him, right? In school. What was he like back then? Did he hang out with perversive types?"

Myron looked at him. "Perversive types?"

"Just answer the question."

"What the hell is this? Perversive types?"

Dimonte turned the ignition key. The sound was loud. He hit the gas a bit, let the engine do the rev thing for a while. The car had been jacked up like a race car. The sound was, like, totally rad, man. No women were in the nearby vicinity to hear this human mating call or they would surely be disrobing by now. Dimonte finally shifted into gear.

"Where we going?" Myron asked.

Dimonte didn't answer. He followed the ramp that leads from the arena to Giants Stadium and the horse track.

"Is this one of those mystery dates?" Myron asked. "I love those."

"Stop fucking around and answer my question."

"What question?"

"What's Downing like? I need to know everything about him."

"You're asking the wrong guy, Rolly. I don't know him that well."

"Tell me what you do know." Dimonte's voice left little room for disagreement. His tone was less fake-macho than usual, and there was a funny quake in it. Myron didn't like it.

"Greg grew up in New Jersey," Myron began. "He's a great basketball player. He's divorced with two kids."

"You dated his wife, right?"

"A long time ago."

"Would you say she was left-wing?"

"Rolly, this is getting too weird."

"Just answer the goddamn question." The tone aimed for angry and impatient, but fear seemed to overlap them. "Would you call her politics radical?"

"No."

"She ever hang out with perversives?"

"Is that even a word? Perversives?"

Dimonte shook his head. "Do I look like I'm in the mood for your shit, Bolitar?"

"Okay, okay." Myron made a surrendering gesture with his hands. The Corvette swerved across the empty stadium lot. "No, Emily did not hang out with perversives, whatever they are."

They headed past the racetrack and took the other ramp back toward the arena. It became apparent to Myron that they were just going to circle the Meadowlands' vast expanse of paved lots. "Let's get back to Downing then."

"I just told you we haven't talked in years."

"But you know about him, right? You've been investigating him; you've probably read stuff about him." Gear shift up. Extra rev power. "Would you say he was a revolutionary?"

Myron could not believe these questions. "No, Mr. Chairman."

"Do you know who he hangs out with?"

"Not really. He's supposed to be closest to his teammates, but Leon White—that's his roommate on the road—seemed less than enamored. Oh, here's something that might interest you: after home games, Greg drives a taxi in the city."

Dimonte looked puzzled. "You mean he picks up fares and stuff?"

"Yes."

"Why the fuck does he do that?"

"Greg is a little"—Myron searched for the word—"off."

"Uh huh." Dimonte rubbed his face vigorously, as if he were polishing a fender with a rag. He did this for several seconds, not looking at the road; fortunately, he was in the middle of an empty parking lot. "Does it make him feel like a regular guy or something? Could that be part of it? Getting closer to the masses?"

"I guess," Myron said.

"Go on. What about his interests? His hobbies?"

"He's a nature boy. He likes to fish and hunt and hike and boat, that goyish stuff."

"A back-to-nature type?"

"Sort of."

"Like maybe an outdoor, communal guy?"

"No. Like maybe an outdoor, loner guy."

"You have any idea where he might be?"

"None."

Dimonte hit the gas and circled the arena. He came to a stop in front of Myron's Ford Taurus and put the car in park. "Okay, thanks for the help. We'll talk later."

"Whoa, hold up a second. I thought we were working together on this."

"You thought wrong."

"You're not going to tell me what's going on?"

His voice was suddenly soft. "No."

Silence. The rest of the players were gone by now. The Taurus stood alone in the still, empty lot.

"It's that bad?" Myron said.

Dimonte kept frighteningly still.

"You know who she is, don't you?" Myron went on. "You got an ID?"

Dimonte leaned back. Again he rubbed his entire face. "Nothing confirmed," he muttered.

"You got to tell me, Rolly."

He shook his head. "I can't."

"I won't say anything. You know—"

"Get the fuck out of my car, Myron." He leaned across Myron's lap and opened the car door. "Now."

Chapter 15

TC lived in a turn-of-the-century, red brick mansion encircled by a six-foot, matching brick fence on one of the better streets of Englewood, New Jersey. Eddie Murphy lived down the block. So did three Forbes 500 CEOs and several major Japanese bankers. There was a security post by the driveway entrance. Myron gave the security guard his name. The guard checked his clipboard.

"Please park along the drive. The party is out back." He raised the yellow-and-black striped gate and waved him through. Myron parked next to a black BMW. There were maybe a dozen other cars, all glistening from fresh washes and waxes or perhaps they were all new. Mostly Mercedes Benzes. A few BMWs. A Bentley. A Jag. A Rolls. Myron's Taurus stood out like a zit in a Revlon commercial.

The front lawn was immaculately manicured. Perfectly pruned shrubs guarded and clung to the brick facade. In stark contrast to this majestic setting was the rap music blaring from the speakers. Awful. The shrubs looked pained by the sound. Myron didn't necessarily hate all rap. He knew there was worse music out there—John Tesh and Yanni proved it every day. Some rap songs Myron found engaging and even profound. He also recognized that rap music had not been written for him; he didn't get it all, but he suspected that he wasn't supposed to.

The party was held in the well-lit pool area. The crowd of about thirty mingled about in a fairly subdued fashion. Myron was wearing a blue blazer, a button-down pinstripe shirt, a flower tie, J. Murphy casual loafers. Bolitar the Prep. Win would be so proud. But Myron felt frighteningly underdressed next to his teammates. At the risk of sounding racist, the black guys on the team—there were only two other white players on the Dragons right now—knew how to dress with style. Not Myron's style (or lack thereof), but definitely with style. The group looked like they were readying themselves for a Milan runway walk. Perfectly tailored suits. Silk shirts buttoned to the neck. No ties. Shoes polished like twin mirrors.

TC reclined in a lounge chair by the shallow end of the pool. He was surrounded by a bunch of white guys who looked like college

students. They were laughing at his every word. Myron also spotted
Audrey in her customary reporter's garb. She had added pearls for
the occasion. Really dressing up. He barely had a chance to step
toward them when a woman in her late thirties/maybe forty approached him. "Hello," the woman said.

"Hi." The Wordsmith Strikes Again.

"You must be Myron Bolitar. My name is Maggie Mason."

"Hi, Maggie." They shook hands. Firm grip, nice smile.

She was dressed conservatively in a white blouse, charcoal-gray
blazer, red skirt, and black pumps. Her hair was down and slightly
mussed, as if she'd just released her bun. She was slim and attractive
and would have been the perfect choice to play the opposing attorney on *L.A. Law.*

She smiled at him. "You don't know who I am, do you?"

"Sorry, I don't."

"They call me Thumper."

Myron waited. When she didn't add anything, he said, "Uh huh."

"Didn't TC tell you about this?"

"He mentioned something about getting thump . . ." He stopped
midword. She just smiled at him and spread her arms. After some
time had passed, hc said, "I don't get it."

"Nothing to get," she said matter-of-factly. "I have sex with all the
guys on the team. You're new to the team. It's your turn."

Myron opened his mouth, closed it, tried again. "You don't look
like a groupie."

"Groupie." She shook her head. "God, I hate that word."

Myron closed his eyes and pinched the bridge of his nose. "Let
me see if I'm getting this."

"Go ahead."

"You've slept with every guy on the Dragons?"

"Yes."

"Even the married ones?"

"Yes," she replied. "Anyone who has been on the team since 1993.
That's when I started with the Dragons. I started with the Giants in
1991."

"Wait a second. You're a groupie for the Giants, too? The football
Giants?"

"I told you. I don't like the term groupie."

"What word would you be more comfortable with?"

She tilted her head a little and kept the smile. "Look, Myron, I'm
an investment banker on Wall Street. I work very hard. I like taking
cooking classes and I'm a step-aerobics nut. All in all I am pretty

normal by this world's standards. I don't hurt anybody. I don't want to get married or have a relationship. But I have this one little fetish."

"You have sex with professional athletes."

She held up her index finger. "Only with the guys on the Giants and Dragons."

"Nice to see team loyalty," Myron said, "in this era of free agency."

Thumper laughed. "That's pretty funny."

"Are you telling me you've slept with every player on the Giants?"

"Just about. I have tickets on the fifty-yard line. After every game, I have sex with two players—one from the defense, and one from the offense."

"Sort of like the game MVPs?"

"Exactly."

Myron shrugged. "Beats getting the game ball, I guess."

"Yes," she said slowly. "It definitely beats getting a game ball."

Myron rubbed his eyes. *Ground control to Major Tom.* He studied her for a moment. She seemed to be doing the same thing to him. "So how did you get the nickname Thumper?" he asked.

"It's not what you think."

"What's not what I think?"

"How I got the nickname. Everyone assumes it has something to do with screwing like a rabbit."

"And it doesn't?"

"No, it doesn't." She looked up in the air. "How do I explain this delicately?"

"You're worried about delicacy?"

She gave him a mildly disapproving look. "Don't be like that."

"Like what?"

"Like some right-wing, narrow-minded, Pat Buchanan–type Neanderthal. I have feelings."

"I didn't say you didn't."

"No, but you're acting like it. I don't hurt anyone. I'm honest. I'm forward. I'm direct. I control what I do and to whom. And I'm happy."

"Not to mention disease-ridden," he heard himself say and immediately regretted it. The words had just slipped out; that happened to him sometimes.

"What?"

"I'm sorry," he said. "That was uncalled for."

But he had hit a nerve. "The men I have sex with always wear condoms," she snapped. "I get tested frequently. I'm clean."

"I'm sorry. I shouldn't have said anything."

She didn't stop. "And I don't sleep with anyone I think might be infected with something. I'm careful that way."

Myron bit his lip this time. No point. "My mistake," he said. "I didn't mean it; I'm sorry. Please accept my apology."

Her chest heaved, but she was calm now. "Okay," she said with an exhale. "Apology accepted."

Her eyes met his again. They smiled at each other for far too long. Myron felt like a game-show contestant. A thought thankfully interrupted the semitrance. "Did you sleep with Greg Downing?" he asked.

"In 1993," she said. "He was one of the first Dragons."

How that must swell his bosom with pride. "You still see him?"

"Sure. We're good friends. I'm friends with most of the guys afterwards. Not all, but most."

"Do you two talk a lot?"

"Sometimes."

"Recently?"

"Not the past month or two."

"Do you know if he's seeing anyone?"

Thumper gave him a curious look. "Why would you want to know about that?"

Myron shrugged. "Just making conversation." The Return of Mr. Lame.

"It's an odd topic," she said.

"I guess I've been thinking about him a lot. All this talk about my being on Greg's team and our history together. It just got me thinking."

"It got you thinking about Greg's love life?" She wasn't buying it.

Myron sort of shrugged and mumbled something even he didn't understand. A laugh broke out from the other side of the pool. A group of his new teammates were enjoying a joke. Leon White was one of them. He met Myron's eye and nodded a hello. Myron nodded back. Myron realized that while no one seemed to be staring at them, all of his teammates had to know why Thumper had approached him. Again he felt like he was back in college, but this time the feeling didn't bring on the same happy nostalgia.

Thumper was busy studying him again, her eyes narrowed and focused. Myron tried to look neutral, but he felt like a doofus. Being so openly inspected did that to him. He tried to meet her gaze.

Thumper suddenly smiled widely and folded her arms. "I get it now," she said.

"What?"

"It's obvious."

"What's obvious?"

"You want revenge," she said.

"Revenge for what?"

The smile grew a bit, then relaxed. "Greg stole Emily from you. Now you want to steal someone back."

"He didn't steal her from me," Myron said quickly. He heard the defensive tone in his voice and didn't like it. "Emily and I broke up before they started dating."

"If you say so."

"I say so." Mr. Snappy Retort.

She let loose a throaty laugh and put a hand on his arm. "Relax, Myron. I'm only teasing you." She looked at him again. All of this eye contact was beginning to give Myron a headache. He stared at her nose instead. "So are we going to do this?" she asked.

"No," Myron said.

"If it's the fear of disease—"

"It's not. I'm involved with someone."

"So?"

"So I don't cheat on her."

"Who wants you to cheat? I just want to have sex with you."

"And you think those two things are mutually exclusive?"

"Of course they are," Thumper said. "Our having sex should have absolutely no effect on your relationship. I don't want you to stop caring about your girlfriend. I don't want to be a part of your life. I don't even want to be intimate."

"Gee, you make it sound so romantic," Myron said.

"But that's just the point. It's not romantic. It's just a physical act. Sure, it feels great, but in the end it's just a physical act. Like shaking hands."

"Shaking hands," Myron repeated. "You should write greeting cards."

"I'm just telling you how it is. Past civilizations—ones far more intellectually advanced than us—understood that pleasure of the flesh was no sin. Associating sex with guilt is a modern, absurd hang-up. This whole concept of tying sex to possession is something we got from uptight Puritans who wanted to maintain control over their major possession: their wife."

A history scholar, Myron thought. Nice to see.

"Where is it written," she continued, "that two people can't reach heights of physical ecstasy without being in love? I mean, think about how ridiculous that is. It's silly, isn't it?"

"Maybe," Myron said. "But I'll still pass, thank you."

She shrugged a suit-yourself. "TC will be very disappointed."

"He'll get over it," he said.

Silence.

"Well," she said, clasping her hands together, "I think I'll mingle. It was nice chatting with you, Myron."

"A true experience," Myron agreed.

Myron mingled a bit, too. He hooked up with Leon for a while. Leon introduced him to his wife, a blond sexpot named Fiona. Very Playmate-like. She had a breathy voice and was one of those women who made even the most casual conversation one long double entendre—so accustomed to using her physical charms that she did not know when to turn them off. Myron chatted with them both briefly and excused himself.

The bartender informed him that they were not stocking any Yoo-Hoo. He took an Orangina instead. Not just orange soda, but Orangina. How European. He took a sip. Pretty good.

A hand slapped Myron's back. It was TC. He had foregone the *GQ*-suit look, opting for white leather pants and a white leather vest. No shirt. He wore dark sunglasses.

"Having a good time?" he asked.

"It's been interesting," Myron said.

"Come on. I'll show you something."

They walked in silence up a grassy hill away from the party. The incline grew steadily steeper, the music fainter. The rap had been replaced with an alternative group called the Cranberries. Myron liked their music. "Zombie" was on right now. Dolores O'Riordan was repeatedly singing, "In your head, in your head," until she got tired and moved to repeating the word, "Zombie, zombie" several hundred times. Okay, the Cranberries could work on their chorus lyrics, but the song still worked. Good stuff.

There were no lights now, but a glow from the ones by the pool provided enough illumination. When they reached the plateau, TC motioned in front of them. "There."

Myron looked out, and the sight nearly took his breath away. They were up high enough to get an unimpeded, spectacular view of the Manhattan skyline. The sea of lights seemed to shimmer like beads of water. The George Washington Bridge looked close enough to touch. They both stood in silence for several moments.

"Nice, huh?" TC said.

"Very."

He took off his sunglasses. "I come up here a lot. By myself. It's a good place to think."

"I would think so."

They looked off again.

"Thumper talk to you yet?" Myron asked.

TC nodded.

"Were you disappointed?"

"No," TC said. "I knew you'd say no."

"How?"

He shrugged. "Just a feeling. But don't let her fool you. Thumper's good people. She's probably the closest thing I got to a friend."

"What about all those guys you were hanging out with?"

TC sort of smiled. "You mean the white boys?"

"Yeah."

"Not friends," he said. "If tomorrow I stopped playing ball, they'd all look at me like I'm pinching on a loaf on their sofa."

"Poetically put, TC."

"Just the truth, man. You in my position, you don't have no friends. Facts of life. White or black, it don't matter. People hang around me because I'm a rich superstar. They figure they can get something for free. That's all."

"And that's okay with you?"

"Don't matter if it's okay," TC said. "It's the way it is. I ain't complaining."

"Do you get lonely?" Myron asked.

"Too many people around to get lonely."

"You know what I mean."

"Yeah, I know what you mean." TC sort of jerked his head from side to side, like he was trying to loosen up his neck before a game. "Folks always talking about the price of fame, but you wanna know the real price? Forget that privacy shit. So I don't go out to the movies as much. Big fucking deal—where I come from you can't afford to go anyway. The real price is you ain't a person anymore. You're just a thing, a shiny thing like one of those Benzes out there. The poor brothers think I'm a golden ladder with goodies at every step up. The rich white boys think I'm a fancy pet. Like with OJ. Remember those guys who hung out in OJ's trophy room?"

Myron nodded.

"Look, I ain't complaining. Don't get me wrong. This is a whole lot better than pumping gas or working in a coal mine or something. But I always got to remember the truth: the only thing that separates me from any nigger on the street is a game. That's it. A knee going pop, like with what happened to you, and I'm back down there. I always remember that. Always." He gave Myron hard eyes, letting his words hang in the crisp air. "So when some hot babe acts like I'm something special, it ain't me she's after. You see what I'm saying? She's blinded by all that money and fame. Everyone is, male or female."

"So you and I could never be friends?" Myron asked.

"Would you be asking me that if I was just some ignorant fool pumping gas?"

"Maybe."

"Bullshit," he said with a smile. "People bitch about my attitude, you know. They say I act like everybody owes me. Like I'm a prima donna. But they just mad because I see through them. I know the truth. They all think I'm some ignorant nigger—the owners, the coaches, whatever—so why should I respect them? Only reason they even talk to me is because I can slam the ball through the hoop. I'm just a monkey making them money. Once I stop, that's it. I'm just another dumb slice of ghetto shit not fit to sit my black ass on their toilet." He stopped then, as though out of breath. He looked back at the skyline. The sight seemed to rejuvenate him. "You ever meet Isiah Thomas?" he asked.

"The Detroit Piston? Yeah, once."

"I heard him doing this interview one time, must have been when the Pistons won those championships. Some guy asked him what he'd be doing if he wasn't a basketball player. You know what Isiah said?"

Myron shook his head.

"He said he'd be a United States senator." TC laughed hard and high-pitched. The sound echoed in the still night. "I mean, is the brother crazy or what? Isiah really believe that shit. A United States senator—who the fuck is he kidding?" He laughed again, but the sound seemed more forced now. "Me, I know what I'd be. I'd be working in a steel mill, the midnight to ten A.M. shift, or maybe I'd be in jail or dead, I don't know." He shook his head. "United States senator. Shit."

"What about the game?" Myron asked.

"What about it?"

"Do you love playing basketball?"

He looked amused. "You do, don't you? You buy all that 'for the love of the game' bullshit."

"You don't?"

TC shook his head. The moon reflected off his shaved pate, giving his head an almost mystical glow. "It was never about that for me," he said. "Basketball was just a means to an end. It's about making money. It's about setting me up for life."

"Did you ever love the game?"

"Sure, I guess I must have. It was a good place to go, you know? But I don't think it was the game—I mean, not the running and jumping and shit. Basketball was just what I was all about. Everywhere else I was just another dumb black boy, but on the basketball court, I was, well, the man. A hero. It's an incredible high, everyone treating you like that. You know what I mean?"

Myron nodded. He knew. "Can I ask you something else?"

"Go ahead."

"What's with all the tattoos and rings?"

He smiled. "They bother you?"

"Not really. I'm just curious."

"Suppose I just like wearing them," TC said. "That enough?"

"Yes," Myron said.

"But you don't believe it, do you?"

Myron shrugged. "I guess not."

"Truth is, I do like them a little. The bigger truth is, it's business."

"Business?"

"Basketball business. Making money. Lots of it. You know how much money I make in endorsements? A shit load. Why? Because outrageousness sells. Look at Deon. Look at Rodman. The more crazy shit I do, the more they pay me."

"So it's just an act?"

"A lot of it, yeah. I like to shock, too, just my way. But mostly I do it for the press."

"But the press is always ripping you apart," Myron said.

"Don't matter. They write about me, they make me more money. Simple as that." He smiled. "Let me clue you in on something, Myron. The press is the dumbest animal on God's green earth. You know what I'm gonna do one day?"

Myron shook his head.

"One day I'll get rid of the rings and shit, and I'll start dressing nice. Then I'll start talking polite, you know, giving them all yes-sirs and yes-ma'ams and start spitting out all that team-effort bullshit

they like to hear. You know what'll happen? These same fucks that
say I'm destroying the integrity of the game will be kissing my black
ass like it's the Blarney Stone. They be talking about how I went
through some sort of miraculous transformation. How now I'm a
hero. But only thing that's really changed is my act." TC gave him a
big smile.

Myron said, "You're a piece of work, TC."

TC turned back to the water. Myron watched him in silence. He
hadn't bought all of TC's rationalizations. There was more at work
here. TC wasn't lying, but he wasn't exactly telling the truth either—
or maybe he couldn't admit the truth even to himself. He hurt. He
truly believed no one could love him, and no matter who you are, that
hurts. It made you insecure. It made you want to hide and build
fences. The sad thing was, TC was at least partially right. Who'd care
about him if he wasn't playing professional basketball? If not for his
ability to play a child's game, where would he be right now? TC was
like the beautiful girl who wanted you to look down deep to find the
soul within—but the only reason you'd bother trying was because
she was beautiful. Get rid of that physical beauty—become the ugly
girl—and nobody gives a damn about scratching the surface to find
the beauty within. Get rid of TC's physical prowess and the same
thing happens.

In the end, TC was not as off-the-wall as he appeared in public nor
was he as put-together as he wanted Myron to think. Myron was no
psychologist, but he was sure that there was more to the tattoos and
body piercing than making money. They were too physically destructive for so pat an explanation. With TC, there were a lot of factors at
work. Being a former basketball star himself, Myron understood
some of them; being that Myron and TC came from completely different worlds, there were others he could not so readily grasp.

TC interrupted their joint solitude. "Now I got a question for
you," he said.

"Shoot."

"Why you really here?" TC asked.

"Here? As in your house—"

"On the team. Look, man, I saw you play when I was in junior
high. In the NCAAs. You were great, okay? But that was a long time
ago. You got to know you can't do it anymore. You had to see that at
practice today."

Myron tried not to look stunned. Had he and TC been at the same
practice? But of course they had, and of course, TC was right. Didn't
Myron remember the days when he was the team's superstar? Didn't

he remember scrimmaging against the last five guys who would play
their butt off while the starting five screwed around and played with
no incentive? Didn't he remember how disillusioned those last five
became, fooling themselves into believing they were just as good as
the first five when the first five were tired from real games and were
just slacking off? And back then, Myron was in college. He played
maybe twenty-five games a season—these guys played almost a hundred against vastly superior competition.

Good enough to play with these guys? Who had he been kidding?

"I'm just giving it a shot," Myron said softly.

"Can't let go, huh?"

Myron said nothing. They fell back into a brief silence.

"Hey, I almost forgot," TC said. "I hear you're good friends with
a big hotshot at Lock-Horne Securities. That true?"

"Yes."

"Was he that slice of white bread you talking with after the
game?"

Myron nodded. "His name is Win."

"You know Thumper works on Wall Street, right?"

"She told me," Myron said.

"Thumper wants to change jobs. Think your friend could talk to
her?"

Myron shrugged. "I could ask him." Win would certainly appreciate her outlook on the role of sex in ancient civilizations. "Who does
she work for now?"

"Small outfit. Called Kimmel Brothers. But she needs to move on,
you know? They won't make her a partner, even though she busts her
butt for them."

TC said something else but Myron was no longer listening. Kimmel Brothers. Myron remembered the name immediately. When he'd
hit the redial button on the phone at Greg's house, a woman had answered and said, "Kimmel Brothers." Yet Thumper had just told Myron she hadn't spoken to Greg in a month or two.

Coincidence? Myron thought not.

Chapter 16

Thumper was gone.

"She came for you," TC said. "When it didn't happen she split. She got work tomorrow morning."

Myron checked his watch. Eleven-thirty. Long day. Time for a little shut-eye. He made his good nights and headed for his car. Audrey was leaning against the hood, her arms folded across her chest, her ankles crossed. Pure casual.

"You going back to Jessica's?" she asked.

"Yes."

"Mind giving me a lift?"

"Hop in."

Audrey gave him the same smile he had seen back at practice. He had thought at the time she had been impressed with his play; now it was clearer that the amusement was more akin to ridicule than appreciation. He unlocked the doors in silence. She took off her blue blazer and laid it on the backseat; he did likewise. She wore a forest green turtleneck underneath it. She adjusted the neck part, folding it back an extra time. She took off the pearls and jammed them in the front pocket of her jeans. Myron started the car.

"I'm starting to put this thing together," Audrey said.

Myron did not like the way she said it. Too much authority in her voice. Audrey hadn't needed a lift home, he was sure of that. She wanted to talk to him alone. That worried him. He gave her the good-natured smile and said, "This doesn't have anything to do with my ass, does it?"

"What?"

"Jessica told me you two were discussing my ass."

She laughed. "Well, I hate to admit this," she said, "but it did look pretty scrumptious."

Myron tried not to look too pleased. "So you doing a story on it?"

"On your ass?"

"Yes."

"Of course," she said. "I was thinking we could give it a big spread."

Myron groaned.

"You're trying to change the subject," she said.

"There was a subject?"

"I was telling you how I was putting this thing together."

"That's a subject?"

He glanced at her. She was sitting with her left knee on the seat and her left ankle tucked under her so her entire body could face him. Audrey had a wide face and a few freckles, though he bet she had a lot more when she was a kid. Remember that tomboy who was kinda cute in your sixth grade class? Here she was all grown up. No beauty certainly. Not in the classic sense. But there was an earthy appeal to Audrey that made you want to reach out and hug her and roll in leaves on a crisp autumn day.

"It shouldn't have taken me so long to figure out," she continued. "It's pretty obvious in hindsight."

"Am I supposed to know what you're talking about?"

"No," she replied. "You're supposed to continue to play dumb for a few more minutes."

"My specialty."

"Good, then just drive and listen." Her hands were in constant gesturing motion, peaking and valleying along with her voice. "See, I was waylaid by the whole poetic irony stuff. That's what I concentrated on. But your backgrounds as rivals is secondary in all this. It's not nearly as important as, say, your past relationship with Emily."

"I have no idea what you're talking about."

"You didn't play AAU. You didn't play in any summer league. You play in pickup games at the Y maybe once a week. Your major workout revolves around Master Kwon's place with Win—and they don't have a basketball court."

"Is there a point?"

Her hands spread in disbelief. "You haven't been honing your skills. You haven't played anyplace where Clip or Calvin or Donny would have seen you play. So why would the Dragons sign you? It doesn't make sense. Was the move strictly P.R.? Unlikely. The positive bump will be minimum, and if you fail—which, let's face it, is very likely—that good publicity will probably be nullified. Ticket sales are good. The team is doing well. They don't need a publicity stunt right now. So there has to be another reason." She stopped and readjusted herself on the car seat. "Enter the timing."

"The timing?"

"Yes," she said. "Why now? Why sign you so late in the season?

The answer is obvious really. There is only one thing about the timing that stands out."

"And that is?"

"Downing's sudden disappearance."

"He didn't disappear," Myron corrected. "He's injured. That's your precious timing. Greg got hurt. A spot opened up. I filled it."

Audrey smiled and shook her head. "Still want to play dumb, huh? Fine, go ahead. You're right. Downing is supposed to be injured and in seclusion. Now I'm good, Myron, and for the life of me I can't find this secluded spot of his. I've called in all my best contacts and I can't get anything. Don't you find that a bit odd?"

Myron shrugged.

"Maybe," she went on, "if Downing really craved seclusion to fix his injured ankle—an injury which doesn't show up on any game tape, by the way—he could find a way. But if all he's doing is working on an injury, why work so hard at it?"

"So pain in the asses like you don't bother him," Myron said.

Audrey almost laughed at that one. "Said with such conviction, Myron. It's almost like you believe it."

Myron said nothing.

"But let me just add a few more points and then you can stop playing dumb." Audrey counted them off on ringless, slightly callused fingers. "One, I know you used to work for the feds. That gives you some background in investigative work. Two, I know Downing has a habit of vanishing. He's done it before. Three, I know Clip's situation with the other owners. The big vote is coming up. Four, I know you visited Emily yesterday and I doubt you were there to restoke the flames."

"How did you know about that?" Myron asked.

She just smiled and put her hand down. "Add them up and there's only one conclusion: you are looking for Greg Downing. He's missing again. This time however the timing is much more critical; Clip's ownership vote and the playoffs are coming up. Your job is to find him."

"You got a hell of an imagination, Audrey."

"I do at that," she agreed, "but we both know I got this right so let's end playing dumb and cut to the heart of it: I want in."

"Want in." Myron shook his head. "You reporters and your lingo."

"I don't want to give you up," she continued. Her knee was still up on the seat. Her face was as bright and expectant as a school kid's waiting for the final bell in May. "I think we should team up. I can help. I got great sources. I can ask questions without worrying about blowing my cover. I know this team inside and out."

"And what exactly do you want for this help?"

"The full story. I'm the first reporter to know where he is, why he vanished, whatever. You promise to tell only me; I get the full exclusive."

They passed several sleazy motels and a potpourri of gas stations on Route 4. No-tell motels in New Jersey always gave themselves lofty names that belied their social station. Right now, for example, they were driving past the "Courtesy Inn." This fine establishment not only gave you courteous attention, but they gave it to you by the hour at a rate, according to the sign, of $19.82. Not twenty dollars, mind you, but $19.82—so priced, Myron guessed, because it was also the year they last changed sheets. The CHEAP BEER DEPOT, according to another sign, was the next building on Myron's right. Truth in advertising. Nice to see. The Courtesy Inn could learn a lesson from them.

"We both know I could report it now," she said. "It'd still be a pretty good scoop—reporting that Downing wasn't really injured and you're just here to find him. But I'd be willing to trade it in for a larger story."

Myron thought it over as he paid the toll. He glanced at her expectant face. She looked wild-eyed and wild-haired, kind of like the refugee women coming off the boat in Palestine in the movie *Exodus*. Ready to do battle to claim her homeland.

"You have to make me a promise," he said.

"What?"

"No matter what—no matter how incredible the story seems—you won't jump the gun. You won't report any of it until he's found."

Audrey nearly leapt from her seat. "What do you mean? How incredible?"

"Forget it, Audrey. Report whatever you want."

"All right, all right, you have a deal," she said quickly, hands raised in surrender. "You had to know saying something like that would pique my interest."

"You promise?"

"Yeah, yeah, I promise. So what's up?"

Myron shook his head. "You first," he said. "Why would Greg vanish?"

"Who knows?" she replied. "The man is a professional flake."

"What can you tell me about his divorce?"

"Just that's it's been acrimonious as all hell."

"What have you heard?"

"They've been battling over the kids. They're both trying to prove the other is an unfit parent."

"Any details on how they're going about that?"

"No. It's been kept pretty hush-hush."

"Emily told me Greg had pulled some sleazy tricks," Myron said. "Do you know anything about that?"

Audrey chewed on her bottom lip for a few moments. "I heard a rumor—a very unsubstantiated rumor—that Greg hired a private eye to follow her."

"Why?"

"I don't know."

"To film her maybe? Catch her with another man?"

She shrugged. "It's just a rumor. I don't know."

"You know the P.I.'s name, or who he works for?"

"Rumor, Myron. Rumor. A pro basketball player's divorce is hardly earth-shattering sports news. I didn't follow it that closely."

Myron made a mental note to check Greg's files for any payment to an investigation firm. "How was Greg's relationship with Marty Felder?"

"His agent? Good, I guess."

"Emily told me Felder had lost Greg millions."

She shrugged. "I've never heard anything about that."

The Washington bridge was fairly clear. They stayed to the left and took the Henry Hudson Parkway south. On their right, the Hudson River sparkled like a blanket of black sequins; on their left was a billboard with Tom Brokaw displaying his friendly yet firm smile. The caption under his picture read: "NBC News—Now More Than Ever." Very dramatic. What the hell did it mean?

"How about Greg's personal life?" Myron continued. "Girlfriends, that kind of thing?"

"You mean a steady?"

"Yes."

She ran her fingers through the thick, curling locks, then rubbed the back of her own neck. "There was this one girl. He kept it kind of secret, but I think they were living together for a while."

"What's her name?"

"He never told me. I saw them together at a restaurant once. A place called the Saddle River Inn. He didn't look happy to see me."

"What did she look like?"

"Nothing special from what I remember. She was a brunette. She was sitting so I couldn't tell you height or weight."

"Age?"

"I don't know. Thirty-ish, I guess."

"What makes you think they were living together?"

It seemed like an easy question, but she stopped and raised her eyes. "Leon let something slip once," she said.

"What did he say?"

"I don't remember anymore. Something about the girlfriend. Then he clammed up."

"How long ago was this?"

"Three, four months ago. Maybe more."

"Leon implied that he and Greg weren't really that close, that the media made a bigger deal out of it than it was."

Audrey nodded. "There is a tension there now, but I think it's just temporary."

"Why would there be a tension?"

"I don't know."

"How long have you noticed the tension?"

"Not long. Within the last two weeks maybe."

"Anything happen recently between Greg and Leon that you're aware of?"

"Nope. They've been friends for a long time. Friends have disagreements. I didn't take it too seriously."

Myron let loose a deep breath. Friends did indeed have disagreements, but the timing was curious. "Do you know Maggie Mason?"

"Thumper? Of course."

"Were she and Greg close?"

"If you mean did they screw—"

"No, I don't mean that."

"Well, they screwed. That I'm sure of. Despite what Thumper claims, not every guy on the team has gotten thumped. Some have turned her down. Not many, I admit. But some. She hit on you yet?"

"Just a few short hours ago."

She smiled. "I assume you joined the few, the proud, the Un-thumped?"

"You assume correctly. But what about her relationship with Greg? Are they close?"

"They're pretty close, I'd say. But Thumper is closest to TC. Those two are very tight. It's not purely sexual either. Don't get me wrong. I'm sure TC and Maggie have had sex and probably still do on occasions. But they're like brother and sister too. It's weird."

"How do TC and Greg get along?" Myron asked.

"Not bad for team superstars. Not great either."

"Care to elaborate?"

She paused, gathered her thoughts. "For five years now, TC and Downing have shared the spotlight. I guess there is a mutual respect for each other on the court, but they don't talk off it. At least, not very much. I'm not saying they dislike each other, but playing basketball is a job like any other. You might be able to stand one another at work, but you don't want to see the person socially." She looked up. "Take the Seventy-ninth Street exit."

"You still live on Eighty-first?"

"Yes."

Myron took the exit and stopped at a traffic light on Riverside Drive.

"Now it's your turn, Myron. Why did they hire you?"

"It's like you said. They want me to find Greg."

"What have you learned so far?"

"Not much."

"So why were you so concerned I'd jump the gun and tell the story early?"

Myron hesitated.

"I promised not to say anything," she reminded him. "You have my word."

Fair is fair. He told her about the blood in Greg's basement. Her mouth dropped open. When he told her about finding Sally/Carla's body, he feared her heart might give out.

"My God," Audrey said when he finished. "You think Downing killed her."

"I didn't say that."

She fell back against the seat. Her head lolled against the headrest as though her neck could no longer support her. "Christ, what a story."

"And one you can't tell."

"Don't remind me." She sat back up again. "Do you think it'll leak soon?"

"It might."

"Why can't I be the recipient of that leak?"

Myron shook his head. "Not yet. We got a lid on this so far. You can't be the one to blow it off."

Her nod was grudging. "Do you think Downing killed her and ran?"

"There is no evidence of that." He pulled up to her building. "One last question," he said. "Was Greg involved in anything unsavory?"

"Like what?"

"Like is there any reason thugs would be after him?"

Again her excitement was palpable. The woman was like an electric current. "What do you mean? What thugs?"

"A couple of thugs were watching Greg's house."

Her face was positively glowing. "Thugs? You mean like professional gangsters?"

"Probably. I don't know for sure yet. Can you think of anything that would connect Greg to thugs or for that matter, the murder of this woman? Drugs maybe?"

Audrey shook her head immediately. "It can't be drugs."

"What makes you so sure?"

"Downing is a health nut, a real Granola head."

"So was River Phoenix."

She shook her head again. "Not drugs. I'm sure of it."

"Look into it," he said. "See what you can come up with."

"Sure," she said. "I'll look into everything we talked about."

"Try to be discreet."

"No problem," she said. She got out of the car. "Good night, Myron. Thanks for trusting me."

"Like I had a choice."

Audrey smiled and closed the car door. He watched her walk into the building. He put the car back in drive and headed back to Seventy-ninth Street. He got back on the parkway and continued south toward Jessica's. He was about to pick up his cellular phone and call her when the phone rang. The dashboard clock read 12:07 A.M. It had to be Jessica.

"Hello?"

It wasn't Jessica. "Right lane, three cars behind you. You're being followed."

It was Win.

Chapter 17

"When did you get back?" Myron asked.

Win ignored the question. "The automobile following you is the same one we spotted at Greg's house. It is registered to a storage facility in Atlantic City. No known mob connections, but that would seem to me to be a safe bet."

"How long have you been following me?"

Again Win ignored him. "The two men who jumped you the other night. What did they look like?"

"Big," Myron said. "One was absolutely huge."

"Crew cut?"

"Yes."

"He's in the car following you. Passenger seat."

Myron didn't bother asking how Win knew about the thugs jumping him. He had a pretty good idea.

"They've been communicating on the telephone quite a bit," Win continued. "I believe they're coordinating with someone else. The phone activity picked up after your stop on Eighty-first Street. Hold on a second. I'll call you right back." He hung up. Myron checked his rearview mirror. The car was still there, right where Win said it was. A minute later the phone rang again.

"What?" Myron said.

"I just spoke to Jessica again."

"What do you mean, again?"

Win sighed impatiently. He hated explanations. "If they are planning to jump you tonight, it is logical to assume it will be by her loft."

"Right."

"Ergo, I called her ten minutes ago. I told her to keep an eye out for anything unusual."

"And?"

"An unmarked white van parked across the street," Win answered. "No one got out."

"So it appears they are going to strike," Myron said.

"Yes," Win said. "Should I preempt it?"

"How?"

"I could disable the car following you."

"No," Myron said. "Let them make their move and see where it leads."

"Pardon?"

"Just back me up. If they grab me, I may be able to get to the boss."

Win made a noise.

"What?" Myron asked.

"You complicate the simple," Win said. "Would it not be easier to simply take out the two in the car? We could then make them tell us about their boss."

"It's that 'make them' part I have trouble with."

"But of course," Win countered. "A thousand pardons for my lack of ethics. Clearly it is far wiser to risk your own life than to make a worthless goon feel momentary discomfort."

Win had a way of putting things that made very frightening sense. Myron had to remind himself that the logical was often more terrifying than the illogical—especially where Win was concerned. "They're just hired help," Myron said. "They're not going to know anything."

Pause. "Fair point," Win conceded. "But suppose they simply shoot you."

"That wouldn't make any sense. The reason they're interested in me is because they think I know where Greg is."

"And dead men tell no tales," Win added.

"Exactly. They want to make me talk. So just follow me. If they take me some place well guarded—"

"I'll get through," Win said.

Myron did not doubt it. He gripped the steering wheel. His pulse began to race. Easy to dismiss the possibility of getting shot by reasonable analysis; it was another thing to have to park a car down the street from men you knew were out to hurt you. Win would have his eye on the van. So would Myron. If a gun came out before a person, the situation would be handled.

He got off the highway. The streets of Manhattan were supposed to be a nice, even grid. Streets ran north/south and east/west. They were numbered. They were straight. But when you got to Greenwich Village and Soho, it was like a grid painted by Dali. Gone were the numerical roads for the most part, except when they twisted and turned between streets with real-live names. Gone was any pretext of straight or systematized.

Luckily Spring Street was a direct run. A bicyclist sped by Myron, but no one else was out. The white van was parked right where it was supposed to be. Unmarked, just as Jessica had said. The windows were tinted so you couldn't look in. Myron didn't see Win's car, but then again he wasn't supposed to. He moved slowly down the street. He passed the van. When he did, the van started its motor. Myron pulled into a spot toward the end of the block. The van pulled out.

Show time.

Myron parked the car, straightened out the steering wheel, turned the engine off. He pocketed the keys. The van inched forward. He took out his revolver and stuck it under the car seat. It wouldn't do him any good right now. If they grabbed him, they would search him. If they started shooting, shooting back would be a waste of time. Win would either remove the threat or not.

He reached for the door handle. Fear nestled into his throat, but he did not stop. He pulled the handle, opened the door, and stepped out. It was dark. The streetlights in Soho were nearly worthless, like pen beams in a black hole. Lights drifting out from nearby windows provided more of an eerie kindle than real illumination. There were plastic garbage bags out on the street. Most had been torn open; the odor of spoiled food wafted through the air. The van slowly cruised toward him. A man stepped out from a doorway and approached without hesitation. The man wore a black turtleneck under a black overcoat. He pointed a gun at Myron. The van stopped, and the side door slid open.

"Get in, asshole," the man with the gun said.

Myron pointed at himself. "You talking to me?"

"Now, asshole. Haul ass."

"Is that a turtleneck or a dickey?"

The man with the gun moved closer. "I said, now."

"It's nothing to get angry about," Myron said, but he stepped toward the van. "If it is a dickey, you can't tell. It's a very sporty look." When Myron got nervous, his mouth went into overdrive. He knew it was self-destructive; Win had pointed that out to him on several occasions. But Myron couldn't stop himself. Diarrhea of the mouth or some such ailment.

"Move."

Myron got in the van. The man with the gun did likewise. There were two more men in the back of the van and one man driving. Everyone was in black, except for one guy who looked to be in charge. He wore a blue pinstripe suit. His Windsor-knotted yellow tie was held in place by a gold tie bar at the collar. Euro-chic. He had long, bleached-blond hair and one of those tans that were a little too perfect to come from the sun. He looked more like an aging surfer boy than a professional mobster.

The van's interior had been custom designed, but not in a good way. All the seats had been ripped out except for the driver's. There was a leather couch in the back along one wall where Pinstripe sat alone. A lime-green shag carpet even Elvis would have found too garish ran along the van's floor and up the sides like a poor man's ivy.

The man in the pinstripe suit smiled; his hands were folded in his lap, very much at ease. The van started moving.

The gunman quickly searched Myron. "Sit, asshole," he said.

Myron sat on the carpeted floor. He ran his hand over the shag. "Lime green," he said to Pinstripe. "Nice."

"It's inexpensive," Pinstripe said. "That way we don't worry about bloodstains."

"Thinking of overhead." Myron nodded coolly, though his mouth felt very dry. "That's smart business."

Pinstripe did not bother with a response. He gave the man with the gun and dickey/turtleneck a look that made the man jolt upward. The man cleared his throat.

"This here is Mr. Baron," the gunman told Myron, indicating Pinstripe. "Everyone calls him the B Man." He cleared his throat again. He spoke like he'd been rehearsing this little speech, which, Myron surmised, was probably likely. "He's called the B Man because he enjoys breaking bones."

"Say, that must woo the women," Myron said.

The B Man smiled with capped teeth as white as anything in those old Pepsodent commercials. "Hold his leg out," he said.

The man with the turtleneck/dickey pressed the gun against Myron's temple hard enough to leave a permanent imprint. He wrapped his other arm around Myron's neck, the inside of his elbow jammed into Myron's windpipe. He lowered his head and whispered, "Don't even flinch, asshole."

He forced Myron into a lying position. The other man straddled Myron's chest and pinned the leg to the floor. Myron had trouble breathing. Panic seized him, but he remained still. Any move at this stage would almost inevitably be the wrong one. He'd have to play it out and see where it went.

The B Man moved off the leather couch slowly. His eyes never left Myron's bad knee; his smile was a happy one. "I'm going to place one hand on the distal femur and the other on your proximal tibia," he explained in the same tone a surgeon might use with a student. "My thumbs will then rest on the medial aspect of the patella. When my thumbs snap forward, I will basically rip off your kneecap laterally." He met Myron's gaze. "This will tear your medial retinaculum and several other ligaments. Tendons will snap. I fear it will be most painful."

Myron didn't even try a wisecrack. "Hey, wait a second," he said quickly. "There's no reason for violence."

The B Man smiled, shrugged. "Why does there have to be a reason?"

Myron's eyes widened. Fear hardened in his belly. "Hold on," he said quickly. "I'll talk."

"I know you will," the B Man replied. "But first you'll jerk us around a bit—"

"No, I won't."

"Please don't interrupt me. It's very rude to interrupt." The smile was gone. "Where was I?"

"First he'll jerk us around," the driver prompted.

"That's right, thank you." He turned the white smile back to Myron. "First, you'll stall. You'll do a song-and-dance. You'll hope we'll take you someplace where your partner can save you."

"Partner?"

"You're still friends with Win, aren't you?"

The man knew Win. This was not a good thing. "Win who?"

"Precisely," B Man said. "This is what I mean by being jerked around. Enough."

He moved closer. Myron started to struggle, but the man jammed the gun in Myron's mouth. It struck teeth and made him gag. The taste was cold and metallic.

"I'll destroy the knee first. Then we'll talk."

The other man pulled Myron's leg straight while the gunman took the revolver out of Myron's mouth and pressed it back against his temple. Their grips grew a bit tighter. The B Man lowered his hands to Myron's knee, his fingers spread like eagle's talons.

"Wait!" Myron shouted.

"No," B Man replied calmly.

Myron started to squirm. He grabbed a loading handle on the floor of the van, the kind of thing used to tie down cargo. He held on and braced himself. He didn't have to wait very long.

The crash jarred them. Myron had been ready for it. No one else had. They all went flying, their grips slackening. Glass shattered. The scream of metal hitting metal filled the air. Brakes screeched. Myron held on until the van slowed. Then he curled into a ball and rolled out of harm's way. There were shouts and a door opened. Myron heard a shot being fired. Voices sounded in a cacophony of confusion. The driver ducked out through his door. The B Man followed, leaping like a grasshopper. The side door opened. Myron looked up as Win stepped in with his gun drawn. The man with the turtleneck/dickey had recovered. He picked up his gun.

"Drop it," Win said.

The man with the turtleneck/dickey didn't. Win shot him in the face. He turned his aim toward the man who had straddled Myron's chest.

"Drop it," Win said.

The man did. Win smiled at him. "Fast learner."

Win's eyes slid smoothly from side to side, never darting. Win barely moved, seeming to glide rather than walk. His movements were short and economical. He returned his eyes to his captive. The one still breathing.

"Talk," Win said.

"I don't know nothing."

"Bad answer," Win said. He spoke with calm authority, his matter-of-fact tone more intimidating than any scream. "If you know nothing, you are useless to me; if you are useless to me, you end up like him." He vaguely motioned toward the still form at his feet.

The man held up his hands. His eyes were round and white. "Hey, wait a sec, okay? It's no secret. Your buddy heard the guy's name. Baron. The guy's name is Baron. But everyone calls him the B Man."

"The B Man works out of the Midwest," Win said. "Who brought him in?"

"I don't know; I swear."

Win moved the gun closer. "You're being useless to me again."

"It's the truth, I'd tell you if I knew. All I know is the B Man flew in late last night."

"Why?" Win asked.

"It's got something to do with Greg Downing. That's all I know, I swear."

"How much does Downing owe?"

"I don't know."

Win moved closer still. He pressed the barrel of the gun between the man's eyes. "I rarely miss from this distance," he said.

The man dropped to his knees. Win followed him down with the gun. "Please." His voice was a pained plea. "I don't know nothing else." His eyes filled with tears. "I swear to God, I don't."

"I believe you," Win said.

"Win," Myron said.

Win's eyes never left the man. "Relax," he said. "I just wanted to make sure our friend here had confessed all. Confession is good for the soul, is it not?"

The man nodded hurriedly.

"Have you confessed all?"

More nods.

"You're sure?"

Nod, nod.

Win lowered the weapon. "Go then," he said. "Now."

The man didn't have to be told twice.

Chapter 18

Win looked down at the dead body as though it were a bag of peat moss. "We best depart."

Myron nodded. He reached into his pants pocket and took out the cellular phone. A relatively new trick of the trade. Neither he nor Win had hung up after their call. The line was left open; Win had been able to hear everything that had gone on in the van. It worked as well as any bug or walkie-talkie.

They stepped into the cool night. They were on Washington Street. During the day the place was popping with delivery trucks, but at night it was completely silent. Someone would find a nasty surprise in the morning.

Win normally drove a Jaguar, but he had smashed a 1983 Chevy Nova into the van. Totaled. Not that it mattered. Win had several such vehicles he kept out in New Jersey to use for surveillance or activities just east of legal. The car was untraceable. The plates and paperwork were all phony. It would never lead back to anyone.

Myron looked at him. "A man of your breeding in a Chevy Nova?" He tsk-tsked.

"I know," Win said. "Sitting in it almost gave me a rash."

"If anyone at the club saw you . . ."

Win shuddered. "Do not even think such a thought."

Myron's legs still felt shaky and numb. Even as the B Man had reached down for his knee, Myron had known that Win would find a way to get to him. But the thought of how close he'd come to being crippled for life kept plucking at the muscles in his calves and thighs. He kept bending down and touching the bad knee, as if he couldn't believe it was still there. Tears brimmed in his eyes as he looked at Win. Win saw them and turned away.

Myron followed behind him. "So how do you know this B Man?" he asked.

"He operates out of the Midwest," Win said. "He is also a superb martial artist. We met in Tokyo once."

"What sort of operation does he run?"

"The usual assorted sundries—gambling, drugs, loan sharking, extortion. A bit of prostitution too."

"So what's he doing here?"

"It appears that Greg Downing owes him money," Win said, "probably from gambling. The B Man specializes in gambling."

"Nice to have a specialty."

"Indeed. I would assume that your Mr. Downing owes them a large sum of money." Win glanced over at Myron. "That's good news for you."

"Why?"

"Because it implies that Downing is on the run rather than dead," Win said. "The B Man is not wasteful. He wouldn't kill someone who owes him a lot of money."

"Dead men pay no debts."

"Precisely," Win said. "On top of that, he is clearly looking for Downing. If he killed him, he wouldn't need you to find him."

Myron considered this for a moment. "It sort of meshes with what Emily told me. She said Greg had no money. Gambling might explain that fact."

Win nodded. "Kindly fill me in on what else has occurred in my absence. Jessica mentioned something about finding a dead woman."

Myron told him everything. As he spoke, new theories rushed forward. He tried to sort through them and organize them a bit. When he finished the recap, Myron went right into the first one.

"Let's assume," he said, "that Downing does owe a lot of money to this B Man. That might explain why he finally agreed to sign an endorsement deal. He needs the money."

Win nodded. "Go on."

"And let's also assume the B Man is not stupid. He wants to collect, right? So he would never really hurt Greg. Greg makes him money through his physical prowess. Broken bones would have an adverse effect on Greg's financial status and thus his ability to pay."

"True," Win said.

"So let's say Greg owes them a lot of money. Maybe the B Man wanted to scare him in another way."

"How?"

"By hurting someone close to him. As a warning."

Win nodded again. "That might work."

"And suppose they followed Greg. Suppose they saw him with Carla. Suppose they figured that Greg and Carla were close." Myron looked up. "Wouldn't killing her be a hell of a warning?"

Win frowned. "You think the B Man killed her to warn Downing?"

"I'm saying it's possible."

"Why wouldn't he just break some of her bones?" Win asked.

"Because the B Man wasn't personally on the scene yet, remember? He got in last night. The murder would have been the work of hired muscle."

Win still didn't like it. "Your theory is improbable, at best. If the murder was indeed a warning, where is Downing now?"

"He ran away," Myron said.

"Why? Because he was afraid for his own life?"

"Yes."

"And did he run away immediately after learning Carla was dead?" Win asked. "On Saturday night?"

"That would be most logical."

"He was frightened off then? By the murder?"

"Yes," Myron said.

"Ah." Win stopped and smiled at Myron.

"What?" Myron asked.

"Pray tell," Win began with a lilt in his voice, "if Carla's body was just discovered today, how did Downing know about the murder last Saturday night?"

Myron felt a chill.

"For your theory to hold up," Win continued, "Greg Downing would have to have done one of three things. One, he witnessed the murder; two, he stumbled into her apartment after the murder; three, he committed the murder himself. Furthermore, there was a great deal of cash in her apartment. Why? What was it doing there? Was this money to help pay back the B Man? If so, why didn't his men take it? Or better yet, why didn't Downing take it back when he was there?"

Myron shook his head. "So many holes," he said. "And we still haven't come up with what connection there is between Downing and this Carla or Sally or whatever her name is."

Win nodded. They continued walking.

"One more thing," Myron said. "Do you really think the mob would kill a woman just because she happened to be with Greg at a bar?"

"Very doubtful," Win agreed.

"So basically, that whole theory is blown to hell."

"Not basically," Win corrected. "Entirely."

They kept walking.

"Of course," Win said, "Carla could have been working for the B Man."

An icy finger poked at Myron. He saw where Win was going but he still said, "What?"

"Perhaps this Carla woman was the B Man's contact. She collected for him. She was meeting Downing because he owed a great deal of money. Downing promises to pay. But he doesn't have the money. He knows they are closing in on him. He has stalled long enough. So he goes back to her apartment, kills her, and runs."

Silence. Myron tried to swallow, but his throat felt frozen. This was good, this talking it through. It helped. His legs were still rubbery from the incident, but what really bothered him now was how easily he had forgotten the dead man lying in the van. True, the man was probably a professional scum bag. True, the man had jammed the barrel of a gun into his mouth and had not dropped his weapon when Win told him to. And true, the world was probably a better place without him. But in the past Myron would have still felt some remorse for this fellow human being; in all honesty, he didn't now. He tried to muster some sympathy, but the only thing he felt sad about was that he didn't feel sad.

Enough self-analysis. Myron shook it off and said, "There are problems with that scenario too."

"Such as?"

"Why would Greg kill her? Why not just run off before the back-booth meeting?"

Win considered this. "Fair point. Unless something happened during their meeting to set him off."

"Like what?"

Win shrugged.

"It all comes back to this Carla," Myron said. "Nothing about her adds up. I mean, even a drug dealer doesn't have a setup like hers—working as a diner waitress, hiding sequentially numbered hundred dollar bills, wearing wigs, having all those fake passports. And on top of that, you should have seen Dimonte this afternoon. He knew who she was and he was in a panic."

"You contacted Higgins at Treasury?" Win asked.

"Yes. He's tracing those serial numbers."

"That could help."

"We also need to get a hold of the telephone records from the Parkview Diner. See who Carla called."

They fell back into silence and kept walking. They didn't want to hail a taxi too close to the scene.

"Win?"

"Yes?"

"Why didn't you want to go to the game the other night?"

Win kept on walking. Myron kept pace. After some time, Win said, "You've never watched a replay of it, have you?"

He knew he meant the knee injury. "No."

"Why not?"

Myron shrugged. "No point."

"No, there is a point." Win kept walking.

"Mind telling me what that is?" Myron said.

"Watching what happened to you might have meant dealing with it. Watching it might have meant closure."

"I don't understand," Myron said.

Win nodded. "I know."

"I remember you watched it," Myron said. "I remember you watched it over and over."

"I did that for a reason," Win said.

"For vengeance."

"To see if Burt Wesson injured you on purpose," Win corrected.

"You wanted to pay him back."

"You should have let me. Then you might have been able to put it behind you."

Myron shook his head. "Violence is always the answer for you, Win."

Win frowned. "Stop sounding melodramatic. A man committed a vile act upon you. Squaring things would have helped put it behind you. It's not about vengeance. It's about equilibrium. It's about man's basic need to keep the scales balanced."

"That's your need," Myron said, "not mine. Hurting Burt Wesson wouldn't have fixed my knee."

"But it might have given you closure."

"What does that mean, closure? It was a freak injury. That's all."

Win shook his head. "You never watched the tape."

"It wouldn't have mattered. The knee was still ruined. Watching a tape wouldn't have changed that."

Win said nothing.

"I don't understand this," Myron continued. "I went on after the injury. I never complained, did I?"

"Never."

"I didn't cry or curse the gods or do any of that stuff."

"Never," Win said again. "You never let yourself be a burden on any of us."

"So why do you think I needed to relive it?"

Win stopped and looked at him. "You've answered your own question, but you choose not to hear it."

"Spare me the Kung-Fu-grasshopper philosophical bullshit," Myron shot back. "Why didn't you go to the game?"

Win started walking again. "Watch the tape," he said.

Chapter 19

Myron didn't watch the tape. But he had the dream.

In the dream he could see Burt Wesson bearing down on him. He could see the gleeful, almost giddy violence in Burt's face as he drew closer and closer. In the dream, Myron had plenty of time to step out of harm's way. Too much time really. But in this dream—as in many—Myron could not move. His legs would not respond, his feet mired in thick, dream-world quicksand while the inevitable approached.

But in reality, Myron had never seen Burt Wesson coming. There had been no warning. Myron had been pivoting on his right leg when the blinding collision befell him. He heard rather than felt a snap. At first there had been no pain, just wide-eyed astonishment. The astonishment had probably lasted less than a second, but it was a frozen second, a snapshot Myron only took out in dreams. Then came the pain.

In the dream Burt Wesson was almost on him now. Burt was a huge man, an enforcer-type player, the basketball equivalent of a hockey goon. He did not have much talent, but he had tremendous bulk and he knew how to use it. It had gotten him far, but this was the pros now. Burt would be cut before the start of the season—poetic irony that neither he nor Myron would play in a real professional basketball game. Until two nights ago anyway.

In the dream Myron watched Burt Wesson approach and waited. Somewhere in his subconscious, he knew that he would awaken before the collision. He always did. He lingered now in that cusp between nightmare and being awake—that tiny window where you are still asleep but you know it is a dream and even though it may be terrifying, you want to go on and see how it will end because it is only a dream and you are safe. But reality would not keep that window open for long. It never did. As Myron swam to the surface, he knew that whatever the answer was, he would not find it in any nocturnal voyage to the past.

"Phone for you," Jessica said.

Myron blinked his eyes and rolled onto his back. Jessica was already dressed. "What time is it?" he asked.

"Nine."

"What? Why didn't you wake me?"

"You needed the sleep." She handed him the phone. "It's Esperanza."

He took it. "Hello."

"Christ, don't you ever sleep in your own bed?" Esperanza said.

He was hardly in the mood. "What is it?"

"Fred Higgins from Treasury is on the line," she said. "I thought you'd want it."

"Pass it through." A click. "Fred?"

"Yeah, how you doing, Myron?"

"I'm okay. You got anything on those serial numbers?"

There was a brief hesitation. "You stumbled into some heavy shit, Myron. Some very heavy shit."

"I'm listening."

"People don't want this out, you understand? I had to jump through all kinds of hoops to get this."

"Mum's the word."

"Okay then." Higgins took a deep breath. "The bills are from Tucson, Arizona," he said. "More specifically, First City National Bank of Tucson, Arizona. They were stolen in an armed bank heist."

Myron shot up in the bed. "When?"

"Two months ago."

Myron remembered a headline, and his blood turned cold.

"Myron?"

"The Raven Brigade," Myron managed. "That was one of theirs, right?"

"Right. You ever work on their case with the feds?"

"No, never." But he remembered. Myron and Win had worked on cases with a special and almost contradictory nature: high profile with the need for undercover. They had been perfect for such situations—who, after all, would suspect a former basketball star and a rich, Main Line prep of being undercover agents? They could travel in whatever circles they wanted to and not raise suspicion. Myron and Win didn't have to create a cover; their reality the best one the agency had. But Myron was never full-time with them. Win was their fair-haired boy; Myron was more a utility fielder Win called in when he thought it necessary.

But of course he knew about the Raven Brigade. Most people with even a passing familiarity with sixties extremism knew about them. Started by a charismatic leader named Cole Whiteman, the Ravens had been yet another splinter group of the Weather Underground. They were very much like the Symbionese Liberation Army, the group that kidnapped Patty Hearst. The Ravens, too, attempted a high-profile kidnapping, but the victim ended up dead. The group had gone underground. Four of them. Despite the FBI's best efforts, the four escapees—including Cole Whiteman, who with his Win-like blond hair and Waspy background never looked the part of an extremist—had remained hidden for nearly a quarter century.

Dimonte's bizarre questions about radical politics and "perversives" no longer seemed so bizarre.

"Was the victim one of the Ravens?" Myron asked.

"I can't say."

"You don't have to," Myron said. "I know it was Liz Gorman."

There was another brief hesitation. Then: "How the hell did you know that?"

"The implants," Myron said.

"What?"

Liz Gorman, a fiery redhead, had been one of the founding members of the Raven Brigade. During their first "mission"—a failed attempt to burn down a university chemistry lab—the police had picked up a code name on the scanner: CD. It was later revealed that the male members of the Brigade called her CD, short for Carpenter's Dream, because she was "flat as a board and easy to screw." Sixties radicals, for all their so-called progressive thoughts, were some of the world's biggest sexists. Now the implants made sense. Everyone Myron had interviewed remembered one thing about "Carla"— her cup size. Liz Gorman had been famous for her flat chest—what better disguise than oversized breast implants?

"The feds and cops are cooperating on this one," Higgins said. "They're trying to keep this quiet for a while."

"Why?"

"They got her place under surveillance. They're hoping to maybe draw out another member."

Myron felt completely numb. He had wanted to learn more about the mystery woman and now he had: she was Liz Gorman, a famous radical who had not been seen since 1975. The disguises, the various passports, the implants—they all added up now. She wasn't a drug dealer, she was a woman on the run.

But if Myron had hoped learning the truth about Liz Gorman would help clarify his own investigation, he had been sadly mistaken. What possible connection could there be between Greg Downing and Liz Gorman? How had a professional basketball player gotten enmeshed with a wanted extremist who had gone underground when Greg was still a kid? It made absolutely no sense.

"How much did they get in the bank heist?" Myron asked.

"Hard to say," Higgins answered. "About fifteen thousand in cash, but they also blew open the safe-deposit boxes. Over a half million in goods have been declared for insurance purposes, but a lot of it is bullshit. A guy gets robbed, all of a sudden he was keeping ten Rolexes in the box instead of one—trying to rip off the insurance company, you know how it is."

"On the other hand," Myron said, "anyone keeping illegal dollars in there wouldn't declare it. They'd just have to swallow the loss." Back to drugs and drug money. The extremists in the underground needed resources. They'd been known to rob banks, blackmail former followers who had gone mainstream, deal drugs, whatever. "So it could have been even more."

"Right, hard to say."

"You got anything else on this?"

"Nothing," Higgins said. "It's being kept sealed tight, and I'm not in the loop. I can't tell you how hard it was to get this, Myron. You owe me big."

"I already promised you the tickets, Fred."

"Courtside?"

"I'll do my best."

Jessica came back into the room. When she saw Myron's face, she stopped and looked a question at him. Myron hung up and told her. She listened. Remembering Esperanza's crack, Myron realized that he had now spent four nights in a row here—a postbreakup world and Olympic record. He worried about that. It wasn't that he didn't like staying here. He did. It wasn't that he feared commitment or any of that other drivel; to the contrary, he craved it. But part of him was still afraid—old wounds that wouldn't heal and all that.

Myron had a habit of exposing too much of himself. He knew that. With Win or Esperanza it was okay. He trusted them absolutely. He loved Jessica with all his heart, but she had hurt him. He wanted to be tentative. He wanted to hold back, to not leave himself so open, but the heart don't know from stop. At least, Myron's didn't. Two primal internal forces were at odds here: his natural instinct to give all he had when it came to love vs. the survival instinct of pain avoidance.

"This whole thing," Jessica said when he had finished, "is just too weird."

"Yep," he said. They had barely talked last night. He had assured her that he was all right and they had both gone to sleep. "I guess I should thank you."

"For what?"

"You were the one who called Win."

She nodded. "After those goons jumped you."

"I thought you said you weren't going to interfere."

"Wrong. I said I wasn't going to try to stop you. There's a difference."

"True enough."

Jessica started chewing on her bottom lip. She was wearing jeans and a Duke sweatshirt several sizes too large on her. Her hair was still wet from a recent shower. "I think you should move in," she said.

Her words hit him square in the jaw. "What?"

"I didn't mean to just blurt it out like that," she said. "I'm not very good at beating around the bush."

"That's my job anyway," he said.

She shook her head. "You pick the strangest times to be crude."

"Yeah, I'm sorry."

"Look, I'm not good at this stuff, Myron. You know that."

He nodded. He knew.

She tilted her head to the side, shrugged, smiled nervously. "It's just that I like having you here. It feels right."

His heart soared and sung and quivered in fear. "It's a big step."

"Not really," she said. "You're here most of the time anyway. And I love you."

"I love you, too."

The pause lingered a bit longer than it should. Jessica jumped into it before it could do irreparable harm. "Don't say anything now," she said, rushing the words out in a gush. "I want you to think about it. It was a dumb time to bring it up, with all this stuff going on. Or maybe that's why I chose now, I don't know. But don't say anything. Just think about it. Don't call me today. Or tonight. I'm going to your game, but then I'm taking Audrey out for a few drinks. It's her birthday. Sleep at your house tonight. Maybe we'll talk tomorrow, okay? Tomorrow?"

"Tomorrow," Myron agreed.

Chapter 20

Big Cyndi sat at the reception desk. "Sat" was probably the wrong word. Talk about the proverbial camel trying to squeeze through the eye of the needle. The desk's four legs were off the floor, the top teetering on Big Cyndi's knees like a seesaw. Her coffee mug disappeared into fleshy hands that resembled couch cushions. Her short spikes of hair had more of a pinkish hue today. Her makeup reminded him of a childhood incident involving melted Crayola crayons. She wore white lipstick, like something out of an Elvis documentary. Her size-3XL T-shirt read CLUB SODA NOT SEALS. It took Myron a few seconds to get it. Politically correct but cute.

Usually she growled when she saw Myron. Today she smiled sweetly and batted her eyes at him. The sight was far more frightening, like Bette Davis in *Whatever Happened to Baby Jane*, only on steroids. Big Cyndi pointed up her middle finger and bounced it up and down.

"Line one?" he tried.

She shook her head. The up and down gesture became more hurried. She looked up at the ceiling. Myron followed her gaze but he saw nothing. Cyndi rolled her eyes. The smile was frozen on her face, like a clown's.

"I don't get it," he said.

"Win wants to see you," she said.

It was the first time Myron had heard her voice, and it startled him. She sounded like one of those perky hostesses on a cable shopping network, the one where people call up and describe in far too much detail how much their lives were improved by purchasing a green vase shaped like Mount Rushmore.

"Where's Esperanza?" he asked.

"Win's cute."

"Is she here?"

"Win seemed to think it was important."

"I'm just—"

"You're going to see Win," Cyndi interrupted. "You're certainly not checking up on your most valued associate." The sweet smile.

"I'm not checking up. I just want to know—"

"Where Win's office is. It's two stories up." She made a sound with her coffee that some might loosely label, "slurping." Moose in the tri-state area scattered in search of mates.

"Tell her I'll be back," Myron said.

"But of course." She batted her eyelashes. They looked like two tarantulas in death throes. "Have a nice day."

Win's corner office faced Fifty-second Street and Park Avenue. Major league view for Lock-Horne Securities' golden boy. Myron sank into one of the lush burgundy leather chairs. There were several paintings of fox hunts on the richly paneled walls. Dozens of manly men on horseback, dressed in black hats, red blazers, white pants, black boots, rode out armed with only rifles and dogs to chase down a small furry creature until they caught and killed it. Ah, gamesman-ship. A tad overkill maybe. Like using a flamethrower to light a cig-arette.

Win typed on a laptop computer that looked lonely on the mono-expanse he called a desk. "I found something of interest on the com-puter disks we made at Greg's house."

"Oh?"

"It appears our friend Mr. Downing had an e-mail address with America Online," Win said. "He downloaded this particular piece of mail on Saturday." Win spun the laptop around so Myron could read the screen:

Subj:	Sex!
Date:	3-11 14:51:36 EST
From:	Sepbabe
To:	Downing22

Meet you tonight at ten. The place we discussed. Come. I promise you the greatest night of ecstasy imaginable.

—F

Myron looked up. "Greatest night of ecstasy imaginable?"

"She has quite the writing flair, no?" Win said.

Myron made a face.

Win put a sincere hand to his heart. "Even if she could not live up to such a promise," he continued, "one has to admire her ability to take risk, her dedication to her craft."

"Uh huh," Myron said. "So who is F?"

"There is no profile for the screen name Sepbabe on line," Win explained. "That doesn't mean anything, of course. Many users don't have a profile. They don't want everyone knowing their real name. I would assume however that F is yet another alias for our dearly departed friend Carla."

"We have Carla's real name now," Myron said.

"Oh?"

"Liz Gorman."

Win arched an eyebrow. "Pardon?"

"Liz Gorman. As in the Raven Brigade." He told Win about Fred Higgins's call. Win leaned back in his chair and steepled his fingers. As usual his face gave away nothing.

When Myron finished, Win said, "Curiouser and curiouser."

"It comes down to this," Myron said. "What connection could there possibly be between Greg Downing and Liz Gorman?"

"A strong one," Win said, nodding toward the screen. "The possibility of the greatest night of ecstasy imaginable, if one is to buy into the hyperbole."

"But with Liz Gorman?"

"Why not?" Win almost sounded defensive. "You shouldn't discriminate on the basis of age or implants. It wouldn't be right."

Mr. Equal Rights. "It's not that," Myron said. "Let's pretend that Greg has the hots for Liz Gorman, even though nobody described her as much of a looker . . ."

"You're so shallow, Myron," Win said with a disenchanted shake of the head. "Did you ever consider the possibility that Greg saw beneath that? She did, after all, have large breasts."

"As usual when discussing sex," Myron replied, "you've missed the point."

"Which is?"

"How would they have hooked up in the first place?"

Win steepled his fingers again, bouncing the tips against his nose. "Ah," he said.

"Right, ah. Here's a woman who's been living underground for more than twenty years. She's traveled all over the world, probably never staying in one spot for very long. She was in Arizona robbing a bank two months ago. She's working as a waitress in a tiny diner on Dyckman Street. How does this woman hook up with Greg Downing?"

"Difficult," Win allowed, "but not impossible. There is plenty of evidence to support that."

"Like?"

Win motioned to the computer screen. "This e-mail is talking about last Saturday night, for one—the same night Greg and Liz Gorman met in a New York City bar."

"In a dive bar," Myron corrected. "Why there? Why not go to a hotel or her place?"

"Perhaps because it is out of the way. Perhaps, as you implied, Liz Gorman would want to keep out of the public eye. Such a bar might be a good alternative." He stopped steepling and lightly drummed his fingers on the desk. "But you, my friend, are forgetting something else."

"What?"

"The woman's clothes in Greg's house," Win said. "Your investigation has led us to conclude that Downing has a lover he was keeping secret. The question, of course is: why? Why would he work so hard to keep a love affair clandestine? One possible explanation is that the secret love was the infamous Liz Gorman."

Myron wasn't sure what to think. Audrey had seen Greg at a restaurant with a woman that did not fit Liz Gorman's description. But what did that mean? It might have been another date. It might have been something innocent. It might have been a side affair, who knows? Still, Myron had trouble buying a romantic entanglement involving Greg Downing and Liz Gorman. Something about it just didn't wash. "There must be a way of tracing down this screen name and finding out the user's real identity," he said. "Let's make sure it checks back to Liz Gorman or one of her aliases."

"I'll see what I can do. I don't have any contacts with America Online, but someone we know must." Win reached behind him. He opened up the paneled door on his minifridge. He tossed Myron a can of Yoo-Hoo and poured himself a Brooklyn Lager. Win never drank beer, only lager. "Greg's money has been difficult to locate," he said. "I'm not sure there is very much."

"That would fit into what Emily said."

"However," Win continued, "I did find one major withdrawal."

"How much?"

"Fifty thousand dollars in cash. It took some time because it came out of an account that Martin Felder holds for him."

"When did he withdraw it?"

"Four days before he disappeared," Win said.

"Paying off a gambling debt?"

"Perhaps."

Win's phone rang. He picked it up and said, "Articulate. Okay, put it through." Two seconds later he handed the phone to Myron.

"For me?" Myron asked.

Win gave him flat eyes. "No," he said. "I'm handing you the phone because it's too heavy for me."

Everyone's a wiseass. Myron took the phone. "Hello?"

"I got a squad car downstairs." It was Dimonte in full bark. "Get your ass in it now."

"What's wrong?"

"I'm at fucking Downing's house, that's what's wrong. I had to practically suck off a judge to get the warrant."

"Nice imagery, Rolly."

"Don't fuck with me, Bolitar. You said there was blood in the house."

"In the basement," Myron corrected.

"Well, I'm in the basement right now," he countered. "And it's as clean as a baby's ass."

Chapter 21

The basement was indeed clean. No blood anywhere.

"There's got to be traces," Myron said.

Dimonte's toothpick looked like it was about to snap between his clenched teeth. "Traces?"

"Yeah. With a microscope or something."

"With a . . ." Dimonte flapped his arms, his face crimson. "What the hell good is traces going to do me? They don't prove a damn thing. You can't test traces."

"It'll prove there was blood."

"So what?" he shouted. "You go through any house in America with a microscope and you're bound to find traces of blood. Who the fuck cares?"

"I don't know what to tell you, Rolly. The blood was there."

There were maybe five lab cops—no uniforms, no marked cars—going through the house. Krinsky was there too. The videocamera in his hand was off right now. He also had what looked like manila files jammed into his armpit. Myron motioned to them. "That the coroner's report?"

Roland Dimonte stepped in to block Myron's view. "That ain't none of your business, Bolitar."

"I know about Liz Gorman, Rolly."

The toothpick hit the floor on that one. "How the hell . . . ?"

"It's not important."

"The fuck it ain't. What else do you know? If you're holding out on me, Bolitar—"

"I'm not holding out on you, but I think I can help."

Dimonte narrowed his eyes. Señor Suspicious. "Help how?"

"Just tell me Gorman's blood type. That's all I want to know. Her blood type."

"Why the hell should I?"

"Because you're not a total numb nut, Rolly."

"Don't give me that shit. Why do you want to know?"

"Remember I told you about finding blood in the basement?" Myron said.

"Yeah."

"I left something out."

Dimonte gave him the glare. "What?"

"We tested some of the blood."

"We? Who the fuck is . . ." His voice trailed off. "Oh Christ, don't tell me that psycho-yuppie is in on all this?"

To know Win was to love him. "I'd like to make a little trade."

"What kind of trade?"

"You tell me the blood type in the report. I tell you the blood type we found in the basement."

"Fuck you, Bolitar. I can arrest your ass for tampering with evidence in a police investigation."

"What tampering? There was no investigation."

"I could still nail your ass for breaking and entering."

"If you could prove it. And if Greg were around to press charges. Look, Rolly—"

"AB positive," Krinsky said. He ignored Dimonte's renewed glare and continued. "It's fairly rare. Four percent of the populace."

They both turned their attention to Myron. Myron nodded. "AB positive. It's the same."

Dimonte put up both hands and scrunched his face into perplexed. "Whoa, hold up here. Just what the fuck are you trying to say? That she was killed down here and moved?"

"I'm not saying anything," Myron said.

"Cause we didn't see any evidence of the body being moved," Dimonte went on. "None at all. Not that we were looking for it. But the bleeding pattern—I mean, if she was killed down here, there wouldn't have been so much blood like that at her apartment. You saw the mess there, right?"

Myron nodded.

Dimonte's eyes darted aimlessly. Myron could practically see the gears inside his head grinding to a halt. "You know what that means, don't you, Bolitar?"

"No, Rolly, why don't you enlighten me?"

"It means the killer came back here after the murder. It's the only explanation. And you know who all this is starting to point to? Your pal Downing. First we found his fingerprints in the victim's apartment—"

"What's this?"

Dimonte nodded. "That's right. Downing's fingerprints were by the door frame."

"But not inside?"

"Yeah, inside. Inside the door frame."

"But nowhere else?"

"What the hell's the difference? The fingerprints prove he was at the scene. What more do you need? Anyway, here's how it must have happened." He stuck a new toothpick in his mouth. New toothpick for a new theory. "Downing kills her. He comes back to his house to pack or something. He's in a rush so he leaves a little mess in the basement. Then he runs away. A few days later he comes back and cleans it up."

Myron shook his head. "Why come down to the basement in the first place?"

"The laundry room," Dimonte answered. "He was coming down here to wash his clothes."

"The laundry room is upstairs off the kitchen," Myron said.

Dimonte shrugged. "So maybe he was getting a suitcase."

"They're in the bedroom closet. This is just a kids' playroom, Rolly. Why did he come down here?"

That stopped Dimonte for a moment. It stopped Myron too. None of this made much sense. Had Liz Gorman been killed here and dragged to her apartment in Manhattan? That didn't seem to make much sense based on the physical evidence. Could she have been injured down here?

Whoa, hold the phone.

Maybe the attack started here. Maybe there had been a scuffle in the basement. In the course of subduing or knocking her out, blood was spilled. But then what? Did the killer stick her in a car and drive to Manhattan? And then—what?—on a fairly active street, the killer parked a car, dragged her injured body up the stairs, entered her apartment, killed her?

Did that make any sense?

From the first level a voice cried down, "Detective! We found something! Quick!"

Dimonte wet his lips. "Turn on the video," he told Krinsky. Videotaping all the relevant moments. Just like Myron had told him. "Stay here, Bolitar. I don't want to have to explain your ugly mug being on the film."

Myron followed but at a discreet distance. Krinsky and Dimonte headed up the stairs into the kitchen. They turned left. The laundry room. Vinyl yellow wallpaper with white chicks blanketed all four walls. Emily's taste? Probably not. Knowing Emily she'd probably never even seen the inside of a laundry room.

"Over here," someone said. Myron stayed back. He could see that the dryer had been pushed away from the wall. Dimonte bent down and looked behind it. Krinsky arched over to make sure the whole thing was being filmed. Dimonte stood back up. He was trying like hell to look grim—a smile wouldn't look good on film—but he was having a rough time of it. He snapped on a pair of rubber gloves and lifted the item into view.

The baseball bat was covered with blood.

Chapter 22

When Myron got back to the office, Esperanza was at the reception desk.

"Where's Big Cyndi?" Myron asked.

"Having lunch."

The image of Fred Flintstone's car tipping over from the weight of his Bronto-ribs flashed in front of Myron's eyes.

"Win filled me in on what's been going on," Esperanza said. She wore an aqua-blue blouse open at the throat. A gold heart on a slender chain dangled proudly against the dark skin of her sternum. Her always-mussed hair was slightly entangled in big hoop earrings. She pushed the hair back with one finger. "So what happened at the house?"

He explained about the cleaned-up blood and the baseball bat. Esperanza usually liked to do other things while she listened. She wasn't right now. She stared square into his eyes. When she looked at you like that, there was such intensity it was sometimes hard to look back.

"I'm not sure I understand," she said. "You and Win found blood in the basement two days ago."

"Right."

"Since then, someone cleaned up that blood—but they left behind the murder weapon?"

"So it appears."

Esperanza considered this for a moment. "Could it have been a maid?"

"The police already checked on that. She hasn't been there in three weeks."

"Do you have a thought?"

He nodded. "Someone is trying to frame Greg. It's the only logical explanation."

She arched a skeptical eyebrow. "By planting and then cleaning up blood?"

"No, let's start from the beginning." He grabbed the chair and sat in front of her. He had been going over it in his mind the whole ride back, and he wanted to talk it out. In the corner on his left, the fax machine sounded its digitally primordial screech. Myron waited for the sound to subside. "Okay," he said, "first I'm going to assume that the killer knew Greg was with Liz Gorman that night—maybe he followed them, maybe he was waiting for them near her apartment. Whatever, he knows they were together."

Esperanza nodded, stood. She walked over to the fax machine to check the incoming transmission.

"After Greg leaves, the killer murders Liz Gorman. Knowing that Downing would make a good fall guy, he takes some blood from the murder scene and plants it at Greg's house. That will raise suspicion. To put the icing on the cake, the killer also takes the murder weapon and plants it behind the dryer."

"But you just said the blood was cleaned up," she interjected.

"Right. Here's where it gets a little tricky. Suppose, for example, I wanted to protect Greg Downing. I go into his house and find the blood. Now remember, I want to protect Greg from a murder rap. So what would I do?"

She squinted at the fax coming through. "Clean up the blood."

"Exactly."

"Wow, thanks. Do I get a gold star? Get on with it already."

"Just bear with me, okay? I would see the blood and clean it up. But—and here's the important part—the first time I was in that house I *never* saw the bat. That's not just in this example. That's real life. Win and I only saw the blood in the basement. No baseball bat."

"Hold on," she said. "You're saying someone cleaned up the blood to protect Greg from a murder rap but didn't know about the bat?"

"Right."

"Who?"

"I don't know."

Esperanza shook her head. She moved back to her desk and hit some keys on her computer keyboard. "It doesn't add up."

"Why not?"

"Suppose I'm madly in love with Greg Downing," she said, moving back to the fax machine. "I'm in his house. For some reason I can't fathom, I'm in his kids' playroom. Doesn't matter where I am. Imagine I'm in my own apartment. Or I'm visiting your house. I could be anywhere."

"Okay."

"I see blood on the floor or on the walls or wherever." She

stopped, looked at him. "What conclusion would you logically expect me to draw?"

Myron shook his head. "I don't understand what you're saying."

Esperanza thought a moment. "Suppose you left here right now," she began, "and went back to the bitch's loft."

"Don't call her that."

"Whatever. Suppose when you walked in, you found blood on her walls. What would be your first reaction?"

Myron nodded slowly. Now he saw what she was getting at. "I'd be worried about Jessica."

"And your second reaction? After you found out she was okay?"

"Curiosity, I guess. Whose blood is it? How did it get there? That sort of thing."

"Right," she said with a quick nod. "Would you think to yourself, 'Gee, I better clean it up before the bitch gets accused of murdering somebody'?"

"Stop calling her that."

Esperanza waved him off. "Would you think that or not?"

"Not in that circumstance, no," Myron said. "So in order for my theory to hold water—"

"Your protector had to know about the murder," she finished for him, back checking her computer for something. "He or she would also have to know that Greg was somehow involved."

Myron's head spun with possibilities. "You think Greg killed her," he said. "You think he went back to his house after the murder and left behind some traces of the crime—like blood in the basement. Then he sent this protector back to the house to help cover his tracks."

Esperanza made a face. "Where the hell did you come up with that?"

"I just—"

"That's not what I think at all," Esperanza said. She stapled the fax pages together. "If Greg sent someone to get rid of the evidence, the weapon would be gone too."

"Right. So that leaves us where?"

Esperanza shrugged, circled something on the fax page with a red marker. "You're the great detective. You figure it out."

Myron thought about it a moment. Another answer—one he prayed was wrong—came to him all at once. "There's another possibility," he said.

"What?"

"Clip Arnstein."

"What about him?"

"I told Clip about the blood in the basement," Myron said.

"When?"

"Two days ago."

"How did he react?"

"He freaked, pretty much," Myron said. "He's also got motive— any scandal will destroy his chances of keeping control of the Dragons. Hell, that's why he hired me. To keep any trouble contained. Nobody else even knew about the blood in the basement." Myron stopped. He leaned back and ran it through his mind again. "Of course I haven't had a chance to tell Clip about Liz Gorman's murder. He didn't even know the blood wasn't Greg's. All he knew was that there was blood in the basement. Would he go that far just on that? Would he still risk covering it all up if he didn't know anything about Liz Gorman?"

Esperanza gave him a small smile. "Maybe he knows more than you think," she said.

"What makes you say that?"

She handed him the fax. "It's the list of long distance calls made from the pay phone at the Parkview Diner," she said. "I already cross-checked it with my computer Rolodex. Look at the number I circled."

Myron saw it. A call lasting twelve minutes had been made from the Parkview Diner four days before Greg's disappearance. The phone number was Clip's.

Chapter 23

"Liz Gorman called Clip?" Myron looked up at Esperanza. "What the hell is going on?"

Esperanza shrugged. "Ask Clip."

"I knew he was keeping something from me," he went on, "but I don't get it. How does Clip fit into this equation?"

"Uh huh." She shuffled through some papers on her desk. "Look, we got a ton of work to do. I mean, sports agent work. You have a game tonight, right?"

He nodded.

"So ask Clip then. In the meantime, we're just going around in circles here."

Myron scanned the sheet. "Any other numbers jump out at you?"

"Not yet," she said. "But I want to talk about something else for a minute."

"What?"

"We have a problem with a client."

"Who?"

"Jason Blair."

"What's wrong?"

"He's pissed off," she said. "He's not happy with me handling his contract negotiations. He said he hired you, not some"—she made quote marks in the air with her fingers—" 'scantily clad wrestler with a nice ass.' "

"He said that?"

"Yep. Nice ass. Didn't even notice my legs." Esperanza shook her head.

Myron smiled. "So what happened?"

Behind them the elevator dinged. Only one hit this part of the floor. The elevator opened directly into the reception area of MB SportsReps. Classy, or so he had been told. When the doors opened, two men came out. Myron recognized them right away. Camouflage Pants and Brick Wall. They were both armed. They aimed their guns at Myron and Esperanza. B Man stepped out behind them like he'd just been introduced on the Leno show. Big smile, acknowledging-the-crowd wave.

"How's the knee, Myron?" he asked.

"Better than your van."

B Man laughed at that one. "That Win," he mused. "The man is always a surprise. How did he know when to hit us?"

No reason not to tell. "We kept the cellular phones on."

B Man shook his head. "Ingenious really. I'm very impressed." He wore one of those suits that are just a tad too shiny and a pink tie. His shirt was french-cuffed and monogrammed with four letters: B MAN. Taking the nickname thing a little far. A thick, ropelike gold bracelet encircled his right wrist.

"How did you get up here?" Myron asked.

"Do you really think a few rent-a-cops are going to stop us?"

"I'd still like to hear," Myron said.

B Man shrugged. "I called Lock-Horne Securities and told them I was looking for a new financial advisor for my millions. An anxious young peon told me to come right up. I hit the twelfth floor on the elevator instead of the fifteenth." He spread his hands. "So here I am." He smiled at Esperanza. What with the too-white teeth and the tan, it looked like he switched on a night-light.

"And who is this fetching creature?" he asked with a wink.

"My," Esperanza said, "what woman doesn't love to be called a creature?"

B Man laughed again. "The little lady has gumption," he said. "I like that. I really do."

"Like I care," Esperanza said.

More laughter. "May I indulge you a moment, Miss . . . ?"

"Money Penny," she finished for him. She said it with her best Sean Connery imitation. No Rich Little, but not bad either.

Another laugh from the B Man. The man was half-hyena. "Would you please call Win down here? On the speakerphone if you don't mind. Tell him to come down unarmed."

She looked at Myron. Myron nodded. She dialed. Over the speakerphone, Win offered up another, "Articulate."

Esperanza said, "Some bottled blond with a bottled tan is down here to see you."

"Ah, I've been expecting him," Win said. "Hello, B Man."

"Hello, Win."

"I assume you are in well-armed company."

"That I am, Win," B Man said. "If you try anything, your friends won't make it out alive."

" 'Won't make it out alive'?" Win repeated. "I expected better from you, B Man, really. I'll be down in a second."

"Come unarmed, Win."

"Not a chance. But there will be no violence. That I promise you." The phone clicked off. For several moments everyone looked at one another as if wondering who was going to take the lead.

"I don't trust him," B Man said. He pointed to Brick Wall. "Take the girl in the other room. Duck down behind a desk or something. You hear any shooting, you blow her head off."

The Brick Wall nodded.

B Man directed his attention to Camouflage Pants. "Keep your gun on Bolitar."

"Right."

B Man took out his own weapon. When the elevator dinged, he squatted and aimed. The doors slid open, but it wasn't Win. Big Cyndi emerged from the elevator, not unlike a dinosaur emerging from its egg.

"Jesus Christ!" Camouflage Pants said. "What the hell is that?"

Big Cyndi growled.

"Who is she, Bolitar?" B Man demanded.

"My new receptionist."

"Tell her to wait in the other room."

Myron nodded to her. "It's okay. Esperanza's in there."

Cyndi growled again, but she listened. She walked past the B Man on her way to Myron's office. His gun looked like a disposable lighter next to her. She opened the door, snarled one last time, and closed it.

Silence.

"Jesus Christ," Camouflage Pants said again.

They waited approximately thirty seconds before the elevator dinged again. B Man got back into his squat and aimed. The doors slid open. Win stepped out. He looked mildly annoyed when he saw the weapon aimed his way. His voice was clipped. "I told you there would be no violence."

"You have information we need," B Man said.

"I'm well aware of that," Win replied. "Now put that gun away and we'll talk civilly."

The B Man kept his weapon on Win. "You armed?"

"Of course."

"Hand over your weapon."

"No," Win said. "And it's not weapon. It's weapons. Plural."

"I said—"

"And I heard you, Orville."

"Don't call me that."

Win sighed. "Fine, *B Man*." He shook his head as he said it. "You are making this far more difficult than it has to be."

"What's that supposed to mean?"

"It means that for an intelligent fellow, you too often forget that brute strength is not the only course. There are situations that call for restraint."

Win lecturing on restraint, Myron thought. What next? Xaviera Hollander lecturing on monogamy?

"Think about what you've already done," Win said. "First, you have Myron roughed up by a pair of amateurs—"

"Amateurs!" Camouflage Pants didn't like that. "Who you calling—"

"Shut up, Tony," B Man said.

"You hear what he called me? An amateur?"

"I said, shut up, Tony."

But Tony The Pants wasn't through yet. "Hey, I got feelings too, B Man."

The B Man gave him hard eyes. "Your left femur, if you don't shut up."

Tony closed his mouth.

The B Man looked back to Win. "Sorry about the interruption."

"Apology accepted."

"Go on."

"As I was saying," Win continued, "first you try to rough Myron up. Then you try to kidnap and cripple him. All for naught."

"Not for naught," B Man countered. "We need to know where Downing is."

"And what makes you think Myron knows?"

"You were both at his house. Then all of a sudden Bolitar is on Downing's team. As a matter of fact, he takes his place on the roster."

"So?"

"So I'm not stupid. You two know something."

"And what if we do?" Win said, hands spread. "Why didn't you just ask? Did you ever even consider that possibility? Did you ever think that maybe the best course of action would be simply to ask?"

"I did ask!" Camouflage Pants jumped in. He was defensive now. "On the street! I asked him where Greg was. He gave me lip."

Win looked at him. "Were you ever in the military?" he asked.

Pants seemed confused. "No."

"You are a worthless punk," Win said in the same tone he might use when discussing a mixed stock report. "A pitiful ectoplasm such as yourself wearing army fatigues is an affront to any man or woman who has ever experienced real combat. If I ever happen across you again donning any similar garb, I will hurt you severely. Do I make myself clear?"

"Hey—"

"You don't know this guy, Tony," B Man interrupted. "Just nod and shut up."

Camouflage Pants looked hurt but he did as he was told.

Win turned his attention back to the B Man. "We can help each other out in this situation," he said.

"How?"

"It just so happens that we, too, are searching for the elusive Mr. Downing. That is why I wish to make a proposal."

"I'm listening."

"First," Win said, "stop aiming the weapons at us."

B Man gave him a funny look. "How do I know I can trust you?"

"If I wanted you dead," Win answered, "I would have killed you last night."

The B Man thought it over, nodded, lowered his weapon. He signaled Camouflage Pants, who then did likewise. "Why didn't you?" B Man asked. "I probably would have killed you in the same situation."

"That's what I mean about brute force," Win said. "About being wasteful. We need each other here. If I had killed you, I wouldn't be able to make this proposal today."

"Fair enough. The floor is yours."

"I assume that Mr. Downing owes you a rather hefty sum."

"Very hefty sum."

"Fine," Win said. "You tell us what you know. We find him, no cost to you. When we do find him, you promise not to hurt him if he pays up."

"And if he doesn't pay up?"

Win grinned and held his hands out, palms up. "Who are we to interfere with the way you conduct your business?"

B Man thought about it, but not for very long. "Okay, I can live with that," he said. "But I don't talk with the hired help around." He turned to Camouflage. "Go sit in the other room."

"Why?"

"Because if someone decides to torture you, you'll know nothing."

That answer seemed to make perfect sense to Camouflage. He went into Myron's office without another word.

"Why don't we sit?" Win suggested.

They did so. B Man crossed his legs and started right in. "Downing is your basic gamble-a-holic," he began. "He had pretty good luck for a long time. That's a bad thing when a man has the itch. When his luck changed—as it must in the long run—he kept thinking he could win it back. They all do. When they have the sort of money that Downing has, I let them go. Let them dig their own grave. It's good for business. But at the same time, you have to keep an eye out. There is a fine line working here. You don't want them to end up digging to China either." He turned and looked at Myron. "You know what I'm saying?"

Myron nodded. "China."

"Right. Anyway, Downing started losing big. I'm talking very big here. He was never a prompt payer, but he was always good for it. I sometimes let the tab run as high as two-fifty or even three."

"Hundred thousand?" Myron asked.

"Yeah." B Man smiled. "You don't know any gamblers, do you?"

Myron kept silent. He wasn't about to tell this slime bucket his life story.

"It's as bad as alcohol or heroin," B Man went on. "They can't stop themselves. In some ways, it's even worse. People drink and do drugs to escape despair. Gambling has that element, too, but it also offers you the friendly hand of hope. You always got hope when you gamble. You always believe that you're just one bet away from turning it all around. It's a catch-twenty-two. If you got hope, you keep on gambling. But with gambling, there's always hope."

"Very deep," Win said. "Let's get back to Greg Downing."

"Simply put, Greg stops paying his tab. It runs up to half a million. I start putting some pressure on him. He tells me he's flat broke, but I shouldn't worry because he's signing some big endorsement deal that will net him zillions."

The Forte deal, Myron thought. Greg's sudden change of heart about endorsement money made more sense now.

"I asked him when this endorsement money will be coming in. He tells me in about six months. Six months? On a half million dollar debt and growing? I told him that's not good enough. He'd have to pay up now. He said he didn't have the money. So I ask for a show of good faith."

Myron knew where this was going. "He shaved points."

"Wrong. He was *supposed* to shave points. The Dragons were favored by eight over Charlotte. Downing was going to see to it that the Dragons won by less than eight. No big deal."

"He agreed?"

"Sure he did. The game was on Sunday. I dumped a ton on Charlotte. A ton."

"And Greg never played," Myron finished for him.

"You got it," B Man said. "The Dragons won by twelve. Okay, I figure Greg got hurt. Like the papers say. A freak injury, that's not his fault. Don't get me wrong. He's still responsible for what I lost. Why should I pay for his freak injury?" He paused to see if anyone was going to argue with his logic. No one bothered. "So I waited for Downing to call me, but he never did. I'm owed close to two million by now. Win, you know I can't just sit back with that kind of thing, right?"

Win nodded.

"When was the last time Greg made a payment to you?" Myron asked.

"It's been a while. I don't know. Five, six months maybe."

"Nothing more recent?"

"Nothing."

They talked a bit more. Esperanza, Big Cyndi, Camouflage, and Brick Wall came back into the room. Win and B Man changed the topic to martial art buddies they had in common. A few minutes later B Man and his entourage left. When the elevator door closed, Big Cyndi turned and smiled widely at Esperanza. Then she began to skip in a circle. The floor shook.

Myron looked a question at Esperanza.

"That big guy," Esperanza said, "the one who was with us in the other room."

"What about him?"

"He asked Cyndi for her phone number."

Big Cyndi continued skipping with childlike abandon. The occupants of the floor beneath them were probably diving for cover like it was the last day of Pompeii. He turned to Win. "Did you catch the fact that Greg hadn't paid anything in months?"

Win nodded. "Clearly the fifty thousand dollars he withdrew before his disappearance was not to pay off gambling debts."

"So what was it for?"

"To run, I imagine."

"So he knew at least four days before the fact that he was going to take off," Myron said.

"It would appear so."

Myron thought about that for a moment. "Then the timing of the murder can't just be a coincidence. If Greg planned to disappear, it can't be a coincidence that the day he takes off is the day Liz Gorman gets killed."

"Doubtful," Win agreed.

"You think Greg killed her?"

"The clues point in that direction," Win said. "I mentioned to you that the money had come from an account handled by Marty Felder. Perhaps Mr. Felder has an answer."

Myron wondered about that. Big Cyndi suddenly stopped skipping. She hugged Esperanza and made a la-la noise. Young love. "If Felder knew Greg was going into hiding," Myron said, "why would he leave those messages on Greg's machine?"

"Perhaps to throw us off. Or perhaps he did not know Greg's intent."

"I'll call him," Myron said. "See if I can make an appointment for tomorrow."

"You have a game tonight, do you not?"

"Yes."

"What time?"

"Seven-thirty." Myron checked his watch. "But I need to leave pretty soon if I want to talk to Clip first."

"I'll drive," Win said. "I'd like to meet this Mr. Arnstein."

After they left, Esperanza went through the messages on the voice mail. Then she straightened out her desk. Her two photographs—one of her bearded collie Chloe getting Best in Breed at the Westchester Dog Show; the other of her as Little Pocahontas and Big Cyndi as Big Chief Mama, holding up their FLOW (Fabulous Ladies Of Wrestling) tag-team title belts—had been knocked askew by Cyndi's knees.

As she stared at the photographs, something Myron said kept needling her. He was worried about timing. The timing of the murder. The timing of Downing's disappearance. But what about Liz Gorman's timing? What about the timing of her arrival in New York City? The bank in Tucson was robbed two months ago; Liz Gorman also started working for the Parkview Diner two months ago. A criminal on the run would want to get far away from the crime scene, yes, but to a place as populated as New York City? Why?

The more Esperanza thought about it, the more she grew bewildered. There had to be a cause and effect at work here. There had to be something about the bank heist that made Liz Gorman come out this way. Esperanza chewed on this for another minute or two. Then she picked up the phone and called one of Myron and Win's closest contacts at the bureau.

"They need everything you got on the Raven Brigade bank heist in Tucson," Esperanza said. "Can you send me a copy of the file?"

"You'll have it by tomorrow morning."

Chapter 24

Win and Myron shared a somewhat unusual passion for Broadway musicals. Right now, the stereo system in Win's Jag was pumping out the soundtrack from *1776*. A Continental Congressman cried out, "Somebody better open up a window!" This led to a fierce argument over the merits of opening said window (it was "hot as hell in Philadelphia") vs. keeping them closed ("too many flies"). Interspersed in this argument, people were telling John Adams to sit down. History.

"Who played the original Thomas Jefferson?" Win asked. He knew the answer. Life with Myron's friends was a nonstop quiz show.

"Movie version or stage?"

Win frowned. "I don't do movie versions."

"Ken Howard," Myron answered.

"Correct. What is Mr. Howard's most famous role?"

"The coach on the *White Shadow*."

"Correct again. The original John Adams?"

"William Daniels."

"Best known as?"

"The obnoxious surgeon on *St. Elsewhere*."

"The actress who portrayed Martha Jefferson?"

"Betty Buckley. Best known as Abby on *Eight Is Enough*."

Win smiled. "You are good."

Myron stared out the window, the buildings and cars blurring into one pulsating mass, and thought about Jessica. Moving in with her. There was no reason not to. He loved her. She loved him. More than that, she had made the first move—the first time he could remember such a thing. In most relationships, one partner has more control than the other. It was just the natural order of things. Perfect balance was a hard thing to find. In their case, Jessica currently had the upper hand. Myron knew that—if he hadn't, Esperanza's constant references to his being "whipped" would surely have made him aware. It didn't mean he loved her more or Jessica loved him less. Or maybe it did. Myron wasn't sure anymore. What he did know for sure was that moments where Jessica made the move—where she was the one exposing herself—were rare. Myron wanted to embrace it, encourage it. He had waited a long time for her to say such words to him. But something held him back. Like with TC, there were a lot of factors pushing and pulling at him.

His mind churned through the pros and cons, but no conclusions spewed forward. What he really wanted was to bounce his thoughts off someone. He deliberated best that way—by thinking out loud with a close friend. The problem was, who? Esperanza, his most dependable confidante, hated Jessica. Win . . . well, when it came to matters of the heart, Win was simply not your man; something in that nether region had shorted out a long time ago.

Still Myron heard himself say, "Jessica asked me to move in."

For a moment Win said nothing. Then: "Do you get a full share of the playoff money?"

"What?"

"You joined the team late. Have you worked out what share of the playoff money you'll be getting?"

"Don't worry. It's taken care of."

Win nodded. His eyes remained on the road. The speedometer hovered around eighty, a swiftness Route 3 was not built to bear. Win swerved lanes constantly. Myron had gotten somewhat used to Win's driving over the years, but he still kept his eyes averted from the front windshield.

"Are you staying for the game?" Myron asked.

"That depends."

"On?"

"On if this Thumper will be there," Win replied. "You said she was seeking employment. Perhaps I can interrogate her at the same time."

"What will you say?"

"That," Win said, "is a dilemma we both face. If you ask her about Downing's call, you blow your cover. If I ask her, she'll want to know the whys and wherefores. Either way, unless this Thumper is brain dead, she will be suspicious. Moreover, if she knows anything significant, she will most probably lie."

"So what do you suggest?"

Win tilted his head as though in deep thought. "Perhaps I'll bed her," he concluded. "Then I can make her talk while lost in the throes of passion."

"She only sleeps with men on the Giants or the Dragons," Myron said. Then he frowned and added, "Bed her?"

Win shrugged. "Just suggesting an alternative to whipping her

with a rubber hose," he said. "Unless, of course, she's into that kind
of thing."

"Any other suggestions?"

"I'm working on it." They took the exit to the Meadowlands in silence. On the CD player, Abigail Adams was telling John Adams that
women in Massachusetts needed pins. Win hummed along with the
music for a moment. Then he spoke. "As far as Jessica goes"—he
took one hand off the wheel and sort of waved it—"I'm not one to
ask about such things."

"I know."

"You were miserable the first time she left," he added. "I don't
know why you would risk going through that again."

Myron looked at him. "You really don't, do you?"

Win said nothing.

"That's sad, Win."

"Yes," he replied. "So very tragic."

"I'm serious," Myron said.

Win put a dramatic forearm to his brow. "Oh, what woe that I may
never experience the depths of misery you plunged to when Jessica
left. Pity this child."

"You know there's more to it than that."

Win put down the arm, shook his head. "No, my friend, there is
not. What was real was your pain. The rest of what you felt is the
stuff of cruel delusion."

"You really feel that way?"

"Yes."

"About all relationships?"

Win shook his head. "I never said that."

"How about our friendship? Is that a cruel delusion too?"

"This isn't about us," Win said.

"I'm just trying to understand—"

"There is nothing to understand," Win interrupted. "Do what you
believe is best. As I said, I am not the one with which to have this discussion."

Silence. The arena loomed in front of them. For years, it had been
called the Brendan Byrne Arena, named for the unpopular governor
who had been in office when the complex had been built. Recently,
however, the sports authority needed to raise funds, so the name had
been changed to the Continental Airlines Arena—not exactly musical, but then again the old name didn't exactly make you want to
break out in song either. Brendan Byrne and his past lackeys cried
foul over this affront. What a disgrace, they shouted with grave in-

dignation. This was Governor Byrne's legacy. How could they sell him out like this? But Myron didn't have a problem with the name change. Which would you rather do—tax the people to collect twenty-seven million dollars or bruise a politician's ego? No contest when you thought about it.

Myron glanced over at Win. Win's eyes were on the road, his fingers tightly wrapped around the wheel. Myron's mind flashed back to the morning after Jessica left five years ago. He'd been moping around his house alone when Win knocked on the door. Myron opened it.

Without preamble, Win said, "Come on. I'll hire you a girl. You need to get laid."

Myron shook his head.

"Are you certain?"

"Yes," Myron said.

"Do me a favor then."

"What?"

"Don't go out and get drunk," Win said. "That would be such a cliché."

"And what, getting laid isn't?"

Win pursed his lips together. "But at least it's a good cliché."

Then Win turned around and left. That had been it. They had never broached the subject of his relationship with Jessica again. It'd been a mistake to have brought it up now. Myron should have known better.

There were reasons Win was the way he was. Myron looked now at his friend and truly did pity him. From Win's vantage point, his life had been one long lesson in how to take care of himself. The results weren't always pretty, but they were usually effective. Win had not severed off his feelings or anything that dramatic, nor was he as robotic as he sometimes wanted people to think. But Win had learned not to trust or depend on others very much. There were not many people he cared about, but those he did were cherished with an intensity few ever experienced. The rest of the world meant very little to him.

"I'll get you a seat near Thumper's," Myron said softly.

Win nodded, pulled into a parking spot. Myron gave his name to Clip's secretary and they were shown into his office. Calvin Johnson was already there, standing to Clip's right. Clip was behind his desk. He looked older today. His cheeks were grayer; and the skin around his jowls seemed looser. When he stood, it seemed to take more effort.

Clip eyed Win for a moment. "This must be Mr. Lockwood."

He even knew about Win—again well prepared. "Yes," Myron said.

"He's helping us with our problem?"

"Yes."

Introductions were made. Hands were shaken. Rear ends were seated. As was his custom in such situations, Win remained silent. His eyes slid from one side of the room to the other, taking in everything. He liked to study people for a while before speaking to them, especially in their home environment.

"So," Clip began, forcing up a tired smile, "what have we got?"

"When you first approached me," Myron began, "you were afraid I'd uncover something unsavory. I'd like to know what that something was."

Clip tried to look amused. "Nothing personal, Myron," he began with a light chuckle, "but if I knew that, I wouldn't have needed to hire you."

Myron shook his head. "Not good enough."

"What?"

"Greg has disappeared before."

"So?"

"So you never suspected anything unsavory then," Myron said. "Why now?"

"I told you. I have the owners' vote coming up."

"That's your only concern?"

"Of course not," Clip said. "I'm worried about Greg too."

"But you never hired anyone to find him before. What are you afraid of?"

Clip shrugged. "Probably nothing. I'm just covering all my bases. Why? What have you found out?"

Myron shook his head. "You never cover all your bases, Clip. You're a risk-taker. Always were. I've seen you trade popular, proven veterans for untested draft picks. I've seen you risk going for the steal rather than hoping your defense holds. You've never been afraid to lean over that edge, to risk it all."

Clip smiled thinly. "The problem with that strategy," he said, "is that you lose too. Sometimes you lose a lot."

"What did you lose this time?" Myron asked.

"Nothing yet," he said. "But if Greg doesn't come back, it might cost my team a championship ring."

"That's not what I meant. There's something more going on."

"I'm sorry," Clip said, spreading his hands. "I really don't know what you're talking about. I hired you because it was the logical thing to do. Greg vanished. Now true, he's vanished before, but never this late in the season and never when we were so close to a championship. This simply isn't like him."

Myron glanced over at Win. Win appeared to be bored.

"Do you know a woman named Liz Gorman?" Myron tried.

In the corner of his eye, Myron saw Calvin sit up a bit.

"No," Clip said. "Should I?"

"How about a woman named Carla or Sally?"

"What? You mean have I ever known a woman named—"

"Recently. Or any woman involved in some way with Greg Downing."

Clip shook his head. "Calvin?" Calvin also shook his head, but the shake was a little too lingering. "Why do you ask?" Clip demanded.

"Because that's whom Greg was with the night he vanished," Myron said.

Clip sat up, his words coming scatter-gun. "Have you located her? Where is she now? Maybe they're together."

Myron looked at Win again. This time, Win nodded ever so slightly. He'd caught it too. "She's dead," Myron said.

Any traces of color on Clip's face drained away. Calvin remained silent, but he crossed his legs. A big move for ol' Frosty. "Dead?"

"Murdered, to be more specific."

"Oh my God . . ." Clip's eyes leapt from one face to another, as though seeking some sort of answer or solace there. He found none.

"Are you sure you don't know the names Liz Gorman, Carla, or Sally?" Myron asked.

Clip opened his mouth, closed it. No sound came out. He tried again. "Murdered?"

"Yes."

"And she was with Greg?"

"He's the last known person to see her alive. His fingerprints are at the murder scene."

"The murder scene?" His voice trembled, his eyes dazed. "My God, the blood you found in the basement," he said. "The body was at Greg's house?"

"No. She was killed in her apartment in New York."

Clip looked puzzled. "But I thought you found blood in Greg's basement. In the playroom."

"Yes. But that blood is gone now."

"Gone?" Clip sounded both confused and annoyed. "What do you mean, gone?"

"I mean somebody cleaned it up." He looked straight at Clip. "I mean somebody entered Greg's house in the past two days and tried to snuff out an unsavory scandal."

Clip startled up at that one. Life came back into the eyes. "You think it was me?"

"You were the only one I told about the blood. You wanted to keep the discovery secret."

"I left that up to you," Clip countered. "I said I thought it was the wrong move, but I'd respect your decision. Of course, I would want to avoid a scandal. Who wouldn't? But I would never do something like that. You know me better than that, Myron."

"Clip," Myron said, "I have the dead woman's phone records. She called you four days before the murder."

"What do you mean she called me?"

"Your office number is in the phone records."

He started to say something, stopped, started again. "Well, maybe she called here, but that doesn't mean she spoke to me." His tone was far from convincing. "Maybe she spoke to my secretary."

Win cleared his throat. Then he spoke for the first time since entering the office. "Mr. Arnstein?" he said.

"Yes."

"With all due respect, sir," Win continued, "your lies are growing tiresome."

Clip's mouth dropped. He was used to underlings kissing his rear, not to being called a liar. "What?"

"Myron has a great deal of respect for you," Win said. "That's admirable. People do not earn Myron's respect easily. But you know the dead woman. You talked to her on the phone. We have proof."

Clip's eyes narrowed. "What kind of proof?"

"The phone records, for one—"

"—but I just told you—"

"And your own words, for another," Win finished.

He slowed down, his expression wary. "What the hell are you talking about?"

Win steepled his fingers. "Earlier in this conversation, Myron asked you if you knew Liz Gorman or a woman named Carla or Sally. Do you recall that?"

"Yes. I told him no."

"Correct. And then he told you—and I quote his exact words because they are relevant—'that's whom Greg was with the night he vanished.' Awkward phrasing, I admit, but with a purpose. Do you recall your next two queries, Mr. Arnstein?"

Clip looked lost. "No."

"They were—and again I quote exact words—'Have you located *her* yet? Where is *she* now?' " Win stopped.

"Yeah, so?"

"You said, *her*. Then you said, *she*. Yet Myron asked you if you knew Liz Gorman or Carla or Sally. From his wording, wouldn't it be natural to assume he was referring to three different women? A *they* rather than a she or her? But you, Mr. Arnstein, immediately concluded that these three names belonged to one woman. Don't you find that odd?"

"What?" But Clip's anger was all bluster now. "You call that evidence?"

Win leaned forward. "Myron is being well compensated for his efforts here. For that reason, I would normally recommend that he continue working for you. I would advise him to mind his own business and take your money. If you wish to muck up your own investigation, who are we to interfere? Not that Myron would listen. He is a nosy man. Worse, he has this warped sense of doing right, even when it is not required."

Win stopped, took a breath, leaned back again. Instead of steepling his fingers, he gently bounced the tips against one another. All eyes were on him. "The problem is," he continued, "a woman has been murdered. On top of that, someone has tampered with a crime scene. Someone has also vanished and may very well be a murderer or another victim. In other words, it is now far too dangerous to remain in such a situation with blinders on. The potential costs outweigh the possible benefits. As a businessman, Mr. Arnstein, you should understand that."

Clip remained silent.

"So let us get to it, shall we?" Win spread his hands, then resteepled. "We know the murder victim spoke to you. Either tell us what she said, or we shake hands and part company."

"She spoke to me first." It was Calvin. He shifted in his seat. He avoided Clip's eyes, but there was no need. Clip did not seem upset by the outburst. He sank farther down in his chair, a balloon continuing to deflate. "She used the name Carla," Calvin continued.

With a small nod, Win settled back into his chair. He had done his part. The reins were back in Myron's hands.

"What did she say?" Myron asked.

"She said she had some kind of dirt on Greg. She said she could destroy the franchise."

"What was the dirt?"

Clip came back into the fold. "We never found out," he chimed in. Clip hesitated a moment—to buy time or gather himself, Myron wasn't sure which. "I didn't mean to lie to you, Myron. I'm sorry. I was just trying to protect Greg."

"You spoke to her too?" Myron asked.

Clip nodded. "Calvin came to me after she called. The next time she called we both spoke to her. She said she wanted money in exchange for silence."

"How much?"

"Twenty thousand dollars. We were supposed to meet on Monday night."

"Where?"

"I don't know," Clip said. "She was going to tell us the locale on Monday morning, but she never called."

Probably because she was dead, Myron thought. Dead people rarely made phone calls. "And she never told you her big secret?"

Clip and Calvin looked a question at each other. Calvin nodded. Then Clip turned back to Myron. "She didn't have to," Clip said with resignation. "We already knew."

"Knew what?"

"Greg gambled. He owed a lot of money to some very bad people."

"You already knew about his gambling?"

"Yes," Clip said.

"How?"

"Greg told me."

"When?"

"About a month ago," Clip said. "He wanted help. I . . . I've always been something of a father figure to him. I care about him. I care about him very much." He looked up at Myron, his eyes raw with pain. "I care about you too, Myron. That's what makes this so hard."

"Makes what so hard?"

But he shook it off. "I wanted to help him. I convinced him to start seeing somebody. A professional."

"Did he listen?"

"Greg started with the doctor just last week. A psychiatrist who specializes in gambling addictions. We also talked about him signing an endorsement deal," he added. "To pay off the gambling debt."

"Did Marty Felder know about the gambling?" Myron asked.

"I can't say for certain," Clip said. "The doctor told me about the amazing lengths gamblers go to keep their addiction a secret. But Marty Felder handled most of Greg's money. If he didn't know, I'd be surprised."

Behind Clip's head was a poster of this year's team. Myron looked at it a moment. The co-captains, TC and Greg, were kneeling in front. Greg smiled widely. TC sneered in typical fashion. "So even when you first hired me," Myron said, "you suspected Greg's disappearance had something to do with his gambling."

"No." Then thinking further, Clip added. "At least not in the way you think. I never thought Greg's bookie would harm him. I figured the Forte deal bought him time."

"Then in what way?"

"I worried about his sanity." Clip motioned to Greg's image on the poster behind him. "Greg is not the most balanced person to begin with, but I wondered how much the pressure from the gambling debt weighed on his already questionable sanity. He loved his image, you know, strange as that might sound. He loved being a fan favorite more than the money. But if his fans learned the truth, who knows how they'd react? So I wondered if all of this pressure was too much for him. If maybe he had snapped."

"And now that a woman is dead," Myron asked, "what do you think?"

Clip shook his head vehemently. "I know Greg better than anyone. When he feels trapped, he runs away. He wouldn't kill anyone. I believe that with all my heart. He is not a violent man. Greg learned the dangers of violence a long time ago."

No one spoke for several moments. Myron and Win both waited for Clip to elaborate. When he didn't, Win said, "Mr. Arnstein, do you have anything else to tell us?"

"No. That's all."

Win rose without another word or gesture and walked out of the office. Myron sort of shrugged and started after him.

"Myron?"

He turned back to Clip. The old man was standing now. His eyes looked moist.

"Have a good game tonight," he said softly. "It's only a game, after all. Remember that."

Myron nodded, discomfited yet again by Clip's demeanor. He jogged ahead and caught up with Win.

"Do you have my ticket?" Win asked.

Myron handed it to him.

"Describe this Thumper person please."

Myron did. When they reached the elevator, Win said, "Your Mr. Arnstein is still not telling us the truth."

"Anything concrete or just a hunch?"

"I don't do hunches," Win said. "Do you believe him?"

"I'm not sure."

"You are fond of Mr. Arnstein, are you not?"

"Yes."

"Even though he has already admitted lying to you?"

"Yes."

"Then let me present you with an interesting scenario," Win said. "Who, besides Greg, has the most to lose if his gambling addiction becomes public knowledge? Who, besides Greg, would have the greatest motive to keep Liz Gorman silent? And finally, if Greg Downing was about to become a terrible embarrassment to the franchise—to the point of devaluating if not destroying Clip Arnstein's chances of maintaining control—who would have the best motive to make sure Greg Downing disappeared?"

Myron did not bother answering.

Chapter 25

The seat next to Thumper was open. Win took it and gave her the full-wattage smile.

"Good evening," he said.

She smiled back. "Hello."

"You must be Ms. Mason."

She nodded. "And you are Windsor Horne Lockwood III. I recognize you from the picture in *Forbes*."

They shook hands, their eyes meeting. Their hands released one another; their eyes didn't. "A pleasure to meet you, Ms. Mason."

"Please call me Maggie."

"Yes, fine." Win upped the smile for a moment. A buzzer sounded on the court. The first quarter was over. He saw Myron stand up to let his teammates sit. Seeing him dressed in a uniform on an NBA court hit Win in a very weird, unpleasant way. He didn't like to watch. He turned back toward Thumper. She looked at him expectantly.

"I understand that you are seeking employment with my firm," Win said.

"Yes."

"Do you mind if I ask you a few questions?"

"Please do." She motioned a welcome with her hand.

"You are currently employed by Kimmel Brothers, are you not?"

"Yes."

"How many traders do they currently engage?" Win asked.

"Less than ten," she said. "We're very small."

"I see." Win did the steepling, feigning consideration of her words. "Do you work there on weekends?"

"Sometimes."

"Weekend evenings?"

Her eyes narrowed just slightly, then relaxed back into place. "Sometimes," she repeated.

"How about last Saturday night?"

"Pardon me?"

"You know Greg Downing, do you not?"

"Of course but—"

"As you are no doubt aware," Win continued, "he has been missing since last Saturday night. Interestingly enough, the last call Mr. Downing made from his home was to your office. Do you recall that phone call?"

"Mr. Lockwood—"

"Please. Call me Win."

"I don't know what you're trying to do here—"

"It's quite simple really," Win interrupted. "Last night, you told my associate Mr. Bolitar that you had not spoken to Greg Downing in several months. Yet, as I have just told you, I have information that contradicts your statement. So there is a discrepancy here—a discrepancy that may cause some to view you, Ms. Mason, as less than honest. I cannot have that at Lock-Horne Securities. My employees must be beyond reproach. For that reason, I'd like you to explain this contradiction."

Win took out a bag of peanuts from his coat pocket. He shelled a few in the neatest manner imaginable, swept the shells with small movements into a second bag, then placed the peanuts into his mouth one at a time.

"How do you know Mr. Downing called my office?" Thumper asked.

"Please," Win said with a side glance. "Let us not waste time with trivialities. His call is an established fact. You know it. I know it. Let us move beyond it."

"I didn't work last Saturday night," she said. "He must have been calling somebody else."

Win frowned. "I grow weary of your tactics, Ms. Mason. As you just admitted to me, yours is a small firm. I could call your employer, if you wish. I am sure he would be glad to tell Mr. Windsor Horne Lockwood III if you were there or not."

Thumper sat back in her chair, folding her arms across her chest, looking out at the game. The Dragons were up 24 to 22. Her eyes followed the course of the ball down the court. "I have nothing more to say to you, Mr. Lockwood."

"Ah. No longer interested in a job?"

"That's right."

"You misunderstand," Win said. "I don't mean just with Lock-Horne Securities. I mean with anybody, including your current employer."

She turned to him. "What?"

"There are two options here," Win said. "Let me spell them out for you clearly, so that you choose the one most suitable for you. One, you tell me why Greg Downing called you on Saturday night. You tell me why you lied to Myron about it. You tell me everything you know about his disappearance."

"What disappearance?" she interrupted. "I thought he was injured."

"Option two," Win went on. "You continue to either stay silent or lie to me, in which case I will begin to circulate a rumor within our industry vis-à-vis your integrity. More specifically, I will let it be known that there are federal authorities looking into serious allegations of embezzlement."

"But . . ." she started, stopped. "You can't do that."

"No?" He made an amused face. "I am Windsor Horne Lockwood III. My word on such matters will not be questioned. You, on the other hand, will have difficulty finding employment as a hat check girl in a roadside Denny's when I'm through." He smiled and tilted the bag her way. "Peanut?"

"You're insane."

"And you are normal," Win countered. He looked down at the court. "Say, that young towel boy is wiping a player's sweat off the floor. That must be worth"—he gave a big shrug—"oh, I don't know. Fellatio at the very least, wouldn't you say?"

Win smiled at her sweetly.

"I'm leaving." She started to stand.

"Would you sleep with me?" he asked.

She looked at him in horror. "What?"

"Would you sleep with me? If you're very good, I may consider employing you at Lock-Horne."

Her teeth were clenched. "I'm not a prostitute," she hissed.

"No, you are not a prostitute," Win said, loud enough so that a few heads turned. "But you are a hypocrite."

"What are you talking about?"

Win motioned to her seat. "Please sit down."

"I'd rather not."

"And I'd rather not have to shout." He motioned again. "Please."

With wary eyes she did as he asked. "What do you want?"

"You find me attractive, do you not?"

She made a face. "I think you are the most repulsive man I have—"

"I am just speaking only about looks here," Win said. "The physical, remember? As you told Myron just last night, having sex is merely a physical thing. Like shaking hands—though with an analogy like that I question your partners' prowess. Now, at the risk of appearing immodest, I know that I am not physically unattractive. When you think back over the many Giants and Dragons you've bedded in your stellar career, surely there must be at least one that was less physically attractive than *moi*."

Her eyes squinted. She looked intrigued and horror-stricken at the same time. "Perhaps," she allowed.

"Yet you will not sleep with me. That, my dear, is hypocritical."

"How so?" Thumper countered. "I'm an independent woman. I choose."

"So you've told me," Win said. "But why do you choose only Giants and Dragons?" When she hesitated a bit too long, he smiled and wagged his finger. "You should at least be honest as to why you made that particular choice."

"You seem to know a lot about me," Thumper said. "Why don't you tell me?"

"Fine. You immediately announce this bizarre rule about Dragons and Giants and whatnot. You set limits. I do not. If I find a woman attractive, that is enough. But you need this random team affiliation. You use it as a fence to separate you."

"Separate me from what?"

"Not from what. Whom. From so-called freewheeling sluts. As you just pointed out to me, you are not a prostitute. You choose, dammit. You are no slut."

"That's right, I'm not."

He smiled. "But what is a slut? A woman who sleeps around? Well, no. That's what you do. You wouldn't criticize a fellow sister to the cause. So what exactly is a slut? Well, by your definition, there is no such thing. Except, of course, you needed to deny being a slut when I questioned you. Why?"

"Don't make it out to be more than it is," Thumper said. "Slut carries with it a negative connotation. That's the only reason I got defensive."

Win spread his hands. "But why should there be any negative connotation? If a slut is, by definition, a so-called loose woman, a woman who sleeps around, why not embrace the term with both legs? Why put up these fences? Why create these artificial limits? You use your team affiliations to announce your independence. But it announces the opposite. It announces that you are unsure and insecure."

"And that's why I'm a hypocrite?"

"Of course. Go back to my request to sleep with you. Either sex is a purely physical act, in which case my brusque behavior with you now should have no bearing on it, or sex is something more than physical. Which is it?"

She smiled, gave a quick head shake. "You're an interesting man, Mr. Lockwood. Maybe I will sleep with you."

"No good," he said.

"What?"

"You'll be doing it simply to prove I'm wrong. That, my dear, is as pathetic and insecure as what you are currently doing. But we are getting sidetracked. That is my fault, I apologize. Are you going to tell me about your conversation with Greg Downing, or do I destroy your reputation?"

She looked dazed. It was what he wanted.

"Of course there is option three," Win continued, "which closely follows option two. That is, on top of having your reputation destroyed you face a murder charge."

That made her eyes widen. "What?"

"Greg Downing is a serious suspect in a murder investigation. If it is discovered that you in some way helped him, that would make you an accessory." He stopped, frowned. "But to be frank, I don't think the D.A. will get a conviction. No matter. I'll start with your reputation. We'll see how it goes from there."

Thumper looked at him steadily. "Mr. Lockwood?"

"Yes."

"Go fuck yourself," she said.

Win rose. "Undeniably a better option than present company." He smiled and bowed. If he had a hat, he would have tipped it. "Good day."

He moved away, head high. There was, of course, a method to such madness. She would not talk. He knew that almost immediately. She was both smart and loyal. A dangerous albeit admirable combination. But what he had said would jar her. Even the best amongst us would panic or at the very least act. He would wait outside and follow her.

He checked the scoreboard. Midway through the second quarter. He had no interest in watching any more of this game. But as he reached the gate, a buzz came over the loudspeaker and then a voice said, "Now coming in for Troy Erickson, Myron Bolitar."

Win hesitated. Then he took another step for the exit. He did not wish to watch. But he stopped again and, still standing, he faced the court.

Chapter 26

Myron sat at the far end of the bench. He knew that he wasn't going to play, but his chest was still wrapped in the steel bands of pregame jitters. In his younger days Myron had enjoyed the pressure of big-time competition, even when the jitters reached a level of near paralysis. They never lasted long after the opening tip. Once he had physical contact with an opponent or chased down a loose ball or shot a fade-away jumper, the butterflies flew off, the crowd's cheers and jeers dissolving into something akin to office background music.

Pregame jitters hadn't been a part of Myron's existence for over a decade, and he knew now what he'd always suspected: this nerve-jangled high was directly connected to basketball. Nothing else. He had never experienced anything similar in his business or personal life. Even violent confrontations—a perverted high if ever there was one—were not exactly like this. He had thought this uniquely sports-related sensation would ebb away with age and maturity, when a young man no longer takes a small event like a basketball game and blows it into an entity of near biblical importance, when something so relatively insignificant in the long run is no longer magnified to epic dimensions through the prism of youth. An adult, of course, can see what is useless to explain to a child—that one particular school dance or missed foul shot would be no more than a pang in the future. Yet here Myron was, comfortably ensconced in his thirties and still feeling the same heightened and raw sensations he had known only in youth. They hadn't gone away with age. They'd just hibernated—as Calvin had warned him—hoping for a chance to stir, a chance that normally never came in one man's lifetime.

Were his friends right? Was this all too much for him? Had he not put this all behind him? He spotted Jessica in the stands. She was watching the action, that funny look of concentration on her face. She alone seemed unconcerned by his return, but then again, she had not been a part of his life in his basketball heyday. Did the woman he love not understand, or did she—?

He stopped.

When you are on the bench, an arena can be a small place. He saw, for example, Win speaking with Thumper. He saw Jessica. He saw the other players' wives and girlfriends. And then, entering from a gate dead straight in front of him, he saw his parents. His eyes quickly fled back to the court. He clapped his hands and yelled out encouragement to his teammates, pretending to be interested in the outcome of the game. His mom and dad. They must have flown in early from their trip.

He risked a quick glance. They sat near Jessica now, in the family and friends section. His mom was staring back at him. Even from the distance he could see the lost look in her glassy eyes. Dad's eyes darted about, his jaw taut, as though he were summoning up a little extra before looking at the court straight on. Myron understood. This was all too familiar, like an old family film coming to life. He looked away again.

Leon White came out of the game. He grabbed an empty seat next to Myron. A towel boy draped his sweat top around his shoulders and gave him a squeeze bottle. Leon guzzled some Gatorade, his body glistened with sweat.

"Saw you talking with Thumper last night," Leon said.

"Yeah."

"You get some?"

Myron shook his head. "I remain thump-less."

Leon chuckled. "Anyone tell you how she got that nickname?"

"No."

"When she gets into it—I mean, when she gets really fired up—she's got this habit of thumping her leg up and down. Left leg. Always her left leg, you know. So she's like on her back and you're pumping her for all you're worth and then all of a sudden her left leg starts bopping up and down. You hear thump-thump, get it?"

Myron nodded. He got it.

"So if she don't do that—if a guy don't get Thumper thumping—it's like you haven't done your duty. You can't show your face. You hang your head." Then he added, "It's a pretty serious tradition."

"Like lighting a menorah on Hanukkah," Myron said.

Leon laughed. "Well, not exactly."

"You ever been thumped, Leon?"

"Sure, once." Then he quickly added, "But that was before I was married."

"How long you been married?"

"Me and Fiona been married a little over a year."

Myron's heart plummeted down an elevator shaft. Fiona. Leon's wife's name was Fiona. He looked up in the stands at the flashy, well-rounded blonde. Fiona began with the letter F.

"Bolitar!"

Myron looked up. It was Donny Walsh, the head coach. "Yeah?"

"Go in for Erickson." Walsh said it like the words were fingernail clippings he needed to spit out. "Take the off guard spot. Put Kiley at the point."

Myron looked at his coach as if he were speaking Swahili. It was the second quarter. The score was tied.

"What the fuck you waiting for, Bolitar? For Erickson. Now."

Leon slapped his back. "Go, man."

Myron stood. His legs felt like strung-out Slinkys. Thoughts of murder and disappearances fled like bats in a spotlight. He tried to swallow but his mouth was bone dry. He jogged over to the scorer's table. The arena spun like the bed of a drunk. Without conscious thought he discarded his sweats on the floor like a snake changing skin. He nodded at the scorer. "For Erickson," he said. Ten seconds later, a buzzer sounded. "Now coming in the game for Troy Erickson, Myron Bolitar."

He jogged out, pointing to Erickson. His teammates looked surprised to see him. Erickson said, "You got Wallace." Reggie Wallace. One of the game's best shooting guards. Myron lined up next to him and prepared. Wallace studied him with an amused smile.

"SWB alert," Reggie Wallace called out with a mocking laugh. "Goddamn SWB alert."

Myron looked at TC. "SWB?"

"Slow White Boy," TC told him.

"Oh."

Everyone else was breathing deeply and coated with sweat. Myron felt stiff and unprepared. His eyes swung back to Wallace. The ball was about to be inbounded. Something caught Myron's eye and he looked up. Win stood near an exit. His arms crossed. Their eyes met for a brief second. Win gave a half nod. The whistle blew. The game began.

Reggie Wallace began the trash talk immediately. "You got to be kidding me," he said. "Old-timer, I'm gonna make you my woman."

"Dinner and a movie first," Myron said.

Wallace looked at him. "Lame retort, old man."

Hard to argue.

Wallace lowered himself to a ready position. He shook his head. "Shit. Might as well have my grandma cover me."

"Speaking of making someone your woman," Myron said.

Wallace looked at him hard, nodded. "Better," he said.

The Pacers inbounded the ball. Wallace tried to post Myron up under the basket. This was a good thing. Physical contact. Nothing unclasped those steel bands like battling for position. Their bodies bounced against one another with small grunts. At six-four, two-twenty, Myron held his ground. Wallace tried digging back with his butt, but Myron held firm, putting a knee into Wallace's backside.

"Man," Wallace said, "you are so strong."

And with that, he made a move Myron barely saw. He spun off Myron's knee so quickly that Myron barely had time to turn his head. Seeming to use Myron for leverage, Wallace leaped high in the air. From Myron's vantage point, it looked like an Apollo spacecraft heading straight out of the arena. He watched helplessly as Wallace's outstretched hands grasped the lob pass at rim level. He seemed to pause in midair, then continue rising as though gravity itself had decided to freeze frame the moment. When Reggie Wallace finally began to descend, he pulled the ball behind his head before throwing it through the cylinder with frightening force.

Slam dunk.

Wallace landed with both arms spread for applause. His taunting chased Myron up court. "Welcome to the NBA, has-been. Or never-was. Or whatever the fuck you are. Oh, man, was that pretty or what? How did I look going up? Be honest. Bottom of my sneakers look sweet, don't they? I'm so pretty. So very pretty. How did it feel when I slammed it in your face? Come on, old-timer, you can tell me."

Myron tried to tune him out. The Dragons came down and missed a quick shot. The Pacers grabbed the rebound and headed back up court. Wallace faked going back in-side and popped way out past the three point circle. He caught the pass and shot in one motion. The ball went in with a swish. Three pointer.

"Whoa, old man, did you hear that sound?" Reggie Wallace went on. "That swish? There is no sweeter sound on earth. You hear me? No sweeter sound at all. Not even a woman crying out in orgasm."

Myron looked at him. "Women have orgasms?"

Wallace laughed. "Touché, old-timer. Touché."

Myron checked the clock. He'd been in for thirty-four seconds and his man had scored five points. Myron did some quick math. At that rate, Myron could hold Reggie Wallace to under six hundred points per game.

The boos started soon after. Unlike his youth, the crowd sounds did not fade into the background. They were not one indistinguishable blur of sound, a home-court cheer to perhaps ride upon the way a surfer picks up a wave. Or a boo in a rival's arena—something you expect and even thrive on in a perverse way. But to hear your own fans boo your specific performance, to hear your home crowd turn against you—Myron had never experienced that before. He heard the crowd now as never before, as a collective entity of derision and as distinct voices making ugly catcalls. "You suck, Bolitar!" "Get that stiff outta there!" "Blow out your other knee and sit down!" He tried to ignore them but each catcall punctured him like a dagger.

Pride took over. He would not let Wallace score. The mind was willing. The heart was willing. But as Myron soon saw, the knee was not. He was simply too slow. Reggie Wallace scored six more points off Myron that period for a total of eleven. Myron scored two off an open jumper. He took to playing what he used to call "appendix" basketball; that is, certain players on the floor are like your appendix—they're either superfluous or they hurt you. He tried to stay out of the way and hit TC down low. He kept passing and moving away from the ball. When he saw a big opening and drove the lane near the end of the quarter, the Pacers' big center swatted the shot into the crowd. The boos were thunderous. Myron looked up. His mom and dad were still as two statues. One box over, a group of well-dressed men were cupping their hands around their mouths and starting a "Bolitar Sucks" chant. Myron saw Win move quickly toward them. Win offered his hand to the cheer's leader. The leader took it. The leader went down.

But the odd thing was, even as Myron stunk up the joint, even as he continued to get beaten on defense and play ineffectively on offense, the old confidence remained. He wanted to stay in the game. He would still look for an opening, relatively unshaken, a man in denial, a man ignoring the mounting evidence that a crowd of 18,812 (according to the loudspeaker) could plainly see. He knew his luck would change. He was a little out of shape, that was all. Soon it would all turn around.

He realized how much that sounded like B Man's description of a compulsive gambler's rationale.

The half ended not long after that. As Myron headed off the court, he looked up again at his parents. They stood and smiled down at him. He smiled and nodded back. He looked toward the group of well-dressed booers. They were nowhere to be seen. Neither was Win.

Nobody spoke to him at halftime, and Myron didn't get in the rest of the game. He suspected that Clip had been behind his playing. Why? What had Clip been trying to prove? The game ended in a two-

point victory for the Dragons. By the time they got into the locker
room and began changing, Myron's performance was forgotten. The
media surrounded TC, who had played a brilliant game, scoring
thirty-three points and grabbing eighteen rebounds. TC slapped Myron's back when he walked past him but said nothing.

Myron unlaced his sneakers. He wondered if his parents were going to wait for him. Probably not. They would figure he would want
to be alone. His parents, for all their butting in, were actually pretty
good at knowing when to make themselves scarce. They'd wait for
him at home, staying up all night if they had to. To this day, his father stayed awake watching TV on the couch until Myron got home.
Once Myron put the key in the lock, his father feigned sleep, his
reading glasses still perched at the end of his nose, the newspaper lying across his chest. Thirty-two years old and his father still waited
up for him. Christ, he was too old for that anymore, wasn't he?

Audrey peered tentatively around the corner and waited. Only
when he signaled with a beckoning wave did she approach. She stuck
her pad and pencil in her purse and shrugged. "Look at the bright
side," she said.

"And that is?"

"You still have a great ass."

"It's these pro shorts," Myron said. "They really mold and hold."

"Mold and hold?"

He shrugged. "Hey, happy birthday."

"Thanks," Audrey said.

" 'Beware the Ides of March,' " Myron pronounced in dramatic
fashion.

"The Ides are the fifteenth," Audrey said. "Today is the seventeenth."

"Yeah, I know. But I never skip an opportunity to quote Shakespeare. Makes me look smart."

"Brains and a good ass," Audrey said. "Who cares if you have no
lateral movement?"

"Funny," Myron said, "Jess never complains about that."

"At least not to your face." Audrey smiled. "Nice to see you so
chipper."

He returned the smile, shrugged.

Audrey looked around to make sure no one was in earshot. "I got
some info for you," she said.

"On?"

"On the private eye in the divorce case."

"Greg hired one?"

"Either him or Felder," she replied. "I have a source who does electronics work for ProTec Investigations. They do all of Felder's work. Now my source doesn't know all the details, but he helped set up a videotaping at the Glenpointe Hotel two months ago. You know the Glenpointe?"

Myron nodded. "The hotel on Route 80? Maybe five miles from here?"

"Right. My source doesn't know what it was for or what ended up on it. He just knows the work was for the Downing divorce. He also confirmed the obvious: this thing is usually done to catch a spouse in *flagrante delicto*."

Myron frowned. "This was two months ago?"

"Yep."

"But Greg and Emily were already separated by then," Myron said. "The divorce was practically finalized. What would be the point?"

"The divorce, yes," she agreed. "But the child custody battle was just starting."

"Yeah, but so what? She was a near-single woman having a sexual encounter. That kind of thing hardly proves parental unfitness in this day and age."

Audrey shook her head. "You are so naive."

"What do you mean?"

"A tape of a mother getting it on with some buck at a motel, doing lord-knows-what? We still live in a sexist society. It would be bound to influence a judge."

Myron mulled it over, but it just wouldn't mesh. "First of all, you're assuming the judge is both male and a Neanderthal. Second"—he sort of held up his hands and shrugged—"it's the nineties for crying out loud. A woman separated from her husband having sex with another man? Hardly earth-shattering stuff."

"I don't know what else to tell you, Myron."

"You got anything else?"

"That's it," she said. "But I'm working on it."

"Do you know Fiona White?"

"Leon's wife? Enough to say hello. Why?"

"She ever model?"

"Model?" She sort of chuckled. "Yeah, I guess you'd call it that."

"She was a centerfold?"

"Yep."

"You know what month?"

"No. Why?"

He told her about the e-mail. He was fairly sure now that Ms. F was Fiona White, that Sepbabe was short for September babe, the month, he bet, that she was a centerfold. Audrey listened raptly. "I can check it out," she said when he finished. "See if she was a September playmate."

"That would help."

"It would explain a lot," Audrey continued. "About the tension between Downing and Leon."

Myron nodded.

"Look, I gotta run. Jess is getting the car around back. Keep me posted."

"Right, have fun."

He finished up, toweled off, started dressing. He thought about Greg's secret girlfriend, the one who had been staying at his house. Could it possibly be Fiona White? If so, that would also explain the need for secrecy. Could Leon White have found out about it? That seemed logical based on his antagonism toward Greg. So where did that leave us? And how did this all tie in with Greg's gambling and Liz Gorman's blackmail scheme?

Whoa, hold the phone.

Forget gambling for a moment. Suppose Liz Gorman had something else on Greg Downing, a revelation equally if not potentially more explosive than laying down a few bets. Suppose she had somehow found out that Greg was having an affair with his best friend's wife. Suppose she had decided to blackmail Greg and Clip with this information. How much would Greg pay to keep his fans and teammates from learning about his betrayal? How much would Clip pay to keep that particular warhead from detonating in the midst of a championship run?

It was worth looking into.

Chapter 27

Myron stopped at the traffic light that divided South Livingston Avenue and the JFK Parkway. This particular intersection had barely changed in the past thirty years. The familiar brick facade of Nero's Restaurant was on his right. It had originally been Jimmy Johnson's Steak House, but that had to be at least twenty-five years ago. The same Gulf station occupied another corner, a small firehouse another, undeveloped land on the last.

He turned onto Hobart Gap Road. The Bolitar family had first moved to Livingston when Myron was six weeks old. Little had changed in comparison to the rest of the world. The familiarity of seeing the same sights over so many years was less comforting now than numbing. You didn't notice anything. You looked but you never saw.

As he turned up the same street where his dad had first taught him to ride that two-wheeler with a Batman reflector on the back, he tried to pay true heed to the homes that had surrounded him all of his life. There had been changes, of course, but in his mind it was still 1970. He and his parents still referred to the neighboring homes by their original owners, as though they were Southern plantations. The Rackins, for example, hadn't lived in the Rackin House for over a decade. Myron didn't know anymore who lived in the Kirschner Place or the Roth House or the Parkers'. Like the Bolitars, the Rackins and the Kirschners and the rest had moved in when the construction was new, when you could still see some remnants of the Schnectman farm, when Livingston was considered the boonies, as far away from New York City at twenty-five miles as western Pennsylvania. The Rackins and the Kirschners and the Roths had lived a big chunk of their lives here. They'd moved in with infant children, raised them, taught them how to ride bicycles on the same streets Myron had learned on, sent them to Burnet Hill elementary school, then Heritage Junior High, finally Livingston High School. The kids had gone off to college, visiting only on college breaks. Not long after, wedding invitations went out. A few started displaying photos of grandchildren, shaking their heads in disbelief at how time flew.

Eventually the Rackins and the Kirschners and the Roths felt out of place. This town designed to raise kids held nothing for them anymore. Their familiar homes suddenly felt too big and too empty, so they put them on the market and sold them to new young families with infant children who would too soon go off to Burnet Hill elementary school, then Heritage Junior High, and finally Livingston High School.

Life, Myron decided, was not that different from one of those depressing life insurance commercials.

Some neighborhood old-timers had managed to hang on. You could usually tell which houses belonged to them because—in spite of the fact that the children were grown—they had built additions and nice porches and kept their lawns well groomed. The Brauns and the Goldsteins were two who had done just that. And of course, Al and Ellen Bolitar.

Myron pulled his Ford Taurus into the driveway, his headlights sweeping across the front yard like searchlights during a prison break. He parked up on the blacktop not far from the basketball hoop. He turned off the ignition. For a moment he just stared at the basket. An image of his father lifting him so he could reach the basket appeared before him. If the image had come from memory or imagination, he could not say. Nor did it matter.

As he moved toward the house, outside lights came on via a motion detector. Though the detectors had been installed three years ago, they were still a source of unbridled awe for his parents, who considered this technological advance on a par with the discovery of fire. When the motion detectors were first put up, Mom and Dad spent blissful hours in disbelief testing the mechanism, seeing if they could duck under its eye or walk superslowly so that the detector would not sense them. Sometimes in life, it's the simple pleasures.

His parents were sitting in the kitchen. When he entered, they both quickly pretended they were doing something.

"Hi," he said.

They looked at him with tilted heads and too-concerned eyes. "Hi, sweetheart," Mom said.

"Hi, Myron," Dad said.

"You're back from Europe early," Myron said.

Both heads nodded like they were guilty of a crime. Mom said, "We wanted to see you play." She said it gently, like she was walking on thin ice with a blowtorch.

"So how was your trip?" Myron asked.

"Wonderful," Dad said.

"Marvelous," Mom added. "The food they served was just ter-
rific."

"Small portions though," Dad said.

"What do you mean, small portions?" Mom snapped.

"I'm just commenting, Ellen. The food was good, but the portions
were small."

"What, did you measure it or something? What do you mean
small?"

"I know a small portion when I see one. These were small."

"Small. Like he needs larger portions. The man eats like a horse.
It wouldn't kill you to lose ten pounds, Al."

"Me? I'm not getting heavy."

"Oh no? Your pants are getting so tight you'd think you were star-
ring in a dance movie."

Dad winked at her. "You didn't seem to have any problem taking
them off on the trip."

"Al!" she shrieked, but there was a smile there too. "In front of
your own child! What's wrong with you?"

Dad looked at Myron, arms spread. "We were in Venice," he said
in a way of explanation. "Rome."

"Say no more," Myron said. "Please."

They laughed. When it died out his mother spoke in a hushed
tone.

"You okay, sweetheart?"

"I'm fine," he said.

"Really?"

"Really."

"I thought you did some good things out there," Dad said. "You
hit TC for a couple of nice passes on the post. Real nice passes. You
showed smarts."

Count on Dad to find the silver lining. "I bit the big one," Myron
said.

Dad gave a staunch head shake and said, "You think I'm saying
this just to make you feel good?"

"I know you're saying this just to make me feel good."

"It doesn't matter," Dad said. "It never mattered. You know that."

Myron nodded. He did know. He had witnessed pushy fathers all
his life, men who tried to live hollow dreams through their offspring,
forcing their sons to carry a burden they themselves could never
carry. But not his father. Never his father. Al Bolitar had never
needed to fill his son with grandiose stories of his athletic prowess.
He never pushed him, possessing the wondrous ability to appear al-

most indifferent while making it clear he cared intensely. Yes, this
was a direct contradiction—sort of a detached attachment—but
somehow Dad pulled it off. Sadly, it was unusual for Myron's generation to admit to such wonderment. His generation had remained un-
defined—shoehorned between the Beat Generation of Woodstock
and the Generation X of MTV, too young when *thirtysomething* had
ruled the airwaves, too old now for *Beverly Hills, 90210,* or *Melrose
Place*. Mostly, it seemed to Myron, he was part of the Blame Generation, where life was a series of reactions and counterreactions. In
the same way those pushy fathers put everything on their sons, the
sons came right back and blamed their future failures on the fathers.
His generation had been taught to look back and pinpoint exact moments when their parents had ruined their lives. Myron never did. If
he looked back—if he studied his parents' past feats—it was only to
try to unravel their secret before he had children of his own.

"I know what it looked like tonight," he said, "but I really don't
feel that bad."

Mom sniffled. "We know." Her eyes were red. She sniffled again.
"You're not crying over—"

She shook her head. "You've grown up. I know that. But when
you ran out on the court again like that, for the first time in so
long . . ."

Her voice died out. Dad looked away. The three of them were all
the same. They were drawn to nostalgia like starlets to paparazzi.

Myron waited until he was sure his voice would be clear. "Jessica
wants me to move in with her," he said.

He expected protests, at least from his mother. Mom had not for-
given Jessica for leaving the first time; Myron doubted that she ever
would. Dad, as was his way, acted like a good news reporter—neutral, but you wondered what opinion he was making under those balanced questions.

Mom looked at Dad. Dad looked back and put a hand on her
shoulder. Then Mom said, "You can always come back," she said.

Myron almost asked for a clarification, but he stopped himself
and simply nodded. The three of them gathered around the kitchen
table and began to talk. Myron made himself a grilled cheese. Mom
didn't do it for him. Dogs were domesticated, she believed, not people. She never cooked anymore, which Myron took as a positive
thing. Her doting was all verbal, and that was all right with him.

They told him about their trip. He briefly and very vaguely
sketched out why he was playing pro basketball again. An hour later
he headed into his room in the basement. He had lived here since he

was sixteen, the year his sister had gone off to college. The basement was subdivided into two rooms—a sitting area he almost never used except for company and hence kept clean, and a bedroom that looked very much like a teenager's. He crawled into bed and looked at the posters on the wall. Most had been up since his adolescence, the colors faded, the corners frayed near the thumbtacks.

Myron had always loved the Celtics—his father had grown up near Boston—and so his two favorite posters were of John Havlicek, the Celtics star of the sixties and seventies, and Larry Bird, the team's star of the eighties. He looked now from Havlicek to Bird. Myron was supposed to have been the next poster on the wall. It had been his boyhood dream. When the Celtics drafted him, it barely surprised him. A higher power was at work. It had been preordained that he would be the next Celtics legend.

Then Burt Wesson slammed into him.

Myron put his hands behind his head. His eyes adjusted to the light. When his phone rang, he reached for it absently.

"We have what you're looking for," an electronically altered voice said.

"Excuse me?"

"The same thing Downing wanted to buy. It'll cost you fifty thousand dollars. Get the money together. We'll call you with instructions tomorrow night."

The caller hung up. Myron tried hitting star-six-nine to ring back, but the call was from out of the area. He lowered his head back to the pillow. Then he stared at the two posters and waited for sleep to claim him.

Chapter 28

Martin Felder's office was on Madison Avenue in midtown, not far from Myron's own. The agency was called Felder Inc., the clever name making it very apparent that Marty wasn't on Madison Avenue as a hotshot advertising exec. A sprightly receptionist was all too happy to show Myron the way to Marty's office.

The door was already open. "Marty, Myron is here to see you."

Marty. Myron. It was one of those kind of offices. Everyone was a first name. Everyone was dressed in that new, neat-casual look. Marty, who Myron guessed was in his mid-fifties, wore one of those blue jean shirts with a bright orange tie. His thinning gray hair was plastered down, almost a comb over but not quite. His pants were Banana Republic green and crisply pressed. His orange socks matched the tie and his shoes looked like Hush Puppies.

"Myron!" he exclaimed, pumping Myron's hand. "Great to see you."

"Thanks for seeing me so soon, Marty."

He waved a dismissing hand. "Myron, please. For you, anytime." They'd met a few times at different sporting and sports representative events. Myron knew that Marty had a solid reputation as a guy who was—to coin a cliché—tough but fair. Marty also had a knack for getting great media coverage for both himself and his athletes. He'd written a couple of how-to-succeed books which helped enhance his name recognition as well as his rep. On top of that, Marty looked like your favorite, self-effacing uncle. People liked him instantly.

"Can I get you a drink?" he asked. "Caffè latte perhaps?"

"No thanks."

He smiled, shook his head. "I've been planning on calling you for the longest time, Myron. Please, have a seat."

The walls were bare except for bizarre sculptures twisted out of neon light. His desk was glass, the built-in shelves fiberglass. There were no visible papers. Everything shone like the inside of a spaceship. Felder gestured to a chair in front of the desk for Myron; then he took the other chair in front of the desk. Two equals chatting it up. No desk to use as a divider or intimidator.

Felder started right in. "I don't have to tell you, Myron, that you are quickly making a name for yourself in this field. Your clients trust you absolutely. Owners and managers respect and fear"—he emphasized the fear part—"you. That's rare, Myron. Very rare." He slapped his palms on his thighs and leaned forward. "Do you enjoy being in sports representation?"

"Yes."

"Good," he said with a sharp nod. "It's important to like what you're doing. Choosing a profession is the most important decision you'll ever make—more important even than choosing a spouse." He looked up at the ceiling. "Who was it that said, you may tire of your relationship with people but never of a job you love?"

"Wink Martindale?" Myron said.

Felder chuckled and offered up a shy, caught-himself smile. "Guess you didn't come here to hear me drone on about my own personal philosophies," he said. "So let me put my cards on the table. Just flat out say it. How would you like to come work for Felder Inc.?"

"Work here?" Myron said. Job Interview Rule #1: Dazzle them with sparkling repartee.

"Here's what I'd like to do," Felder said. "I want to make you a senior vice president. Your salary would be generous. You'd still be able to give all your clients the personal Bolitar attention they've come to expect, plus you'll have all the resources of Felder Inc. at your command. Think about it, Myron. We employ over one hundred people here. We have our own travel agency to handle all those arrangements for you. We have—well, let's call them what they are, shall we?—gofers who can deal with all those details that are so necessary in our business, freeing you up to tackle important tasks." He raised a hand as if to stop Myron, though Myron hadn't moved. "Now I know you have an associate, Miss Esperanza Diaz. She'd come aboard too, of course. At a higher salary. Plus I understand she's finishing up law school this year. There'll be plenty of room for advancement here." He gestured with his hands before adding, "So what do you think?"

"I'm very flattered—"

"Don't be," Felder interrupted. "It's a sound business decision for me. I know good stock when I see it." He leaned forward with a sincere smile. "Let someone else be the client's errand boy, Myron. I want to free you up to do what you do best—recruit new clients and negotiate deals."

Myron had no interest in giving up his company, but the man knew how to make it sound attractive. "May I think about it?" he asked.

"Of course," Felder said, raising his hands in surrendered agreement. "I don't want to pressure you, Myron. Take your time. I certainly don't expect an answer today."

"I appreciate that," Myron said, "but I actually wanted to talk to you about another matter."

"Please." He leaned back, folded his hands on his lap, smiled. "Go right ahead."

"It's about Greg Downing."

The smile didn't budge, but the light behind it flickered a bit. "Greg Downing?"

"Yes. I have a few questions."

Still smiling. "You realize, of course, that I cannot reveal anything that may fall under what I consider privileged."

"Of course," Myron agreed. "I was wondering if you could tell me where he is."

Marty Felder waited a beat. This was no longer a sales pitch meeting. It was now a negotiation. A good negotiator is frighteningly patient. Like a good interrogator, he must above all else be a listener. He must make his opponent do the talking. After several seconds, Felder asked, "Why do you want to know that?"

"I need to speak with him," Myron said.

"May I ask what this is about?"

"I'm afraid it's confidential."

They looked at each other, both faces open and friendly, but now they were two card sharks who didn't want to show their hands. "Myron," Felder began, "you have to understand my position here. I don't feel comfortable divulging this type of information without having at least some hint as to why you want to see him."

Time to jar something loose. "I didn't join the Dragons to make a comeback," Myron said. "Clip Arnstein hired me to find Greg."

Felder's eyebrows dropped to half mast. "Find him? But I thought he went into seclusion to heal an ankle injury."

Myron shook his head. "That was the story Clip told the press."

"I see." Felder put a hand to his chin and nodded slowly. "And you're trying to locate him?"

"Yes."

"Clip hired you? He chose you himself? It was his idea?"

Myron answered in the affirmative. There was a faint smile on Felder's face now, like he was enjoying an inside joke. "I'm sure Clip already told you that Greg had done this kind of thing before."

"Yes," Myron said.

"So I don't see why you should be all that concerned," Felder said. "Your help is appreciated, Myron, but it is really not necessary."

"You know where he is?"

Felder hesitated. "Again, Myron, I ask you to put yourself in my position. If one of your clients wanted to stay hidden, would you go against his wishes or respect his rights?"

Myron smelled a bluff. "That would depend," he said. "If the client was in big trouble, I'd probably do whatever I could to help him."

"What sort of big trouble?" Felder asked.

"Gambling, for one. Greg owes a lot of money to some awfully unpleasant fellows." Still no reaction from Felder. In this case, Myron read it as a good thing. If most people had just heard that a client owed money to mobsters, they would show some sort of surprise. "You know about his gambling, don't you, Marty?"

Felder's words were slow, as if he were weighing each one separately with a hand scale. "You are still new in this business, Myron. With that comes a certain enthusiasm that is not always well placed. I am Greg Downing's sports representative. That gives me certain responsibilities. It is not a carte blanche to run his life. What he or any other client does on his own time is not, should not, and cannot be my concern. For all our sakes. We care about every client, but we are not parental substitutes or life managers. It's important to learn this early on."

The Cliff Notes summary: he knew about the gambling.

Myron asked, "Why did Greg withdraw fifty thousand dollars ten days ago?"

Again Felder showed no reaction. He was either beyond being surprised by what Myron knew or he had the ability to shut off any connection between his brain and facial muscles. "You know I can't discuss that with you—or even confirm that such a withdrawal took place." He slapped his palms against his thighs again and mounted a smile. "Do us both a favor, Myron. Think about my offer and drop this other matter. Greg will pop up soon. He always does."

"I wouldn't be so sure," Myron said. "He's in real trouble this time."

"If you are talking about his alleged gambling debts—"

Myron shook his head. "I'm not."

"Then what?"

So far, the man had given Myron nothing. Letting on that he knew about the gambling problem was a lay-up. He had realized Myron knew about it. To deny it would make him look either incompetent for not knowing or dishonest for making a strong denial. Marty Felder was shrewd. He would not misstep. Myron tried shifting direction. "Why did you videotape Greg's wife?"

He blinked. "Pardon?"

"ProTec. That's the name of the agency you hired. They set up a videotape surveillance at the Glenpointe Hotel. I'd like to know why."

Felder looked almost amused. "Help me understand this, Myron. First you say that my client is in deep trouble. You claim you want to help him. Then you start making allegations about a videotape. I'm having trouble following you."

"I'm just trying to help your client."

"The best thing you can do for Greg is to tell me all you know. I am his advocate, Myron. I am truly interested in doing what's best for him—not what might be best for the Dragons or Clip or anybody else. You said he was in trouble. Tell me how."

Myron shook his head. "First you tell me about the videotape."

"No."

There you have it. Top-notch negotiating getting down to basics. Soon they'd be sticking tongues out at each other, but for now both faces remained pleasant. They were playing the waiting game. Who would be the first to crack? Myron ran down the situation in his mind. The cardinal rule of negotiating: Don't lose sight of what you want and what your opponent wants. Okay. So what did Felder have that Myron wanted? Information on the fifty thousand dollars, the videotape, and maybe some other stuff. What did Myron have that Felder wanted? Not much. Myron had made him curious when he mentioned big trouble. Felder might already know what trouble Greg was in, but he would still want to know what Myron knew. End analysis: Myron needed the information more. He would have to move. Time to up the ante. And no more delicacy.

"I don't have to be the one asking you these questions," Myron said.

"What do you mean?"

"I could have a homicide detective ask them."

Felder barely moved, but his pupils expanded in a funny way. "What?"

"A certain homicide detective is this close"—Myron held up his thumb and index finger close together—"to putting out an APB on Greg."

"A homicide detective?"

"Yes."

"But who was killed?"

Myron shook his head. "First the videotape."

Felder was not a man to jump. He refolded his hands on his lap, looked up, tapped his foot. He took his time, considering the pros and cons, the costs and benefits, all that. Myron half-expected him to start charting graphs.

"You never practiced as an attorney, did you, Myron?"

Myron shook his head. "I passed the bar. That's about it."

"You're lucky," he said. He sighed and made a tired gesture with his hands. "You know why people make all the jokes about lawyers being scum? It's because they are. It's not their fault. Not really. It's the system. The system encourages cheating and lying and basic scummy behavior. Suppose you were at a Little League game. Suppose you told the kids that there were no umpires today—that they were to umpire themselves. Wouldn't that lead to some pretty unethical behavior? Probably. But then tell the little tykes that they must win, no matter what. Tell them that their only obligation is to winning and that they should forget about things like fair play and sportsmanship. That's what our judicial system is like, Myron. We allow for deceit in the name of an abstract greater good."

"Bad analogy," Myron said.

"Why's that?"

"The part about no umpires. Lawyers have to face judges."

"Not many of them. Most cases are settled before a judge sees it. You know that. But no matter, my point is made. The system encourages attorneys to lie and distort under the guise of the client's best interest. That best-interest crap has become an all-purpose excuse for anything goes. It's ruining our judicial system."

"Fascinating, really," Myron said. "And all this relates to the videotape . . . ?"

"Very directly," Felder said. "Emily Downing's lawyer lied and distorted the truth. She did it to an unethical and unnecessary extreme."

"Are you talking about the child custody case?" Myron asked.

"Yes."

"What did she do?"

He smiled. "I'll give you a hint. This particular claim is made now in one out of every three child custody cases in the United States. It has become almost standard practice, tossed about like rice was at the actual wedding, though it destroys lives."

"Child abuse?"

Felder did not bother with an answer. "We felt that we needed to quell these malicious and dangerous untruths. To balance the scales, so to speak. I'm not proud of that. None of us are. But I'm not ashamed either. You can't fight fair if your opponent insists on using brass knuckles. You must do what you can to survive."

"What did you do?"

"We videotaped Emily Downing in a rather delicate situation."

"When you say delicate, what exactly do you mean?"

Felder stood up and took a key from his pocket. He unlocked a cabinet and pulled out a videotape. Then he opened another cabinet. A TV and VCR faced them. He placed the tape in the machine and picked up the remote. "Your turn now," he said. "You said Greg was in big trouble."

It was time for Myron to give a little. Another cardinal rule of negotiation: don't be a pig and just take. It'll backfire in the long run. "We believe a woman may have been blackmailing Greg," he said. "She has several aliases. Usually Carla but she may have used the names Sally or Liz. She was murdered last Saturday night."

That one stunned him. Or at least he acted stunned. "Surely the police don't suspect Greg—"

"Yes," Myron said.

"But why?"

Myron kept it vague. "Greg was the last person seen with her the night of the murder. His fingerprints were at the murder scene. And the police found the murder weapon at his house."

"They searched his house?"

"Yes."

"But they can't do that."

Already playing the ready-to-distort lawyer. "They got a warrant," Myron said. "Do you know this woman? This Carla or Sally?"

"No."

"Do you have any idea where Greg is?"

"None."

Myron watched him, but he couldn't tell if he was lying or not. Except in very rare instances, you can never tell if a person is lying by watching their eyes or their body language or any of that stuff. Nervous, fidgety people tell the truth too, and a good liar could look as sincere as Alan Alda at a telethon. So-called "students of body language" were usually just fooled with more certainty. "Why did Greg take out fifty thousand dollars in cash?" Myron asked.

"I didn't ask," Felder said. "As I just explained to you, such matters were not my concern."

"You thought it was for gambling."

Again Felder didn't bother responding. He lifted his eyes from the floor. "You said this woman was blackmailing him."

"Yes," Myron said.

He looked at Myron steadily. "Do you know what she had on him?"

"Not for sure. The gambling, I think."

Felder nodded. With his eyes looking straight ahead, he pointed the remote control at the television behind him and pressed some buttons. The screen brightened into gray static. Then a black and white image appeared. A hotel room. The camera seemed to be shooting from the ground up. No one was in the room. A digital counter showed the time. The setup reminded Myron of those tapes of Marion Barry smoking a crack pipe.

Uh oh.

Could that be it? Having sex would hardly be grounds to show unfitness as a parent, but what about drugs? What better way to balance the scales, as Felder had put it, than to show the mother smoking or snorting or shooting up in a hotel room? How would that work on a judge?

But as Myron was about to see, he was wrong.

The hotel room door opened. Emily entered alone. She looked around tentatively. She sat on the bed, but then got back up. She paced. She sat down again. She paced again. She checked the bathroom, came right back out, paced. Her fingers picked up whatever object they could find—hotel brochures, room services menus, a television guide.

"Is there any sound?" Myron asked.

Marty Felder shook his head no. He was still not looking at the screen.

Myron watched transfixed as Emily continued to go through her nervous ritual. Suddenly she froze in place and turned to the door. Must have heard a knock. She approached tentatively. Looking for Mr. Goodbar? Probably, Myron surmised. But when Emily turned the knob and let the door swing open, Myron realized he was wrong again. It was not Mr. Goodbar who entered the hotel room.

It was Ms. Goodbar.

The two women talked for a bit. They had a drink from the room's minibar. Then they began to undress. Myron's stomach coiled. By the time they moved to the bed, he had seen more than enough.

"Turn it off."

Felder did so, still not looking at the screen. "I meant what I said before. I'm not proud of that."

"What a guy," Myron said.

So now he understood Emily's ferocious hostility. She had indeed been taped in *flagrante delicto*—not with another man, but with a woman. Certainly no law against it. But most judges would be influenced. It was the way of the world. And speaking of the way of the world, Myron knew Ms. Goodbar by another nickname:

Thumper.

Chapter 29

Myron walked back to his office, wondering what it all meant. For one thing, it meant that Thumper was more than a harmless diversion in all this. But what exactly was she? Had she set up Emily or had she, too, been taped unaware? Were they steady lovers or participants in a one-night stand? Felder claimed he didn't know. On the tape, the two women hadn't appeared to be all that familiar with each other—at least, not in the small portion he had watched—but he was hardly an expert on the subject.

Myron cut east on 50th Street. An albino wearing a Mets cap and yellow boxer shorts on the outside of ripped jeans played an Indian sitar. He was singing the seventies classic "The Night Chicago Died" in a voice that reminded Myron of elderly Chinese women in the back of a laundromat. The albino also had a tin cup and a stack of cassettes. A sign read "The Original Benny and His Magical Sitar, only $10." The original. Oh. Wouldn't want that imitation albino, sitar, AM seventies music, no sir.

Benny smiled at him. When he reached the part of the song where the son learns a hundred cops are dead—maybe even the boy's father—Benny began to weep. Moving. Myron stuffed a dollar into the cup. He crossed the street, his thoughts reverting back to the videotape of Emily and Thumper. He wondered now about the relevance. He'd felt like a dirty voyeur for watching the tape in the first place, and now he felt that way for rehashing it in his mind. It was, after all, probably no more than a bizarre aside. What possible connection could there be in all this to the murder of Liz Gorman? None that he could see; then again he still had trouble seeing how Liz Gorman fit in with Greg's gambling or how she fit in at all.

Still, the video undoubtedly raised a few fairly major issues. For one thing, there was the abuse allegations made against Greg. Was there anything to them, or as Marty Felder had indicated, was Emily's attorney just playing hardball? And hadn't Emily told Myron she would do anything to keep her kids? Even kill. How did Emily react when she learned about the videotape? Spurred on by this awful violation, how far would Emily go?

Myron entered his office building on Park Avenue. He exchanged a brief elevator smile with a young woman in a business suit. The elevator reeked of drugstore cologne, the kind where some guy decides that taking a shower is too time-consuming so he opts for sprinkling himself with enough cologne to glaze a wedding cake. The young woman sniffed and looked at Myron.

"I don't wear cologne," he said.

She didn't seem convinced. Or perhaps she was condemning the gender in general for this affront. Understandable under these circumstances.

"Try holding your breath," he said.

She looked at him, her face a seaweed green.

When he entered his office, Esperanza smiled and said, "Good morning."

"Oh no," Myron said.

"What?"

"You've never said good morning to me before. Ever."

"I have, too."

Myron shook his head. "*Et tu*, Esperanza?"

"What are you talking about?"

"You heard about what happened last night. You're trying to be—dare I say it?—nice to me."

The fire in her eyes flamed up. "You think I give a shit about that game? That you got your butt burned at every turn?"

Myron shook his head. "Too late," he said. "You care."

"I do not. You sucked. Get over it."

"Nice try."

"What, nice try? You sucked. S-U-C-K-E-D. A pitiful display. I was embarrassed to know you. I hid my head in shame when I came in."

He bent down and kissed her cheek.

Esperanza wiped it off with the back of her hand. "Now I got to get a cootie shot."

"I'm fine," he said. "Really."

"Like I care. Really."

The phone rang. She picked it up. "MB SportsReps. Why yes, Jason, he is here. Hold on a moment." She put a hand over the receiver. "It's Jason Blair."

"The vermin who said you had a nice ass?"

She nodded. "Remind him about my legs."

"I'll take it in my office." A photograph on the top of a stack of papers on her desk caught his eye. "What's this?"

"The Raven Brigade file," she said.

He picked up a grainy photo of the group taken in 1973, the only shot of the seven of them together. He quickly found Liz Gorman. He hadn't gotten a good look at her, but from what he saw, there was no way anyone would ever imagine that Carla and Liz Gorman were one and the same. "Mind if I keep this for a few minutes?" he asked.

"Suit yourself."

He moved into his office and picked up the phone. "What's up, Jason?"

"Where the fuck have you been?"

"Not much. How about you?"

"Don't play smart guy with me. You put that little lady on my contract and she fucked it all up. I got half a mind to leave MB."

"Calm down, Jason. How did she fuck it up?"

His voice cracked with incredulity. "You don't know?"

"No."

"Here we are, hot in the middle of negotiating with the Red Sox, right?"

"Right."

"I want to stay in Boston. We both know that. But we have to make a lot of noise like I'm leaving. That's what you said to do. Make them think you want to switch teams. To up the money. I'm a free agent. This is what we got to do, right?"

"Right."

"We don't want them to know I want to be on the team again, right?"

"Right. To a degree."

"Fuck to a degree," he snapped. "The other day my neighbor gets a mailing from the Sox, asking him to renew his season tickets. Guess whose picture is on the brochure saying I'm gonna be back? Go ahead. Guess."

"Would that be yours, Jason?"

"Damn straight mine! So I call up little Miss Nice Ass—"

"She's got great legs too."

"What?"

"Her legs. She's not that tall, so they're not very long. But they're nicely toned."

"Will you quit fucking around here, Myron? Listen to me. She tells me the Sox called up and asked if they could use my picture in the ad, even though I wasn't signed. She tells them to go ahead! Go right fucking ahead! Now what are those Red Sox assholes supposed to think, huh? I'll tell you what. They think I'm gonna sign with them no matter what. We lost all our leverage because of her."

Esperanza opened the door without knocking. "This came in this morning." She tossed a contract on Myron's desk. It was Jason's. Myron began to skim through it. Esperanza said, "Put the pea brain on the speakerphone."

Myron did.

"Jason."

"Oh Christ, Esperanza, get the fuck off the line. I'm talking to Myron here."

She ignored him. "Even though you don't deserve to know, I finalized your contract. You got everything you wanted and more."

That slowed him down. "Four hundred thou more per year?"

"Six hundred thousand. Plus an extra quarter million on the signing bonus."

"How the . . . what . . . ?"

"The Sox screwed up," she said. "Once they printed your picture in that mailer, the deal was as good as done."

"I don't get it."

"Simple," she said. "The mailer went out with your picture on it. People bought tickets based on that. Meanwhile I called the front office and said that you'd decided to sign with the Rangers down in Texas. I told them the deal was almost final." She shifted in the chair. "Now, Jason, pretend you are the Red Sox for a moment. What are you going to do? How are you going to explain to all those ticket holders that Jason Blair, whose picture was on your latest mailer, won't be around because the Texas Rangers outbid them?"

Silence. Then: "To hell with your ass and legs," Jason said. "You got the most gorgeous set of brains I ever laid eyes on."

Myron said, "Anything else, Jason?"

"Go practice, Myron. After the way you played last night, you need it. I want to talk over the details with Esperanza."

"I'll take it at my desk," Esperanza said.

Myron put him back on hold. "Nice move," he said to her.

She shrugged. "Some kid in the Sox marketing department screwed up. It happens."

"You read it very well."

Her tone was exaggerated monotone. "My heaving bosom is swelling with pride."

"Forget I said anything. Go take the call."

"No, really, my goal in life is to be just like you."

Myron shook his head. "You'll never have my ass."

"There's that," she agreed before leaving.

Left alone, Myron picked up the Raven Brigade photo. He located the three members still at large—Gloria Katz, Susan Milano, and the Raven's enigmatic leader and most famous member, Cole Whiteman. No one had drawn the press's attention and ire more than Cole Whiteman. Myron had been in elementary school when the Ravens went into hiding, yet he still remembered the stories. For one thing, Cole could have passed for Win's brother—blond, patrician-featured, well-to-do family. While everyone else in the picture was scraggly and long haired, Cole was fresh shaven with a conservative haircut, his one sixties concession being sideburns that went down a tad too far. Hardly your Hollywood-cast, radical leftist. But as Myron had learned from Win, looks could often be deceiving.

He put down the photograph and dialed Dimonte's line at One Police Plaza. After Dimonte snarled a hello, Myron asked him if he had anything new.

"You think we're partners now, Bolitar?"

"Just like Starsky and Hutch," Myron said.

"God, I miss those two," Dimonte said. "That hot car. Hanging out with Fuzzy Bear."

"Huggy Bear," Myron said.

"What?"

"His name was Huggy Bear, not Fuzzy Bear."

"Really?"

"Time's short, Rolly. Let me help if I can."

"You first. What have you got?"

Another negotiation. Myron told him about Greg's gambling. Figuring that Rolly had the phone records too, he also told him about the suspected blackmail scheme. He didn't tell him about the videotape. It wouldn't be fair, not until he spoke to Emily first. Dimonte asked a few questions. When he was satisfied, he said, "Okay, what do you want to know?"

"Did you find anything else at Greg's house?"

"Nothing," Dimonte said. "And I mean, nothing. Remember how you told me you found some feminine doo-dads in the bedroom? Some woman's clothes or lotions or something?"

"Yes."

"Well, someone got rid of them too. No sign of any female apparel."

So, Myron thought, the lover theory rears its ugly head once again. The lover comes back to the house and cleans up the blood to protect Greg. Then she covers her own tracks too, making sure that their relationship remains a secret. "How about witnesses?" Myron asked. "Anybody in Liz Gorman's building see anything?"

"Nope. We canvassed the whole neighborhood. No one saw nada. Everybody was studying or something. Oh, another thing: the press picked up the murder. The story hit the morning editions."

"You gave them her real name?"

"You crazy? Of course not. They think it's just another breaking and entering homicide. But get this. We got an anonymous tip called in this morning. Someone suggested we check out Greg Downing's house."

"You're kidding."

"Nope. Female voice."

"He's being set up, Rolly."

"No shit, Sherlock. By a chick nonetheless. And the murder didn't exactly make a big news splash. It was stuck in the back pages like every other unspectacular homicide in this cesspool. Got a little extra juice because it was so close to a college campus."

"Have you looked into that connection?" Myron asked.

"What connection?"

"Columbia University being so close by. Half of the sixties movements started there. They must still have some sympathizers in the ranks. Maybe someone there helped Liz Gorman."

Dimonte gave a dramatic sigh. "Bolitar, do you think all cops are morons?"

"No."

"You think you're the only who thought of that?"

"Well," Myron said, "I have been called gifted."

"Not in today's sports section."

Touché. "So what did you find out?"

"She rented the place from some whacko, fanatic, leftist, commie, pinko so-called Columbia professor named Sidney Bowman."

"You're so tolerant, Rolly."

"Yeah, well, I lose touch when I keep missing those ACLU meetings. Anyway, this pinko won't talk. He says she just rented from him and paid in cash. We all know he's lying. The feds grilled him, but he got a team of faggot, liberal lawyers down here to spring him. Called us a bunch of Nazi pigs and stuff."

"That's not a compliment, Rolly. In case you don't know."

"Thanks for clueing me in. I got Krinsky tailing him right now, but he's got nothing. I mean, this Bowman's not a retard. He's got to know we're watching."

"What else have you got on him?"

"Divorced. No kids. He teaches a class in existential, worthless-in-the-real-world bullshit. According to Krinsky he spends most of his time helping the homeless. That's supposed to be his daily ritual—hanging out with hobos in parks and shelters. Like I said, a whacko."

Win entered the office without knocking. He headed straight for the corner and opened the closet door, revealing a full-length mirror. He checked his hair. Patted it though every strand was perfect. Then he spread his legs a bit and put his arms straight down. Pretending to be gripping a golf club. Win slowly began to turn into a backswing, watching his motion in the mirror, making sure the front arm remained straight, the grip relaxed. He did this all the time, sometimes stopping in front of store windows while walking down the street. This was the golf equivalent, Myron surmised, to the weight lifters who flex whenever they happen past their reflection. It was also annoying as all hell.

"Got anything else, Rolly?"

"No. You?"

"Nothing. I'll talk to you later."

"Can hardly wait, Hutch," Dimonte said. "You know something? Krinsky's so young he doesn't even remember the show. Sad, ain't it?"

"Today's youth," Myron said. "They got no culture."

Myron hung up. Win continued to study his shot in the mirror. "Fill me in please," he said. Myron did. When he finished, Win said, "This Fiona, the ex-playmate. She sounds like a perfect candidate for a Windsor Horne Lockwood III interrogation."

"Uh huh," Myron said. "But why don't you first tell me about the Windsor Horne Lockwood III interrogation of Thumper?"

Win frowned at the mirror, adjusted his grip. "She is rather closed mouthed," he said. "So I took a distinctive tack."

"What tack is that?"

Win told him about their conversation. Myron just shook his head. "So you followed her?"

"Yes."

"And?"

"And there is not much to report. She went to TC's house after the game. She slept over. No calls of any consequence were made from his residence. Either she was not rattled by our conversation, or she doesn't know anything."

"Or," Myron added, "she knew she was being followed."

Win frowned again. He either didn't like Myron's suggestion or he'd spotted a problem with his swing. Probably the latter. He turned away from the mirror and glanced at Myron's desk. "Is that the Raven Brigade?"

"Yes. One of them looks like you." Myron pointed to Cole White-man.

Win studied it for a moment. "While the man is indeed hand-some, he lacks both my sense of style and my striking, debonair good looks."

"Not to mention your humility."

Win put out his hand. "Then you understand."

Myron looked at the picture again. He thought again about what Dimonte said about Professor Sidney Bowman's daily routine. Then it came to him all at once. Ice flooded his veins in a gush. In his mind he changed around Cole's features a bit, imagined distortions from plastic surgery and twenty years of aging. It didn't fit exactly, but it was close enough.

Liz Gorman had disguised herself by perverting her most distin-guishing characteristic. Wouldn't it make sense to assume that Cole Whiteman had done the same?

"Myron?"

He looked up. "I think I know where to find Cole Whiteman."

Chapter 30

Hector was not thrilled to see Myron back at the Parkview Diner.

"We think we found Sally's accomplice," Myron said.

Hector cleaned the counter with a rag.

"His name is Norman Lowenstein. Do you know him?"

Hector shook his head.

"He's a homeless man. He hangs out in the back and uses your pay phone."

Hector stopped cleaning. "You think I'd let a homeless man in my kitchen?" he said. "And we don't even have a back. Take a look."

The answer did not surprise Myron. "He was sitting at the counter when I was here the other day," he tried. "Unshaven. Long black hair. Tattered beige overcoat."

Still working the rag over the Formica, Hector nodded. "I think I know who you mean. Black sneakers?"

"Right."

"He comes in a lot. But I don't know his name."

"Did you ever see him talk to Sally?"

Hector shrugged. "Maybe. When she was his waitress. I really don't know."

"When was he here last?"

"I haven't seen him since the day you came in," Hector said.

"And you never met him?"

"No."

"Or know anything about him?"

"No."

Myron wrote down his phone number on a scrap of paper. "If you see him, please call. There's a thousand dollar reward."

Hector studied the phone number. "This your work number? At AT&T?"

"No. It's my personal phone."

"Uh huh," Hector said. "I called AT&T after you left last time. There's no such thing as Y511 and there's no employee named Bernie Worley." He did not look particularly upset, but he wasn't dancing the hula either. He just waited, watching Myron with steady eyes.

"I lied to you," Myron said. "I'm sorry."

"What's your real name?" he asked.

"Myron Bolitar." He gave the man one of his cards. Hector studied it for a moment.

"You're a sports agent?"

"Yes."

"What does a sports agent have to do with Sally?"

"It's a long story."

"You shouldn't have lied like that. It wasn't right."

"I know," Myron said. "I wouldn't have done it if it wasn't important."

Hector put the card in his shirt pocket. "I have customers." He turned away. Myron debated explaining further, but there was no point.

Win was waiting for him on the sidewalk. "Well?"

"Cole Whiteman is a homeless man who calls himself Norman Lowenstein."

Win waved down a taxi. A driver in a turban slowed down. They got in. Myron told him where to go. The driver nodded; as he did, his turban buffed the taxi's ceiling. Sitar music blew forth from the front speakers, plucking at the air with razor-sharp nails. Awful. It made Benny and His Magical Sitar sound like Itzhak Perlman. Still it was preferable to Yanni.

"He looks nothing like that old picture," Myron said. "He's had plastic surgery. He grew his hair and dyed it jet black."

They waited at a traffic light. A blue TransAm pulled up next to them, one of those souped up models that hip-hopped up and down while playing music loud enough to crack the earth's core. The taxi actually started shaking from the decibel level. The light turned green. The TransAm sped ahead.

"I started thinking about how Liz Gorman had disguised herself," Myron continued. "She'd taken her defining attribute and stood it on its head. Cole was the well-bred, clean-cut, rich boy. What better way to stand that on its head than to become an unkempt vagrant?"

"A *Jewish*, unkempt vagrant," Win corrected.

"Right. So when Dimonte told me that Professor Bowman liked to hang out with the homeless, something clicked."

The turban barked, "Route."

"What?"

"Route. Henry Hudson or Broadway."

"Henry Hudson," Win replied. He glanced over at Myron. "Continue."

"This is what I think happened," Myron said. "Cole Whiteman suspected Liz Gorman was in some kind of trouble. Maybe she hadn't called him or met up with him. Something. The problem was, he couldn't check it out himself. Whiteman hasn't survived underground all these years by being stupid. He knew that if the police found her, they'd set a trap for him—the way they're doing right now."

"So," Win said, "he gets you to go in for him."

Myron nodded. "He hangs around the diner, hoping to hear something about 'Sally.' When he overhears me talking to Hector, he figures I'm his best bet. He gives me this weird story about how he knows her from using the phone at the diner. Claimed they were lovers. The story didn't really mesh, but I didn't bother questioning it. Anyway, he takes me to her place. Once I'm inside, he hides and waits to see what happens. He sees the cops come. He probably even sees the body being taken out—all from a safe distance. It confirms what he probably suspected all along. Liz Gorman is dead."

Win thought about it a moment. "And now you think Professor Bowman may be contacting him when he visits with the homeless?"

"Yes."

"So our next goal is to find Cole Whiteman."

"Yes."

"Amongst the wretched unbathed in some godforsaken shelter?"

"Yes."

Win looked pained. "Oh, goodie."

"We could try to set a trap for him," Myron said. "But I think it'll take too long."

"Set a trap how?"

"I think he's the one who called me on the phone last night," Myron said. "Whatever blackmail scheme Liz Gorman was running, it's natural to think that Whiteman was in on it too."

"But why you?" Win asked. "If he has dirt on Greg Downing, why would you be the target of his extortion?"

It was a question that had been gnawing at Myron too. "I'm not sure," he said slowly. "The best guess I can come up with is that Whiteman recognized me at the diner. He probably figures that I'm closely connected to Greg Downing. When he couldn't reach Greg, he decided to try me."

Myron's cellular phone rang. He flicked it on and said hello.

"Hey, Starsky." It was Dimonte.

"I'm Hutch," Myron said. "You're Starsky."

"Either way," Dimonte said, "I think you'll want to get your butt over to the precinct pronto."

"You got something?"

"Only if you call a picture of the killer leaving Gorman's apartment something," Dimonte said.

Myron almost dropped the phone. "For real?"

"Yep. And you'll never guess what."

"What?"

"It's a she."

Chapter 31

"Here's the deal," Dimonte said. They were threading their way through a veritable United Nations of cops, witnesses, and whatnots. Win was waiting outside. He didn't like cops, and they didn't exactly feel like taking him out for ice cream. Best for all if he kept his distance. "We got a partial image of the perp on a videotape. Problem is, it's not enough to make an ID. I thought maybe you'd recognize her."

"What kind of videotape?"

"There's a shipping garage on Broadway between One Hundred Tenth and One Hundred Eleventh streets, east side of the block," Dimonte said. He remained a pace ahead of Myron, moving briskly. He kept turning behind him to make sure Myron was keeping up. "They handle home electronics. You know how that is—every worker steals like it's a Constitutional right. So the company set up surveillance cameras all over the place. Videotape everything." Still moving he shook his head, awarded Myron a toothpick-less smile and added, "Good old big brother. Every once in a while somebody tapes a crime instead of a bunch of cops beating up a perp, you know what I'm saying?"

They entered a small interrogation room. Myron looked into a mirror. He knew it was one-way glass—so did anybody with even a passing knowledge of cop shows or movies. Myron doubted anybody was on the other side, but he stuck his tongue out just in case. Mr. Mature. Krinsky was standing by a television and a VCR. For the second time today, Myron was going to watch a video. He trusted this one would be more tame.

"Hey, Krinsky," Myron said.

Krinsky barely nodded. Mr. Loquacious.

Myron looked over at Dimonte. "I still don't see how a shipping garage camera could have gotten the killer on tape."

"One of the cameras is by the truck entrance," Dimonte explained. "Just to make sure nothing falls off the truck as it's leaving, if you know what I mean. The camera catches part of the sidewalk. You can see people walking by." He leaned up against the wall and motioned Myron to sit in a chair. "You'll see what I mean."

Myron sat. Krinsky hit the play button. Black and white again. No sound again. But this time the shot was from above. Myron saw the front end of a truck and behind it, a glimpse of the sidewalk. Not many people walked by; the ones that did were barely more than distant silhouettes.

"How did you come up with this?" Myron asked.

"With what?"

"This tape."

"I always check for this stuff," Dimonte said, hitching up his pants by belt loops. "Parking garages, storage houses, any of those places. They all have surveillance cameras nowadays."

Myron nodded. "Good work, Rolly. I'm impressed."

"Wow," Dimonte said, "now I can die happy."

Everyone's a wiseass. Myron turned his attention back to the screen. "So how long is each tape?"

"Twelve hours," Dimonte replied. "They change them at nine A.M. and P.M. Eight camera set-up. They keep each tape for three weeks. Then they tape over them." He pointed his fingers. "Here she comes now. Krinsky."

Krinsky pressed a button and the tape froze.

"The woman who just entered the picture. On the right. Heading south, which would be away from the scene."

Myron saw a blurry image. He couldn't see a face or even gather much about her height. She wore high heels and a long overcoat with a frilly neck. Hard to tell much about her weight either. The hair however was familiar. He kept his tone neutral. "Yeah, I see her."

"Look at her right hand," he said.

Myron did. There was something dark and long in it. "I can't make it out."

"We got it blown up. Krinsky."

Krinsky handed Myron two large black and white photographs. The woman's head was enlarged in the first one, but you still couldn't see any facial features. In the second picture, the long, dark object in her hand was clearer.

"We think it's a plastic garbage bag wrapped around something," Dimonte said. "Kind of an odd shape, wouldn't you say?"

Myron looked at the photo and nodded. "You figure it's covering up a baseball bat."

"Don't you?"

"Yeah," Myron said.

"We found plastic garbage bags just like that one in Gorman's kitchen."

"And probably half the kitchens in New York City," Myron added.

"True enough. Now look at the date and time on the screen."

On the top left-hand side of the screen, a digital clock read 02:12.32 A.M. The date was early Sunday morning. Just hours after Liz Gorman had been at the Swiss Chalet bar with Greg Downing.

"Did the camera get her coming the other way?" Myron asked.

"Yeah, but it's not too clear. Krinsky."

Krinsky hit the rewind button. Several seconds later, he stopped and the picture came back on. The time now read 01:41.12. A little more than thirty minutes earlier.

"Coming now," Dimonte said.

The image almost flew past. Myron only recognized the woman by the long overcoat with the frilly neck. This time, she was carrying nothing in her hand. Myron said, "Let me see the other part again. All the way through."

Dimonte nodded at Krinsky. Krinsky found it and hit play. While Myron still couldn't see the woman's face, her walk was another matter. And a person's walk could be fairly distinctive. Myron felt his heart crawl up into his throat.

Dimonte was studying him through squinting eyes. "You recognize her, Bolitar?"

Myron shook his head. "No," he lied.

Chapter 32

Esperanza liked to make lists.

With the Raven Brigade file in front of her, she jotted down the three most important factors in chronological order:

1) The Raven Brigade robs a bank in Tucson.

2) Within days, at least one of the Ravens (Liz Gorman) was in Manhattan.

3) Soon after, Liz Gorman made contact with a high profile professional basketball player.

It didn't flow.

She opened the file and briefly scanned the "brigade's" history. In 1975 the Ravens had kidnapped Hunt Flootworth, the twenty-two-year-old son of publishing giant Cooper Flootworth. Hunt had been a classmate at San Francisco State of several of the Ravens, including both Cole Whiteman and Liz Gorman. The famous Cooper Flootworth, never one to sit around idly and let others handle his affairs, hired mercenaries to rescue his son. During their raid, young Hunt was shot at point-blank range in the head by one of the Ravens. No one knew which one. Of all the brigade members at the scene, four managed to escape.

Big Cyndi skipped into the office. The vibrations rolled Esperanza's pens off the desk.

"Sorry," Cyndi said.

"It's okay."

"Timmy called me," Cyndi said. "We're going out Friday night."

Esperanza made a face. "His name is Timmy?"

"Yeah," Cyndi said. "Isn't that sweet?"

"Adorable."

"I'll be in the conference room," Cyndi said.

Esperanza turned back to the file. She flipped ahead to the Tucson bank heist—the group's first in more than five years. The robbery took place as the bank was closing. The feds believed one of the security guards was in on it, but so far they had nothing more than the guard's left-leaning background. About $15,000 in cash was taken, but the robbers took the time to blow the safe deposit boxes. Risky.

The feds theorized that the Ravens had somehow found out that drug money was stored there. The bank cameras showed two people dressed head to toe in black with black ski masks. No fingerprints or hairs or fibers. Nada.

Esperanza read through the file again, but nothing new exploded from the pages. She tried to imagine what the past twenty years had been like for the surviving Ravens, constantly on the run, never sleeping in the same place very long, leaving and reentering the country, relying on old sympathizers you were never sure you could completely trust. She grabbed her piece of paper and made some more notes:

Liz Gorman——>Bank Robbery——>Blackmail

Okay, she thought, follow the arrows. Liz Gorman and the Ravens needed funds, so they robbed the bank. That worked out. It explained the first arrow. That was a gimme anyway. The real problem was that second connection:

Bank Robbery——>Blackmail.

Simply put, what about the bank robbery had led her to the East Coast and her scheme to blackmail Greg Downing? She tried to write down possibilities.

1) Downing was involved in the bank robbery.

She looked up. It was possible, she surmised. He needed the money for gambling debts. He might do something illegal. But this hypothesis still did not answer the biggest question in all this: how did they meet? How did Liz Gorman and Greg Downing hook up in the first place?

That, she felt, was the key.

She wrote a number two. And waited.

What other link could there be?

Nothing came to mind so she decided to try it from the opposite end. Start with the blackmail and go back. In order to blackmail Downing, Liz Gorman had to have stumbled across something incriminating. When? Esperanza drew another arrow:

Bank Robbery<——>Blackmail

Esperanza felt something like a tiny pinprick. The bank robbery. Something they found at the bank robbery led to the blackmail scheme.

She quickly shuffled through the file, but she already knew that it wasn't there. She picked up the phone and dialed. When the man answered, she said, "Do you have a list of the people who were renting safe-deposit boxes?"

"Somewhere, I guess," he replied. "Why, you need it?"

"Yes."

Deep sigh. "All right, I'll start looking. But tell Myron he owes me for this. Owes me big."

When Emily opened the door, Myron said, "Are you alone?"

"Why, yes," she replied with a coy smile. "What do you have in mind?"

He shoved past her. Emily stumbled back, her mouth an open circle of surprise. He headed straight for the foyer closet and opened it.

"What the hell are you doing?"

Myron did not bother answering. His hands pushed hangers left and right in a frenzy. It didn't take long. He pulled the long overcoat with the frilly neck into view. "Next time you commit a murder," he said, "dispose of the clothes you wore."

She took two steps back, her hand fluttering toward her mouth. "Get out," she hissed.

"I'm giving you one chance to tell the truth."

"I don't care what you're giving. Get the fuck out of my house."

He held up the coat. "You think I'm the only who knows? The police have a videotape of you at the murder scene. You were wearing this coat."

Her body slackened. Her face looked like she'd been on the receiving end of a palm strike to the solar plexus.

Myron lowered the coat to his side. "You planted the murder weapon at your old house," he said. "You smeared blood in the basement." He turned and half-pounced into the living room. The pile of tabloids was still there. He pointed at it. "You kept searching the papers for the story. When you read about the body being found, you made an anonymous call to the police."

He glanced back at Emily. Her eyes were unfocused and glazed.

"I kept wondering about the playroom," Myron said. "Why, I kept asking myself, would Greg go down there of all places after the murder? But of course that was the point. He wouldn't. The blood could remain undetected for weeks if need be."

Emily made two fists at her sides. She shook her head, finally finding her voice. "You don't understand."

"Then tell me."

"He wanted my kids."

"So you framed him for murder."

"No."

"This isn't the time to lie, Emily."

"I'm not lying, Myron. I didn't frame him."

"You planted the weapon—"

"Yes," she interrupted, "you're right about all that. But I didn't frame him." Her eyes closed and reopened, almost like she was doing a minimeditation. "You can't frame somebody for something they did."

Myron stiffened. Emily stared at him stone faced. Her hands were still tightened into small balls. "Are you saying Greg killed her?"

"Of course." She moved toward him, taking her time, using the seconds the way a boxer uses an eight count after a surprise left hook. She took the coat from his hands. "Should I really destroy it, or can I trust you?"

"I think you better explain first."

"How about some coffee?"

"No," Myron said.

"I need some. Come on. We'll talk in the kitchen."

She kept her head high and walked the same walk Myron had watched on the tape. He followed her into a bright white kitchen. The kitchen gleamed in tiled splendor. Most people probably thought the decor was to die for; Myron thought it resembled a urinal at a fancy restaurant.

Emily took out one of those new coffee presses people were using. "You sure you won't have some? It's Starbucks. Kona Hawaiian blend."

Myron shook his head. Emily had regained her senses now. She was back in control; he'd let her stay there. A person in control talks more and thinks less.

"I'm trying to figure out where to begin," she said, adding hot water to the press. The rich aroma immediately filled the air. If this was a coffee commercial, one of them would be saying "Ahhhh" right about now. "And don't tell me to begin at the beginning or I'll scream."

Myron held up his hands to show he would do no such thing.

Emily pushed a little on the plunger, met resistance, pushed again. "She came up to me one day in the supermarket of all places," she said. "Out of the blue. I'm reaching for some frozen bagels, and this woman tells me she has uncovered something that could destroy my husband. She tells me that if I don't pay up, she's going to call the papers."

"What did you say?"

"I asked her if she'd need a quarter for the phone." Emily chuckled, stopped pressing, stood upright. "I figured it was a joke. I told her to go ahead and destroy the bastard. She just nodded and said she'd be in touch."

"That was it?"

"Yep."

"When was this?"

"I don't know. Two, three weeks ago."

"So when did you hear from her next?"

Emily opened a cabinet and took out a coffee mug. The mug had a picture of some cartoon character. The words WORLD'S GREATEST MOM was emblazoned on the side. "I'm making enough for two," she said.

"No thank you."

"You sure?"

"Yes," Myron said. "What happened next?"

She bent down and peered into the coffee press like it was a crystal ball. "A few days after this, Greg did something to me. . . ." She stopped. Her tone was different now, the words coming slower and with more care. "It's like I told you last time you were here. He did something awful. The details aren't important."

Myron nodded but said nothing. No reason to raise the videotape now and knock her off stride. Facilitate her—that was the key.

"So when she came back and told me Greg was willing to pay big for her silence, I told her I'd pay more to make her talk. She told me it would cost a lot. I told her I didn't care how much. I tried to appeal to her as a woman. I went so far as to tell her about my situation, how Greg was trying to take my kids away from me. She seemed to sympathize, but she also made it clear that she couldn't afford to be philanthropic. If I wanted the information, I'd have to pay up."

"Did she tell you how much?"

"One hundred thousand dollars."

Myron held back a whistle. Serious double dipping. Liz Gorman's strategy was probably to keep collecting from both of them, bleeding them both for as long as she thought it was safe. Or maybe she was hitting hard and fast because she knew she would have to go underground again. Either way, it made sense from Liz Gorman's perspective to collect from all interested parties—Greg, Clip, and Emily. Take money for silence. Take money to sing. Blackmailers have the loyalty of election-year politicians.

"Do you know what she had on Greg?" he asked.

Emily shook her head. "She wouldn't tell me."

"But you were prepared to pay her a hundred grand?"

"Yes."

"Even though you didn't know what it was for?"

"Yes."

Myron gestured with both hands. "How did you know she wasn't just a crackpot?"

"The truth? I didn't know. But I was going to lose my kids, for chrissake. I was desperate."

And, Myron thought, Emily had shown that desperation to Liz Gorman who, in turn, took full advantage of it. "So you still have no idea what she had on him?"

Emily shook her head. "None."

"Could it have been Greg's gambling?"

Her eyes narrowed in confusion. "What about it?"

"Did you know Greg gambled?"

"Sure. But so what?"

"Do you know how much he gambled?" Myron asked.

"Just a little," she said. "A trip to Atlantic City once in a while. Maybe fifty dollars on a football game."

"Is that what you thought?"

Her eyes moved over his face, trying to read it. "What are you saying?"

Myron looked out the back window. The pool was still covered, but some of the robins had returned from the yearly aliya to the south. A dozen or so crowded a bird feeder, heads down, wings flapping happily like dog tails. "Greg is a compulsive gambler," Myron said. "He's lost away millions over the years. Felder didn't embezzle money—Greg lost it gambling."

Emily gave him a little head shake. "That can't be," she said. "I lived with him for almost ten years. I would have seen something."

"Gamblers learn how to hide it," Myron said. "They lie and cheat and steal—anything to keep on betting. It's an addiction."

Something in her eyes seemed to spark up. "And that's what this woman had on Greg? The fact that he gambled?"

"I think so," Myron said. "But I can't say for sure."

"But Greg definitely gambled, right? To the point where he lost all his money?"

"Yes."

The answer kindled Emily's face with hope. "Then no judge in the world would award him custody," she said. "I'll win."

"A judge is more likely to give the kids to a gambler than a murderer," Myron said. "Or someone who plants false evidence."

"I told you already. It's not false."

"So you say," Myron said. "But let's get back to what happened with the blackmailer. You were saying she wanted a hundred grand."

Emily moved back to her coffee press. "That's right."

"How were you to pay her?"

"She told me to wait by a pay phone outside a Grand Union supermarket on Saturday night. I was supposed to get there at midnight and have the money ready. She called at midnight on the dot and gave me an address on One Hundred Eleventh Street. I was supposed to get there at two in the morning."

"So you drove to One Hundred Eleventh Street at two in the morning with one hundred thousand dollars?" He tried not to sound too incredulous.

"I could only raise sixty thousand," she corrected.

"Did she know that?"

"No. Look, I know this all sounds crazy, but you don't understand how desperate I was. I would have done anything at this point."

Myron understood. He had seen up-close how far mothers would go. Love twists; maternal love twists absolutely. "Go on," he said.

"When I turned the corner, I saw Greg come out of the building," Emily said. "I was stunned. He had his collar up, but I could still see his face." She looked up at Myron. "I was married to him a long time, but I've never seen his face like this."

"Like what?"

"So filled with terror," she replied. "He practically sprinted toward Amsterdam Avenue. I waited until he turned the corner. Then I approached the door and pressed her apartment button. Nobody answered. I started pressing other buttons. Somebody finally buzzed me in. I went upstairs and knocked on her door for a while. Then I tried the knob. It was unlocked. So I opened the door."

Emily stopped. A trembling hand brought the cup up to her lips. She took a sip.

"This is going to sound awful," she went on, "but I didn't see a dead human being lying there. I only saw my last hope of keeping my kids."

"So you decided to plant evidence."

Emily put down the cup and looked at him. Her eyes were clear. "Yes. And you were right about everything else, too. I chose the playroom because I knew he'd never go down there. I figured that when Greg got back home—I didn't know he'd run—the blood would be safe. Look, I know I went too far, but it's not like I was lying. He killed her."

"You don't know that."

"What?"

"He might have stumbled across the body the same way you did."

"Are you serious?" Her tone was sharp now. "Of course Greg killed her. The blood on the floor was still fresh. He was the one who had everything to lose. He had motive, opportunity."

"Just as you do," Myron said.

"What motive?"

"You wanted to set him up for murder. You wanted to keep your children."

"That's ridiculous."

"Do you have any proof your story is true?" Myron asked.

"Do I have what?"

"Proof. I don't think the police are going to buy it."

"Do you buy it?" she asked him.

"I'd like to see proof."

"What do you mean, proof?" she snapped. "Like what? It's not like I took pictures."

"Any facts that back up your story?"

"Why would I kill her, Myron? What possible motive could I have? I needed her alive. She was my best chance of keeping my kids."

"But let's assume for a moment that this woman did indeed have something on Greg," Myron said. "Something concrete. Like a letter he wrote or a videotape"—he watched for a reaction—"or something like that."

"All right," she said with a nod. "Go ahead."

"And suppose she double-crossed you. Suppose she sold the incriminating evidence to Greg. You admit Greg was there before you. Maybe he paid her enough so that she'd back out of your agreement. Then you go into her apartment. You find out what she's done. You realize your one chance at keeping your kids is gone. So you kill her and pin it on the man who had seemed to have the most to gain from her death: Greg."

Emily shook her head. "That's nuts."

"You hated Greg enough," Myron continued. "He played dirty with you; you'd play dirty back."

"I didn't kill her."

Myron took another look at the robins, but they were gone. The yard looked barren now, stripped of any life. He waited a few seconds before he turned back toward her. "I know about the videotape of you and Thumper."

A quick bolt of anger hit Emily's eyes. Her fingers clutched the coffee mug. Myron half-expected her to throw it at him. "How the hell . . . ?" Then her grip suddenly slackened. She backed away. She sort of shrugged into a slouch. "It doesn't matter."

"It must have made you furious," he said.

She shook her head. A small sound like a chuckle escaped from her lips. "You just don't get it, do you, Myron?"

"Don't get what?"

"I wasn't looking for revenge. The only thing that mattered was that the tape could take away my kids."

"No, I do get it," Myron countered. "You'd do anything to keep your kids."

"I didn't kill her."

Myron shifted gears. "Tell me about you and Thumper," he said.

Emily snorted a derisive laugh. "I didn't think you were that type, Myron."

"I'm not."

She picked up her coffee mug and took a deep sip. "Did you watch the whole tape from beginning to end?" she asked in a tone somewhere between flirtatious and furious. "Did you hit the slow motion button a few times, Myron? Rewind and replay certain parts over and over? Drop your pants to your knees?"

"No to all of the above."

"How much did you see?"

"Just enough to know what was going on."

"Then you stopped?"

"Then I stopped."

She regarded him from behind the mug. "You know something? I actually believe you. You're that kind of goody two-shoes."

"Emily, I'm trying to help."

"Help me or Greg?"

"Help get to the truth. I assume you want that too."

She shrugged noncommittally.

"So when did you and Thumper . . . ?" He made vague coming-together motions with his hand.

She laughed at his discomfort. "It was the first time," she replied. "In all respects."

"I'm not judging—"

"I don't care if you are or not. You want to know what happened, right? It was my first time. That little whore set me up."

"How?"

"What do you mean, how?" she countered. "You want me to go

into details—how many drinks I had, how I was feeling lonely, how her hand started up my leg?"

"I guess not."

"Then let me give you the quick capsule: she seduced me. We'd flirted innocently a few times in the past. She invited me to the Glenpointe for drinks. It was like a dare on myself—I was drawn and repelled, but I knew I wouldn't go through with it. One thing led to another. We went upstairs. End of capsule."

"So you're saying Thumper knew you were being filmed?"

"Yes."

"How do you know? Did she say anything?"

"She didn't say anything. But I know."

"How?"

"Myron, please stop asking so many goddamn questions. I just know, okay? How else would anyone know to set up a camera in that room? She set me up."

That made sense, Myron thought. "But why would she do it?"

Her face registered her exasperation. "Christ, Myron, she's the team whore. Didn't she fuck you yet? Or no, let me guess. You refused, right?"

Emily stormed away into the living room and collapsed on a couch. "Get me the aspirin," she said. "They're in the bathroom. In the medicine chest."

Myron shook out two tablets and filled a cup with water. When he came back, he said, "I have to ask you about one more thing."

She sighed. "What?"

"I understand you made allegations against Greg," he said.

"My attorney made allegations."

"Were they true?"

She put the pills on her tongue, took some water, swallowed. "Some of them."

"How about the ones about him abusing the children?"

"I'm tired, Myron. Can we talk more later?"

"Were they true?"

Emily looked into Myron's eyes, and a cold gust of air blew across his heart. "Greg wanted to take my kids away from me," she said slowly. "He had money, power, prestige on his side. We needed something."

Myron broke the eye contact. He walked toward the door. "Don't destroy that coat."

"You have no right to judge me."

"Right now," he said, "I don't want to be near you."

Chapter 33

Audrey was leaning against his car. "Esperanza told me you'd be here."

Myron nodded.

"Jesus, you look like hell," she said. "What happened?"

"Long story."

"And one that you will soon tell me in riveting detail," Audrey added. "But I'll go first. Fiona White was indeed a Miss September in 1992—or as that particular rag calls it, the September Babe-A-Rama."

"You're kidding."

"Nope. Fiona's turn-ons include moonlit walks on the beach and cozy nights by a fireplace."

He smiled in spite of himself. "My, what originality."

"Her turn-offs include shallow men who only care about looks. And men with back hair."

"Did they list her favorite movies?"

"Schindler's List," Audrey said. "And *Cannonball Run II.*"

He laughed. "You're making this up."

"All except the part about being the September Babe-A-Rama in 1992."

Myron shook his head. "Greg Downing and his best friend's wife," he sighed. In a way, the news sort of buoyed him. Myron's ten-year-old indiscretion with Emily no longer seemed quite so bad. He knew that he shouldn't find comfort in such logic, but man takes solace where he can find it.

Audrey motioned toward the house. "So what's up with the ex?"

"Long story."

"You said that already. I got time."

"I don't."

She held up her palm like a cop directing traffic. "Not fair, Myron. I've been a good girl. I've been running your errands and keeping my big mouth shut. Not to mention the fact that I got zippo from you for my birthday. Please don't make me start with the exposure threats again."

She was right. Myron gave her an abbreviated update, leaving out two parts: the Thumper videotape (no reason anyone had to know about that) and the fact that Carla was the infamous Liz Gorman (it was simply too big a story; no reporter could be trusted to keep it off the record).

Audrey listened intently. Her page-boy cut had grown a little too long in the front. Hairs dangled close to her eyes. She kept sticking out her lower lip and blowing strands off her forehead. Myron had never before seen this particular gesture done by anybody over the age of eleven. It was kind of sweet.

"Do you believe her?" Audrey asked, motioning again to Emily's house.

"I'm not sure," he replied. "Her story sort of makes sense. She had no motive to kill the woman, except to frame Greg and that's reaching."

Audrey tilted her head as if to say, maybe yes—maybe no.

"What?" he asked.

"Well," she began, "isn't there's a chance that we're looking at this from the wrong perspective?"

"What do you mean?"

"We assume that this blackmailer had dirt on Downing," Audrey said. "But maybe she had dirt on Emily."

Myron stopped, looked back at the house as though it held some answers, looked back at Audrey.

"According to Emily," Audrey went on, "the blackmailer approached her. But why? She and Greg aren't together anymore."

"Carla didn't know that," Myron replied. "She figured Emily was his wife and would want to protect him."

"That's one possibility," Audrey agreed. "But I'm not sure it's the best one."

"Are you saying that they were blackmailing her, not Greg?"

Audrey turned her palms skyward. "All I'm saying is that it could work the other way too. The blackmailer might have had something on Emily—something Greg would want to use against her in the child custody case."

Myron folded his arms and leaned against the car. "But what about Clip?" he asked. "If they had something on Emily, why would he be interested?"

"I don't know." Audrey shrugged. "Maybe she had dirt on both of them."

"Both of them?"

"Sure. Something that could destroy them both. Or maybe Clip thought whatever it was—even if it was about Emily—would distract Greg."

"Any guesses?"

"Not a one," Audrey said.

Myron mulled it over for a few seconds, but nothing came to him. "There's a chance," he said, "we'll find out tonight."

"How?"

"The blackmailer called. He wants to sell me the information."

"Tonight?"

"Yep."

"Where?"

"I don't know yet. He's going to call. I got my home line forwarded to the cellular."

As if on cue, the cellular rang. Myron took it out of his pocket.

It was Win. "The dear professor's schedule was posted on his office door," he said. "He is in class for another hour. After that, he has open office hours so the kiddies can whine about grades."

"Where are you?"

"On Columbia's campus," Win replied. "By the way, Columbia women are fairly attractive. I mean, for the Ivy Leagues and all."

"Glad you haven't lost your powers of observation."

"Indeed," Win said. "Have you finished speaking to our girl?"

Our girl was Emily. Win did not trust cellular phones with names. "Yes," he said.

"Goodie. What time should I expect you then?"

"I'm on my way."

Chapter 34

Win was sitting on a bench near the Columbia gate on 116th Street. He was wearing Eddie Bauer khakis, Top-Siders without socks, a blue button-down Oxford, and a power tie.

"I'm blending in," Win explained.

"Like a Hasid at Christmas mass," Myron agreed. "Is Bowman still in class?"

Win nodded. "He should be exiting that door in ten minutes."

"Do you know what he looks like?"

Win handed him a faculty handbook. "Page two ten," he said. "So tell me about Emily."

Myron did. A tall brunette dressed in a black, skintight cat suit strolled by with her books pressed up against her chest. Julie Newmar on Batman. Win and Myron watched her closely. Meow.

When Myron finished, Win didn't bother with any questions. "I have a meeting at the office," he said as he stood. "Do you mind?"

Myron shook his head and sat down. Win left. Myron kept his eye on the door. Ten minutes later students began to file out the door. Two minutes after that, Professor Sidney Bowman followed suit. He had the same unkempt, academic beard as in the photo. He was bald but kept his fringe hair ridiculously long. He wore jeans, Timberland boots, and a red flannel shirt. He was either trying to look like a working stiff or Jerry Brown on the campaign trail.

Bowman pushed up his spectacles and kept walking. Myron waited until he was out of sight before following. No rush. The good professor was indeed heading for his office. He crossed the grassy commons and disappeared into yet another brick building. Myron found a bench and sat down.

An hour passed. Myron watched the students and felt very old. He should have brought a newspaper. Sitting for an hour without reading material meant he had to think. His mind kept conjuring up new possibilities and then dismissing them. He knew he was missing something, could see it bobbing in the distance, but every time he reached out it ducked back down below the surface.

He suddenly remembered that he had not checked Greg's answering machine today. He took out his cellular phone and dialed the number. When Greg's voice came on, he pressed 317, the code numbers Greg had programmed into the machine. There was only one message on the tape, but it was a doozy.

"Don't fuck with us," the electronically altered voice said. "I've spoken to Bolitar. He's willing to pay. Is that what you want?"

End of message.

Myron sat very still. He stared at a brick, ivyless wall. He listened to a tone for a few seconds and did nothing. What the hell . . . ?

"*. . . He's willing to pay. Is that what you want?*"

Myron pressed the star button to have the message replayed. Then he did it again. He probably would have listened for a fourth time, had Professor Bowman not suddenly appeared at the door.

Bowman stopped to chat with a couple of students. The conversation grew animated, all three displaying fervent, academic earnest. College. Continuing their undoubtedly weighty discourse, they walked off campus and down Amsterdam Avenue. Myron pocketed the phone and kept his distance. At 112th Street, the group separated. The two students continued south. Bowman crossed the street and headed toward the Cathedral of St. John the Divine.

St. John the Divine's was a massive structure and interestingly enough, the largest cathedral in the world in terms of cubic square feet (St. Peter's in Rome is considered a basilica by this statistic, not a cathedral). The edifice was like the city that housed it: awe-inspiring yet worn. Towering columns and gorgeous stained-glass windows were surrounded by signs like HARD HAT AREA (though it dated back to 1892, St. John the Divine's has never been completed) and THE CATHEDRAL IS PATROLLED AND ELECTRONICALLY MONITORED FOR YOUR PROTECTION. Wooden planks plugged holes in the granite facade. On the left side of this architectural wonder were two prefab aluminum storage barracks that brought back memories of the opening credits of *Gomer Pyle*. On the right was the Children's Sculpture Garden featuring the Peace Fountain, an enormous sculpture that inspired several moods, none of them peaceful. Images of severed heads and limbs, lobster claws, hands reaching out from the dirt as though trying to escape hell, a man twisting the neck of a deer all whirled together to create an atmosphere that was more Dante meets Goya than languid tranquillity.

Bowman headed down the driveway on the cathedral's right. Myron knew that there was a homeless shelter down that way. He crossed the street and tried to keep his distance. Bowman passed a group of apparently homeless men—all dressed in threadbare synthetics and pants with plunging butt-lines. Some waved and called out to Bowman. Bowman waved back. Then he disappeared through a door. Myron debated what to do. There was no choice really. Even if it meant blowing his cover, he had to go in.

He passed the men, nodded, smiled. They nodded and smiled back. The shelter entrance was a double black door with chintzy lace curtains. Not far from it were two signs—one reading SLOW CHIL-DREN AT PLAY and the other CATHEDRAL SCHOOL. A homeless shelter and a children's school side by side—an interesting yet working combo. Only in New York.

Myron entered. The room was packed with frayed mattresses and men. A smell like a used bong after an all-nighter singed his nostril hairs. Myron tried not to make a face. He spotted Bowman talking to several men in one corner. None of them was Cole Whiteman aka Norman Lowenstein. Myron glanced about the unshaven faces and hollow eyes, his gaze swinging left to right.

They spotted each other at exactly the same time.

From across the room, their eyes locked for perhaps a second, but that was long enough. Cole Whiteman turned and ran. Myron fol-lowed, threading his way through the throngs. Professor Bowman spotted the disturbance. Eyes afire, he jumped in Myron's path. My-ron lowered his shoulder and flattened him without breaking stride. Just like Jim Brown. Except Jim Brown had to do it against guys like Dick Butkus and Ray Nitschke opposed to a fifty-year-old college professor who probably didn't weigh 180 even with the soft gut. Still.

Cole Whiteman disappeared out a back door, slamming it behind him. Myron went through it not long after. They were outside now, but only briefly. Whiteman disappeared up a metal stairway and back into the main chapel. Myron followed. The inside was very much like the outside—spectacular examples of art and architecture mixed in with the tattered and tacky. The pews, for example, were cheap folding chairs. Lush tapestries hung upon granite walls with seem-ingly no organization. Ladders were melded into thick columns.

Myron spotted Cole heading back out a nearby door. He sprinted after him, his heels echoing up through the giant arched ceiling. They were back outside. Cole headed down below the cathedral and through heavy fire doors. A sign read A.C.T. PROGRAM. It looked like a basement school or daycare center. Both men raced down a hallway lined with beat-up, metallic lockers. Cole turned right and disap-peared behind a wooden door.

When Myron pushed the door open, a darkened stairway greeted him. He heard footsteps below him. He trotted down, the light from above dwindling with each step. He was descending deep into the cathedral's subdwelling now. The walls were cement and clammy to the touch. He wondered if he was entering a crypt or tomb or something equally creepy, if indeed there was equally creepy. Did American cathedrals have crypts, or was that only in Europe?

By the time he reached the bottom step, Myron was bathed in darkness, the light from above little more than distant glint. Great. He stepped into a black hole of a room. He cocked his head, listening for a sound like a dog on a hunt. Nothing. He felt for a light switch. Again nothing. The room had a bone-chilling, windless cold. A damp smell permeated his surroundings. He didn't like it down here. He didn't like it at all.

He inched forward blindly, his arms outstretched like Frankenstein's monster. "Cole," he called out. "I just want to talk to you."

His words echoed hard before fading out like a song on the radio.

He kept going. The room was still as . . . well, as a tomb. He had moved about five feet when his outstretched fingers hit something. Myron kept his hand on the smooth, cold surface. Like marble, he thought. He traced down. It was a statue of some sort. He felt the arm, the shoulder, to the back, down a marble wing. He wondered if it was some kind of tombstone decoration and quickly withdrew his hand.

He stayed perfectly still and tried to listen again. The only sound was a rushing in his ears, like seashells were pressed against them. He debated going back upstairs, but there was no way he could do that. Cole knew now that his identity was in danger. He would go into hiding again and not resurface. This was Myron's only chance.

He took another step, leading now with his foot. His toe hit something hard and unyielding. Marble again, he figured. He circled around it. Then a sound—a scurrying sound—made him freeze in his tracks. It had come from the ground. Not a mouse. Too big for a mouse. He cocked his head again and waited. His pulse raced. His eyes were just beginning to adjust to the darkness, and he could make out a few shadowy, tall figures. Statues. Lowered heads. He imagined the serene expressions of religious art on their faces, looking down at him with the knowledge they were embarking on a journey to a better place than the one in which they dwelled.

He took another step, and cold fingers of flesh grabbed his ankle. Myron screamed.

The hand pulled and Myron fell hard against the cement. He kicked his leg loose and scrambled backward. His back slammed into more marble. A man giggled madly. Myron felt the hairs on the nape of his neck stand up. Another man giggled. Then another. Like a group of hyenas were encircling him.

Myron tried to get to his feet, but midway up, the men suddenly pounced. He didn't know how many. Hands dragged him back to the floor. He threw a blind fist and connected square into a face. Myron heard a crunching sound and a man fell. But others reached their target. He found himself sprawled on the wet cement, fighting blindly and frantically. He heard grunts. The stench of body odor and alcohol was suffocating, inescapable. The hands were everywhere now. One ripped off his watch. One grabbed his wallet. Myron threw another punch. It hit ribs. Another grunt and another man fell.

Somebody turned on a flashlight and shone it into his eyes. It looked like a train heading toward him.

"Okay," a voice said, "back off him."

The hands slid off like wet snakes. Myron tried to sit up.

"Before you get any cute ideas," the voice behind the flashlight said, "take a look at this."

The voice put a gun in front of the flashlight.

Another voice said, "Sixty bucks? That's fuckin' all? Shit."

Myron felt the wallet hit him in the chest.

"Put your hands behind your back."

He did as the voice asked. Someone grabbed the forearms, pulling them closer together, tearing at the shoulder tendons. A pair of handcuffs were snapped on his wrists.

"Leave us," the voice said. Myron heard the rustling movements. The air cleared. Myron heard a door open, but the flashlight in his eyes prevented him from seeing anything. Silence followed. After some time passed, the voice said, "Sorry to do this to you, Myron. They'll let you go in a few hours."

"How long you going to keep running, Cole?"

Cole Whiteman chuckled. "Been running a long time," he said. "I'm used to it."

"I'm not here to stop you."

"Imagine my relief," he said. "So how did you figure out who I was?"

"It's not important," Myron said.

"It is to me."

"I don't have any interest in bringing you down," Myron said. "I just want some information."

There was a pause. Myron blinked into the light. "How did you get involved in all this?" Cole asked.

"Greg Downing vanished. I was hired to find him."

"You?"

"Yes."

Cole Whiteman laughed deep and hearty. The sound bounced around like balls of Silly Putty, the volume reaching a frightening crescendo before mercifully fading away.

"What's so funny?" Myron asked.

"Inside joke." Cole stood, the flashlight rising with him. "Look, I have to go. I'm sorry."

More silence. Cole flicked off the flashlight, plunging Myron back into total blackness. He heard footsteps receding.

"Don't you want to know who killed Liz Gorman?" Myron called out.

The footsteps continued unimpeded. Myron heard a switch and a dim lightbulb came on. Maybe forty watts. It didn't come close to fully illuminating the place, but it was a hell of an improvement. Myron blinked away black spots left over from the flashlight assault and examined his surroundings. The room was jammed with marble statues, lined and piled up without reason or logic, some tilted over. It wasn't a tomb, after all. It was some bizarre, church-art storage room.

Cole Whiteman came back over to him. He sat cross-legged directly in front of Myron. The white stubble was still there—thick in some spots, completely missing in others. His hair jutted up and out in every direction. He lowered the gun to his side.

"I want to know how Liz died," he said softly.

"She was bludgeoned with a baseball bat," Myron said.

Cole's eyes closed. "Who did it?"

"That's what I'm trying to find out. Right now, Greg Downing is the main suspect."

Cole Whiteman shook his head. "He wasn't there long enough."

Myron felt a knot in his stomach. He tried to lick his lips but his mouth was too dry. "You were there?"

"Across the street behind a garbage can. Like Oscar the fucking Grouch." His lips smiled, but there was nothing behind it. "You want no one to notice you? Pretend you're homeless." He stood up in one fluid motion, like some kind of yoga master. "A baseball bat," he said. He pinched the bridge of his nose, turned away, and lowered his chin to his chest. Myron could hear small sobs.

"Help me find her killer, Cole."

"Why the fuck should I trust you?"

"Me or the police," Myron said. "It's up to you."

That slowed him. "The cops won't do shit. They think she's a murderer."

"Then help me," Myron said.

He sat back down on the floor and inched a bit closer to Myron. "We're not murderers, you know. The government labeled us that and now everyone believes it. But it's not true. You understand?"

Myron nodded. "I understand."

Cole gave him a hard look. "You patronizing me?"

"No."

"Don't patronize me," Cole said. "You want me to stay and talk, don't you dare patronize me. You stay honest—I'll stay honest."

"Fine," Myron said. "But then don't hand me the 'we're not killers, we're freedom fighters' line. I'm not in the mood for a verse of 'Blowin' in the Wind.' "

"You think that's what I'm talking about?"

"You're not being prosecuted by a corrupt government," Myron said. "You kidnapped and killed a man, Cole. You can dress it up in all the fancy language you want, but that's what you did."

Cole almost smiled. "You really believe that."

"Wait, don't tell me; let me guess," Myron said. He feigned looking up in thought. "The government brainwashed me, right? This whole thing has been a CIA plot to crush a dozen college students who threatened to undermine our government."

"No," he said. "But we didn't kill Hunt."

"Who did?"

Cole hesitated. He looked up and blinked back what looked like tears. "Hunt shot himself."

His reddening eyes looked to Myron for a reaction. Myron remained still.

"The kidnapping was a hoax," Cole went on. "The whole thing was Hunt's idea. He wanted to hurt his old man so he figured what better way than to take his money and then embarrass the shit out of him? But then those assholes surprised us and Hunt chose another revenge." Cole's breathing grew deep and erratic. "He ran outside with the gun. He screamed, 'Fuck you, Dad.' Then he blew his own head off."

Myron said nothing.

"Look at our history," Cole Whiteman said, his voice a semiplea. "We were a harmless group of stragglers. We protested at antiwar rallies. We got stoned a lot. We never committed one act of violence. None of us even had a gun, except for Hunt. He was my roommate and best friend. I could never hurt him."

Myron didn't know what to believe; more to the point, he didn't have time now to worry about a twenty-year-old homicide. He waited for Cole to continue, to let him talk out the past, but Cole remained still. Finally, Myron tried to update the subject. "You saw Greg Downing go into Liz Gorman's building?"

Cole nodded slowly.

"She was blackmailing him?"

"Not just her," he corrected. "It was my idea."

"What did you have on Greg?"

Cole shook his head. "Not important."

"She was probably killed over it."

"Probably," Cole agreed. "But you don't need to know the specifics. Trust me."

Myron was in no position to push it. "Tell me about the night of the murder."

Cole scratched at his stubble hard, like a cat on a post. "Like I said," he began, "I was across the street. When you live underground, you have certain rules you live by—rules that have kept us alive and free for the last twenty years. One of them is that after we commit a crime, we never stay together. The feds look for us in groups, not individuals. Since we've been in the city, Liz and I have made sure we were never together. We only communicated by pay phone."

"What about Gloria Katz and Susan Milano?" Myron asked. "Where are they?"

Cole smiled without mirth or humor. Myron saw the missing teeth and wondered if they were part of the disguise or something more sinister. "I'll tell you about them another time," he said.

Myron nodded. "Go on," he said.

The lines in Cole's face seemed to deepen and darken in the bare light. He took his time before continuing. "Liz was all packed and ready to go," he said finally. "We were going to score the cash and get out of the city, just like I planned. I was just waiting across the street for her signal."

"What signal?"

"After all the money was collected, she'd flicker the lights three times. That meant she'd be down in ten minutes. We were going to meet at One Hundred Sixteenth Street and take the One train out of here. But the signal never came. In fact, her light never went off at all. I was afraid to go check on her for obvious reasons. We got rules about that, too."

"Who was Liz supposed to collect from that night?"

"Three people," Cole said, holding up the pointer, middle man, and ring man. "Greg Downing"—he dropped ring man—"his wife what's-her-name—"

"Emily."

"Right, Emily." The middle finger went down. "And the old guy who owns the Dragons." His hand made a fist now.

Myron's heart contracted. "Wait a second," he said. "Clip Arnstein was supposed to show up?"

"Not supposed to," Cole corrected. "He did."

A black coldness seeped into Myron's bones. "Clip was there?"

"Yes."

"And the other two?"

"All three showed up. But that wasn't the plan. Liz was supposed to meet Downing at a bar downtown. They were going to make the transaction there."

"A place called the Swiss Chalet?"

"Right."

"But Greg showed up at the apartment too?"

"Later on, yeah. But Clip Arnstein arrived first."

Win's warning about Clip came back to him. You like him too much. You're not being objective. "How much was Clip supposed to pay?"

"Thirty thousand dollars."

"The police only found ten thousand in her apartment," Myron said. "And those bills were from the bank robbery."

Cole shrugged. "Either the old man didn't pay her or else the killer took the money." Then, thinking it through a little more he added, "Or maybe Clip Arnstein killed her. But he seems kind of old, don't you think?"

Myron didn't answer. "How long was he inside?"

"Ten, fifteen minutes."

"Who came by next?"

"Greg Downing. I remember he had a satchel. I figured it had the money in it. He was in and out fast—couldn't have been more than a minute. And he still had the satchel on him when he came out. That's when I started to worry."

"Greg could have killed her," Myron said. "It doesn't take long to hit someone with a baseball bat."

"But he wasn't carrying a bat," Cole said. "The satchel wasn't big enough for one. And Liz had a bat in her apartment. She hated guns, so she kept it for protection."

Myron knew that no bat had been found at Gorman's apartment.

That meant the killer must have used Liz's. Could Greg have gone upstairs, entered her apartment, found the bat, killed her with it, ran out—all in such a short time?

It seemed doubtful.

"What about Emily?" Myron asked.

"She came in last," Cole said.

"How long was she there?"

"Five minutes. Something like that."

Time enough to gather the evidence to plant. "Did you see anybody else go in and out of the building?"

"Sure," Cole said. "Lot of students live there."

"But we can assume that Liz was already dead by the time Greg Downing arrived, right?"

"Right."

"So the question is, who do you remember going in between the time she got back from the Swiss Chalet and the time Greg arrived? Besides Clip Arnstein."

Cole thought about it and shrugged. "Mostly students, I guess. There was a real tall guy—"

"How tall?"

"I don't know. Very."

"I'm six-four. Taller than me?"

"Yeah, I think so."

"Was he black?"

"I don't know. I was across the street and the light wasn't too good. I wasn't watching that closely. He might have been black. But I don't think he's our man."

"Why do you say that?"

"I watched the building until the next morning. He never came back out. He must have lived there or at least stayed with someone overnight. I doubt the killer would've hung around like that."

Tough to argue, Myron thought. He tried to process what he was hearing in a cold, computerlike way, but the circuits were starting to overload. "Who else did you remember seeing? Anybody stand out?"

Cole thought again, his eyes wandering aimlessly. "There was one woman who went in not long before Greg got there. Now that I think of it, she left before he got there too."

"What did she look like?"

"I don't remember."

"Blond, brunette?"

Cole shook his head. "I only remember her because she wore a long coat. The students all wear windbreakers or sweatshirts or something like that. I remember thinking she looked like an adult."

"Was she carrying anything? Did she—"

"Look, Myron, I'm sorry. I gotta get moving." He stood and looked down at Myron with a hollow, lost expression. "Good luck finding the son of a bitch," he said. "Liz was a good person. She never hurt anyone. None of us did."

Before he could turn away, Myron asked, "Why did you call me last night? What were you going to sell me?"

Cole smiled sadly and began to walk away. He stopped before he reached the door and turned back around. "I'm alone now," he said. "Gloria Katz was shot in the initial attack. She died three months later. Susan Milano died in a car crash in 1982. Liz and I kept their deaths a secret. We wanted the feds searching for four of us, not two. We thought it would help us stay hidden. So you see, there is only one of us left now."

He had the bone-weary look of a survivor who wasn't so sure the dead weren't the lucky ones. He rambled back over toward Myron and unlocked the handcuffs. "Go," he said.

Myron rose, rubbing his wrists. "Thank you," he said.

Cole merely nodded.

"I won't tell anyone where you are."

"Yeah," Cole said. "I know."

Chapter 35

Myron sprinted to his car and dialed Clip's number. Clip's secretary answered and told him that Mr. Arnstein was not in at the moment. He asked her to transfer the call to Calvin Johnson. She put him on hold. Ten seconds later, the call was put through.

"Hey, Myron," Calvin said, "what's up?"

"Where's Clip?"

"He should be here in a couple of hours. By game time anyway."

"Where is he now?"

"I don't know."

"Find him," Myron said. "When you do, call me back."

"What's going on?" Calvin asked.

"Just find him."

Myron disconnected the call. He opened the car window and took deep breaths. It was a few minutes after six. Most of the guys would already be at the arena warming up. He headed up Riverside Drive and crossed the George Washington Bridge. He dialed Leon White's number. A woman answered.

"Hello?"

Myron disguised his voice. "Is this Mrs. Fiona White?" he asked.

"Yes, it is."

"Would you like to subscribe to *Popular Mechanics*? We have a special going on for a limited time."

"No, thank you." She hung up.

Conclusion: Fiona White, the Sepbabe and promisor of night ecstasy, was home. Time to pay her a little visit.

He took Route 4 and got off at Kindermack Road. Five minutes later, he was there. The house was a semi-nouveau ranch with orange-tinged brick and diamond-shaped windows. This particular architectural look was all the rage for maybe a two-month span in 1977, and it had aged about as well as the leisure suit. Myron parked in the driveway. On either side of the cement walkway were low-rise iron fences with plastic ivy snaked through them. Classy.

He rang the bell. Fiona White opened the door. Her green, flower-print blouse hung open over a white leotard. Her bleached-blonde hair was tied in a bun that was falling apart, spare strands dangling down over her eyes and ears. She looked at Myron and frowned. "Yes?"

"Hi, Fiona. I'm Myron Bolitar. We met the other night at TC's house."

The frown was still there. "Leon isn't here."

"I wanted to talk to you."

Fiona sighed and crossed her arms under the ample bosom. "What about?"

"Can I come inside?"

"No. I'm busy right now."

"I think it would be better in private."

"This is private," she said, her face unyielding. "What do you want?"

Myron shrugged, conjured up his most charming smile, saw it would take him nowhere. "I want to know about you and Greg Downing."

Fiona White's arms dropped to her side. She suddenly looked horror-stricken. "What?"

"I know about your e-mail to him. Sepbabe. You were supposed to meet last Saturday for the"—Myron made quote marks with his fingers—"'greatest night of ecstasy imaginable.' Do you recall that?"

Fiona White went to close the door. Myron stuck his foot in the way.

"I've got nothing to say to you," she said.

"I'm not trying to expose you."

She pushed the door against his foot. "Get out."

"I'm just trying to find Greg Downing."

"I don't know where he is."

"Were you having an affair with him?"

"No. Now leave."

"I saw the e-mail, Fiona."

"Think what you want. I'm not talking to you."

"Fine," Myron said, moving back and throwing up his hands. "I'll talk to Leon instead."

Her cheeks flushed. "Do whatever you want," she said. "I did not have an affair with him. I did not see him last Saturday night. I don't know where he is."

She slammed the door.

Gee, that went well.

Myron headed back to his car. As he reached the door, a black

BMW with tinted windows rocketed up the street and screeched to a halt in the driveway. The driver's door opened and Leon flew out like an escaped bird.

"What the fuck you doing here?" he snapped.

"Take it easy, Leon."

"Fuck take it easy," he shouted. Leon ran up and stuck his face within an inch of Myron's. "What the fuck you doing around here, huh?"

"I came by to see you."

"Bullshit." The spittle hit Myron's cheeks. "We're supposed to be at the arena in twenty minutes." He pushed Myron in the chest. Myron stumbled back. "Why you here, huh?" Leon pushed again. "What are you sniffing after?"

"Nothing."

"You think you'd find my wife alone?"

"It's nothing like that."

Leon lined himself up for another push. Myron was ready. When Leon's hand reached him, Myron's right forearm shot across his body, pinning Leon's hands helplessly against Myron's chest. Myron bent at the waist, bending Leon's wrists back the wrong way. The pressure forced Leon to drop to one knee. Myron's right hand slid until it met Leon's left. He grabbed it and quickly executed an elbow lock. Leon winced.

"You calm?" Myron asked.

"Motherfucker."

"That doesn't sound like calm, Leon." Myron applied a little pressure to the elbow. Joint locks were about controlled pain. They worked by bending joints in ways they were never intended to bend. The more the bend, the more the pain. But go too far and the joint dislocated or a bone broke. Myron was careful.

"Greg is missing again," Myron said. "That's why I'm on the team. I'm supposed to find him."

Leon was still on his knees, his arm locked and upright. "So what does that have to do with me?"

"You two have had a falling out," Myron said. "I want to know why."

Leon looked up at him. "Let go of me, Myron."

"If you attack me again—"

"I won't. Just let go already."

Myron waited another second or two, then did as Leon asked. Leon rubbed his arm and stood. Myron eyed him.

Leon said, "You're here because you think Greg and Fiona were getting it on."

"Were they?"

He shook his head. "Not from a lack of trying though."

"What do you mean?"

"He's supposed to be my best friend. But he's not. He's just another fucking superstar who takes what he wants."

"Including Fiona."

"He tried. Tried like hell. But she's not like that."

Myron said nothing. Not his place.

"Guys are always hitting on Fiona," he went on. "Because of the way she looks. And the whole racial thing. So when I saw you here when you figured I wouldn't be around . . ." He shrugged into silence.

"Did you ever confront Greg?" Myron asked.

"Yeah," he said. "A couple of weeks ago."

"What did you say to him?"

Leon's eyes narrowed, suddenly wary. "What does this have to do with finding him?" he asked, suspicious now. "You trying to pin this on me?"

"Pin what on you?"

"You said he's disappeared. You trying to pin that on me?"

"I'm just trying to find out where he is."

"I got nothing to do with it."

"I didn't say you did. I just want to know what happened when you confronted him."

"What do you think happened?" Leon countered. "The motherfucker denied it. He made this big point of swearing he'd never sleep with any married woman—especially his best friend's wife."

Myron sort of gulped at that one. "But you didn't believe him."

"He's a superstar, Myron."

"That doesn't make him a liar."

"No, but it makes him something different. Guys like Greg and Michael Jordan and Shaq and TC . . . they ain't like the rest of us. They got their own thing going. Everyone else is a fucking underling to them. The whole planet is set up to cater to their whims, you know what I'm saying?"

Myron nodded. In college he had been one of those who got to breathe the rarefied air of superstardom. He thought again about the bonds superstars shared. He and Greg had not exchanged more than five words before Greg visited him in the hospital, but there had been a bond. They both knew. Superstars share that rarefied air with very few. As TC had told him, it does indeed isolate in a very bizarre, often unhealthy way.

And with that thought came something of a revelation. Myron took a step back.

He'd always thought that if Greg was in trouble, he'd go to his closest friend for help. But that wasn't the case. If Greg had indeed stumbled across the dead body and panicked, if he had seen all his problems—the gambling debts, the threat of exposure, the divorce, the child custody case, the blackmail, the probability of being a suspect in a murder—closing in on him, who would he go to for help?

He'd go to the guy who understood him best.

He'd go to the guy who could best relate to the unique troubles of superstardom.

He'd go to the guy who shared that rarefied air with him.

Chapter 36

Myron wasn't sure what to do next.

In truth, he had nothing more than a suspicion. There was no proof. No real evidence. But it could potentially answer a lot of questions. Why, for example, had Thumper helped set up Emily on videotape? By all accounts, she was not particularly close to Greg.

But she was to TC.

Again the superstar bond. Greg had feared losing his kids in a custody battle. That's about as big a worry as a person can have. So whom did he turn to for help?

TC.

When Win had leaned on Thumper last night, letting her know that he was searching for Greg, whom had she warned?

TC.

No proof, of course. But it felt very right.

Myron could now put a lot of it together. Greg was under incredible strain—not the best situation for a man of his questionable mental fortitude to be ensnared. What had gone through his mind when he saw Liz Gorman dead on the floor? He'd have to have known that he would be the prime suspect in her murder. As Emily had pointed out, Greg had motive, opportunity, and was at the murder scene. Emily saw that. It was why she set him up. Greg must have seen it too.

So what did he do?

He ran.

Seeing Liz Gorman dead had been the final straw. But Greg had also known that he could not do it alone. People would be looking for him this time. He needed help. He needed time and space.

So whom did Greg reach out to?

The guy who understood him best. Who could relate to the unique troubles of superstardom. Who shared that rarefied air with him.

Myron stopped at a red light. He was close, so goddamn close. TC was helping Greg hide; he was sure of it. But of course, TC was only part of the solution. None of this answered the central question in all this:

Who killed Liz Gorman?

He put his mind on rewind and reviewed the night of the murder. He thought about Clip being the first of the three to arrive. In many ways, Clip was now his best suspect. But Myron still saw big problems with that scenario. What was Clip's motive, for example? Yes, Liz Gorman's information may have been detrimental to the team. The information may have even been potent enough for him to lose the vote. But would Clip pick up a baseball bat and murder a woman over that? People kill for money and power all the time. Would Clip?

But there was still a larger problem at work here, one that Myron could not get around no matter how hard he tried. Emily was the one who planted the blood and murder weapon at Greg's house. That was established and that made sense. Okay, fine. We know who planted the evidence . . .

. . . but who cleaned it up?

There were only three logical choices: 1) Greg Downing, 2) someone trying to protect Greg, or 3) the killer.

But it couldn't have been Greg. Even if you accept the semi-impossible premise that Greg went back into his house after going into hiding, how did he find the blood? Did he just happen to go down into his playroom? No. It was too ridiculous. The only way Greg would have gone down there was if he'd known the blood had been planted.

Myron froze.

That was it. Whoever had cleaned up the blood had known what Emily had done. They didn't just stumble across it by accident. So how did they find out? From Emily? Uh uh, no way. Emily would be the last person to say anything. Could she have been spotted in the act? Again, the answer was a resounding no. If that had been the case, the bat would have been removed too. More to the point, the blood would have been cleaned up right away—*before* Myron and Win found it. The timing of the clean-up was crucial—it'd happened after Myron and Win had revealed their discovery. That meant Myron and Win were the leak.

So who had they told?

The finger pointed back to Clip.

He turned on Route 3 and entered the Meadowlands complex. The arena loomed before him like a large UFO on a white landing pad. Did Clip Arnstein murder Liz Gorman and clean up the blood? Myron wrestled with the possibility, but he didn't like it. How had Clip gotten inside Greg's house? There were no signs of forced entry. Had he picked the lock? Doubtful. Did he have a key? Doubtful. Did he

hire a professional? Still doubtful. Clip hadn't even let a private investigator do a simple credit card check on Greg for fear word would
get out. Whom would he trust to clean up the blood of a person he
murdered?

And something else still jabbed at Myron with a sharpened, steel
point: the woman's clothes in the bedroom. They had been packed
away too. Why would Clip remove all traces of a secret girlfriend?
Why would anybody?

The different scenarios swirled in Myron's head like rubber ducks
in a whirlpool. He concentrated again on the mystery girlfriend.
Could it have been Fiona White? She wasn't talking, but Myron
firmly believed that she was not the one. How could Fiona have lived
with Greg and kept it hidden from a husband as obsessively jealous
as Leon? Perhaps there had been some entanglement between Greg
and Fiona—a casual fling in a motel room or something—but Myron no longer believed even that. The more he thought about it, the
"greatest night of sexual ecstasy" epistle was more of a come-on
than the talk of two familiar lovers. It seemed more logical that Greg
was telling Leon the truth when he said he would never sleep with
another man's wife. The thought gave Myron's old shame new life.

A commercial came on the radio. A very hip man and a very hip
woman were enjoying a Molson's Golden far too much. They spoke
in low voices and laughed at each other's lame jokes. Myron
switched it off.

He still had more questions than answers. But when he picked up
his cellular phone to check Greg's answering machine, his fingers began to tremble. Something tightened his chest, making it hard to
breathe. This feeling, however, was not like pregame jitters. In fact,
it was the furthest thing from them.

Chapter 37

Myron rushed by Clip's secretary.

"He's not in there," she cried.

Ignoring her, he opened the office door. The lights were off and the room was empty. He spun back toward the secretary. "Where is he?"

The secretary, a classic battle-ax who had probably been with Clip since the Coolidge Administration, put her hands on her hips. "I don't have the slightest idea," she huffed.

Calvin Johnson came out of the adjoining office. Myron approached him. He waited until they were inside Calvin's office and the door was closed. "Where is he?"

Calvin held up his hands. "I don't know. I tried his house, but there was no answer."

"Does he have a car phone?"

"No."

Myron shook his head and began pacing. "He lied to me," Myron said. "The son of a bitch lied."

"What?"

"He met with the blackmailer."

Calvin raised an eyebrow. He moved to the chair behind his desk and sat down. "What are you talking about?"

"The night she was murdered," Myron said, "Clip went to her apartment."

"But she wasn't supposed to meet with us until Monday," Calvin said.

"Did you hear her say that?"

Calvin plucked at his chin with his thumb and pointer. The track lights from above his desk reflected off the receding forehead. His face remained the ever placid pool. "No," he said slowly. "Clip told me."

"He lied to you."

"But why?"

"Because he's hiding something."

"Do you know what?"

"No," Myron said. "But I intend to find out tonight."

"How?"

"The blackmailer still wants to sell," Myron said. "I'm his new buyer."

Calvin tilted his head. "I thought you said the blackmailer was dead."

"She had a partner."

"I see," Calvin said with a slow nod. "And you're meeting tonight?"

"Yep. But I don't know when or where. He's supposed to call."

"I see," Calvin said again. He made a neat fist and coughed into it. "If it's something damaging. I mean, something that could affect the outcome of the vote tomorrow. . . ."

"I'll do whatever is right, Calvin."

"Of course. I didn't mean to imply otherwise."

Myron rose. "Let me know when he gets here."

"Sure."

Myron entered the locker room. TC was in his pregame pose—sprawled on a chair in the corner with a Walkman plugged into his ears, his eyes blazing straight ahead and unmoving. He did not acknowledge Myron. Leon was also there. He, too, studiously avoided Myron's gaze. Not surprising.

Audrey approached. "How did it go with—?"

Myron shook his head to silence her. She nodded, understanding. "You okay?" she asked.

"Fine."

"You think they can hear us?"

"I'm not taking any chances."

Audrey looked left, then right. "You find something new?"

"Plenty," Myron said. "You should have your story tonight. And then some."

The gleam in her eye expanded. "You know where he is?"

Myron nodded. The locker room door opened. Calvin popped his head in. He leaned over and spoke to the Kipper for a moment. When he left, Myron noticed that he turned right, which led to the exit, as opposed to left which would have taken him back to his office.

The cellular phone in Myron's pocket rang. He looked up at Audrey. Audrey looked back. He moved closer to the corner and picked it up.

"Hello?"

An electronically altered voice said, "You got the money?"

"You got lousy timing," Myron said.

"Answer my question."

Leon pulled up his gym shorts. TC stood and bobbed his head in rhythm to the music.

"I have it," Myron said. "I also have a game tonight."

"Forget the game. Do you know Overpeck Park?"

"The one in Leonia? Yeah, I know it."

"Turn in the right side off Route Ninety-five. Then go down a quarter mile and make another right. You'll see a cul-de-sac. Park there and look for a flashlight. Approach with both your hands raised."

"Do I get to say a password?" Myron asked. "I love passwords."

"Fifteen minutes. Don't be late. And for the record, I know your superhero partner is in his Park Avenue office. I have a man watching it. If he leaves between now and then, the deal is off."

Myron turned off the phone. It was coming to a head now. In fifteen minutes it would all be over—one way or another. "Could you hear?" he asked.

Audrey nodded. "Most of it."

"There's going to be some weird stuff going down," Myron said. "I need an unbiased journalist to record it. You want to come along?"

She smiled. "That was a rhetorical question, right?"

"You'll have to keep on the floor in the backseat," he went on. "I can't risk having you spotted."

"No problem," she said. "It'll remind me of my high school dates."

Myron turned toward the door. His nerves were as frayed as an old horse whip. He tried to look nonchalant as they exited. Leon was lacing up his sneakers. TC remained still, but this time his eyes followed them out.

Chapter 38

Rain beat down, blackening the pavement. Cars were just starting to enter the arena lot in force. Myron took the back exit over the New Jersey Turnpike and onto the northbound lanes just past the final toll booth. He veered to the right, staying on Route 95.

"So what's going on?" Audrey asked.

"The man I am about to meet," he said, "killed Liz Gorman."

"Who's Liz Gorman?"

"The blackmailer who was murdered."

"I thought her name was Carla."

"That was an alias."

"Wait a minute. Isn't Liz Gorman the name of some sixties radical?"

Myron nodded. "It's a long story; I don't have time to go into details. Suffice to say the guy we're about to meet was part of the blackmail scheme. Something went awry. She ended up dead."

"Do you have evidence?" Audrey asked.

"Not really. That's what I need you for. You have your microcassette player?"

"Sure."

"Let me have it."

Audrey reached into her purse and handed it up front.

"I'm going to try to get him to talk," Myron said.

"How?"

"By pushing the right buttons."

She frowned. "You think he'll fall for that?"

"Yeah, I do. If I push the right ones." He picked up the car phone. "I have two separate phones here: the car phone and the cellular in my pocket. I'm going to dial the car phone with the cellular and keep the line open. This way, you can listen in. I want you to take down every word. If something happens to me, go to Win. He'll know what to do."

She leaned forward and nodded. The windshield wipers whipped shadows across her face. The rain picked up its tempo, glistening the road in front of them. Myron took the next exit. A sign reading Overpeck Park greeted them a quarter mile later.

"Get down," he said.

She disappeared from view. He made the right turn. Another sign told him the park was closed. He ignored it and proceeded ahead. It was too dark to see anything, but he knew there were woods on his left and a horse stables straight ahead. He made the first right. The car's headlights danced across a picnic area, illuminating tables, benches, garbage cans, a swing set, a sliding board. He reached the cul-de-sac and stopped the car. He killed the lights, turned off the engine, and dialed the car's number on his cellular. He answered with the car's speakerphone so Audrey could listen in. Then he waited.

For several minutes nothing happened. The rain pelted down on the roof like tiny pebbles. Audrey remained still in the back. Myron put his hands back on the wheel and felt his grip tighten. He could hear his heart thumping in his chest.

Without warning, a beacon of light sliced through the night like a reaper's scythe. Myron shaded his eyes with his hand and squinted. He slowly opened the car door. The wind had picked up now, spraying the rain into his face. He hefted himself out of the car.

A male voice, distorted by the elements, shouted, "Put your hands up."

Myron raised them above his head.

"Open your coat. I know you're carrying a gun in a shoulder holster. Take it out with two fingers and toss it onto the seat of the car."

Keeping one hand in the air, Myron unbuttoned his coat. He was already drenched from the rain, his hair matted against his forehead. He took out the gun and put in on his car seat.

"Close the door."

Again Myron obeyed the voice.

"Do you have the money?"

"First I want to see what you brought," Myron said.

"No."

"Hey, be reasonable here. I don't even know what I'm buying."

A brief hesitation. "Come closer."

Myron stepped toward the light, ignoring the symbolism. "Whatever you're selling," he said, "how do I know you haven't made copies?"

"You don't," the voice said. "You'll have to trust me."

"Who else knows about this?"

"I'm the only one," the voice said, "who is still alive."

Myron picked up the pace. His hands were still in the air. The wind whipped into his face. His clothes were sopping. "How do I know you won't talk?"

"Again, you don't. Your money buys my silence."

"Until someone ups the bid."

"No. I'm leaving after this. You won't hear from me again." The flashlight flickered. "Please stop."

Ten feet in front of him stood a man wearing a ski mask. He had a flashlight in one hand and a box in the other. He nodded at Myron and lifted the box. "Here."

"What is it?"

"First, the money."

"For all I know, the box is empty."

"Fine. Go back to your car and leave then." The man in the ski mask turned around.

"No, wait," Myron said. "I'll get the money."

The ski mask faced Myron again. "No games."

Myron headed back to the car. He had moved about twenty paces when he heard the gunshots. Three of them. The noises did not startle him. He slowly turned around. The man with the ski mask was down. Audrey was running toward the still body. She was carrying Myron's gun.

"He was going to kill you," Audrey cried. "I had to shoot."

Audrey kept running. When she reached the still body, she ignored it and scooped up the box. Myron slowly walked toward her.

"Open it," he said.

"Let's get out of this rain first. The police—"

"Open it."

She hesitated. No thunder bellowed. No lightning struck.

"You were right before," Myron said.

Audrey looked puzzled. "About what?"

"I was looking at this the wrong way."

"What are you talking about?"

Myron took another step toward her. "When I asked myself who knew about the blood in the basement," he began, "I only remembered Clip and Calvin. I forgot I told you. When I wondered why Greg's lover would have to keep her identity a secret, I thought about Fiona White and Liz Gorman. Again I forgot about you. It's hard enough for a woman to get respect as a female sports reporter. Your career would be ruined if anybody found out you were dating one of the players you covered. You had to keep it quiet."

She looked at him, her face a wet, white blank.

"You're the only one who fits, Audrey. You knew about the blood in the basement. You had to keep a relationship with Greg a secret. You had a key to his house so access would be no problem. And you were the one who had a motive to clean up the blood in order to protect him. After all, you killed to protect him. What's cleaning up some blood?"

She brushed her hair away from her eyes and blinked into the rain. "You can't seriously believe that I—"

"That night after TC's party," Myron interrupted, "when you told me how you had put it all together. I should have wondered then. Sure, my joining the team was unusual. But only somebody with a personal connection—somebody who truly knew that Greg had vanished and why—would have been able to come up with it so fast. You were the mystery lover, Audrey. And you don't know where Greg is either. You cooperated with me not because you wanted the story, but because you wanted to find Greg. You're in love with him."

"That's ridiculous," she said.

"The police will comb the house, Audrey. They'll find hairs."

"That doesn't mean anything," she said. "I interviewed him a couple of times—"

"In his bedroom? In his bathroom? In his shower?" Myron shook his head. "They'll also comb the murder scene now that they know about you. There'll be evidence there too. A hair or something." He took another step toward her. Audrey raised the gun with a quivering hand.

"Beware the Ides of March," Myron said.

"What?"

"You were the one who pointed it out to me. The ides are the fifteenth of March. Your birthday was the seventeenth. March seventeenth. Three-one-seven. The code Greg set on his answering machine."

She pointed the gun at his chest. "Turn off the tape recorder," she said. "And the phone."

Myron reached into his pocket and did as she asked.

Tears and rain mixed together and cascaded down her cheeks. "Why couldn't you just keep your mouth shut?" she wailed. She pointed to the still body on the wet grass. "You heard what he said: no one else knows. All the blackmailers are dead. I could have destroyed this thing"—she held up the box—"once and for all. I wouldn't have had to hurt you. It would have finally been over."

"And what about Liz Gorman?"

Audrey made a scoffing noise. "That woman was nothing more than a conniving blackmailer," she said. "She couldn't be trusted. I told Greg that. What was to stop her from making copies and bleeding him dry? I even went to her house that night and pretended I was an ex-girlfriend with an ax to grind. I told her I wanted to buy a copy. She said sure. Don't you see? Paying her off would do no good. There was only one way to keep her quiet."

He nodded. "You had to kill her."

"She was just a low-life criminal, Myron. She'd robbed a bank, for chrissake. Greg and I . . . we were perfect together. You were right about my career. I had to keep our relationship a secret. But not much longer. I was going to get transferred to another beat. Baseball. The Mets or Yankees. Then we could be open about it. It was going so well, Myron, and then this low-life bitch comes along. . . ." Her voice drifted off with a hard shake of the head. "I had to think about our future," she said. "Not just Greg's. Not just mine. But our baby's too."

Myron's eyes closed in pain. "You're pregnant," he said softly.

"Now do you see?" Her wide-eyed enthusiasm was back, though it took on a more twisted dimension now. "She wanted to destroy him. Destroy us. What choice did I have? I'm not a killer but it was either us or her. And I know how it looks—Greg running off and not telling me. But it's just the way he is. We've been together for more than six months. I know he loves me. He just needed time."

Myron swallowed. "It's over now, Audrey."

She shook her head and held the gun with both hands. "I'm sorry, Myron. I don't want to do it. I'd almost rather die first."

"It doesn't matter." Myron took another step. She moved back. The gun trembled in her hand. "They're blanks," he said.

Her eyes squinted in confusion. The man in the ski mask sat up like Bela Lugosi in an old Dracula film. He pulled off the mask and showed his badge. "Police," Dimonte shouted. Win and Krinsky came over the crest. Audrey's mouth formed a perfect circle. Win had made the fake blackmailer call; Myron had set his cellular phone's volume on high to be sure Audrey overheard it. The rest was easy.

Dimonte and Krinsky made the arrest. Myron watched, no longer feeling the rain. After Audrey was put into the back of a cruiser, he and Win walked toward the car.

"Superhero partner?" Myron said.

Win shrugged.

Chapter 39

Esperanza was still in the office when the fax machine rang. She crossed the room and watched the machine begin to spew out paper. The facsimile was addressed to her attention, from the FBI:

Re: FIRST CITY NATIONAL BANK—TUCSON, ARIZONA

Subject: Renters of Safe-Deposit Boxes.

She'd been waiting for this transmission all day.

Esperanza's theory on the blackmail plot had gone something like this: The Raven Brigade robbed the bank. They hit the safe-deposit boxes. People keep all kinds of things in those. Money, jewelry, important documents. That was what hooked the timing together. Simply put, the Raven Brigade had found something in one of those boxes that was damaging to Greg Downing. Then they hatched their little blackmail scheme.

The names came out in alphabetical order. Esperanza read down the list while the paper was still being transmitted. The first page ended in the Ls. No name was familiar. The second page ended in the Ts. No name was familiar. On the third page, when she reached the Ws, her heart leaped into her throat. Her hand fluttered to her mouth, and for a moment she feared that she might scream.

It took several hours to sort through the mess. Statements had to be taken. Explanations made. Myron told Dimonte practically the whole story. He left out the videotape of Thumper and Emily. Again, it was nobody's business. He also left out the part about meeting up with Cole Whiteman. Myron somehow felt he owed him. For her part, Audrey would not talk at all, except to ask for a lawyer.

"Do you know where Downing is?" Dimonte asked Myron.

"I think so."

"But you don't want to tell me."

Myron shook his head. "He's not your business."

"Ain't that the truth," Dimonte agreed. "Go on. Get out of here."

They were downtown at One Police Plaza. Myron and Win walked out in the city night. Large municipal structures consumed the neighboring area. Modern bureaucracy in its most extreme and intimidating form. Even this late at night, you could visualize lines of people heading out the door.

"It was a good plan," Win said.

"Audrey is pregnant."

"I heard."

"Her baby will be born in jail."

"Not your doing."

"She thought it was her only way out," Myron said.

Win nodded. "She saw a blackmailer who stood in the way of all her dreams. I'm not so sure I would have behaved any differently."

"You don't commit murder to stave off life's inconveniences," Myron said.

Win didn't argue, but he didn't agree either. They kept walking. When they reached the car, Win said, "So where does that leave us?"

"With Clip Arnstein," Myron said. "He has some explaining to do."

"You want me to come along?"

"No. I want to talk to him alone."

Chapter 40

By the time Myron arrived at the arena, the game was over. Cars tapped the exits, making it hard to go the opposite way. Myron managed to weave through. He showed his ID to the guard and drove into the players' lot.

He ran to Clip's office. Someone called his name. He ignored it. When he reached the outer office door, he tried the knob. It was locked. He was tempted to break it down.

"Yo, Myron."

It was one of the towel boys. Myron forgot the kid's name. "What's up?" he said.

"This came for you."

The kid handed Myron a manila envelope.

"Who dropped this off?" Myron asked.

"Your uncle."

"My uncle?"

"That's what the guy said."

Myron looked at the envelope. His name was scrawled across the front in giant block letters. He tore it open and turned it upside down. First, a letter slid out. He shook again and a black cassette tape fell into the palm of his hand. He put the cassette down and unfolded the letter:

Myron,

I should have given this to you at the cathedral. I'm sorry I didn't, but I got too caught up in Liz's murder. I wanted you to concentrate on catching the killer, not on this tape. I was afraid it would distract you. I still think it will, but that doesn't give me the right to keep it from you. I just hope you stay focused enough to find the bastard who killed Liz. She deserves justice.

I also wanted to tell you that I'm thinking about turning myself in. Now that Liz is gone, there's no reason to keep hiding. I spoke to some old lawyer buddies about it. They've already started reaching out to all the mercenaries Hunt's father hired. They're sure one of them will corroborate my story. We'll see.

Don't listen to this tape alone, Myron. Listen to it with a friend.
Cole

Myron folded the letter. He had no idea what to think. He glanced down the corridor. No sign of Clip. He jogged toward the exit. Most of the players had already left the arena. TC, of course. Last in, first out. Myron got in his car and turned the key. Then he stuck the tape into the car's player and waited.

Esperanza tried dialing Myron's car phone. No answer. Then his cellular. Same deal. He always carried his cellular. If he wasn't picking up, it was because he didn't want to. She quickly dialed Win's cellular. He picked up on the second ring.

"Do you know where Myron is?" she asked.

"He went to the arena."

"Go find him, Win."

"Why? What's wrong?"

"The Raven Brigade robbed the safe-deposit boxes. That's where they got the information they used to blackmail Downing."

"What did they find?"

"I don't know," she said, "but I have a list of the people who rented the boxes."

"So?"

"One was rented to a Mr. and Mrs. B. Wesson."

Silence.

Win said, "Are you sure it's the same B. Wesson who injured Myron?"

"I already checked," she said. "The B stands for Burt, listed on his application as a thirty-three-year-old high school basketball coach. It's him, Win. It's the same Burt Wesson."

Chapter 41

Nothing.

Myron fiddled with the volume knob. Static feedback screeched through the car speakers. He turned it down a second, then back up. He heard muffled sounds, but he had no idea what they were. Then the sounds faded away.

Silence.

Two minutes of blank tape passed before Myron finally heard voices. His ears perked up, but he couldn't make out much. Then the voices grew a little louder, a little clearer. He leaned closer to the speaker and suddenly he heard a gruff voice with frightening clarity:

"You have the money?"

A hand reached into Myron's chest, grabbed his heart, and squeezed. He hadn't heard the voice in ten years, but recognition was instantaneous. It was Burt Wesson. What the hell—?

Then the second voice jarred him like a body blow:

"I got half now. A thousand dollars now. You get the other half when he goes down. . . ."

Myron's entire body shuddered. A flash of rage unlike anything he had ever known warmed and then engulfed him. His hands tightened into fists. Tears forced their way forward. He remembered wondering why the blackmailers had contacted him to buy the dirt on Greg; he remembered Cole Whiteman's laugh and Marty Felder's ironic smile when they'd learned that he'd been hired to find Greg Downing; he remembered the voice on Greg's answering machine saying, "He's willing to pay. Is that what you want?"; and most of all, he remembered Greg's pained face at the hospital all those years ago. It hadn't been a bond that brought Greg to Myron's bedside.

It'd been guilt.

"Don't hurt him too bad, Burt. I just want Bolitar banged up for a few games . . ."

Something in the deep recesses of Myron's mind snapped like a dry twig. Without conscious thought, Myron shifted into reverse.

"Look, I really need the money. Can't you give me another five

hundred? They're going to cut me soon. It's my last scrimmage and then I'm unemployed . . ."

He straightened out his car and shifted into drive. His foot pressed down upon the pedal. The speedometer climbed. Myron's face twisted into a mask of incognizant fury. Tears sheeted down his cheeks but no sound came with them. He drove without really seeing.

When he reached the Jones Road exit, Myron wiped his face with his sleeve. He turned into TC's driveway. The security gate blocked his path.

The guard stepped out of his little hut. Myron waved him closer to the car. When the guard was fully out of the box, Myron showed the gun.

"Move and I'll blow your head off."

The guard's hands went up. Myron got out of the car and opened the gate. He ordered the guard inside the car. The car roared up the driveway. Myron slammed on the brake just feet before the front door. He jumped out on the run and without hesitating, he kicked in TC's front door. He ran into the den.

The television was on. TC looked up, startled. "What the fuck—?"

Myron bounded across the room, grabbed TC's arm, twisted it behind his back.

"Hey—"

"Where is he?" Myron demanded.

"I don't know what—"

Myron pulled up on the arm. "Don't make me break it, TC. Where is he?"

"What the fuck are you—?"

Myron silenced him by pushing the arm farther up his back. TC cried out, his huge frame bent at the waist to lessen the pressure. "Last time I ask," Myron said. "Where's Greg?"

"I'm here."

Myron let go and spun toward the voice. Greg Downing stood in the doorway. Myron did not hesitate. Letting out a guttural scream, he pounced.

Greg put up his hands, but it was like quieting a volcano with a squirt gun. Myron's fist landed square in Greg's face. Greg toppled back from the assault. Myron fell on him, his knee landing in his ribs. Something cracked. He straddled Greg's chest and threw another punch.

"Stop!" TC shouted, "You're gonna kill him."

Myron barely heard him.

He cocked his other fist, but TC was on him before he could throw it. Myron rolled with the tackle, digging his elbow into TC's solar plexus. When they hit the wall, the air whooshed out of TC, his eyes bulging as he gasped for air. Myron rose. Greg was scrambling away. Myron vaulted over the couch. He grabbed Greg by the leg and pulled him toward him.

"You fucked my wife!" Greg shouted. "You think I didn't know? You fucked my wife!"

The words slowed Myron, but they didn't stop him. Through his tears, he threw another punch. Greg's mouth filled with blood. Myron cocked his fist again. A hand of iron reached out and grabbed his arm, holding it in place.

"Enough," Win said.

Myron looked up, his face distorted by confusion and rage. "What?"

"He's had enough."

"But it's like you said," Myron pleaded. "Wesson did do it on purpose. Greg hired him."

"I know," Win said. "But he's had enough."

"What the hell are you talking about? If it was you—"

"I'd probably kill him," Win finished for him. He looked down and something flickered in his eyes. "But you wouldn't."

Myron swallowed. Win nodded again and let go of Myron's wrist. Myron let his arm fall to his side. He got off Greg Downing.

Greg sat up, coughing blood into his hand. "I followed Emily that night," Greg managed through the hacks. "I saw you two . . . I just wanted payback, that's all. You weren't supposed to get hurt that bad."

Myron swallowed and breathed deeply. The adrenaline rush would soon ebb, but for now it was still there. "You been hiding here since the beginning?"

Greg touched part of his face, winced, then nodded. "I was afraid they'd think I killed that woman," he said. "And I had the mob chasing me and the custody battle and my girlfriend is pregnant." He looked up. "I just needed some time."

"Do you love Audrey?"

Greg said, "You know?"

"Yes."

"Yeah," Greg said, "I love her a lot."

"Then give her a call," Myron said. "She's in jail."

"What?"

Myron didn't elaborate. He'd hoped throwing that in Greg's face would give him some sort of perverse pleasure, but it didn't. All it did was remind him that he was far from blameless in this.

He turned and walked away.

Myron found Clip alone in that same corporate skybox they'd met in when this all began. He was looking down at the empty court, his back to Myron. He didn't move when Myron cleared his throat.

"You knew all along," Myron said.

Clip said nothing.

"You went to Liz Gorman's apartment that night," Myron continued. "She played the tape for you, didn't she?"

Clip clasped his hands behind his back. Then he nodded.

"That's why you hired me. This wasn't all a coincidence. You wanted me to find out the truth."

"I didn't know how else to tell you." Clip finally turned and faced Myron. His eyes were dazed and hazy. All color was gone from his face. "It wasn't an act, you know. The emotion at the press conference . . ." He lowered his head, gathered himself, raised it again. "You and I lost touch after your injury. I wanted to call you a thousand times, but I understood. You wanted to stay away. The injury never leaves the great ones, Myron. I knew it would never leave you."

Myron opened his mouth but nothing came out. His entire being felt exposed and raw. Clip came closer. "I thought this would be a way for you to learn the truth," Clip said. "I also hoped this would be something of a catharsis. Not a complete one. Like I said, it never leaves the great ones."

For several moments, they both just stood and stared.

"You told Walsh to play me the other night," Myron said.

"Yes."

"You knew I wouldn't be able to match up."

Clip nodded slowly.

Myron felt the tears come back to his eyes. He blinked them down.

Clip set his jaw. There were tiny tremors in his face, but he stood rigid. "I wanted to help you," he said, "but my reasons for hiring you were not all altruistic. I knew, for example, that you'd always been a team player. You loved that aspect of basketball, Myron—being part of a team."

"So?"

"My plan included making you feel like a member of the team. A real member. So much so that you would never hurt us."

Myron understood. "You figured that if I bonded with my team-mates, I wouldn't blow the whistle when I learned the truth."

"It's not in your nature," Clip said.

"But it will come out," Myron said. "There's no way to avoid it now."

"I know that."

"You could lose the team."

Clip smiled, shrugged. "There are worse things," he said. "Just as you now know there are worse things than never being able to play again."

"I always knew," Myron said. "I just maybe needed a reminder."

Chapter 42

He and Jessica sat on the couch in her loft. He told her everything. Jess hugged her knees and rocked back and forth. Her eyes looked pained.

"She was my friend," Jessica said.

"I know."

"I wonder."

"What?"

"What would I have done in the same situation? To protect you."

"You wouldn't have killed."

"No," she said. "I guess not."

Myron watched her. She looked on the verge of tears. He said, "I think I learned something about us in all this."

She waited for him to elaborate.

"Win and Esperanza didn't want me to play again. But you never tried to stop me. I was afraid that maybe you didn't understand me as well as they do. But that wasn't the case at all. You saw what they couldn't."

Jessica studied his face with a penetrating gaze. She let go of her knees and slid her feet to the floor. "We've never really talked about this before," she said.

He nodded.

"The truth is, you never mourned the end of your career," Jessica went on. "You never showed weakness. You stuffed it all in some internal suitcase and moved on. You tackled everything else in your life with a smothering desperation. You didn't wait. You seized whatever was left and pressed it against you, afraid your whole world was as fragile as that knee. You rushed off to law school. You ran off and helped Win. You frantically clung to whatever you could." She stopped.

"Including you," he finished.

"Yes. Including me. Not just because you loved me. Because you were afraid of losing more than you already had."

"I did love you," he said. "I still do."

"I know. I'm not trying to put this all on you. I was an idiot. It was mostly my fault. I admit that. But your love back then bordered on the desperate. You channeled your grief into a grasping need. I was afraid of suffocating. I don't want to sound like an amateur shrink, but you needed to mourn. You needed to put it behind you, not suppress it. But you wouldn't face it."

"You thought my playing again would make me face it," he said.

"Yes."

"It's not like this was a cure-all."

"I know," she said. "But I think it helped you let go a little."

"And that's why you think now is a good time for me to move in."

Jessica swallowed hard. "If you want," she said. "If you feel ready."

He looked up in the air and said, "I'll need more closet space."

"Done," she whispered. "Whatever you want."

She snuggled into him. He put his arms around her, pulled her close, and felt very much at home.

It was a sweltering morning in Tucson, Arizona. A big man opened his front door.

"Are you Burt Wesson?"

The big man nodded. "Can I help you with something?"

Win smiled. "Yes," he said. "I think you can."

ONE
FALSE
MOVE

In memory of my parents,
Corky and Carl Coben

and in celebration of their grandchildren,
Charlotte, Aleksander, Benjamin, and Gabrielle

ACKNOWLEDGMENTS

I wrote this book alone. Nobody helped me. But if mistakes were made, I wish to keep in the long-standing American tradition of passing the buck. So with that in mind, the author would like to thank the following wonderful people: Aaron Priest, Lisa Erbach Vance, and everyone at the Aaron Priest Literary Agency; Carole Baron, Leslie Schnur, Jacob Hoye, Heather Mongelli, and everyone at Dell Publishing; Maureen Coyle of the New York Liberty; Karen Ross, ME of the Dallas County Institute of Forensic Science; Peter Roisman of Advantage International; Sergeant Jay Vanderbeck of the Livingston Police Department; Detective Lieutenant Keith Killion of the Ridgewood Police Department; Maggie Griffin, James Bradbeer, Chip Hinshaw, and of course, Dave Bolt. Again I repeat: any errors—factual or otherwise—are totally the fault of these people. The author is not to blame.

Prologue

SEPTEMBER 15

The cemetery overlooked a schoolyard.

Myron pushed at the loose dirt with the toe of his Rockport. There was no stone here yet, just a metal marker holding a plain index card with a name typed in capital letters. He shook his head. Why was he standing here like some cliché from a bad TV show? In his mind's eye Myron could see how the whole scene should be played out. Torrential rain should be pounding on his back, but he would be too bereaved to notice. His head should be lowered, tears glistening in his eyes, maybe one running down his cheek, blending in with the rain. Cue the stirring music. The camera should move off his face and pull back slowly, very slowly, showing his slumped shoulders, the rain driving harder, more graves, no one else present. Still pulling back, the camera eventually shows Win, Myron's loyal partner, standing in the distance, silently understanding, giving his buddy time alone to grieve. The TV image should suddenly freeze and the executive producer's name should flash across the screen in yellow caps. Slight hesitation before the viewers are urged to stay tuned for scenes from next week's episode. Cut to commercial.

But that would not happen here. The sun shone like it was the first day and the skies had the hue of the freshly painted. Win was at the office. And Myron would not cry.

So why was he here?

Because a murderer would be coming soon. He was sure of it.

Myron searched for some kind of meaning in the landscape but only came up with more clichés. It had been two weeks since the funeral. Weeds and dandelions had already begun to break through the dirt and stretch toward the heavens. Myron waited for his inner voice-over to spout the standard drivel about weeds and dandelions representing cycles and renewal and life going on, but the voice was mercifully mute. He sought irony in the radiant innocence of the schoolyard—the faded chalk on black asphalt, the multicolor three-wheelers, the slightly rusted chains for the swings—cloaked in the shadows of tombstones that watched over the children like silent sentinels, patient and almost beckoning. But the irony would not hold. Schoolyards were not about innocence. There were bullies down there too and sociopaths-in-waiting and burgeoning psychoses and young minds filled prenatally with undiluted hate.

Okay, Myron thought, *enough abstract babbling for one day.*

On some level, he recognized that this inner dialogue was merely a distraction, a philosophical sleight of hand to keep his brittle mind from snapping like a dry twig. He wanted so very much to cave in, to let his legs give way, to fall to the ground and claw at the dirt with his bare hands and beg forgiveness and plead for a higher power to give him one more chance.

But that too would not happen.

Myron heard footsteps coming up from behind him. He closed his eyes. It was as he expected. The footsteps came closer. When they stopped, Myron did not turn around.

"You killed her," Myron said.

"Yes."

A block of ice melted in Myron's stomach. "Do you feel better now?"

The killer's tone caressed the back of Myron's neck with a cold, bloodless hand. "The question is, Myron, do you?"

Chapter 1

AUGUST 30

Myron hunched his shoulders and slurred his words. "I am not a baby-sitter," he said. "I am a sports agent."

Norm Zuckerman looked pained. "Was that supposed to be Bela Lugosi?"

"The Elephant Man," Myron said.

"Damn, that was awful. And who said anything about being a baby-sitter? Did I say the word *baby-sitter* or *baby-sitting* or for that matter any form of the verb *to baby-sit* or noun or even the word *baby* or the word *sit* or *sat* or—"

Myron held up a hand. "I get the point, Norm."

They sat under a basket at Madison Square Garden in those cloth-and-wood directors' chairs that have stars' names on the back. Their chairs were set high so that the net from the basket almost tickled Myron's hair. A model shoot was going on at half-court. Lots of those umbrella lights and tall, bony women-cum-children and tripods and people huffing and fluffing about. Myron waited for someone to mistake him for a model. And waited.

"A young woman may be in danger," Norm said. "I need your help."

Norm Zuckerman was approaching seventy and as CEO of Zoom, a megasize sports manufacturing conglomerate, he had more money than Trump. He looked, however, like a beatnik trapped in a bad acid trip. Retro, Norm had explained earlier, was cresting, and he was catching the wave by wearing a psychedelic poncho, fatigue pants, love beads, and an earring with a dangling peace sign. Groovy, man. His black-to-gray beard was unruly enough to nest beetle larvae, his hair newly curled like something out of a bad production of *Godspell*.

Che Guevara lives and gets a perm.

"You don't need me," Myron said. "You need a bodyguard."

Norm waved a dismissing hand. "Too obvious."

"What?"

"She'd never go for it. Look, Myron, what do you know about Brenda Slaughter?"

"Not much," Myron said.

He looked surprised. "What do you mean, not much?"

"What word are you having trouble with, Norm?"

"For crying out loud, you were a basketball player."

"So?"

"So Brenda Slaughter may be the greatest female player of all time. A pioneer in her sport—not to mention the pinup girl, pardon the political insensitivity, for my new league."

"That much I know."

"Well, know this: I'm worried about her. If something happens to Brenda Slaughter, the whole WPBA—and my substantial investment—could go right down the toilet."

"Well, as long as it's for humanitarian reasons."

"Fine, I'm a greedy capitalist pig. But you, my friend, are a sports agent. There is not a greedier, sleazier, slimier, more capitalist entity in existence."

Myron nodded. "Suck up to me," he said. "That'll work."

"You're not letting me finish. Yes, you're a sports agent. But a damn fine one. The best, really. You and the Spanish shiksa do incredible work for your clients. Get the most for them. More than they should get really. By the time you finish with me, I feel violated. Hand to God, you're that good. You come into my office, you rip off my clothes and have your way with me."

Myron made a face. "Please."

"But I know your secret background with the feds."

Some secret. Myron was still hoping to bump into someone above the equator who didn't know about it.

"Just listen to me for a second, Myron, okay? Hear me out. Brenda is a lovely girl, a wonderful basketball player—and a pain in my left *tuchis*. I don't blame her. If I grew up with a father like that, I'd be a pain in the left *tuchis* too."

"So her father is the problem?"

Norm made a yes-and-no gesture. "Probably."

"So get a restraining order," Myron said.

"Already done."

"Then what's the problem? Hire a private eye. If he steps within a hundred yards of her, call the cops."

"It's not that easy." Norm looked out over the court. The workers involved in the shoot darted about like trapped particles under sudden heat. Myron sipped his coffee. Gourmet coffee. A year ago he never drank coffee. Then he started stopping into one of the new coffee bars that kept cropping up like bad movies on cable. Now Myron could not go through a morning without his gourmet coffee fix.

There is a fine line between a coffee break and a crack house.

"We don't know where he is," Norm said.

"Excuse me?"

"Her father," Norm said. "He's vanished. Brenda is always looking over her shoulder. She's terrified."

"And you think the father is a danger to her?"

"This guy is the Great Santini on steroids. He used to play ball himself. Pac Ten, I think. His name is—"

"Horace Slaughter," Myron said.

"You know him?"

Myron nodded very slowly. "Yeah," he said. "I know him."

Norm studied his face. "You're too young to have played with him."

Myron said nothing. Norm did not catch the hint. He rarely did.

"So how do you know Horace Slaughter?"

"Don't worry about it," Myron said. "Tell me why you think Brenda Slaughter is in danger."

"She's been getting threats."

"What kind of threats?"

"Death."

"Could you be a little more specific?"

The photo shoot frenzy continued to whirl. Models sporting the latest in Zoom wear and oodles of attitude cycled through poses and pouts and postures and pursed lips. Come on and vogue. Someone called out for Ted, where the hell is Ted, that prima donna, why isn't Ted dressed yet, I swear, Ted will be the death of me yet.

"She gets phone calls," Norm said. "A car follows her. That kind of thing."

"And you want me to do what exactly?"

"Watch her."

Myron shook his head. "Even if I said yes—which I'm not—you said she won't go for a bodyguard."

Norm smiled and patted Myron's knee. "Here's the part where I lure you in. Like a fish on a hook."

"Original analogy."

"Brenda Slaughter is currently unagented."

Myron said nothing.

"Cat got your tongue, handsome?"

"I thought she signed a major endorsement deal with Zoom."

"She was on the verge when her old man disappeared. He was her manager. But she got rid of him. Now she's alone. She trusts my judgment, to a point. This girl is no fool, let me tell you. So here's my plan: Brenda will be here in a couple of minutes. I recommend you to her. She says hello. You say hello. Then you hit her with the famed Bolitar charm."

Myron arched one eyebrow. "Set on full blast?"

"Heavens, no. I don't want the poor girl disrobing."

"I took an oath to only use my powers for good."

"This is good, Myron, believe me."

Myron remained unconvinced. "Even if I agreed to go along with this cockamamy scheme, what about nights? You expect me to watch her twenty-four hours a day?"

"Of course not. Win will help you there."

"Win has better things to do."

"Tell that goy boy-toy it's for me," Norm said. "He loves me."

A flustered photographer in the great Eurotrash tradition hurried over to their perch. He had a goatee and spiky blond hair like Sandy Duncan on an off day. Bathing did not appear to be a priority here. He sighed repeatedly, making sure all in the vicinity knew that he was both important and being put out. "Where is Brenda?" he whined.

"Right here."

Myron swiveled toward a voice like warm honey on Sunday pancakes. With her long, purposeful stride—not the shy-girl walk of the too-tall or the nasty strut of a model—Brenda Slaughter swept into the room like a radar-tracked weather system. She was very tall, over six feet for sure, with skin the color of Myron's Starbucks Mocha Java with a hefty splash of skim milk. She wore faded jeans that hugged deliciously but without obscenity and a ski sweater that made you think of cuddling inside a snow-covered log cabin.

Myron managed not to say wow out loud.

Brenda Slaughter was not so much beautiful as electric. The air around her crackled. She was far too big and broad-shouldered to be a model. Myron knew some professional models. They were always throwing themselves at him—snicker—and were ridiculously thin, built like strings with helium balloons on top. Brenda was no size six. You felt strength with this woman, substance, power, a force if you will, and yet it was all completely feminine, whatever that meant, and incredibly attractive.

Norm leaned over and whispered, "See why she's our poster girl?"

Myron nodded.

Norm jumped down from the chair. "Brenda, darling, come over here. I want you to meet someone."

The big brown eyes found Myron's, and there was a hesitation. She smiled a little and strode toward them. Myron rose, ever the gentleman. Brenda headed straight for him and stuck out her hand. Myron shook it. Her grip was strong. Now that they were both standing, Myron could see he had an inch or two on her. That made her six-two, maybe six-three.

"Well, well," Brenda said. "Myron Bolitar."

Norm gestured as if he were pushing them closer together. "You two know each other?"

"Oh, I'm sure Mr. Bolitar doesn't remember me," Brenda said. "It was a long time ago."

It took Myron only a few seconds. His brain immediately realized that had he met Brenda Slaughter before, he would have undoubtedly remembered. The fact that he didn't meant their previous encounter was under very different circumstances. "You used to hang out at the courts," Myron said. "With your dad. You must have been five or six."

"And you were just entering high school," she added. "The only white guy that showed up steadily. You made all-state out of Livingston High, became an all-American at Duke, got drafted by the Celtics in the first round—"

Her voice dovetailed. Myron was used to that. "I'm flattered you remembered," he said. Already wowing her with the charm.

"I grew up watching you play," she went on. "My father followed your career like you were his own son. When you got hurt—" She broke off again, her lips tightening.

He smiled to show he both understood and appreciated the sentiment.

Norm jumped into the silence. "Well, Myron is a sports agent now. A damn good one. The best, in my opinion. Fair, honest, loyal as hell—" Norm stopped suddenly. "Did I just use those words to describe a sports agent?" He shook his head.

The goateed Sandy Duncan bustled over again. He spoke with a French accent that sounded about as real as Pepe LePew's. "*Monsieur* Zuckermahn?"

Norm said, *"Oui."*

"I need your help, *s'il vous plaît.*"

"Oui," Norm said.

Myron almost asked for an interpreter.

"Sit, both of you," Norm said. "I have to run a sec." He patted the empty chairs to drive home the point. "Myron is going to help me set up the league. Kinda like a consultant. So talk to him, Brenda. About your career, your future, whatever. He'd be a good agent for you." He winked at Myron. Subtle.

When Norm left, Brenda high-stepped into the director's chair. "So was all that true?" she asked.

"Part of it," Myron said.

"What part?"

"I'd like to be your agent. But that's not why I'm really here."

"Oh?"

"Norm is worried about you. He wants me to watch out for you."

"Watch out for me?"

Myron nodded. "He thinks you're in danger."

She set her jaw. "I told him I didn't want to be watched."

"I know," Myron said. "I'm supposed to be undercover. Shh."

"So why are you telling me?"

"I'm not good with secrets."

She nodded. "And?"

"And if I'm going to be your agent, I'm not sure it pays to start our relationship with a lie."

She leaned back and crossed legs longer than a DMV line at lunchtime. "What else did Norm tell you to do?"

"To turn on my charm."

She blinked at him.

"Don't worry," Myron said. "I took a solemn oath to only use it for good."

"Lucky me." Brenda brought a long finger up to her face and tapped it against her chin a few times. "So," she said at last, "Norm thinks I need a baby-sitter."

Myron threw up his hands and did his best Norm impression. "Who said anything about a baby-sitter?" It was better than his Elephant Man, but nobody was speed-dialing Rich Little either.

She smiled. "Okay," she said with a nod. "I'll go along with this."

"I'm pleasantly surprised."

"No reason to be. If you don't do it, Norm might hire someone else who might not be so forthcoming. This way I know the score."

"Makes sense," Myron said.

"But there are conditions."

"I thought there might be."

"I do what I want when I want. This isn't carte blanche to invade my privacy."

"Of course."

"If I tell you to get lost for a while, you ask how lost."

"Right."

"And no spying on me when I don't know about it," she continued.

"Okay."

"You keep out of my business."

"Agreed."

"I stay out all night, you don't say a thing."

"Not a thing."

"If I choose to participate in an orgy with pygmies, you don't say a thing."

"Can I at least watch?" Myron asked.

That got a smile. "I don't mean to sound difficult, but I have enough father figures in my life, thank you. I want to make sure you know that we're not going to be hanging out with each other twenty-four a day or anything like that. This isn't a Whitney Houston–Kevin Costner movie."

"Some people say I look like Kevin Costner." Myron gave her a quick flash of the cynical, rogue smile, à la Bull Durham.

She looked straight through him. "Maybe in the hairline."

Ouch. At half-court the goateed Sandy Duncan started calling for Ted again. His coterie followed suit. The name Ted bounced about the arena like rolled-up balls of Silly Putty.

"So do we understand each other?" she asked.

"Perfectly," Myron said. He shifted in his seat. "Now do you want to tell me what's going on?"

From the right, Ted—it simply had to be a guy named Ted—finally made his entrance. He wore only Zoom shorts, and his abdomen was rippled like a relief map in marble. He was probably in his early twenties, model handsome, and he squinted like a prison guard. As he sashayed toward the shoot, Ted kept running both hands through his Superman blue-black hair, the movement expanding his chest and shrinking his waist and demonstrating shaved underarms.

Brenda muttered, "Strutting peacock."

"That's totally unfair," Myron said. "Maybe he's a Fulbright scholar."

"I've worked with him before. If God gave him a second brain, it would die of loneliness." Her eyes veered toward Myron. "I don't get something."

"What?"

"Why you? You're a sports agent. Why would Norm ask you to be my bodyguard?"

"I used to work"—he stopped, waved a vague hand—"for the government."

"I never heard about that."

"It's another secret. Shh."

"Secrets don't stay secret much around you, Myron."

"You can trust me."

She thought about it. "Well, you were a white man who could jump," she said. "Guess if you can be that, you could be a trustworthy sports agent."

Myron laughed, and they fell into an uneasy silence. He broke it by trying again. "So do you want to tell me about the threats?"

"Nothing much to tell."

"This is all in Norm's head?"

Brenda did not reply. One of the assistants applied oil to Ted's hairless chest. Ted was still giving the crowd his tough guy squint. Too many Clint Eastwood movies. Ted made two fists and continuously flexed his pecs. Myron decided that he might as well beat the rush and start hating Ted right now.

Brenda remained silent. Myron decided to try another approach. "Where are you living now?" he asked.

"In a dorm at Reston University."

"You're still in school?"

"Medical school. Fourth year. I just got a deferment to play pro ball."

Myron nodded. "Got a specialty in mind?"

"Pediatrics."

He nodded again and decided to wade in a bit deeper. "Your dad must be very proud of you."

A flicker crossed her face. "Yeah, I guess." She started to rise. "I better get dressed for this shoot."

"You don't want to tell me what's going on first?"

She stayed in her seat. "Dad is missing."

"Since when?"

"A week ago."

"Is that when the threats started?"

She avoided the question. "You want to help? Find my father."

"Is he the one threatening you?"

"Don't worry about the threats. Dad likes control, Myron. Intimidation is just another tool."

"I don't understand."

"You don't have to understand. He's your friend, right?"

"Your father? I haven't seen Horace in more than ten years."

"Whose fault is that?" she asked.

The words, not to mention the bitter tone, surprised him. "What's that supposed to mean?"

"Do you still care about him?" she asked.

Myron didn't have to think about it. "You know I do."

She nodded and jumped down from the chair. "He's in trouble," she said. "Find him."

Chapter 2

Brenda reappeared in Lycra Zoom shorts and what was commonly called a sports bra. She was limbs and shoulders and muscles and substance, and while the professional models glared at her size (not her height—most of them were six-footers too), Myron thought that she stood out like a bursting supernova next to, well, gaseous entities.

The poses were risqué, and Brenda was clearly embarrassed by them. Not so Ted. He undulated and squinted at her in what was supposed to be a look of smoldering sexuality. Twice Brenda broke out and laughed in his face. Myron still hated Ted, but Brenda was starting to grow on him.

Myron picked up his cellular phone and dialed Win's private line. Win was a big-time financial consultant at Lock-Horne Securities, an old-money financial firm that first sold equities on the *Mayflower.* His office was in the Lock-Horne Building on Park Avenue and Forty-seventh Street in midtown Manhattan. Myron rented space there from Win. A sports agent on Park Avenue—now that was class.

After three rings the machine picked up. Win's annoyingly superior accent said, "Hang up without leaving a message and die." Beep. Myron shook his head, smiled, and, as always, left a message.

He hit the switch and dialed his office. Esperanza answered. "MB SportsReps."

The *M* was for Myron, the *B* for Bolitar, and the *SportsReps* because they Represented people in the world of Sports. Myron had come up with the name with no help from professional marketing personnel. Despite the obvious accolades, Myron remained humble.

"Any messages?" he asked.

"About a million."

"Anything crucial?"

"Greenspan wanted your take on interest rate hikes. Outside of that, no." Esperanza, ever the wiseass. "So what did Norm want?"

Esperanza Diaz—the "Spanish shiksa," in Norm's words—had been at MB SportsReps since its inception. Before that, she had wrestled professionally under the moniker Little Pocahontas; put simply, she wore a bikini reminiscent of Raquel Welch in *One Million Years B.C.* and groped other women in front of a drooling horde. Esperanza considered her career shift to representing athletes as something of a step down.

"It involves Brenda Slaughter," he began.

"The basketball player?"

"Yes."

"I've seen her play a couple of times," Esperanza said. "On TV she looks hot."

"In person too."

There was a pause. Then Esperanza said, "Think she participates in the love that dare not speaketh its name?"

"Huh?"

"Does she swing the way of the woman?"

"Gee," Myron said, "I forgot to check for the tattoo."

Esperanza's sexual preference flip-flopped like a politician in a nonelection year. Currently she seemed to be on a man kick, but Myron guessed that was one of the advantages of bisexuality: love everyone. Myron had no problem with it. In high school he had dated almost exclusively bisexual girls—he'd mention sex, the girls would say "bye." Okay, old joke, but the point remained.

"Doesn't matter," Esperanza said. "I really like David." Her current beau. It wouldn't last. "But you got to admit, Brenda Slaughter is steaming."

"So admitted."

"It might be fun for a night or two."

Myron nodded into the phone. A lesser man might mentally conjure up a few choice images of the lithe, petite Hispanic beauty in the throes of passion with the ravishing black Amazon in the sports bra. But not Myron. Too worldly.

"Norm wants us to watch her," Myron said. He filled her in. When he finished, he heard her sigh.

"What?" he said.

"Jesus Christ, Myron, are we a sports agency or Pinkertons?"

"It's to get clients."

"Keep telling yourself that."

"What the hell does that mean?"

"Nothing. So what do you need me to do?"

"Her father is missing. His name is Horace Slaughter. See what you can dig up on him."

"I'll need help here," she said.

Myron rubbed his eyes. "I thought we were going to hire someone on a permanent basis."

"Who has the time?"

Silence.

"Fine," Myron said. He sighed. "Call Big Cyndi. But make sure
she knows it's just on a trial basis."

"Okey-dokey."

"And if any client comes in, I want Cyndi to hide in my office."

"Yeah, fine, whatever."

She hung up the phone.

When the photo shoot ended, Brenda Slaughter approached him.

"Where does your father live now?" Myron asked.

"Same place."

"Have you been there since he disappeared?"

"No."

"Then let's start there," Myron said.

Chapter 3

Newark, New Jersey. The bad part. Almost a redundancy.

Decay was the first word that came to mind. The buildings were more than falling apart—they actually seemed to be breaking down, melting from some sort of acid onslaught. Here urban renewal was about as familiar a concept as time travel. The surroundings looked more like a war newsreel—Frankfurt after the Allies' bombing—than a habitable dwelling.

The neighborhood was even worse than he remembered. When Myron was a teenager, he and his dad had driven down this very street, the car doors suddenly locking as though even they sensed oncoming danger. His father's face would tighten up. "Toilet," he would mutter. Dad had grown up not far from here, but that had been a long time ago. His father, the man Myron loved and worshiped like no other, the most gentle soul he had ever known, would barely contain his rage. "Look what they did to the old neighborhood," he would say.

Look what they did.

They.

Myron's Ford Taurus slowly cruised by the old playground. Black faces glared at him. A five-on-five was going on with plenty of kids sprawled on the sidelines waiting to take on the winners. The cheap sneakers of Myron's day—Thom McAn or Keds or Kmart—had been replaced with the hundred-dollar-plus variety these kids could ill afford. Myron felt a twinge. He would have liked to take a noble stand on the issue—the corruption of values and materialism and such—but as a sports agent who made money off sneaker deals, such perceptions paid his freight. He didn't feel good about that, but he didn't want to be a hypocrite either.

Nobody wore shorts anymore either. Every kid was dressed in blue or black jeans that journeyed far south of baggy, like something a circus clown might sport for an extra laugh. The waist drooped below the butt, revealing designer boxer shorts. Myron did not want to sound like an old man, grousing over the younger generation's fashion sense, but these made bell-bottoms and platforms seem practical.

How do you play your best when you're constantly pausing to pull up your pants?

But the biggest change was in those glares. Myron had been scared when he first came down here as a fifteen-year-old high school student, but he had known that if he wanted to rise to the next level, he had to face down the best competition. That meant playing here. He had not been welcomed at first. Not even close. But the looks of curious animosity he received back then were nothing compared with the dagger-death glares of these kids. Their hatred was naked, up front, filled with cold resignation. Corny to say, but back then—less than twenty years ago—there had been something different here. More hope maybe. Hard to say.

As though reading his thoughts, Brenda said, "I wouldn't even play down here anymore."

Myron nodded.

"It wasn't easy on you, was it? Coming down here to play."

"Your father made it easy," he said.

She smiled. "I never understood why he took such a liking to you. He usually hated white people."

Myron feigned a gasp. "I'm white?"

"As Pat Buchanan."

They both forced out a laugh. Myron tried again. "Tell me about the threats."

Brenda stared out the window. They passed a place that sold hubcaps. Hundreds, if not thousands, of hubcaps gleamed in the sun. Weird business when you thought about it. The only time people need a new hubcap is when one of theirs is stolen. The stolen ones end up in a place like this. A mini fiscal cycle.

"I get calls," she began. "At night mostly. One time they said they were going to hurt me if they didn't find my father. Another time they told me I better keep Dad as my manager or else." She stopped.

"Any idea who they are?"

"No."

"Any idea why someone would want to find your father?"

"No."

"Or why your father would disappear?"

She shook her head.

"Norm said something about a car following you."

"I don't know anything about that," she said.

"The voice on the phone," Myron said. "Is it the same one every time?"

"I don't think so."

"Male, female?"

"Male. And white. Or at least, he sounds white."

Myron nodded. "Does Horace gamble?"

"Never. My grandfather gambled. Lost everything he had, which wasn't much. Dad would never go near it."

"Did he borrow money?"

"No."

"Are you sure? Even with financial aid, your schooling had to cost."

"I've been on scholarship since I was twelve."

Myron nodded. Up ahead a man stumbled about the sidewalk. He was wearing Calvin Klein underwear, two different ski boots, and one of those big Russian hats like Dr. Zhivago. Nothing else. No shirt, no pants. His fist gripped the top of a brown paper bag like he was helping it cross the street.

"When did the calls start?" Myron asked.

"A week ago."

"When your dad disappeared?"

Brenda nodded. She had more to say. Myron could see it in the way she stared off. He kept silent and waited her out.

"The first time," she said quietly, "the voice told me to call my mother."

Myron waited for her to say more. When it was apparent she wouldn't, he said, "Did you?"

She smiled sadly. "No."

"Where does your mother live?"

"I don't know. I haven't seen her since I was five years old."

"When you say 'haven't seen her'—"

"I mean just that. She abandoned us twenty years ago." Brenda finally turned toward him. "You look surprised."

"I guess I am."

"Why? You know how many of those boys back there had their fathers abandon them? You think a mother can't do the same thing?"

She had a point, but it sounded more like hollow rationalization than true conviction. "So you haven't seen her since you were five?"

"That's right."

"Do you know where she lives? A city or state or anything?"

"No idea." She tried hard to sound indifferent.

"You've had no contact with her?"

"Just a couple of letters."

"Any return address?"

Brenda shook her head. "They were postmarked in New York City. That's all I know."

"Would Horace know where she lives?"

"No. He's never so much as spoken her name in the past twenty years."

"At least not to you."

She nodded.

"Maybe the voice on the phone didn't mean your mother," Myron said. "Do you have a stepmother? Did your father remarry or live with someone—"

"No. Since my mother there has been no one."

Silence.

"So why would someone be asking about your mother after twenty years?" Myron asked.

"I don't know."

"Any ideas?"

"None. For twenty years she's been a ghost to me." She pointed up ahead. "Make a left."

"Do you mind if I get a trace put on your phone? In case they call again?"

She shook her head.

He steered the car per her instructions. "Tell me about your relationship with Horace," he said.

"No."

"I'm not asking to be nosy—"

"It's irrelevant, Myron. If I loved him or hated him, you still need to find him."

"You got a restraining order to keep him away from you, right?"

She said nothing for a moment. Then: "Do you remember how he was on the court?"

Myron nodded. "A madman. And maybe the best teacher I ever had."

"And the most intense?"

"Yes," Myron said. "He taught me not to play with so much finesse. That wasn't always an easy lesson."

"Right, and you were just some kid he took a liking to. But imagine being his own child. Now imagine that on-court intensity mixed with his fear that he would lose me. That I would run away and leave him."

"Like your mother."

"Right."

"It would be," Myron said, "stifling."

"Try suffocating," she corrected. "Three weeks ago we were play-ing a promotional scrimmage at East Orange High School. You know it?"

"Sure."

"A couple of guys in the crowd were getting rowdy. Two high school kids. They were on the basketball team. They were drunk or high, or maybe they were just punks. I don't know. But they started yelling things out at me."

"What kind of things?"

"Graphic and ugly things. About what they'd like to do to me. My father stood up and went after them."

"I can't say I blame him," Myron said.

She shook her head. "Then you're another Neanderthal."

"What?"

"Why would you have gone after them? To defend my honor? I'm a twenty-five-year-old woman. I don't need any of that chivalry crap."

"But—"

"But nothing. This whole thing, your being here—I'm not a radi-cal feminist or anything, but it's a load of sexist bullshit."

"What?"

"If I had a penis between my legs, you wouldn't be here. If my name was Leroy and I got a couple of weird phone calls, you wouldn't be so hot to protect poor little me, would you?"

Myron hesitated a second too long.

"And," she continued, "how many times have you seen me play?"

The change of subject caught him off guard. "What?"

"I was the number one collegiate player three years in a row. My team won two national championships. We were on ESPN all the time, and during the NCAA finals we were on CBS. I went to Reston University, which is only half an hour from where you live. How many of my games did you see?"

Myron opened his mouth, closed it, said, "None."

"Right. Chicks' basketball. It's not worth the time."

"That's not it. I don't watch much sports anymore." He realized how lame he sounded.

She shook her head and grew quiet.

"Brenda—"

"Forget I said anything. It was dumb to raise the subject."

Her tone left little room for follow-up. Myron wanted to defend himself, but he had no idea how. He opted for silence, an option he should probably exercise more often.

"Take your next right," she said.

"So what happened next?" he asked.

She looked at him.

"To the punks who called you names. What happened after your father went after them?"

"The security guards broke it up before anything really happened. They threw the kids out of the gym. Dad too."

"I'm not sure I see the point of this story."

"It's not over yet." Brenda stopped, looked down, summoned up a little something, raised her head again. "Three days later the two boys—Clay Jackson and Arthur Harris—were found on the roof of a tenement building. Someone had tied them up and cut their Achilles tendon in half with pruning shears."

Myron's face lost color. His stomach took a nosedive. "Your father?"

Brenda nodded. "He's been doing stuff like that my whole life. Never this bad. But he's always made people who cross me pay. When I was a little girl with no mother, I almost welcomed the protection. But I'm not a little girl anymore."

Myron absently reached down and touched the back of his ankle. Cut the Achilles tendon in half. With pruning shears. He tried not to look too stunned. "The police must have suspected Horace."

"Yes."

"So how come he wasn't arrested?"

"Not enough evidence."

"Couldn't the victims identify him?"

She turned back to the window. "They're too scared." She pointed to the right. "Park there."

Myron pulled over. People toddled about the street. They stared at him as though they had never seen a white man; in this neighborhood that was entirely possible. Myron tried to look casual. He nodded a polite hello. Some people nodded back. Some didn't.

A yellow car—nay, a speaker on wheels—cruised by, blaring a rap tune. The bass was set so high that Myron felt the vibrations in his chest. He could not make out the lyrics, but they sounded angry. Brenda led him to a stoop. Two men were sprawled on the stairs like war wounded. Brenda stepped over them without a second glance. Myron followed. He suddenly realized that he had never been here before. His relationship with Horace Slaughter had been strictly basketball. They had always hung out on the playground or in a gym or maybe grabbing a pizza after a game. He had never been in Horace's home, and Horace had never been in his.

There was no doorman, of course, no lock or buzzers or any of that. The lighting was bad in the corridor, but not bad enough to conceal the paint flaking off like the walls had psoriasis. Most of the mailboxes were doorless. The air felt like a beaded curtain.

She climbed up the cement stairs. The railing was industrial metal. Myron could hear a man coughing as if he were trying to dislodge a lung. A baby cried. Then another joined in. Brenda stopped on the second floor and turned right. Her keys were already in her hand and at the ready. The door too was made of some sort of reinforced steel. There was a peephole and three bolt locks.

Brenda unlocked the three bolts first. They jerked back noisily, like the prison scene in a movie where the warden yells, "Lockdown!" The door swung open. Myron was hit by two thoughts at exactly the same time. One was how nice Horace's setup was. Whatever was outside this apartment, whatever grime and rot were on the streets or even in his corridor, Horace Slaughter had not allowed to sneak past the steel door. The walls were as white as a hand cream commercial. The floors looked newly buffed. The furniture was a mix of what looked like fixed-up family pieces and newer Ikea acquisitions. It was indeed a comfortable home.

The other thing Myron noticed as soon as the door was open was that someone had trashed the room.

Brenda rushed in. "Dad?"

Myron followed, wishing that he had his gun. This scene called for a gun. He would signal her to be quiet, take it out, have her stand behind him, creep through the apartment with her clutching on to his free arm in fear. He would do that gun swing thing into each room, his body crouched and prepared for the worst. But Myron did not regularly carry a gun. It was not that he disliked guns—when in trouble, in fact, he rather enjoyed their company—but a gun is bulky and chafed like a tweed condom. And let's face it, for most prospective clients, a sports agent packing heat does not inspire confidence, and for those it does, well, Myron would rather do without them.

Win, on the other hand, always carried a gun—at least two, actually, not to mention a prodigious potpourri of concealed weaponry. The man was like a walking Israel.

The apartment consisted of three rooms and a kitchen. They hurried through them. Nobody. And no body.

"Anything missing?" Myron asked.

She looked at him, annoyed. "How the hell would I know?"

"I mean, anything noticeable. The TV is here. So is the VCR. I want to know if you think it's a robbery."

She glanced about the living room. "No," she said. "It doesn't look like a robbery."

"Any thoughts on who did this or why?"

Brenda shook her head, her eyes still taking in the mess.

"Did Horace hide money someplace? A cookie jar or under a floorboard or something?"

"No."

They started in Horace's room. Brenda opened up his closet. For a long moment she stood and said nothing.

"Brenda?"

"A lot of his clothes are missing," she said softly. "His suitcase too."

"That's good," Myron said. "It means he probably ran; it makes it less likely that he met up with foul play."

She nodded. "But it's creepy."

"How so?"

"It's just like my mother. I can still remember Dad just standing here, staring at the empty hangers."

They moved back into the living room and then into a small bedroom.

"Your room?" Myron asked.

"I'm not here very much, but yeah, this is my room."

Brenda's eyes immediately fell on a spot near her night table. She gave a little gasp and dived to the floor. Her hands began to paw through her effects.

"Brenda?"

Her pawing grew more intense, her eyes aflame. After a few minutes she got up and ran to her father's room. Then the living room. Myron kept back.

"They're gone," she said.

"What?"

Brenda looked at him. "The letters my mother wrote me. Someone took them."

Chapter 4

Myron parked the car in front of Brenda's dorm room. Except for monosyllabic directions, Brenda had not spoken during the drive. Myron did not push it. He stopped the car and turned toward her. She continued to stare ahead.

Reston University was a place of green grass and big oaks and brick buildings and Frisbees and bandannas. Professors still had long hair and unkempt beards and tweed jackets. There was such a feeling of innocence here, of make-believe, of youth, of startling passion. But that was the beauty of such a university: students debating over life-and-death issues in an environment as insulated as Disney World. Reality had nothing to do with the equation. And that was okay. In fact, that was how it should be.

"She just left," Brenda said. "I was five years old, and she just left me alone with him."

Myron let her speak.

"I remember everything about her. The way she looked. The way she smelled. The way she'd come home from her job so tired she could barely put her feet up. I don't think I've talked about her five times in the past twenty years. But I think about her every day. I think about why she gave me up. And I think about why I still miss her."

She put her hand to her chin then and turned away. The car stayed silent.

"You good at this, Myron?" she asked. "At investigating?"

"I think so," he said.

Brenda grabbed the door handle and pulled. "Could you find my mother?"

She did not wait for a response. She hurried out of the car and up the steps. Myron watched her disappear into the colonial brick building. Then he started up the car and headed home.

Myron found a spot on Spring Street right outside Jessica's loft. He still referred to his new dwelling as Jessica's loft, even though he now lived here and paid half the rent. Weird how that worked.

Myron took the stairs to the third floor. He opened the door and immediately heard Jessica yell out, "Working."

He did not hear any clacking on the computer keyboard, but that didn't mean anything. He made his way into the bedroom, closed the door, and checked the answering machine. When Jessica was writing, she never answered the phone.

Myron hit the play button. "Hello, Myron? This is your mother." Like he wouldn't recognize the voice. "God, I hate this machine. Why doesn't she pick up? I know she's there. Is it so hard for a human being to pick up a phone and say hello and take a message? I'm in my office, my phone rings, I pick it up. Even if I'm working. Or I have my secretary take a message. Not a machine. I don't like machines, Myron, you know that." She continued on in a similar vein for some time. Myron longed for the old days when there was a time limit on answering machines. Progress was not always a good thing.

Finally Mom began to wind down. "Just calling to say hello, doll face. We'll talk later."

For the first thirty-plus years of his life, Myron had lived with his parents in the New Jersey suburb of Livingston. As an infant he'd started life in the small nursery upstairs on the left. From the age of three to sixteen, he lived in the bedroom upstairs on the right; from sixteen to just a few months ago, he'd lived in the basement. Not all the time, of course. He went to Duke down in North Carolina for four years, spent summers working basketball camps, stayed on occasion with Jessica or Win in Manhattan. But his true home had always been, well, with Mommy and Daddy—by choice, strangely enough, though some might suggest that serious therapy would unearth deeper motives.

That changed several months ago, when Jessica asked him to move in with her. This was a rarity in their relationship, Jessica making the first move, and Myron had been deliriously happy and heady and scared out of his mind. His trepidation had nothing to do with fear of commitment—that particular phobia plagued Jessica, not him—but there had been rough times in the past, and to put it simply, Myron never wanted to be hurt like that again.

He still saw his folks once a week or so, going out to the house for dinner or having them make the trip into the Big Apple. He also spoke to either his mom or his dad nearly every day. Funny thing is, while they were undoubtedly pests, Myron liked them. Crazy as it might sound, he actually enjoyed spending time with his parents. Uncool? Sure. Hip as a polka accordionist? Totally. But there you go.

He grabbed a Yoo-Hoo from the refrigerator, shook it, popped the top, took a big swig. Sweet nectar. Jessica yelled in, "What are you in the mood for?"

"I don't care."

"You want to go out?"

"Do you mind if we just order in?" he asked.

"Nope." She appeared in the doorway. She wore his oversize Duke sweatshirt and black knit pants. Her hair was pulled back in a ponytail. Several hairs had escaped and fell in front of her face. When she smiled at him, he still felt his pulse quicken.

"Hi," he said. Myron prided himself on his clever opening gambits.

"You want Chinese?" she asked.

"Whatever, sure. Hunan, Szechwan, Cantonese?"

"Szechwan," she said.

"Okay. Szechwan Garden, Szechwan Dragon, or Empire Szechwan?"

She thought a moment. "Dragon was greasy last time. Let's go with Empire."

Jessica crossed the kitchen and kissed him lightly on the cheek. Her hair smelled like wildflowers after a summer storm. Myron gave her a quick hug and grabbed the delivery menu from the cabinet. They figured out what they'd get—the hot and sour soup, one shrimp entrée, one vegetable entrée—and Myron called it in. The usual language barriers applied—why don't they ever hire a person who speaks English at least to take the phone order?—and after repeating his telephone number six times, he hung up.

"Get much done?" he asked.

Jessica nodded. "The first draft will be finished by Christmas."

"I thought the deadline was August."

"Your point being?"

They sat at the kitchen table. The kitchen, living room, dining room, TV room were all one big space. The ceiling was fifteen feet high. Airy. Brick walls with exposed metal beams gave the place a look that was both artsy and railroad station–like. The loft was, in a word, neat-o.

The food arrived. They chatted about their day. Myron told her about Brenda Slaughter. Jessica sat and listened in that way of hers. She was one of those people who had the ability to make any speaker feel like the only person alive. When he finished, she asked a few questions. Then she stood up and poured a glass of water from their Brita pitcher.

She sat back down. "I have to fly out to L.A. on Tuesday," Jessica said.

Myron looked up. "Again?"

She nodded.

"For how long?"

"I don't know. A week or two."

"Weren't you just out there?"

"Yeah, so?"

"For that movie deal, right?"

"Right."

"So why are you going out again?" he asked.

"I got to do some research for this book."

"Couldn't you have done both when you were there last week?"

"No." Jessica looked at him. "Something wrong?"

Myron fiddled with a chopstick. He looked at her, looked away, swallowed, and just said it: "Is this working?"

"What?"

"Our living together."

"Myron, it's just for a couple of weeks. For research."

"And then it's a book tour. Or a writer's retreat. Or a movie deal. Or more research."

"What, you want me to stay home and bake cookies?"

"No."

"Then what's going on here?"

"Nothing," Myron said. Then: "We've been together a long time."

"On and off for ten years," she added. "So?"

He was not sure how to continue. "You like traveling."

"Hell, yes."

"I miss you when you're gone."

"I miss you too," she said. "And I miss you when you go away on business too. But our freedom—that's part of the fun, isn't it? And besides"—she leaned forward a little—"I give great reunion."

He nodded. "You do at that."

She put her hand on his forearm. "I don't want to do any pseudo-analysis, but this move has been a big adjustment for you. I understand that. But so far I think it's working great."

She was, of course, right. They were a modern couple with sky-rocketing careers and worlds to conquer. Separation was part of that. Whatever nagging doubts he had were a by-product of his innate pessimism. Things were indeed going so well—Jessica had come back, she had asked him to move in—that he kept waiting for something to go wrong. He had to stop obsessing. Obsession does not seek out problems and correct them; it manufactures them out of nothing, feeds them, makes them stronger.

He smiled at her. "Maybe this is all a cry for attention," he said.

"Oh?"

"Or maybe it's a ploy to get more sex."

She gave him a look that curled his chopsticks. "Maybe it's working," she said.

"Maybe I'll slip into something more comfortable," he said.

"Not that Batman mask again."

"Aw, c'mon, you can wear the utility belt."

She thought about it. "Okay, but no stopping in the middle and shouting, 'Same Bat Time, same Bat Channel.' "

"Deal."

Jessica stood, walked over to him, and sat on his lap. She hugged him and lowered her lips toward his ear. "We've got it good, Myron. Let's not fuck it up."

She was right.

She got off his lap. "Come on, let's clear the table."

"And then?"

Jessica nodded. "To the Batpoles."

Chapter 5

As soon as Myron hit the street the next morning, a black limousine pulled in front of him. Two mammoth men—muscle-headed, neckless wonders—lumbered out of the car. They wore ill-fitted business suits, but Myron did not fault their tailor. Guys built like that always looked ill fitted. They both had Gold's Gym tans, and though he could not confirm this by sight, Myron bet that their chests were as waxed as Cher's legs.

One of the bulldozers said, "Get in the car."

"My mommy told me to never get in a car with strangers," Myron said.

"Oh," the other bulldozer said, "we got ourselves a comedian here."

"Yeah?" The bulldozer tilted his head at Myron. "That right? You a comedian?"

"I'm also an exciting vocalist," Myron said. "Want to hear my much-loved rendition of 'Volare'?"

"You'll be singing out the other end of your ass if you don't get in the car."

"Other end of my ass," Myron said. He looked up as though in deep thought. "I don't get it. Out of the end of my ass, okay, that makes sense. But out of the *other* end? What does that mean exactly? I mean, technically, if we follow the intestinal tract, isn't the other end of your ass simply your mouth?"

The bulldozers looked at each other, then at Myron. Myron was not particularly scared. These thugs were delivery boys; the package was not supposed to be delivered bruised. They would take a little needling. Plus, you never show these guys fear. They smell fear, they swarm in and devour you. Of course Myron could be wrong. They might be unbalanced psychotics who'd snap at the slightest provocation. One of life's little mysteries.

"Mr. Ache wants to see you," Bulldozer One said.

"Which one?"

"Frank."

Silence. This was not good. The Ache brothers were leading mob figures in New York. Herman Ache, the older brother, was the leader, a man responsible for enough suffering to make a third world dictator envious. But next to his whacked-out brother Frank, Herman Ache was about as scary as Winnie-the-Pooh.

The muscleheads cracked their necks and smiled at Myron's silence. "Not so funny now, are you, smart guy?"

"Testicles," Myron said, stepping toward the car. "They shrink when you use steroids."

It was an old Bolitar rejoinder, but Myron never got tired of the classics. He had no choice really. He had to go. He slid into the backseat of the stretch limo. There was a bar and a television tuned in to Regis and Kathie Lee. Kathie Lee was regaling the audience with Cody's most recent exploits.

"No more, I beg you," Myron said. "I'll tell you everything."

The bulldozers did not get it. Myron leaned forward and snapped the television off. No one protested.

"We going to Clancy's?" Myron asked.

Clancy's Tavern was the Aches' hangout. Myron had been there with Win a couple of years back. He had hoped never to return.

"Sit back and shut up, asshole."

Myron kept still. They took the West Side Highway north—in the opposite direction of Clancy's Tavern. They turned right at Fifty-seventh Street. When they hit a Fifth Avenue parking garage, Myron realized where they were headed.

"We're going to TruPro's office," he said out loud.

The bulldozers said nothing. Didn't matter. He had not said it for their benefit anyway.

TruPro was one of the larger sports agencies in the country. For years it'd been operated by Roy O'Connor, a snake in a suit, who had been nothing if not an expert in how to break the rules. O'Connor was the master of illegally signing athletes when they were barely out of diapers, using payoffs and subtle extortion. But like so many who flitted in and out of the world of corruption, Roy inevitably got nuked. Myron had seen it happen before. A guy figures he can be a "little pregnant," a tad enmeshed with the underworld. But the mob does not work that way. You give them an inch, they take the whole damn yardstick. That was what had happened to TruPro. Roy owed money, and when he couldn't pay up, the appropriately named Ache brothers took control.

"Move it, asshole."

Myron followed Bubba and Rocco—if those weren't their names, they should have been—into the elevator. They got out on the eighth floor and headed past the receptionist. She kept her head down but sneaked a glance. Myron waved to her and kept moving. They stopped in front of an office door.

"Search him."

Bulldozer One started patting him down.

Myron closed his eyes. "God," he said. "This feels good. A little left."

Bulldozer stopped, threw him a glare. "Go in."

Myron opened the door and entered the office.

Frank Ache spread his arms and stepped toward him. "Myron!"

Whatever fortune Frank Ache had amassed, the man never did spend it on clothes. He favored chintzy velour sweat suits, like something the guys on *Lost in Space* might consider casual wear. The one Frank sported today was burnt orange with yellow trim. The top was zippered lower than a *Cosmo* cover, his gray chest hair so thick it looked like a natty sweater. He had a huge head, tiny shoulders, and a spare tire that was the envy of the Michelin man—an hourglass figure with all the time run out. He was big and puffy and the kind of bald where the top of the head looks like it exploded through the hair during an earthquake.

Frank gave Myron a ferocious bear hug. Myron was taken aback. Frank was usually about as cuddly as a jackal with shingles.

He pulled Myron to arm's length. "Sheesh, Myron, you're looking good."

Myron tried not to wince. "Thanks, Frank."

Frank offered him a big smile—two rows of corn-kernel teeth jam-packed together. Myron tried not to flinch. "How long's it been?"

"A little over a year."

"We were at Clancy's, right?"

"No, Frank, we weren't."

Frank looked puzzled. "Where were we?"

"On a road in Pennsylvania. You shot out my tires, threatened to kill members of my family, and then you told me to get out of your car before you used my nuts for squirrel food."

Frank laughed and clapped Myron on the back. "Good times, eh?"

Myron kept very still. "What can I do for you, Frank?"

"You in a rush?"

"Just wanted to get to the heart of it."

"Hey, Myron." Frank opened his arms wide. "I'm trying to be friendly here. I'm a changed man. It's a whole new me."

"Find religion, did you, Frank?"

"Something like that."

"Uh-huh."

Frank's smile slowly faded. "You like my old ways better?"

"They're more honest."

The smile was gone completely now. "You're doing it again, My-ron."

"What?"

"Crawling up the crack of my ass," he said. "It cozy up there?"

"Cozy," Myron said with a nod. "Yeah, Frank, that's the word I'd use."

The door behind them opened. Two men came in. One was Roy O'Connor, the figurative president of TruPro. He crept in silently, as though waiting for permission to exist. Probably was. When Frank was around, Roy probably raised his hand before going to the bathroom. The second guy was in his mid-twenties. He was immaculately dressed and looked like an investment banker fresh off his M.B.A.

Myron gave a big wave. "Hi, Roy. Looking good."

Roy nodded stiffly, sat down.

Frank said, "This here's my kid, Frankie Junior. Call him FJ."

"Hi," Myron said. FJ?

The kid gave him a hard glare and sat down.

"Roy here just hired FJ," Frank said.

Myron smiled at Roy O'Connor. "The selection process must have been hell, Roy. Combing through all those résumés and every-thing."

Roy said nothing.

Frank waddled around the desk. "You and FJ got something in common, Myron."

"Oh?"

"You went to Harvard, right?"

"For law school," Myron said.

"FJ got his M.B.A. there."

Myron nodded. "Like Win."

His name quieted the room. Roy O'Connor crossed his legs. His face lost color. He had experienced Win up close, but they all knew him. Win would be pleased by the reaction.

The room started up again slowly. Everyone took seats. Frank put two hands the size of canned hams on the desk. "We hear you're rep-resenting Brenda Slaughter," he said.

"Where did you hear that?"

Frank shrugged as if to say, silly question.

"Is it true, Myron?"

"No."

"You're not repping her?"

"That's right, Frank."

Frank looked at Roy. Roy sat like hardening plaster. Then he looked at FJ, who was shaking his head.

"Is her old man still her manager?" Frank asked.

"I don't know, Frank. Why don't you ask her?"

"You were with her yesterday," Frank said.

"So?"

"So what were you two doing?"

Myron stretched out his legs, crossing the ankles. "Tell me something, Frank. What's your interest in all this?"

Frank's eyes widened. He looked at Roy, then at FJ; then he pointed a meaty finger at Myron. "Pardon my fucking French," he said, "but do I look like I'm here to answer your fucking questions?"

"The whole new you," Myron said. "Friendly, changed."

FJ leaned forward and looked in Myron's eyes. Myron looked back. There was nothing there. If the eyes were indeed the window to the soul, these read NO VACANCY. "Mr. Bolitar?" FJ's voice was soft and willowy.

"Yes?"

"Fuck you."

He whispered the words with the strangest smile on his face. He did not lean back after he said it. Myron felt something cold scramble up his back, but he did not look away.

The phone on the desk buzzed. Frank hit a button. "Yeah?"

"Mr. Bolitar's associate on the line," a female voice said. "He wanted to speak with you."

"With me?" Frank said.

"Yes, Mr. Ache."

Frank looked confused. He shrugged his shoulders and hit a button.

"Yeah," he said.

"Hello, Francis."

The room became still as a photograph.

Frank cleared his throat. "Hello, Win."

"I trust that I am not interrupting," Win said.

Silence.

"How is your brother, Francis?"

"He's good, Win."

"I must give Herman a call. We haven't hit the links together in ages."

"Yeah," Frank said, "I'll tell him you asked for him."

"Fine, Francis, fine. Well, I must be going. Please give my best to Roy and your charming son. How rude of me not to have said hello earlier."

Silence.

"Hey, Win?"

"Yes, Francis."

"I don't like this cryptic shit, you hear?"

"I hear everything, Francis."

Click.

Frank Ache gave Myron a hard glare. "Get out."

"Why are you so interested in Brenda Slaughter?"

Frank lifted himself out of the chair. "Win's scary," he said. "But he ain't bulletproof. Say one more word, and I'll tie you to a chair and set your dick on fire."

Myron did not bother with good-byes.

Myron took the elevator down. Win—real name Windsor Horne Lockwood III—stood in the lobby. He was dressed this morning in Late American Prep. Blue blazer, light khakis, white button-down Oxford shirt, loud Lilly Pulitzer tie, the kind with more colors than a gallery at a golf course. His blond hair was parted by the gods, his jaw jutting in that way of his, his cheekbones high and pretty and porcelain, his eyes the blue of ice. To look at Win's face, Myron knew, was to hate him, was to think elitism, class-consciousness, snobbery, anti-Semitism, racism, old-world money earned from the sweat of other men's brows, all that. People who judged Windsor Horne Lockwood III solely by appearance were always mistaken. Often dangerously so.

Win did not glance in Myron's direction. He looked out as though posing for a park statue. "I was just thinking," Win said.

"What?"

"If you clone yourself, and then have sex with yourself, is it incest or masturbation?"

Win.

"Good to see you're not wasting your time," Myron said.

Win looked at him. "If we were still at Duke," he said, "we'd probably discuss the dilemma for hours."

"That's because we'd be drunk."

Win nodded. "There's that."

They both switched off their cellular phones and started heading down Fifth Avenue. It was a relatively new trick that Myron and Win used with great effect. As soon as the Hormonal He-Men pulled up, Myron had switched on the phone and hit the programmed button for Win's cellular. Win had thus heard every word. That was why Myron had commented out loud on where they were heading. That was how Win knew exactly where he was and exactly when to call. Win had nothing to say to Frank Ache; he just wanted to make sure that Frank knew that Win knew where Myron was.

"Tie you to a chair and set your dick on fire," Win repeated. "That would sting."

Myron nodded. "Talk about having a burning sensation when you urinate."

"Indeed. So tell me."

Myron started talking. Win, as always, did not appear to be listening. He never glanced in Myron's direction, his eyes searching the streets for beautiful women. Midtown Manhattan during work hours was full of them. They wore business suits and silk blouses and white Reebok sneakers. Every once in a while Win would reward one with a smile; unlike almost anybody else in New York, he was often rewarded with one in return.

When Myron told him about bodyguarding Brenda Slaughter, Win suddenly stopped and broke out in song: *"AND I-I-I-I-I-I WILL ALWAYS LOVE YOU-OU-OU-OU-OU-OU-OU."*

Myron looked at him. Win stopped, put his face back in place, continued walking. "When I sing that," Win said, "it's almost like Whitney Houston is in the room."

"Yeah," Myron said. "Or something."

"So what is the Aches' interest in all this?"

"I don't know."

"Perhaps TruPro just wishes to represent her."

"Doubtful. She'll make somebody money but not enough for pulling this."

Win thought about it, nodded his agreement. They headed east on Fiftieth Street. "Young FJ might pose a problem."

"Do you know him?"

"A bit. He is something of an intriguing story. Daddy groomed him to go legit. He sent him to Lawrenceville, then to Princeton, finally Harvard. Now he's setting him up in the business of representing athletes."

"But."

"But he resents it. He is still Frank Ache's son and thus wants his approval. He needs to show that despite the upbringing, he's still a tough guy. Worse, he is genetically Frank Ache's son. My guess? If you trample through FJ's childhood, you'll stumble across many a legless spider and wingless fly."

Myron shook his head. "This is definitely not a good thing."

Win said nothing. They hit the Lock-Horne Building on Forty-seventh Street. Myron got off the elevator on the twelfth floor. Win stayed in, his office being two flights up. When Myron looked at the reception desk—the place where Esperanza usually sat—he nearly jumped back. Big Cyndi sat silently watching him. She was far too big for the desk—far too big for the building, really—and the desk actually teetered on her knees. Her makeup would be labeled "too garish" by members of Kiss. Her hair was short and seaweed green. The T-shirt she wore had the sleeves ripped off, revealing biceps the size of basketballs.

Myron gave her a tentative wave. "Hello, Cyndi."

"Hello, Mr. Bolitar."

Big Cyndi was six-six, three hundred pounds and had been Esperanza's tag team wrestling partner, known in the ring as Big Chief Mama. For years Myron had only heard her growl, never speak. But her voice could be anything she wanted. When she worked as a bouncer at Leather-N-Lust on Tenth Street, she put on an accent that made Arnold Schwarzenegger sound like a Gabor sister. Right now, she was doing her perky Mary-Richards-off-decaf.

"Is Esperanza here?" he asked.

"Miss Diaz is in Mr. Bolitar's office." She smiled at him. Myron tried not to cringe. Forget what he'd said about Frank Ache—this smile made his fillings hurt.

He excused himself and headed into his office. Esperanza was at his desk, talking on the phone. She wore a bright yellow blouse against the olive skin that always made him think of stars shimmering off the warm water in the Amalfi bay. She looked up at him, signaled to give her a minute with a finger, and kept on talking. Myron sat down across from her. It was an interesting perspective, seeing what clients and corporate sponsors saw when they sat in his office. The Broadway musical posters behind his chair—too desperate, he decided. Like he was trying to be irreverent for irreverence sake.

When she finished the call, Esperanza said, "You're late."

"Frank Ache wanted to see me."

She crossed her arms. "He need a fourth for mah-jongg?"

"He wanted to know about Brenda Slaughter."

Esperanza nodded. "So we got trouble."

"Maybe."

"Dump her."

"No."

She looked at him with flat eyes. "Tattoo me surprised."

"Did you get anything on Horace Slaughter?"

She grabbed a piece of paper. "Horace Slaughter. None of his credit cards have been used in the past week. He has one bank account at Newark Fidelity. Balance: zero dollars."

"Zero?"

"He cleaned it out."

"How much?"

"Eleven grand. In cash."

Myron whistled and leaned back. "So he was planning on running. That fits with what we saw in his apartment."

"Uh-huh."

"I got a harder one for you," Myron said. "His wife, Anita Slaughter."

"They still married?"

"I don't know. Maybe legally. She ran away twenty years ago. I don't think they ever bothered with a divorce."

She frowned. "Did you say twenty years ago?"

"Yes. Apparently no one has seen her since then."

"And what exactly are we trying to find?"

"In a word: her."

"You don't know where she is?"

"Not a clue. Like I said, she's been missing for twenty years."

Esperanza waited a beat. "She could be dead."

"I know."

"And if she's managed to stay hidden this long, she could have changed her name. Or left the country."

"Right."

"And there'd be few records, if any, from twenty years ago. Certainly nothing on the computer."

Myron smiled. "Don't you hate it when I make it too easy?"

"I realize I'm only your lowly assistant—"

"You're not my lowly assistant."

She gave him a look. "I'm not your partner either."

That quieted him.

"I realize that I'm only your lowly assistant," she said again, "but do we really have time for this bullshit?"

"Just do a standard check. See if we get lucky."

"Fine." Her tone was like a door slamming shut. "But we got other things to discuss here."

"Shoot." .

"Milner's contract. They won't renegotiate."

They dissected the Milner situation, batted it around a bit, developed and fine-tuned a strategy, and then concluded that their strategy would not work. Behind them Myron could hear the construction starting. They were cutting space out of the waiting area and conference room to make a private office for Esperanza.

After a few minutes Esperanza stopped and stared at him.

"What?"

"You're going to follow through with this," she said. "You're going to search for her parents."

"Her father is an old friend of mine."

"Oh Christ, please don't say, 'I owe him.' "

"It's not just that. It's good business."

"It's not good business. You're out of the office too much. Clients want to talk to you directly. So do the sponsors."

"I have my cellular."

Esperanza shook her head. "We can't keep going on like this."

"Like what?"

"Either you make me a partner or I walk."

"Don't hit me with that now, Esperanza. Please."

"You're doing it again."

"What?"

"Stalling."

"I'm not stalling."

She gave him a look that was half harsh, half pity. "I know how you hate change—"

"I don't hate change."

"—but one way or the other, things are going to be different. So get over it."

Part of him wanted to yell, Why? Things were good the way they were. Hadn't he been the one who encouraged her to get a law degree in the first place? A change, sure, he expected that after her graduation. He had been slowly giving her new responsibilities. But a partnership?

He pointed behind him. "I'm building you an office," he said.

"So?"

"So doesn't that scream commitment? You can't expect me to rush this. I'm taking baby steps here."

"You took one baby step, and then you fell on your ass." She stopped, shook her head. "I haven't pushed you on this since we were down at Merion." The golf U.S. Open in Philadelphia. Myron was in the midst of finding a kidnap victim when she hit him with her partnership demands. Since then, he had been, well, er, stalling.

Esperanza stood. "I want to be a partner. Not full. I understand that. But I want equity." She walked to the door. "You have a week."

Myron was not sure what to say. She was his best friend. He loved her. And he needed her here. She was a part of MB. A big part. But things were not that simple.

Esperanza opened the door and leaned against the frame. "You going to see Brenda Slaughter now?"

He nodded. "In a few minutes."

"I'll start the search. Call me in a few hours."

She closed the door behind her. Myron went around to his chair and picked up the phone. He dialed Win's number.

Win picked up on the first ring. "Articulate."

"You got plans for tonight?"

"*Moi?* But of course."

"Typical evening of demeaning sex?"

"Demeaning sex," Win repeated. "I told you to stop reading Jessica's magazines."

"Can you cancel?"

"I could," he said, "but the lovely lass will be very disappointed."

"Do you even know her name?"

"What? Off the top of my head?"

One of the construction workers started hammering. Myron put a hand over his free ear. "Could we meet at your place? I need to bounce a few things off you."

Win did not hesitate. "I am but a brick wall awaiting your verbal game of squash."

Myron guessed that meant yes.

Chapter 6

Brenda Slaughter's team, the New York Dolphins, practiced at Englewood High School in New Jersey. Myron felt a tightness in his chest when he entered the gym. He heard the sweet echo of dribbling basketballs; he savored the high school gym scent, that mix of strain and youth and uncertainty. Myron had played in huge venues, but whenever he walked into a new gymnasium, even as a spectator, he felt as if he'd been dropped through a time portal.

He climbed up the steps of one of those wooden space-saving pull-out stands. As always, it shook with each step. Technology may have made advancements in our daily lives, but you wouldn't know it from a high school gymnasium. Those velvet banners still hung from one wall, showing a variety of state or country or group championships. There was a list of track and field records down one corner. The electric clock was off. A tired janitor swept the hardwood floor, moving in a curling up-and-down pattern like a Zamboni on a hockey rink.

Myron spotted Brenda Slaughter shooting foul shots. Her face was lost in the simple bliss of this purest of motions. The ball backspun off her fingertips; it never touched the rim, but the net jumped a bit at the bottom. She wore a sleeveless white T-shirt over what looked like a black tube top. Sweat shimmered on her skin.

Brenda looked over at him and smiled. It was an unsure smile, like a new lover on that first morning. She dribbled the ball toward him and threw him a pass. He caught it, his fingers automatically finding the grooves.

"We need to talk," he said.

She nodded and sat next to him on the bench. Her face was wide and sweaty and real.

"Your father cleared out his bank account before he disappeared," Myron said.

The serenity fled from her face. Her eyes flicked away, and she shook her head. "This is too weird."

"What?" Myron said.

She reached toward him and took the ball from his hands. She held on to it as though it might grow wings and fly off. "It's so like my mother," she said. "First the clothes gone. Now the money."

"Your mother took money?"

"Every dime."

Myron looked at her. She kept her eyes on the ball. Her face was suddenly so guileless, so frail, Myron felt something inside him crumble. He waited a moment before changing the subject. "Was Horace working before he disappeared?"

One of her teammates, a white woman with a ponytail and freckles, called out to her and clapped her hands for the ball. Brenda smiled and led her with a one-armed pass. The ponytail bounced up and down as the woman speed-dribbled toward the basket.

"He was a security guard at St. Barnabas Hospital," Brenda said. "You know it?"

Myron nodded. St. Barnabas was in Livingston, his hometown.

"I work there too," she said. "In the pediatric clinic. Sort of a work-study program. I helped him get the job. That's how I first knew he was missing. His supervisor called me and asked where he was."

"How long had Horace been working there?"

"I don't know. Four, five months."

"What's his supervisor's name?"

"Calvin Campbell."

Myron took out a notecard and wrote it down.

"Where else does Horace hang out?"

"Same places," she said.

"The courts?"

Brenda nodded. "And he still refs high school games twice a week."

"Any close friends who might help him out?"

She shook her head. "No one in particular."

"How about family members?"

"My aunt Mabel. If there is anyone he'd trust, it's his sister Mabel."

"She live near here?"

"Yeah. In West Orange."

"Could you give her a call for me? Tell her I'd like to drop by."

"When?"

"Now." He looked at his watch. "If I hurry, I can be back before practice is over."

Brenda stood. "There's a pay phone in the hallway. I'll call her."

Chapter 7

On the ride to Mabel Edwards's house, Myron's cellular phone rang. It was Esperanza. "Norm Zuckerman is on the line," she said.

"Patch it through."

There was a click.

"Norm?" Myron said.

"Myron, sweetie, how are you?"

"Fine."

"Good, good. You learn anything yet?"

"No."

"Good, okay, fine." Norm hesitated. His jocular tone was a little off, forced. "Where are you?"

"In my car."

"I see, I see, okay. Look, Myron, you going to go over to Brenda's practice?"

"I just came from there."

"You left her alone?"

"She's at practice. A dozen people are there with her. She'll be fine."

"Yeah, I guess you're right." He didn't sound convinced. "Look, Myron, we need to talk. When can you get back to the gym?"

"I should be back in an hour. What's this about, Norm?"

"An hour. I'll see you then."

Aunt Mabel lived in West Orange, a suburb outside Newark. West Orange was one of those "changing" suburbs, the percentage of white families sinking bit by bit. It was the spreading effect. Minorities scratched their way out of the city and into the nearest suburbs; the whites then wanted out of said suburbs and moved still farther away from the city. In real estate terms this was known as progress.

Still, Mabel's tree-lined avenue seemed a zillion light-years from the urban blight that Horace called home. Myron knew the town of West Orange well. His own hometown of Livingston bordered it. Livingston too was starting to change. When Myron was in high school, the town had been white. Very white. Snow white. It had been so white that of the six hundred kids in Myron's graduating class, only one was black—and he was on the swim team. Can't get much whiter than that.

The house was a one-level structure—fancier folks might call it a ranch—the kind of place that probably had three bedrooms, one and a half baths, and a finished basement with a used pool table. Myron parked his Ford Taurus in the driveway.

Mabel Edwards was probably late forties, maybe younger. She was a big woman with a fleshy face, loosely curled hair, and a dress that looked like old drapes. When she opened the door, she gave Myron a smile that turned her ordinary features into something almost celestial. A pair of half-moon reading glasses hung from a chain, resting on her enormous chest. There was a puffiness in her right eye, remnants of a contusion maybe. She gripped some sort of knitting project in her hand.

"Goodness me," she said. "Myron Bolitar. Come in."

Myron followed her inside. The house had the stale smell of a grandparent. When you're a kid, the smell gives you the creeps; when you're an adult, you want to bottle it and let it out with a cup of co-coa on a bad day.

"I put coffee on, Myron. Would you like some?"

"That would be nice, thank you."

"Sit down over there. I'll be right back."

Myron grabbed a seat on a stiff sofa with a flowered print. For some reason he put his hands in his lap. As if he were waiting for a schoolteacher. Myron glanced about. There were African sculptures made of wood on the coffee table. The fireplace mantel was lined with family photographs. Almost all of them featured a young man who looked vaguely familiar. Mabel Edwards's son, he guessed. It was the standard parental shrine—that is, you could follow the off-spring's life from infancy through adulthood with the images in these frames. There was a baby photo, those school portraits with the rain-bow background, a big Afro playing basketball, a tuxedo-and-date prom, a couple of graduations, blah, blah, blah. Corny, yes, but these photo montages always touched Myron, exploiting his overtuned sensitivity like a sappy Hallmark commercial.

Mabel Edwards came back into the living room with a tray. "We met once before," she said.

Myron nodded, trying to remember. Something played along the edges, but it wouldn't come into focus.

"You were in high school." She handed him a cup on a saucer. Then she pushed the tray with cream and sugar toward him. "Horace took me to one of your games. You were playing Shabazz."

It came back to Myron. Junior year, the Essex County tournament. Shabazz was short for Malcolm X Shabazz High School of Newark. The school had no whites. Its starting five featured guys named Rhahim and Khalid. Even back then Shabazz High had been surrounded by a barbwire fence with a sign that read GUARD DOGS ON DUTY.

Guard dogs at a high school. Think about it.

"I remember," Myron said.

Mabel burst into a short laugh. When she did, every part of her jiggled. "Funniest thing I ever saw," she said. "All these pale boys walking in scared out of their wits, eyes as big as saucers. You were the only one at home, Myron."

"That's because of your brother."

She shook her head. "Horace said you were the best he ever worked with. He said nothing would have stopped you from being great." She leaned forward. "You two had something special, didn't you?"

"Yes, ma'am."

"Horace loved you, Myron. Talked about you all the time. When you got drafted, I tell you, it was the happiest I'd seen him in years. You called him, right?"

"As soon as I heard."

"I remember. He came over and told me all about it." Her voice was wistful. She paused and adjusted herself in the seat. "And when you got hurt, well, Horace cried. Big, tough man came to this house and sat right where you are now, Myron, and he cried like a little baby."

Myron said nothing.

"You want to know something else?" Mabel continued. She took a sip of her coffee. Myron held his cup, but he could not move. He managed a nod.

"When you tried that comeback last year, Horace was so worried. He wanted to call you, talk you out of it."

Myron's voice was thick. "So why didn't he?"

Mabel Edwards gave him a gentle smile. "When was the last time you spoke to Horace?"

"That phone call," Myron said. "Right after the draft."

She nodded as though that explained everything. "I think Horace knew you were hurting," she said. "I think he figured you'd call when you were ready."

Myron felt something well up in his eyes. Regrets and could-have-beens tried to sneak in, but he shoved them away. No time for

this now. He blinked a few times and put the coffee to his lips. After
he had taken a sip, he asked, "Have you seen Horace lately?"

She put her cup down slowly and studied his face. "Why do you
want to know?"

"He hasn't shown up for work. Brenda hasn't seen him."

"I understand that," Mabel continued, her voice set on caution
now, "but what's your interest in this?"

"I want to help."

"Help what?"

"Find him."

Mabel Edwards waited a beat. "Don't take this the wrong way,
Myron," she said, "but how does this concern you?"

"I'm trying to help Brenda."

She stiffened slightly. "Brenda?"

"Yes, ma'am."

"Do you know she got a court order to keep her father away from
her?"

"Yes."

Mabel Edwards slipped on the half-moon glasses and picked up
her knitting. The needles began to dance. "I think maybe you should
stay out of this, Myron."

"Then you know where he is?"

She shook her head. "I didn't say that."

"Brenda is in danger, Mrs. Edwards. Horace might be connected."

The knitting needles stopped short. "You think Horace would hurt
his own daughter?" Her voice was a little sharp now.

"No, but there might be a connection. Somebody broke into Horace's apartment. He packed a bag and cleared out his bank account.
I think he may be in trouble."

The needles started again. "If he is in trouble," she said, "maybe
it's best that he stay hid."

"Tell me where he is, Mrs. Edwards. I'd like to help."

She stayed silent for a long time. She pulled at the yarn and kept
knitting. Myron looked around the room. His eyes found the photographs again. He stood and studied them.

"Is this your son?" he asked.

She looked up over her glasses. "That's Terence. I got married
when I was seventeen, and Roland and I were blessed with him a
year later." The needles picked up speed. "Roland died when Terence
was a baby. Shot on the front stoop of our home."

"I'm sorry," Myron said.

She shrugged, managed a sad smile. "Terence is the first college graduate in our family. That's his wife on the right. And my two grandsons."

Myron lifted the photograph. "Beautiful family."

"Terence worked his way through Yale Law School," she continued. "He became a town councilman when he was just twenty-five." That was probably why he looked familiar, Myron thought. Local TV news or papers. "If he wins in November, he'll be in the state senate before he's thirty."

"You must be proud," Myron said.

"I am."

Myron turned and looked at her. She looked back.

"It's been a long time, Myron. Horace always trusted you, but this is different. We don't know you anymore. These people who are looking for Horace"—she stopped and pointed to the puffy eye— "you see this?"

Myron nodded.

"Two men came by here last week. They wanted to know where Horace was. I told them I didn't know."

Myron felt his face flush. "They hit you?"

She nodded, her eyes on his.

"What did they look like?"

"White. One was a big man."

"How big?"

"Maybe your size."

Myron was six-four, two-twenty. "How about the other guy?"

"Skinny. And a lot older. He had a tattoo of a snake on his arm." She pointed to her own immense biceps, indicating the spot.

"Please tell me what happened, Mrs. Edwards."

"It's just like I said. They came into my house and wanted to know where Horace was. When I told them I didn't know, the big one punched me in the eye. The little one, he pulled the big one away."

"Did you call the police?"

"No. But not because I was afraid. Cowards like that don't scare me. But Horace told me not to."

"Mrs. Edwards," Myron said, "where is Horace?"

"I've already said too much, Myron. I just want you to understand. These people are dangerous. For all I know, you're working for them. For all I know, your coming here is just a trick to find Horace."

Myron was not sure what to say. To protest his innocence would do little to assuage her fears. He decided to switch tracks and head in a completely different direction. "What can you tell me about Brenda's mother?"

Mabel Edwards stiffened. She dropped the knitting into her lap, the half-moon glasses falling back to her bosom. "Why on earth would you ask about that?"

"A few minutes ago I told you that somebody broke into your brother's apartment."

"I remember."

"Brenda's letters from her mother were missing. And Brenda has been receiving threatening phone calls. One of them told her to call her mother."

Mabel Edwards's face went slack. Her eyes began to glisten.

After some time had passed, Myron tried again. "Do you remember when she ran away?"

Her eyes regained focus. "You don't forget the day your brother dies." Her voice was barely a whisper. She shook her head. "I can't see how any of this matters. Anita's been gone for twenty years."

"Please, Mrs. Edwards, tell me what you remember."

"Not much to tell," Mabel said. "She left my brother a note and ran away."

"Do you remember what the note said?"

"Something about how she didn't love him anymore, how she wanted a new life." Mabel Edwards stopped, waved her hand as though making space for herself. She took a handkerchief out of her bag and just held it in a tight ball.

"Could you tell me what she was like?"

"Anita?" She smiled now, but the handkerchief remained at the ready. "I introduced them, you know. Anita and I worked together."

"Where?"

"The Bradford estate. We were maids. We were young girls then, barely in our twenties. I only worked there for six months. But Anita, she stayed on for six years, slaving for those people."

"When you say the Bradford estate—"

"I mean, *the* Bradfords. Anita was a servant really. For the old lady mostly. That woman must be eighty by now. But they all lived there. Children, grandchildren, brothers, sisters. Like on *Dallas*. I don't think that's healthy, do you?"

Myron had no comment on that.

"Anyway, when I met Anita, I thought she was a fine young woman except"—she looked in the air as though searching for the right words, then shook her head because they weren't there—"well, she was just too beautiful. I don't know how else to say it. Beauty like that warps a man's brain, Myron. Now Brenda, she's attractive,

I guess. Exotic, I think they call it. But Anita . . . hold on. I'll find you a picture."

She stood fluidly and semiglided out of the room. Despite her size, Mabel moved with the unlabored grace of a natural athlete. Horace too moved like that, blending bulk with finesse in an almost poetic way. She was gone for less than a minute, and when she returned, she handed him a photograph. Myron looked down.

A knockout. A pure, undiluted, knee-knocking, breath-stealing knockout. Myron understood the power a woman like that had over a man. Jessica had that kind of beauty. It was intoxicating and more than a little scary.

He studied the photograph. A young Brenda—no more than four or five years old—held her mother's hand and smiled brightly. Myron tried to imagine Brenda smiling like that now, but the image would not form. There was a resemblance between mother and daughter, but as Mabel had pointed out, Anita Slaughter was certainly more beautiful—at least in the conventional sense—her features sharper and more defined where Brenda's seemed large and almost mismatched.

"Anita put a dagger through Horace when she ran off," Mabel Edwards continued. "He never recovered. Brenda neither. She was only a little girl when her mama left. She cried every night for three years. Even when she was in high school, Horace said she'd call out for her mama in her sleep."

Myron finally looked up from the picture. "Maybe she didn't run away," he said.

Mabel's eyes narrowed. "What do you mean?"

"Maybe she met up with foul play."

A sad smile crossed Mabel Edwards's face. "I understand," she said gently. "You look at that picture and you can't accept it. You can't believe a mother would abandon that sweet little child. I know. It's hard. But she did it."

"The note could have been a forgery," Myron tried. "To throw Horace off the track."

She shook her head. "No."

"You can't be sure—"

"Anita calls me."

Myron froze. "What?"

"Not often. Maybe once every two years. She'd ask about Brenda. I'd beg her to come back. She'd hang up."

"Do you have any idea where she was calling from?"

Mabel shook her head. "In the beginning it sounded like long distance. There'd be static. I always figured she was overseas."

"When was the last time she called you?"

There was no hesitation. "Three years ago. I told her about Brenda getting accepted to medical school."

"Nothing since?"

"Not a word."

"And you're sure it was her?" Myron realized that he was reaching.

"Yes," she said. "It was Anita."

"Did Horace know about the calls?"

"At first I told him. But it was like ripping at a wound that wasn't closing anyhow. So I stopped. But I think maybe she called him too."

"What makes you say that?"

"He said something about it once when he had too much to drink. When I asked him about it later, he denied it, and I didn't push him. You have to understand, Myron. We never talked about Anita. But she was always right there. In the room with us. You know what I'm saying?"

The silence moved in like a cloud covering. Myron waited for it to disperse, but it hung there, thick and heavy.

"I'm very tired, Myron. Can we talk more about this another time?"

"Of course." He rose. "If your brother calls again—"

"He won't. He thinks maybe they bugged the phone. I haven't heard from him in almost a week."

"Do you know where he is, Mrs. Edwards?"

"No. Horace said it'd be safer that way."

Myron took a business card and a pen. He jotted down the number of his cellular phone. "I can be reached at this number twenty-four hours a day."

She nodded, drained, the simple act of reaching for the card suddenly a chore.

Chapter 8

"I wasn't totally honest with you yesterday."

Norm Zuckerman and Myron sat alone in the top row of the stands. Below them the New York Dolphins scrimmaged five-on-five. Myron was impressed. The women moved with finesse and strength. Being something of the semisexist Brenda had described, he had expected their movements to be more awkward, more the old stereotype of "throwing like a girl."

"You want to hear something funny?" Norm asked. "I hate sports. Me, owner of Zoom, the sports apparel king, detests anything to do with a ball or a bat or a hoop or any of that. Know why?"

Myron shook his head.

"I was always bad at them. A major spaz, as the kids say today. My older brother, Herschel, now he was an athlete." He looked off. When he started speaking again, his voice was throaty. "So gifted, sweet Heshy. You remind me of him, Myron. I'm not just saying that. I still miss him. Dead at fifteen."

Myron did not need to ask how. Norm's entire family had been slaughtered in Auschwitz. They all went in; only Norm came out. Today was warm, and Norm was wearing short sleeves. Myron could see his concentration camp tattoo and no matter how many times he saw one, he always fell into a respectful hush.

"This league"—Norm motioned toward the court—"it's a long shot. I understood that from the start. It's why I link so much of the league promotion with the clothing. If the WPBA goes down the tubes, well, at least Zoom athletic wear would have gotten a ton of exposure out of it. You understand what I'm saying?"

"Yes."

"And let's face it: without Brenda Slaughter, the investment is shot. The league, the endorsements, the tie-in with the clothing, the whole thing goes kaput. If you wanted to destroy this enterprise, you would go through her."

"And you think someone wants to do that?"

"Are you kidding? Everybody wants to do that. Nike, Converse, Reebok, whoever. It's the nature of the beast. If the sneaker were on the other foot, so to speak, I would want the same thing. It's called capitalism. It's Economics one-oh-one. But this is different, Myron. Have you heard of the PWBL?"

"No."

"You aren't supposed to. Yet. It stands for the Professional Women's Basketball League."

Myron sat up a bit. "A second women's basketball league?"

Norm nodded. "They want to start up next year."

On the court Brenda got the ball and drove hard baseline. A player jumped up to block the shot. Brenda pump-faked, glided under the basket, and made a reverse layup. Improvised ballet.

"Let me guess," Myron said. "This other league. It's being set up by TruPro."

"How did you know that?"

Myron shrugged. Things were beginning to click.

"Look, Myron, it's like I said before: Women's basketball is a tough sell. I'm promoting it a ton of different ways—to sports nuts, women eighteen to thirty-five, families who want something more genteel, fans who want more access to athletes—but at the end of the day there is one problem that this league will never overcome."

"What's that?"

Again Norm motioned to the court below them. "They're not as good as the men. I'm not being a chauvinist here. It's a fact. The men are better. The best player on this team could never compete against the worst player in the NBA. And when people watch professional sports, they want to watch the best. I'm not saying that the problem destroys us. I think we can build a nice fan base. But we have to be realistic."

Myron massaged his face with his hands. He felt a headache coming on. TruPro wanted to start a women's basketball league. It made sense. Sports agencies were moving in that direction, aiming to corner markets. IMG, one of the world's biggest agencies, ran entire golf events. If you can own an event or run a league, you can make money a dozen different ways—not to mention how many clients you'd pick up. If a young golfer, for example, wanted to qualify for the big moneymaking IMG events, wouldn't he naturally want to have IMG as his sports rep?

"Myron?"

"Yes, Norm."

"Do you know this TruPro well?"

Myron nodded. "Oh, yeah."

"I got hemorrhoids older than this kid they're making league commissioner. You should see him. He comes up to me and shakes my hand and gives me this icy smile. Then he tells me they're going to wipe me out. Just like that. Hello, I'm going to wipe you off the face of the earth." Norm looked at Myron. "Are they, you know, connected?" He bent his nose with his index fingers in case Myron did not get the drift.

"Oh, yeah," Myron said again. Then he added, "Very."

"Great. Just great."

"So what do you want to do, Norm?"

"I don't know. I don't run and hide—I had enough of that in my life—but if I'm putting these girls in danger—"

"Forget they're women."

"What?"

"Pretend it's a men's league."

"What, you think this is about sex? I wouldn't want men in danger either, okay?"

"Okay," Myron said. "Has TruPro said anything else to you?"

"No."

"No threats, nothing?"

"Just this kid and his wipeout stuff. But don't you think they're probably the ones making the threats?"

It made sense, Myron guessed. Old gangsters had indeed moved into more legitimate enterprises—why limit yourself to prostitution and drugs and loan sharking when there were so many other ways to turn a buck?—but even with the best of intentions, it never worked out. Guys like the Aches couldn't help themselves really. They'd start out legit, but once things got the slightest bit tough, once they lost out on a contract or a sale or something, they reverted back to their old ways. Couldn't help it. Corruption too was a terrible addiction, but where were the support groups?

In this case TruPro would quickly realize that it needed to get Brenda away from its competition. So it started applying pressure. It put the screws to her manager—her father—and then moved on to Brenda herself. It was a classic scare tactic. But that scenario was not without problems. The phone call that mentioned Brenda's mother, for example—how did that fit in?

The coach blew the whistle ending practice. She gathered her players around, reminded them that they needed to be back in two hours for the second session, thanked them for their hustle, dismissed them with a clap.

Myron waited for Brenda to shower and get dressed. It didn't take

her long. She came out in a long red T-shirt and black jeans, her hair
still wet.

"Did Mabel know anything?" she asked.

"Yes."

"Has she heard from Dad?"

Myron nodded. "She says he's on the run. Two men came to her
house looking for him. They roughed her up a bit."

"My God, is she okay?"

"Yes."

She shook her head. "What's he on the run from?"

"Mabel doesn't know."

Brenda looked at him, waited a beat. "What else?" she said.

Myron cleared his throat. "Nothing that can't wait."

She kept looking at him. Myron turned and headed for his car.
Brenda followed.

"So where we going?" she asked.

"I thought we'd stop by St. Barnabas and talk to your father's supervisor."

She caught up to him. "You think he knows something?"

"Highly doubtful. But this is what I do. I go poking around and
hope something stirs."

They reached the car. Myron unlocked the doors, and they both
got in.

"I should be paying you for your time," she said.

"I'm not a private investigator, Brenda. I don't work by the hour."

"Still. I should be paying you."

"Part of client recruitment," Myron said.

"You want to represent me?"

"Yes."

"You haven't made much of a sales pitch or applied any pressure."

"If I had," he said, "would it have worked?"

"No."

Myron nodded and started up the car.

"Okay," she said. "We've got a few minutes. Tell me why I should
choose you and not one of the big boys. Personal service?"

"Depends on your definition of personal services. If you mean
someone always following you around with lips firmly planted on
your buttocks, then no, the big boys are better at puckering. They
have the staff for it."

"So what does Myron Bolitar offer? A little tongue with those
lips?"

He smiled. "A total package designed to maximize your assets while allowing room for integrity and a personal life."

She nodded. "What a crock."

"Yeah, but it sounds good. In truth, MB SportsReps is a three-prong system. Prong one is earning money. I'm in charge of negotiating all contracts. I will continually seek out new endorsement deals for you and whenever possible get a bidding war going for your services. You'll make decent money playing for the WPBA, but you'll make a hell of a lot more on endorsements. You got a lot of pluses in that department."

"Such as?"

"Three things off the top of my head. One, you're the best female player in the country. Two, you're studying to be a doctor—a pediatrician, no less—so we can play up the whole role model thing. And three, you're not hard on the eyes."

"You forgot one."

"What?"

"Four, that perennial white man favorite: well spoken. You ever notice that no one ever describes a white athlete as well spoken?"

"As a matter of fact, I have. It's why I left it off the list. But the truth is, it helps. I'm not going to get into a debate on Ebonics and the like, but if you are what is commonly referred to as well spoken, it adds revenue. Simple as that."

She nodded. "Go on."

"In your case we need to design a strategy. Clearly you would have tremendous appeal to clothing and sneaker companies. But food products would love you too. Restaurant chains."

"Why?" she asked. "Because I'm big?"

"Because you're not waiflike," Myron corrected. "You're real. Sponsors like real—especially when it comes in an exotic package. They want someone attractive yet accessible—a contradiction, but there you go. And you have it. Cosmetic companies will want to get in on this too. We could also pick up a lot of local deals, but I would advise against it in the beginning. Try to stick with the national markets where we can. It doesn't pay to go after every dime out there. But that will be up to you. I'll present them to you. The final decision is always yours."

"Okay," she said. "Give me prong two."

"Prong two is what you do with your money after you earn it. You've heard of Lock-Horne Securities?"

"Sure."

"All of my clients are required to set up a long-term financial plan with their top man, Windsor Horne Lockwood the Third."

"Nice name."

"Wait till you meet him. But ask around. Win is considered one of the best financial advisers in the country. I insist that every client meet with him quarterly—not by fax or phone but in person—to go over their portfolios. Too many athletes get taken advantage of. That won't happen here, not because Win or I am watching your money but because you are."

"Impressive. Prong three?"

"Esperanza Diaz. She is my right hand and handles everything else. I mentioned before that I'm not the best with ass kissing. That's true. But the reality of this business means I have to wear a lot of hats—travel agent, marriage counselor, limo driver, whatever."

"And this Esperanza helps out with all that?"

"She's crucial."

Brenda nodded. "Sounds like you give her the shit detail."

"Esperanza just graduated law school, as a matter of fact." He tried not to sound too defensive, but her words had struck bone. "She takes on more responsibility every day."

"Okay, one question."

"What?" Myron asked.

"What aren't you telling me about your visit to Mabel?"

Myron said nothing for a moment.

"It's about my mother, isn't it?"

"Not really. It's just . . ." He let his voice drift off before starting up again. "Are you sure you want me to find her, Brenda?"

She crossed her arms and slowly shook her head. "Cut it out."

"What?"

"I know you think protecting me is sweet and noble. But it's not. It's annoying and insulting. So stop it. Now. If your mother ran away when you were five, wouldn't you want to know what happened?"

Myron thought about it, nodded. "Point taken. I won't do it again."

"Fine. So what did Mabel say?"

He recounted his conversation with her aunt. Brenda stayed still. She reacted only when he mentioned the phone calls Mabel and perhaps her father had received from her mother.

"They never told me," she said. "I suspected as much, but"—she looked at Myron—"looks like you weren't the only one who thought I couldn't handle the truth."

They fell into silence and continued the drive. Before making the left off Northfield Avenue, Myron noticed a gray Honda Accord in the rearview mirror. At least it looked like a Honda Accord. All cars pretty much looked the same to Myron, and there was no vehicle more unassuming than a gray Honda Accord. No way to tell for sure, but Myron thought that maybe they were being followed. He slowed down, memorized the license plate. New Jersey plate. 890UB3. When he entered the St. Barnabas Medical Center lot, the car drove on. Didn't mean anything. If the guy doing the tailing was good, he'd never pull in behind him.

St. Barnabas was bigger than when he was a kid, but what hospital wasn't? His dad had taken Myron here several times when he was a kid, for sprains and stitches and X rays and even one ten-day stint for rheumatic fever when he was twelve.

"Let me talk to this guy alone," Myron said.

"Why?"

"You're the daughter. He may speak more freely without you there."

"Yeah, okay. I have some patients I'm following on the fourth floor anyway. I'll meet you back down in the lobby."

Calvin Campbell was in full uniform when Myron found him in the security office. He sat behind a high counter with several dozen TV monitors running. The pictures were in black and white and, from what Myron could see, completely uneventful. Campbell's feet were up. He was downing a submarine sandwich slightly longer than a baseball bat. He took off his policelike cap to reveal tightly curled white hair.

Myron asked him about Horace Slaughter.

"He didn't show for three straight days," Calvin said. "No call, no nothing. So I fired his ass."

"How?" Myron asked.

"What?"

"How did you fire him? In person? On the phone?"

"Well, I tried to call him. But nobody answered. So I wrote a letter."

"Return receipt?"

"Yes."

"Did he sign it?"

He shrugged. "Haven't gotten it back yet, if that's what you mean."

"Was Horace a good worker?"

Calvin's eyes narrowed. "You a private eye?"

"Something like that."

"And you're working for the daughter?"

"Yes."

"She got juice."

"Huh?"

"Juice," Calvin repeated. "I mean, I never wanted to hire the man in the first place."

"So why did you?"

He scowled. "Don't you listen? His daughter got juice. She's tight with some of the bigwigs here. Everybody likes her. So you start hearing things. Rumors, you know. So I figured, what the hell. Being a security guard ain't brain surgery. I hired him."

"What kind of rumors?"

"Hey, don't get me in the middle here." He held his palms as though pushing trouble back. "People talk, is all I'm saying. I've been here eighteen years. I ain't one to make waves. But when a guy don't show for work, well, I have to draw the line."

"Anything else you can tell me?"

"Nope. He came. He did his job okay, I guess. Then he didn't show and I fired him. End of story."

Myron nodded. "Thank you for your time."

"Hey, man, can you do me a favor?"

"What?" Myron asked.

"See if his daughter can clear out his locker. I got a new man coming on board, and I could use the space."

Myron took the elevator up to the pediatric floor. He circled the nurses' station and spotted Brenda through a big window. She was sitting on the bed of a little girl who could not have been more than seven. Myron stopped and watched for a moment. Brenda had put on a white coat, a stethoscope draped around her neck. The little girl said something. Brenda smiled and put the stethoscope on the little girl's ears. They both laughed. Brenda beckoned behind her, and the girl's parents joined them on the bed. The parents had gaunt faces—the sunken cheeks, hollow eyes of the terminally harrowed. Brenda said something to them. More laughter. Myron continued to watch, mesmerized.

When she finally came out, Brenda walked straight to him. "How long have you been standing here?"

"Just a minute or two," he said. Then he added, "You like it here."

She nodded. "It's even better than being on the court."

Enough said.

"So what's up?" she asked.

"Your father has a locker here."

They took the elevator to the basement. Calvin Campbell was waiting for them. "Do you know the combination?" he asked.

Brenda said no.

"No problem." Calvin had a lead pipe in his hand. With practiced precision he belted the combination lock. It shattered like glass. "You can use that empty carton in the corner," he said. Then he sauntered out.

Brenda looked at Myron. He nodded. She reached out and opened the locker. An odor like oft-soiled socks popped out. Myron made a face and looked in. Using his index finger and thumb like a pair of tweezers, he lifted a shirt into view. The shirt looked like the before picture in a Tide commercial.

"Dad wasn't great with laundry," Brenda said.

Or with throwing away garbage, from the looks of things. The entire locker resembled a condensed frat house. There were dirty clothes and empty cans of beer and old newspapers and even a pizza box. Brenda brought over the carton, and they began to load stuff in. Myron started with a pair of uniform pants. He wondered if Horace owned them or if they belonged to the hospital, and then he wondered why he was wondering about something so irrelevant. He searched through the pockets and pulled out a crumpled ball of paper.

Myron smoothed it out. An envelope. He plucked out a sheet of paper and began to read.

"What is it?" Brenda asked.

"A letter from an attorney," Myron said.

He handed it to her:

Dear Mr. Slaughter:

We are in receipt of your letters and are aware of your constant communications with this office. As explained to you in person, the matter you are asking about is confidential. We ask you to kindly stop contacting us. Your behavior is fast approaching harassment.

Sincerely,

Thomas Kincaid

"Do you know what he's talking about?" Myron asked.

She hesitated. "No," she said slowly. "But that name—Thomas Kincaid—it rings a bell. I just can't place it."

"Maybe he did work for your dad before."

Brenda shook her head. "I don't think so. I can't remember my father ever hiring a lawyer. And if he had, I doubt he would have gone to Morristown."

Myron took out his cellular phone and dialed the office. Big Cyndi answered and transferred the call to Esperanza.

"What?" Esperanza said. Always with the pleasantries.

"Did Lisa fax over Horace Slaughter's phone bill?"

"It's right in front of me," Esperanza said. "I was just working on it."

Scary as it might sound, getting a list of someone's long-distance calls had always been fairly easy. Almost every private investigator has a source at the phone company. All it takes is a little grease.

Myron signaled that he wanted the letter back. Brenda handed it to him. Then she knelt and extracted a plastic bag from the back of the locker. Myron looked at the phone number for Kincaid's office on the letter.

"Is five-five-five–one-nine-zero-eight on there?" he asked.

"Yeah. Eight times. All less than five minutes."

"Anything else?"

"I'm still tracking down all the numbers."

"Anything stick out?"

"Maybe," Esperanza said. "For some reason he called Arthur Bradford's gubernatorial headquarters a couple of times."

Myron felt a familiar, not unpleasant jolt. The Bradford name rears its ugly head yet again. Arthur Bradford, one of two prodigal sons, was running for governor in November. "Okay, good. Anything else?"

"Not yet. And I found nothing—I mean, *nada*—on Anita Slaughter."

No surprise there. "Okay, thanks."

He hung up.

"What?" Brenda asked.

"Your father has been calling this Kincaid guy a lot. He's also called Arthur Bradford's campaign headquarters."

She looked confused. "So what does that mean?"

"I don't know. Was your dad political at all?"

"No."

"Did he know Arthur Bradford or anybody connected with the campaign?"

"Not that I'm aware of." Brenda opened the garbage bag and peered inside. Her face went slack. "Oh Christ."

Myron dropped down next to her. Brenda spread open the top of the bag so he could see the contents. A referee's shirt, black and white striped. On the right breast pocket was a patch reading "New Jersey Basketball Referee Association." On the left breast was a big crimson stain.

A bloodstain.

Chapter 9

"We should call the police," Myron said.

"And tell them what?"

Myron was not sure. The bloody shirt didn't have a hole in it—there were no rips or tears visible—and the stain was a concentrated fan shape over the left breast. How had it gotten there? Good question. Not wanting to contaminate any possible clues, Myron gave the shirt a quick, gentle once-over. The stain was thick and looked a bit sticky, if not wet. Since the shirt had been wrapped in a plastic bag, it was hard to say how long the blood had been there. Probably not long, though.

Okay, good. Now what?

The position of the stain itself was puzzling. If Horace had been wearing the shirt, how could the blood have ended up on just that one spot? If, for example, he had a bloody nose, the stain would be more widespread. If he had been shot, well, there'd be a hole in the shirt. If he had hit somebody else, again the stain would probably be more like a spray or at least more dispersed than this.

Why was the stain so concentrated in that one spot?

Myron studied the shirt again. Only one scenario fit: Horace had *not* been wearing the shirt when the injury occurred. Strange but probably true. The shirt had been used to stave off blood flow, like a bandage. That would explain both the placement and concentration. The fan shape indicated it had probably been pressed against a bleeding nose.

Okey-dokey, we're on a roll. It didn't help him in any way, shape, or form. But rolling was good. Myron liked to roll.

Brenda interrupted his thoughts. "What are we going to tell the police?" she asked again.

"I don't know."

"You think he's on the run, right?"

"Yes."

"Then maybe he doesn't want to be found."

"Almost definitely."

"And we know he ran away by his own volition. So what are we going to tell them? That we found some blood on a shirt in his locker? You think the police are going to give a rat's ass?"

"Not even one cheek," Myron agreed.

They finished clearing out the locker. Then Myron drove her to the late practice. He kept his eye on the rearview mirror, looking for the gray Honda Accord. There were many, of course, but none with the same license plate.

He dropped her off at the gym, and then he took Palisades Avenue toward the Englewood Public Library. He had a couple of hours to kill, and he wanted to do some research on the Bradford family.

The Englewood Library sat on Grand Avenue off Palisades Avenue like a clunky spaceship. When it was erected in 1968, the building had probably been praised for its sleek, futuristic design; now it looked like a rejected movie prop for *Logan's Run*.

Myron quickly found a reference librarian who was straight from central casting: gray bun, glasses, pearls, boxy build. The nameplate on her desk read "Mrs. Kay." He approached her with his boyish grin, the one that usually made such ladies pinch his cheek and offer him hot cider.

"I hope you can help me," he said.

Mrs. Kay looked at him in that way librarians often do, wary and tired, like cops who know you're going to lie about how fast you were driving.

"I need to look up articles from the *Jersey Ledger* from twenty years ago."

"Microfiche," Mrs. Kay said. She rose with a great sigh and led him to a machine. "You're in luck."

"Why's that?"

"They just computerized an index. Before that you were on your own."

Mrs. Kay taught him how to use the microfilm machine and the computer indexing service. It looked pretty standard. When she left him alone, Myron first typed in the name Anita Slaughter. No hits. Not a surprise, but hey, you never know. Sometimes you get lucky. Sometimes you plug in the name, and an article comes up and says, "I ran away to Florence, Italy. You can find me at the Plaza Lucchesi hotel on the Arno River, room 218." Well, not often. But sometimes.

Typing in the Bradford name would produce ten zillion hits. Myron was not sure what he was looking for exactly. He knew who the Bradfords were, of course. They were New Jersey aristocracy, the closest thing the Garden State had to the Kennedys. Old Man Bradford had been the governor in the late sixties, and his older son,

Arthur Bradford, was the current front-runner for the same office. Arthur's younger brother, Chance—Myron would have made fun of the name, but when your name is Myron, well, glass houses and big stones and all that—was his campaign manager and—to keep within the Kennedy metaphor—played Robert to Arthur's Jack.

The Bradfords had started modestly enough. Old Man Bradford had come from farm stock. He had owned half the town of Livingston, considered the boonies in the sixties, and sold it in small pieces over the years to developers, who built split-levels and colonials for baby boomers escaping Newark and Brooklyn and the like. Myron in fact had grown up in a split-level that had been built on what had formerly been Bradford farmland.

But Old Man Bradford had been smarter than most. For one thing, he reinvested his money in strong local businesses, mostly malls, but more important, he sold his land slowly, over time, not immediately cashing in. By holding on a bit longer, he became a true baron as the price for land increased at an alarming rate. He married a blue blood aristocrat from Connecticut. She redid the old farmhouse and made it something of a monument to excess. They stayed in Livingston, in the original spot of the old farmhouse, fencing off an enormous chunk of real estate. They were the mansion on the hill, surrounded by hundreds of middle-class cookie-cut houses: feudal lords overlooking the serfdom. Nobody in town really knew the Bradfords. When Myron was a kid, he and his friends just referred to them as the millionaires. They were the stuff of legends. Supposedly, if you climbed their fence, armed guards shot at you. Two sixth graders gave a wide-eyed Myron this stern warning when he was seven years old. He of course believed it absolutely. Outside of the Bat Lady, who lived in a shack near the Little League field and kidnapped and then ate little boys, no one was more feared than the Bradfords.

Myron tried limiting the search on the Bradfords to 1978, the year Anita Slaughter disappeared, but there were still a ton of hits. Most, he noticed, were from March, while Anita had run off in November. A vague memory prodded him, but he couldn't conjure up more than a glimpse. He'd been just starting high school then, but there had been something in the news about the Bradfords. A scandal of some sort. He threaded microfilm into the machine. He was a tad spastic with anything mechanical—something he blamed on his ancestry—so it took him longer than it should have. After a few screeching false starts, Myron managed to look up a couple of articles. In fairly short order he stumbled across the obituary. *"Elizabeth Bradford. Age thirty. Daughter of Richard and Miriam Worth. Wife of Arthur Bradford. Mother of Stephen Bradford . . ."*

No cause of death given. But now Myron remembered the story. It had, in fact, been rehashed a bit recently, what with the press on the gubernatorial race. Arthur Bradford was now a fifty-two-year-old widower who, if the accounts were to be believed, still pined for his dead love. He dated, sure, but the spin was that he had never gotten over the devastating heartbreak of losing his young bride; it made for a nice, too-neat contrast with his thrice-married gubernatorial opponent, Jim Davison. Myron wondered if there was any truth in the spin. Arthur Bradford was perceived as a little too mean, a little Bob Dole. Sick as it sounded, what better way to offset that image than resurrecting a dead wife?

But who knew for sure? Politics and the press: two cherished institutions that spoke with tongues so forked they could double for fine dinnerware. Arthur Bradford refused to talk about his wife, and that could reflect either genuine pain or clever media manipulation. Cynical, but there you have it.

Myron continued to review the old articles. The story had made the front page on three consecutive dates in March 1978. Arthur and Elizabeth Bradford had been college sweethearts and married six years. Everyone described them as a "loving couple," one of those media buzz phrases that meant as much as calling a dead youth an honor student. Mrs. Bradford had fallen off a third-level balcony at the Bradford mansion. The surface below was brick, and Elizabeth Bradford had landed on her head. There was not much in the way of details. A police investigation stated unequivocally that the death had been a tragic accident. The balcony was tiled and slippery. It had been raining and dark. A wall was being replaced and thus not secure in certain spots.

Awfully clean.

The press played very fair with the Bradfords. Myron now recalled the obvious rumors that had gone around the schoolyard. What the heck was she doing out on her balcony in March? Was she drunk? Probably. How else do you fall off your own balcony? Naturally some of the guys speculated that she'd been pushed. It made for interesting high school cafeteria fodder for at least, oh, two days. But this was high school. Hormones inevitably recaptured the flag, and everybody returned to panicking about the opposite sex. Ah, the sweet bird of youth.

Myron leaned back and stared at the screen. He thought again about Arthur Bradford's refusal to comment. Maybe it had nothing to do with genuine grief or media manipulation; maybe Bradford refused to talk because he didn't want something brought to light after twenty years.

Hmm. Right, Myron, sure. And maybe he had kidnapped the Lindbergh baby. Stick to the facts. One, Elizabeth Bradford had been dead for twenty years. Two, there was not a scintilla of evidence that her death was anything but an accident. Three—and most important to Myron—this had all happened a full nine months before Anita Slaughter ran away.

Conclusion: There was not even the flimsy hint of a connection.

At least not right then.

Myron's throat went dry. He'd continued to read the article from the March 18, 1978, issue of the *Jersey Ledger.* The page one story finished up on page eight. Myron played with the knob on the microfiche machine. It screamed in protest but trudged forward.

There it was. Near the bottom right-hand corner. One line. That was all. Nothing that anybody would notice: *"Mrs. Bradford's body was first discovered on the brick back porch of the Bradford estate at 6:30 A.M. by a maid arriving for work."*

A maid arriving for work. Myron wondered what the maid's name was.

Chapter 10

Myron immediately called Mabel Edwards. "Do you remember Elizabeth Bradford?" he asked.

There was a brief hesitation. "Yes."

"Did Anita find her body?"

A longer hesitation. "Yes."

"What did she tell you about it?"

"Wait a second. I thought you were trying to help Horace."

"I am."

"So why are you asking about that poor woman?" Mabel sounded slightly put out. "She died more than twenty years ago."

"It's a little complicated."

"I bet it is." He heard her take a deep breath. "I want the truth now. You're looking for her too, aren't you? For Anita?"

"Yes, ma'am."

"Why?"

Good question. But when you stripped it bare, the answer was pretty simple. "For Brenda."

"Finding Anita ain't gonna help that girl."

"You tell her that."

She chuckled without humor. "Brenda can be headstrong," Mabel said.

"I think it runs in the family."

"Guess it does at that," she said.

"Please tell me what you remember."

"Not much to it, I guess. She came to work, and the poor woman was lying there like a broken rag doll. That's all I know."

"Anita never said anything else about it?"

"No."

"Did she seem shaken up?"

"Of course. She worked for Elizabeth Bradford for almost six years."

"No, I mean beyond the shock of finding the body."

"I don't think so. But she never talked about it. Even when the reporters called, Anita just hung up the phone."

Myron computed this information, sorted in through his brain cells, came up with zippo. "Mrs. Edwards, did your brother ever mention a lawyer named Thomas Kincaid?"

She thought a moment. "No, I don't think so."

"Were you aware of him seeking legal advice on anything?"

"No."

They said their good-byes, and then he hung up. The phone was barely disconnected when it rang again. "Hello?"

"Got something strange here, Myron."

It was Lisa from the phone company.

"What's up?"

"You asked me to put a tracer on the phone in Brenda Slaughter's dorm."

"Right."

"Someone beat me to it."

Myron nearly slammed on the brake. "What?"

"There's already a tap on her phone."

"For how long?"

"I don't know."

"Can you trace it back? See who put it on?"

"Nope. And the number is blocked out."

"What does that mean?"

"I can't read anything on it. I can't get a trace or even look at old bills on the computer. My guess is, someone in law enforcement is behind it. I can poke around, but I doubt I'll come up with anything."

"Please try, Lisa. And thanks."

He hung up. A missing father, threatening phone calls, a possible car tail, and now a phone tap: Myron was starting to get nervous here. Why would someone—someone with authority—have a tap on Brenda's phone? Was that person part of the group making the threatening phone calls? Were they tapping her phone to track down her father or—

Hold the phone.

Hadn't one of the threatening calls told Brenda to call her mother? Why? Why would someone have said that? More important, if Brenda had obeyed the call—and if she had indeed known where her mother was hiding—the people behind the trace would have been able to find Anita too. Was that what this was really all about?

Was someone looking for Horace . . . or Anita?

"We have a problem," Myron told her.

They sat in the car. Brenda turned toward him and waited.

"Your phone is bugged," he said.

"What?"

"Someone has been listening in to your calls. You're also being tailed by someone."

"But—" Brenda stopped, shrugged. "Why? To find my father?"

"That's the best bet, yes. Someone is anxious to get to Horace. They've already attacked your aunt. You might be next on their list."

"So you think I'm in danger."

"Yes."

She watched his face. "And you have a suggested course of action."

"I do," he said.

"I'm listening."

"First, I'd like to have your dorm room swept for bugs."

"I have no problem with that."

"Second, you have to get out of your dorm room. You're not safe there."

She considered this for a moment. "I can stay with a friend. Cheryl Sutton. She's the other captain of the Dolphins."

Myron shook his head. "These people know you. They've been following you, listening to your phone calls."

"Meaning?"

"Meaning they probably know who your friends are."

"Including Ms. Sutton."

"Yes."

"And you think they'll look for me there?"

"It's a possibility."

Brenda shook her head and faced forward. "This is spooky."

"There's more."

He told her about the Bradford family and about her mother finding the body.

"So what does that mean?" Brenda asked when he finished.

"Probably nothing," Myron said. "But you wanted me to tell you everything, right?"

"Right." She leaned back and chewed at her lower lip. After some time had passed, she asked, "So where do you think I should stay?"

"Do you remember my mentioning my friend Win?"

"The guy who owns Lock-Horne Securities?"

"His family does, right. I'm supposed to go to his place tonight to discuss a business problem. I think you should come too. You can stay at his apartment."

"You want me to stay with him?"

"Just for tonight. Win has safe houses all over. We'll find you someplace."

She made a face. "A preppy Mainliner who knows about safe houses?"

"Win," Myron said, "is more than he appears."

She crossed her arms under her chest. "I don't want to act like a jackass and hand you that phony crap about how I'm not going to let this interfere with my life. I know you're helping me, and I want to cooperate."

"Good."

"But," she added, "this league means a lot to me. So does my team. I'm not going to just walk away from that."

"I understand."

"So whatever we do, will I be able to go to practice? Will I be able to play in the opener Sunday?"

"Yes."

Brenda nodded. "Okay then," she said. "And thank you."

They drove to her dorm room. Myron waited downstairs while she packed a bag. She had her own room, but she wrote a note to her suite mate that she was staying with a friend for a few days. The whole enterprise took her less than ten minutes.

She came down with two bags over her shoulders. Myron relieved her of one. They were heading out the door when Myron spotted FJ standing next to his car.

"Stay here," he told her.

Brenda ignored him and kept pace. Myron looked to his left. Bubba and Rocco were there. They waved at him. Myron did not wave back. That'll show them.

FJ leaned against the car, completely relaxed, almost too relaxed, like an old movie drunk against a lamppost.

"Hello, Brenda," FJ said.

"Hello, FJ."

Then he nodded toward Myron. "And you too, Myron."

His smile did more than lack warmth. It was the most purely physical smile Myron had ever seen, a by-product strictly of the brain giving specific orders to certain muscles. It touched no part of him but his lips.

Myron circled the car and feigned inspecting it. "Not a bad job, FJ. But next time put a little muscle into the hubcaps. They're filthy."

FJ looked at Brenda. "This the famed Bolitar rapier wit I've heard so much about?"

She shrugged sympathetically.

Myron motioned at them with his hands. "You two know each other?"

"But of course," FJ said. "We went to prep school together. At Lawrenceville."

Bubba and Rocco lumbered a few steps closer. They looked like Luca Brasi Youth.

Myron eased between Brenda and FJ. The protective move would probably piss her off, but tough. "So what can we do for you, FJ?"

"I just want to make sure that Ms. Slaughter is honoring her contract with me."

"I don't have a contract with you," Brenda said.

"Your father—one Horace Slaughter—is your agent, no?"

"No," Brenda said. "Myron is."

"Oh?" FJ's eyes slithered toward Myron. Myron kept up the eye contact, but there was still nothing there, like looking into the windows of an abandoned building. "I'd been informed otherwise."

Myron shrugged. "Life is change, FJ. Gotta learn to adapt."

"Adapt," FJ said, "or die."

Myron nodded and said, "Oooo."

FJ kept the stare going a few more seconds. He had skin that looked like wet clay, as if it might dissolve under heavy rains. He turned back to Brenda. "Your father used to be your agent," he said. "Before Myron."

Myron handled that one. "And what if he was?"

"He signed with us. Brenda was going to bow out of the WPBA and join the PWBL. It's all spelled out in the contract."

Myron looked at Brenda. She shook her head. "You have Ms. Slaughter's signature on those contracts?" he asked.

"Like I said, her father—"

"Who has no legal standing in this matter whatsoever. Do you have Brenda's signature or not?"

FJ looked rather displeased. Bubba and Rocco moved closer still. "We do not."

"Then you have nothing." Myron unlocked his car door. "But we've all enjoyed this too brief time together. I know I'm a better person for it."

Bubba and Rocco started toward him. Myron opened the car door. His gun was under his car seat. He debated making a move. It would be dumb, of course. Someone—probably Brenda or Myron—would get hurt.

FJ lifted a hand, and the two men stopped as though they'd been

sprayed by Mr. Freeze. "We're not mobsters," FJ said. "We're busi-
nessmen."

"Right," Myron said. "And Bubba and Rocco over there—they
your CPAs?"

A tiny smile came to FJ's lips. The smile was strictly reptilian,
meaning it was far warmer than his other ones. "If you are indeed her
agent," FJ said, "then it would behoove you to speak with me."

Myron nodded. "Call my office, make an appointment," he said.

"We'll talk soon then," FJ said.

"Looking forward to it. And keep using the word *behoove*. It
really impresses people."

Brenda opened her car door and got in. Myron did likewise. FJ
came around to Myron's window and knocked on the glass. Myron
lowered the window.

"Sign with us or don't sign with us," FJ said quietly. "That's business. But when I kill you, well, that will be for fun."

Myron was about to crack wise again, but something—probably
a fly-through of good sense—made him pause. FJ moved away then.
Rocco and Bubba followed. Myron watched them disappear, his
heart flapping in his chest like a caged condor.

Chapter 11

They parked on a lot on Seventy-first Street and walked to the Dakota. The Dakota remains one of New York's premier buildings, though it's still best known for John Lennon's assassination. A fresh bouquet of roses marked the spot where his body had fallen. Myron always felt a little weird crossing over it, as if he were trampling on a grave or something. The Dakota doorman must have seen Myron a hundred times by now, but he always pretended otherwise and buzzed up to Win's apartment.

Introductions were brief. Win found Brenda a place to study. She broke out a medical textbook the size of a stone tablet and made herself comfortable. Win and Myron moved back into a living room semidecorated in the manner of Louis the Somethingteenth. There was a fireplace with big iron tools and a bust on the mantel. The substantial furniture looked, as always, freshly polished yet plenty old. Oil paintings of stern yet effeminate men stared down from the walls. And just to keep things in the proper decade, there was a big-screen TV and VCR front and center.

The two friends sat and put their feet up.

"So what do you think?" Myron asked.

"She's too big for my tastes," Win said. "But nicely toned legs."

"I mean, about protecting her."

"We'll find a place," Win said. He laced his hands behind his neck. "Talk to me."

"Do you know Arthur Bradford?"

"The gubernatorial candidate?"

"Yes."

Win nodded. "We've met several times. I played golf with him and his brother once at Merion."

"Can you set up a meet?"

"No problem. They've been hitting us up for a sizable donation." He crossed his ankles. "So how does Arthur Bradford fit into all this?"

Myron recapped the day's developments: the Honda Accord following them, the phone taps, the bloody clothes, Horace Slaughter's phone calls to Bradford's office, FJ's surprise visit, Elizabeth Bradford's murder, and Anita's role in finding the body.

Win looked unimpressed. "Do you really see a link between the Bradfords' past and the Slaughters' present?"

"Yeah, maybe."

"Then let me see if I can follow your rationale. Feel free to correct me if I'm wrong."

"Okey-dokey."

Win dropped his feet to the floor and steepled his fingers, resting his indexes against his chin. "Twenty years ago Elizabeth Bradford died under somewhat murky circumstances. Her death was ruled an accident, albeit a bizarre one. You do not buy that one. The Bradfords are rich, and thus you are extra-suspicious of the official rendering—"

"It's not just that they're rich," Myron interrupted. "I mean, falling off her own balcony? Come on."

"Yes, fine, fair enough." Win did the hand-steeple again. "Let us pretend that you are correct in your suspicions. Let us assume that something unsavory did indeed occur when Elizabeth Bradford plunged to her death. And I am further going to assume—as you no doubt have—that Anita Slaughter, in her capacity as maid or servant or what have you, happened upon the scene and witnessed something incriminating."

Myron nodded. "Continue."

Win spread his hands. "Well, my friend, that is where you reach an impasse. If the dear Ms. Slaughter did indeed see something that she was not supposed to, the issue would have been resolved immediately. I know the Bradfords. They are not people who take chances. Anita Slaughter would have been killed or forced to run immediately. But instead—and here is the rub—she waited a full nine months before disappearing. I therefore conclude that the two incidents are unrelated."

Behind them Brenda cleared her throat. They both turned to the doorway. She stared straight at Myron. She did not look happy.

"I thought you two were discussing a business problem," she said.

"We are," Myron said quickly. "I, uh, mean we're going to. That's why I came here. To discuss a business problem. But we just started talking about this first, and well, you know, one thing led to another. But it wasn't intentional or anything. I mean, I came here to discuss a business problem, right, Win?"

Win leaned forward and patted Myron's knee. "Smooth," he said.

She crossed her arms. Her eyes were two drill bits—say, three-sixteenths of an inch, quarter inch tops.

"How long have you been standing there?" Myron asked.

Brenda gestured toward Win. "Since he said I had nicely toned legs," she said. "I missed the part about being too big for his tastes."

Win smiled. Brenda did not wait to be asked. She crossed the room and grabbed an open chair. She kept her eyes on Win. "For the record, I don't buy any of this either," Brenda said to him. "Myron has trouble believing a mother would just abandon her little daughter. He has no trouble believing a father would do the same, just not a mother. But as I've explained to him, he's something of a sexist."

"A snorting pig," Win agreed.

"But," she continued, "if you two are going to sit here and play Holmes and Watson, I do see a way around your"—she made quote marks with her finger—"impasse."

"Do tell," Win said.

"When Elizabeth Bradford fell to her death, my mother may have seen something that appeared innocuous at first. I don't know what. Something bothersome maybe but nothing to get excited about. She continues to work for these people, scrubbing their floors and toilets. And maybe one day she opens a drawer. Or a closet. And maybe she sees something that coupled with what she saw the day Elizabeth Bradford died leads her to conclude that it wasn't an accident after all."

Win looked at Myron. Myron raised his eyebrows.

Brenda sighed. "Before you two continue your patronizing glances—the ones that say, 'Golly gee, the woman is actually capable of cogitation'—let me add that I'm just giving you a way around the impasse. I don't buy it for a second. It leaves too much unexplained."

"Like what?" Myron asked.

She turned to him. "Like why my mother would run away the way she did. Like why she would leave that cruel note for my father about another man. Like why she left us penniless. Like why she would leave behind a daughter she theoretically loved."

There was no quiver in the voice. Just the opposite, in fact. The tone was far too steady, straining too hard for normality.

"Maybe she wanted to protect her daughter from harm," Myron said. "Maybe she wanted to discourage her husband from looking for her."

She frowned. "So she took all his money and faked running away with another man?" Brenda looked at Win. "Does he really believe this crap?"

Win held his hands palms up and nodded apologetically.

Brenda turned back to Myron. "I appreciate what you're trying to do here, but it just doesn't add up. My mother ran away twenty years ago. Twenty years. In all that time couldn't she have done more than write a couple of letters and call my aunt? Couldn't she have figured out a way to see her own daughter? To set up a meet? At least once in twenty years? In all that time couldn't she have gotten herself settled and come back for me?"

She stopped as though out of breath. She hugged her knees to her chest and turned away. Myron looked at Win. Win kept still. The silence pressed against the windows and doors.

Win was the one who finally spoke. "Enough speculating. Let me call Arthur Bradford. He'll see us tomorrow."

Win left the room. With some people, you might be skeptical or at least wonder how they could be so sure a gubernatorial candidate would see them on such short notice. Not so when it came to Win.

Myron looked over at Brenda. She did not look back. A few minutes later Win returned.

"Tomorrow morning," Win said. "Ten o'clock."

"Where?"

"The estate at Bradford Farms. In Livingston."

Brenda stood. "If we're finished with this topic, I'll leave you two alone." She looked at Myron. "To discuss a business problem."

"There is one more thing," Win said.

"What?"

"The question of a safe house."

She stopped and waited.

Win leaned back. "I am inviting both you and Myron to stay here if you're comfortable. As you can see, I have plenty of room. You can use the bedroom at the end of the corridor. It has its own bathroom. Myron will be across the hallway. You'll have the security of the Dakota and easy, close proximity to the two of us."

Win glanced at Myron, who tried to hide his surprise. Myron frequently stayed overnight—he even kept clothes and a bunch of toiletries here—but Win had never made an offer like this before. He usually demanded total privacy.

Brenda nodded and said, "Thank you."

"The only potential problem," Win said, "is my private life."

Uh-oh.

"I may bring in a dizzying array of ladies for a variety of purposes," he went on. "Sometimes more than one. Sometimes I film them. Does that bother you?"

"No," she said. "As long as I can do the same with men."

Myron started coughing.

Win remained unfazed. "But of course. I keep the video camera in that cabinet."

She turned to the cabinet and nodded. "Got a tripod?"

Win opened his mouth, closed it, shook his head. "Too easy," he said.

"Smart man." Brenda smiled. "Good night, guys."

When she left, Win looked at Myron. "You can close your mouth now."

Win poured himself a cognac. "So what business problem did you want to discuss?"

"It's Esperanza," Myron said. "She wants a partnership."

"Yes, I know."

"She told you?"

Win swirled the liquid in the snifter. "She consulted me. On the hows mostly. The legal setup for such a change."

"And you never told me?"

Win did not reply. The answer was obvious. Win hated stating the obvious. "Care for a Yoo-Hoo?"

Myron shook his head. "The truth is, I don't know what to do about it."

"Yes, I know. You've been stalling."

"Did she tell you that?"

Win looked at him. "You know her better than that."

Myron nodded. He did know better. "Look, she's my friend—"

"Correction," Win interrupted. "She's your best friend. More so, perhaps, than even I. But you must forget that for now. She is just an employee—a great one perhaps—but your friendship must be meaningless in this decision. For your sake as well as hers."

Myron nodded. "Yeah, you're right, forget I said that. And I do understand where she's coming from. She's been with me since the beginning. She's worked hard. She's finished law school."

"But?"

"But a partnership? I'd love to promote her, give her her own office, give her more responsibility, even work out a profit-sharing program. But she won't accept that. She wants to be a partner."

"Has she told you why?"

"Yeah," Myron said.

"And?"

"She doesn't want to work for anyone. It's as simple as that. Not even me. Her father worked menial jobs for scumbags his whole life. Her mother cleaned other people's houses. She swore that one day she would work for herself."

"I see," Win said.

"And I sympathize. Who wouldn't? But her parents probably worked for abusive ogres. Forget our friendship. Forget the fact that I love Esperanza like a sister. I'm a good boss. I'm fair. Even she'd have to admit that."

Win took a deep sip. "But clearly that is not enough for her."

"So what am I supposed to do? Give in? Business partnerships between friends or family never work. Never. It's just that simple. Money screws up every relationship. You and I—we work hard to keep our businesses linked but separate. That's why we get away with it. We have similar goals, but that's it. There is no money connection. I know a lot of good relationships—and good businesses—that have been destroyed over something like this. My father and his brother still don't talk because of a business partnership. I don't want that to happen here."

"Have you told Esperanza this?"

He shook his head. "But she's given me a week to make a decision. Then she walks."

"Tough spot," Win said.

"Any suggestions?"

"Not a one." Then Win tilted his head and smiled.

"What?"

"Your argument," Win said. "I find it ironic."

"How so?"

"You believe in marriage and family and monogamy and all that nonsense, correct?"

"So?"

"You believe in raising children, the picket fences, the basketball pole in the driveway, peewee football, dance classes, the whole suburbia scene."

"And again I say, so?"

Win spread his arms. "So I would argue that marriages and the like never work. They inevitably lead to divorce or disillusionment or the deadening of dreams or at the very least, bitterness and resentment. I might—similar to you—point to my own family as an example."

"It's not the same thing, Win."

"Oh, I recognize that. But the truth is, we all take facts and compute them through our own experiences. You had a wonderful family life; thus you believe as you do. I am of course the opposite. Only a leap of faith could change our positions."

Myron made a face. "Is this supposed to be helping?"

"Heavens, no," Win said. "But I do so enjoy philosophical folly."

Win picked up the remote and switched on the television. Nick at Night. *Mary Tyler Moore* was on. They grabbed fresh drinks and settled back to watch.

Win took another sip, reddening his cheeks. "Maybe Lou Grant will have your answer."

He didn't. Myron imagined what would happen if he treated Esperanza the same way Lou treated Mary. If Esperanza were in a good mood, she'd probably tear out his hair until he looked like Murray.

Bedtime. On his way to his room, Myron checked on Brenda. She was sitting lotus style on the antique Queen Something-or-other bed. The large textbook was open in front of her. Her concentration was total, and for a moment he just watched her. Her face displayed the same serenity he'd seen on the court. She wore flannel pajamas, her skin still a little wet from a recent shower, a towel wrapped around her hair.

Brenda sensed him and looked up. When she smiled at him, he felt something tighten in his stomach.

"You need anything?" he asked.

"I'm fine," she said. "You solve your business problem?"

"No."

"I didn't mean to eavesdrop before."

"Don't worry about it."

"I meant what I said earlier. I'd like you to be my agent."

"I'm glad."

"You'll draw up the papers?"

Myron nodded.

"Good night, Myron."

"Good night, Brenda."

She looked down and turned a page. Myron watched her for another second. Then he went to bed.

Chapter 12

They took Win's Jaguar to the Bradford estate because, as Win explained, people like the Bradfords "don't do Taurus." Neither did Win.

Win dropped Brenda off at practice and headed down Route 80 to Passaic Avenue, which had finally completed a widening program that began when Myron was in high school. They finished up on Eisenhower Parkway, a beautiful four-lane highway that ran for maybe five miles. Ah, New Jersey.

A guard with enormous ears greeted them at the gate of, as the sign said, Bradford Farms. Right. Most farms are known for their electronic fences and security guards. Wouldn't want anyone getting into the carrots and corn. Win leaned out the window, gave the guy the snooty smile, and was quickly waved through. A strange pang struck Myron as they drove through. How many times had he gone past the gate as a kid, trying to peer through the thick shrubs for a glance at the proverbial greener grass, dreaming up scenarios for the lush, adventure-filled life that lay within these manicured grounds?

He knew better now, of course. Win's familial estate, Lockwood Manor, made this place look like a railroad shanty, so Myron had seen up close how the superrich lived. It was indeed pretty, but pretty doesn't mean happy. Wow. That was deep. Maybe next time Myron would conclude that money can't buy happiness. Stay tuned.

Scattered cows and sheep helped keep the farm illusion—for the purpose of nostalgia or a tax write-off, Myron could not say, though he had his suspicions. They pulled up to a white farmhouse that had undergone more renovations than an aging movie queen.

An old black man wearing gray butler's tails answered the door. He gave them a slight bow and asked them to follow him. In the corridor were two goons dressed like Secret Service men. Myron glanced at Win. Win nodded. Not Secret Service guys. Goons. The bigger of the two smiled at them like they were cocktail franks heading back to the kitchen. One big. One skinny. Myron remembered Mabel Edwards's descriptions of her attackers. Not much to go on if he couldn't check for a tattoo, but worth keeping in mind.

The butler or manservant or whatever led them into the library. Rounded walls of books climbed three stories high, topped by a glass cupola that let in the proper amount of fresh light. The room might have been a converted silo, or maybe it just looked that way. Hard to tell. The books were leather and in series and untouched. Cherry mahogany dominated the scene. Paintings of old sailing vessels were framed under portrait lamps. There was a huge antique globe in the center of the room, not unlike the one Win had in his own office. Rich people like old globes, Myron surmised. Maybe it has something to do with the fact that they are both expensive and utterly useless.

The chairs and couches were leather with gold buttons. The lamps were Tiffany. A book lay strategically open on a coffee table next to a bust of Shakespeare. Rex Harrison was not sitting in the corner wearing a smoking jacket, but he should have been.

As though on cue, a door on the other side of the room—a bookshelf actually—swung open. Myron half expected Bruce Wayne and Dick Grayson to storm into the room calling for Alfred, maybe tilt back the head of Shakespeare, and turn a hidden knob. Instead it was Arthur Bradford, followed by his brother, Chance. Arthur was very tall, probably six-six, thin, and stooped a bit the way tall people over the age of fifty are. He was bald, his fringe hair trimmed short. Chance was under six feet with wavy brown hair and the kind of boyish good looks that made it impossible to tell his age, though Myron knew from the press clippings that he was forty-nine, three years younger than Arthur.

Playing the part of the perfect politician, Arthur beelined toward them, a fake smile at the ready, hand extended in such a way as either to shake hands or to imply that the extended hand hoped to touch more than just flesh.

"Windsor!" Arthur Bradford exclaimed, grasping Win's hand as if he'd been searching for it all his life. "How wonderful to see you."

Chance headed toward Myron like it was a double date and he had gotten stuck with the ugly girl and was used to it.

Win flashed the vague smile. "Do you know Myron Bolitar?"

The brothers switched handshaking partners with the practiced proficiency of experienced square dancers. Shaking Arthur Bradford's hand was like shaking hands with an old, unoiled baseball glove. Up close, Myron could see that Arthur Bradford was big-boned and rough-hewn and large-featured and red-faced. Still the farm boy under the suit and manicure.

"We've never met," Arthur said through the big smile, "but everyone in Livingston—heck, all of New Jersey—knows Myron Bolitar."

Myron made his aw-shucks face but refrained from batting his eyes.

"I've been watching you play ball since you were in high school," Arthur continued with great earnestness. "I'm a big fan."

Myron nodded, knowing that no Bradford had ever stepped foot in Livingston High School's gymnasium. A politician who stretched the truth. What a shock.

"Please, gentlemen, sit down."

Everyone grabbed smooth leather. Arthur Bradford offered coffee. Everyone accepted. A Latina woman opened the door. Arthur Bradford said to her, *"Café, por favor."* Another linguist.

Win and Myron were on a couch. The brothers sat across from them in matching wingback chairs. Coffee was wheeled in on something that could have doubled as a coach for a palace ball. The coffee was poured and milked and sugared. Then Arthur Bradford, the candidate himself, took over and actually handed Myron and Win their beverages. Regular guy. Man of the people.

Everyone settled back. The servant faded away. Myron raised the cup to his lips. The problem with his new coffee addiction was that he drank only coffee-bar coffee, the potent "gourmet" stuff that could eat through driveway sealant. The at-home brews tasted to his suddenly picky palate like something sucked through a sewer grate on a hot afternoon—this coming from a man who could not tell the difference between a perfectly aged Merlot and a recently stomped Manischewitz. But when Myron took a sip from the Bradfords' fine china, well, the rich have their ways. The stuff was ambrosia.

Arthur Bradford put down his Wedgwood cup and saucer. He leaned forward, his forearms resting on his knees, his hands in a quiet clasp. "First, let me tell you how thrilled I am to have you both here. Your support means a great deal to me."

Bradford turned toward Win. Win's face was totally neutral, patient.

"I understand Lock-Horne Securities wants to expand its Florham Park office and open a new one in Bergen County," Bradford went on. "If I can be of any help at all, Windsor, please let me know."

Win gave a noncommittal nod.

"And if there are any state bonds Lock-Horne has any interest in underwriting, well, again I would be at your disposal."

Arthur Bradford sat up on his haunches now, as though waiting for a scratch behind the ears. Win rewarded him with another noncommittal nod. Good doggie. Hadn't taken Bradford long to start with the graft, had it? Bradford cleared his throat and turned his attention to Myron.

"I understand, Myron, that you own a sports representation company."

He tried to imitate the Win nod, but he went too far. Not subtle enough. Must be something in the genes.

"If there is anything I can do to help, please do not hesitate to ask."

"Can I sleep in the Lincoln bedroom?" Myron asked.

The brothers froze for a moment, looked at each other, then exploded into laughter. The laughs were about as genuine as a televangelist's hair. Win looked over at Myron. The look said, go ahead.

"Actually, Mr. Bradford—"

Through his laugh he stuck up a hand the size of a throw pillow and said, "Please, Myron, call me Arthur."

"Arthur, right. There is something you can do for us."

Arthur and Chance's laughter segued into chuckles before fading away like a song on the radio. Their faces grew harder now. Game time. They both leaned into the strike zone a bit, signaling to one and all that they were going to listen to Myron's problem with four of the most sympathetic ears in existence.

"Do you remember a woman named Anita Slaughter?" Myron asked.

They were good, both of them thoroughbred politicians, but their bodies still jolted as if they'd been zapped with a stun gun. They recovered fast enough, busying themselves with the pretense of scouring for a recollection, but there was no doubt. A nerve had been jangled big time.

"I can't place the name," Arthur said, his face twisted as though he'd given this thought process an effort equal to childbirth. "Chance?"

"The name is not unfamiliar," Chance said, "but . . ." He shook his head.

Not unfamiliar. You gotta love it when they speak politicianese.

"Anita Slaughter worked here," Myron said. "Twenty years ago. She was a maid or house servant of some kind."

Again the deep, probing thought. If Rodin were here, he'd break out the good bronze for these guys. Chance kept his eyes on his brother, waiting for his stage cue. Arthur Bradford held the pose for a few more seconds before he suddenly snapped his fingers.

"Of course," he said. "Anita. Chance, you remember Anita."

"Yes, of course," Chance chimed in. "I guess I never knew her last name."

They were both smiling now like morning anchors during a sweeps week.

"How long did she work for you?" Myron asked.

"Oh, I don't know," Arthur said. "A year or two, I guess. I really don't remember. Chance and I weren't responsible for household help, of course. That was more Mother's doing."

Already with the "plausible deniability." Interesting. "Do you remember why she left your family's employ?"

Arthur Bradford's smile stayed frozen, but something was happening to his eyes. His pupils were expanding, and for a moment it looked like he was having trouble focusing. He turned to Chance. They both looked uncertain now, not sure how to handle this sudden frontal assault, not wanting to answer but not wanting to lose the potentially massive Lock-Horne Securities support either.

Arthur took the lead. "No, I don't remember." When in doubt, evade. "Do you, Chance?"

Chance spread his hands and gave them the boyish smile. "So many people in and out." He looked to Win as if to say, You know how it is. But Win's eyes, as usual, offered no solace.

"Did she quit or was she fired?"

"Oh, I doubt she was fired," Arthur said quickly. "My mother was very good to the help. She rarely, if ever, fired anyone. Not in her nature."

The man was pure politician. The answer might be true or not—that was pretty much irrelevant to Arthur Bradford—but under any circumstances, a poor black woman fired as a servant by a wealthy family would not play well in the press. A politician innately sees this and calculates his response in a matter of seconds; reality and truth must always take a backseat to the gods of sound bite and perception.

Myron pressed on. "According to her family, Anita Slaughter worked here until the day she disappeared."

They both were too smart to bite and say, "Disappeared?," but Myron decided to wait them out anyway. People hate silence and often jump in just to break it. This was an old cop trick: Say nothing and let them dig their own graves with explanations. With politicians the results were always interesting: They were smart enough to know they should keep their mouths shut, yet genetically incapable of doing so.

"I'm sorry," Arthur Bradford said at last. "As I explained earlier, Mother handled these matters."

"Then maybe I should talk to her," Myron said.

"Mother is not well, I'm afraid. She's in her eighties, poor dear."

"I'd still like to try."

"I'm afraid that won't be possible."

There was just a hint of steel in his voice now.

"I see," Myron said. "Do you know who Horace Slaughter is?"

"No," Arthur said. "I assume he's a relative of Anita's?"

"Her husband." Myron looked over at Chance. "You know him?"

"Not that I recall," Chance said. Not that I recall. Like he was on a witness stand, needing to leave himself the out.

"According to his phone records, he's been calling your campaign headquarters a lot lately."

"Many people call our campaign headquarters," Arthur said. Then he added with a small chuckle, "At least I hope they do."

Chance chuckled too. Real yucksters, these Bradford boys.

"Yeah, I guess." Myron looked at Win. Win nodded. Both men stood up.

"Thank you for your time," Win said. "We'll show ourselves out."

The two politicians tried not to look too stunned. Chance finally cracked a bit. "What the hell is this?" Arthur silenced him with a look. He rose to shake hands, but Myron and Win were already at the door.

Myron turned and did his best Columbo. "Funny."

"What?" Arthur Bradford said.

"That you don't remember Anita Slaughter better. I thought you would."

Arthur turned his palms upward. "We've had lots of people work here over the years."

"True," Myron said, stepping through the portal. "But how many of them found your wife's dead body?"

The two men turned to marble—still and smooth and cool. Myron did not wait for more. He released the door and followed Win out.

Chapter 13

As they drove through the gate, Win said, "What exactly did we just accomplish?"

"Two things. One, I wanted to find out if they had something to hide. Now I know they do."

"Based on?"

"Their outright lies and evasiveness."

"They're politicians," Win said. "They'd lie and evade if you asked them what they had for breakfast."

"You don't think there's something there?"

"Actually," Win said, "I do. And thing two?"

"I wanted to stir them up."

Win smiled. He liked that idea. "So what next, Kemo Sabe?"

"We need to investigate Elizabeth Bradford's premature demise," Myron said.

"How?"

"Hop onto South Livingston Avenue. I'll tell you where to make the turn."

The Livingston Police Station sat next to the Livingston Town Hall and across the street from the Livingston Public Library and Livingston High School. A true town center. Myron entered and asked for Officer Francine Neagly. Francine had graduated from the high school across the street the same year as Myron. He'd hoped to get lucky and catch her at the station.

A stern-looking desk sergeant informed Myron that Officer Neagly was "not present at this particular time"—that's how cops talk—but that she had just radioed in for her lunch break and would be at the Ritz Diner.

The Ritz Diner was truly ugly. The formerly workmanlike brick structure had been spray-painted seaweed green with a salmon pink door—a color scheme too gaudy for a Carnival Cruise ship. Myron hated it. In its heyday, when Myron was in high school, the diner had been a run-of-the-mill, unpretentious eatery called the Heritage. It'd been a twenty-four-hour spot back then, owned by Greeks naturally—this seemed to be a state law—and frequented by high school kids grabbing burgers and fries after a Friday or Saturday night of doing nothing. Myron and his friends would don their varsity jackets, go out to a variety of house parties, and end up here. He tried now to remember what he did at those parties, but nothing specific came to mind. He didn't imbibe in high school—alcohol made him sick—and was prudish to the point of Pollyanna when it came to the drug scene. So what did he do at these things? He remembered the music, of course, blaring the Doobie Brothers and Steely Dan and Supertramp, gleaning deep meaning from the lyrics of Blue Oyster Cult songs ("Yo, man, what do you think Eric *really* means when he says, 'I want to do it to your daughter on a dirt road'?"). He remembered occasionally making out with a girl, rarely more, and then their avoiding each other at all costs for the rest of their scholastic lives. But that was pretty much it. You went to the parties because you were afraid you'd miss something. But nothing ever happened. They were all an indistinguishable, monotonous blur now.

What he did remember—what, he guessed, would always remain vivid in the old memory banks—was coming home late and finding his dad feigning sleep in the recliner. It didn't matter what time it was. Two, three in the morning. Myron did not have a curfew. His parents trusted him. But Dad still stayed up every Friday and Saturday night and waited in that recliner and worried and when Myron put his key in the lock, he faked being asleep. Myron knew he was faking. His dad knew Myron knew. But Dad still tried to pull it off every time.

Win elbowed him back to reality. "Are you going to go in, or are we just going to marvel at this monument to *nouveau* tackiness?"

"My friends and I used to hang out here," Myron said. "When I was in high school."

Win looked at the diner, then at Myron. "You guys were the balls."

Win waited in the car. Myron found Francine Neagly at the counter. He sat on the stool next to her and fought off the desire to spin it.

"That police uniform," Myron said, and gave a little whistle. "It's quite the turn-on."

Francine Neagly barely looked up from her burger. "Best part is, I can also use it to strip at bachelor parties."

"Saves on the overhead."

"Right-o." Francine took a bite out of a burger so rare it screamed ouch. "As I live and breathe," she said, "the local hero appears in public."

"Please don't make a fuss."

"Good thing I'm here, though. If the women get out of control, I can shoot them for you." She wiped very greasy hands. "I heard you moved out of town," she said.

"I did."

"Been the opposite around here lately." She grabbed another napkin out of the dispenser. "Most towns, all you hear about is how people want to grow up and move away. But here, well, everyone's coming back to Livingston and raising their own families. Remember Santola? He's back. Three kids. And Friedy? He lives in the Weinbergs' old house. Two kids. Jordan lives by St. Phil's. Fixed up some old piece of shit. Three kids, all girls. I swear, half our class got married and moved back to town."

"How about you and Gene Duluca?" Myron asked with a little smile.

She laughed. "Dumped him my freshman year of college. Christ, we were gross, huh?"

Gene and Francine had been the class couple. They spent lunch hours sitting at a table, French-kissing while eating cafeteria food, both wearing debris-enmeshed braces.

"Gross City," Myron agreed.

She took another bite. "Wanna order something gooey and suck face? See what it was like?"

"If only I had more time."

"That's what they all say. So what can I do for you, Myron?"

"Remember that death at the Bradford place when we were in high school?"

She stopped mid-bite. "A little," she said.

"Who would've handled it for the department?"

She swallowed. "Detective Wickner."

Myron remembered him. Ever-present reflector sunglasses. Very active in Little League. Cared about winning waaaaay too much. Hated the kids once they got into high school and stopped worshiping him. Big on speeding tickets for young drivers. But Myron had always liked the man. Old Americana. As dependable as a good tool set.

"He still on the force?"

Francine shook her head. "Retired. Moved to a lake cabin upstate. But he still comes to town a lot. Hangs out at the fields and shakes hands. They named a backstop after him. Had a big ceremony and everything."

"Sorry I missed that," Myron said. "Would the case file still be at the station?"

"How long ago this happen?"

"Twenty years."

Francine looked at him. Her hair was shorter than in high school, and the braces were gone, but other than that, she looked exactly the same. "In the basement maybe. Why?"

"I need it."

"Just like that."

He nodded.

"You're serious?"

"Yep."

"And you want me to get it for you."

"Yep."

She wiped her hands with a napkin. "The Bradfords are powerful folks."

"Don't I know it."

"You looking to embarrass him or something? He running for governor and all."

"No."

"And I guess you have a good reason for needing it?"

"Yep."

"You want to tell me what it is, Myron?"

"Not if I don't have to."

"How about a teensy-weensy hint?"

"I want to verify that it was an accident."

She looked at him. "You have anything that says otherwise?"

He shook his head. "I barely have a suspicion."

Francine Neagly picked up a fry and examined it. "And if you do find something, Myron, you'll come to me, right? Not the press. Not the bureau boys. Me."

"Deal," Myron said.

She shrugged. "Okay. I'll take a look for it."

Myron handed her his card. "Good seeing you again, Francine."

"Likewise," she said, swallowing another bite. "Hey, you involved with anyone?"

"Yeah," Myron said. "You?"

"No," she said. "But now that you mention it, I think I kinda miss Gene."

Chapter 14

Myron hopped back into the Jaguar. Win started it up and pulled out.

"Your Bradford plan," Win said. "It involved prodding him into action, did it not?"

"It did."

"Then congratulations are in order. The two gentlemen from the Bradfords' foyer did a pass by while you were inside."

"Any sign of them now?"

Win shook his head. "They're probably covering the ends of the road. Someone will pick us up. How would you like to play it?"

Myron thought a moment. "I don't want to tip them off yet. Let them follow us."

"Where to, O wise one?"

Myron checked his watch. "What's your schedule look like?"

"I need to get back to the office by two."

"Can you drop me off at Brenda's practice? I'll get a ride back."

Win nodded. "I live to chauffeur."

They took Route 280 to the New Jersey Turnpike. Win turned on the radio. A commercial voice-over sternly warned people not to buy a mattress over the phone but, rather, to go to Sleepy's and "consult your mattress professional." Mattress professional. Myron wondered if that was a master's program or what.

"Are you armed?" Win asked.

"I left my gun in my car."

"Open the glove compartment."

Myron did. There were three guns and several boxes of ammunition. He frowned. "Expecting an armed invasion?"

"My, what a clever quip," Win said. He gestured to a weapon. "Take the thirty-eight. It's loaded. There's a holster under the car seat."

Myron feigned reluctance, but the truth was, he should have been carrying all along.

Win said, "You realize, of course, that young FJ will not back down."

"Yeah, I know."

"We have to kill him. There is no choice."

"Kill Frank Ache's son? Not even you could survive that."

Win sort of smiled. "Is that a challenge?"

"No," Myron said quickly. "Just don't do anything yet. Please. I'll come up with something."

Win shrugged.

They paid a toll and drove past the Vince Lombardi rest stop. In the distance Myron could still see the Meadowlands Sports Complex. Giants Stadium and the Continental Arena floated above the vast swampland that was East Rutherford, New Jersey. Myron stared off at the arena for a moment, silent, remembering his recent shot at playing pro basketball again. It hadn't worked out, but Myron was over that now. He had been robbed of playing the game he loved, but he'd accepted it, come to terms with reality. He'd put it behind him, had moved on, had let go of his anger.

So what if he still thought about it every day?

"I've done a bit of digging," Win said. "When young FJ was at Princeton, a geology professor accused him of cheating on an exam."

"And?"

"Na, na, na. Na, na, na. Hey, hey, hey. Good-bye."

Myron looked at him. "You're kidding, right?"

"Never found the body," Win said. "The tongue, yes. It was sent to another professor, who'd been considering leveling the same charges."

Myron felt something flitter in his throat. "Might have been Frank, not FJ."

Win shook his head. "Frank is psychotic but not wasteful. If Frank had handled it, he would have used a few colorful threats perhaps punctuated by a few well-placed blows. But this kind of overkill—it's not his style."

Myron thought about it. "Maybe we can talk to Herman or Frank," he said. "Get him off our back."

Win shrugged. "Easier to kill him."

"Please don't."

Another shrug. They kept driving. Win took the Grand Avenue exit. On the right was an enormous complex of town houses. During the mid-eighties, approximately two zillion such complexes had mushroomed across New Jersey. This particular one looked like a staid amusement park or the housing development in *Poltergeist*.

"I don't want to sound maudlin," Myron said, "but if FJ does manage to kill me—"

"I'll spend several fun-filled weeks spreading slivers of his genitalia throughout New England," Win said. "After that, I'll probably kill him."

Myron actually smiled. "Why New England?"

"I like New England," Win said. Then he added, "And I would be lonely in New York without you."

Win pushed the MODE button, and the CD player spun to life. The music from *Rent*. The lovely Mimi was asking Roger to light her candle. Great stuff. Myron looked at his friend. Win said nothing more. To most people, Win seemed about as sentimental as a meat locker. But the fact was, Win just cared for very few people. With those select few, he was surprisingly open; much like his lethal hands, Win struck deep and hard and then backed off, ready to elude.

"Horace Slaughter only had two credit cards," Myron said. "Could you check them out?"

"No ATM?"

"Only off his Visa."

Win nodded, took the card numbers. He dropped Myron off at Englewood High School. The Dolphins were running through a one-on-one defensive drill. One player dribbled in a zigzag formation up the court while the defender bent low and worked on containment. Good drill. Tiring as all hell, but it worked the quads like no other.

There were about a half dozen people in the stands now. Myron took a seat in the front row. Within seconds the coach beelined toward him. She was husky with neatly trimmed black hair, a knit shirt with the New York Dolphins logo on the breast, gray sweatpants, a whistle, and Nike high-tops.

"You Bolitar?" the coach barked.

Her spine was a titanium bar, her face as unyielding as a meter maid's.

"Yes."

"Name's Podich. Jean Podich." She spoke like a drill sergeant. She put her hands behind her back and rocked on her heels a bit. "Used to watch you play, Bolitar. Friggin' awesome."

"Thank you." He almost added *sir*.

"Still play at all?"

"Just pickup games."

"Good. Had a player go down with a twisted ankle. Need someone to fill in for the scrimmage."

"Pardon me?" Coach Podich was not big on using pronouns.

"Got nine players here, Bolitar. Nine. Need a tenth. Plenty of gym clothes in the equipment room. Sneakers too. Go suit up."

This was not a request.

"I need my knee brace," Myron said.

"Got that too, Bolitar. Got it all. The trainer will wrap you up good and tight. Now hustle, man."

She clapped her hands at him, turned, walked away. Myron stayed still for a second. Great. This was just what he needed.

Podich blew her whistle hard enough to squeeze out an internal organ. The players stopped. "Shoot foul shots, take ten," she said. "Then scrimmage."

The players drifted off. Brenda jogged toward him.

"Where you going?" she asked.

"I have to suit up."

Brenda stifled a smile.

"What?" he said.

"The equipment room," Brenda said. "All they have is yellow Lycra shorts."

Myron shook his head. "Then somebody should warn her."

"Who?"

"Your coach. I put on tight yellow shorts, no way anybody's going to concentrate on basketball."

Brenda laughed. "I'll try to maintain a professional demeanor. But if you post me down low, I may be forced to pinch your butt."

"I'm not just a plaything," Myron said, "here for your amusement."

"Too bad." She followed him into the equipment room. "Oh, that lawyer who wrote to my dad," she said. "Thomas Kincaid."

"Yes."

"I remember where I heard his name before. My first scholarship. When I was twelve years old. He was the lawyer in charge."

"What do you mean, in charge?"

"He signed my checks."

Myron stopped. "You received checks from a scholarship?"

"Sure. The scholarship covered everything. Tuition, board, schoolbooks. I wrote out my expenses, and Kincaid signed the checks."

"What was the name of the scholarship?"

"That one? I don't remember. Outreach Education or something like that."

"How long did Kincaid administer the scholarship?"

"It covered through my high school years. I got an athletic scholarship to college, so basketball paid the freight."

"What about medical school?"

"I got another scholarship."

"Same deal?"

"It's a different scholarship, if that's what you mean."

"Does it pay for the same stuff? Tuition, board, the works?"

"Yep."

"Handled by a lawyer again?"

She nodded.

"Do you remember his name?"

"Yeah," she said. "Rick Peterson. He works out of Roseland."

Myron thought about this. Something clicked.

"What?" she asked.

"Do me a favor," he said. "I got to make a couple of calls. Can you stall Frau Brucha for me?"

She shrugged. "I can try."

Brenda left him alone. The equipment room was enormous. An eighty-year-old guy worked the desk. He asked Myron for his sizes. Myron told him. Two minutes later the old man handed Myron a pile of clothes. Purple T-shirt, black socks with blue stripes, white jockstrap, green sneakers, and, of course, yellow Lycra shorts.

Myron frowned. "I think you missed a color," he said.

The old man gave him the eye. "I got a red sports bra, if you're interested."

Myron thought about it but ultimately declined.

He slipped on his shirt and jock. Pulling on the shorts was like pulling on a wet suit. Everything felt compressed—not a bad feeling, actually. He grabbed his cellular phone and hurried to the trainer's room. On the way he passed a mirror. He looked like a box of Crayolas left too long on a windowsill. He lay on a bench and dialed the office. Esperanza answered.

"MB SportsReps."

"Where's Cyndi?" Myron asked.

"At lunch."

A mental image of Godzilla snacking on Tokyo's citizenry flashed in front of his eyes.

"And she doesn't like to be called just Cyndi," Esperanza added. "It's Big Cyndi."

"Pardon my overabundance of political sensitivity. Do you have the list of Horace Slaughter's phone calls?"

"Yes."

"Any to a lawyer named Rick Peterson?"

The pause was brief. "You're a regular Mannix," she said. "Five of them."

Wheels were beginning to churn in Myron's head. Never a good thing. "Any other messages?"

"Two calls from the Witch."

"Please don't call her that," Myron said.

Witch was actually an improvement over what Esperanza usually called Jessica (hint: rhymes with *Witch* but starts with the letter *B*). Myron had recently hoped for a thawing between the two—Jessica had invited Esperanza to lunch—but he now recognized that nothing short of a thermonuclear meltdown would soften that particular spread of earth. Some mistook this for jealousy. Not so. Five years ago Jessica had hurt Myron. Esperanza had watched it happen. She had seen up close the devastation.

Some people held grudges; Esperanza clutched them and tied them around her waist and used cement and Krazy glue to hold them steady.

"Why does she call here anyway?" Esperanza half snapped. "Doesn't she know your cellular number?"

"She only uses it for emergencies."

Esperanza made a noise like she was gagging on a soup ladle. "You two have such a mature relationship."

"Can I just have the message please?"

"She wants you to call her. At the Beverly Wilshire. Room six-one-eight. Must be the Bitch Suite."

So much for improvement. Esperanza read off the number. Myron jotted it down.

"Anything else?"

"Your mom called. Don't forget dinner tonight. Your dad is barbecuing. A potpourri of aunts and uncles will be in attendance."

"Okay, thanks. I'll see you this afternoon."

"Can't wait," she said. Then she hung up.

Myron sat back. Jessica had called twice. Hmm.

The trainer tossed Myron a leg brace. Myron strapped it on, fastening it with Velcro. The trainer silently worked on the knee, starting with stretch wrap. Myron debated calling Jessica back right now and decided he still had time. Lying back with his head on a sponge pillow of some sort, he dialed the Beverly Wilshire and asked for Jessica's room. She picked up as though she'd had her hand on the receiver.

"Hello?" Jessica said.

"Hello there, gorgeous," he said. Charm. "What are you doing?"

"I just spread out a dozen snapshots of you on the floor," she said.

"I was about to strip naked, coat my entire body with some type of oil, and then undulate on them."

Myron looked up at the trainer. "Er, can I have an ice pack?"

The trainer looked puzzled. Jessica laughed.

"Undulate," Myron said. "That's a good word."

"Me a writer," Jessica said.

"So how's the left coast?" Left coast. Hip lingo.

"Sunny," she said. "There's too much damn sun here."

"So come home."

There was a pause. Then Jessica said, "I have some good news."

"Oh?"

"Remember that production company that optioned *Control Room*?"

"Sure."

"They want me to produce it and cowrite the screenplay. Isn't that cool?"

Myron said nothing. A steel band wrapped around his chest.

"It'll be great," she continued, forcing pseudojocularity into the cautious tone. "I'll fly home on weekends. Or you can fly out here sometimes. Say, you can do some recruiting out here, nab some West Coast clients. It'll be great."

Silence. The trainer finished up and left the room. Myron was afraid to speak. Seconds passed.

"Don't be like that," Jessica said. "I know you're not happy about this. But it'll work out. I'll miss you like mad—you know that—but Hollywood always screws up my books. It's too big an opportunity."

Myron opened his mouth, closed it, started again. "Please come home."

"Myron . . ."

He closed his eyes. "Don't do this."

"I'm not doing anything."

"You're running away, Jess. It's what you do best."

Silence.

"That's not fair," she said.

"Screw fair. I love you."

"I love you too."

"Then come home," he said.

Myron's grip on the phone was tight. His muscles were tensing. In the background he heard Coach Podich blow that damn whistle.

"You still don't trust me," Jessica said softly. "You're still afraid."

"And you've done so much to assuage my fears, right?" He was surprised by the edge in his voice.

The old image jarred him anew. Doug. A guy named Doug. Five years ago. Or was he a Dougie? Myron bet he was. He bet his friends called him Dougie. Yo, Dougie, wanna party, man? Probably called her Jessie. Dougie and Jessie. Five years ago. Myron had walked in on them, and his heart had crumbled as though it'd been molded in ash.

"I can't change what happened," Jessica said.

"I know that."

"So what do you want from me?"

"I want you to come home. I want us to be together."

More cellular static. Coach Podich called out his name. Myron could feel something vibrating in his chest like a tuning fork.

"You're making a mistake," Jessica said. "I know I've had some trouble with commitment before—"

"*Some* trouble?"

"—but this isn't like that. I'm not running away. You're pushing on the wrong issue."

"Maybe I am," he said. He closed his eyes. It was hard for him to breathe. He should hang up now. He should be tougher, show some pride, stop wearing his heart on his sleeve, hang up. "Just come home," he said. "Please."

He could feel their distance, a continent separating them, their voices bypassing millions of people.

"Let's both take a deep breath," she said. "Maybe this isn't for the phone anyway."

More silence.

"Look, I got a meeting," she said. "Let's talk later, okay?"

She hung up then. Myron held the empty receiver. He was alone. He stood. His legs were shaky.

Brenda met him at the doorway. A towel was draped around her neck. Her face was shiny from sweat. She took one look at him and said, "What's wrong?"

"Nothing."

She kept her eyes on him. She didn't believe him, but she wouldn't push either.

"Nice outfit," she said.

Myron looked down at his clothing. "I was going to wear a red sports bra," he said. "It throws the whole look together."

"Yummy," she said.

He managed a smile. "Let's go."

They started heading down the corridor.

"Myron?"

"Yeah?"

"We talk a lot about me." She continued walking, not looking at him. "Wouldn't kill either of us to switch roles now and again. Might even be nice."

Myron nodded, said nothing. Much as he might wish to be more like Clint Eastwood or John Wayne, Myron was not the silent type, not a macho tough guy who kept all his problems inside him. He confided to Win and Esperanza all the time. But neither one of them was helpful when it came to Jessica. Esperanza hated her so much that she could never think rationally on the subject. And in Win's case, well, Win was simply not the man to discuss matters of the heart. His views on the subject could conservatively be called "scary."

When they reached the edge of the court, Myron pulled up short. Brenda looked at him questioningly. Two men stood on the sidelines. Ragged brown suits, totally devoid of any sense of style or fashion. Weary faces, short hair, big guts. No doubt in Myron's mind.

Cops.

Somebody pointed at Myron and Brenda. The two men sauntered over with a sigh. Brenda looked puzzled. Myron moved a little closer to her. The two men stopped directly in front of them.

"Are you Brenda Slaughter?" one asked.

"Yes."

"I am Detective David Pepe of the Mahwah Police Department. This is Detective Mike Rinsky. We'd like you to come with us please."

Chapter 15

Myron stepped forward. "What's this about?"

The two cops looked at him with flat eyes. "And you are?"

"Myron Bolitar."

The two cops blinked. "And Myron Bolitar is?"

"Miss Slaughter's attorney," Myron said.

One cop looked at the other. "That was fast."

Second cop: "Wonder why she called her attorney already."

"Weird, huh?"

"I'd say." He looked the multicolored Myron up and down. Smirked. "You don't dress like an attorney, Mr. Bolitar."

"I left my gray vest at home," Myron said. "What do you guys want?"

"We would like to bring Miss Slaughter to the station," the first cop said.

"Is she under arrest?"

First Cop looked at Second Cop. "Don't lawyers know that when we arrest people, we read them their rights?"

"Probably got his degree at home. Maybe from that Sally Struthers school."

"Got his law degree and VCR repairman certificate in one."

"Right. Like that."

"Or maybe he went to that American Bartenders Institute. They got a competitive program, I hear."

Myron crossed his arms. "Whenever you guys are through. But please keep going. You're both extremely amusing."

First Cop sighed. "We'd like to bring Miss Slaughter to the station," he said again.

"Why?"

"To talk."

Boy, this was moving along nicely. "Why do you want to talk to her?" Myron tried.

"Not us," Second Cop said.

"Right, not us."

"We're just supposed to pick her up."

"Like escorts."

Myron was about to make a comment on their being male escorts, but Brenda put her hand on his forearm. "Let's just go," she said.

"Smart lady," First Cop said.

"Needs a new lawyer," Second Cop added.

Myron and Brenda sat in the back of an unmarked police car that a blind man could tell was an unmarked police car. It was a brown sedan, the same brown as the cops' suits, a Chevrolet Caprice with simply too much antenna.

For the first ten minutes of the ride nobody spoke. Brenda's face was set. She moved her hand along the seat closer until it touched his. Then she left it there. She looked at him. The hand felt warm and nice. He tried to look confident, but he had a terrible sinking feeling in the pit of his stomach.

They drove down Route 4 and up Route 17. Mahwah. Nice suburb, almost on the New York border. They parked behind the Mahwah municipal building. The entrance to the station was in the back. The two cops led them into an interrogation room. There was a metal table bolted to the floor and four chairs. No hot lamp. A mirror took up half a wall. Only a moron who never, ever watched television didn't know that it was a one-way mirror. Myron often wondered if anybody was fooled by that anymore. Even if you never watched TV, why would the police need a giant mirror in an interrogation room? Vanity?

They were left alone.

"What do you think this is about?" Brenda asked.

Myron shrugged. He had a pretty good idea. But speculating at this stage was worthless. They would find out soon enough. Ten minutes passed. Not a good sign. Another five. Myron decided to call their bluff.

"Let's go," he said.

"What?"

"We don't have to wait around here. Let's go."

As if on cue, the door opened. A man and a woman entered. The man was big and barrellike with explosions of hair everyplace. He had a mustache so thick it made Teddy Roosevelt's look like a limp eyelash. His hairline was low, the kind of low where you can't tell where the eyebrow ends and the actual hairline begins. He looked like a member of the Politburo. His pants were stretched tautly in the front, creasing obscenely, yet his lack of an ass made them too big in the back. His shirt was also too tight. The collar strangled him. The rolled-up sleeves worked the forearms like tourniquets. He was red-faced and angry.

For those with a scorecard, this would be your Bad Cop.

The woman wore a gray skirt with her detective shield on the waistband and a high-neck white blouse. She was early thirties, blond with freckles and pink cheeks. Healthy-looking. If she were a veal entrée, the menu would describe her as "milk-fed."

She smiled at them warmly. "Sorry to keep you waiting." Nice, even teeth. "My name is Detective Maureen McLaughlin. I'm with the Bergen County Prosecutor's Office. This is Detective Dan Tiles. He works for the Mahwah Police Department."

Tiles did not say anything. He folded his arms and glowered at Myron like he was a vagrant urinating in his garden. Myron looked up at him.

"Tiles," Myron repeated. "As in the porcelain things in my bathroom?"

McLaughlin kept up the smile. "Miss Slaughter—may I call you Brenda?"

Already with the friendly.

Brenda said, "Yes, Maureen."

"Brenda, I'd like to ask you a few questions, if that's okay."

Myron said, "What's this all about?"

Maureen McLaughlin flashed him the smile now. With the freckles it made for a very pert look. "Can I get either of you something? A coffee maybe? A cold beverage?"

Myron stood. "Let's go, Brenda."

"Whoa," McLaughlin said. "Settle down a second, okay? What's the problem?"

"The problem is you won't tell us why we're here," Myron said. "Plus you used the word *beverage* in casual conversation."

Tiles spoke for the first time. "Tell them," he said. His mouth never moved. But the shrub below his nose bounced up and down. Kinda like Yosemite Sam.

McLaughlin suddenly looked distraught. "I can't just blurt it out, Dan. That wouldn't—"

"Tell them," Tiles said again.

Myron motioned at them. "You guys rehearse this?" But he was flailing now. He knew what was coming. He just did not want to hear it.

"Please," McLaughlin said. The smile was gone. "Please sit down."

They both slid slowly back into their seats. Myron folded his hands and put them on the table.

McLaughlin seemed to be considering her words. "Do you have a boyfriend, Brenda?"

"You running a dating service?" Myron said.

Tiles stepped away from the wall. He reached out and picked up Myron's right hand for a moment. He dropped it and picked up his left. He studied it, looked disgusted, put it back down.

Myron tried not to look confused. "Palmolive," he said. "More than just mild."

Tiles moved away, recrossed his arms. "Tell them," he said again.

McLaughlin's eyes were only on Brenda now. She leaned forward a little and lowered her voice. "Your father is dead, Brenda. We found his body three hours ago. I'm sorry."

Myron had steeled himself, but the words still hit like a falling meteorite. He gripped the table and felt his head spin. Brenda said nothing. Her face didn't change, but her breathing became shallow gulps.

McLaughlin did not leave much time for condolences. "I realize that this is a very tough time, but we really need to ask you a few questions."

"Get out," Myron said.

"What?"

"I want you and Stalin to get the hell out of here right now. This interview is over."

Tiles said, "You got something to hide, Bolitar?"

"Yeah, that's it, wolf boy. Now get out."

Brenda still had not moved. She looked at McLaughlin and uttered one word. "How?"

"How what?"

Brenda swallowed. "How was he murdered?"

Tiles almost leaped across the room. "How did you know he was murdered?"

"What?"

"We didn't say anything about murder," Tiles said. He looked very pleased with himself. "Just that your father was dead."

Myron rolled his eyes. "You got us, Tiles. Two cops drag us in here, play Sipowicz and Simone, and somehow we figure that her father didn't die of natural causes. Either we're psychic or we did it."

"Shut up, asshole."

Myron stood up quickly, knocking over his chair. He went eyeball to eyeball with Tiles. "Get out."

"Or?"

"You want a piece of me, Tiles?"

"Love it, hotshot."

McLaughlin stepped between them. "You boys sprinkle on a little extra testosterone this morning? Back off, both of you."

Myron kept his eyes on Tiles's. He took several deep breaths. He was acting irrationally. He knew that. Stupid to lose control. He had to get his act together. Horace was dead. Brenda was in trouble. He had to keep calm.

Myron picked up his chair and sat back down. "My client will not talk to you until we confer."

"Why?" Brenda said to him. "What's the big deal?"

"They think you did it," Myron said.

That surprised her. Brenda turned to McLaughlin. "Am I a suspect?"

McLaughlin gave a friendly, on-your-side shrug. "Hey, it's too early to rule anybody in or out."

"That's cop-speak for yes," Myron said.

"Shut up, asshole." Tiles again.

Myron ignored him. "Answer her question, McLaughlin. How was her father killed?"

McLaughlin leaned back, weighing her options. "Horace Slaughter was shot in the head."

Brenda closed her eyes.

Dan Tiles moved in again. "At close range," he added.

"Right, close range. Back of the head."

"Close range," Tiles repeated. He put his fists on the table. Then he leaned in closer. "Like maybe he knew the killer. Like maybe it was somebody he trusted."

Myron pointed at him. "You got some food stuck in your mustache. Looks like scrambled eggs."

Tiles leaned in closer until their noses almost touched. He had big pores. Really big pores. Myron almost feared he'd fall into one. "I don't like your attitude, asshole."

Myron leaned in a bit too. Then he gently shook his head from side to side, nose tip making contact with nose tip. "If we were Eskimos," Myron said, "we'd be engaged right now."

That backed Tiles up. When he recovered, he said, "Your acting like an ass doesn't change the facts: Horace Slaughter was shot at close range."

"Which means squat, Tiles. If you were part of a real force, you'd know that most assassins for hire shoot their victims at close range.

Most family members don't." Myron had no idea if that was true, but it sounded good.

Brenda cleared her throat. "Where was he shot?"

"Excuse me?" McLaughlin said.

"Where was he shot?"

"I just told you. In the head."

"No, I mean where. What city?"

But of course they had known that she meant that. They did not want to tell her, hoping to trip her up.

Myron answered the question. "He was found here in Mahwah." Then he looked at Tiles. "And before Magnum PI pounces again, I know that because we're in the Mahwah police station. The only reason for that is that the body was found here."

McLaughlin did not respond directly. She folded her hands in front of her. "Brenda, when was the last time you saw your father?"

"Don't answer," Myron said.

"Brenda?"

Brenda looked at Myron. Her eyes were wide and unfocused. She was fighting to hold it all back, and the strain was starting to show. Her voice was almost a plea. "Let's just get through this, okay?"

"I'm advising you against it."

"Good advice," Tiles said. "If you got something to hide."

Myron looked at Tiles. "I can't tell. Is that a mustache or really long nostril hair?"

McLaughlin remained overly earnest, a perp's dearest chum. "It's like this, Brenda. If you can answer our questions now, we can end this. If you clam up, well, we'll have to wonder why. It won't look good, Brenda. It'll look like you've got something to hide. And then there's the media."

Myron put his hand out. "What?"

Tiles handled this one. "Simple, asshole. You lawyer her up, we tell the media she's a suspect and that she wouldn't cooperate." He smiled. "Miss Slaughter here will be lucky to endorse condoms."

Momentary silence. Striking an agent where he lives.

"When did you last see your father, Brenda?"

Myron was about to interrupt, but Brenda silenced him by putting her hand on his forearm. "Nine days ago."

"Under what circumstances?"

"We were in his apartment."

"Please continue."

"Continue with what?" Myron interrupted. Rule twenty-six of

lawyering: Never let the interrogator—cop or fellow attorney—get a rhythm. "You asked her when she last saw her father. She told you."

"I asked under what circumstances," McLaughlin replied. "Brenda, please tell me what occurred during your visit."

"You know what occurred," Brenda said.

That put her a step ahead of Myron.

Maureen McLaughlin nodded. "I have in my possession a sworn complaint." She slid a piece of paper across the metal table. "Is that your signature, Brenda?"

"Yes."

Myron took the sheet and began to skim it.

"Does that accurately describe your last meeting with your father?"

Brenda's eyes were hard now. "Yes."

"So on this occasion at your father's apartment—the last time you saw him—your father assaulted you both physically and verbally. Is that correct?"

Myron kept still.

"He shoved me," Brenda said.

"Hard enough for you to want a restraining order, isn't that correct?"

Myron tried to keep pace, but he was starting to feel like a buoy in rough waters. Horace had assaulted his own daughter and was now dead. Myron had to get a handle on this, get back into the fray.

"Stop badgering," he said, his voice sounding weak and forced. "You have the documentation, so let's get on with it."

"Brenda, please tell me about your father's assault."

"He pushed me," she said.

"Can you tell me why?"

"No."

"No, you won't tell me. Or no, you don't know."

"No, I don't know."

"He just shoved you?"

"Yes."

"You walked into his apartment. You said, 'Hi, Dad.' Then he cursed at you and assaulted you. Is that what you're telling us?"

Brenda was trying to keep her face steady, but there was shaking near the fault lines. The facade was about to crack.

"That's enough," Myron said.

But McLaughlin moved in. "Is that what you're trying to tell us, Brenda? Your father's attack was completely unprovoked?"

"She's not telling you anything, McLaughlin. Back off."

"Brenda—"

"We're out of here." Myron took hold of Brenda's arm and half dragged her to a standing position. Tiles moved to block the door.

McLaughlin kept talking. "We can help you, Brenda. But this is your last chance. You walk out of here, you're talking a murder indictment."

Brenda seemed to snap out of whatever trance she'd been in. "What are you talking about?"

"They're bluffing," Myron said.

"You know how this looks, don't you?" McLaughlin continued. "Your father has been dead awhile. We haven't done an autopsy yet, but I'd bet he's been dead for close to a week. You're a smart girl, Brenda. You put it together. The two of you had problems. We have your own list of serious grievances right here. Nine days ago he assaulted you. You went to court to get him to keep away from you. Our theory is that your father did not obey that order. He was clearly a violent man, probably angered beyond control by what he perceived as your disloyalty. Is that what happened, Brenda?"

Myron said, "Don't answer."

"Let me help you, Brenda. Your father didn't listen to the court order, right? He came after you, didn't he?"

Brenda said nothing.

"You were his daughter. You disobeyed him. You publicly humiliated him, so much so that he decided to teach you a lesson. And when he came after you—when that big, scary man was going to attack you again—you had no choice. You shot him. It was self-defense, Brenda. I understand that. I would have done the same thing. But if you walk out that door, Brenda, I can't help you. It moves from something justifiable to cold-blooded murder. Plain and simple."

McLaughlin took her hand. "Let me help you, Brenda."

The room went still. McLaughlin's freckled face was totally earnest, the perfect mask of concern and trust and openness. Myron glanced over at Tiles. Tiles quickly diverted his gaze.

Myron didn't like that.

McLaughlin had laid out a neat little theory. It made sense. Myron could see why they would believe it. There was bad blood between father and daughter. A well-documented history of abuse. A court order . . .

Hold the phone.

Myron looked back over at Tiles. Tiles would still not meet his eyes.

Then Myron remembered the blood on the shirt in the locker. The cops didn't know about that, couldn't know about it. . . .

"She wants to see her father," Myron blurted out.

Everybody looked at him. "Excuse me?"

"His body. We want to see Horace Slaughter's body."

"That won't be necessary," McLaughlin said. "We've positively identified him through fingerprints. There's no reason to put—"

"Are you denying Miss Slaughter the opportunity to view her father's body?"

McLaughlin backpedaled a bit. "Of course not. If that's what you really want, Brenda—"

"That's what we want."

"I'm speaking to Brenda—"

"I'm her attorney, Detective. You speak to me."

McLaughlin stopped. Then she shook her head and turned to Tiles. Tiles shrugged.

"Okay then," McLaughlin said. "We'll drive you over."

Chapter 16

The Bergen County Medical Examiner's Office looked like a small elementary school. It was one level, red brick, right angles, and as unassuming a building as one could construct, but then again, what did you want in a morgue? The waiting room chairs were molded plastic and about as comfortable as a pinched nerve. Myron had been here once before, not long after Jessica's father had been murdered. The memory was not a pleasant one.

"We can go in now," McLaughlin said.

Brenda stayed close to Myron as they all walked down a short corridor. He put his arm around her waist. She moved in a touch. He was comforting her. He knew that. He also knew that it shouldn't have felt so right.

They entered a room of gleaming metal and tile. No big storage drawers or anything like that. Clothes—a security guard's uniform—was in a plastic bag in one corner. All the instruments and utensils and what-have-you's were in another corner, covered by a sheet. So was the table in the center. Myron could see right away that the body underneath it belonged to a big man.

They paused at the door before gathering around the gurney. With minimum fanfare, a man—Myron assumed he was the medical examiner—pulled the sheet back. For the briefest of moments, Myron thought that maybe the cops had screwed up the ID. It was a whimsical hope, he realized, not anything based on fact. He was sure it ran through every person's mind who came here to identify someone, even when he knew the truth, a last gasp, a fantasy that a wonderful, beautiful mistake had been made. It was only natural.

But there was no mistake here.

Brenda's eyes filled. She tilted her head and screwed up her mouth. Her hand reached out and brushed the still cheek.

"That's enough," McLaughlin said.

The medical examiner started pulling the sheet back. But Myron reached his hand out and stopped him. He looked down at the remains of his old friend. He felt tears sting his own eyes, but he forced them back. Now was not the time. He had come here for a purpose.

"The bullet wound," Myron said, his voice thick. "It's in the back of the head?"

The medical examiner glanced at McLaughlin. McLaughlin nodded. "Yes," the medical examiner said. "I cleaned him up when I heard you were coming."

Myron pointed to Horace's right cheek. "What's that?"

The medical examiner looked nervous. "I have not yet had the time to properly analyze the body."

"I didn't ask you for an analysis, Doctor. I asked you about this."

"Yes, I understand that. But I do not wish to make any suppositions until I perform a complete autopsy."

"Well, Doctor, it's a bruise," Myron said. "And it happened premortem. You can tell by the lividity and coloring." Myron had no idea if that was true, but he ran with it. "His nose also appears to be broken, does it not, Doctor?"

"Don't answer that," McLaughlin said.

"He doesn't have to." Myron started leading Brenda away from the shell that was once her father. "Nice try, McLaughlin. Call us a taxi. We're not saying another word to you."

When they were alone outside, Brenda said, "Do you want to tell me what that was all about?"

"They were trying to con you."

"How?"

"For the sake of argument, let's say you did murder your father. The police are questioning you. You're nervous. Suddenly they give you the perfect out."

"That self-defense stuff."

"Right. Justifiable homicide. They pretend they're on your side, that they understand. You as the killer would jump at the chance, right?"

"If I were the killer, yeah, I guess I would."

"But you see, McLaughlin and Tiles knew about those bruises."

"So?"

"So if you shot your father in self-defense, why was he beaten beforehand?"

"I don't understand."

"Here's how it works. They get you to confess. You follow their lead, come up with a story about how he attacked you and how you had to shoot him. But the problem is, if that's the case, where did the facial bruises come from? All of a sudden, McLaughlin and Tiles produce this new physical evidence that contradicts your version of the events. So what are you left with? A confession you can't retract. With that in hand, they use the bruises to show it wasn't self-defense. You've screwed yourself."

Brenda chewed that over. "So they figure someone beat him right before he was killed?"

"Right."

She frowned. "But do they really believe I could have beaten him up like that?"

"Probably not."

"So how are they figuring?"

"Maybe you surprised him with a baseball bat or something. But more likely—and this is the tricky part—they think you had an accomplice. You remember how Tiles checked my hands?"

She nodded.

"He was looking for bruised knuckles or some other telltale sign of trauma. When you punch somebody, your hand usually shows it."

"And that's also why she asked me about a boyfriend?"

"Right."

The sun was starting to weaken a bit. Traffic whizzed by. There was a parking lot across the street. A sprinkling of men and women in business suits trudged to their cars after a day of unnatural office light, their faces pale, their eyes blinking.

"So they believe that Dad was beaten right before he was shot," she said.

"Yes."

"But we know that it probably isn't true."

Myron nodded. "The blood in the locker. My guess is, your father was beaten a day or two before. Either he got away or the beating was just a warning. He went to his locker at St. Barnabas to clean up. He used a shirt to stop the blood flowing out of his nose. Then he ran away."

"And someone found him and shot him."

"Yes."

"Shouldn't we tell the police about the bloody shirt?"

"I'm not sure. Think about it a second. The cops firmly believe you did it. Now you produce a shirt with your dad's blood on it. Is that going to help us or hurt us?"

Brenda nodded and suddenly turned away. Her breathing became funny again. Too much too fast, Myron thought. He stayed back and gave her a little space. His heart started swelling up. Mother and father both gone, no sisters or brothers. What must that feel like?

A taxi pulled up a few minutes later. Brenda faced him again.

"Where do you want to be dropped off?" Myron asked. "A friend's house? Your aunt's?"

She thought about it. Then she shook her head and met his gaze. "Actually," she said, "I'd like to stay with you."

Chapter 17

The taxi pulled up to the Bolitar house in Livingston.

"We can go somewhere else," he tried again.

She shook her head. "Just do me one favor."

"What?"

"Don't tell them about my father. Not tonight."

He sighed. "Yeah, okay."

Uncle Sidney and Aunt Selma were already there. So were Uncle Bernie and Aunt Sophie and their boys. Other cars pulled up as he paid the taxi driver. Mom sprinted down the driveway and hugged Myron as though he'd just been released by Hamas terrorists. She also hugged Brenda. So did everyone else. Dad was in the back at the barbecue. A gas grill now, thank goodness, so Dad could stop loading on the lighter fluid with a hose. He wore a chef's hat somewhat taller than a control tower and an apron that read REFORMED VEGE-TARIAN. Brenda was introduced as a client. Mom quickly grabbed her away from Myron, threading her arm through Brenda's, and led her into the house for a tour. More people came. The neighbors. Each with a pasta salad or fruit salad or something. The Dempseys and the Cohens and the Daleys and the Weinsteins. The Brauns had finally surrendered to the warm allure of Florida, and a couple younger than Myron with two kids had moved in. They came over too.

The festivities began. A Wiffle ball and bat were produced. Teams were chosen. When Myron swung and missed, everyone fell down as though from the breeze. Funny. Everyone talked with Brenda. They wanted to hear about the new women's league, but they were far more impressed when they heard Brenda was going to be a doctor. Dad even let Brenda take over the grill for a while, a move for Dad tantamount to donating a kidney. The smell of charred foods filled the air. Chicken and burgers and hot dogs from Don's deli (Mom bought her hot dogs only from Don) and shish kebabs and even a few salmon steaks for the health-conscious.

Myron kept meeting Brenda's eye. Brenda kept smiling.

Kids, all dutifully wearing helmets, parked their bikes at the end of the driveway. The Cohens' kid had gotten an earring. Everyone ribbed him about it. He slumped his head and smiled. Vic Ruskin gave Myron a stock tip. Myron nodded and promptly forgot it. Fred Dempsey grabbed a basketball from the garage. The Daley girl picked teams. Myron had to play. So did Brenda. Everyone laughed. Myron downed a cheeseburger between points. Delicious. Timmy Ruskin fell down and cut his knee. He cried. Brenda bent down and examined the cut. She put on a Band-Aid and smiled at Timmy. Timmy beamed.

Hours passed. Darkness crept in slowly as it does in suburban summer skies. People began to drift home. Cars and bikes faded away. Fathers threw their arms around sons. Little girls rode home on shoulders. Everyone kissed Mom and Dad good-bye. Myron looked at his parents. They were the only original family left in the neighborhood now, the surrogate grandparents of the block. They suddenly looked old to Myron. That scared him.

Brenda came up behind him. "This is wonderful," she said to him.

And it was. Win might poke fun at it. Jessica did not care for scenes like these—her own family had created the perfect Rockwellian facade to hide the rot below—and rushed back to the city as though it held an antidote. Myron and Jess often drove back from such events in total silence. Myron thought about that. And he thought again what Win had said about taking leaps of faith.

"I miss your father," Myron said. "I haven't talked to him in ten years. But I still miss him."

She nodded. "I know."

They helped clean up. Not much to it. They'd used only paper plates and cups and plastic utensils. Brenda and Mom laughed the whole time. Mom kept sneaking glances at Myron. The looks were a little too knowing.

"I always wanted Myron to be a doctor," Mom said. "Isn't that a shock? A Jewish mother who wants her son to be a doctor?"

Both women laughed.

"But he faints at the sight of blood," Mom continued. "Can't stand it. Myron wouldn't even go to an R-rated movie until he was in college. Slept with a night-light until he was—"

"Mom."

"Oh, I'm embarrassing him. I'm your mother, Myron. I'm supposed to embarrass you. Isn't that right, Brenda?"

"Definitely, Mrs. Bolitar."

"For the tenth time, it's Ellen. And Myron's father is Al. Everyone calls us El Al. Get it? Like the Israeli airline."

"Mom."

"Shush, you, I'm going. Brenda, you'll stay tonight? The guest room is all ready for you."

"Thank you, Ellen. That would be very nice."

Mom turned. "I'll leave you kids alone." Her smile was too happy.

The backyard fell silent. A full moon was the only source of illumination. Crickets hummed. A dog barked. They started walking. They talked about Horace. Not about the murder. Not about why he vanished or about Anita Slaughter or FJ or the league or the Bradfords or any of that. Just about Horace.

They reached Burnet Hill, Myron's elementary school. A few years ago the town had closed down half the building because of its proximity to high-tension electromagnetic wires. Myron had spent three years under those wires. Might explain a few things.

Brenda sat on a swing. Her skin glistened in the moonlight. She started swinging, kicking her legs high. He sat on the swing next to her and joined her in the air. The metal apparatus was strong, but it still started swaying a bit under their onslaught.

They slowed.

"You haven't asked about the assault," she said.

"There will be time."

"It's a pretty simple story," she said.

Myron said nothing, waited.

"I came to Dad's apartment. He was drunk. Dad didn't drink much. When he did, it really hit him. He was barely coherent when I opened the door. He started cursing me. He called me a little bitch. Then he pushed me."

Myron shook his head, not sure what to say.

Brenda stopped the swing. "He also called me Anita," she said.

Myron's throat went dry. "He thought you were your mother?"

Brenda nodded. "He had such hate in his eyes," she said. "I've never seen him look like that."

Myron stayed still. A theory had been slowly taking shape in his mind. The blood in the locker at St. Barnabas. The call to the lawyers and to the Bradfords. Horace's running away. His being murdered. It all sort of fit. But right now, it was just a theory based on the purest of speculation. He needed to sleep on it, marinate the whole thing in the brain fridge for a while, before he dared articulate it.

"How far is it to the Bradfords' place?" Brenda asked.

"Half a mile maybe."

She looked away from him. "Do you still think my mom ran away because of something that happened in that house?"

"Yes."

She stood. "Let's walk over there."

"There's nothing to see. A big gate and some shrubs."

"My mother walked through those gates for six years. That'll be enough. For now."

They took the path between Ridge Drive and Coddington Terrace—Myron could not believe it was still here after all these years—and made a right. The lights on the hill were visible from here. Not much else. Brenda approached the gate. The security guard squinted at her. She stopped in front of the iron bars. She stared for several seconds.

The guard leaned out. "Can I help you, ma'am?"

Brenda shook her head and moved away.

They got back to the house late. Myron's father was feigning sleep in the recliner. Some habits die hard. Myron "woke" him up. He startled to consciousness. Pacino never overacted this much. He smiled good night at Brenda. Myron kissed his father on the cheek. The cheek felt rough and smelled faintly of Old Spice. As it should.

The bed was made in the downstairs guest room. The maid must have been in that day because Mom stayed away from domestic chores as though they were radioactive. She had been a working mother, one of the most feared defense attorneys in the state, since the days before Gloria Steinem.

His parents saved toiletry bags from first-class flights. He gave one to Brenda. He also found her a T-shirt and pajama bottoms.

When she kissed him hard on the mouth, he felt every part of him stir. The excitement of a first kiss, the brand-newness of it, the wondrous taste and smell of her. Her body, substantial and hard and young, pressed against his. Myron had never felt so lost, so heady, so weightless. When their tongues met, Myron felt a jolt and heard himself groan.

He pulled back. "We shouldn't. Your father just died. You—"

She shut him up with another kiss. Myron cupped the back of her head with his palm. He felt tears come to his eyes as he held on.

When the kiss ended, they held each other tightly, gasping.

"If you tell me I'm doing this because I'm vulnerable," she said, "you're wrong. And you know you're wrong."

He swallowed. "Jessica and I are going through a rough patch right now."

"This isn't about that either," she said.

He nodded. He did know that. And after a decade of loving the same woman, maybe that was what scared him most of all. He stepped back.

"Good night," he managed.

Myron rushed downstairs to his old room in the basement. He crawled under the sheets and pulled them up to his neck. He stared up at the frayed posters of John Havlicek and Larry Bird. Havlicek, the old Celtic great, had been on his wall since he was six years old. Bird had joined him in 1979. Myron sought comfort and maybe escape in his old room, in surrounding himself with familiar images.

He found none.

Chapter 18

The ring of the phone and the muffled voices invaded his sleep, becoming part of his dream. When Myron opened his eyes, he remembered little. He'd been younger in the dream, and he felt a deep sadness as he'd floated up toward consciousness. He closed his eyes again, trying to claw back into that warm, nocturnal realm. The second ring blew away the fading images like so much cloud dust.

He reached for his cell phone. As it had for the past three years, the bedside clock blinked 12:00 A.M. Myron checked his watch. Almost seven in the morning.

"Hello?"

"Where are you?"

It took Myron a moment to place the voice. Officer Francine Neagly, his old high school buddy.

"Home," he croaked.

"Remember the Halloween scare?"

"Yeah."

"Meet me there in a half hour," she said.

"Did you get the file?"

Click.

Myron hung up the phone. He took a few deep breaths. Great. Now what?

Through the vents he heard the muffled voices again. They were coming from the kitchen. Years down here had given him the ability to tell by the echo in what room of the house a certain sound originated—not unlike the Indian brave in an old western who puts his ear to the ground to calculate the distance of incoming hoofbeats.

Myron swung his legs out of the bed. He massaged his face with his palms. He threw on a velour bathrobe circa 1978, gave the teeth a quick brush, the hair a quick pat, and headed to the kitchen.

Brenda and Mom sipped coffee at the kitchen table. Instant coffee, Myron knew. *Muy* watery. Mom wasn't big on better coffees. The wondrous smell of fresh bagels, however, jump-started his stomach. A bowlful of them along with an assortment of spreads and sev-

eral newspapers adorned the tabletop. A typical Sunday morning at
the Bolitar homestead.

"Good morning," Mom said.

"Morning."

"Want a cup of coffee?"

"No, thanks." New Starbucks in Livingston. He'd check it out on
the way to Francine.

Myron looked at Brenda. She looked back steadily. No embarrassment. He was glad.

"Good morning," he said to her. Sparkling morning-after repartee
was Myron's forte.

She nodded a good morning back.

"There are bagels," Mom said, in case both his eyes and olfactory
nerves had shorted out. "Your father picked them up this morning.
From Livingston Bagels, Myron. Remember? The one on Northfield
Avenue? Near Two Gondoliers Pizzeria?"

Myron nodded. His dad had bought bagels from the same store
for thirty years, yet his mother still felt a constant need to entice him
with this tidbit. He joined them at the table.

Mom folded her hands in front of her. "Brenda was filling me in
on her situation," she said. Her voice was different now, more
lawyerly, less maternal. She pushed a newspaper in front of Myron.
The murder of Horace Slaughter had made page one, left-hand column, the spot usually reserved for whatever teen had thrown her
newborn out with the morning trash.

"I'd represent her myself," Mom continued, "but with your involvement, it might look like a conflict of interest. I was thinking of
Aunt Clara."

Clara was not really his aunt, just an old friend of the family and,
like Mom, an awesome attorney.

"Good idea," Myron said.

He picked up the paper and scanned the article. Nothing surprising. The article mentioned the fact that Brenda had recently gotten a
restraining order against her father, that she had accused him of as-
saulting her, and that she was wanted for further questioning but
could not be reached. Detective Maureen McLaughlin gave the standard spiel about its being "too early to rule anybody in or out." Right.
The police were controlling the story, leaking just enough to incriminate and put pressure on one person: Brenda Slaughter.

There was a photograph of Horace and Brenda. She was wearing
her college basketball uniform, and he had his arm around her. Both
were smiling, but the smiles looked more of the "say cheese" variety

than anything approaching genuine joy. The caption read something about the father and daughter during "a happier time." Media melodrama.

Myron turned to page A-9. There was a smaller photograph of Brenda and then, more interestingly, a photograph of Horace Slaughter's nephew, Terence Edwards, candidate for state senate. According to the caption, the photograph had been taken at "a recent campaign stop." Hmm. Terence Edwards looked pretty much as he had in the photographs at his mother's house. With one important difference: In this picture Terence was standing next to Arthur Bradford.

Hello.

Myron showed Brenda the photograph. She looked at it a moment. "Arthur Bradford seems to pop up frequently," she said.

"Yes."

"But how does Terence fit into this? He was a kid when my mother ran off."

Myron shrugged. He checked the kitchen clock. Time to meet Francine. "I have to run a quick errand," he said vaguely. "I shouldn't be long."

"An errand?" Mom frowned. "What kind of errand?"

"I'll be back soon."

Mom magnified the frown, getting her eyebrows into the act. "But you don't even live here anymore, Myron," she went on. "And it's only seven in the morning." In the morning. In case he mistook it for being seven at night. "Nothing's even open at seven in the morning."

Mother Bolitar, Mossad Interrogation.

Myron stood through the grilling. Brenda and Mom weighed him with their eyes. He shrugged and said, "I'll tell you about it when I come back." He hurried off, showered, dressed in record time, and jumped into his car.

Francine Neagly had mentioned the Halloween scare. He surmised that this was a kind of code. When they were in high school, about a hundred of their classmates had gone to see the movie *Halloween*. It was a new movie then, just out, and it scared the piss out of everyone. The next day Myron and his friend Eric had dressed up like the murderous Michael Myers—i.e., in black and wearing a goalie mask—and hidden in the woods during the girls' gym class. They never approached, just popping into sight every once in a while. A few of the kids freaked out and started screaming.

Hey, it was high school. Cut him some slack, okay?

Myron parked the Taurus near the Livingston football field. AstroTurf had replaced grass almost a decade earlier. AstroTurf at a high school. Was that necessary? He climbed through the woods. Sticky dew. His sneakers got wet. He quickly found the old path. Not far from this very spot Myron had made out—necked, to use his parents' terminology—with Nancy Pettino. Sophomore year. Neither one of them liked the other very much, but all their friends had paired up, and they'd both been bored and figured what the hell.

Ah, young love.

Francine sat in full uniform on the same big rock the two fake Michael Myers had stood upon nearly two decades ago. Her back was to him. She did not bother to turn around when he approached. He stopped a few feet from her.

"Francine?"

She let out a deep breath and said, "What the hell is going on, Myron?"

In their high school days Francine had been something of a tomboy, the kind of fierce, spunky competitor you could not help envying. She tackled everything with energy and relish, her voice daunting and confident. Right now she was balled up on the rock, hugging her knees to her chest and rocking back and forth.

"Why don't you tell me?" Myron said.

"Don't play games with me."

"I'm not playing games."

"Why did you want to see that file?"

"I told you. I'm not sure it was an accident."

"What makes you unsure?"

"Nothing concrete. Why? What happened?"

Francine shook her head. "I want to know what's going on," she said. "The whole story."

"Nothing to tell."

"Right. Yesterday you woke up and you said to yourself, 'Hey, that accidental death that occurred twenty years ago, I bet it wasn't an accident at all. So I'll go ask my old buddy Francine to get the police file for me.' That what happened, Myron?"

"No."

"So start talking."

Myron hesitated a moment. "Let's say that I'm right, that Elizabeth Bradford's death was not an accident. And let's say there is something in those files that proves it. That would mean the police covered it up, right?"

She shrugged, still not looking at him. "Maybe."

"And maybe they would want it to stay buried."

"Maybe."

"So maybe they would want to know what I know. Maybe they would even send an old friend to make me talk."

Francine's head snapped around as if someone had pulled a string. "You accusing me of something, Myron?"

"No," he said. "But if there's a cover-up going on, how do I know I can trust you?"

She rehugged her knees. "Because there is no cover-up," she said. "I saw the file. A little thin, but nothing unusual. Elizabeth Bradford fell. There were no signs of a struggle."

"They did an autopsy?"

"Yep. She landed on her head. The impact crushed her skull."

"Tox screen?"

"They didn't run one."

"Why not?"

"She died from a fall, not an overdose."

"But a tox screen would have shown if she'd been drugged," Myron said.

"So?"

"There were no signs of a struggle, okay, but what would have prevented someone from drugging her and then dumping her over the side?"

Francine made a face. "And maybe little green men pushed her."

"Hey, if this was a poor couple and the wife had accidentally fallen off her fire escape—"

"But this wasn't a poor couple, Myron. It was the Bradfords. Did they get preferential treatment? Probably. But even if Elizabeth Bradford had been drugged, it still doesn't add up to murder. Quite the opposite, in fact."

Now it was Myron's turn to look confused. "How do you figure?"

"The fall was only three stories," Francine said. "A short three stories."

"So?"

"So a murderer who pushed her off that terrace could not have counted on that low a fall killing her. More likely she would have just broken a leg or something."

Myron stopped. He had not thought of that. But it made sense. Pushing someone off a third-floor balcony with the hopes that she would land on her head and die was risky at best. Arthur Bradford did not hit Myron as a man who took risks.

So what did that mean?

"Maybe she was hit over the head beforehand," Myron tried.

Francine shook her head. "The autopsy didn't show any signs of

an earlier blow. And they also checked the rest of the house. There
was no blood anywhere. They might have cleaned it up, of course,
but I doubt we'll ever know."

"So there's absolutely nothing suspicious in the report?"

"Nothing," she said.

Myron raised his hands. "So why are we out here? Trying to recapture our lost youth?"

Francine looked at him. "Somebody broke into my house."

"What?"

"After I read the file. It was supposed to look like a burglary, but
it was a search. A thorough one. The place is trashed. Then right after that Roy Pomeranz calls me. Remember him?"

"No."

"He was Wickner's old partner."

"Oh, right," Myron said, "an early musclehead?"

"That's him. He's chief of detectives now. So yesterday he calls
me into his office, something he's never done before. He wants to
know why I was looking at the old Bradford file."

"What did you tell him?"

"I made up some bullshit story about studying old police tech-
niques."

Myron made a face. "And Pomeranz bought that?"

"No, he didn't buy it," Francine snapped. "He wanted to slam me
against a wall and shake the truth out of me. But he was afraid. He
was pretending like his questions were just routine, no big deal, but
you should have seen his face. He looked maybe half an egg sandwich away from a coronary. He claimed that he was worried about
the implications of what I was doing because it was an election year.
I nodded a lot and apologized and bought his story about as much as
he bought mine. When I drove home, I spotted a tail. I shook it this
morning, and here we are."

"And they trashed your place?"

"Yup. The work of professionals." Francine stood now and moved
closer to him. "So now that I've stepped into a pail of snakes for you,
you want to tell me why I'm taking all these bites?"

Myron considered his options, but there weren't any. He had indeed gotten her into this mess. She had a right to know.

"You read this morning's paper?" he asked.

"Yes."

"You see the story on the murder of Horace Slaughter?"

"Yes." Then she held a hand out as though to silence him. "There was a Slaughter in the file. But it was a woman. A maid or something. She found the body."

"Anita Slaughter. The victim's wife."

Her face lost a little color. "Oh, Christ, I don't like the sound of this. Go on."

So he did. He told her the whole story. When he finished, Francine looked down below them at the patch of grass where she had captained the field hockey team. She chewed on her lower lip.

"One thing," she said. "I don't know if it's important or not. But Anita Slaughter had been assaulted before Elizabeth Bradford's death."

Myron took a step back. "What do you mean, assaulted?"

"In the report. Wickner wrote that the witness, Anita Slaughter, still displayed abrasions from the earlier assault."

"What assault? When?"

"I don't know. That's all it said."

"So how do we find out?"

"There might be a police report on it in the basement," she said. "But—"

"Right, you can't risk it."

Francine checked her watch. She moved toward him. "I got some errands to run before I start my shift."

"Be careful," he said. "Assume your phone is tapped and your house bugged. Assume at all times you're being followed. If you spot a tail, call me on the cell phone."

Francine Neagly nodded. Then she looked down at the field again. "High school," she said softly. "Ever miss it?"

Myron looked at her.

She smiled. "Yeah, me neither."

Chapter 19

On the ride back to his house the cell phone rang. Myron picked it up.

"I got the information on Slaughter's credit card." Win. Another one who loved to exchange pleasantries. It was still before eight in the morning.

Myron said, "You're awake?"

"My God, man." Win waited a beat. "What gave it away?"

"No, I mean, you usually sleep late."

"I haven't gone to bed yet."

"Oh." Myron almost asked what he'd been doing, but he knew better. When it came to Win and the night, ignorance was quite often bliss.

"Only one charge in the past two weeks," Win said. "A week ago Thursday Horace used his Discover card at the Holiday Inn in Livingston."

Myron shook his head. Livingston. Again. The day before Horace vanished. "How much?"

"Twenty-six dollars even."

Curious amount. "Thanks."

Click.

Livingston. Horace Slaughter had been in Livingston. Myron replayed the theory that had been rumbling in his head since last night. It was looking better and better.

By the time he got back to his house, Brenda was showered and dressed. The cornrows in her hair cascaded down her shoulders in a wondrous dark wave. The *café con leche* skin was luminous. She gave him a smile that corkscrewed right through his heart.

He wanted very much to hold her.

"I called Aunt Mabel," Brenda said. "People are gathering at her house."

"I'll drop you off."

They said good-bye to Mom. Mom warned them sternly not to talk to the police without an attorney present. And to wear seat belts.

When they got in the car, Brenda said, "Your parents are great."

"Yeah, I guess they are."

"You're lucky."

He nodded.

Silence. Then Brenda said, "I keep waiting for one of us to say, 'About last night.' "

Myron smiled. "Me too."

"I don't want to forget it."

Myron swallowed. "Neither do I."

"So what do we do?"

"I don't know."

"Decisiveness," she said. "I love that in a man."

He smiled again and turned right on Hobart Gap Road.

Brenda said, "I thought West Orange was the other way."

"I want to make a quick stop, if you don't mind."

"Where?"

"The Holiday Inn. According to your father's charge cards, he was there a week ago Thursday. It was the last time he used any of his cards. I think he met someone for a meal or drinks."

"How do you know he didn't stay overnight?"

"The charge was for twenty-six dollars even. That's too low for a room yet too high for a meal for one. It's also a straight twenty-six dollars. No cents. When people tip, they often round off. Best guess is that he met someone there for lunch."

"So what are you going to do?"

Myron gave a half shrug. "I have the photograph of Horace from the paper. I'm going to show it around and see what happens."

On Route 10 he made a left and pulled into the Holiday Inn lot. They were less than two miles from Myron's house. The Holiday Inn was a typical two-level highway motel. Myron had last been here four years ago. An old high school buddy's bachelor party. Someone had hired a black hooker aptly named Danger. Danger put on a supposed "sex show" far closer to freaky than erotic. She also handed out business cards. They read: "FOR A GOOD TIME, CALL DANGER." Original. And now that Myron thought about it, he bet that Danger was not even her real name.

"You want to wait in the car?" he asked.

Brenda shook her head. "I'll walk around a little."

The lobby had prints of flowers on the wall. The carpet was pale green. The reception desk was on the right. A plastic sculpture that looked like two fish tails stuck together was on the left. Serious ugly.

Breakfast was still being served. Buffet-style. Dozens of people jockeyed about the spread, moving as though choreographed—step forward, spoon food onto plate, step back, step right, step forward again. Nobody bumped into anyone else. Hands and mouths were a blur. The whole thing looked a bit like a Discovery Channel special on the anthill.

A perky hostess stepped up to him. "How many?"

Myron put on his best cop face, adding just a hint of a smile. From his Peter Jennings line—professional yet accessible. He cleared his throat and asked, "Have you seen this man?" Just like that. No preamble.

He held up the photograph from the newspaper. The perky hostess studied it. She did not ask who he was; as he had hoped, his demeanor made her assume that he was someone official.

"I'm not the one to ask," the hostess said. "You should speak to Caroline."

"Caroline?" Myron Bolitar, Parrot Investigator.

"Caroline Gundeck. She was the one who had lunch with him."

Every once in a while you just get lucky.

"Would that have been last Thursday?" he asked.

The hostess thought about it a moment. "I think so, yeah."

"Where can I find Miss Gundeck?"

"Her office is on levcl B. Down at the end of the corridor."

"Caroline Gundeck works here?" He'd been told that Caroline Gundeck has an office on level B, and just like that he'd deduced that she worked here. Sherlock reincarnated.

"Caroline's worked here forever," the hostess said with a friendly eye roll.

"What's her title?"

"Food and beverage manager."

Hmm. Her occupation was not enlightening—unless Horace had been planning to throw a party before his murder. Doubtful. Nonetheless, this was a solid clue. He took the steps down to the basement and quickly found her office. But his luck did not hold. A secretary informed him that Miss Gundeck was not in today. Was she expected? The secretary would not say. Could he get her home number? The secretary frowned. Myron did not push it. Caroline Gundeck had to live in the area. Getting her phone number and address would be no problem.

Back in the corridor Myron dialed information. He asked for Gundeck in Livingston. Nothing. He asked for Gundeck in East Hanover or the area. Bingo. There was a C Gundeck in Whippany. Myron dialed the number. After four rings a machine picked up. Myron left a message.

When he came back up to the lobby, he found Brenda standing alone in a corner. Her face looked drained, her eyes wide as though someone had just poked her hard in the solar plexus. She did not move or even glance his way as he approached.

"What is it?" he asked.

Brenda gulped some air and turned to him. "I think I've been here before," she said.

"When?"

"A long time ago. I don't remember really. It's just a feeling . . . or maybe I'm just imagining. But I think I was here as a little kid. With my mother."

Silence.

"Do you remember—"

"Nothing," Brenda interrupted him. "I'm not even sure it was here. Maybe it was another motel. It's not like this one is special. But I think it was here. That weird sculpture. It's familiar."

"What were you wearing?" he tried.

She shook her head. "I don't know."

"What about your mother? What was she wearing?"

"What are you, a fashion consultant?"

"I'm just trying to jar something loose."

"I don't remember anything. She vanished when I was five. How much do you remember from back then?"

Point taken. "Let's walk around a little," he suggested. "See if something comes back to you."

But nothing surfaced, if indeed there was anything there to surface. Myron had not expected anything anyway. He was not big on repressed memory or any of that stuff. Still the whole episode was curious, and once again it fit into his scenario. As they made their way back to Myron's car, he decided that it was time to voice his theory.

"I think I know what your father was doing."

Brenda stopped and looked at him. Myron kept moving. He got into the car. Brenda followed. The car doors closed.

Myron said, "I think Horace was looking for your mother."

The words took a moment to sink in. Then Brenda leaned back and said, "Tell me why."

He started up the car. "Okay, but remember I used the word *think*. I *think* that's what he was doing. I don't have any real proof."

"Okay, go ahead."

He took a deep breath. "Let's start with your father's phone records. One, he calls Arthur Bradford's campaign headquarters sev-

eral times. Why? As far as we know, there is only one connection between your father and Bradford."

"The fact that my mother worked in his house."

"Right. Twenty years ago. But here's something else to consider.
When I started searching for your mother, I stumbled upon the Bradfords. I thought they might somehow be connected. Your father
might have come to the same conclusion."

She looked less than impressed. "What else?"

"The phone records again. Horace called the two attorneys who
handled your scholarships."

"So?"

"So why would he call them?"

"I don't know."

"Your scholarships are strange, Brenda. Especially the first one.
You weren't even a basketball player yet and you get a vague aca-
demic scholarship to a ritzy private school plus expenses? It doesn't
make sense. Scholarships just don't work that way. And I checked.
You are the only recipient of the Outreach Education scholarship.
They only awarded it that one year."

"So what are you getting at?"

"Somebody set up those scholarships with the sole intent of helping you, with the sole intent of funneling you money." He made the
U-turn by Daffy Dan's, a discount clothing store, and started heading back down Route 10 toward the circle. "In other words, somebody was trying to help you out. Your father may have been trying to
find out who that was."

He glanced over at her, but she would not face him now. Her
voice, when she finally spoke, was throaty. "And you think it was my
mother?"

Myron tried to tread gently. "I don't know. But why else would
your father call Thomas Kincaid so many times? The man had not
handled your scholarship money since you left high school. You read
that letter. Why would Horace pester him to the point of near harassment? The only thing I can think of is that Kincaid had information
that your father wanted."

"Where the scholarship money originated from?"

"Right. My guess is, if we can trace that back"—again, tread gently—"we would find something very interesting."

"Can we do that?"

"I'm not sure. The attorneys will undoubtedly claim privilege.
But I'm going to put Win on it. If it involves money, he'll have the
connections to track it down."

Brenda sat back and tried to digest all this. "Do you think my father traced it back?"

"I doubt it, but I don't know. Either way your father was starting to make some noise. He hit up the lawyers, and he even went so far as to start questioning Arthur Bradford. That was where he probably went too far. Even if there'd been no wrongdoing, Bradford would not be happy with someone poking into his past, raising old ghosts, especially during an election year."

"So he killed my father?"

Myron was not sure how to answer that one. "It's too early to say for sure. But let's assume for a second that your father did a little too much poking. And let's also assume the Bradfords scared him off with a beating."

Brenda nodded. "The blood in the locker."

"Right. I keep wondering why we found the blood there, why Horace didn't go home to change or recuperate. My guess is he was beaten near the hospital. In Livingston, at the very least."

"Where the Bradfords live."

Myron nodded. "And if Horace escaped from the beating or if he was just afraid they'd come after him again, he wouldn't go home. He'd probably change at the hospital and run. In the morgue I noticed clothes in the corner—a security guard uniform. It was probably what he changed into when he got to the locker. Then he hit the road and—"

Myron stopped.

"And what?" she asked.

"Damn," Myron said.

"What?"

"What's Mabel's phone number?"

Brenda gave it to him. "Why?"

Myron switched on the cell phone and dialed Lisa at Bell Atlantic. He asked her to check the number. It took Lisa about two minutes.

"Nothing official on it," Lisa said. "But I checked the line. There's a noise there."

"Meaning?"

"Someone's probably got a tap on it. Internal. You'd have to send someone by there to be sure."

Myron thanked her and hung up. "They have Mabel's phone tapped too. That's probably how they found your father. He called your aunt, and they traced it."

"So who's behind the tap?"

"I don't know," Myron said.

Silence. They passed the Star-Bright Pizzeria. In Myron's youth it was rumored that a whorehouse operated out of the back. Myron had gone several times there with his family. When his dad went to the bathroom, Myron followed. Nothing.

"There's something else that doesn't make sense," Brenda said.

"What?"

"Even if you're right about the scholarships, where would my mother get that kind of money?"

Good question. "How much did she take from your dad?"

"Fourteen thousand, I think."

"If she invested well, that might be enough. There were seven years between the time she disappeared and the first scholarship payment, so . . ." Myron calculated the figures in his head. Fourteen grand to start. Hmm. Anita Slaughter would have had to score big to make the money last this long. Possible, sure, but even in the Reagan years, not likely.

Hold the phone.

"She may have found another way to get money," he said slowly.

"How?"

Myron stayed quiet for a moment. The head gears were churning again. He checked his rearview mirror. If there was a tail, he didn't spot it. But that did not mean much. A casual glance rarely gave it away. You had to watch the cars, memorize them, study their movements. But he could not concentrate on that. Not right now.

"Myron?"

"I'm thinking."

She looked like she was about to say something but then thought better of it.

"Suppose," Myron continued, "your mother did learn something about the death of Elizabeth Bradford."

"Didn't we already try this?"

"Just stay with me a second, okay? Before, we came up with two possibilities. One, she was scared and ran. Two, they tried to hurt her and she ran."

"And now you have a third?"

"Sort of." He drove past the new Starbucks on the corner of Mount Pleasant Avenue. He wanted to stop—his caffeine craving worked like a magnetic pull—but he pushed on. "Suppose your mother did run away. And suppose once she was safe, she demanded money to keep quiet."

"You think she blackmailed the Bradfords?"

"More like compensation." He spoke even as the ideas were still forming. Always a dangerous thing. "Your mother sees something. She realizes that the only way to guarantee her safety, and her family's safety, is to run away and hide. If the Bradfords find her, they'll kill her. Plain and simple. If she tries to do something cute—like hide evidence in a safety-deposit box in the event she disappears or something like that—they'll torture her until she tells them where it is. Your mother has no choice. She has to run. But she wants to take care of her daughter too. So she makes sure that her daughter gets all the things she herself could never have provided for her. A top-quality education. A chance to live on a pristine campus instead of the bowels of Newark. Stuff like that."

More silence.

Myron waited. He was voicing theories too fast now, not giving his brain a chance to process or even to inspect his words. He stopped now, letting everything settle.

"Your scenarios," Brenda said. "You're always looking to put my mother in the best light. It blinds you, I think."

"How so?"

"I'll ask you again: If all that is true, why didn't she take me with her?"

"She was on the run from killers. What kind of mother would want to put her child in that kind of danger?"

"And she was so paranoid that she could never call me? Or see me?"

"Paranoid?" Myron repeated. "These guys have a tap on your phone. They have people tailing you. Your father is dead."

Brenda shook her head. "You don't get it."

"Get what?"

Her eyes were watery now, but she kept her tone a little too even. "You can make all the excuses you want, but you can't get around the fact that she abandoned her child. Even if she had good reason, even if she was this wonderful self-sacrificing mother who did all this to protect me, why would she let her daughter go on believing that her own mother would abandon her? Didn't she realize how this would devastate a five-year-old girl? Couldn't she have found some way to tell her the truth—even after all these years?"

Her child. *Her* daughter. Tell *her* the truth. Never *I* or *me*. Interesting. But Myron kept silent. He had no answer to that one.

They drove past the Kessler Institute and hit a traffic light. After some time had passed, Brenda said, "I still want to go to practice this afternoon."

Myron nodded. He understood. The court was comfort.

"And I want to play in the opener."

Again Myron nodded. It was probably what Horace would have wanted too.

They made the turn near Mountain High School and arrived at Mabel Edwards's house. There were at least a dozen cars parked on the road, most American-made, most older and beaten up. A formally dressed black couple stood by the door. The man pressed the bell. The woman held a platter of food. When they spotted Brenda, they glared at her and then turned their backs.

"They've read the papers, I see," Brenda said.

"No one thinks you did it."

Her look told him to stop with the patronizing.

They walked her to the front door and stood behind the couple. The couple huffed and looked away. The man tapped his foot. The woman made a production out of sighing. Myron opened his mouth, but Brenda closed it with a firm shake of her head. Already she was reading him.

Someone opened the door. There were lots of people already inside. All nicely dressed. All black. Funny how Myron kept noticing that. A black couple. Black people inside. Last night at the barbecue he had not found it strange that everyone except Brenda was white. In fact, Myron could not recall a black person ever attending one of the neighborhood barbecues. So why should he be surprised to be the only white person here? And why should it make him feel funny?

The couple disappeared inside as though sucked up by a vortex. Brenda hesitated. When they finally stepped through the doorway, it was like something out of a saloon scene in a John Wayne film. The low murmurs ceased as if somebody had snapped off a radio. Everyone turned and glowered. For a half a second Myron thought it was a racial thing—he being the only white guy—but then he saw the animosity was aimed directly at the grieving daughter.

Brenda was right. They thought she did it.

The room was crowded and sweltering. Fans whirred impotently. Men were hooking fingers into collars to let in air. Sweat coated faces. Myron looked at Brenda. She looked small and alone and scared, but she would not look away. He felt her take his hand. He gripped back. She stood ramrod straight now, her head high.

The crowd parted a bit, and Mabel Edwards stepped into view. Her eyes were red and swollen. A handkerchief was balled up in her fist. They all swung their gazes toward Mabel now, awaiting her reaction. When Mabel saw her niece, she spread her hands and beckoned Brenda forward. Brenda did not hesitate. She sprinted into the thick, soft arms, lowered her head onto Mabel's shoulder, and for the first time truly sobbed. Not cried. These were gut-wrenching sobs.

Mabel rocked her niece back and forth and patted her back and cooed comfort. At the same time, Mabel's eyes scanned the room, mother wolf–protective, challenging and then extinguishing any glare that might be aimed in the direction of her niece.

The crowd turned away, and the murmur returned to normal. Myron felt the stomach knots begin to loosen. He scanned the room for familiar faces. He recognized a couple of the ballplayers from his past, guys he had played against on the playground or in high school. A couple nodded hellos. Myron nodded back. A little boy just past the toddler stage sprinted through the room imitating a siren. Myron recognized him from the pictures on the mantel. Mabel Edwards's grandson. Terence Edwards's son.

Speaking of whom, where was candidate Edwards?

Myron scanned the room again. No sign of him. In front of him Mabel and Brenda finally broke their hold. Brenda wiped her eyes. Mabel pointed her toward a bathroom. Brenda managed a nod and hurried off.

Mabel approached him, her gaze on him and unwavering. Without preamble she asked, "Do you know who killed my brother?"

"No."

"But you're going to find out."

"Yes."

"Do you have a thought?"

"A thought," Myron said. "Nothing more."

She nodded again. "You're a good man, Myron."

There was a shrine of some sort on the fireplace. A photograph of a smiling Horace was surrounded by flowers and candles. Myron looked at the smile he had not seen in ten years and would never see again.

He did not feel like a good man.

"I'll need to ask you some more questions," Myron said.

"Whatever it takes."

"About Anita too."

Mabel's eyes stayed on him. "You still think she's connected in all this?"

"Yes. I'd also like to send a man around to check your phone."

"Why?"

"I think it's tapped."

Mabel looked confused. "But who would tap my phone?"

Better not to speculate right now. "I don't know," Myron said.

"But when your brother called, did he mention the Holiday Inn in Livingston?"

Something happened to her eyes. "Why do you want to know that?"

"Evidently Horace had lunch with a manager there the day before he disappeared. It was the last charge on his credit card. And when we stopped by, Brenda thought she recognized it. That she may have been there with Anita."

Mabel closed her eyes.

"What?" Myron asked.

More mourners entered the house, all carrying platters of food. Mabel accepted their words of sympathy with a kind smile and a firm hand grasp. Myron waited.

When there was a free second, Mabel said, "Horace never mentioned the Holiday Inn on the phone."

"But there's something else," Myron said.

"Yes."

"Did Anita ever take Brenda to the Holiday Inn?"

Brenda stepped back into the room and looked at them. Mabel put her hand on Myron's arm. "Now is not the time for this," Mabel said to him.

He nodded.

"Tonight maybe. Do you think you can come alone?"

"Yes."

Mabel Edwards left him then to attend to Horace's family and friends. Myron felt like an outsider again, but this time it had nothing to do with skin color.

He left quickly.

Chapter 20

Once on the road Myron switched his cellular phone back on. Two incoming calls. One was from Esperanza at the office, the other from Jessica in Los Angeles. He briefly debated what to do. No question really. He dialed Jessica's hotel suite. Was it wimpy to call her right back? Maybe. But Myron looked at it as one of his more mature moments. Call him whipped, but engaging in head games had never been his style.

The hotel operator connected him, but there was no answer. He left a message. Then he dialed the office.

"We got a big problem," Esperanza said.

"On Sunday?" Myron said.

"The Lord may take it off, but not team owners."

"Did you hear about Horace Slaughter?" he asked.

"Yes," she said. "I'm sorry about your friend, but we still got a business to run. And a problem."

"What?"

"The Yankees are going to trade Lester Ellis. To Seattle. They've scheduled a news conference first thing tomorrow morning."

Myron rubbed the bridge of his nose with his pointer and thumb. "How did you hear?"

"Devon Richards."

Reliable source. Damn. "Does Lester know?"

"Nope."

"He'll have a fit."

"Don't I know it."

"Suggestions?"

"Not a one," Esperanza said. "A fringe benefit of being the underling."

The call waiting clicked. "I'll call you back." He switched lines and said hello.

Francine Neagly said, "I'm being tailed."

"Where are you?"

"The A and P off the circle."

"What kind of car?"

"Blue Buick Skylark. Few years old. White top."

"Got a plate?"

"New Jersey, four-seven-six–four-five T."

Myron thought a moment. "When do you start your shift?"

"Half an hour."

"You working the car or the desk?"

"Desk."

"Good, I'll pick him up there."

"Pick him up?"

"If you're staying in the station, he's not going to waste a beautiful Sunday hanging outside it. I'm going to follow him."

"Tail the tailer?"

"Right. Take Mount Pleasant to Livingston Avenue. I'll pick him up there."

"Hey, Myron?"

"Yeah."

"If something big goes down, I want in."

"Sure."

They hung up. Myron backtracked to Livingston. He parked along Memorial Circle near the turnoff to Livingston Avenue. Good view of the police station and easy access to all routes. Myron kept the car running and watched the townsfolk handle Memorial Circle's half-mile perimeter. A tremendous variety of Livingstonites frequented "the circle." There were old ladies pacing slowly, usually in twos, some of the more adventurous swinging tiny barbells. There were couples in their fifties and sixties, many in matching sweat suits. Cute, sort of. Teenagers ambled, their mouths getting a far better workout than any extremity or cardiovascular muscle. Hard-core joggers raced past them all with nary a glance. They wore sleek sunglasses and firm faces and sported bare midriffs. Bare midriffs. Even the men. What was up with that?

He forced himself not to think about kissing Brenda. Or how it felt when she smiled at him across the picnic table. Or how her face flushed when she got excited. Or how animated she'd gotten when talking to people at the barbecue. Or how tender she'd been with Timmy when she put on that bandage.

Good thing he wasn't thinking about her.

For a brief moment he wondered if Horace would approve. Strange thought, really. But there it was. Would his old mentor approve? He wondered. He wondered what it would be like to date a black woman. Was there attraction in the taboo? Repulsion? Concern for the future? He pictured the two of them living in the suburbs, the pediatrician and the sports agent, a mixed couple with similar dreams, and then he realized how dumb it was for a man in love with a woman in Los Angeles to think such nonsense about a woman he'd only known for two days.

Dumb. Yup.

A blond hard-core jogger dressed in tight magenta shorts and a much-tested white sports bra jogged by his car. She looked inside and smiled at him. Myron smiled back. The bare midriff. You take the good with the bad.

Across the street Francine Neagly pulled into the police station driveway. Myron shifted into drive and kept his foot on the brake. The Buick Skylark passed the station without slowing down. Myron had tried to trace the license plate from his source at the Department of Motor Vehicles, but hey, it was Sunday, it was the DMV, you put it together.

He pulled onto Livingston Avenue and followed the Buick south. He kept four cars back and craned his neck. Nobody was pushing hard on the accelerator. Livingston took its time on Sunday. But that was okay. The Buick came to a stop at a traffic light at Northfield Avenue. On the right was a brick minimall of some sort. When Myron had been growing up, the same building had been Roosevelt Elementary School; twenty-some-odd years ago someone decided what New Jersey really needed were fewer schools and more malls. Foresight.

The Skylark turned right. Myron kept back and did likewise. They were heading toward Route 10 again, but before they had gone even half a mile, the Skylark made a left onto Crescent Road. Myron frowned. Small suburban street, mostly used to cut through to Hobart Gap Road. Hmm. It probably meant that Mr. Skylark knew the town fairly well and was not an outsider.

A quick right followed the left. Myron knew now where the Skylark was headed. There was only one thing nestled into this suburban landscape besides the split-level homes and a barely flowing brook. A Little League field.

Meadowbrook Little League field. Two fields actually. Sunday and sun meant the road and parking lot were packed with vehicles. So-called utility trucks and minivans had replaced the wood-paneled station wagons of Myron's youth, but little else had changed. The lot was still unpaved gravel. The concession booth was still white cement with green trim and run by volunteer moms. The stands were still metal and rickety and filled with parents cheering a tad too loudly.

The Buick Skylark grabbed an illegal space near the backstop.

Myron slowed the car and waited. When the door of the Skylark opened and Detective Wickner, the lead officer in the Elizabeth Bradford "accident," swept out of the car in grand style, Myron was not really surprised. The retired officer took off his sunglasses with a snap and tossed them back into the car. He put on a baseball cap, green with the letter *S* on it. You could almost see Wickner's lined face slacken as though the field's sunlight were the most gentle masseur. Wickner waved to some guys standing behind the backstop—the Eli Wickner Backstop, according to the sign. The guys waved back. Wickner bounded toward them.

Myron stayed where he was for a moment. Detective Eli Wickner had hung out in the same spot since before the days Myron had frequented this field. Wickner's Throne. People greeted him here. They came up and slapped his back and shook his hand; Myron half expected them to kiss his ring. Wickner was beaming now. At home. In paradise. In the place where he was still a big man.

Time to change that.

Myron found a parking spot a block away. He hopped out of the car and approached. His feet crunched the gravel. He traveled back to a time when he walked upon this same surface with soft kid cleats. Myron had been a good Little League player—no, he'd been a *great* player—until the age of eleven. It'd been right here, on Field Two. He'd led the league in home runs and seemed on the verge of breaking the all-time Livingston American League Little League record. He needed to hit two more homers with four games left. Twelve-year-old Joey Davito was pitching. Davito threw hard and with no control. The first pitch hit Myron square on the forehead, right under the brim of the helmet. Myron went down. He remembered blinking when he landed on his back. He remembered looking up into the glare of the sun. He remembered seeing the face of his coach, Mr. Farley. And then his father was there. Dad blinked back tears and scooped him up in his strong arms, gently cradling Myron's head with his large hand. He'd gone to the hospital, but there was no lasting damage. At least not physical. But after that Myron had never been able to stop from bailing out on an inside pitch. Baseball was never the same to him. The game had hurt him, had lost its innocence.

He stopped playing for good a year later.

There were half a dozen guys with Wickner. They all wore baseball caps sitting high and straight, no breaks in the brims, like you see with the kids. White T-shirts were stretched across bellies that resembled swallowed bowling balls. Bodies by Budweiser. They leaned against the fence, elbows draped over the top like they were taking a Sunday ride in a car. They commented on the kids, inspecting them, dissecting their games, predicting their futures—as though their opinions mattered a rat's ass.

There is a lot of pain in Little League. Much has been written in recent years criticizing the pushy Little League parents—deservedly so—but the namby-pamby, politically correct, everybody equal, semi–New Age alternative was not much better. A kid hits a weak grounder. Disappointed, he sighs and walks toward first. He is thrown out by a mile and sulks straight to the dugout. The New Age coach yells, "Good hustle!" But of course it wasn't good hustle. So what message are you sending? The parents pretend that winning is irrelevant, that the best player on the team should not get more playing time or a better batting position than the worst. But the problem with all this—besides the obvious fact that it's a lie—is that the kids are not fooled. Kids aren't dumb. They know that they are being patronized with all this "as long as he's having fun" talk. And they resent it.

So the pain remains. It probably would always be there.

Several people recognized Myron. They tapped their neighbors' shoulders and pointed. There he is. Myron Bolitar. The greatest basketball player this town ever produced. Would have been a top pro if . . . If. Fate. The knee. Myron Bolitar. Half legend, half a warning to today's youth. The athletic equivalent to the smashed-up car they used to demonstrate the dangers of drunk driving.

Myron headed straight for the men along the backstop. Livingston fans. The same guys went to all the football games and basketball games and baseball games. Some were nice. Some were blowhards. All of them recognized Myron. They greeted him warmly. Detective Wickner stayed silent, his eyes glued to the field, studying the play with a little too much intensity, especially since it was between innings.

Myron tapped Wickner on the shoulder.

"Hello, Detective."

Wickner turned slowly. He'd always had these piercing gray eyes, but right now they were heavily tinged with red. Conjunctivitis maybe. Or allergies. Or booze. Your choice. His skin was tan to the point of rawhide. He wore a yellow collared shirt with a little zipper in the front. The zipper was down. He had on a thick gold chain. New probably. Something to jazz up retirement. It didn't work on him.

Wickner mustered up a smile. "You're old enough to call me Eli now, Myron."

Myron tried it. "How are you, Eli?"

"Not bad, Myron. Retirement's treating me good. I fish a lot. How about yourself? Saw you try that comeback. Sorry it didn't work out."

"Thanks," Myron said.

"You still living at your folks'?"

"No, I'm in the city now."

"So what brings you out this way? Visiting the family?"

Myron shook his head. "I wanted to talk to you."

They drifted about ten feet from the entourage. No one followed, their body language working as a force field.

"What about?" Wickner asked.

"An old case."

"A police case?"

Myron looked at him steadily. "Yes."

"And what case would that be?"

"The death of Elizabeth Bradford."

To Wickner's credit, he skipped the surprise act. He took the baseball cap off his head and smoothed down the gray flyaways. Then he put the cap back on. "What do you want to know?"

"The bribe," Myron said. "Did the Bradfords pay you off in a lump sum, or did they set up a more long-term payout with interest and stuff?"

Wickner took the blow but stayed upright. There was a quiver on the right side of his mouth like he was fighting back tears. "I don't much like your attitude, son."

"Tough." Myron knew that his only chance here was a direct, no-barred frontal assault; dancing around or subtle interrogation would get him squat. "You've got two choices, Eli. Choice one, you tell me what really happened to Elizabeth Bradford and I try to keep your name out of it. Choice two, I start screaming to the papers about a police cover-up and destroy your reputation." Myron gestured to the field. "By the time I'm done with you, you'll be lucky to hang out in the Eli Wickner Urinal."

Wickner turned away. Myron could see his shoulders rising and falling with the labored breaths. "I don't know what you're talking about."

Myron hesitated a beat. Then he kept his voice soft. "What happened to you, Eli?"

"What?"

"I used to look up to you," Myron said. "I used to care what you thought."

The words struck home. Wickner's shoulders began to hitch a bit. He kept his face low. Myron waited. Wickner finally turned to face him. The rawhide skin looked drier now, sapped, more brittle. He was working up to saying something. Myron gave him space and waited.

From behind him Myron felt a large hand squeeze his shoulder.

"There a problem here?"

Myron spun around. The hand belonged to Chief of Detectives Roy Pomeranz, the musclehead who used to be Wickner's partner. Pomeranz wore a white T-shirt and white shorts that rode so high it looked like someone was giving him a power wedgie. He still had the he-man physique, but he was totally bald now, his head completely smooth as though waxed.

"Get your hand off my shoulder," Myron said.

Pomeranz ignored the request. "Everything okay here?"

Wickner spoke up. "We were just talking, Roy."

"Talking about what?"

Myron handled that one. "About you."

Big smile. "Oh?"

Myron pointed. "We were just saying that if you got a hoop earring, you'd be the spitting image of Mr. Clean."

Pomeranz's smile vanished.

Myron lowered his voice. "I'll tell you one more time. Move your hand, or I'll break it in three places." Note the three-places reference. Specific threats were always the best. He'd learned that from Win.

Pomeranz kept the hand there a second or two longer—to keep face—and then he slid it off.

"You're still on the force, Roy," Myron said. "So you got the most to lose. But I'll make you the same offer. Tell me what you know about the Bradford case, and I'll try to keep your name out of it."

Pomeranz smirked at him. "Funny thing, Bolitar."

"What?"

"You digging into all this in an election year."

"Your point being?"

"You're working for Davison," he said. "You're just trying to drag down a good man like Arthur Bradford for that scum sucker."

Davison was Bradford's opponent for governor. "Sorry, Roy, that's incorrect."

"Yeah? Well, either way, Elizabeth Bradford died from a fall."

"Who pushed her?"

"It was an accident."

"Someone accidentally pushed her?"

"Nobody pushed her, wise guy. It was late at night. The terrace was slippery. She fell. It was an accident. Happens all the time."

"Really? How many deaths has Livingston had in the past twenty years where a woman accidentally fell to her death from her own balcony?"

Pomeranz crossed his arms over his chest. His biceps bulged like baseballs. The guy was doing one of those subtle flexes, where you're trying to look like you're not flexing. "Accidents in the home. You know how many people die in home accidents every year?"

"No, Roy, how many?"

Pomeranz didn't answer. Big surprise. He met Wickner's eye. Wickner remained silent. He looked vaguely ashamed.

Myron decided to go for the whammy. "And what about the assault on Anita Slaughter? Was that an accident too?"

Stunned silence. Wickner involuntarily groaned a little. Pomeranz's thigh-thick arms dropped back to his sides.

Pomeranz said, "I don't know what you're talking about."

"Sure you do, Roy. Eli even alluded to it in the police file."

Angry smirk. "You mean the file that Francine Neagly stole from the records room?"

"She didn't steal it, Roy. She looked at it."

Pomeranz smiled slowly. "Well, it's missing now. She had it last. We firmly believe that Officer Neagly stole it."

Myron shook his head. "Not that easy, Roy. You can hide that file. You can even hide the file on the Anita Slaughter assault. But I already got my hand on the hospital file. From St. Barnabas. They keep records, Roy."

More stunned looks. It was a bluff. But it was a good one. And it drew blood.

Pomeranz leaned very close to Myron, his breath reeking of a poorly digested meal. He kept his voice low. "You're poking your nose where it don't belong."

Myron nodded. "And you're not brushing after every meal."

"I'm not going to let you drag down a good man with false innuendos."

"Innuendos," Myron repeated. "You been listening to vocabulary tapes in the squad car, Roy? Do the taxpayers know about this?"

"You're playing a dangerous game, funny man."

"Oooo, I'm so scared." When short a comeback, fall back on the classics.

"I don't have to start with you," Pomeranz said. He leaned back a bit, the smile returning. "I got Francine Neagly."

"What about her?"

"She had no business with that file. We believe that someone in Davison's campaign—probably you, Bolitar—paid her to steal it. To gather any information that can be used in a distorted fashion to hurt Arthur Bradford."

Myron frowned. "Distorted fashion?"

"You think I won't do it?"

"I don't even know what that means. Distorted fashion? Was that on one of your tapes?"

Pomeranz stuck a finger in Myron's face. "You think I won't suspend her sorry ass and ruin her career?"

"Pomeranz, not even you can be that dumb. You ever heard of Jessica Culver?"

The finger came down. "She's your girlfriend, right?" Pomeranz said. "She's a writer or something."

"A big writer," Myron said. "Very well respected. And you know what she would love to do? A big exposé on sexism in police departments. You do anything to Francine Neagly, you so much as demote her or give her one shit detail or breathe on her between meals, and I promise you that when Jessica gets done, you'll make Bob Packwood look like Betty Friedan."

Pomeranz looked confused. Probably didn't know who Betty Friedan was. Maybe he should have said Gloria Steinem. To his credit, Pomeranz took his time. He fought for recovery, offering up an almost sweet smile.

"Okay," he said, "so it's the cold war all over again. I can nuke you, you can nuke me. It's a stalemate."

"Wrong, Roy. You're the one with the job, the family, the rep, and maybe a looming jail term. Me, I got nothing to lose."

"You can't be serious. You're dealing with the most powerful family in New Jersey. Do you really think you've got nothing to lose?"

Myron shrugged. "I'm also crazy," he said. "Or to put it another way, my mind works in a distorted fashion."

Pomeranz looked over at Wickner. Wickner looked back. There was a crack of the bat. The crowd got to its feet. The ball hit the fence. "Go, Billy!" Billy rounded second and slid into third.

Pomeranz walked away without another word.

Myron looked at Wickner for a long time. "Are you a total sham, Detective?"

Wickner said nothing.

"When I was eleven, you spoke to my fifth-grade class and we all thought you were the coolest guy we'd ever seen. I used to look for you at games. I used to want your approval. But you're just a lie."

Wickner kept his eyes on the field. "Let it go, Myron."

"I can't."

"Davison is a scum. He's not worth it."

"I'm not working for Davison. I'm working for Anita Slaughter's daughter."

Wickner kept his eyes on the field. His mouth was set, but Myron could see the tremor starting back up in the corner of his mouth. "All you're going to do is hurt a lot of people."

"What happened to Elizabeth Bradford?"

"She fell," he said. "That's all."

"I'm not going to stop digging," Myron said.

Wickner adjusted his cap again and began to walk away. "Then more people are going to die."

There was no threat in his tone, just the stilted, pained timber of inevitability.

Chapter 21

When Myron headed back to his car, the two goons from Bradford Farms were waiting for him. The big one and the skinny, older guy. The skinny guy wore long sleeves so Myron could not see if there was a snake tattoo, but the two looked right from Mabel Edwards's description.

Myron felt something inside him start to simmer.

The big guy was show. Probably a wrestler in high school. Maybe a bouncer at a local bar. He thought he was tough; Myron knew that he would be no problem. The skinny, older guy was hardly a formidable physical specimen. He looked like an aged version of the puny guy who gets the sand kicked on him in the old Charles Atlas cartoon. But the face was so ferretlike, the eyes so beady that he made you pause. Myron knew better than to judge on appearance, but this guy's face was simply too thin and too pointed and too cruel.

Myron spoke to the Skinny Ferret. "Can I see your tattoo?" Direct approach.

The big guy looked confused, but Skinny Ferret took it all in stride.

"I'm not used to guys using that line on me," Skinny said.

"Guys," Myron repeated. "But with your looks, the chicks must be asking all the time."

If Skinny was offended by the crack, he was laughing his way through it. "So you really want to see the snake?"

Myron shook his head. The snake. The question had been answered. These were the right guys. The big one had punched Mabel Edwards in the eye.

The simmer flicked up a notch.

"So what can I do for you fellas?" Myron said. "You collecting donations for the Kiwanis Club?"

"Yeah," the big guy said. "Blood donations."

Myron looked at him. "I'm not a grandmother, tough guy."

Big said, "Huh?"

Skinny cleared his throat. "Governor-to-be Bradford would like to see you."

"Governor-to-be?"

The Skinny Ferret shrugged. "Confidence."

"Nice to see. So why doesn't he call me?"

"The next governor thought it would be best if we accompanied you."

"I think I can manage to drive the mile by myself." Myron looked at the big guy again and spoke slowly. "After all, I'm not a grand-mother."

The big guy sniffed and rolled his neck. "I can still beat you like one."

"Beat me as you would a grandmother," Myron said. "Gee, what a guy."

Myron had read recently about self-help gurus who taught their students to picture themselves successful. Visualize it, and it will happen or some such credo. Myron was not sure, but he knew that it worked in combat. If the chance presents itself, picture how you will attack. Imagine what countermoves your opponent might make and prepare yourself for them. That was what Myron had been doing since Skinny had admitted to the tattoo. Now that he saw that no one was in sight, he struck.

Myron's knee landed squarely in the big guy's groin. The big guy made a noise like he was sucking through a straw that still had drops of liquid in it. He folded like an old wallet. Myron pulled out his gun and pointed it at the Skinny Ferret. The big guy's body melted to the pavement and formed a puddle.

The Skinny Ferret had not moved. He looked slightly amused.

"Wasteful," Skinny said.

"Yeah," Myron agreed. "But I feel much better." He looked at the big guy. "That was for Mabel Edwards."

Skinny shrugged. Not a care in the world. "So now what?"

"Where's your car?" Myron asked.

"We were dropped off. We're supposed to go back to the house with you."

"I don't think so."

The big guy writhed and tried to suck in a breath. Neither stand-ing man cared. Myron put away his gun.

"I'll drive myself over, if you don't mind."

The skinny guy spread his arms. "Suit yourself."

Myron started to get into his Taurus.

"You don't know what you're up against," Skinny said.

"I keep hearing that."

"Maybe," he said. "But now you've heard it from me."

Myron nodded. "Consider me scared."

"Ask your father, Myron."

That made him pull up. "What about my father?"

"Ask him about Arthur Bradford." The smile of a mongoose gnawing on a neck. "Ask him about me."

Icy water flooded Myron's chest. "What does my father have to do with any of this?"

But Skinny was not about to answer. "Hurry now," he said. "The next governor of New Jersey is waiting for you."

Chapter 22

Myron put a call in to Win. He quickly told him what'd happened.

"Wasteful," Win agreed.

"He hit a woman."

"Then shoot him in the knee. Permanently injure him. A kick in the scrotum is wasteful."

Proper Payback Etiquette by Windsor Horne Lockwood III. "I'm going to leave the cellular on. Can you get down here?"

"But of course. Please refrain from further violence until I am present."

In other words: Save some for me.

The guard at Bradford Farms was surprised to see Myron alone. The gate was open, probably in expectation of a threesome. Myron did not hesitate. He drove through without stopping. The guard panicked. He jumped out of his booth. Myron gave him a little finger wave, like Oliver Hardy used to do. He even scrunched up his face into that same Hardy smile. Heck, if he had a bowler, he would have gotten that into the act too.

By the time Myron parked at the front entrance, the old butler was already standing in the doorway. He bowed slightly.

"Please follow me, Mr. Bolitar."

They headed down a long corridor. Lots of oils on the walls, mostly of men on horses. There was one nude. A woman, of course. No horse in this one. Catherine the Great was truly dead. The butler made a right at the hallway. They entered a glass corridor that resembled a passageway in the Biosphere or maybe Epcot Center. Myron figured that they must have traveled close to fifty yards already.

The manservant stopped and opened a door. His face was perfect butler deadpan.

"Please enter, sir."

Myron smelled the chlorine before he heard the tiny splashes.

The manservant waited.

"I didn't bring my bathing suit," Myron said.

The manservant looked at him blankly.

"I usually wear a thong," Myron said. "Though I can make due with bikini mesh."

The manservant blinked.

"I can borrow yours," Myron continued, "if you have an extra."

"Please enter, sir."

"Right, well, let's stay in touch."

The butler or whatever left. Myron went inside. The room had that indoor-pool mustiness. Everything was done in marble. Lots of plant life. There were statues of some goddess at each corner of the pool. What goddess, Myron did not know. The goddess of indoor pools, he surmised. The pool's sole occupant sliced through the water with nary a ripple. Arthur Bradford swam with easy, almost lazy movements. He reached the edge of the pool near Myron and stopped. He was wearing swimming goggles with dark blue lenses. He took them off and ran his hand across his scalp.

"What happened to Sam and Mario?" Bradford asked.

"Mario." Myron nodded. "That has to be the big guy, right?"

"Sam and Mario were supposed to escort you here."

"I'm a big boy, Artie. I don't need an escort." Bradford had of course sent them to intimidate; Myron needed to show him that the move had not produced the desired effect.

"Fine then," Bradford replied, his voice crisp. "I have six more laps to go. Do you mind?"

Myron waved a dismissal. "Hey," he said. "Please go ahead. I can think of nothing that would give me greater pleasure than watching another man swim. Hey, here's an idea. Why not film a commercial here? Slogan: Vote for Art, He's Got an Indoor Pool."

Bradford almost smiled. "Fair enough." He pushed himself out of the pool in one lax motion. His body was long and lean and looked sleek when wet. He grabbed a towel and signaled to two chaise longues. Myron sat in one but did not lean back. Arthur Bradford did likewise.

"It's been a long day," Arthur said. "I've already made four campaign stops, and I have three more this afternoon."

Myron nodded through the small talk, encouraging Bradford to move on. Bradford picked up the hint. He slapped his thighs with his palms. "Well, then, you're a busy man. I'm a busy man. Shall we get to it?"

"Sure."

Bradford leaned in a bit. "I wanted to talk to you about your previous visit here."

Myron tried to keep his face blank.

"You'll agree, will you not, that it was all rather bizarre?"
Myron made a noise. Sort of like "Uh-huh" but more neutral.
"Put simply, I'd like to know what you and Win were up to."
"I wanted the answers to some questions," Myron said.
"Yes, I realize that. My question is, why?"
"Why what?"
"Why were you asking about a woman who hasn't been in my employ for twenty years?"
"What's the difference? You barely remember her, right?"
Arthur Bradford smiled. The smile said that they both knew better. "I would like to help you," Bradford said. "But I must first question your motives." He opened his arms. "This is, after all, a major election."
"You think I'm working for Davison?"
"You and Windsor come to my home under false pretenses. You start asking bizarre questions about my past. You pay off a police officer to steal a file on my wife's death. You are connected with a man who recently tried to blackmail me. And you've been seen conversing with known criminal associates of Davison's." He gave the political smile, the one that couldn't help being a touch condescending. "If you were I, what would you think?"
"Back up," Myron said. "One, I didn't pay off anybody to steal a file."
"Officer Francine Neagly. Do you deny meeting with her at the Ritz Diner?"
"No." Too long to explain the truth, and what was the point? "Okay, forget that one for now. Who tried to blackmail you?"
The manservant entered the room. "Iced tea, sir?"
Bradford thought it over. "Lemonade, Mattius. Some lemonade would be divine."
"Very well, sir. Mr. Bolitar?"
Myron doubted that Bradford stocked much Yoo-Hoo. "Same here, Mattius. But make mine *extra* divine."
Mattius the Manservant nodded. "Very well, sir." He slid back out the door.
Arthur Bradford wrapped a towel around his shoulders. Then he lay back on the chaise. The lounges were long so that his legs would not hang over the ends. He closed his eyes. "We both know that I remember Anita Slaughter. As you implied, a man does not forget the name of the person who found his wife's body."
"That the only reason?"
Bradford opened one eye. "Excuse me?"

"I've seen pictures of her," Myron said simply. "Hard to forget a woman who looked like that."

Bradford reclosed the eye. For a moment he did not speak. "There are plenty of attractive women in the world."

"Uh-huh."

"You think I had a relationship with her?"

"I didn't say that. I just said she was attractive. Men remember attractive women."

"True," Bradford agreed. "But you see, that is the sort of false rumor Davison would love to get his hands on. Do you understand my concern? This is politics, and politics is spin. You wrongly think that my concerns for this matter prove that I have something to hide. But that's not the case. The truth is, I am worried about perception. Just because I didn't do anything does not mean my opponent won't try to make it look like I did. Do you follow?"

Myron nodded. "Like a politician after graft." But Bradford had a point. He was running for governor. Even if there were nothing there, he would snap into a defensive stance. "So who tried to blackmail you?"

Bradford waited a second, internally calculating, adding up the pros and cons of telling Myron. The internal computer worked down the scenarios. The pros won.

"Horace Slaughter," he said.

"With what?" Myron asked.

Bradford didn't answer the question directly. "He called my campaign headquarters."

"And he got through to you?"

"He said he had incriminating information about Anita Slaughter. I figured it was probably a crackpot, but the fact that he knew Anita's name bothered me."

I bet, Myron thought. "So what did he say?"

"He wanted to know what I'd done with his wife. He accused me of helping her run away."

"Helping her how?"

He waved his hands. "Supporting her, helping her, chasing her away. I don't know. He was rambling."

"But what did he say?"

Bradford sat up. He swung his legs across the side of the chaise. For several seconds he looked at Myron as if he were a hamburger he wasn't sure it was time to flip. "I want to know your interest in this."

Give a little, get a little. Part of the game. "The daughter."

"Excuse me?"

"Anita Slaughter's daughter."

Bradford nodded very slowly. "Isn't she a basketball player?"

"Yes."

"Do you represent her?"

"Yes. I was also friendly with her father. You heard he was murdered?"

"It was in the newspaper," Bradford said. In the newspaper. Never a straight yes or no with this guy. Then he added, "So what is your connection with the Ache family?"

Something in the back of Myron's head clicked. "Are they Davison's 'criminal associates'?" Myron asked.

"Yes."

"So the Aches have an interest in his winning the election?"

"Of course. That's why I'd like to know how you're connected to them."

"No connection," Myron said. "They're setting up a rival women's basketball league. They want to sign Brenda." But now Myron was wondering. The Aches had been meeting with Horace Slaughter. According to FJ, he had even signed his daughter to play with them. Next thing you know, Horace was pestering Bradford about his deceased wife. Could Horace have been working with the Aches? Fodder for thought.

Mattius returned with the lemonades. Fresh squeezed. Cold. Delicious, if not divine. Again the rich. When Mattius left the room, Bradford fell into the feigning-deep-thought look he'd displayed so often at their previous meeting. Myron waited.

"Being a politician," Bradford began, "it's a strange thing. All creatures fight to survive. It's instinctive, of course. But the truth is, a politician is colder about it than most. He can't help it. A man has been murdered here, and all I see is the potential for political embarrassment. That's the plain truth. My goal is simply to keep my name out of it."

"That's not going to happen," Myron said. "No matter what you or I might want."

"What makes you say that?"

"The police are going to link you into this the same way I did."

"I'm not following you."

"I came to you because Horace Slaughter called you. The police will see those same phone records. They'll have to follow up."

Arthur Bradford smiled. "Don't worry about the police."

Myron remembered Wickner and Pomeranz and the power of this

family. Bradford might be right. Myron thought about this. And decided to turn it to his advantage.

"So you're asking me to keep quiet?" Myron said.

Bradford hesitated. Chess time. Watching the board and trying to figure out Myron's next move. "I am asking you," he said, "to be fair."

"Meaning?"

"Meaning you have no real evidence that I am involved in anything illicit."

Myron tilted his head back and forth. Maybe yes, maybe no.

"And if you are telling the truth, if you do not work for Davison, then you would have no reason to damage my campaign."

"I'm not sure that's true," Myron said.

"I see." Again Bradford tried to read the tea leaves. "I assume then that you want something in exchange for your silence."

"Perhaps. But it's not what you think."

"What is it then?"

"Two things. First, I want the answer to some questions. The real answers. If I suspect you are lying or worried about how it will look, I'll hang you out to dry. I'm not out to embarrass you. I don't care about this election. I just want the truth."

"And the second thing?"

Myron smiled. "We'll get to that. First I need the answers."

Bradford waited a beat. "But how can you expect me to agree to a condition I don't even know?"

"Answer my questions first. If I am convinced that you are telling the truth, then I'll give you the second condition. But if you're evasive, the second condition becomes irrelevant."

Bradford didn't like it. "I don't think I can agree to that."

"Fine." Myron rose. "Have a nice day, Arthur."

His voice was sharp. "Sit down."

"Will you answer my questions?"

Arthur Bradford looked at him. "Congressman Davison is not the only one who has unsavory friends."

Myron let the words hang in the air.

"If you are to survive in politics," Bradford continued, "you must align yourself with some of the state's more sordid elements. That's the ugly truth, Myron. Am I making myself clear?"

"Yes," Myron said. "For the third time in the past hour someone is threatening me."

"You don't appear too frightened."

"I don't scare easily." Half truth. Showing fear was unhealthy; you show fear, you're dead. "So let's cut the crap. There are questions here. I can ask them. Or the press can."

Bradford took his time again. The man was nothing if not careful. "I still don't understand," he said. "What's your interest in this?"

Still stalling with questions. "I told you. The daughter."

"And when you came here the first time, you were looking for her father?"

"Yes."

"And you came to me because this Horace Slaughter had called my office?"

Myron nodded. Slowly.

Bradford threw on the baffled face again. "Then why on God's green earth did you ask about my wife? If indeed you were solely interested in Horace Slaughter, why were you so preoccupied with Anita Slaughter and what happened twenty years ago?"

The room fell silent, save for the gentle whisper of the pool waves. Light reflected off the water, bouncing to and fro like an erratic screen saver. They were at the crux of it now, and both men knew it. Myron thought about it a moment. He kept his eyes on Bradford's and wondered how much to say and how he could use it. Negotiating. Life was like being a sports agent, a series of negotiations.

"Because I wasn't just looking for Horace Slaughter," Myron said slowly. "I was looking for Anita Slaughter."

Bradford wrestled to maintain control over his facial expressions and body language. But Myron's words still caused a sharp intake of air. His complexion lost a bit of color. He was good, no doubt about it, but there was something there.

Bradford spoke slowly. "Anita Slaughter disappeared twenty years ago, did she not?"

"Yes."

"And you think she's still alive?"

"Yes."

"Why?"

To get information, you had to give it. Myron knew that. You had to prime the pump. But Myron was flooding it now. Time to stop and reverse the flow. "Why would you care?"

"I don't." Bradford hardly sounded convincing. "But I assumed that she was dead."

"Why?"

"She seemed like a decent woman. Why would she have run off and abandoned her child like that?"

"Maybe she was afraid," Myron said.

"Of her husband?"

"Of you."

That froze him. "Why would she be afraid of me?"

"You tell me, Arthur."

"I have no idea."

Myron nodded. "And your wife accidentally slipped off that terrace twenty years ago, right?"

Bradford did not reply.

"Anita Slaughter just came to work one morning and found your wife dead from a fall," Myron continued. "She'd slipped off her own balcony in the rainy dark and no one noticed. Not you. Not your brother. No one. Anita just happened by her dead body. Isn't that what happened?"

Bradford wasn't cracking, but Myron could sense some fault lines starting to open a touch. "You don't know anything."

"Then tell me."

"I loved my wife. I loved her with everything I had."

"So what happened to her?"

Bradford took a few breaths, tried to regain control. "She fell," he said. Then, thinking further, he asked, "Why would you think that my wife's death has anything to do with Anita's disappearance?" His voice was stronger now, the timbre coming back. "In fact, if I recall correctly, Anita stayed on after the accident. She left our employ well after Elizabeth's tragedy."

True enough. And a point that kept irritating Myron like a grain of sand in the retina.

"So why do you keep harping on my wife's death?" Bradford pressed.

Myron had no answer, so he parried with a couple of questions. "Why is everyone so concerned about that police file? Why are the cops so worried?"

"The same reason I am," he said. "It's an election year. Looking into old files is suspicious behavior. That's all there is to it. My wife died in an accident. End of story." His voice was growing stronger still. Negotiation can have more momentum shifts than a basketball game. If so, the Big Mo' was back on Bradford's side. "Now you answer a question for me: Why do you think Anita Slaughter is still alive? I mean, if the family hasn't heard from her in twenty years?"

"Who says they haven't heard from her?"

He arched an eyebrow. "Are you saying they have?"

Myron shrugged. He had to be oh-so-careful here. If Anita Slaughter were indeed hiding from this guy—and if Bradford did in-

deed believe she was dead—how would he react to evidence that she
was still alive? Wouldn't he logically try to find her and silence her?
Interesting thought. But at the same time, if Bradford had been se-
cretly paying her off, as Myron had earlier theorized, he would know
she was alive. At the very least he would know that she had run away
instead of having met up with foul play.

So what was going on here?

"I think I've said enough," Myron said.

Bradford took a long pull on his lemonade glass, draining it. He
stirred the pitcher and poured himself another. He gestured toward
Myron's glass. Myron shook him off. Both men settled back.

"I would like to hire you," Bradford said.

Myron tried a smile. "As?"

"An adviser of sorts. Security, perhaps. I want to hire you to keep
me up-to-date on your investigation. Hell, I have enough morons on
the payroll in charge of damage control. Who better than the inside
man? You'll be able to prepare me for a potential scandal. What do
you say?"

"I think I'll pass."

"Don't be so hasty," Bradford said. "I will pledge my cooperation
as well as that of my staff's."

"Right. And if something bad turns up, you squash it."

"I won't deny that I'll be interested in making sure the facts are
put in the proper light."

"Or shade."

He smiled. "You're not keeping your eyes on the prize, Myron.
Your client is not interested in me or my political career. She is interested in finding her mother. I'd like to help."

"Sure, you would. After all, helping people is why you got into
politics in the first place."

Bradford shook his head. "I'm making you a serious offer, and
you choose to be glib."

"It's not that." Time to shift the momentum again. Myron chose
his words carefully. "Even if I wanted to," he said, "I can't."

"Why not?"

"I mentioned a second condition before."

Bradford put a finger to his lips. "So you did."

"I already work for Brenda Slaughter. She must remain my pri-
mary concern in this matter."

Bradford put his hand behind his neck. Relaxed. "Yes, of course."

"You read the papers. The police think she did it."

"Well, you'll have to admit," Bradford said, "she makes a good suspect."

"Maybe. But if they arrest her, I'll have to act in her best interest." Myron looked straight at him. "That means I'll have to toss out any information that will lead the police to look at other potential suspects."

Bradford smiled. He saw where this was going. "Including me."

Myron turned both palms up and shrugged. "What choice would I have? My client must come first." Slight hesitation. "But of course none of that will occur if Brenda Slaughter remains free."

Still the smile. "Ah," Bradford said.

Myron kept still.

Bradford sat up and put up both hands in stop position. "Say no more."

Myron didn't.

"It'll be dealt with." Bradford checked his watch. "Now I must get dressed. Campaign obligations."

They both rose. Bradford stuck out his hand. Myron shook it. Bradford had not come clean, but Myron had not expected him to. They'd both learned a bit here. Myron was not sure who had gotten the better of the deal. But the first rule of any negotiation is not to be a pig. If you just keep taking, it will backfire in the long run.

Still he wondered.

"Good-bye," Bradford said, still shaking the hand. "I do hope you'll keep me up-to-date on your progress."

The two men released their grips. Myron looked at Bradford. He didn't want to, but he couldn't stop himself from asking:

"Do you know my father?"

Bradford angled his head and smiled. "Did he tell you that?"

"No. Your friend Sam mentioned it."

"Sam has worked for me a long time."

"I didn't ask about Sam. I asked about my father."

Mattius opened the door. Bradford motioned to it.

"Why don't you ask your father, Myron? Maybe it will help clarify the situation."

Chapter 23

As Mattius the Manservant led Myron back down the long corridor, the same two words kept rocking through Myron's bone-dry skull:

My father?

Myron searched for a memory, a casual mention of the Bradford name in the house, a political tête-à-tête surrounding Livingston's most prominent resident. Nothing came to him.

So how did Bradford know his father?

Big Guy Mario and Skinny Sam were in the foyer. Mario stamped back and forth as though the very floor had pissed him off. His arms and hands gestured with the subtlety of a Jerry Lewis flick. If he had been a cartoon character, smoke would have been power-shooting out of both ears.

Skinny Sam pulled on a Marlboro, leaning against the banister like Sinatra waiting for Dino. Sam had that ease. Like Win. Myron could engage in violence, and he was good at it, but there were adrenal spikes and tingling legs and postcombat cold sweats when he did so. That was normal, of course. Only a rare few had the ability to disconnect, to remain calm in the eye, to view the outbursts in slow motion.

Big Guy Mario stormed toward Myron. His fists were clenched at his sides. His face was contorted like it'd been pressed up against a glass door. "You're dead, asshole. You hear me? Dead. Dead and buried. I'm gonna take you outside and—"

Myron snapped up the knee again. And again it found its target. Big Dope Mario landed hard on the cool marble and thrashed around like a dying fish.

"Today's friendly tip," Myron said. "A protective cup is a worthwhile investment, though not as a drinking receptacle."

Myron looked over at Sam. Sam still rested on the banister. He took another drag of the cigarette and let the smoke ease out of his nostrils.

"New guy," Sam said in way of explanation.

Myron nodded.

"Sometimes you just want to scare stupid people," Sam said. "Stupid people are scared by big muscles." Another drag. "But don't let his incompetence get you cocky."

Myron looked down. He was about to crack wise, but he stopped himself and shook his head. Cocky, a knee in the balls.

Too easy.

Win waited by Myron's car. He was bent slightly at the waist, practicing his golf swing. He did not have a club or a ball, of course. Remember blasting rock music and jumping on your bed and playing air guitar? Golfers do the same thing. They hear some internal sounds of nature, step on imaginary first tees, and swing air clubs. Air woods usually. Sometimes, when they want more control, they take air irons out of their air bags. And like teens with air guitars, golfers like to watch themselves in mirrors. Win, for example, often checks out his reflection in store windows. He stops on the sidewalk, makes sure his grip is right, checks his backswing, recocks his wrists, whatever.

"Win?"

"A moment."

Win had repositioned Myron's passenger side mirror for a better full-body view. He stopped mid-swing, spotted something in the reflection, frowned.

"Remember," Myron said. "Objects in the mirror may appear smaller than they are."

Win ignored him. He readdressed the, uh, ball, selected an air sand wedge, and tried a little air chip. From the look on Win's face the, uh, ball landed on the green and rolled within three feet of the cup. Win smiled and put up a hand to acknowledge the, uh, appreciative crowd.

Golfers.

"How did you get here so fast?" Myron asked.

"Batcopter."

Lock-Horne Securities had a helicopter and a landing pad on the roof. Win had probably flown to a nearby field and jogged over.

"So you heard everything?"

Win nodded.

"What do you think?"

"Wasteful," Win said.

"Right, I should have shot him in the knee."

"Well, yes, there is that. But in this instance I am referring to the entire matter."

"Meaning?"

"Meaning that Arthur Bradford may be on to something. You are not keeping your eyes on the prize."

"And what is the prize?"

Win smiled. "Exactly."

Myron nodded. "Yet again, I have no idea what you're talking about."

He unlocked the car doors, and the two men slid into their seats. The Leatherette was hot from the sun. The air conditioner sputtered out something close to warm spit.

"On occasion," Win said, "we have performed extracurricular duties for one reason or another. But there was, for the most part, a purpose. A goal, if you will. We knew what we were trying to accomplish."

"And you don't think that's the case here?"

"Correct."

"I'll give you three goals then," Myron said. "One, I'm trying to find Anita Slaughter. Two, I'm trying to find Horace Slaughter's killer. Three, I'm trying to protect Brenda."

"Protect her from what?"

"I don't know yet."

"Ah," Win said. "And—let me make sure I understand you here—you feel that the best way to protect Ms. Slaughter is to agitate police officers, the most powerful family in the state, and known mobsters?"

"That can't be helped."

"Well, yes, of course you're right about that. And we also have your other two goals to consider." Win lowered the visor and checked his hair in the mirror. Not a blond hair out of place. He still patted about, frowning. When he finished, he snapped the visor back into place. "Let's start with finding Anita Slaughter, shall we?"

Myron nodded, but he knew that he was not going to like where this was going.

"That is the core of the matter, is it not? Finding Brenda's mother?"

"Right," Myron said.

"So—and again let me make sure I comprehend completely—you are taking on police officers, the most powerful family in the state, and known mobsters to find a woman who ran off twenty years ago?"

"Yes."

"And the reason for this search?"

"Brenda. She wants to know where her mother is. She has the right—"

"Bah," Win interrupted.

"Bah?"

"What are you, the ACLU? What right? Brenda has no right here. Do you believe Anita Slaughter is being held against her will?"

"No."

"Then what, pray tell, are you trying to accomplish here? If Anita Slaughter craved a reconciliation with her daughter, she would seek it. Clearly she has opted not to do that. We know that she ran away twenty years ago. We know that she has worked hard to stay hidden. What we don't know, of course, is why. And instead of respecting her decision, you choose to ignore it."

Myron said nothing.

"Under normal circumstances," Win continued, "this search would be a close call. But when you add in the mitigating factors— the obvious danger upsetting these particular adversaries—the call is an easy one. Simply put, we are taking a tremendous risk for very little reason."

Myron shook his head, but he saw the logic. Had he not wondered about these same issues himself? He was doing his tightrope act again, this time over a raging inferno, and he was dragging others, including Francine Neagly, with him. And for what? Win was right. He was pissing off powerful people. He might even be inadvertently helping those who wished Anita Slaughter great harm, flushing her out into the open where they could set their sights with greater ease. He knew that he had to step carefully here. One false move and ka-pow.

"There's more to it," Myron tried. "A crime may have been covered up."

"Are you speaking now of Elizabeth Bradford?"

"Yes."

Win frowned. "So is that what you're after, Myron? You're risking lives in order to give her justice after twenty years? Elizabeth Bradford is calling out to you from the grave or some such thing?"

"There's also Horace to think about."

"What about him?"

"He was my friend."

"And you believe that finding his killer will ease your guilt over not talking to him in ten years?"

Myron swallowed at that one. "Low blow, Win."

"No, my friend, I am merely trying to pull you back from the abyss. I am not saying that there is no value in what you are doing here. We have worked for questionable profit before. But you have to calculate some sort of cost-benefit analysis. You are trying to find a woman who does not want to be found. You are pushing against forces more powerful than you and me combined."

"You almost sound afraid, Win."

Win looked at him. "You know better."

Myron looked at the blue eyes with the flecks of silver. He nodded. He did know better.

"I'm talking about pragmatism," Win continued, "not fear. Pushing is fine. Forcing confrontation is fine. We've done that plenty of times before. We both know that I rarely back away from such instances, that I perhaps enjoy them too much. But there was always a goal. We were looking for Kathy to help clear a client. We were looking for Valerie's killer for the same reason. We searched for Greg because you were well compensated monetarily. The same could be said about the Coldren boy. But the goal here is too hazy."

The volume switch on the car radio was set low, but Myron could still hear Seal "compare" his love to "a kiss from the rose on the grave." Romance.

"I have to stick with this," Myron said. "For a little while longer anyway."

Win said nothing.

"And I'd like your help."

Still nothing.

"There were scholarships set up to help Brenda," Myron said. "I think her mother may have been funneling money to her through them. Anonymously. I want you to try to track the money trail."

Win reached forward and turned off the radio. Traffic was almost nonexistent. The air conditioner hummed, but otherwise the silence was heavy. After a couple of minutes, Win broke it.

"You're in love with her, aren't you?"

The question hit him by surprise. Myron opened his mouth, closed it. Win had never asked a question like this before; he did, in fact, all he could do to avoid the subject. Explaining love relationships to Win had always seemed akin to explaining jazz music to a lawn chair.

"I think I might be," Myron said.

"It's affecting your judgment," Win said. "Emotion may be ruling over pragmatism."

"I won't let it."

"Pretend you are not in love with her. Would you still pursue this?"

"Does it matter?"

Win nodded. He understood better than most. Hypotheticals had nothing to do with reality. "Fine then," he said. "Give me the information on the scholarships. I'll see what I can find."

They both settled into silence. Win as always looked perfectly relaxed and in a state of total readiness.

"There is a very fine line between relentless and stupid," Win said. "Try to stay on the right side of it."

Chapter 24

The Sunday afternoon traffic remained light. The Lincoln Tunnel was a breeze. Win fiddled with the buttons on Myron's new CD player, settling on a recently purchased compilation CD of AM seventies classics. They listened to "The Night Chicago Died." Then "The Night the Lights Went Out in Georgia." Nights, Myron surmised, were a dangerous time in the seventies. Then the theme song to the movie *Billy Jack* blasted its peace on earth message. Remember the Billy Jack movies? Win did. A little too well, in fact.

The final song was a classic seventies tearjerker called "Shannon." Shannon dies pretty early in the song. In a very high pitch, we are told that Shannon is gone, that she drifted out to sea. Sad. The song always moved Myron. Mother is heartbroken at the loss. Dad always seems tired now. Nothing is the same without Shannon.

"Did you know," Win said, "that Shannon was a dog?"

"You're kidding."

Win shook his head. "If you listen closely to the chorus, you can tell."

"I can only make out the part about Shannon being gone and drifting out to sea."

"That is followed by the hopes that Shannon will find an island with a shady tree."

"A shady tree?"

Win sang, "Just like the one in our backyard."

"That doesn't mean it's a dog, Win. Maybe Shannon liked sitting under a tree. Maybe they had a hammock."

"Perhaps," Win said. "But there is one other subtle giveaway."

"What's that?"

"The CD liner notes say the song is about a dog."

Win.

"Do you want me to drop you off at home?" Myron asked.

Win shook his head. "I have paperwork," he said. "And I think it best if I stay close."

Myron did not argue.

"You have the weapon?" Win asked.

"Yes."

"Do you want another?"

"No."

They parked at the Kinney lot and took the elevator up together. The high-rise was silent today, the ants all away from the hill. The effect was sort of eerie, like one of those end-of-the-earth apocalypse movies where everything is abandoned and ghostlike. The dinging of the elevator echoed in the still air like a thunderclap.

Myron got off at the twelfth floor. Despite its being Sunday, Big Cyndi was at her desk. As always, everything around Big Cyndi looked tiny, like that episode of *The Twilight Zone* where the house starts shrinking or like someone had jammed a large stuffed animal into Barbie's pink Corvette. Big Cyndi was wearing a wig today that looked like something stolen from Carol Channing's closet. Bad hair day, Myron supposed. She stood and smiled at him. Myron kept his eyes open and was surprised when he didn't turn to stone.

Big Cyndi was normally six-six, but she was wearing high heels today. Pumps. The heels cried out in agony as she stood. She was dressed into what some might consider a business suit. The shirt was French-Revolution frilly, the jacket solid gray with a fresh tear along the shoulder stitch.

She raised her hands and twirled for Myron. Picture Godzilla rearing back after getting nailed by a Taser gun.

"Like it?" she asked.

"Very much," Myron said. *Jurassic Park III: The Fashion Show.*

"I bought it at Benny's."

"Benny's?"

"Down in the Village," Big Cyndi explained. "It's a clothing store for transvestites. But lots of us big girls shop there too."

Myron nodded. "Practical," he said.

Big Cyndi sniffled once, then suddenly began to cry. She still had on waaaay too much makeup, none of it waterproof, and she quickly started to look like a lava lamp left in the microwave.

"Oh, Mr. Bolitar!"

She ran toward him, her arms spread, the floor creaking from the thumping. An image of one of those cartoon scenes where characters keep falling through floors, forming cutout silhouettes in each floor as they pass through it, came to him.

Myron put up his hands. *No! Myron good! Myron like Cyndi! Cyndi no hurt Myron!* But the gesture was useless.

She embraced him, wrapping both arms around him and lifting

him off his feet. It felt as though a water bed had come to life and attacked him. He closed his eyes and tried to ride it out.

"Thank you," she whispered through her tears.

Out of the corner of his eye he spotted Esperanza. She watched the scene with crossed arms, smiling slightly. The new job, Myron suddenly remembered. Rehiring her full-time.

"You're welcome," he managed.

"I won't let you down."

"Could you at least put me down?"

Big Cyndi made a noise that might have been a giggle. Children in the tristate area screamed and reached for Mommy's hand.

She lowered him gently back to the floor like a child placing a block on the top of a pyramid. "You won't be sorry. I'll work night and day. I'll work weekends. I'll pick up your laundry. I'll make coffee. I'll fetch Yoo-Hoos. I'll even give you backrubs."

The image of a steamroller approaching a bruised peach flashed through his mind.

"Er, a Yoo-Hoo would be great."

"Right away." Big Cyndi bounced toward the refrigerator.

Myron moved toward Esperanza.

"She does give a great backrub," Esperanza said.

"I'll take your word for it."

"I told Big Cyndi you were the one who wanted to hire her full-time."

Myron nodded. "Next time," he said, "just let me pull a thorn out of her paw, okay?"

Big Cyndi held up the can of Yoo-Hoo. "Do you want me to shake it for you, Mr. Bolitar?"

"I'll handle that, Cyndi, thanks."

"Yes, Mr. Bolitar." She hopped back over, and Myron was reminded of the scene where the boat flips over in the *Poseidon Adventure.* She handed him the Yoo-Hoo. Then she smiled again. And the gods shielded their eyes.

Myron spoke to Esperanza. "Any more word on Lester's trade?"

"No."

"Get me Ron Dixon on the phone. Try his home number."

Big Cyndi took that one. "Right away, Mr. Bolitar."

Esperanza shrugged. Big Cyndi dialed and used her English accent. She sounded like Maggie Smith in a Noël Coward play. Myron and Esperanza went into his office. The call was transferred.

"Ron? It's Myron Bolitar, how are you?"

"I know who the hell this is, moron. Your receptionist told me. It's

Sunday, Myron. Sunday is my day off. Sunday is my family day. My quality time. My chance to get to know the kids better. So why are you calling me on a Sunday?"

"Are you trading Lester Ellis?"

"That's why you're calling me at home on a Sunday?"

"Is it true?"

"No comment."

"You told me you wouldn't trade him."

"Wrong. I told you I wouldn't actively put him on the block. If you recall, Mr. Super Agent, you wanted to put in a trade approval clause in his contract. I said, no, unless you wanted to shave fifty grand off his salary. You refused. Now it's coming back and biting your ass cheek, ain't it, hotshot?"

Myron shifted in his seat. Sore ass cheek and all. "Who are you getting for him?"

"No comment."

"Don't do this, Ron. He's a great talent."

"Yeah. Too bad he's not a great baseball player."

"You're going to look foolish. Remember Nolan Ryan for Jim Fregosi? Remember Babe Ruth, uh"—Myron forgot who they got in the trade—"being traded by the Red Sox?"

"Now Lester Ellis is Babe Ruth?"

"Let's talk about this."

"Nothing to talk about, Myron. And now, if you'll excuse me, the wife is calling me. It's strange."

"What's that?"

"This quality time stuff. This getting to know my children better. You know what I've learned, Myron?"

"What?"

"I hate my kids."

Click.

Myron looked up at Esperanza.

"Get me Al Toney at the *Chicago Tribune.*"

"He's being traded to Seattle."

"Trust me here."

Esperanza gestured to the phone. "Don't ask me. Ask Big Cyndi."

Myron hit the intercom. "Big Cyndi, could you please get me Al Toney? He should be at his office."

"Yes, Mr. Bolitar."

A minute later Big Cyndi beeped in. "Al Toney on line one."

"Al? Myron Bolitar here."

"Hey, Myron, what's up?"

"I owe you one, right?"

"At least one."

"Well, I got a scoop for you."

"My nipples are hardening as we speak. Talk dirty to me, baby."

"You know Lester Ellis? He's being traded tomorrow to Seattle. Lester is thrilled. He's been bugging the Yankees to trade him all year. We couldn't be happier."

"That's your big scoop?"

"Hey, this is an important story."

"In New York or Seattle maybe. But I'm in Chicago, Myron."

"Still. I thought you might want to know."

"No good. You still owe me."

Myron said, "You don't want to check with your nipples first?"

"Hold on." Pause. "Soft as overripe grapes already. But I could check again in a few minutes, if you'd like."

"Pass, Al, thanks. Frankly I didn't think it would fly with you, but it was worth a try. Between you and me, the Yankees are pushing hard on this trade. They want me to put on the best spin. I thought you could help."

"Why? Who they getting?"

"I don't know."

"Lester's a pretty good player. Raw but good. Why the Yankees so interested in getting rid of him?"

"You won't print this?"

Pause. Myron could almost hear Al's brain awhirring. "Not if you tell me not to."

"He's hurt. Home accident. Damaged the knee. They're keeping it quiet, but Lester will need surgery after the season."

Silence.

"You can't print it, Al."

"No problem. Hey, I gotta go."

Myron smiled. "Later, Al."

He hung up.

Esperanza looked at him. "Are you doing what I think you're doing?"

"Al Toney is the master of the loophole," Myron explained. "He promised *he* wouldn't print it. He won't. But he works by trading favors. He's the best barterer in the business."

"So?"

"So now he'll call a friend at the *Seattle Times* and barter. The injury rumor will spread. If it gets public before the trade is announced, well, it's doomed."

Esperanza smiled. "Highly unethical."

Myron shrugged. "Let's just say it's fuzzy."

"I still like it."

"Always remember the MB SportsReps credo: The client comes first."

She nodded and added, "Even in sexual liaisons."

"Hey, we're a full-service agency." Myron looked at her for a long moment. Then he said, "Can I ask you something?"

She tilted her head. "I don't know. Can you?"

"Why do you hate Jessica?"

Esperanza's face clouded over. She shrugged. "Habit, I guess."

"I'm serious."

She crossed her legs, uncrossed them. "Let me just stick to taking cheap potshots, okay?"

"You're my best friend," he said. "I want to know why you don't like her."

Esperanza sighed, crossed the legs again, tucked a loose strand behind her ear. "Jessica is bright, smart, funny, a great writer, and I wouldn't throw her out of bed for eating crackers."

Bisexuals.

"But she hurt you."

"So? She's not the first woman to commit an indiscretion."

"True enough," Esperanza agreed. She slapped her knees and stood. "Guess I'm wrong. Can I go now?"

"So why do you still hold a grudge?"

"I like grudges," Esperanza said. "They're easier than forgiveness."

Myron shook his head, signaled her to sit.

"What do you want me to say, Myron?"

"I want you to tell me why you don't like her."

"I'm just being a pain in the ass. Don't take it seriously."

Myron shook his head again.

Esperanza put her hand to her face. She looked away for a moment. "You're not tough enough, okay?"

"What do you mean?"

"For that kind of hurt. Most people can take it. I can. Jessica can. Win certainly can. But you can't. You're not tough enough. You're just not built that way."

"Then maybe that's my fault."

"It is your fault," Esperanza said. "At least in part. You idealize relationships too much, for one thing. And you're too sensitive. You used to expose yourself too much. You used to leave yourself too open."

"Is that such a bad thing?"

She hesitated. "No. In fact, it's a good thing, I guess. A bit naive, but it's a lot better than those assholes who hold everything back. Can we stop talking about this now?"

"I still don't think you've answered my question."

Esperanza raised her palms. "That's as good as I can do."

Myron flashed back to Little League again, to being hit by Joey Davito's pitch, to never planting his feet in the batter's box the same again. He nodded. Used to expose, Esperanza had said. "Used to." A curious use of words.

Esperanza took advantage of the silence and changed subjects. "I checked into Elizabeth Bradford for you."

"And?"

"There's nothing there that would suggest her death was anything other than an accident. You can take a run at her brother, if you want. He lives in Westport. He's also closely aligned to his old brother-in-law, so I doubt you'll get anywhere."

Waste of time. "Any other family?"

"A sister who also lives in Westport. But she's spending the summer on the Côte d'Azur."

Strike two.

"Anything else?"

"One thing bothered me a little," Esperanza said. "Elizabeth Bradford was clearly a social animal, a society dame of the first order. Barely a week went by when her name wasn't in the paper for some function or other. But about six months before she fell off the balcony, mentions of her stopped."

"When you say 'stopped'—"

"I mean, completely. Her name was nowhere, not even in the town paper."

Myron thought about this. "Maybe she was on the Côte d'Azur."

"Maybe. But her husband wasn't there with her. Arthur was still getting plenty of coverage."

Myron leaned back and spun his chair around. He checked out the Broadway posters behind his desk again. Yep, they definitely had to go. "You said there were a lot of stories on Elizabeth Bradford before that?"

"Not stories," Esperanza corrected. "Mentions. Her name was almost always preceded by 'Hosting the event was' or 'Attendees included' or 'Pictured from right to left are.'"

Myron nodded. "Were these in some kind of column or general articles or what?"

"The *Jersey Ledger* used to have a social column. It was called 'Social Soirees.'"

"Catchy." But Myron remembered the column vaguely from his childhood. His mother used to skim it, checking out the boldface names for a familiar one. Mom had even been listed once, referred to as "prominent local attorney Ellen Bolitar." That was how she wanted to be addressed for the next week. Myron would yell down, "Hey, Mom!" and she would reply, "That's Prominent Local Attorney Ellen Bolitar to you, Mr. Smarty Pants."

"Who wrote the column?" Myron asked.

Esperanza handed him a sheet of paper. There was a head shot of a pretty woman with an overstylized helmet of hair, à la Lady Bird Johnson. Her name was Deborah Whittaker.

"Think we can get an address on her?"

Esperanza nodded. "Shouldn't take long."

They looked at each other for a long moment. Esperanza's deadline hung over them like a reaper's scythe.

Myron said, "I can't imagine you not in my life."

"Won't happen," Esperanza replied. "No matter what you decide, you'll still be my best friend."

"Partnerships ruin friendships."

"So you tell me."

"So I know." He had avoided this conversation long enough. To use basketball vernacular, he had gone into four corners, but the twenty-four-second clock had run down. He could no longer delay the inevitable in the hope that the inevitable would somehow turn to smoke and vanish in the air. "My father and my uncle tried it. They ended up not talking to each other for four years."

She nodded. "I know."

"Even now their relationship is not what it was. It never will be. I know literally dozens of families and friends—good people, Esperanza—who tried partnerships like this. I don't know one case where it worked in the long run. Not one. Brother against brother. Daughter against father. Best friend against best friend. Money does funny things to people."

Esperanza nodded again.

"Our friendship could survive anything," Myron said, "but I'm not sure it can survive a partnership."

Esperanza stood again. "I'll get you an address on Deborah Whittaker," she said. "It shouldn't take long."

"Thanks."

"And I'll give you three weeks for the transition. Will that be long enough?"

Myron nodded, his throat dry. He wanted to say something more, but whatever came to mind was even more inane than what preceded it.

The intercom buzzed. Esperanza left the room. Myron hit the button.

"Yes?"

Big Cyndi said, "The *Seattle Times* on line one."

Chapter 25

The Inglemoore Convalescent Home was painted bright yellow and cheerfully maintained and colorfully landscaped and still looked like a place you went to die.

The inner lobby had a rainbow on one wall. The furniture was happy and functional. Nothing too plush. Didn't want the patrons having trouble getting out of chairs. A table in the room's center had a huge arrangement of freshly cut roses. The roses were bright red and strikingly beautiful and would die in a day or two.

Myron took a deep breath. *Settle, boy, settle.*

The place had a heavy cherry smell like one of those dangling tree-shaped car fresheners. A woman dressed in slacks and a blouse—what you'd call "nice casual"—greeted him. She was in her early thirties and smiled with the genuine warmth of a Stepford Wife.

"I'm here to see Deborah Whittaker."

"Of course," she said. "I think Deborah is in the rec room. I'm Gayle. I'll take you."

Deborah. Gayle. Everyone was a first name. There was probably a Dr. Bob on the premises. They headed down a corridor lined with festive murals. The floors sparkled, but Myron could still make out fresh wheelchair streaks. Everyone on staff had the same fake smile. Part of the training, Myron supposed. All of them—orderlies, nurses, whatever—were dressed in civilian clothes. No one wore a stethoscope or beeper or name tag or anything that implied anything medical. All buddies here at Inglemoore.

Gayle and Myron entered the rec room. Unused Ping-Pong tables. Unused pool tables. Unused card tables. Oft-used television.

"Please sit down," Gayle said. "Becky and Deborah will be with you momentarily."

"Becky?" Myron asked.

Again the smile. "Becky is Deborah's friend."

"I see."

Myron was left alone with six old people, five of whom were women. No sexism in longevity. They were neatly attired, the sole

man in a tie even, and all were in wheelchairs. Two of them had the
shakes. Two were mumbling to themselves. They all had skin a color
closer to washed-out gray than any flesh tone. One woman waved at
Myron with a bony, blue-lined hand. Myron smiled and waved back.

Several signs on the wall had the Inglemoore slogan:
INGLEMOORE—NO DAY LIKE TODAY.

Nice, Myron guessed, but he couldn't help but think up a more ap-
propriate one:
INGLEMOORE—BETTER THAN THE ALTERNATIVE.

Hmm. He'd drop it in the suggestion box on the way out.

"Mr. Bolitar?"

Deborah Whittaker shuffled into the room. She still had Le Helmet de Hair from the newspaper portrait—black as shoe polish and
shellacked on until it resembled fiberglass—but the overall effect
was still like something out of Dorian Gray, as though she had aged
a zillion years in one fell swoop. Her eyes had that soldier's thou-
sand-yard stare. She had a bit of a shake in her face that reminded
him of Katharine Hepburn. Parkinson's maybe, but he was no expert.

Her "friend" Becky had been the one who called his name. Becky
was maybe thirty years old. She too was dressed in civilian clothes
rather than whites, and while nothing about her appearance suggested nursing, Myron still thought of Louise Fletcher in *One Flew
over the Cuckoo's Nest*.

He stood.

"I'm Becky," the nurse said.

"Myron Bolitar."

Becky shook his hand and offered him a patronizing smile. Probably couldn't help it. Probably couldn't smile genuinely until she was
out of here for at least an hour. "Do you mind if I join you two?"

Deborah Whittaker spoke for the first time. "Go away," she
rasped. Her voice sounded like a worn tire on a gravel road.

"Now, Deborah—"

"Don't 'now Deborah' me. I got myself a handsome gentleman
caller, and I'm not sharing him. So buzz off."

Becky's patronizing smile turned a bit uncertain. "Deborah," she
said in a tone that aimed for amiable but landed smack on, well, patronizing, "do you know where we are?"

"Of course," Deborah snapped. "The Allies just bombed Munich.
The Axis has surrendered. I'm a USO girl standing by the south pier
in Manhattan. The ocean breeze hits my face. I wait for the sailors to
arrive so I can lay a big, wet kiss on the first guy off the boat."

Deborah Whittaker winked at Myron.

Becky said, "Deborah, it's not 1945. It's—"

"I know, dammit. For crying out loud, Becky, don't be so damn gullible." She sat down and leaned toward Myron. "Truth is, I go in and out. Sometimes I'm here. Sometimes I time travel. When my grandpa had it, they called it hardening of the arteries. When my mother had it, they called it senility. With me, it's Parkinson's and Alzheimer's." She looked at her nurse, her facial muscles still doing the quivers. "Please, Becky, while I'm still lucid, get the hell out of my face."

Becky waited a second, holding the uncertain smile as best she could. Myron nodded at her, and she moved away.

Deborah Whittaker leaned a little closer. "I love getting ornery with her," she whispered. "It's the only fringe benefit of old age." She put her hands on her lap and managed a shaky smile. "Now I know you just told me, but I forgot your name."

"Myron."

She looked puzzled. "No, that's not it. André maybe? You look like André. He used to do my hair."

Becky kept a watchful eye on the corner. At the ready.

Myron decided to dive right in. "Mrs. Whittaker, I wanted to ask you about Elizabeth Bradford."

"Lizzy?" The eyes flared up and settled into a glisten. "Is she here?"

"No, ma'am."

"I thought she died."

"She did."

"Poor thing. She threw such wonderful parties. At Bradford Farm. They'd string lights across the porch. They'd have hundreds of people. Lizzy always had the best band, the best caterer. I had such fun at her parties. I used to dress up and . . ." A flicker hit Deborah Whittaker's eyes, a realization perhaps that the parties and invitations would never come again, and she stopped speaking.

"In your column," Myron said, "you used to write about Elizabeth Bradford."

"Oh, of course." She waved a hand. "Lizzy made good copy. She was a social force. But—" She stopped again and looked off.

"But what?"

"Well, I haven't written about Lizzy in months. Strange really. Last week Constance Lawrence had a charity ball for the St. Sebastian's Children's Care, and Lizzy wasn't there again. And that used to be Lizzy's favorite event. She ran it the past four years, you know."

Myron nodded, trying to keep up with the changing eras. "But Lizzy doesn't go to parties anymore, does she?"

"No, she doesn't."

"Why not?"

Deborah Whittaker sort of half startled. She eyed him suspiciously. "What's your name again?"

"Myron."

"I know that. You just told me. I mean, your last name."

"Bolitar."

Another spark. "Ellen's boy?"

"Yes, that's right."

"Ellen Bolitar," she said with a spreading smile. "How's she doing?"

"She's doing well."

"Such a shrewd woman. Tell me, Myron. Is she still ripping apart opposing witnesses?"

"Yes, ma'am."

"So shrewd."

"She loved your column," Myron said.

Her face beamed. "Ellen Bolitar, the attorney, reads my column?"

"Every week. It was the first thing she read."

Deborah Whittaker settled back, shaking her head. "How do you like that? Ellen Bolitar reads my column." She smiled at Myron. Myron was getting confused by the verb tenses. Bouncing in time. He'd just have to try to stay with her. "We're having such a nice visit, aren't we, Myron?"

"Yes, ma'am, we are."

Her smile quivered and faded. "Nobody in here remembers my column," she said. "They're all very nice and sweet. They treat me well. But I'm just another old lady to them. You reach an age, and suddenly you become invisible. They only see this rotting shell. They don't realize that this mind inside used to be sharp, that this body used to go to the fanciest parties and dance with the handsomest men. They don't see that. I can't remember what I had for breakfast, but I remember those parties. Do you think that's strange?"

Myron shook his head. "No, ma'am, I don't."

"I remember Lizzy's final soiree like it was last night. She wore a black, strapless Halston with white pearls. She was tan and lovely. I wore a bright pink summer dress. A Lilly Pulitzer, as a matter of fact, and let me tell you, I was still turning heads."

"What happened to Lizzy, Mrs. Whittaker? Why did she stop going to parties?"

Deborah Whittaker stiffened suddenly. "I'm a social columnist," she said, "not a gossip."

"I understand that. I'm not asking to be nosy. It may be important."

"Lizzy is my friend."

"Did you see her after that party?"

Her eyes had the faraway look again. "I thought she drank too much. I even wondered if maybe she had a problem."

"A drinking problem?"

"I don't like to gossip. It's not my way. I write a social column. I don't believe in hurting people."

"I appreciate that, Mrs. Whittaker."

"But I was wrong anyway."

"Wrong?"

"Lizzy doesn't have a drinking problem. Oh, sure, she might have a social drink, but she's too proper a hostess to go beyond her limit."

Again with the verb tenses. "Did you see her after that party?"

"No," she said softly. "Never."

"Did you talk to her on the phone maybe?"

"I called her twice. After she missed the Woodmeres' party and then Constance's affair, well, I knew something had to be very wrong. But I never spoke to her. She was either out or couldn't come to the phone." She looked up at Myron. "Do you know where she is? Do you think she'll be all right?"

Myron was not sure how to respond. Or in what tense. "Are you worried about her?"

"Of course I am. It's as though Lizzy just vanished. I've asked all her close friends from the club, but none of them has seen her either." She frowned. "Not friends really. Friends don't gossip like that."

"Gossip about what?"

"About Lizzy."

"What about her?"

Her voice was a conspiratorial whisper. "I thought she was acting strange because she drank too much. But that wasn't it."

Myron leaned in and matched her tone. "What was it then?"

Deborah Whittaker gazed at Myron. The eyes were milky and cloudy, and Myron wondered what reality they were seeing. "A breakdown," she said at last. "The ladies at the club were whispering that Lizzy had a breakdown. That Arthur had sent her away. To an institution with padded walls."

Myron felt his body go cold.

"Gossip," Deborah Whittaker spit. "Ugly rumors."

"You didn't believe it?"

"Tell me something." Deborah Whittaker licked lips so dry they looked like they might flake off. She sat up a bit. "If Elizabeth Bradford had been locked away in an institution," she said, "how come she fell at her own home?"

Myron nodded. Food for thought.

Chapter 26

He stayed for a while and talked with Deborah Whittaker about people and a time period he never knew. Becky finally called a halt to the visit. Myron promised that he would visit again. He said that he'd try to bring his mother. And he would. Deborah Whittaker shuffled off, and Myron wondered if she would still remember his visit by the time she got to her room. Then he wondered if it mattered.

Myron headed back to his car and called Arthur Bradford's office. His "executive secretary" told him that the "next governor" would be in Belleville. Myron thanked her and hung up. He checked his watch and started on his way. If he didn't hit any traffic, he'd make it in time.

When he hit the Garden State Parkway, Myron called his father's office. Eloise, Dad's longtime secretary, said the same thing she'd said every time he'd called for the past twenty-five years: "I'll patch you through immediately, Myron." It didn't matter if Dad was busy. It didn't matter if he was on the phone or if someone was in the office with him. Dad had left instructions long ago: When his son called, he was always to be disturbed.

"No need," Myron said. "Just tell him I'll be dropping by in a couple of hours."

"Here? My God, Myron, you haven't been here in years."

"Yeah, I know."

"Is anything wrong?"

"Nothing, Eloise. I just want to talk to him. Tell him it's nothing to worry about."

"Oh, your father will be so pleased."

Myron was not so sure.

Arthur Bradford's tour bus had red and blue stripes and big white stars. "BRADFORD FOR GOVERNOR" was painted in a hip, slanted font with 3-D letters. The windows were tinted black so none of the great unwashed could look in on their leader. Quite the homespun touch.

Arthur Bradford stood by the bus door, microphone in hand. Brother Chance was behind him, smiling in that the-camera-might-

be-on-me, gee-isn't-the-candidate-brilliant mode of the political underling. On his right was Terence Edwards, Brenda's cousin. He too
beamed with a smile about as natural as Joe Biden's hairline. Both of
them were wearing those goofy political Styrofoam hats that looked
like something a barbershop quartet might sport.

The crowd was sparse and mostly old. Very old. They looked dis-
tracted, glancing about as if someone had enticed them here with the
promise of free food. Other people slowed and meandered over to
take a look, not unlike pedestrians who stumbled across a fender
bender and were now hoping a fight would break out. Bradford's
handlers blended into the crowd and passed out big signs and buttons
and even those goofy Styrofoam hats, all with the same hip "BRAD-
FORD FOR GOVERNOR" lettering. Every once in a while the interspersed handlers would break into applause, and the rest of the
crowd would lazily follow suit. There was also a sprinkling of media
and cable stations, local political correspondents who looked visibly
pained by what they were doing, wondering what was worse: covering yet another canned political speech or losing a limb in a machin-
ery mishap. Their expressions indicated a toss-up.

Myron eased into the crowd and slid up toward the front.

"What we need in New Jersey is a change," Arthur Bradford bellowed. "What we need in New Jersey is daring and brave leadership.
What we need in New Jersey is a governor who will not cave in to
special interests."

Oh, boy.

The handlers loved that line. They burst into applause like a porno
starlet faking an orgasm (er, or so Myron imagined). The crowd was
more tepid. The handlers started a chant: "Bradford . . . Bradford . . .
Bradford." Original. Another voice came over the loudspeaker.
"Once again, ladies and gentlemen, the next governor of New Jersey,
Arthur Bradford! What we need in New Jersey!"

Applause. Arthur waved at the common folk. Then he stepped
down from his perch and actually touched a chosen few.

"I'm counting on your support," he said after each handshake.

Myron felt a tap on his shoulder. He turned around. Chance was
there. He was still smiling and wearing the goofy Styrofoam hat.
"What the hell do you want?"

Myron pointed at his head. "Can I have your hat?"

Still smiling. "I don't like you, Bolitar."

Myron mirrored the smile. "Ouch, that hurt."

They both stayed with the frozen smiles. If one of them were female, they could have hosted one of those *Hard Copy* rip-offs.

"I need to talk to Art," Myron said.

Still smiling. Best buddies. "Get on the bus."

"Sure thing," Myron said. "But once inside, can I stop smiling? My cheeks are starting to hurt."

But Chance was already moving away. Myron shrugged and hopped on board. The carpet on the bus floor was thick and maroon. The regular seats had been ripped out and replaced with what looked like lounge chairs. There were several overhead televisions, a bar with a minifridge, telephones, computer terminals.

Skinny Sam was the sole occupant. He sat up front and read a copy of *People* magazine. He looked at Myron, then back at his magazine.

"Top fifty most intriguing people," Sam said. "And I'm not one of them."

Myron nodded sympathetically. "It's based on connections, not merit."

"Politics," Sam agreed. He flipped the page. "Head to the back, bucko."

"On my way."

Myron settled into a pseudofuturistic swivel chair that looked like something from the set of *Battlestar Galactica*. He didn't have to wait long. Chance hopped on first. He was still smiling and waving. Terence Edwards came in next. Then Arthur. The driver pressed a button, and the door slid closed. So did all three faces, their smiles thrown aside like itchy masks.

Arthur signaled for Terence Edwards to sit in the front. He obeyed like, well, a political underling. Arthur and Chance moved to the back of the bus. Arthur looked relaxed. Chance looked constipated.

"Nice to see you," Arthur said.

"Yeah," Myron said, "always a pleasure."

"Would you care for a drink?"

"Sure."

The bus pulled out. The crowd gathered around the bus and waved into the one-way glass. Arthur Bradford looked at them with utter disdain. Man of the people. He tossed Myron a Snapple and popped one open for himself. Myron looked at the bottle. Diet Peach Iced Tea. Not bad. Arthur sat down, and Chance sat next to him.

"What did you think of my speech?" Arthur asked.

"What we need in New Jersey," Myron said, "is more political clichés."

Arthur smiled. "You'd prefer a more detailed discussion on the issues, is that it? In this heat? With that crowd?"

"What can I say? I still like 'Vote for Art, He's Got an Indoor Pool.' "

Bradford waved the comment away. "Have you learned something new about Anita Slaughter?"

"No," Myron said. "But I've learned something new about your late wife."

Arthur frowned. Chance's face reddened. Arthur said, "You're supposed to be trying to find Anita Slaughter."

"Funny thing that," Myron said. "When I look into her disappearance, your wife's death keeps popping up. Why do you think that is?"

Chance piped up. "Because you're a goddamn idiot."

Myron looked at Chance. Then he put his finger to his lips. "Shhh."

"Useless," Arthur said. "Utterly useless. I have told you repeatedly that Elizabeth's death has nothing to do with Anita Slaughter."

"Then humor me," Myron said. "Why did your wife stop going to parties?"

"Pardon me?"

"During the last six months of her life none of your wife's friends saw her. She never went to parties anymore. She never even went to her club." Whatever club that might have been.

"Who told you that?"

"I've spoken to several of her friends."

Arthur smiled. "You've spoken," he said, "to one senile old goat."

"Careful, Artie. Senile goats have the right to vote." Myron paused. "Hey, that rhymes. You may have another campaign slogan on your hands: 'Senile Goats, We Need Your Votes.' "

No one reached for a pen.

"You're wasting my time and I'm through with trying to cooperate," Arthur said. "I'll have the driver drop you off."

"I can still go to the press," Myron said.

Chance jumped on that one. "And I can put a bullet through your heart."

Myron put his finger to his lips again. "Shhh."

Chance was about to add something, but Arthur took the helm. "We had a deal," he said. "I help keep Brenda Slaughter out of jail. You search for Anita Slaughter and keep my name out of the papers. But you insist on delving into peripheries. That's a mistake. Your pointless digging will eventually draw my opponent's attention and give him fresh fodder to use against me."

He waited for Myron to say something. Myron didn't.

"You leave me no choice," Arthur continued. "I will tell you what you want to know. You will then see that it is irrelevant to the issues at hand. And then we will move on."

Chance did not like that. "Arthur, you can't be serious—"

"Sit up front, Chance."

"But—" Chance was sputtering now. "He could be working for Davison."

Arthur shook his head. "He's not."

"But you can't know—"

"If he was working for Davison, they'd have ten guys following up on this by now. And if he continues to dig into this, he will most certainly be noticed by Davison's people."

Chance looked at Myron. Myron winked.

"I don't like it," Chance said.

"Sit up front, Chance."

Chance rose with as much dignity as he could muster, which was absolutely none, and skulked to the front of the bus.

Arthur turned to Myron. "It goes without saying that what I'm about to tell you is strictly confidential. If it's repeated . . ." He decided not to finish the sentence. "Have you spoken to your father yet?"

"No."

"It will help."

"Help with what?"

But Arthur did not reply. He sat in silence and looked out the window. The bus stopped at a traffic light. A group of people waved at the bus. Arthur looked right through them.

"I loved my wife," he began. "I want you to understand that. We met in college. I saw her walking across the commons one day and . . ." The light turned green. The bus started up again. "And nothing in my life was ever the same." Arthur glanced at Myron and smiled. "Corny, isn't it?"

Myron shrugged. "Sounds nice."

"Oh, it was." He tilted his head at a memory, and for a moment the politician was replaced with a real human being. "Elizabeth and I got married a week after graduation. We had a huge wedding at Bradford Farms. You should have seen it. Six hundred people. Our families were both thrilled, though that didn't matter a hoot to us. We were in love. And we had the certainty of the young that nothing would ever change."

He looked off again. The bus whirred. Someone flipped on a television and then muted the sound.

"The first blow came a year after we wed. Elizabeth learned that

she could not have children. Some sort of weakness in her uterine
walls. She could get pregnant, but she couldn't carry past the first
trimester. It's strange when I think about it now. You see, from the beginning Elizabeth had what I thought of as quiet moments—bouts of
melancholy, some might call them. But they didn't seem like melancholy to me. They seemed more like moments of reflection. I found
them oddly appealing. Does that make any sense to you?"

Myron nodded, but Arthur was still looking out the window.

"But now the bouts came more often. And they were deeper. Natural, I suppose. Who wouldn't be sad under our circumstances? Today, of course, Elizabeth would have been labeled a manic depres-
sive." He smiled. "They say it's all physiological. That there is simply
a chemical imbalance in the brain or some such thing. Some even
claim that outside stimuli are irrelevant, that even without the uterine problem Elizabeth would have been equally ill in the long run."
He looked at Myron. "Do you believe that?"

"I don't know."

He didn't seem to hear. "I guess it's possible. Mental illnesses are
so strange. A physical problem we can understand. But when the
mind works irrationally, well, by its very definition, the rational mind
cannot truly relate. We can pity. But we cannot fully grasp. So I
watched as her sanity began to peel away. She grew worse. Friends
who had thought Elizabeth eccentric began to wonder. At times she
got so bad that we would feign a vacation and keep her in the house.
This went on for years. Slowly the woman I had fallen in love with
was eaten away. Well before her death—five, six years before—she
was already a different person. We tried our best, of course. We gave
her the best medical care and propped her up and sent her back out.
But nothing stopped the slide. Eventually Elizabeth could not go out
at all."

Silence.

"Did you institutionalize her?" Myron asked.

Arthur took a swig of his Snapple. His fingers started playing
with the bottle's label, pulling up the corners. "No," he said at last.
"My family urged me to have her committed. But I couldn't do it.
Elizabeth was no longer the woman I loved. I knew that. And maybe
I could go on without her. But I could not abandon her. I still owed
her that much, no matter what she'd become."

Myron nodded, said nothing. The TV was off now, but a radio up
front blasted an all-news station: You give them twenty-two minutes,
they'll give you the world. Sam read his *People*. Chance kept glancing over his shoulder, his eyes thin slits.

"I hired full-time nurses and kept Elizabeth at home. I continued to live my life while she continued to slide toward oblivion. In hindsight, of course, my family was right. I should have had her committed."

The bus lurched to a stop. Myron and Arthur lurched a bit too.

"You can probably guess what happened next. Elizabeth grew worse. She was nearly catatonic by the end. Whatever evil had entered her brain now moved in and laid total claim. You were right, of course. Her fall was not accidental. Elizabeth jumped. It was not bad luck that she landed on her head. It was intentional on her part. My wife committed suicide."

He put his hand to his face and leaned back. Myron watched him. It might be an acting job—politicians make awfully good thespians—but Myron thought that he spotted genuine guilt here, that something had indeed fled from this man's eyes and left nothing in their wake. But you never know for sure. Those who claim they can spot a lie are usually just fooled with greater conviction.

"Anita Slaughter found her body?" Myron asked.

He nodded. "And the rest is classic Bradford. The cover-up began immediately. Bribes were made. You see, a suicide—a wife so crazy that a Bradford man had driven her to kill herself—would simply not do. We would have kept Anita's name out of it too, but her name went over the radio dispatch. The media picked it up."

That part certainly made sense. "You mentioned bribes."

"Yes."

"How much did Anita get?"

He closed his eyes. "Anita wouldn't take any money."

"What did she want?"

"Nothing. She wasn't like that."

"And you trusted her to keep quiet."

Arthur nodded. "Yes," he said. "I trusted her."

"You never threatened her or—"

"Never."

"I find that hard to believe."

Arthur shrugged. "She stayed on for nine more months. That should tell you something."

That same point again. Myron mulled it over a bit. He heard a noise at the front of the bus. Chance had stood up. He stormed to the back and stood over them. Both men ignored him.

After several moments Chance said, "You told him?"

"Yes," Arthur said.

Chance spun toward Myron. "If you breathe a word of this to any-one, I'll kill—"

"Shhh."

Then Myron saw it.

Hanging there. Just out of sight. The story was partially true—the best lies always are—but something was missing. He looked at Arthur. "You forgot one thing," Myron said.

Arthur's brow lines deepened. "What's that?"

Myron pointed to Chance, then back at Arthur. "Which one of you beat up Anita Slaughter?"

Stone silence.

Myron kept going. "Just a few weeks before Elizabeth's suicide, someone assaulted Anita Slaughter. She was taken to St. Barnabas Hospital and still had abrasions when your wife jumped. You want to tell me about it?"

Lots of things started happening seemingly all at once. Arthur Bradford gave a small head nod. Sam put down his copy of *People* and stood. Chance turned apoplectic.

"He knows too much!" Chance shouted.

Arthur paused, considering.

"We have to take him out!"

Arthur was still thinking. Sam started moving toward them.

Myron kept his voice low. "Chance?"

"What?"

"Your fly's undone."

Chance looked down. Myron already had the thirty-eight out. Now he pressed it firmly against Chance's groin. Chance jumped back a bit, but Myron kept the muzzle in place. Sam took out his gun and pointed it at Myron.

"Tell Sam to sit down," Myron said, "or you'll never have trouble fitting a catheter again."

Everybody froze. Sam kept the gun on Myron. Myron kept his gun against Chance's groin. Arthur still seemed lost in thought. Chance started shaking.

"Don't pee on my gun, Chance." Tough guy talk. But Myron did not like this. He knew Sam's type. And he knew Sam might very well take the risk and shoot.

"There's no need for the gun," Arthur said. "No one is going to harm you."

"I feel better already."

"To put it simply, you are worth more to me alive than dead. Otherwise Sam would have blown your head off by now. Do you understand?"

Myron said nothing.

"Our deal remains unchanged: You find Anita, Myron, I'll keep Brenda out of jail. And both of us will leave my wife out of this. Do I make myself clear?"

Sam kept the gun at eye level and smiled a little.

Myron gestured with his head. "How about a show of good faith?"

Arthur nodded. "Sam."

Sam put away the gun. He walked back to his seat and picked up his *People*.

Myron pressed the gun a little harder. Chance yelped. Then Myron pocketed his weapon.

The bus dropped him off back by his car. Sam gave Myron a little salute as he stepped off. Myron nodded in return. The bus continued down the street and disappeared around the corner. Myron realized that he had been holding his breath. He tried to relax and think straight.

"Fitting a catheter," he said out loud. "Awful."

Chapter 27

Dad's office was still a warehouse in Newark. Years ago they had actually made undergarments here. Not anymore. Now they shipped in finished products from Indonesia or Malaysia or someplace else that employed child labor. Everybody knew that abuses occurred and everybody still used them and every customer still bought the goods because it saved a couple of bucks, and to be fair, the whole issue was morally hazy. Easy to be against children working in factories; easy to be against paying a twelve-year-old twelve cents an hour or whatever; easy to condemn the parents and be against such exploitation. Harder when the choice is twelve cents or starvation, exploitation or death.

Easiest still not to think too much about it.

Thirty years ago, when they actually made the undergarments in Newark, Dad had lots of inner-city blacks working for him. He thought that he was good to his workers. He thought that they viewed him as a benevolent leader. When the riots broke out in 1968, these same workers burned down four of his factory buildings. Dad had never looked at them the same again.

Eloise Williams had been with Dad since before the riots. "As long as I breathe," Dad often said, "Eloise will have a job." She was like a second wife to him. She took care of him during his workday. They argued and fought and got grumpy with each other. There was genuine affection. Mom knew all this. "Thank God Eloise is uglier than a cow living near Chernobyl," Mom liked to say. "Or I might wonder."

Dad's plant used to consist of five buildings. Only this warehouse still stood. Dad used it as a storage facility for the incoming shipments from overseas. His office was smack in the middle and raised to almost the ceiling. All four walls were made of glass, giving Dad the chance to watch over his stock like a prison guard in the main tower.

Myron trotted up the metal stairs. When he reached the top, Eloise greeted him with a big hug and a cheek pinch. He half expected her to take out a little toy from her desk drawer. When he'd visit as a child, she would always be ready for him with a popgun or one of those snap-together gliders or a comic book. But Eloise just gave him a hug this time, and Myron was only mildly disappointed.

"Go right in," Eloise said. No buzzing in. No checking with Dad first.

Through the glass Myron could see that his father was on the phone. Animated. As always. Myron stepped in. His father held up a finger to him. "Irv, I said, tomorrow. No excuses. Tomorrow, do you hear?"

Sunday and everyone was still doing business. The shrinking leisure time of the late twentieth century.

Dad hung up the phone. He looked at Myron, and his whole being just beamed. Myron came around the desk and kissed his father's cheek. As always, his skin felt a little like sandpaper and smelled faintly like Old Spice. Just as it should.

His father was dressed like a member of the Israeli Knesset: charcoal slacks with a white dress shirt opened at the neck and a T-shirt underneath. White chest hair popped out of the space between neck and T-shirt front collar. Dad was clearly a Semite—thick dark olive skin and a nose that polite people called prominent.

"Remember Don Rico's?" Dad asked.

"That Portuguese place we used to go?"

Dad nodded. "Gone. As of last month. Manuel ran the place beautifully for thirty-six years. He finally had to give it up."

"Sorry to hear that."

Dad made a scoffing noise and waved him off. "Who the hell cares? I'm just making silly small talk because I'm a little worried here. Eloise said you sounded funny on the phone." His voice went soft. "Everything okay?"

"I'm fine."

"You need money or something?"

"No, Dad, I don't need money."

"But something is wrong, no?"

Myron took the plunge. "Do you know Arthur Bradford?"

Dad's face lost color—not slowly but all at once. He started fiddling with things on his desk. He readjusted the family photographs, taking a little extra time with the one of Myron holding aloft the NCAA trophy after leading Duke to the title. There was an empty box of Dunkin' Donuts. He picked it up and dropped it into a wastepaper basket.

Finally Dad said, "Why would you ask that?"

"I'm tangled up in something."

"And it involves Arthur Bradford?"

"Yes," Myron said.

"Then get untangled. Fast."

Dad lifted one of those traveling coffee cups to his lips and craned his neck. The cup was empty.

"Bradford told me to ask you about him," Myron said. "He and this guy who works for him."

Dad's neck snapped back into place. "Sam Richards?" His tone was quiet, awe-filled. "He's still alive?"

"Yes."

"Jesus Christ."

Silence. Then Myron asked, "How do you know them?"

Dad opened his drawer and fumbled about for something. Then he yelled for Eloise. She came to the door. "Where's the Tylenol?" he asked her.

"Bottom right-hand drawer. Left side toward the back. Under the box of rubber bands." Eloise turned to Myron. "Would you like a Yoo-Hoo?" she asked.

"Yes, please." Stocking Yoo-Hoos. He had not been to his father's office in almost a decade, but they still stocked his favorite drink. Dad found the bottle and played with the cap. Eloise closed the door on her way out.

"I've never lied to you," Dad said.

"I know."

"I've tried to protect you. That's what parents do. They shelter their children. When they see danger coming, they try to step in the way and take the hit."

"You can't take this hit for me," Myron said.

Dad nodded slowly. "Doesn't make it any easier."

"I'll be okay," Myron said. "I just need to know what I'm up against."

"You're up against pure evil." Dad shook out two tablets and swallowed them without water. "You're up against naked cruelty, against men with no conscience."

Eloise came back in with the Yoo-Hoo. Reading their faces, she silently handed Myron the drink and slipped back out. In the distance a forklift started beeping out the backup warning.

"It was a year or so after the riots," Dad began. "You're probably too young to remember them, but the riots ripped this city apart. To this day the rip has never healed. Just the opposite, in fact. It's like one of my garments." He gestured to the boxes below. "The garment rips near the seam, and then nobody does anything so it just keeps ripping until the whole thing falls apart. That's Newark. A shredded garment.

"Anyway, my workers finally came back, but they weren't the same people. They were angry now. I wasn't their employer anymore. I was their oppressor. They looked at me like I was the one who dragged their ancestors across the ocean in chains. Then troublemakers started prodding them. The writing was already on the wall, Myron. The manufacturing end of this business was going to hell. Labor costs were too high. The city was just imploding on itself. And then the hoodlums began to lead the workers. They wanted to form a union. Demanded it, actually. I was against the idea, of course."

Dad looked out his glass wall at the endless rows of boxes. Myron wondered how many times his father had looked out at this same view. He wondered what his father had thought about when looking out, what he dreamed about over the years in this dusty warehouse. Myron shook the can and popped the top. The sound startled Dad a bit. He looked back at his son and managed a smile.

"Old Man Bradford was hooked in to the mobsters who wanted to set up the union. That's who was involved in this: mobsters, hoodlums, punks who ran everything from prostitutes to numbers; all of a sudden they're labor experts. But I still fought them. And I was winning. So one day Old Man Bradford sends his son Arthur to this very building. To have a chat with me. Sam Richards is with him— the son of a bitch just leans against the wall and says nothing. Arthur sits down and puts his feet on my desk. I'm going to agree to this union, he says. I'm going to support it, in fact. Financially. With generous contributions. I tell the little snotnose there's a word for this. It's called extortion. I tell him to get the hell out of my office."

Beads of sweat popped up on Dad's forehead. He took a hankie and blotted them a few times. There was a fan in the corner of the office. It oscillated back and forth, teasing you with moments of comfort followed by stifling heat. Myron glanced at the family photos, focusing in on one of his parents on a Caribbean cruise. Maybe ten years ago. Mom and Dad were both wearing loud shirts and looked healthy and tan and much younger. It scared him.

"So what happened then?" Myron asked.

Dad swallowed away something and started speaking again. "Sam finally spoke. He came over to my desk and looked over the family photos. He smiled, like he was an old friend of the family. Then he tossed these pruning shears on my desk."

Myron started to feel cold.

His father kept talking, his eyes wide and unfocused. " 'Imagine what they could do to a human being,' Sam says to me. 'Imagine snipping away a piece at a time. Imagine not how long it would take to die but how long you could keep someone alive.' That's it. That's all he said. Then Arthur Bradford started laughing, and they both left my office."

Dad tried the cup of coffee again, but it was still empty. Myron held up the Yoo-Hoo, but Dad shook his head.

"So I go home and try to pretend that everything is hunky-dory. I try to eat. I try to smile. I play with you in the yard. But I can't stop thinking about what Sam said. Your mother knew something was wrong, but for once even she didn't push it. Later I go to bed. I can't sleep at first. It was like Sam said: I kept imagining. About cutting off little pieces of a human being. Slowly. Each cut causing a new scream. And then the phone rang. I jumped up and looked at my watch. It was three in the morning. I picked up the phone, and no one spoke. They were there. I could hear them breathing. But nobody spoke. So I hung up the phone and got out of bed."

Dad's breathing was shallow now. His eyes were welling up. Myron rose toward him, but Dad held up a hand to stop him.

"Let me just get through this, okay?"

Myron nodded, sat back down.

"I went into your room." His voice was more monotone now, lifeless and flat. "You probably know that I used to do that a lot. Sometimes I would just sit in awe and watch you sleep."

Tears started racing down his face. "So I stepped in the room. I could hear your deep breathing. The sound comforted me immediately. I smiled. And then I walked over to tuck you in a little better. And that's when I saw it."

Dad put a fist to his mouth as though stifling a cough. His chest started hitching. His words came in a sputter.

"On your bed. On top of the cover. Pruning shears. Someone had broken into your room and left pruning shears on your bed."

A steel hand started squeezing Myron's insides.

Dad looked at him with reddening eyes. "You don't fight men like that, Myron. Because you can't win. It's not a question of bravery. It's a question of caring. You have people you care about, that are connected to you. These men don't even understand that. They don't feel. How do you hurt a person who can't feel?"

Myron had no answer.

"Just walk away," Dad said. "There's no shame in that."

Myron stood up then. So did Dad. They hugged, gripping each

other fiercely. Myron closed his eyes. His father cupped the back of his head and then smoothed his hair. Myron snuggled in and stayed there. He inhaled the Old Spice. He traveled back, remembering how this same hand had cradled his head after Joey Davito had hit him with a pitch.

Still comforting, he thought. After all these years, this was still the safest place to be.

Chapter 28

Pruning shears.

It couldn't be a coincidence. He grabbed his cellular and called the Dragons' practice site. After a few minutes Brenda came on the line.

"Hey," Brenda said.

"Hey."

They both fell silent.

"I love a smooth-talking man," she said.

"Uh-huh," Myron said.

Brenda laughed. The sound was melodious, plucking at his heart.

"How are you doing?" he asked.

"Good," she said. "Playing helps. I've also been thinking about you a lot. That helps too."

"Mutual," Myron said. Killer lines, one after another.

"Are you coming to the opener tonight?" Brenda asked.

"Sure. You want me to pick you up?"

"No, I'll take the team bus."

"Got a question for you," Myron said.

"Shoot."

"What are the names of the two boys who had their Achilles tendons sliced in half?"

"Clay Jackson and Arthur Harris."

"They were cut with pruning shears, right?"

"Right."

"And they live in East Orange?"

"Yeah, why?"

"I don't think Horace was the one who hurt them."

"Then who?"

"Long story. I'll tell you about it later."

"After the game," Brenda suggested. "I'll have some media stuff to do, but maybe we can grab a bite and go back to Win's."

"I'd like that," Myron said.

Silence.

Brenda said, "I sound too eager, don't I?"

"Not at all."

"I should be playing harder to get."

"No."

"It's just that"—she stopped, started again—"it feels right, you know?"

He nodded into the phone. He knew. He thought about what Esperanza had said, about how he "used to" leave himself totally exposed, keeping his feet planted with nary a worry of getting beaned on the head.

"I'll see you at the game," he said.

Then he hung up.

He sat and closed his eyes and thought about Brenda. For a moment he didn't push the thoughts away. He let them cascade over him. His body tingled. He started smiling.

Brenda.

He opened his eyes and came out of it. He switched on the car phone again and dialed Win's number.

"Articulate."

"I need some backup," Myron said.

"Bitching," Win said.

They met up at the Essex Green Mall in West Orange.

"How far is the ride?" Win asked.

"Ten minutes."

"Bad area?"

"Yes."

Win looked at his precious Jag. "We'll take your car."

They got into the Ford Taurus. The late-summer sun still cast long, thin shadows. Heat rose from the sidewalk in lazy tendrils, dark and smoky. The air was so thick that an apple falling from a tree would take several minutes to hit the ground.

"I looked into the Outreach Education scholarship," Win said. "Whoever set up the fund had a great deal of financial acumen. The money was dumped in from a foreign source, more specifically the Cayman Islands."

"So it's untraceable?"

"Almost untraceable," Win corrected. "But even in places like the Caymans a greased palm is a greased palm."

"So who do we grease?"

"Already done. Unfortunately the account was in a dummy name and closed four years ago."

"Four years ago," Myron repeated. "That would be right after

Brenda received her last scholarship. Before she started medical school."

Win nodded. "Logical," he said. Like he was Spock.

"So it's a dead end."

"Temporarily, yes. Someone could prowl through old records, but it will take a few days."

"Anything else?"

"The scholarship recipient was to be chosen by certain attorneys rather than any educational institution. The criteria were vague: academic potential, good citizenship, that type of thing."

"In other words, it was fixed so the attorneys would select Brenda. Like we said before, it was a way of funneling her money."

Another nod. "Logical," he repeated.

They started moving from West Orange into East Orange. The transformation was gradual. The fine suburban homes turned into gated condo developments. Then the houses came back—smaller now, less land, more worn and crowded together. Abandoned factories started popping up. Subsidy housing too. It was a butterfly in reverse, turning back into a caterpillar.

"I also received a call from Hal," Win said. Hal was an electronics expert they had worked with during their days working for the government. He'd been the one Myron had sent to check for phone taps.

"And?"

"All the residences contained telephone listening devices and traces—Mabel Edwards's, Horace Slaughter's, and Brenda's dorm room."

"No surprise," Myron said.

"Except for one thing," Win corrected. "The devices in the two households—that is, Mabel's and Horace's homes—were old. Hal estimated that they had been present for at least three years."

Myron's head started spinning again. "Three years?"

"Yes. It's an estimate, of course. But the pieces were old and in some cases crusted over from dirt."

"What about the tap on Brenda's phone?"

"More recent. But she's only lived there a few months. And Hal also found listening devices in Brenda's room. One under her desk in her bedroom. Another behind a sofa in the common room."

"Microphones?"

Win nodded. "Someone was interested in more than Brenda's telephone calls."

"Jesus Christ."

Win almost smiled. "Yes, I thought you might find it odd."

Myron tried to enter the new data into his brain. "Someone has obviously been spying on the family for a long time."

"Obviously."

"That means that it has to be somebody with resources."

"Indeed."

"Then it has to be the Bradfords," Myron said. "They're looking for Anita Slaughter. For all we know, they've been looking for twenty years. It's the only thing that makes sense. And you know what else this means?"

"Do tell," Win said.

"Arthur Bradford has been conning me."

Win gasped. "A less than truthful politician? Next you'll tell me there's no Easter Bunny."

"It's like we thought from the start," Myron said. "Anita Slaughter ran because she was scared. And that's why Arthur Bradford is being so cooperative. He wants me to find Anita Slaughter for him. So he can kill her."

"And then he'll try to kill you," Win added. He studied his hair in the visor mirror. "Being this handsome. It is not easy, you realize."

"And yet you suffer without complaint."

"That is my way." Win took one last look before snapping the visor back in place.

Clay Jackson lived in a row of houses whose backyards sat above Route 280. The neighborhood looked like working poor. The homes were all two-family, except for several corner residences that doubled as taverns. Tired neon Budweiser signs flickered through murky windows. Fences were all chain-link. So many overgrown weeds had popped through the sidewalk cracks that it was impossible to tell where pavement ended and lawn began.

Again all the inhabitants appeared to be black. Again Myron felt his customary and seemingly inexplicable discomfort.

There was a park across the street from Clay Jackson's house. People were setting up for a barbecue. A softball game was going on. Loud laughter exploded everywhere. So did a boom box. When Myron and Win got out of the car, all eyes swerved in their direction. The boom box went suddenly silent. Myron forced up a smile. Win remained completely unbothered by the scrutiny.

"They're staring," Myron said.

"If two black men pulled up to your house in Livingston," Win said, "what sort of reception would they receive?"

Myron nodded. "So you figure the neighbors are calling the cops and describing two 'suspicious youths' prowling the streets?"

Win raised an eyebrow. "Youths?"

"Wishful thinking."

"Yes, I'd say."

They headed up a stoop that looked like the one on Sesame Street. A man poked through a nearby garbage can, but he looked nothing like Oscar the Grouch. Myron knocked on the door. Win started with the eyes, the gliding movement, taking it all in. The softballers and barbecuers across the street were still staring. They did not seem pleased with what they saw.

Myron knocked again.

"Who is it?" a woman's voice called.

"My name is Myron Bolitar. This is Win Lockwood. We'd like to see Clay Jackson if he's available."

"Could you hold on a second?"

They held on for at least a full minute. Then they heard a chain rattle. The knob turned, and a woman appeared in the doorway. She was black and maybe forty years old. Her smile kept flickering like one of those neon Budweiser signs in the tavern windows. "I'm Clay's mother," she said. "Please come in."

They followed her inside. Something good was cooking on the stove. An old air-conditioning unit roared like a DC-10, but it worked. The coolness was most welcome, though short-lived. Clay's mother quickly hustled them through a narrow corridor and back out the kitchen door. They were outside again, in the backyard now.

"Can I get you a drink?" she asked. She had to yell over the sounds of traffic.

Myron looked at Win. Win was frowning. Myron said, "No, thank you."

"Okay." The smile flickered faster now, almost like a disco strobe light. "Let me just go get Clay. I'll be right back." The screen door slammed shut.

They were alone outside. The yard was tiny. There were flower boxes bursting with colors and two large bushes that were dying. Myron moved to the fence and looked down at Route 280. The four-lane highway was moving briskly. Car fumes drifted slowly in this humidity, hanging there, not dissipating; when Myron swallowed, he could actually taste them.

"This isn't good," Win said.

Myron nodded. Two white men show up at your house. You don't know either one. You don't ask for ID. You just show them in and leave them out back. Something was definitely not right here.

"Let's just see how it plays out," Myron said.

It did not take long. Eight large men came from three different directions. Two burst through the back door. Three circled in from the right side of the house. Three more from the left. They all carried aluminum baseball bats and let's-kick-some-ass scowls. They fanned out, encircling the yard. Myron felt his pulse race. Win folded his arms; only his eyes moved.

These were not street punks or members of a gang. They were the softball players from across the street, grown men with bodies hardened by daily labor—dockworkers and truck loaders and the like. Some held their bats in a ready-to-swing position. Others rested them on their shoulders. Still others bounced them gently against their legs, like Joe Don Baker in *Walking Tall*.

Myron squinted into the sun. "You guys finish your game?" he asked.

The biggest man stepped forward. He had an enormous iron-cauldron gut, callused hands, and the muscular yet unchiseled arms of someone who could crush Nautilus equipment like so many Styrofoam cups. His Nike baseball cap was set on the largest size, but it still fitted him like a yarmulke. His T-shirt had a Reebok logo. Nike cap, Reebok T-shirt. Confusing brand loyalties.

"Game is just beginning, fool."

Myron looked at Win. Win said, "Decent deliver, but the line lacked originality. Plus, tagging the word *fool* on the end—that seemed forced. I'll have to give him a thumbs-down, but I look forward to his next work."

The eight men looped around Myron and Win. Nike/Reebok, the obvious leader, gestured with the baseball bat. "Hey, Wonder bread, get your ass over here."

Win looked at Myron. Myron said, "I think he means you."

"Must be because I help build strong bodies in twelve ways." Then Win smiled, and Myron felt his heart stutter. People always did that. They always homed in on Win. At five-ten Win was a half foot shorter than Myron. But it was more than that. The blond, pale-faced, blue-veined, china-boned exterior brought out the worst in people. Win appeared soft, unlabored, sheltered—the kind of guy you hit and he shatters like cheap porcelain. Easy prey. Everyone likes easy prey.

Win stepped toward Nike/Reebok. He arched an eyebrow and gave him his best Lurch. "You rang?"

"What's your name, Wonder bread?"

"Thurgood Marshall," Win said.

That reply didn't sit well with the crowd. Murmurs began. "You making a racist crack?"

"As opposed to, say, calling someone Wonder bread?"

Win glanced at Myron and gave him a thumbs-up. Myron returned the gesture. If this were a school debate, Win would be up a point.

"You a cop, Thurgood?"

Win frowned. "In *this* suit?" He pulled at his own lapels. "Puleeze."

"So what do you want here?"

"We wish to speak with one Clay Jackson."

"What about?"

"Solar energy and its role in the twenty-first century."

Nike/Reebok checked his troops. The troops tightened the noose. Myron felt a rushing in his ears. He kept his eyes on Win and waited.

"Seems to me," the leader continued, "that you white boys are here to hurt Clay again." Moving closer. Eye to eye. "Seems to me that we have the right to use lethal force to protect him. That right, fellas?"

The troops grunted their agreement, raising their bats.

Win's move was sudden and unexpected. He simply reached out and snatched the bat away from Nike/Reebok. The big man's mouth formed an O of surprise. He stared at his hands as though he expected the bat to rematerialize at any moment. It wouldn't. Win chucked the bat into the corner of the yard.

Then Win beckoned the big man forward. "Care to tango, pumpernickel bread?"

Myron said, "Win."

But Win kept his eyes on his opponent. "I'm waiting."

Nike/Reebok grinned. Then he rubbed his hands together and wet his lips. "He's all mine, fellas."

Yep, easy prey.

The big man lunged forward like a Frankenstein monster, his thick fingers reaching for Win's neck. Win remained motionless until the last possible moment. Then he darted inside, his fingertips pressed together, transforming his hand into something of a spear. The fingertips struck deep and quick at the big man's larynx, the movement like a bird doing a fast peck. A gagging sound not unlike a dental sucking machine forced its way out the big man's mouth; his hands instinctively flew up to his throat. Win ducked low and whipped his foot around. The heel swept Nike/Reebok's legs. The big man flipped midair and landed on the back of his head.

Win jammed his .44 into the man's face. He was still smiling.

"Seems to me," Win said, "that you just attacked me with a base-ball bat. Seems to me that shooting you in the right eye would be viewed as perfectly justifiable."

Myron had his gun out too. He ordered everyone to drop his bat. They did so. Then he had them lie on their stomachs, hands behind their heads, fingers locked. It took a minute or two, but everyone obeyed.

Nike/Reebok was now on his stomach too. He craned his neck and croaked, "Not again."

Win cupped his ear with his free hand. "Pardon *moi*?"

"We ain't gonna let you hurt that boy again."

Win burst out laughing and nudged the man's head with his toe. Myron caught Win's eye and shook his head. Win shrugged and stopped.

"We don't want to hurt anyone," Myron said. "We're just trying to find out who attacked Clay on that rooftop."

"Why?" a voice asked. Myron turned to the screen door. A young man hobbled out on crutches. The cast protecting the tendon looked like some puffy sea creature in the process of swallowing his entire foot.

"Because everyone thinks Horace Slaughter did it," Myron said.

Clay Jackson balanced himself on one leg. "So?"

"So did he?"

"Why do you care?"

"Because he's been murdered."

Clay shrugged. "So?"

Myron opened his mouth, closed it, sighed. "It's a long story, Clay. I just want to know who cut your tendon."

The kid shook his head. "I ain't talking about it."

"Why not?"

"They told me not to."

Win spoke to the boy for the first time. "And you have chosen to obey them?"

The boy faced Win now. "Yeah."

"The man who did this," Win continued. "You find him scary?"

Clay's Adam's apple danced. "Shit, yeah."

Win grinned. "I'm scarier."

No one moved.

"Would you care for a demonstration?"

Myron said, "Win."

Nike/Reebok decided to take a chance. He started to scramble up on his elbows. Win raised his foot and slammed an ax kick into the spot where the spine met the neck. Nike/Reebok slumped back to the ground like wet sand, his arms splayed. He did not move at all. Win rested his foot on the back of the man's skull. The Nike hat slipped off. Win pushed the still face into the muddy ground as though he were grinding out a cigarette.

Myron said, "Win."

"Stop it!" Clay Jackson cried. He looked to Myron for help, his eyes wide and desperate. "He's my uncle, man. He's just looking out for me."

"And doing a wonderful job," Win added. He stepped up, gaining leverage. The uncle's face sank deeper into the soft earth. His features were fully embedded in the mud now, his mouth and nose clogged.

The big man could no longer breathe.

One of the other men started to rise. Win leveled his gun at the man's head. "Important note," Win said. "I'm not big on warning shots."

The man slinked back down.

With his foot still firmly planted on the man's head, Win turned his attention to Clay Jackson. The boy was trying to look tough, but he was visibly quaking. So, quite frankly, was Myron.

"You fear a possibility," Win said to the boy, "when you should fear a certainty."

Win raised his foot, bending his knee. He angled himself for the proper heel strike.

Myron started to move toward him, but Win froze him with a glance. Then Win gave that smile again, the little one. It was casual, slightly amused. The smile said that he would do it. The smile hinted that he might even enjoy it. Myron had seen the smile many times, yet it never failed to chill his blood.

"I'll count to five," Win told the boy. "But I'll probably crush his skull before I reach three."

"Two white guys," Clay Jackson said quickly. "With guns. A big guy tied us up. He was young and looked like he worked out. The little old guy—he was the leader. He was the one who cut us."

Win turned to Myron. He spread his hands. "Can we go now?"

Chapter 29

Back in the car, Myron said, "You went too far."

"Uh-hmm."

"I mean it, Win."

"You wanted the information. I got it."

"Not like that I didn't."

"Oh, please. The man came at me with a baseball bat."

"He was scared. He thought we were trying to hurt his nephew."

Win played the air violin.

Myron shook his head. "The kid would have told us eventually."

"Doubtful. This Sam character had the boy scared."

"So you had to scare him more?"

"That would be a yes," Win said.

"You can't do that again, Win. You can't hurt innocent people."

"Uh-hmm," Win said again. He checked his watch. "Are you through now? Is your need to feel morally superior satiated?"

"What the hell does that mean?"

Win looked at him. "You know what I do," he said slowly. "Yet you always call on me."

Silence. The echo of Win's words hung in the air, caught in the humidity like the car fumes. Myron gripped the steering wheel. His knuckles turned white.

They did not speak again until they reached Mabel Edwards's house.

"I know you're violent," Myron said. He put the car in park and looked at his friend. "But for the most part you only hurt people who deserve it."

Win said nothing.

"If the boy hadn't talked, would you have gone through with your threat?"

"Not an issue," Win said. "I knew the boy would talk."

"But suppose he hadn't."

Win shook his head. "You are dealing with something out of the realm of possibility."

"Humor me then."

Win thought about it for a moment. "I never intentionally hurt innocent people," he said. "But I never threaten idly either."

"That's not an answer, Win."

Win looked at Mabel's house. "Go inside, Myron. Time's awasting."

Mabel Edwards sat across from him in a small den. "So Brenda remembers the Holiday Inn," she said.

A small yellowish trace of the bruise remained around her eye, but hey, it would go away before the soreness in Big Mario's groin did. Mourners were still milling about, but the house was hushed now; reality set in with the darkness. Win was outside, keeping watch.

"Very vaguely," Myron replied. "It was more like déjà vu than anything concrete."

Mabel nodded as though this made sense. "It was a long time ago."

"Then Brenda was at the hotel?"

Mabel looked down, smoothed the bottom of her dress, reached for her cup of tea. "Brenda was there," she said, "with her mother."

"When?"

Mabel held the cup in front of her lips. "The night Anita disappeared."

Myron tried not to look too confused. "She took Brenda with her?"

"At first, yes."

"I don't understand. Brenda never said anything—"

"Brenda was five years old. She doesn't remember. Or at least that's what Horace thought."

"But you didn't say anything before."

"Horace didn't want her knowing about it," Mabel said. "He thought it would hurt her."

"But I still don't get it. Why did Anita take Brenda to a hotel?"

Mabel Edwards finally took a sip of the tea. Then she set it back down gently. She smoothed the dress again and fiddled with the chain around her neck. "It's like I told you before. Anita wrote Horace a note saying she was running away. She cleared out all his money and took off."

Myron saw it now. "But she planned on taking Brenda with her."

"Yes."

The money, Myron thought. Anita's taking all of it had always bothered him. Running away from danger is one thing. But leaving

your daughter penniless—that seemed unusually cruel. But now
there was an explanation: Anita had intended to take Brenda.

"So what happened?" Myron asked.

"Anita changed her mind."

"Why?"

A woman poked her head through the doorway. Mabel fired a
glare, and the head disappeared like something in a shooting gallery.
Myron could hear kitchen noises, family and friends cleaning up to
prepare for another day of mourning. Mabel looked like she'd aged
since this morning. Fatigue emanated from her like a fever.

"Anita packed them both up," she managed. "She ran away and
checked them into that hotel. I don't know what happened then.
Maybe Anita got scared. Maybe she realized how impossible it
would be to run away with a five-year-old. No matter. Anita called
Horace. She was crying and all hysterical. It was all too much for
her, she said. She told Horace to come pick up Brenda."

Silence.

"So Horace went to the Holiday Inn?" Myron asked.

"Yes."

"Where was Anita?"

Mabel shrugged. "She'd run off already, I guess."

"And this all happened the first night she ran away?"

"Yes."

"So Anita could not have been gone for more than a few hours,
right?"

"That's right."

"So what made Anita change her mind so fast?" Myron asked.
"What could possibly have made her decide to give up her daughter
that quickly?"

Mabel Edwards rose with a great sigh and made her way to the
television set. Her normally supple, fluid movements had been stiffened by her grief. She reached out with a tentative hand and plucked
a photograph off the top. Then she showed it to Myron.

"This is Terence's father, Roland," she said. "My husband."

Myron looked at the black-and-white photograph.

"Roland was shot coming home from work. For twelve dollars.
Right on our front stoop. Two shots in the head. For twelve dollars."
Her voice was a monotone now, dispassionate. "I didn't handle it
well. Roland was the only man I ever loved. I started drinking. Terence was only a little boy, but he looked so much like his father I
could barely stand to look at his face. So I drank some more. And

then I took some drugs. I stopped taking care of my son. The state came and put him in a foster home."

Mabel looked at Myron for a reaction. He tried to keep his face neutral.

"Anita was the one who saved me. She and Horace sent me away to get clean. It took me a while, but I straightened myself out. Anita took care of Terence in the meantime, so the state wouldn't take him away from me." Mabel lifted the reading glasses off her chest and put them on her nose. Then she stared at the image of her dead husband. The longing in her face was so raw, so naked, that Myron felt a tear push into his own eye.

"When I needed her most," Mabel said, "Anita was there for me. Always."

She looked at Myron again.

"Do you understand what I'm telling you?"

"No, ma'am, I don't."

"Anita was there for me," Mabel repeated. "But when she was in trouble, where was I? I knew she and Horace were having problems. And I ignored it. She disappeared, and what did I do? I tried to forget her. She ran off, and I bought this nice house away from the slums and tried to put it all behind me. If Anita had just left my brother, well, that would have been awful. But something scared Anita so bad she abandoned her own child. Just like that. And I keep asking myself what that something was. What could have scared her so bad that twenty years later she still won't come back?"

Myron shifted in the chair. "Have you come up with any answers?"

"Not on my own," she said. "But I asked Anita once."

"When?"

"Fifteen years ago, I guess. When she called to check up on Brenda. I asked why she wouldn't come back and see her own daughter."

"What did she say?"

Mabel looked him straight in the eye. "She said, 'If I come back, Brenda dies.' "

Myron felt a cold gust chill his heart. "What did she mean by that?"

"Like it was just a given. Like one and one equals two." She put the photograph back on top of the television. "I never asked Anita again," she said. "The way I see it, there are some things you're just better off never knowing."

Chapter 30

Myron and Win took separate cars back to New York City. Brenda's game started in forty-five minutes. Just enough time to run into the loft and change clothes.

He double-parked on Spring Street and left his key in the ignition. The car was safe: Win was waiting in the Jag for him. Myron took the elevator up. He opened the door. And Jessica was standing there.

He froze.

Jessica looked at him. "I'm not running away," she said. "Not ever again."

Myron swallowed, nodded. He tried to step forward, but his legs had other ideas.

"What's wrong?" she asked.

"A lot," he said.

"I'm listening."

"My friend Horace was murdered."

Jessica closed her eyes. "I'm sorry."

"And Esperanza's leaving MB."

"You couldn't work something out?"

"No."

Myron's cellular phone rang. He snapped the power off. They stood there, neither of them moving.

Then Jessica said, "What else?"

"That's it."

She shook her head. "You can't even look at me."

So he did. Myron lifted his head and stared right at her for the first time since entering the loft. Jessica was, as always, achingly beautiful. He felt something inside him start to rip.

"I almost slept with someone else," he said.

Jessica did not move. "Almost?"

"Yes."

"I see," she said. Then: "So why almost?"

"Pardon?"

"Did she stop it? Or did you?"

"I did."

"Why?" she asked.

"Why?"

"Yes, Myron, why didn't you consummate the act?"

"Jesus, that's a hell of a question."

"No, not really. You were tempted, right?"

"Yes."

"More than tempted even," she added. "You wanted to go through with it."

"I don't know."

Jessica made a buzzing noise. "Liar."

"Fine, I wanted to go through with it."

"Why didn't you?"

"Because I'm involved with another woman," he said. "In fact, I'm in love with another woman."

"How chivalrous. So you held back for me?"

"I held back for us."

"Another lie. You held back for you. Myron Bolitar, the perfect guy, the one-woman wonder."

She made a fist and put it to her mouth. Myron stepped toward her, but she backed away.

"I've been dumb," Jessica said. "I admit that. I've done so many dumb things it's a wonder you haven't dumped me. Maybe I did all those dumb things because I knew I could. You'd always love me. No matter how dumb I acted, you'd always love me. So maybe I'm owed a little payback."

"This isn't about payback," Myron said.

"I know, goddamn it." She wrapped her arms around herself. As though the room had suddenly gone very cold. As though she needed a hug. "That's what terrifies me."

He kept still and waited.

"You don't cheat, Myron. You don't fool around. You don't have flings. Hell, you don't even get tempted much. So the question is, How much do you love her?"

Myron held up his hands. "I barely know her."

"You think that matters?"

"I don't want to lose you, Jess."

"And I'm not about to give you up without a fight. But I want to know what I'm up against."

"It's not like that."

"So what's it like?"

Myron opened his mouth, closed it. Then he said, "Do you want to get married?"

Jessica blinked, but she didn't step back. "Is this a proposal?"

"I'm asking you a question. Do you want to get married?"

"If that's what it takes, yeah, I want to get married."

Myron smiled. "My, what enthusiasm."

"What do you want me to say, Myron? Whatever you want me to say, I'll say. Yes, no, whatever will keep you here with me."

"This isn't a test, Jess."

"Then why are you raising marriage all of a sudden?"

"Because I want to be with you forever," he said. "And I want to buy a house. And I want to have kids."

"So do I," she said. "But life is so good right now. We've got our careers, our freedom. Why spoil it? There'll be time for all that later."

Myron shook his head.

"What?" she said.

"You're stalling."

"No, I'm not."

"Having a family is not something I want to fit into a convenient time block."

"But now?" Jessica put up her hands. "Right now? This is what you really want? A house in the suburbs like your parents? The Saturday night barbecues? The backyard hoop? The PTA meetings? The back-to-school shopping at the mall? That's what you really want?"

Myron looked at her, and he felt something deep within him crumble. "Yes," he said. "That's exactly what I want."

They both stood and stared at each other. There was a knock on the door. Neither one of them moved. Another knock. Then Win's voice: "Open it."

Win was not one for casual interruptions. Myron did as he asked. Win glanced at Jessica and gave her a slight nod. He handed Myron his cellular. "It's Norm Zuckerman," Win said. "He's been trying to reach you."

Jessica turned and left the room. Quickly. Win watched her, but he kept his expression even. Myron took the phone. "Yeah, Norm."

Norm's voice was pure panic. "It's almost game time."

"So?"

"So where the hell is Brenda?"

Myron felt his heart leap into his throat. "She told me she was riding on the team bus."

"She never got on it, Myron."

Myron flashed back to Horace on the morgue slab. His knees almost buckled. Myron looked at Win.

"I'll drive," Win said.

Chapter 31

They took the Jag. Win did not slow for red lights. He did not slow for pedestrians. Twice Win veered up on sidewalks to bypass heavy traffic.

Myron looked straight ahead. "What I said before. About your going too far."

Win waited.

"Forget it," Myron said.

For the rest of the ride, neither man spoke.

Win screeched the car into an illegal spot on the southeast corner of Thirty-third Street and Eighth Avenue. Myron sprinted toward the Madison Square Garden employee entrance. A police officer sauntered toward Win with major attitude. Win ripped a hundred-dollar bill and handed one half to the officer. The officer nodded and tipped his cap. No words needed to be exchanged.

The guard at the employee entrance recognized Myron and waved him through.

"Where's Norm Zuckerman?" Myron asked.

"Press room. Other side of the—"

Myron knew where it was. As he bounded up the stairs, he could hear the pregame hum of the crowd. The sound was oddly soothing. When he reached court level, he veered to his right. The press room was on the other side of the floor. He ran out onto the playing surface. The crowd, he was surprised to see, was enormous. Norm had told him how he planned to darken and close off the top sections— that is, drape a black curtain over the unused seats so as to give the arena a more crowded yet intimate feel. But sales had far surpassed expectations. A sellout crowd was finding its seats. Many fans held up banners: DAWN OF AN ERA, BRENDA RULES, WELCOME TO THE HOUSE OF BRENDA, NOW IT'S OUR TURN, SISTERS ARE DOING IT FOR THEMSELVES, YOU GO, GIRLS! Stuff like that. Sponsors' logos dominated the landscape like the work of a mad graffiti artist. Giant images of a stunning Brenda flashed across the overhead scoreboard. A highlight reel of some kind. Brenda in her college uniform. Loud music started up. Hip music. That was what Norm wanted. Hip. He'd been generous with the comp tickets too. Spike Lee was courtside. So were Jimmy Smits and Rosie O'Donnell and Sam Waterston and Woody Allen and Rudy Giuliani. Several ex-MTV hosts, the biggest sort of has-beens, mugged for cameras, desperate to be seen. Supermodels wore wire-rimmed glasses, trying a little too hard to look both beautiful and studious.

They were all here to toast New York's latest phenom: Brenda Slaughter.

This was supposed to be her night, her chance to shine in the pro arena. Myron had thought that he understood Brenda's insistence on playing the opener. But he hadn't. This was more than a game. More than her love for basketball. More than a personal tribute. This was history. Brenda had seen that. In this era of jaded superstars she relished the chance to be a role model and shape impressionable kids. Corny, but there you have it. Myron paused for a moment and looked at the Jumbo-tron screen above his head. The digitally enlarged Brenda was driving hard to the hoop, her face a mask of determination, her body and movements fiercely splendid and graceful and purposeful.

Brenda would not be denied.

Myron picked up the sprint again. He left the court and dipped down the ramp and back into a corridor. In a matter of moments he reached the press room. Win was coming up behind him. Myron opened the door. Norm Zuckerman was there. So were Detectives Maureen McLaughlin and Dan Tiles.

Tiles made a point of checking his watch. "That was fast," he said. He may have been smirking under the hinterlands that doubled as his mustache.

"Is she here?" Myron asked.

Maureen McLaughlin gave him the on-your-side smile. "Why don't you sit down, Myron?"

Myron ignored her. He turned to Norm. "Has Brenda shown up?"

Norm Zuckerman was dressed like Janis Joplin guest-starring on *Miami Vice.* "No," he said.

Win trotted in behind Myron. Tiles didn't like the intrusion. He crossed the room and gave Win the tough guy scrutiny. Win let him. "And who might this be?" Tiles asked.

Win pointed at Tiles's face. "You got some food stuck in your mustache. Looks like scrambled eggs."

Myron kept his eyes on Norm. "What are they doing here?"

"Sit down, Myron." It was McLaughlin again. "We need to chat."

Myron glanced over at Win. Win nodded. He moved toward Norm

Zuckerman and put his arm around his shoulders. The two of them headed for a corner.

"Sit," McLaughlin said again. There was just a hint of steel this time.

Myron slid into a chair. McLaughlin did likewise, maintaining oodles of eye contact along the way. Tiles stayed standing and glared down at Myron. He was one of those idiots who believed that head level equaled intimidation.

"What happened?" Myron asked.

Maureen McLaughlin folded her hands. "Why don't you tell us, Myron?"

He shook his head. "I don't have time for this, Maureen. Why are you here?"

"We're looking for Brenda Slaughter," McLaughlin said. "Do you know where she is?"

"No. Why are you looking for her?"

"We'd like to ask her some questions."

Myron looked around the room. "And you figured the best time to ask them would be right before the biggest game of her life?"

McLaughlin and Tiles sneaked an obvious glance. Myron checked out Win. He was still whispering with Norm.

Tiles stepped up to the plate. "When did you last see Brenda Slaughter?"

"Today," Myron said.

"Where?"

This was going to take too long. "I don't have to answer your questions, Tiles. And neither does Brenda. I'm her attorney, remember? You got something, let me know. If not, stop wasting my time."

Tiles's mustache seemed to curl up in a grin. "Oh, we got something, smart guy."

Myron did not like the way he said that. "I'm listening."

McLaughlin leaned forward, again with the earnest eyes. "We got a search warrant this morning for the college dormitory of Brenda Slaughter." Her tone was all police official now. "We found on the premises one weapon, a Smith and Wesson thirty-eight, the same caliber that killed Horace Slaughter. We're waiting for a ballistics test to see if it's the murder weapon."

"Fingerprints?" Myron asked.

McLaughlin shook her head. "Wiped clean."

"Even if it is the murder weapon," Myron said, "it was obviously planted."

McLaughlin looked puzzled. "How do you know that, Myron?"

"Come on, Maureen. Why would she wipe the weapon clean and then leave it where you could find it?"

"It was hidden under her mattress," McLaughlin countered.

Win stepped away from Norm Zuckerman. He started dialing on his cell phone. Someone answered. Win kept his voice low.

Myron shrugged, feigning nonchalance. "Is that all you got?"

"Don't try to snow us, asshole." Tiles again. "We have a motive: she feared her father enough to get a restraining order. We found the murder weapon hidden under her own mattress. And now we have the fact that she's clearly on the lam. That's a shitload more than enough to make an arrest."

"So that's why you're here?" Myron countered. "To arrest her?"

Again McLaughlin and Tiles exchanged a glance. "No," McLaughlin said as though pronouncing the word took great effort. "But we would very much like to speak with her again."

Win disconnected the call. Then he beckoned Myron with a nod. Myron rose. "Excuse me."

Tiles said, "What the hell!"

"I need to converse with my associate for a moment. I'll be right back."

Myron and Win ducked into a corner. Tiles lowered his eyebrows to half-mast and put his fists on his hips. Win stared back for a moment. Tiles kept up the scowl. Win put his thumbs in his ears, stuck out his tongue, wiggled his fingers. Tiles did not follow suit.

Win spoke softly and quickly. "According to Norm, Brenda received a call at practice. She took the call and ran out. The team bus waited awhile, but Brenda ended up being a no-show. When the bus left, an assistant coach waited with her car. The coach is still at the practice site. That's all Norm knew. I then called Arthur Bradford. He knew about the search warrant. He claimed that by the time you two made your arrangement vis-à-vis protecting Brenda, the warrant had been acted upon and the gun had been found. He has since contacted some friends in high places, and they have agreed to move very slowly on Ms. Slaughter."

Myron nodded. That explained the semidiplomacy going on here. McLaughlin and Tiles clearly wanted to arrest her, but the higher-ups were holding them back. "Anything else?"

"Arthur was very concerned about Brenda's disappearance."

"I bet."

"He wants you to call him immediately."

"Well, we don't always get what we want," Myron said. He glanced back at the two detectives. "Okay, I got to clear out of here."

"You have a thought?"

"The detective from Livingston. A guy named Wickner. He almost cracked at the Little League field."

"And you think perhaps he'll crack this time?"

Myron nodded. "He'll crack."

"Would you like me to come along?"

"No, I'll handle it. I need you to stay here. McLaughlin and Tiles can't legally hold me, but they might try. Stall them for me."

Win almost smiled. "No problem."

"See also if you can find the guy who answered the phone at the practice. Whoever called Brenda might have identified themselves. Maybe one of her teammates or coaches saw something."

"I'll look into it." Win handed Myron the ripped hundred and his car keys. He motioned toward his cell phone. "Keep the line open."

Myron did not bother with good-byes. He suddenly bounded out of the room. He heard Tiles call after him, "Stop! Son of a—" Tiles started running after him. Win stepped in front of him, blocking his path. "What the f—" Tiles never finished the expletive. Myron continued to run. Win closed the door. Tiles would not get out.

Once out on the street, Myron tossed the bill to the waiting cop and hopped into the Jag. Eli Wickner's lake house was listed in directory assistance. Myron dialed the number. Wickner answered on the first ring.

"Brenda Slaughter is missing," Myron told him.

Silence.

"We need to talk, Eli."

"Yes," the retired detective said. "I think we do."

Chapter 32

The ride took an hour. Night had firmly set in by now, and the lake area seemed extra dark, the way lake areas often do. There were no streetlights. Myron slowed the car. Old Lake Drive was narrow and only partially paved. At the end of the road his headlights crossed a wooden sign shaped like a fish. The sign said THE WICKNERS. Wickners. Myron remembered Mrs. Wickner. She had overseen the food stand at the Little League field. Her semiblond hair had been overtreated to the point where it resembled hay, her laugh a constant, deep throttle. Lung cancer had claimed her ten years ago. Eli Wickner had retired to this cabin alone.

Myron pulled into the driveway. His tires chewed the gravel. Lights came on, probably by motion detector. Myron stopped the car and stepped into the still night. The cabin was what was often called saltbox. Nice. And right on the water. There were boats in the dock. Myron listened for the sound of the lapping water, but there was none. The lake was incredibly calm, as if someone had put a glass top on it for night protection. Scattered lights shone off the glacial surface, still and without deviation. The moon dangled like a loose earring. Bats stood along a tree branch like the Queen's Guards in miniature.

Myron hurried to the front door. Lamps were on inside, but Myron saw no movement. He knocked on the door. No answer. He knocked again. Then he felt the shotgun barrel against the back of his skull.

"Don't turn around," Eli said.

Myron didn't.

"You armed?"

"Yes."

"Assume the position. And don't make me shoot you, Myron. You've always been a good kid."

"There's no need for the gun, Eli." It was a dumb thing to say, of course, but he had not said it for Wickner's benefit. Win was listening in on the other end. Myron did some quick calculating. It had taken him an hour to get here. It would take Win maybe half that.

He needed to stall.

As Wickner patted him down, Myron smelled alcohol. Not a good sign. He debated making a move, but this was an experienced cop, and he was, per Wickner's request, in the position. Hard to do much from there.

Wickner found Myron's gun immediately. He emptied the bullets onto the ground and pocketed the gun.

"Open the door," Wickner said.

Myron turned the knob. Wickner gave him a little nudge. Myron stepped inside. And his heart dropped to his knees. Fear constricted his throat, making it very hard to breathe. The room was decorated as one might expect a fishing cabin to be decorated: taxidermy catches above a fireplace, wood-paneled walls, a wet bar, cozy chairs, firewood piled high, a worn semishag carpet of beige. What wasn't expected, of course, were the dark red boot prints slashing a path through the beige.

Blood. Fresh blood that filled the room with a smell like wet rust.

Myron turned to look at Eli Wickner. Wickner kept his distance. The shotgun was leveled at Myron's chest. Easiest target. Wickner's eyes were open a bit too wide and even more red-rimmed than at the Little League field. His skin was like parchment paper. Spider veins had nestled into his right cheek. There may have been spider veins on his left cheek too, but it was hard to tell with the spray of blood on it.

"You?"

Wickner remained silent.

"What's going on, Eli?"

"Walk into the back room," Wickner said.

"You don't want to do this."

"I know that, Myron. Now just turn around and start walking."

Myron followed the bloody prints as though they'd been painted there for this reason—a macabre Freedom Trail or something. The wall was lined with Little League team photographs, the early ones dating back some thirty-odd years. In each picture Wickner stood proudly with his young charges, smiling into the powerful sun on a clear day. A sign held by two boys in the front row read FRIENDLY'S ICE CREAM SENATORS or BURRELLES PRESS CLIPPING TIGERS or SEYMOUR'S LUNCHEONETTE INDIANS. Always sponsors. The children squinted and shifted and smiled toothlessly. But they all basically looked the same. Over the past thirty years the kids had changed shockingly little. But Eli had aged, of course. Year by year the photographs on the wall checked off his life. The effect was more than a little eerie.

They headed into the back room. An office of some kind. There were more photos on the wall. Wickner receiving Livingston's Big L Award. The ribbon cutting when the backstop was named after him. Wickner in his police uniform with ex-Governor Brendan Byrne. Wickner winning the Raymond J. Clarke Policeman of the Year award. A smattering of plaques and trophies and mounted baseballs. A framed document entitled "What Coach Means to Me" given to him by one of his teams. And more blood.

Cold fear wrapped around Myron and drew tight.

In the corner, lying on his back, his arms extended as though readying himself for crucifixion, was Chief of Detectives Roy Pomeranz. His shirt looked like someone had squeezed out a bucket of syrup over it. His dead eyes were frozen open and sucked dry.

"You killed your own partner," Myron said. Again for Win. In case he arrived too late. For posterity or to incriminate or some such nonsense.

"Not more than ten minutes ago," Wickner said.

"Why?"

"Sit down, Myron. Right there, if you don't mind."

Myron sat in an oversize chair with wooden slats.

Keeping the gun at chest level, Wickner moved to the other side of a desk. He opened a drawer, dropped Myron's gun in it, then tossed Myron a set of handcuffs. "Cuff yourself to the side arm. I don't want to have to concentrate so hard on watching you."

Myron looked at his surroundings. It was pretty much now or never. Once the cuffs were in place, there would not be another chance. He looked for a way. Nothing. Wickner was too far away, and a desk separated them. Myron spotted a letter opener on the desk. Oh, right, like maybe he would just reach out and throw it like some martial arts death star and hit the jugular. Bruce Lee would be so proud.

As though reading his mind, Wickner raised the gun a bit.

"Put them on now, Myron."

No chance. He would just have to stall. And hope Win arrived in time. Myron clicked the cuff on his left wrist. Then he closed the other end around the heavy chair arm.

Wickner's shoulders slumped, relaxing a bit. "I should have guessed they'd have a tap on the phone," he said.

"Who?"

Wickner seemed not to hear him. "Thing is, you can't approach this house without my knowing. Forget the gravel out there. I got motion sensors all over the place. House lights up like a Christmas tree if you approach from any direction. Use it to scare away the animals—otherwise they get in the garbage. But you see, they knew that. So they sent someone I would trust. My old partner."

Myron was trying to keep up. "Are you saying Pomeranz came here to kill you?"

"No time for your questions, Myron. You wanted to know what happened. Now you will. And then . . ." He looked away, the rest of the sentence vaporizing before reaching his lips.

"The first time I encountered Anita Slaughter was at the bus stop on the corner of Northfield Avenue, where Roosevelt School used to be." His voice had fallen into a cop monotone, almost as though he were reading back a report. "We'd gotten an anonymous call from someone using the phone booth at Sam's across the street. They said a woman was cut up bad and bleeding. Check that. They said a *black* woman was bleeding. Only place you saw black women in Livingston was by the bus stop. They came in to clean houses, or they didn't come here at all. Just that simple. If they were there for other reasons in those days, well, we politely pointed out the errors in their ways and escorted them back on the bus.

"Anyway, I was in the squad car. So I took the call. Sure enough, she was bleeding pretty good. Someone had given her a hell of a beating. But I tell you what struck me right away. The woman was gorgeous. Dark as coal, but even with all those scratches on her face, she was simply stunning. I asked her what happened, but she wouldn't tell me. I figured it was a domestic dispute. A spat with the husband. I didn't like it, but back in those days you didn't do anything about it. Hell, not much different today. Anyway I insisted on taking her to St. Barnabas. They patched her up. She was pretty shook up, but she was basically okay. The scratches were pretty deep, like she'd been attacked by a cat. But hey, I did my bit and forgot all about it—until three weeks later, when I got the call about Elizabeth Bradford."

A clock chimed and echoed. Eli lowered the shotgun and looked off. Myron checked his cuffed wrist. It was secure. The chair was heavy. Still no chance.

"Her death wasn't an accident, was it, Eli?"

"No," Wickner said. "Elizabeth Bradford committed suicide." He reached out on his desk and picked up an old baseball. He stared at it like a Gypsy reading fortunes. A Little League ball, the awkward signature of twelve-year-olds scrawled over the surface.

"Nineteen seventy-three," the old coach said with a pained smile. "The year we won the state championship. Hell of a team." He put down the ball. "I love Livingston. I dedicated my life to that town. But every good place has a Bradford family in it. To add temptation, I guess. Like the serpent in the Garden of Eden. It starts small, you know? You let a parking ticket go. Then you see one of them speeding and you turn the other way. Like I said, small. They don't openly bribe you, but they have ways of taking care of people. They start at the top. You drag a Bradford in for drunk driving, someone above you just springs them anyway, and you get unofficially sanctioned. And other cops get pissed off because the Bradfords gave all of us tickets to a Giants game. Or they paid for a weekend retreat. Stuff like that. But underneath we all know it's wrong. We justify it away, but the truth is, we did wrong. I did wrong." He motioned to the mass of flesh on the ground. "And Roy did wrong. I always knew it would come back and get us one day. Just didn't know when. Then you tapped me on the shoulder at the ball field, and well, I knew."

Wickner stopped, smiled. "Getting off the subject a bit, aren't I?"

Myron shrugged. "I'm not in any hurry."

"Unfortunately I am." Another smile that twisted Myron's heart. "I was telling you about the second time I encountered Anita Slaughter. Like I said, it was the day Elizabeth Bradford committed suicide. A woman identifying herself as a maid called the station at six in the morning. I didn't realize it was Anita until I arrived. Roy and I were in the midst of the investigation when the old man called us into that fancy library. You ever seen it? The library in the silo?"

Myron nodded.

"The three of them were there—the old man, Arthur, and Chance. Still in these fancy silk pajamas and bathrobes, for chrissake. The old man asked us for a little favor. That's what he called it. A little favor. Like he was asking us to help him move a piano. He wanted us to report the death as an accident. For the family reputation. Old Man Bradford wasn't crass enough to put a dollar amount on doing this, but he made it clear we would be well compensated. Roy and I figured, What's the harm? Accident or suicide—in the long run, who really cares? That kind of stuff is changed all the time. No big deal, right?"

"Then you believed them?" Myron said.

The question nudged Wickner out of his daze. "What do you mean?"

"That it was a suicide. You took their word?"

"It was a suicide, Myron. Your Anita Slaughter confirmed it."

"How?"

"She saw it happen."

"You mean she found the body."

"No, I mean she saw Elizabeth Bradford leap."

That surprised him.

"According to Anita's statement, she arrived at work, walked up the driveway, spotted Elizabeth Bradford standing alone on the ledge, and watched her dive on her head."

"Anita could have been coached," Myron said.

Wickner shook his head. "Nope."

"How can you be so sure?"

"Because Anita Slaughter made this statement *before* the Bradfords got to her—both on the phone and when we first got there. Hell, most of the Bradfords were still getting out of bed. Once the spin control began, Anita changed her story. That's when she came up with that stuff about finding the body when she arrived."

Myron frowned. "I don't get it. Why change the time of the jump? What difference could it make?"

"I guess they wanted it to be at night so it would look more like an accident. A woman inadvertently slipping off a wet balcony late at night is an easier sell than at six in the morning."

Myron thought about this. And didn't like it.

"There was no sign of a struggle," Wickner continued. "There was even a note."

"What did it say?"

"Mostly gibberish. I don't really remember. The Bradfords kept it. Claimed it was private thoughts. We were able to confirm it was her handwriting. That's all I cared about."

"You mentioned in the police report that Anita still showed signs of the earlier assault."

Wickner nodded.

"So you must have been suspicious."

"Suspicious of what? Sure, I wondered. But I didn't see any connection. A maid suffers a beating three weeks before the suicide of her employer. What's one thing got to do with the other?"

Myron nodded slowly. It made sense, he guessed. He checked the clock behind Wickner's head. Fifteen minutes more, he estimated. And then Win would have to approach carefully. Making his way around the motion detectors would take time. Myron took a deep breath. Win would make it. He always did.

"There's more," Wickner said.

Myron looked at him and waited.

"I saw Anita Slaughter one last time," Wickner said. "Nine months later. At the Holiday Inn."

Myron realized that he was holding his breath. Wickner put down the weapon on the desk—well out of Myron's reach—and grabbed hold of a whiskey bottle. He took a swig and then picked up the shotgun again.

He aimed it at Myron.

"You're wondering why I'm telling you all this." Wickner's words came out a bit more slurred now. The barrel was still pointed at Myron, growing larger, an angry dark mouth trying to swallow him whole.

"The thought crossed my mind," Myron said.

Wickner smiled. Then he let loose a deep breath, lowered his aim a bit, and started in again. "I wasn't on duty that night. Neither was Roy. He called me at home and said the Bradfords needed a favor. I told him the Bradfords could go to hell, I wasn't their personal security service. But it was all bluster.

"Anyway, Roy told me to put on a uniform and meet him at the Holiday Inn. I went, of course. We hooked up in the parking lot. I asked Roy what was up. He said that one of the Bradford kids had screwed up again. I said, screwed up how? Roy said he didn't know the details. It was girl trouble. He had gotten fresh, or they had taken too many drugs. Something like that. Understand now that this was twenty years ago. Terms like date rape didn't exist back then. You go back to a hotel room with a guy, well, let's just say you got what you got. I'm not defending it. I'm just saying it was the way that it was.

"So I asked him what we were supposed to do. Roy said that we just had to seal off the floor. See, there was a wedding going on and a big convention. The place was mobbed, and the room was in a fairly public spot. So they needed us to keep people away so they could clean up whatever mess there was. Roy and I positioned ourselves at either end of the corridor. I didn't like it, but I didn't really think I had much of a choice. What was I going to do, report them? The Bradfords already had their hooks into me. The payoff for fixing the suicide would come out. So would all the rest. And not just about me but about my buddies on the force. Cops react funny when they're threatened." He pointed to the floor. "Look what Roy was willing to do to his own partner."

Myron nodded.

"So we cleared the floor. And then I saw Old Man Bradford's so-called security expert. Creepy little guy. Scared the piss out of me. Sam something."

"Sam Richards," Myron said.

"Yeah, right, Richards. That's the guy. He spewed out the same dribble I'd already heard. Girl trouble. Nothing to worry about. He'd clean it up. The girl was a little shaky, but they'd get her patched up and pay her off. It would all go away. That's how it is with the rich. Money cleans all spills. So the first thing this Sam guy does is carry the girl out. I wasn't supposed to see it. I was supposed to stay down at the end of the corridor. But I looked anyway. Sam had her wrapped in a sheet and carried her over his shoulder like a fireman. But for a split second I saw her face. And I knew who it was. Anita Slaughter. Her eyes were closed. She hung over his shoulder like a bag of oats."

Wickner took a plaid handkerchief out of his pocket. He unfolded it slowly and wiped his nose as if he were buffing a fender. Then he folded it up again and put it back in his pocket. "I didn't like what I saw," he said. "So I ran over to Roy and told him we had to stop it. Roy said, how would we explain even being here? What would we say, that we were helping Bradford cover up a smaller crime? He was right, of course. There was nothing we could do. So I went back to the end of the corridor. Sam was back in the room by now. I heard him using a vacuum. He took his time and cleaned the entire room. I kept telling myself it was no big deal. She was just a black woman from Newark. Hell, they all did drugs, right? And she was gorgeous. Probably partying with one of the Bradford boys and it got out of hand. Maybe she OD'd. Maybe Sam was going to take her someplace and get her some help and give her money. Just like he said. So I watched Sam finish cleaning up. I saw him get in the car. And I saw him drive away with Chance Bradford."

"Chance?" Myron repeated. "Chance Bradford was there?"

"Yes. Chance was the boy in trouble." Wickner sat back. He stared at the gun. "And that's the end of my tale, Myron."

"Wait a second. Anita Slaughter checked into that hotel with her daughter. Did you see her there?"

"No."

"Do you have any idea where Brenda is now?"

"She probably got tangled up with the Bradfords. Like her mother."

"Help me save her, Eli."

Wickner shook his head. "I'm tired, Myron. And I got nothing more to say."

Eli Wickner lifted the shotgun.

"It's going to come out," Myron said. "Even if you kill me, you can't cover it all up."

Wickner nodded. "I know." He didn't lower the weapon.

"My telephone is on," Myron continued quickly. "My friend has heard every word. Even if you kill me—"

"I know that too, Myron." A tear slid out of Eli's eye. He tossed Myron a small key. For the handcuffs. "Tell everyone I'm sorry."

Then he put the shotgun in his mouth.

Myron tried to bolt from the chair, the cuff holding him back. He yelled, "No!" But the sound was drowned out by the blast of the shotgun. Bats squealed and flew away. Then all was silent again.

Chapter 33

Win arrived a few minutes later. He looked down at the two bodies and said, "Tidy."

Myron did not reply.

"Did you touch anything?"

"I already wiped the place down," Myron said.

"A request," Win said.

Myron looked at him.

"Next time a gun is fired under similar circumstances, say something immediately. A good example might be 'I'm not dead.' "

"Next time," Myron said.

They left the cabin. They drove to a nearby twenty-four-hour supermarket. Myron parked the Taurus and got in the Jag with Win.

"Where to?" Win asked.

"You heard what Wickner said?"

"Yes."

"What do you make of it?"

"I'm still processing," Win said. "But clearly the answer lies within Bradford Farms."

"So most likely does Brenda."

Win nodded. "If she's still alive."

"So that's where we should go."

"Rescuing the fair maiden from the tower?"

"If she's even there, which is a big if. And we can't go in with guns blazing. Someone might panic and kill her." Myron reached for his phone. "Arthur Bradford wants an update. I think I'll give him one. Now. In person."

"They may very well try to kill you."

"That's where you come in," Myron said.

Win smiled. "Bitching." His word of the week.

They turned onto Route 80 and headed east.

"Let me bounce a few thoughts off you," Myron said.

Win nodded. He was used to this game.

"Here's what we know," Myron said. "Anita Slaughter is assaulted. Three weeks later she witnesses Elizabeth Bradford's sui-

cide. Nine months pass. Then she runs away from Horace. She emp-
ties out the bank account, grabs her daughter, and hides out at the
Holiday Inn. Now here is where things get murky. We know that
Chance Bradford and Sam end up there. We know they end up taking an injured Anita off the premises. We also know that sometime
before that Anita calls Horace and tells him to pick up Brenda—"

Myron broke off and looked at Win. "What time would that have
been?"

"Pardon?"

"Anita called Horace to pick up Brenda. That had to be before
Sam arrived on the scene, right?"

"Yes."

"But here's the thing. Horace told Mabel that Anita called him.
But maybe Horace was lying. I mean, why would Anita call Horace?
It makes no sense. She's running away from the man. She's taken all
his money. Why would she then call Horace and give away her loca-
tion? She might call Mabel, for example, but never Horace."

Win nodded. "Go on."

"Suppose . . . suppose we're looking at this all wrong. Forget the
Bradfords for the moment. Take it from Horace's viewpoint. He gets
home. He finds the note. Maybe he even learns that his money is
gone. He'd be furious. So suppose Horace tracked Anita down at the
Holiday Inn. Suppose he went there to take back his child and his
money."

"By force," Win added.

"Yes."

"Then he killed Anita?"

"Not killed. But maybe he beat the hell out of her. Maybe he even
left her for dead. Either way, he takes Brenda and the money back.
Horace calls his sister. He tells her that Anita called him to pick up
Brenda."

Win frowned. "And then what? Anita hides from Horace for
twenty years—lets him raise her daughter by himself—because she
was scared of him?"

Myron didn't like that. "Maybe," he said.

"And then, if I follow your logic, twenty years later Anita becomes aware that Horace is looking for her. So is she the one who
killed him? A final showdown? But then who grabbed Brenda? And
why? Or is Brenda in cahoots with her mother? And while we've dismissed the Bradfords for the sake of hypothesizing, how do they fac-
tor into all this? Why would they be concerned enough to cover up

Horace Slaughter's crime? Why was Chance Bradford at the hotel that night in the first place?"

"There are holes," Myron admitted.

"There are chasms of leviathan proportions," Win corrected.

"There's another thing I don't get. If the Bradfords have had a tap on Mabel's phone this whole time, wouldn't they have been able to trace Anita's calls?"

Win mulled that one over. "Maybe," he said, "they did."

Silence. Myron flipped on the radio. The game was in the second half. The New York Dolphins were getting crushed. The announcers were speculating on the whereabouts of Brenda Slaughter. Myron turned the volume down.

"We're still missing something," Myron said.

"Yes, but we're getting close."

"So we still try the Bradfords."

Win nodded. "Open the glove compartment. Arm yourself like a paranoid despot. This may get ugly."

Myron did not argue. He dialed Arthur's private line. Arthur answered midway through the first ring. "Have you found Brenda?" Arthur asked.

"I'm on my way to your house," Myron said.

"Then you've found her?"

"I'll be there in fifteen minutes," Myron said. "Tell your guards."

Myron hung up. "Curious," he said to Win.

"What?"

And then it hit Myron. Not slowly. But all at once. A tremendous avalanche buried him in one fell swoop. With a trembling hand Myron dialed another number into the cell phone.

"Norm Zuckerman, please. Yes, I know he's watching the game. Tell him it's Myron Bolitar. Tell him it's urgent. And tell him I want to talk with McLaughlin and Tiles too."

Chapter 34

The guard at Bradford Farms shone a flashlight into the car. "You alone, Mr. Bolitar?"

"Yes," Myron said.

The gate went up. "Please proceed to the main house."

Myron drove in slowly. Per their plan, he slowed on the next curve. Silence. Then Win's voice came through the phone: "I'm out."

Out of the trunk. So smooth Myron had not even heard him.

"I'm going on mute," Win said. "Let me know where you are at all times."

The plan was simple: Win would search the property for Brenda while Myron tried not to get himself killed.

He continued up the drive, both hands on the wheel. Part of him wanted to stall; most of him wanted to get at Arthur Bradford immediately. He knew the truth now. Some of it anyway. Enough to save Brenda.

Maybe.

The grounds were silk black, the farm animals silent. The mansion loomed above him, floating almost, only tenuously connected with the world beneath it. Myron parked and got out of the car. Before he reached the door, Mattius the Manservant was there. It was ten o'clock at night, but Mattius still displayed full butler garb and rigid spine. He said nothing, waiting with almost inhuman patience.

When Myron reached him, Mattius said, "Mr. Bradford will see you in the library."

Myron nodded. And that was when someone hit him in the head. There was a thud, and then a thick, blackening numbness swam through him. His skull tingled. Still reeling, Myron felt a bat smash the back of his lower thighs. His legs buckled, and he dropped to his knees.

"Win," he managed.

A boot stomped him hard between the shoulder blades. Myron crashed facefirst into the ground. He felt the air whoosh out of him. There were hands on him now. Searching. Grabbing out the weapons.

"Win," he said again.

"Nice try." Sam stood over him. He was holding Myron's phone. "But I hung it up, I Spy."

Two other men lifted Myron by the armpits and quickly dragged him into the foyer and down the corridor. Myron tried to blink out the fuzzies. His entire body felt like a thumb hit with a hammer. Sam walked in front of him. He opened a door, and the two men tossed Myron in like a sack of peat moss. He started to roll down steps, but he managed to stop his descent before he hit bottom.

Sam stepped inside. The door closed behind him.

"Come on," Sam said. "Let's get this done."

Myron managed to sit up. A basement, Myron realized. He was on the steps of a basement.

Sam walked toward him. He reached out a hand. Myron took it and pulled himself to his feet. The two men walked down the steps.

"This section of the basement is windowless and cement-lined," Sam said. Like he was giving a house tour. "So the only way in or out is through that door. Understand?"

Myron nodded.

"I got two men at the top of the steps. They're going to spread out now. And they're pros, not like that Mario asswipe. So no one is getting through that door. Understand?"

Another nod.

Sam took out a cigarette and put it between his lips. "Lastly, we saw your buddy jump out of the trunk. I got two marine sharpshooters hidden out there. Persian Gulf War vets. Your friend comes anywhere near the house, he's toast. The windows are all alarmed. The motion detectors are set. I'm in radio contact with all four of my men under four different frequencies." He showed Myron a walkie-talkie of some kind with a digital readout.

"Different frequencies," Myron repeated. "Wow."

"I say all this not to impress you but to stress how dumb a flight attempt would be. Do you understand?"

One more nod.

They were in a wine cellar now. It smelled as robust and oaky as, well, a perfectly aged chardonnay. Arthur was there. His face was skull-like, his skin drawn up tautly against his cheekbones. Chance was there too. He was sipping red wine, studying the color, trying very hard to look casual.

Myron glanced about the wine cellar. Lots of bottles in crisscrossed shelves, all tilted slightly forward so the corks would remain properly moist. A giant thermometer. A few wooden barrels, mostly for show. There were no windows. No doors. No other visible entranceways. In the center of the room was a hefty mahogany table. The table was bare except for a gleaming set of pruning shears. Myron looked back at Sam. Sam smiled, still holding a gun.

"Label me intimidated," Myron said.

Sam shrugged.

"Where is Brenda?" Arthur demanded.

"I don't know," Myron said.

"And Anita? Where is she?"

"Why don't you ask Chance?" Myron said.

"What?"

Chance sat up. "He's crazy."

Arthur stood. "You're not leaving here until I'm satisfied that you're not holding out on me."

"Fine," Myron said. "Then let's get to it, Arthur. You see, I've been dumb about this whole thing. I mean, the clues were all there. The old phone taps. Your keen interest in all this. The earlier assault on Anita. Ransacking Horace's apartment and taking Anita's letters. The cryptic calls telling Brenda to contact her mother. Sam cutting those kids' Achilles tendons. The scholarship money. But you know what finally gave it away?"

Chance was about to say something, but Arthur waved him into silence. He strummed his chin with his index finger. "What?" he asked.

"The timing of Elizabeth's suicide," Myron said.

"I don't understand."

"The timing of the suicide," Myron repeated, "and more important, your family's attempt to alter it. Why would Elizabeth kill herself at six in the morning—at the exact moment Anita Slaughter was coming to work? Coincidence? Possibly. But then why did you all work so hard to change the time? Elizabeth could have just as easily had her accident at six A.M. as midnight. So why the change?"

Arthur kept his back straight. "You tell me."

"Because the timing was not incidental," Myron said. "Your wife committed suicide when she did and how she did for a reason. She wanted Anita Slaughter to see her jump."

Chance made a noise. "That's ridiculous."

"Elizabeth was depressed," Myron continued, looking straight at Arthur. "I don't doubt that. And I don't doubt that you once loved her. But that was a long time ago. You said she hadn't been herself for years. I don't doubt that either. But three weeks before her suicide Anita was assaulted. I thought one of you beat her. Then I thought that maybe Horace did it. But the most noticeable injuries were scratches. Deep scratches. Like a cat, Wickner said." Myron looked at Arthur. Arthur seemed to be shrinking in front of him, being sucked dry by his own memories.

"Your wife was the one who attacked Anita," Myron said. "First she attacked her, and then three weeks later, still despondent, she committed suicide in front of her—because Anita was having an affair with her husband. It was the final mental straw that broke her, wasn't it, Arthur? So how did it happen? Did Elizabeth walk in on you two? Did she seem so far gone that you got careless?"

Arthur cleared his throat. "As a matter of fact, yes. That's pretty much how it happened. But so what? What does that have to do with the present?"

"Your affair with Anita. How long did it last?"

"I don't see the relevance of that."

Myron looked at him for a long moment. "You're an evil man," he said. "You were raised by an evil man, and you have much of him in you. You've caused great suffering. You've even had people killed. But this wasn't a fling, was it? You loved her, didn't you, Arthur?"

He said nothing. But something behind the facade began to cave in.

"I don't know how it happened," Myron continued. "Maybe Anita wanted to leave Horace. Or maybe you encouraged her. It doesn't matter. Anita decided to run away and start new. Tell me what the plan was, Arthur. Were you going to set her up in an apartment? A house out of town? Surely no Bradford was going to marry a black maid from Newark."

Arthur made a noise. Half scoff. Half groan. "Surely," he said.

"So what happened?"

Sam kept several steps back, his gaze moving from the basement door to Myron. He whispered into his walkie-talkie every once in a while. Chance sat frozen, both nervous and comforted; nervous about what was being unearthed; comforted because he believed it would never leave this cellar. Perhaps he was right.

"Anita was my last hope," Arthur said. He bounced two fingers off his lips and forced up a smile. "It's ironic, don't you think? If you come from a disadvantaged home, you can blame the environment for your sinful ways. But what about an omnipotent household? What about those who are raised to dominate others, to take what they want? What about those who are raised to believe that they are special and that other people are little more than window dressing? What about those children?"

Myron nodded. "Next time I'm alone," he said, "I'll weep for them."

Arthur chuckled. "Fair enough," he said. "But you have it wrong. I was the one who wanted to run away. Not Anita. Yes, I loved her. When I was with her, every part of me soared. I can't explain it any other way."

He didn't have to. Myron thought of Brenda. And he understood.

"I was going to leave Bradford Farms," he continued. "Anita and I were going to run away together. Start on our own. Escape this prison." He smiled again. "Naive, wouldn't you say?"

"So what happened?" Myron asked.

"Anita changed her mind."

"Why?"

"There was someone else."

"Who?"

"I don't know. We were supposed to meet up in the morning, but Anita never showed. I thought maybe her husband had done something to her. I kept an eye on him. And then I got a note from her. She said she needed to start new. Without me. And she sent back the ring."

"What ring?"

"The one I gave her. An unofficial engagement ring."

Myron looked over at Chance. Chance said nothing. Myron kept his eyes on him for a few more seconds. Then he turned back to Arthur.

"But you didn't give up, did you?"

"No."

"You searched for her. The phone taps. You've had the taps in place all these years. You figured Anita would call her family one day. You wanted to be able to trace the call when she did."

"Yes."

Myron swallowed hard and hoped he would be able to keep his voice from cracking. "And then there were the microphones in Brenda's room," he said. "And the scholarship money. And the severed Achilles tendons."

Silence.

Tears welled up in Myron's eyes. Same with Arthur's. Both men knew what was coming. Myron pressed on, struggling to maintain an even and steady tone.

"The microphones were there so that you could keep an eye on Brenda. The scholarships were set up by someone with a great deal of money and financial expertise. Even if Anita had gotten her hands on cash, she wouldn't have known how to funnel it through the Cayman Islands. You, on the other hand, would. And lastly the Achilles tendons. Brenda thought it was her father who did it. She thought her father was being overprotective. And she was right."

More silence.

"I just called Norm Zuckerman and got Brenda's blood type from the team medical records. The police had Horace's blood type from the autopsy report. They weren't related, Arthur." Myron thought of Brenda's light coffee skin next to the far darker tones of her parents. "That's why you've been so interested in Brenda. That's why you were so quick to help keep her out of prison. That's why you're so worried about her right now. Brenda Slaughter is your daughter."

Tears were streaming down Arthur's face now. He did nothing to stop it.

Myron went on. "Horace never knew, did he?"

Arthur shook his head. "Anita got pregnant early in our relationship. But Brenda still ended up dark enough to pass. Anita insisted we keep it a secret. She didn't want our child stigmatized. She also— she also didn't want our daughter raised in this house. I understood."

"So what happened to Horace? Why did he call you after twenty years?"

"It was the Aches, trying to help Davison. Somehow they found out about the scholarship money. From one of the lawyers, I think. They wanted to cause mischief for me in the governor's race. So they told Slaughter about it. They thought he'd be greedy and follow the money line."

"But he didn't care about the money," Myron said. "He wanted to find Anita."

"Yes. He called me repeatedly. He came to my campaign headquarters. He wouldn't let go. So I had Sam discourage him."

The blood in the locker. "He was beaten?"

Arthur nodded. "But not badly. I wanted to scare him off, not hurt him. A long time ago Anita made me promise never to harm him. I tried my best to keep that promise."

"Sam was supposed to keep an eye on him?"

"Yes. To make sure he didn't cause any trouble. And, I don't know, maybe I had hopes he would find Anita."

"But he ran."

"Yes."

It made sense, Myron thought. Horace had gotten a bloody nose. He had gone to nearby St. Barnabas after the beating. He cleaned himself up. Sam had scared him, yes, but only enough to convince

Horace that he had to go into hiding. So he cleared out his bank account and disappeared. Sam and Mario searched. They followed Brenda. They visited Mabel Edwards and threatened her. They checked the tap on her phone. Eventually Horace called her.

And then?

"You killed Horace."

"No. We never found him."

A hole, Myron thought. There were still a few of them he hadn't plugged. "But you did have your people make cryptic calls to Brenda."

"Just to see if she knew where Anita was. The other calls—the threatening ones—came from the Aches. They wanted to find Horace and finalize the contract before the opener."

Myron nodded. Again it made sense. He turned and stared down Chance. Chance met the gaze and held it. He had a small smile on his face.

"Are you going to tell him, Chance?"

Chance rose and went face-to-face with Myron. "You're a dead man," he said, almost leering. "All you've done here is dig your own grave."

"Are you going to tell him, Chance?"

"No, Myron." He gestured to the pruning shears and leaned closer. "I'm going to watch you suffer and then die."

Myron reared back and head-butted Chance square on the nose. He held back at the last moment. If you head-butt at full strength, you could literally kill a person. The head is both heavy and hard; the face being hit is neither. Picture a wrecking ball heading for a bird's nest.

Still, the blow was effective. Chance's nose did the equivalent of a gymnastic split. Myron felt something warm and sticky on his hair. Chance fell back. His nose gushed. His eyes were wide and shocked. No one rushed to his aid. Sam in fact seemed to be smiling.

Myron turned to Arthur. "Chance knew about your affair, didn't he?"

"Yes, of course."

"And he knew about your plans to run away?"

This time the answer came slower. "Yes. But what of it?"

"Chance has been lying to you for twenty years. So has Sam."

"What?"

"I just spoke to Detective Wickner. He was there that night too. I don't know what happened exactly. Neither did he. But he saw Sam carry Anita out of the Holiday Inn. And he saw Chance in the car."

Arthur glared at his brother. "Chance?"

"He's lying."

Arthur took out a gun and pointed it at his brother. "Tell me."

Chance was still trying to stem the blood flow. "Who are you going to believe? Me or—"

Arthur pulled the trigger. The bullet smashed Chance's knee, splintering the joint. Blood spurted. Chance howled in agony. Arthur aimed the gun at the other knee.

"Tell me," he said.

"You were insane!" Chance shouted. Then he gritted his teeth. His eyes grew small yet strangely clear, as though the pain were sweeping the debris away. "Did you really think Father was going to let you just run off like that? You were going to destroy everything. I tried to make you see that. I talked to you. Like a brother. But you didn't want to listen. So I went to see Anita. Just to talk. I wanted her to see how destructive this whole idea was. I meant her no harm. I was just trying to help."

Chance's face was a bloody mess, but Arthur's was a far more horrid sight. The tears were still there, still flowing freely. But he was not crying. His skin was gray-white, his features contorted like a death mask. Something behind his eyes had been short-circuited by his rage. "What happened?"

"I found her room number. And when I got there, the door was ajar. I swear, Anita was like that when I arrived. I swear it, Arthur. I didn't touch her. At first I thought maybe you had done it. That maybe you two had a fight. But either way, I knew it would be a mess if it leaked out. There were too many questions, too many loose ends. So I called Father. He arranged the rest. Sam came over. He cleaned the place up. We took the ring and forged that note. So you'd stop looking."

"Where is she now?" Myron asked.

Chance looked at him, puzzled. "What the hell are you talking about?"

"Did you take her to a doctor? Give her money? Did you—"

"Anita was dead," Chance said.

Silence.

Arthur let out a harrowing, primitive wail. He collapsed to the floor.

"She was dead when I got there, Arthur. I swear it."

Myron felt his heart sink into deep mud. He tried to speak, but no words came out. He looked over at Sam. Sam nodded. Myron met his eye. "Her body?" he managed.

"I get rid of something," Sam said, "it's gone for good."

Dead. Anita Slaughter was dead. Myron tried to take it in. All these years Brenda had felt unworthy for nothing.

"So where is Brenda?" Myron asked.

The adrenaline was starting to wear off, but Chance still managed to shake his head. "I don't know."

Myron looked over at Sam. Sam shrugged.

Arthur sat up. He hugged his knees and lowered his head. He began to cry.

"My leg," Chance said. "I need a doctor."

Arthur did not move.

"We also need to kill him," Chance said through a clenched jaw. "He knows too much, Arthur. I know you're grief-stricken, but we can't let him ruin everything."

Sam nodded at that. "He's right, Mr. Bradford."

Myron said, "Arthur."

Arthur looked up.

"I'm your daughter's best hope."

"I don't think so," Sam said. He aimed the gun. "Chance is right, Mr. Bradford. It's too risky. We just admitted covering up a murder. He has to die."

Sam's walkie-talkie suddenly squeaked. Then a voice came through the tinny speaker: "I wouldn't do that if I were you."

Win.

Sam frowned at the walkie-talkie. He turned a knob, changed frequency. The red digital readout changed numbers. Then he pressed the talk button. "Someone got to Forster," Sam said. "Move in and take him out."

The response was Win's best *Star Trek* Scottie: "But I can't hold her, Captain. She's breaking up!"

Sam remained calm. "How many radios you got, buddy?"

"Collect all four, now in specially marked packages."

Sam whistled his appreciation. "Fine," he said. "So we got ourselves a stalemate. Let's talk it through."

"No." This time it wasn't Win speaking. It was Arthur Bradford. He fired twice. Both bullets hit Sam in the chest. Sam slumped to the floor, twitched, and then lay still.

Arthur looked at Myron. "Find my daughter," he said. "Please."

Chapter 35

Win and Myron rushed back to the Jag. Win drove. Myron did not ask about the fate of the men who once possessed those four walkie-talkies. He didn't much care.

"I searched the entire grounds," Win said. "She's not here."

Myron sat and thought. He remembered telling Detective Wickner at the Little League field that he would not stop digging. And he remembered Wickner's response: *"Then more people are going to die."*

"You were right," Myron said.

Win kept driving.

"I didn't keep my eye on the prize. I pushed too hard."

Win said nothing.

When Myron heard the first ring, he reached for his cellular. Then he remembered that Sam had taken it from him back at the estate. The ringing was coming from Win's car phone. Win answered it. He said, "Hello." He listened for a full minute without nodding or speaking or making any noise whatsoever. Then he said, "Thank you," and hung up. He slowed the car's speed and pulled over to the side of the road. The car glided to a stop. He shifted into park and snapped off the ignition.

Win turned toward Myron, his gaze as heavy as the ages.

For a fleeting moment Myron was puzzled. But only for a moment. Then his head fell to one side, and he let out a small groan. Win nodded. And something inside Myron's chest dried up and blew away.

Chapter 36

Peter Frankel, a six-year-old boy from Cedar Grove, New Jersey, had been missing for eight hours. Frantic, Paul and Missy Frankel, the boy's parents, called the police. The Frankels' backyard was up against a wooded water reservation area. The police and neighbors formed search parties. Police dogs were brought in. Neighbors even brought their own dogs along. Everyone wanted to help.

It did not take long to find Peter. Apparently the boy had crawled into a neighbor's toolshed and fallen asleep. When he woke up, he pushed at the door, but it was stuck. Peter was scared, of course, but no worse for wear. Everyone was relieved. The town fire whistle blew, signaling that all searchers should return.

One dog didn't heed the whistle. A German shepherd named Wally ran deeper into the woods and barked steadily until Officer Craig Reed, new with the canine corps, came to see what had upset Wally so.

When Reed arrived, he found Wally barking over a dead body. The medical examiner was called in. His conclusion: The victim, a female in her twenties, had been dead less than twenty-four hours. Cause of death: two contact gunshot wounds to the back of the head.

An hour later Cheryl Sutton, cocaptain of the New York Dolphins, positively identified the body as belonging to her friend and teammate Brenda Slaughter.

The car was still parked in the same place.

"I want to take a drive," Myron said. "Alone."

Win wiped his eyes with two fingers. Then he stepped out of the car without a word. Myron slid into the driver's seat. His foot pressed down on the accelerator. He passed trees and cars and signs and shops and homes and even people taking late-night walks. Music came from the car speakers. Myron did not bother turning it off. He kept driving. Images of Brenda tried to infiltrate, but Myron parried and sidestepped.

Not yet.

By the time he reached Esperanza's apartment, it was one in the morning. She sat alone on the stoop, almost as though she were expecting him. He stopped and stayed in the car. Esperanza approached. He could see that she had been crying.

"Come inside," she said.

Myron shook his head. "Win talked about leaps of faith," he began.

Esperanza stayed still.

"I didn't really understand what he meant. He kept talking about his own experiences with families. Marriage led to disaster, he said. It was that simple. He had seen countless people get married, and in almost every case they ended up crippling one another. It would take a huge leap of faith to make Win believe otherwise."

Esperanza looked at him and kept crying. "You loved her," she said.

He closed his eyes hard, waited, opened them. "I'm not talking about that. I'm talking about us. Everything I know—all my past experience—tells me that our partnership is doomed. But then I look at you. You are the finest person I know, Esperanza. You are my best friend. I love you."

"I love you too," she said.

"You're worth taking the leap. I want you to stay."

She nodded. "Good, because I can't leave anyway." She stepped closer to the car. "Myron, please come inside. We'll talk, okay?"

He shook his head.

"I know what she meant to you."

Again he closed his eyes tight. "I'll be at Win's in a few hours," he said.

"Okay. I'll wait for you there."

He drove off before she could say more.

Chapter 37

By the time Myron reached his third destination, it was almost four in the morning. A light was still on. No surprise really. He rang the doorbell. Mabel Edwards opened it. She was wearing a terrycloth robe over a flannel nightgown. She started crying and reached out to hug him.

Myron stepped back.

"You killed them all," he said. "First Anita. Then Horace. And then Brenda."

Her mouth dropped open. "You don't mean that."

Myron took out his gun and placed it against the older woman's forehead. "If you lie to me, I'll kill you."

Mabel's gaze veered quickly from shock to cold defiance. "You wired, Myron?"

"No."

"Doesn't matter. You have a gun pointed to my head. I'll say whatever you want."

The gun nudged her back into the house. Myron closed the door. The photograph of Horace was still on the fireplace mantel. Myron looked at his old friend for a brief moment. Then he turned back to Mabel.

"You lied to me," he said. "From the very beginning. Everything you told me was a lie. Anita never called you. She's been dead for twenty years."

"Who told you that?"

"Chance Bradford."

She made a scoffing noise. "You shouldn't believe a man like that."

"The phone taps," Myron said.

"What?"

"Arthur Bradford tapped your phone. For the last twenty years. He hoped Anita might call you. But we all know she never did."

"That doesn't mean anything," Mabel said. "Maybe he just missed those calls."

"I don't think so. But there's more. You told me that Horace called you last week while he was hiding. He gave you this dire warning about not trying to look for him. But again Arthur Bradford had a tap on your phone. He was looking for Horace. Why didn't he know anything about it?"

"Guess he messed up again."

Myron shook his head. "I just paid a visit to a dumb thug named Mario," he went on. "I surprised him while he was sleeping, and I did some things to him I'm not proud of. By the time I was through, Mario admitted to all kinds of crimes—including trying to get information from you with his skinny partner, just like you told me. But he swears he never punched you in the eye. And I believe him. Because it was Horace who hit you."

Brenda had called him a sexist, and he had been wondering lately about his own race issues. Now he saw the truth. His semilatent prejudices had twisted on him like a snake seizing its own tail. Mabel Edwards. The sweet old black lady. Butterfly McQueen. Miss Jane Pittman. Knitting needles and reading glasses. Big and kind and matronly. Evil could never lurk in so politically correct a form.

"You told me you moved into this house shortly after Anita disappeared. How did a widow from Newark afford it? You told me that your son worked his way through Yale Law School. Sorry, but part-time jobs do not pay that kind of money anymore."

"So?"

He kept the gun trained on her. "You knew Horace wasn't Brenda's father from the beginning, didn't you? Anita was your closest friend. You were still working at the Bradfords' home. You must have known."

She did not back down. "And what if I did?"

"Then you knew Anita ran away. She would have confided in you. And if she had run into a problem at the Holiday Inn, she would have called you, not Horace."

"Could be," Mabel said. "If you're talking hypothetically, I guess this is all possible."

Myron pressed the gun against her forehead, pushing her onto the couch. "Did you kill Anita for the money?"

Mabel smiled. Physically it was that same celestial smile, but now Myron thought he could see at least a hint of the decay looming beneath it. "Hypothetically, Myron, I guess I could have a bunch of motives. Money, yes—fourteen thousand dollars is a lot of money. Or sisterly love—Anita was going to leave Horace brokenhearted, right? She was going to take away the baby girl he thought was his. Maybe she was even going to tell Horace the truth about Brenda's father.

And maybe Horace would know that his only sister had helped keep the secret all those years." She glared up at the gun. "Lots of motives, I'll give you that."

"How did you do it, Mabel?"

"Go home, Myron."

Myron lifted the muzzle and poked her forehead with it. Hard. "How?"

"You think I'm scared of you?"

He poked her again with the muzzle. Harder. Then again. "How?"

"What do you mean, how?" She was spitting words now. "It would have been easy, Myron. Anita was a mother. I would have quietly shown her the gun. I would have told her if she didn't do exactly as I said, I would kill her daughter. So Anita, the good mother, would have listened. She would have given her daughter a last hug and told her to wait in the lobby. I would have used a pillow to muffle the shot. Simple, no?"

A fresh flash of rage surged through him. "Then what happened?"

Mabel hesitated. Myron hit her with the gun again.

"I drove Brenda back to her house. Anita had left a note telling Horace she was running away and that Brenda wasn't his child. I tore it up and wrote another."

"So Horace never even knew that Anita had planned on taking Brenda."

"That's right."

"And Brenda never said anything?"

"She was five years old, Myron. She didn't know what was going on. She told her daddy how I picked her up and took her away from Mommy. But she didn't remember anything about a hotel. At least that's what I thought."

Silence.

"When Anita's body vanished, what did you think happened?"

"I figured that Arthur Bradford had shown up, found her dead, and did what that family always did: threw out the trash."

Another rage flash. "And you found a way to use that. With your son, Terence, and his political career."

Mabel shook her head. "Too dangerous," she said. "You don't want to stir up those Bradford boys with blackmail. I had nothing to do with Terence's career. But truth be told, Arthur was always willing to help Terence. Terence was, after all, his daughter's cousin."

The anger swelled, pressing against his skull. He wanted so much simply to pull the trigger and end this. "So what happened next?"

"Oh, come now, Myron. You know the rest of the story, don't you?

Horace started looking for Anita again. After all these years. He had a lead, he said. He thought he could find her. I tried to talk him out of it, but, well, love is a funny thing."

"Horace found out about the Holiday Inn," Myron said.

"Yes."

"He spoke to a woman named Caroline Gundeck."

Mabel shrugged. "I never heard the woman's name."

"I just woke Ms. Gundeck out of a sound sleep," Myron said. "Scared her half to death. But she talked to me. Just like she talked to Horace. She was a maid back then, and she knew Anita. You see, Anita used to work hotel functions to make a little extra money. Caroline Gundeck remembered seeing Anita there that night. She was surprised because Anita checked in as a guest, not a worker. She also remembered seeing Anita's little daughter. And she remembered seeing Anita's daughter leave with another woman. A strung-out drug addict is how she described the woman. I wouldn't have guessed it was you. But Horace would have."

Mabel Edwards said nothing.

"Horace figured it out after hearing that. So he came charging over here. Still in hiding. Still with all that money on him—eleven grand. And he hit you. He got so angry that he punched you in the eye. And then you killed him."

She shrugged again. "It almost sounds like self-defense."

"Almost," Myron agreed. "With Horace, it was easy. He was on the run already. All you had to do was continue to make it look like he was in hiding. He would be a black man on the run, not a homicide. Who would care? It was like Anita all over again. All these years you did the little things to make people think she was still alive. You wrote letters. You faked phone calls. Whatever. So you decided to do the same again. Hell, it worked once, right? But the problem was, you weren't as good at getting rid of the dead as Sam."

"Sam?"

"The man who worked for the Bradfords," Myron said. "My guess is that Terence helped you move the bodies."

She smiled. "Don't underestimate my strength, Myron. I'm not helpless."

He nodded. She was right. "I keep giving you these other motives, but my guess is that it was mostly about money. You got fourteen thousand from Anita. You got eleven thousand from Horace. And your own husband, dear, sweet Roland whose picture you wept over, had an insurance policy, I'd bet."

She nodded. "Only five thousand dollars, poor soul."

"But enough for you. Shot in the head near his very own home. No witnesses. And the police had arrested you three times the previous year—twice for petty theft and once for drug possession. Seems your downward spiral began before Roland was killed."

Mabel sighed. "Are we done now?"

"No," he said.

"I think we covered everything, Myron."

He shook his head. "Not Brenda."

"Oh, right, of course." She leaned back a bit. "You seem to have all the answers, Myron. Why did I kill Brenda?"

"Because," Myron said, "of me."

Mabel actually smiled. He felt his finger tighten on the trigger.

"I'm right, aren't I?"

Mabel just kept smiling.

"As long as Brenda didn't remember the Holiday Inn, she wasn't a threat. But I was the one who told you about our visit there. I was the one who told you she was having memories. And that's when you knew you had to kill her."

She just kept smiling.

"And with Horace's body found and Brenda already a murder suspect, your job became easier. Frame Brenda and make her disappear. You kill two birds with one stone. So you planted the gun under Brenda's mattress. But again you had trouble getting rid of the body. You shot her and dumped her in the woods. My guess is that you planned on coming back another day when you had more time. What you didn't count on was the search party finding her so soon."

Mabel Edwards shook her head. "You sure can spin a tale, Myron."

"It's not a tale. We both know that."

"And we both know you can't prove any of this."

"There will be fibers, Mabel. Hairs, threads, something."

"So what?" Again her smile poked his heart like a pair of knitting needles. "You saw me hug my niece right here in this very room. If her body has fibers or threads, they'd be from that. And Horace visited me before he was murdered. I told you that. So maybe that's how he got hairs or fibers on him—if they even found any."

A hot bolt of fury exploded inside his head, almost blinding him. Myron pressed the barrel hard against her forehead. His hand started quaking. "How did you do it?"

"Do what?"

"How did you get Brenda to leave practice?"

She didn't blink. "I said I'd found her mother."

Myron closed his eyes. He tried to hold the gun steady. Mabel stared at him.

"You won't shoot me, Myron. You're not the kind of man who shoots a woman in cold blood."

He didn't pull the gun away.

Mabel reached up with her hand. She pushed the barrel away from her face. Then she got up, tightened her robe, and walked away.

"I'm going to bed now," she said. "Close the door on your way out."

He did close the door.

He drove back to Manhattan. Win and Esperanza were waiting for him. They did not ask him where he'd been. And he did not tell them. In fact, he never told them.

He called Jessica's loft. The machine answered. When the beep sounded, he said that he planned on staying with Win for a while. He didn't know for how long. But awhile.

Roy Pomeranz and Eli Wickner were found dead in the cabin two days later. An apparent murder-suicide. Livingstonites speculated, but no one ever knew what had driven Eli over the edge. The Eli Wickner Little League backstop was immediately renamed.

Esperanza went back to work at MB SportsReps. Myron did not.

The homicides of Brenda Slaughter and Horace Slaughter remain unsolved.

Nothing that happened at Bradford Farms that night was ever reported. A publicist for the Bradford campaign confirmed that Chance Bradford had recently undergone knee surgery to repair a nagging tennis injury. He was recovering nicely.

Jessica did not return the phone message.

And Myron told only one person about his final meeting with Mabel Edwards.

Epilogue

SEPTEMBER 15
Two Weeks Later

The cemetery overlooked a schoolyard.

There is nothing as heavy as grief. Grief is the deepest pit in the blackest ocean, the bottomless ravine. It is all-consuming. It suffocates. It paralyzes as no severed nerve could.

He spent much time here now.

Myron heard footsteps coming up behind him. He closed his eyes. It was as he expected. The footsteps came closer. When they stopped, Myron did not turn around.

"You killed her," Myron said.

"Yes."

"Do you feel better now?"

Arthur Bradford's tone caressed the back of Myron's neck with a cold, bloodless hand. "The question is, Myron, do you?"

He did not know.

"If it means anything to you, Mabel Edwards died slowly."

It didn't. Mabel Edwards had been right that night: He was not the type to shoot a woman in cold blood. He was worse.

"I've also decided to quit the gubernatorial race," Arthur said. "I'm going to try to remember how I felt when I was with Anita. I'm going to change."

He wouldn't. But Myron didn't care.

Arthur Bradford left then. Myron stared at the mound of dirt for a while longer. He lay down next to it and wondered how something so splendid and alive could be no more. He waited for the school's final bell, and then he watched the children rush out of the building like bees from a poked hive. Their squeals did not comfort him.

Clouds began to blot the blue, and then rain began to fall. Myron almost smiled. Yes, rain. That was fitting. Much better than the earlier clear skies. He closed his eyes and let the drops pound him—rain on the petals of a crushed rose.

Eventually he stood and trekked down the hill to his car. Jessica was there, looming before him like a translucent specter. He had not seen or spoken to her in two weeks. Her beautiful face was wet—from the rain or tears, he could not say.

He stopped short and looked at her. Something else inside him shattered like a dropped tumbler.

"I don't want to hurt you," Myron said.

Jessica nodded. "I know."

He walked away from her then. Jessica stood and watched him in silence. He got in his car and turned the ignition. Still, she did not move. He started driving, keeping his eye on the rearview mirror. The translucent specter grew smaller and smaller. But it never totally disappeared.

HARLAN COBEN, winner of the Edgar Award, the Shamus Award, and the Anthony Award, is the author of nine critically acclaimed novels: *Drop Shot, Deal Breaker, Fade Away, Back Spin, One False Move, The Final Detail, Darkest Fear, Tell No One,* and *Gone For Good.* He lives in New Jersey with his wife and four children. Visit his website at www.harlancoben.com.